THE HILLS OF THE SHATEMUC.

BY THE

AUTHOR OF THE "WIDE, WIDE WORLD."

A wise man is strong.
PROVERBS xxiv, 5.

NEW YORK:
D. APPLETON AND COMPANY,
346 & 348 BROADWAY.
1856.

CONTENTS.

THE HILLS OF THE SHATEMUC.

CHAPTER I.

Low stirrings in the leaves, before the wind
Wakes all the green strings of the forest lyre.
LOWELL.

THE light of an early Spring morning, shining fair on upland and lowland, promised a good day for the farmer's work. And where a film of thin smoke stole up over the tree-tops, into the sunshine which had not yet got so low, there stood the farmer's house.

It was a little brown house, built surely when its owner's means were not greater than his wishes, and probably some time before his family had reached the goodly growth it boasted now. All of them were gathered at the breakfast-table.

"Boys, you may take the oxen, and finish ploughing that upland field—I shall be busy all day sowing wheat in the bend meadow."

"Then I'll bring the boat for you, papa, at noon," said a child on the other side of the table.

"And see if you can keep those headlands as clean as I have left them."

"Yes, sir. Shall you want the horses, father, or shall we take both the oxen?"

"Both?—both *pairs*, you mean—yes; I shall want the horses. I mean to make a finish of that wheat lot."

"Mamma, you must send us our dinner," said a fourth speaker, and the eldest of the boys;—"it'll be too confoundedly hot to come home."

"Yes, it's going to be a warm day," said the father.

"Who's to bring it to you, Will?" said the mother.

"Asahel—can't he—when he brings the boat for papa?"

"The boat won't go to the top of the hill," said Asahel; "and it's as hot for me as for other folks, I guess."

"You take the young oxen, Winthrop," said the farmer, pushing back his chair from the table.

"Why, sir?" said the eldest son promptly.

"I want to give you the best," answered his father, with a touch of comicality about the lines of his face.

"Are you afraid I shall work them too hard?"

"That's just what I'm afraid they'd do for you."

He went out; and his son attended to his breakfast in silence, with a raised eyebrow and a curved lip.

"What do you want, Winthrop?" the mother presently called to her second son, who had disappeared, and was rummaging somewhere behind the scenes.

"Only a basket, mamma,"—came from the pantry.

His mother got up from table, and basket in hand followed him, to where he was busy with a big knife in the midst of her stores. Slices of bread were in course of buttering, and lay in ominous number piled up on the yellow shelf. Hard by stood a bowl of cold boiled potatoes. He was at work with dexterity as neat-handed and as quick as a woman's.

"There's no pork there, Governor," his mother whispered as he stooped to the cupboard,—"your father made an end of that last night;—but see—here ——"

And from another quarter she brought out a pie. Being made of dried apples, it was not too juicy to cut; and being cut into huge pieces they were stowed into the basket, lapping over each other, till little room was left; and cheese and gingerbread went in to fill that. And then as her hands pressed the lid down and his hands took the basket, the eyes met, and a quick little smile of great brilliancy, that entirely broke up the former calm lines of his face, answered her; for he said nothing. And the mother's "Now go!"—was spoken as if she had enough of him left at home to keep her heart warm for the rest of the day.

The two ploughmen set forth with their teams. Or ploughboys rather; for the younger of them as yet had seen not sixteen years. His brother must have been several in advance of him.

The farmhouse was placed on a little woody and rocky promontory jutting out into a broad river from the east shore. Above it, on the higher grounds of the shore, the main body of the farm lay, where a rich tableland sloped back to a mountainous ridge that framed it in, about half a mile from the water. Cultivation had stretched its hands near to the top of this ridge and driven back the old forest, that yet stood and looked over from the other side. One or two fields were but newly cleared, as the black stumps witnessed. Many another told of good farming, and of a substantial reward for the farmer; at what cost obtained they did not tell.

Towards one of these upland fields, half made ready for a crop of spring grain, the boys took their way. On first leaving the house, the road led gently along round the edge of a little bay, of which the promontory formed the northern horn. Just before reaching the head of the bay, where the road made a sharp turn and began to ascend to the tableland, it passed what was called the *bend meadow.*

It was a very lovely morning of early Spring, one of those days when nature seems to have hushed herself to watch the buds she has set a swelling. Promising to be warm, though a little freshness from the night still lingered in the air. Everywhere on the hills the soft colours of the young Spring-time were starting out, that delicate livery which is so soon worn. They were more soft to-day under a slight sultry haziness of the atmosphere—a luxurious veil that Spring had coyly thrown over her face; she was always a shy damsel. It soothed the light, it bewitched the distance, it lay upon the water like a foil to its brightness, it lay upon the mind with a subtle charm winning it to rest and enjoy. It etherealized Earth till it was no place to work in. But there went the oxen, and the ploughmen.

The one as silently as the other; till the bay was left behind and they came to the point where the road began to go up to the tableland. Just under the hill here was a spring of delicious water, always flowing; and filling a little walled up basin.

Will, or Will Rufus, as his father had long ago called him, had passed on and begun to mount the hill. Winthrop stopped his oxen till he should fill a large stone jug for the day. The jug had a narrow neck, and he was stooping at the edge of the basin, waiting for the water to flow in, when his head and shoulders made a sudden plunge and the jug and he soused in together. Not for any want of steadiness in either of them; the cause of the plunge was a worthless fellow who was coming by at the moment. He had a house a little way off on the bay. He lived by fishing and farming alternately; and was often, and was then, employed by Mr. Landholm as an assistant in his work. He was on his way to the bend meadow, and passing close by Winthrop at the spring, the opportunity was too good to be resisted; he tipped him over into the water.

The boy soon scrambled out, and shaking himself like a great water-dog, and with about as much seeming concern, fixed a calm eye on his delighted enemy.

"Well, Sam Doolittle,—what good has that done anybody?"

"Ha'n't it done you none, Governor?"

"What do you think?"

"Well! I think you be a cool one—and the easiest customer ever *I* see."

"I've a mind it shall do somebody good; so see you don't give my father any occasion to be out with you; for if you do, I'll give him more."

"Ay, ay," said the man comfortably, "you won't tell on me. Hi! here's somebody!"

It was Rufus who suddenly joined the group, whip in hand, and looking like a young Achilles in ploughman's coat and trousers. Not Achilles' port could be more lordly; the very fine bright hazel eye was on fire; the nostril spoke, and the lip quivered; though he looked only at his brother.

"What's the matter, Winthrop?"

"I've been in the water, as you see," said his brother composedly. "I want a change of clothes, rather."

"How did you get into the water?"

"Why, head foremost—which wasn't what I meant to do."

"Sam, you put him in!"

"He, he!—well, Mr. Rufus, maybe I helped him a leetle."

"You scoundrel!" said Rufus, drawing the whip through his fingers; "what did you do it for?"

"He, he!—I didn't know but what it was you, Will."

For all answer, the ox-whip was laid about Sam's legs, with the zest of furious indignation; a fury there was no standing against. It is true, Rufus's frame was no match for the hardened one of Mr. Doolittle, though he might be four or five years the elder of the two boys; but the spirit that was in him cowed Sam, in part, and in part amused him. He made no offer to return the blows; he stood, or rather jumped, as the whip slung itself round his legs, crying out,

"Lay it on, Will!—Lay it on! Hi—That's right—Tuck it on, Will!——"

Till Will's arm was tired; and flinging away from them, in a towering passion still, he went up the hill after his oxen. Sam rubbed his legs.

"I say, Governor, we're quits now, ben't we?" he said in a sort of mock humble good-humour, as Winthrop was about to follow his brother.

"Yes, yes. Be off with yourself!"

"I wish it had ha' been 'tother one, anyhow," muttered Sam.

Not a word passed between the brothers about either the ducking or the flagellation. They spoke not but to their oxen. Rufus's mouth was in the heroic style yet, all the way up the hill; and the lips of the other only moved once or twice to smile.

The day was sultry, as it had promised, and the uphill lay of the ground made the ploughing heavy, and frequent rests of the oxen were necessary. Little communication was held between the ploughmen nevertheless; the day wore on, and each kept steadily to his work and seemingly to his own thoughts. The beautiful scene below them, which they were alternately facing and turning their backs upon, was too well known even to delay their attention; and for the greater part of the day probably neither of them saw much beyond his plough and his furrow.

They were at work on a very elevated point of view, from which the channel of the river and the high grounds on the other side were excellently seen. Valley there was hardly any; the up-springing walls of green started from the very border of the broad white stream which made its way between them. They were nowhere less than two hundred feet high; above that, moulded in all manner of heights and hollows; sometimes reaching up abruptly to twelve or fourteen hundred feet, and sometimes stretching away in long gorges and gentle declivities,—hills grouping behind hills. In Summer all these were a mass of living green, that the eye could hardly arrange; under Spring's delicate marshalling every little hill took its own place, and the soft swells of ground stood back the one from the other, in more and more tender colouring. The eye leapt from ridge to ridge of beauty; not green now, but in the very point of the bursting leaf, taking what hue it pleased the sun. It was a dainty day; and it grew more dainty as the day drew towards its close and the lights and shadows stretched athwart the landscape again. The sun-touched lines and spots of the mountains now, in some places, were of a bright orange, and the shadows between them deep neutral tint or blue. And the river, apparently, had stopped running to reflect.

The oxen were taking one of their rests, in the latter part of the day, and Winthrop was sitting on the beam of his plough, when for the first time Rufus came and joined him. He sat down in silence and without so much as looking at his brother; and both in that warm and weary day sat a little while quietly looking over the water; or perhaps at the little point of rest, the little brown spot among the trees on the promontory, where home and mother and little baby sister, and the end of the day, and the heart's life, had their sole abiding-place. A poor little shrine, to hold so much!

Winthrop's eyes were there, his brother's were on the distance. When did such two ever sit together on the beam of one plough, before or since! Perhaps the eldest might have seen nineteen summers; but his face had nothing of the boy, beyond the fresh colour and fine hue of youth. The features were exceedingly noble, and even classically defined; the eye as beautiful now in its grave thoughtfulness as it had been a few hours before in its fire. The mouth was never at rest; it was twitching or curving at the corners now with the working of some hidden cogitations. The frame of the younger brother was less developed; it promised to be more athletic than that of the elder, with perhaps somewhat less grace of outline; and the face was not so regularly handsome. A very cool and clear grey eye aided the impression of strength; and the mouth, less beautifully moulded than that of Rufus, was also infinitely less demonstrative. Rufus's mouth, in silence, was for ever saying something. Winthrop's for the most part kept its fine outlines unbroken, though when they did give way it was to singular effect. The contrast between the faces was striking, even now when both were in repose.

The elder was the first to break silence, speaking slowly and without moving his eye from its bent.

"Governor,—what do you suppose lies behind those mountains?"

"What? '—said Winthrop quickly.

The other smiled.

"Your slow understanding can make a quick leap now and then."

"I can generally understand you," said his brother quietly.

Rufus added no more for a little, and Winthrop let him alone.

"We've got the farm in pretty good order now," he remarked presently in a considerate tone, folding his arms and looking about him.

"Papa has," observed Winthrop. "Yes—if those stumps were out once. We ought to have good crops this year, of most things."

"I am sure I have spent four or five years of *my* life in hard work upon it," said the other.

"Your life ain't much the worse of it," said Winthrop, laughingly.

Rufus did not answer the laugh. He looked off to the hills again, and his lips seemed to close in upon his thoughts.

"Papa has spent more than that," said the younger brother gravely. "How hard he has worked—to make this farm!"

"Well, he has made it."

"Yes, but he has paid a dozen years of *his* life for it. And mamma!——"

"It was a pretty tough subject to begin with," said the elder, looking about him again. "But it's a nice farm now;—it's the handsomest farm in the county;—it ought to pay considerable now, after this."

"It hasn't brought us in much so far," observed Winthrop, "except just to keep along;—and a pretty tight fit at that."

"The house ought to be up here," said Rufus, considering the little distant brown speck;—"it would be worth twice as much."

"What would?"

"Why!—the farm!"

"The house wouldn't," said Winthrop,—"not to my notions."

"It's confoundedly out of the way, down there, a mile off from the work."

"Only a quarter of that, and a little better," said Winthrop calmly.

"A little worse!—There's a great loss of time. There would be twice as much work done if the house was up here."

"*I* couldn't stand it," said Winthrop. "How came it the house was put down there?"

"Papa bought the point first and built the house, before ever he pushed his acquirements so far as this. He would be wise, now, to let that, and build another up here somewhere."

"It wouldn't pay," said the younger brother; "and for one, I'm not sorry."

"If the farm was clear," said the elder, "I'd stand the chance of it's paying; it's that keeps us down."

"What?"

"That debt."

"What debt?"

"Why, the interest on the mortgage."

"I don't know what you are talking of."

"Why," said Rufus a little impatiently, "don't you know that when papa bought the property he couldn't pay off the whole price right down, and so he was obliged to leave the rest owing, and give security."

"What security?"

"Why, a mortgage on the farm, as I told you."

"What do you mean by a mortgage?"

"Why he gave a right over the farm—a right to sell the farm at a certain time, if the debt was not paid and the interest upon it."

"What is the debt?"

"Several thousands, I believe."

"And how much does he have to pay upon that every year?"

"I don't know exactly—one or two, two or three hundred dollars; and that keeps us down, you see, till the mortgage is paid off."

"I didn't know that."

They sat silent a little time. Then Winthrop said,

"You and I must pay that money off, Will."

"Ay——but still there's a question which is the best way to do it," said Rufus.

"The best way, I've a notion," said Winthrop looking round at his cattle,—"is not to take too long noon-spells in the afternoon."

"Stop a bit. Sit down!—I want to speak to you. Do you want to spend all your life following the oxen?"

Winthrop stopped certainly, but he waited in silence.

"*I* don't!"

"What do you want to do?"

"I don't know—something——"

"What is the matter, Will?"

"Matter?"—said the other, while his fine features shewed the changing lights and shadows of a summer day,—"why Winthrop, that I am not willing to stay here and be a ploughman all my life, when I might be something better!"

The other's heart beat. But after an instant he answered calmly,

"How can you be anything better, Will?"

"Do you think all the world lies under the shadow of Wut-a-qut-o?"

"What do you mean?"

"Do you think all the world is like this little world which those hills shut in?"

"No,"—said Winthrop, his eye going over to the blue depths and golden ridge-tops, which it did not see; "—but——"

"Where does that river lead to?"

"It leads to Mannahatta. What of that?"

"There is a world there, Winthrop,—another sort of world,—where people know something; where other things are to be done than running plough furrows; where men may distinguish themselves!—where men may read and write; and do something great; and grow to be something besides what nature made them! —I want to be in that world."

They both paused.

"But what will you do, Rufus, to get into that world?—we are shut in here."

"*I* am not shut in!" said the elder brother; and brow and lip and nostril said it over again;—"I will live for something greater than this!"

There was a deep-drawn breath from the boy at his side.

"So would I, if I could. But what can we do?"

How difficult it was to do anything, both felt. But after a deliberate pause of some seconds, Rufus answered,

"There is only one thing to do.—I shall go to College."

"To College!—Will?"

The changes in the face of the younger boy were sudden and startling. One moment the coronation of hope; the next moment despair had thrown the coronet off; one more, and the hand of determination,—like Napoleon's,—had placed it firmly on his brow, and it was never shaken again. But he said nothing; and both waited a little, till thoughts could find words.

"Rufus,—do papa and mamma know about this?"

"Not yet."

"What will they think of it?"

I don't know—they *must* think of it as I do. My mind is made up. I can't stay here."

"But some preparation is necessary, Rufus, ain't it?—we must know more than we do before we can go to College, mustn't we? How will you get that?"

"I don't know, I will get it. Preparation!—yes!"

"Father will want us both at home this summer."

"Yes—this summer—I suppose we must. We must do something——we must talk to them at home about it,—gradually."

"If we had books, we could do a great deal at home."

"Yes, if,——But we haven't. And we must have more time. We couldn't do it at home."

"Papa wants us this summer.—And I don't see how he can spare us at all, Rufus."

"I am sure he will let us go," said the other steadily, though with a touch of trouble in his face.

"We are just beginning to help him."

"We can help him much better the other way," said Rufus quickly. "Farming is the most miserable slow way of making money that ever was contrived."

"How do *you* propose to make money?" inquired his brother coolly.

"I don't know! I am not thinking of making money at present!"

"It takes a good deal to go to College, don't it?"

"Yes."

And again there was a little silence. And the eyes of both were fixed on the river and the opposite hills, while they saw only that distant world and the vague barrier between.

"But I intend to go, Winthrop," said his brother looking at him, with fire enough in his face to *burn up* obstacles.

"Yes, you will go," the younger said calmly. The cool grey eye did not speak the internal, "So will I!"—which stamped itself upon his heart. They got up from the plough beam.

"I'll try for't," was Rufus's conclusion, as he shook himself.

"*You'll get it*," said Winthrop.

There was much love as well as ambition in the delighted look with which his brother rewarded him. They parted to their work. They ploughed the rest of their field:—what did they turn over besides the soil?

They wended their slow way back with the oxen when the evening fell; but the yoke was off their own necks. The lingering western light coloured another world than the morning had shined upon. No longer bondsmen of the soil, they trode it like masters. They untackled their oxen and let them out, with the spirit of men whose future work was to be in a larger field. Only Hope's little hand had lifted the weight from their heads. And Hope's only resting point was determination.

CHAPTER II.

A quiet smile played round his lips,
As the eddies and dimples of the tide
Play round the bows of ships,
That steadily at anchor ride.
And with a voice that was full of glee,
He answered, "ere long we will launch
A vessel as goodly, and strong, and stanch,
As ever weathered a wintry sea.

LONGFELLOW.

"THE ploughing's all done; thank fortune!" exclaimed Rufus as he came into the kitchen.

"Well, don't leave your hat there in the middle of the floor," said his mother.

"Yes, it just missed knocking the tea-cups and saucers off the table," said little Asahel.

"It hasn't missed knocking you off your balance," said his brother tartly. "Do you know where your own hat is?"

"It hain't knocked me off anything!" said Asahel. "It didn't touch me!"

"Do you know where your own hat is?"

"No."

"What does it matter, Will?" said his mother.

"It's hanging out of doors, on the handle of the grindstone."

"It ain't!"

"Yes it is;—on the grindstone."

"No it isn't," said Winthrop coming in, "for I've got it here. There—see to it Asahel. Mamma, papa's come. We've done ploughing."

And down went his hat, but not on the floor.

"Look at Winifred, Governor—she has been calling for you all day."

The boy turned to a flaxen-haired, rosy-cheeked, little toddling thing of three or four years old, at his feet, and took her up, to the perfect satisfaction of both parties. Her head nestled in his neck and her little hand patted his cheek with great approval and contentment.

"Mamma," said Asahel, "what makes you call Winthrop Governor?—he isn't a governor."

"Ask your father. And run and tell him tea's just ready."

The father came in; and the tea was made, and the whole party sat down to table. A homely, but a very cheerful and happy board. The supper was had in the kitchen; the little remains of the fire that had boiled the kettle were not amiss after the damps of evening fell; and the room itself, with its big fireplace, high dark-painted wainscoting, and even the clean board floor, was not the least agreeable in the house. And the faces and figures that surrounded the table were manly, comely, and intelligent, in a high degree.

"Well,—I've got through with that wheat field," said Mr. Landholm, as he disposed of a chicken bone.

"Have you got through sowing?" said his wife.

"Sowing!—no!—Winthrop, I guess you must go into the garden to-morrow—I can't attend to anything else till I get my grain in."

"Won't you plant some sweet corn this year, Mr. Landholm?—it's a great deal better for cooking."

"Well, I dont know—I guess the field corn's sweet enough. I haven't much time to attend to sugar things. What *I* look for is substantials."

"Aren't sweet things substantial, sir?" said Winthrop.

"Well—yes,—in a sort they are," said his father laughing, and looking at the little fat creature who was still in her brother's arms and giving him the charge of her supper as well as his own. "I know *some* sweet things I shouldn't like to do without."

"Talking of substantials," said Mrs. Landholm, "there's wood wanting to be got. I am almost out. I had hardly enough to cook supper."

"Don't want much fire in this weather," said the father. "However—we can't get along very well without supper.—Rufus, I guess you'll have to go up into the woods to-morrow with the ox-sled—you and Sam Doolittle—back of the pine wood—you'll find enough dead trees there, I guess."

"I think," said Rufus, "that if you think of it, what are called substantial things are the least substantial of any—they are only the scaffolding of the other."

"Of what other?" said his father.

"Of the things which really last, sir,—the things which belong to the *mind*—things which have to do with something besides the labour of to-day and the labour of to-morrow."

"The labour of to-day and the labour of to-morrow are pretty necessary though," said his father dryly; "we must eat, in the first place. You must keep the body alive before the mind can do much—at least I have found it so in my own experience."

"But you don't think the less of the other kind of work, sir, do you?" said Winthrop looking up;—"when one can get at it?"

"No my boy," said the father,—"no, Governor; no man thinks more highly of it than I do. It has always been my desire that you and Will should be better off in this respect than I have ever been;—my great desire; and I haven't given it up, neither."

A little silence of all parties.

"What are the things which 'really last,' Rufus?" said his mother.

Rufus made some slight and not very direct answer, but the question set Winthrop to thinking.

He thought all the evening; or rather thought and fancy took a kind of whirligig dance, where it was hard to tell which was which. Visions of better opportunities than his father ever had;—of reaching a nobler scale of being than his own early life had promised him;—of higher walks than his young feet had trod: they made his heart big. There came the indistinct possibility of raising up with him the little sister he held in his arms, not to the life of toil which their mother had led, but to some airy unknown region of cultivation and refinement and elegant leisure;—hugely unknown, and yet surely laid hold of by the mind's want. But though fancy saw her for a moment in some strange travestie of years and education and circumstances, that was only a flash of fancy—not dwelt upon. Other thoughts were more near and pressing, though almost as vague. In vain he endeavoured to calculate expenses that he did not know, wants that he could not estimate, difficulties that loomed up with no certain outline, means that were far beyond ken. It was but confusion; except his purpose, clear and steady as the sun, though as yet it lighted not the way but only the distant goal; *that* was always in sight. And under all these thoughts, little looked at yet fully recognized, his mother's question; and a certain security that *she* had that which would 'really last.' He knew it. And oddly enough, when he took his candle from her hand that night, Winthrop, though himself no believer unless with head belief, thanked God in his heart that his mother was a Christian.

Gradually the boys disclosed their plan; or rather the elder of the boys; for Winthrop being so much the younger, for the present was content to be silent. But their caution was little needed. Rufus was hardly more ready to go than his parents were to send him,—if they could; and in their case, as in his, the lack of power was made up by will. Rufus should have an education. He should go to College. Not more cheerfully on his part than on theirs the necessary privations were met, the necessary penalty submitted to. The son should stand on better ground than the father, though the father were himself the stepping-stone that he might reach it.

It had nothing to do with Winthrop, all this. Nothing was said of him. To send one son to College was already a great stretch of effort, and of possibility; to send *two* was far beyond both. Nobody thought of it. Except the one left out of their thoughts.

The summer passed in the diligent companionship of the oxen and Sam Doolittle. But when the harvests were gathered, and the fall work was pretty well done; the winter grain in the ground, and the November winds rustling the dry leaves from the trees,—the strongest branch was parted from the family tree, in the hope that it might take root and thrive better on its own stock elsewhere. It was cheerfully done, all round. The father took bravely the added burden with the lessened means; the mother gave her strength and her eyesight to make the needed preparations; and to supply the means for them, all pinched themselves; and Winthrop had laid upon him the threefold charge of his own, his brother's, and his father's duty. For Mr. Landholm had been chosen a member of the State Legislature; and he too would be away from home all winter. What sort of a winter it would be, no one stopped to think, but all were willing to bear.

The morning came of the day before the dreaded Saturday, and no one cared to look at another. It was a relief, though a hated one, to see a neighbour come in. Even that, Winthrop shunned; he was cleaning the harness of the wagon, and he took it out into the broad stoop outside of the kitchen door. His mother and brother and the children soon scattered to other parts of the house.

"So neighbour," said Mr. Underhill,—"I hear tell one of your sons is goin' off, away from you?"

"Yes,"—said Mr. Landholm, pride and sorrow struggling together in his manner,—"I believe he is."

"Where's he goin'?"

"To Asphodel—in the first place."

"Asphodel, eh?—What's at Asphodel?"

"What do you mean?"

"What's he goin' there for?"

"To pursue his studies—there's an Academy at Asphodel."

"An Academy.—Hum.—And so he's goin' after larnin' is he? And what'll the farmer do without him to hum?"

"Do the best I can—send for you, neighbour Underhill."

"Ha, ha!—well, I reckon I've got enough to do to attend to my own."

"I guess you don't do much but fish, do you?—there under the mountain?"

"Well, you see, I hain't a great deal of ground. You can't run corn *straight* up a hill, can you?—without somethin' to stand on?"

"Not very well."

"There be folks that like that kind o' way o' farming—but I never did myself."

"No, I'll warrant you," said Mr. Landholm, with a little attempt at a laugh.

"Well—you say there's an Academy at Asphodel;—then he aint going to—a—what do you call it?—Collegiate Institution?"

"No, not just yet; by and by he'll go to College, I expect.—That's what he wants to do."

"And you want it too, I suppose?"

"Yes—I'll do the best I can by my children. I can't do as I would by them all," said the father, with a mixture of pride expressed and pride not expressed,—"but I'll try to make a man of Will!"

"And t'other 'll make a man of himself," said Mr. Underhill, as he saw Winthrop quit the stoop. "*He'll* never run a plough up the side of a house. But what kind of a man are you going to make of Will?—a great man?"

"Ah, I don't know!" said Mr. Landholm with a sigh. "That must be as Providence directs."

"Hum—I should say that Providence directs you to keep 'em both to hum," said Mr. Underhill;—"but that's not my affair. Well, I'm going.—I hear you are goin' to be in Vantassel this winter?"

"Yes—I'm going to make laws for you," Mr. Landholm answered laughing.

"Well—" said Mr. Underhill taking his hat,—"I wish they'd put you up for President—I'd vote for you!"

"Thank you. Why?"

"'Cause I should expect you'd give me somethin' nother and make a great man of *me!*"

With a laugh at his own wit, Mr. Underhill departed.

CHAPTER III.

> But who shall so forecast the years,
> And find in loss a gain to match?
> Or reach a hand through time to catch
> The far-off interest of tears?
>
> TENNYSON.

THE day came.

The farewell dinner was got ready—the best of the season it must be, for the honour of all parties and the love of one; but it mocked them. Mrs. Landholm's noble roast pig, and sweet chickens, and tea and fine bread; they were something to be remembered, not enjoyed, and to be remembered for ever, as part of one strong drop of life's bittersweet mixture. The travellers, for Mr. Landholm was to accompany his son, had already dressed themselves in their best; and the other eyes, when they could, gazed with almost wondering pride on the very fine and graceful figure of the young seeker of fortune. But eyes could do little, and lips worse than little. The pang of quitting the table, and the hurried and silent good-byes, were over at last; and the wagon was gone.

It seemed that the whole household was gone. The little ones had run to some corner to cry; Winthrop was nowhere; and the mother of the family stood alone and still by the table in the kitchen where they had left her.

An old black woman, the sole house servant of the family, presently came in, and while taking up two or three of the plates, cast looks of affectionate pity at her mistress and friend. She had been crying herself, but her sorrow had taken a quiet form.

"Don't ye!" she said in a troubled voice, and laying her shrivelled hand timidly on Mrs. Landholm's shoulder,—"don't ye, Mis' Landholm. He's in the Lord's hand,—and just you let him be there."

Mrs. Landholm threw her apron over her face and went out of the kitchen into her own room. The old woman continued to go round the table, gathering the plates, but very evidently busy with something else; and indeed humming or talking to herself, in a voice far from steady.

" 'There is a happy land,
Where parting is unknown——' "

She broke off and sat down and put her face in her hands and wept.

" Oh Lord!—oh good Lord!—I wish I was there!—Be still Karen—that's very wicked—wait, wait. 'They shall not be ashamed that wait for him,' he said,—They will not be ashamed," she repeated, looking up, while the tears streamed down her cheeks. "I will wait. But oh!—I wisht I had patience! I want to get straight out of trouble,—I do. Not yet, Karen,—not yet. 'When *he* giveth quietness, then who can make trouble?' That's it—that's my way."

She went about her business and quietly finished it.

It had long been done, and the afternoon was wearing well on, when Mrs. Landholm came into the kitchen again. Karen had taken care of the children meanwhile. But where was Winthrop? The mother, now quite herself, bethought her of him. Karen knew he was not about the house. But Mrs. Landholm saw that one of the big barn doors was open, and crossed over to it. A small field lay between that and the house. The great barn floor was quite empty, as she entered, except of hay and grain, with which the sides were tightly filled up to the top; the ends were neatly dressed off; the floor left clean and bare. It oddly and strongly struck her, as she saw it, the thought of the hands that had lately been so busy there; the work left, the hands gone; and for a few moments she stood absolutely still, feeling and putting away the idea that made her heart ache. She had a battle to fight before she was mistress of herself and could speak Winthrop's name. Nobody answered; and scolding herself for the tone of her voice, Mrs. Landholm spoke again. A little rustling let her know that she was heard; and presently Winthrop made his appearance from below or from some distant corner behind the hay, and came to meet her. He could not command his face to his mother's eyes, and sorrow for Will for a moment was half forgotten in sorrow for him. As they met she put both hands upon his shoulders, and said wistfully, "My son?"—But that little word silenced them both. It was only to throw their arms about each other and hide their faces in each other's neck, and cry strange tears; tears that are drawn from the heart's deepest well. Slight griefs flow over the surface, with fury perhaps; but the purest and the sweetest waters are drawn silently.

Winthrop was the first to recover himself, and was kissing his mother with manly quietness before she could raise her head at all. When she did, it was to return his kisses, first on one cheek and then on the other and then on his forehead, parting the hair from it with both hands for the purpose. It seemed as if she would have spoken, but she did not, then, not in words.

"My boy," she said at last, "you have too hard measure laid on you!"

"No, mother—I don't think it so;—there is nothing to make me sorry in that."

"Will has got his wish," she observed presently.

"Don't you approve of it mother?"

"Yes—" she said, but as if there were many a thought before and behind.

"*Don't* you approve of it mother?" Winthrop asked quickly.

"Yes, yes—I do,—in itself; but you know there is one wish before all others in my mind, for him and for you, Winthrop."

He said nothing.

"Come," she said a moment after more cheerfully, "we must go in and see how cosy and sociable we can make ourselves alone. We must practise,"—for next winter, she was going to say, but something warned her to stop. Winthrop turned away his face, though he answered manfully,

"Yes mother—I must just go over to the bank field and see what Sam Doolittle has been at; and I've got to cut some wood; then I'll be in."

"Will you be back by sundown?"

"I'll not be long after."

The mother gave a look towards the sun, already very near the high western horizon, and another after Winthrop who was moving off at a good pace; and then slowly walked back to the house, one hand clasping its fellow in significant expression.

Karen was sitting in her clean kitchen with little Winifred on her knees, and singing to her in a very sweet Methodist tune,

"There fairer flowers than Eden's bloom,
Nor sin nor sorrow know.
Blest seats!—through rude and stormy seas,
I onward press to you."

The mother stooped to take up the child.

"What put that into your head, Karen?"

"Everything puts it in my head, missus," said the old woman with a smiling look at her; "sometimes when I see the sun go down, I think by'm-by I won't see him get up again; and times when I lose something, I think by'm-by I won't want it; and sometimes when somebody goes away, I think by'm-by we'll be all gone, and then we'll be all together again; only I'd like sometimes to be all together without going first."

"Will you get down, Winnie?" said her mother, "and let mamma make a cake for brother Winthrop?"

"A cake?—for Governor?"

"Yes, get down, and I'll make one of Governor's hoe-cakes."

The spirit of love and cheerfulness had got the upper hand when the little family party gathered again; at least that spirit had rule of all that either eyes or ears could take note of. They gathered in the 'keeping-room,' as it was called; the room used as a common sitting room by the family, though it served also the purpose of a sleeping chamber, and a bed accordingly in one corner formed part of the furniture. Their eyes were accustomed to that. It did not hurt the general effect of comfort. There the supper-table was set this evening; the paper window-curtains were let down, and a blazing fire sparkled and crackled; while before it, on the approved oaken barrel-head set up against the andirons, the delicate rye and indian hoe-cake was toasting into sweetness and brownness. Asahel keeping watch on one side of the fire, and Winifred at the other burning her little fair cheek in premature endeavours to see whether the cake was ready to be turned.

"What's going on here!" said Winthrop, catching her up in his arms as he came in.

Winifred laughed and kissed him, and then with an earnest slap of her little hand on his cheek requested to be set down, that she might see, "if that side wasn't done."

"Yes, to be sure it's done," said Asahel. "Where's mamma to turn it?"

"Here," said Winthrop, taking up the barrel cover,—"do you think nobody can turn a cake but mamma?"

"*You* can't," said Asahel,—"you'll let it fall in the ashes,—you will!—"

But the slice of half baked dough was cleverly and neatly slipped off the board and happily put in its place again with the right side out; and little Winifred, who had watched the operation anxiously, said with a breath of satisfaction and in her slow utterance,

"There—Governor can do anything!"

There were several cakes to take the benefit of the fire, one after the other, and then to be split and buttered, and then to be eaten; and cakes of Winthrop's baking and mamma's buttering, the children pronounced "as good as could be." Nothing could have better broken up the gloom of their little tea party than Winthrop's hoe-cakes; and then the tea was so good, for nobody had eaten much dinner.

The children were in excellent spirits, and Winthrop kept them in play; and the conversation went on between the three for a large part of the evening. When the little ones were gone to bed, then indeed it flagged; Winthrop and his mother sat awhile silently musing, and then the former bade her good night.

It was long before Mrs. Landholm thought of going to bed, or thought of anything around her; the fire was dead and her candle burnt out, when at length she roused herself. The cold wind made itself felt through many a crevice in the wooden frame house; and feeling too much of its work upon her, she went into the kitchen to see if there were not some warmth still lingering about the covered-up fire. To her surprise, the fire was not covered up; a glow came from it yet; and Winthrop sat there on the hearth, with his head leaning against the jamb and his eyes intently studying the coals. He started, and jumped up.

"Winthrop!—what are you here for, my dear?"

"I came out to warm myself."

"Haven't you been to bed?

"No ma'am."

"Where have you been?"

"Only in my room, mother."

'Doing what, my son?"

"Thinking—" he said a little unwillingly.

"Sit down and warm yourself," said his mother placing his chair again;—"Why, your hands are warm now?"

"Yes ma'am—I have been here a good while."

He sat down, where she had put his chair in front of the fire-place; and she stood warming herself before it, and looking at him. His face was in its usual calmness, and she thought as she looked it was an excellent face. Great strength of character—great truth—beneath the broad brow high intellectual capacity, and about the mouth a certain sweet self-possession; to the ordinary observer more cool than sweet, but his mother knew the sweetness.

"What are you thinking about, Winthrop?" she said softly, bending down near enough to lay a loving hand on his brow.

He looked up quickly and smiled, one of those smiles which his mother saw oftener than anybody, but she not often,—a smile very revealing in its character,—and said,

"Don't ask me, mamma."

"Who should ask you, if not I?"

"There is no need to trouble you with it, mother."

"You can't help that—it will trouble me now, whether I know it or not; for I see it is something that troubles you."

"You have too good eyes, mother," he said smiling again, but a different smile.

"My ears are just as good."

"Mamma, I don't want to displease you," he said looking up.

"You can't do that—you never did yet, Winthrop, my boy," she answered, bending down again and this time her lips to his forehead. "Speak—I am not afraid."

He was silent a moment, and then mastering himself as it were with some difficulty, he said,

"Mamma, I want to be somebody!"

The colour flushed back and forth on his face, once and again, but beyond that, every feature kept its usual calm.

A shadow fell on his mother's face, and for several minutes she stood and he sat in perfect silence; he not stirring his eyes from the fire, she not moving hers from him. When she spoke, the tone was changed, and though quiet he felt the trouble in it.

"What sort of a somebody, Winthrop?"

"Mamma," he said, "I can't live here! I want to know more and to be more than I can here. I can, I am sure, if I only can find a way; and I am sure I can find a way. It is in me, and it will come out. I don't want anybody to give me any help, nor to think of me; I can work my own way, if you'll only let me and not be troubled about me."

He had risen from his chair to speak this. His mother kept her face in the shadow and said quietly,

"What way will you take, Winthrop?"

"I don't know, ma'am, yet; I haven't found out."

"Do you know the difficulties in the way?"

"No, mother."

It was said in the tone not of proud but of humble determination.

"My boy, they are greater than you think for, or than I like to think of at all."

"I dare say, mother."

"I don't see how it is possible for your father to do more than put Will in the way he has chosen."

"I know that, mother," Winthrop replied, with again the calm face but the flushing colour;—"he said yesterday—I heard him—"

"What?"

"He said he would try to make a man of Rufus! I must do it for myself, mother. And I will."

His mother hardly doubted it. But she sighed as she looked, and sighed heavily.

"I ought to have made you promise not to be troubled, mamma," he said with a relaxing face.

"I am more careful of my promises than that," she answered. "But Winthrop, my boy, what do you want to do first?"

"To learn, mamma!" he said, with a singular flash of fire in his usual cool eye. "To get rid of ignorance, and then to get the power that knowledge gives. Rufus said the other day that knowledge is power, and I know he was right. I feel like a man with his hands tied, because I am so ignorant."

"You are hardly a man yet, Winthrop; you are only a boy in years."

"I am almost sixteen, mother, and I haven't taken the first step yet."

What should the first step be? A question in the minds of both; the answer—a blank.

"How long have you been thinking of this?"

"Since last spring, mother."

"Didn't Will's going put it in your head?"

"That gave me the first thought; but it would have made no difference, mother; it would have come, sooner or later. I know it would, by my feeling ever since."

Mrs. Landholm's eye wandered round the room, the very walls in their humbleness and roughness reminding her anew of the labour and self-denial it had cost to rear them, and then to furnish them, and that was now expended in keeping the inside warm. Every brown beam and little window-sash could witness the story of privation and struggle, if she would let her mind go back to it; the associations were on every hand; neither was the struggle over. She turned her back upon the room, and sitting down in Winthrop's chair bent her look as he had done into the decaying bed of coals.

He was standing in the shadow of the mantelpiece, and looking down in his turn scanned her face and countenance as a little while before she had scanned his. Hers was a fine face, in some of the finest indications. It had not, probably it never had, the extreme physical beauty of her first-born, nor the mark of intellect that was upon the features of the second. But there was the unmistakable writing of calm good sense, a patient and possessed mind, a strong power for the right, whether doing or suffering, a pure spirit; and that nameless beauty, earthly and unearthly, which looks out of the eyes of a mother; a beauty like which there is none. But more; toil's work, and care's, were there, very plain, on the figure and on the face, and on the countenance too; he could not overlook it; work that years had not had time to do, nor sorrow permission. His heart smote him.

"Mamma," he said, "you have left out the hardest difficulty of all.—How can I go and leave you and papa without me?"

"How can you? My child, I can bear to do without you in *this* world, if it is to be for your good or happiness. There is only one thing, Winthrop, I cannot bear."

He was silent.

"I could bear anything—it would make my life a garden of roses—if I were sure of having you with me in the next world."

"Mamma—you know I would——"

"I know you would, I believe, give your life to serve me, my boy. But till you love God as well as that,—you may be my child, but you are not his."

He was silent still; and heaving a sigh, a weary one, that came from very far down in her heart, she turned away again and sat looking towards the fireplace. But not at it, nor at anything else that mortal eyes could see. It was a look that left the things around her, and passing present wants and future contingencies, went beyond, to the issues, and to the secret springs that move them. An earnest and painful look; a look of patient care and meek reliance; so earnest, so intent, so distant in its gaze, that told well it was a path the mind often travelled and often in such wise, and with the self-same burden. Winthrop watched the gentle grave face, so very grave then in its gentleness, until he could not bear it; her cheek was growing pale, and whether with cold or with thinking he did not care to know.

He came forward and gently touched his cheek to the pale one.

"Mamma, do not look so for me!" he whispered.

She pulled him down beside her on the hearth, and nestled her face on his shoulder and wrapped her arms round him. And they strained him close, but he could not speak to her then.

"For whom should I look? or for what do I live? My boy! I would *die* to know that you loved Christ;—that my dear Master was yours too!"

The gently-spoken words tied his tongue. He was mute; till she had unloosed her arms from about him and sat with her face in her hands. Then his head sought her shoulder.

"Mamma, I know you are right. I will do anything to please you—anything that I can," he said with a great force upon himself.

"What *can* you do, Winthrop?"

He did not answer again, and she looked up and looked into his face.

"Can you take God for your God? and give your heart and your life,—all the knowledge you will ever get and all the power it will ever give you,—to be used for him?"

"For him, mamma?—"

"In doing his work—in doing his pleasure?"

"Mamma—I am not a Christian," he said hesitatingly and his eye falling.

"And now you know what a Christian is. Till you can do this, you do nothing. Till you are Christ's after this whole-hearted fashion you are not mine as I wish to see you,—you are not mine for ever,—my boy—my dear Winthrop—" she said, again putting her arm round him and bowing her face to his breast.

Did he ever forget the moment her head lay there? the moment when his arms held the dearest earthly thing life ever had for him? It was a quiet moment; she was not crying; no tears had been dropped at all throughout their conversation; and when she raised her face it was to kiss him quietly,—but twice, on his lips and on his cheek,—and bid him good night. But his soul was full of one meaning, as he shut his little bedroom door, —that that face should never be paler or more care-worn for anything of his doing;—that he would give up anything, he would never go from home sooner than grieve her heart in a feather's weight; nay, that rather than grieve her, he would *become a Christian.*

CHAPTER IV.

A lonely dwelling, where the shore
Is shadowed with rocks, and cypresses
Cleave with their dark green cones the silent skies,
And with their shadows the clear depths below.
SHELLEY.

THE winter was a long one to the separated family. Quietly won through, and busily. The father in the distant legislature; the brother away at his studies; and the two or three lonely people at home;—each in his place was earnestly and constantly at work. No doubt Mr. Landholm had more time to play than the rest of them, and his business cares did not press quite so heavily; for he wrote home of gay dinings-out, and familiar intercourse with this and that member of the Senate and Assembly, and hospitable houses that were open to him in Vantassel, where he had pleasant friends and pleasant times. But the home cares were upon him even then; he told how he longed for the Session to be over, that he might be with his family; he sent dear love to little Winifred and Asahel, and postscripts of fatherly charges to Winthrop, recommending to him particularly the care of the young cattle and to go on dressing the flax. And Winthrop, through the long winter, had taken care of the cattle and dressed the flax in the same spirit with which he shut his bedroom door that night; a little calmer, not a whit the less strong.

He filled father's and brother's place—his mother knew how well. Sam Doolittle knew, for he declared "there wa'n't a stake in the fences that wa'n't looked after, as smart as if the old chap was to hum." The grain was threshed as duly as ever, though a boy of sixteen had to stand in the shoes of a man of forty. Perhaps Sam and Anderese wrought better than their wont, in shame or in admiration. Karen never had so good a woodpile, Mrs. Landholm's meal bags were never better looked after; and little

Winifred and Asahel never wanted their rides in the snow, nor had more nuts cracked o' nights; though they had only one tired brother at home instead of two fresh ones. Truth to tell, however, one ride from Winthrop would at any time content them better than two rides from Will. Winthrop never allowed that he was tired, and never seemed so; but his mother and Karen were resolved that tired he must be.

"He had pretty strength to begin with," Karen said; "that was a good thing; and he seemed to keep it up too; he was shootin' over everything."

If Winthrop kept his old plans of self-aggrandizement, it was at the bottom of his heart; he looked and acted nothing but the farmer, all those months. There was a little visit from Rufus too, at mid-winter, which *must* have wakened the spirit of other things, if it had been at all laid to sleep. But if it waked it kept still. It did not so much as shew itself. Unless indirectly.

"What have you been doing all to-day, Governor?" said his little sister, meeting him with joyful arms as he came in one dark February evening.

"What have *you* been about all day?" said her brother, taking her up to his shoulder. "Cold, isn't it? Have you got some supper for me?"

"No, *I* hav'n't,—" said the little girl. "Mamma!—Governor wants his supper!"

"Hush, hush. Governor's not in a hurry."

"Where have you been all day?" she repeated, putting her little hand upon his cold face with a sort of tender consideration.

"In the snow, and out of it."

"What were you doing in the snow?"

"Walking."

"Was it cold?"

"Stinging."

"*What* was stinging?"

"Why, the cold!"

She laughed a little, and went on stroking his face.

"What were you doing when you wa'n't in the snow?"

"What do you want to know for?"

"Tell me!"

"I was scutching flax."

"What is that?"

"Why, don't you know?—didn't you see me beating flax in the barn the other day?—beating it upon a board, with a bat?—that was scutching."

"That day when mamma said,—mamma said, you were working too hard?"

"I think it is very likely."

"I thought we were done dressing flax?" remarked Asahel.

"*We!*—well, I suppose you have, for this season."

"Well, ain't *you* done dressing flax?"

"No sir."

"I thought you said the flax was all done, Winthrop?" said his mother.

"My father's is all done, ma'am."

"And yet you have been dressing flax to-day?" said Asahel; while his mother looked.

"Mamma," said Winthrop, "I wish Asahel was a little older.—He would be a help."

"Who have you been working for?" said the child.

"For myself."

"Where have you been, Winthrop?" said his mother in a lower tone of inquiry.

"I have been over the mountain, mamma,—to Mr. Upshur's."

"Dressing flax?"

"Yes ma'am."

"And you have come over the mountain to-night?"

"Yes, mother."

She stooped in silence to the fire to take up her tea-pot; but Asahel exclaimed,

"It ain't right, mamma, is it, for Winthrop to be dressing flax for anybody else?"

"What's the wrong?" said his brother.

"Is it, mamma?"

But mamma was silent.

"What's the wrong?" repeated Winthrop.

"Because you ought to be doing your own business."

"Never did, if I didn't to-day," Winthrop remarked as he came to the table.

"For shame Asahel!" put in little Winifred with her childish voice;—"*you* don't know. Governor always is right."

It was a very cold February, and it was a very bleak walk over the mountain; but Winthrop took it many a time. His mother now and then said when she saw him come in or go out, "Don't overtry yourself, my son!—" but he answered her always with his usual composure, or with one of those deep breaking-up looks which acknowledged only her care—not the need for it.

As Karen said, "he had a pretty strength to begin with;" and it was so well begun that all the exposure and hardship served rather to its development and maturing.

The snow melted from off the hills, and the winter blasts came more fitfully, and were changed for soft south airs between times. There was an end to dressing flax. The spring work was opening; and Winthrop had enough to do without working on his own score. Then Mr. Landholm came home; and the energies of both the one and the other were fully taxed, at the plough and the harrow, in the barnyard and in the forest, where in all the want of Rufus made a great gap. Mrs. Landholm had more reason now to distress herself, and distressed herself accordingly, but it was of no use. Winthrop wrought early and late, and threw himself into the gap with a desperate ardour that meant—his mother knew what.

They all wrought cheerfully and with good heart, for they were together again; and the missing one was only thought of as a stimulus to exertion, or its reward. Letters came from Rufus, which were read and read, and though not much talked about, secretly served the whole family for dessert at their dinner and for sweetmeats to their tea. Letters which shewed that the father's end was gaining, that the son's purpose was accomplishing; Rufus would be a man! They were not very frequent, for they avoided the post-office to save expense, and came by a chance hand now and then;—"Favoured by Mr. Upshur,"— or, "By Uncle Absalom." They were written on great uncouth sheets of letter-paper, yellow and coarse; but the handwriting grew bold and firm, and the words and the thoughts were changing faster yet, from the rude and narrow mind of the boy, to the polish and the spread of knowledge. Perhaps the letters might be boyish yet, in another contrast; but the home circle could not see it; and if they could, certainly the change already made was so swift as shewed a great readiness for more. Mr. Landholm said little about these letters; read them sometimes to Mr. Upshur, read them many times to himself; and for his family, his face at those times was comment enough.

"Well!—" he said one day, as he folded up one of the uncouth great sheets and laid it on the table,—"the man that could write *that*, was never made to hoe corn—that's certain."

Winthrop heard it.

At midsummer Rufus came home for a little. He brought news. He had got into the good graces of an uncle, a brother of his father's, who lived at Little River, a town in the interior, forty miles off. This gentleman, himself a farmer extremely well to do in the world, and with a small family, had invited Rufus to come to his house and carry on his studies there. The invitation was pressed, and accepted, as it would be the means of a great saving of outlay; and Rufus came home in the interval to see them all, and refit himself for the winter campaign.

No doubt he was changed and improved, like his letters; and fond eyes said that fond hopes had not been mistaken. If they looked on him once with pride, they did now with a sort of insensible wonder. His whole air was that of a different nature, not at all from affectation, but by the necessity of the case; and as noble and graceful as nature intended him to be, they delightedly confessed that he was. Perhaps by the same necessity, *his* view of things was altered a little, as their view of him; a little unconscious change, it might be; that nobody quarrelled with except the children; but certain it is that Winifred did not draw up to him, and Asahel stood in great doubt.

"Mamma," said he one day, "I wish Rufus would pull off his fine clothes and help Winthrop."

"Fine clothes, my dear!" said his mother; "I don't think your brother's clothes are very fine; I wish they were finer. Do you call patches fine?"

"But anyhow they are better than Winthrop's?"

"Certainly—when Winthrop is at his work."

"Well, the other day he said they were too good for him to help Winthrop load the cart; and I think he should pull them off!"

"Did Winthrop ask him?"

"No; but he knew he was going to do it."

"Rufus must take care of his clothes, or he wouldn't be fit to go to Little River, you know."

"Then he ought to take them off," said Asahel.

"He did cut wood with Winthrop all yesterday."

Asahel sat still in the corner, looking uncomfortable.

"Where are they now, mamma?"

"Here they are," said Mrs. Landholm, as Rufus and Winthrop opened the door.

The former met both pair of eyes directed to him, and instantly asked,

"What are you talking of?"

"Asahel don't understand why you are not more of a farmer, when you are in a farmhouse."

"Asahel had better mind his own business," was the somewhat sharp retort; and Rufus pulled a lock of the little boy s hair in a manner to convey a very decided notion of his judgment. Asahel, resenting this handling, or touched by it, slipped off his chair and took himself out of the room.

"He thinks you ought to take off your fine clothes and help Winthrop more than you do," said his mother, going on with a shirt she was ironing.

"Fine clothes!" said the other with a very expressive breath,—"I shall feel fine when I get that on, mother. Is that mine?"

"Yes."

"Couldn't Karen do that?"

"No," said Mrs. Landholm, as she put down her iron and took a hot one. The tone said, "Yes—but not well enough."

He stood watching her neat work.

"I am ashamed of myself, mother, when I look at you."

"Why?"

"Because I don't deserve to have you do this for me."

She looked up and gave him one of her grave clear glances, and said,

"*Will* you deserve it, Will?"

He stood with full eyes and hushed tongue by her table, for the space of five minutes. Then spoke with a change of tone.

"Well, I'm going down to help Winthrop catch some fish for supper; and you sha'n't cook 'em, mamma, nor Karen neither. Karen's cooking is not perfection. By the by, there's one thing more I do want,—and confoundedly too,—a pair of boots;—I really don't know how to do without them."

"Boots?"—said his mother, in an accent that sounded a little dismayful.

"Yes.—I can get capital ones at Asphodel—really stylish ones—for five dollars;—boots that would last me handsome a great while; and that's a third less than I should have to give anywhere else,—for such boots. You see I shall want them at Little River—I shall be thrown more in the way of seeing people—there's a great deal of society there. I don't see that I can get along without them."

His mother was going on with her ironing.

"I don't know," she said, as her iron made passes up and down,—"I don't know whether you can have them or not."

"I know," said Winthrop. "But I don't see the sense of getting them at Asphodel."

"Because I tell you they are two dollars and a half cheaper.'

"And how much more will it cost you to go round by the way of Asphodel than to go straight to Little River?"

"I don't know," said the other, half careless, half displeased;—"I really haven't calculated."

"Well, if you can get them for five dollars," said Winthrop, "you shall have them. I can lend you so much as that."

"How did you come by it?" said his brother looking at him curiously.

"I didn't come by it at all."

"Where did it come from?"

"Made it."

"How?"

"What do you want to know for? I beat it out of some raw flax."

"And carried it over the mountain, through the snow, winter nights," added his mother.

"You didn't know you were doing it for me," Rufus said laughing as he took the money his brother handed him. But it was a laugh assumed to hide some feeling. "Well, it shall get back to you again somehow, Winthrop. Come—are we ready for this piscatory excursion?"

"For what?" said his mother.

"A Latin word, my dear mother, which I lately picked up somewhere."

"Why not use English?" said his mother.

A general little laugh, to which many an unexpressed thought and feeling went, broke up the conference; and the two fishers set forth on their errand; Rufus carrying the basket and fishing-poles, and Winthrop's shoulder bearing the oars. As they went down in front of the house, little Winifred ran out.

"Governor, mayn't I go?"

"No!" said Rufus.

"We are going to Point Bluff, Winnie," said Winthrop stopping to kiss her,—"and I am afraid you would roll off on one side while I was pulling up a fish on the other."

She stood still, and looked after her two brothers as they went down to the water.

The house stood in a tiny little valley, a little basin in the rocks, girdled about on all sides with low craggy heights covered with evergreens. On all sides but one. To the south the view opened full upon the river, a sharp angle of which lay there in a nook like a mountain lake; its further course hid behind a headland of the western shore; and only the bend and a little bit before the bend could be seen from the valley. The level spot about the house gave perhaps half an acre of good garden ground; from the very edge of that, the grey rising ledges of granite and rank greensward between held their undisputed domain. There the wild roses planted themselves; there many a flourishing sweet-briar flaunted in native gracefulness, or climbed up and hung about an old cedar as if like a wilful child determined that only itself should be seen. Nature grew them and nature trained them; and sweet wreaths, fluttering in the wind, gently warned the passer-by that nature alone had to do there. Cedars, as soon as the bottom land was cleared, stood the denizens of the soil on every side, lifting their soft heads into the sky. Little else was to be seen. Here and there, a little further off, the lighter green of an oak shewed itself, or the tufts of a yellow pine; but near at hand the cedars held the ground, thick pyramids or cones of green, from the very soil, smooth and tapered as if a shears had been there; but only nature had managed it. They hid all else that they could; but the grey rocks peeped under, and peeped through, and here and there broke their ranks with a huge wall or ledge of granite, where no tree could stand. The cedars had climbed round to the top and went on again above the ledge, more mingled there with deciduous trees, and losing the exceeding beauty of their supremacy in the valley. In the valley it was not unshared; for the Virginia creeper and cat-briar mounted and flung their arms about them, and the wild grape-vines took wild possession; and in the day of their glory they challenged the bystander to admire anything without them. But the day of their glory was not now; it came when Autumn called them to shew themselves; and Autumn's messenger was far off. The cedars had it, and the roses, and the eglantine, under Summer's rule.

It was in the prime of summer when the two fishers went down to their boat. The valley level was but a few feet above the river; on that side, with a more scattering growth of cedars, the rocks and the greensward gently let themselves down to the edge of the water. The little dory was moored between two uprising heads of granite just off the shore. Stepping from rock to rock the brothers reached her. Rufus placed himself in the stern with the fishing tackle, and Winthrop pushed off.

There was not a stir in the air; there was not a ripple on the water, except those which the oars made, and the long widening mark of disturbance the little boat left behind it. Still—still,—surely it was Summer's siesta; the very birds were still; but it was not the oppressive rest before a thunderstorm, only the pleasant hush of a summer's day. The very air seemed blue—blue against the mountains, and kept back the sun's fierceness with its light shield; and even the eye was bid to rest, the distant landscape was so hidden under the same blue.

No distant landscape was to be seen, until they had rowed for several minutes. Winthrop had turned to the north and was coasting the promontory edge, which in that direction stretched along for more than a quarter of a mile. It stretched west as well as north, and the river's course beyond it was in a northeasterly line; so that keeping close under the shore as they were, the up view could not be had till the point was turned. First they passed the rock-bound shore which fenced in the home valley; then for a space the rocks and the heights fell back and several acres of arable ground edged the river, cut in two by a small belt of woods. These acres were not used except for grazing cattle; the first field was occupied with a grove of cylindrical cedars; in the second a soft growth of young pines sloped up towards the height; the ground there rising fast to a very bluff and precipitous range which ended the promontory, and pushed the river boldly into a curve, as abrupt almost as the one it took in an opposite direction a quarter of a mile below. Here the shore was bold and beautiful. The sheer rock sprang up two hundred feet from the very bosom of the river, a smooth perpendicular wall; sometimes broken with a fissure and an out-jutting ledge, in other parts only roughened with lichens; then breaking away into a more irregular and wood-lined shore; but with this variety keeping its bold front to the river for many an oar's length. Probably as bold and more deep below the surface, for in this place was the strength of the channel. The down tides rushed by here furiously; but it was still water now, and the little boat went smoothly and quietly on, the sound of the oars echoing back in sharp quick return from the rock. It was all that was heard; the silence had made those in the boat silent; nothing but the dip of the oars and that quick mockery of the rowlocks from the wall said that anything was moving.

But as they crept thus along the foot of the precipice, the other shore was unfolding itself. One huge mountain had been all along in sight, over against them, raising its towering head straight up some fourteen hundred feet from the water's edge; green, in the thick luxuriance of summer's clothing, except where here and there a blank precipice of many hundred feet shewed the solid stone. Now the fellow mountain, close beyond, came rapidly in view, and, as the point of the promontory was gained, the whole broad north scene opened upon the eye. Two hills of equal height on the east shore looked over the river at their neighbours. Above them, on both shores, the land fell, and at the distance of about eight miles curved round to the east in an amphitheatre of low hills. There the river formed a sort of inland sea, and from thence swept down queen-like between its royal handmaids on the right hand and on the left, till it reached the promontory point. This low distant shore and water was now masked with blue, and only the nearer highlands shewed under the mask their fine outlines, and the Shatemuc its smooth face.

At the point of the promontory the rocky wall broke down to a low easy shore, which stretched off easterly in a straight line for half a mile, to the bottom of what was called the north bay. Just beyond the point, a rounded mass of granite pushed itself into the water out of reach of the trees and shewed itself summer and winter barefacedly. This rock was known at certain states of the tide to be in the way of the white mackerel. Winthrop made fast his little skiff between it and the shore, and climbing upon the rock, he and Rufus sat down and fell to work; for to play they had not come hither, but to catch their supper.

The spirit of silence seemed to have possessed them both, for with very few words they left the boat and took their places, and with no words at all for some time the hooks were baited and the lines thrown. Profound stillness—and then the flutter of a poor little fish as he struggled out of his element, or the stir made by one of the fishers in reaching after the bait-basket—and then all was still again. The lines drooped motionless in the water; the eyes of the fishers wandered off to the distant blue, and then came back to their bobbing corks. Thinking, both the young men undoubtedly were, for it could not have been the mackerel that called such grave contemplation into their faces.

"It's confoundedly hot!" said Rufus at length very expressively.

His brother seemed amused.

"What are you laughing at?" said Rufus a little sharply.

"Nothing—I was thinking you had been in the shade lately. We've got 'most enough, I guess."

"Shade!—I wish there was such a thing. This is a pretty place though, if it wasn't August,—and if one was doing anything but sitting on a rock fishing."

"Isn't it better than Asphodel?" said Winthrop.

"Asphodel!—When are you going to get away from here Winthrop?"

"I don't know."

"Has anything been done about it?"

"No."

"It is time, Winthrop."

Winthrop was silent.

"We must manage it somehow. You ought not to be fishing here any longer. I want you to get on the way."

"Ay—I must wait awhile," said the other with a sigh. "I shall go—that's all I know, but I can't see a bit ahead. I'm round there under the point now, and there's a big headland in the way that hides the up view."

Again the eyes of the fishers were fixed on their corks, gravely, and in the case of Rufus with a somewhat disturbed look.

"I wish I was clear of the headlands too," said he after a short silence; "and there's one standing right across my way now."

"What's that?"

"Books."

"Books?" said Winthrop.

"Yes—books which I haven't got."

"Books!" said his brother in astonishment.

"Yes—why?"

"I thought you said *boots*," the other remarked simply, as he disengaged a fish from the hook.

"Well," said Rufus sharply, "what then? what if I did? Can't a man want to furnish both ends of his house at once?"

"I have heard of a man in his sleep getting himself turned about with his head in the place of his feet. I thought he was dreaming."

"You may have your five dollars again, if you think them ill-bestowed," said the other putting his hand in his pocket;—"There they are!—I don't want them—I will find a way to stand on my own legs—with boots or without, as the case may be."

"I don't know who has better legs," said Winthrop. "I can't pity you."

"But seriously, Winthrop," said Rufus, smiling in spite of himself,—"a man may go empty-headed, but he cannot go barefooted into a library, nor into society."

"Did you go much into society at Asphodel?" asked Winthrop.

"Not near so much as I shall—and that's the very thing. I *can't do* without these things, you see. They are necessary to me. Even at Asphodel—but that was nothing. Asphodel will be a very good place for you to go to in the first instance. You won't find yourself a stranger."

"Will you be ready for college next year?"

"Hum—don't know—it depends. I am not anxious about it—I shall be all the better prepared if I wait longer, and I should like to have you with me. It will make no difference in the end, for I can enter higher, and that will save expense. Seriously Winthrop, you *must* get away."

"I *must* catch that fish," said Winthrop,—"if I can—"

"You won't—"

"I've got him."

"There's one place at Asphodel where I've been a good deal—Mr. Haye's—he's an old friend of my father and thinks a world of him. You'll like him—he's been very kind to me."

"What shall I like him for—besides that?" said Winthrop.

"O he's a man of great wealth, and has a beautiful place there, and keeps a very fine house, and he's very hospitable. He's always very glad to see me; and it's rather a pleasant change from Glanbally's *vis-à-vis* and underdone apple-pies. He is one of the rich, rich Mannahatta merchants, but he has a taste for better things too. Father knows him—they met some years ago in the Legislature, and father has done him some service or other since. He has no family—except one or two children not grown up—his wife is dead—so I suppose he was glad of somebody to help him eat his fine dinners. He said some very handsome things to encourage me. He might have offered me the use of his library—but he did not."

"Perhaps he hasn't one."

"Yes he has—a good one."

"It's got into the wrong hands, I'm afraid," said Winthrop.

"He has a *little* the character of being hard-fisted. At least I think so. He has a rich ward that he is bringing up with his daughter,—a niece of his wife's—and people say he will take his commission out of her property; and there is nobody to look after it."

"Well I shan't take the office," said Winthrop, getting up "If the thought of Mr. Haye's fine dinner hasn't taken away your appetite, suppose we get home and see how these mackerel will look fried."

"It's just getting pleasant now," said Rufus as he rose to his feet. "There might be a worse office to take, for she will have a pretty penny, they say."

"Do you think of it yourself?"

"There's two of them," said Rufus smiling.

"Well, you take one and I'll take the other," said Winthrop gravely. "That's settled. And here is something you had better put in your pocket as we go—it may be useful in the meanwhile."

He quietly gathered up the five dollars from the rock and slipped them into the pocket of Rufus's jacket as he spoke; then slipped himself off the rock, took the fishing tackle and baskets into the boat, and then his brother, and pushed out into the tide. There was a strong ebb, and they ran swiftly down past rock and mountain and valley, all in a cooler and fairer beauty than a few hours before when they had gone up. Rufus took off his hat and declared there was no place like home; and Winthrop sometimes pulled a few strong strokes and then rested on his oars and let the boat drop down with the tide.

"Winthrop,"—said Rufus, as he sat paddling his hands in the water over the side of the boat,—"you're a tremendous fine fellow!"

"Thank you.—I wish you'd sit a little more in the middle."

"This is better than Asphodel just now," Rufus remarked as he took his hands out and straightened himself.

"How do you like Mr. Glanbally?"

"Well enough—he's a very good man—not too bright; but he's a very good man. He does very well. I must get you there, Winthrop."

Winthrop shook his head and turned the conversation; and Rufus in fact went away from home without finding a due opportunity to speak on the matter. But perhaps other agency was at work.

The summer was passed, and the fall nearly; swallowed up in farm duty as the months before had been. The cornstalks were harvested and part of the grain threshed out. November was on its way.

"Governor," said his father one night, when Winthrop was playing "even or odd" with Winifred and Asahel, a great handful of chestnuts being the game,—"Governor, have you a mind to take Rufus's place at Asphodel for a while this fall?"

The blood rushed to Winthrop's face; but he only forgot his chestnuts and said, "Yes, sir."

"You may go, if you've a mind to, and as soon as you like.—It's better travelling now than it will be by and by. I can get along without you for a spell, I guess."

" Thank you, father."

But Winthrop's eyes sought his mother's face. In vain little Winifred hammered upon his hand with her little doubled up fist, and repeated, "even or odd ? " He threw down the chestnuts and quitted the room hastily.

CHAPTER V

> The wind blew hollow frae the hills,
> By fits the sun's departing beam
> Looked on the fading yellow woods
> That waved o'er Lugar's winding stream.
>
> BURNS.

THE five dollars were gone. No matter—they could be wanted. They must be. Winthrop had no books either. What had he? A wardrobe large enough to be tied up in a pocket-handkerchief; his father's smile; his mother's tremulous blessing; and the tears of his little brother and sister.

He set out with his wardrobe in his hand, and a dollar in his pocket, to walk to Asphodel. It was a walk of thirteen miles. The afternoon was chill, misty and lowering; November's sad-colour in the sky, and Winter's desolating heralds all over the ground. If the sun shone anywhere, there was no sign of it; and there was no sign of it either in the traveller's heart. If fortune had asked him to play "even or odd," he could hardly have answered her.

He was leaving home. *They* did not know it, but he did. It was the first step over home's threshold. This little walk was the beginning of a long race, of which as yet he knew only the starting-point; and for love of that starting-point and for straitness of heart at turning his back upon it, he could have sat down under the fence and cried. How long this absence from home might be, he did not know. But it was the snapping of the tie,—that he knew. He was setting his face to the world; and the world's face did not answer him very cheerfully. And that poor little pocket-handkerchief of things, which his mother's hands had tied up, he hardly dared glance at it; it said so pitifully how much they would, how little they had the power to do for him; she and his father; how little way that heart of love could reach, when once he had set out on the cold journey of life He had set out now, and he felt alone,—alone;—his best company was the remembrance of that whispered blessing; and that, he knew, would abide with him. If the heart could have coined the treasure it sent back, his mother would have been poor no more.

He did not sit down, nor stop, nor shed a tear. It would have gone hard with him if he had been obliged to speak to anybody; but there was nobody to speak to. Few were abroad, at that late season and unlovely time. Comfort had probably retreated to the barns and farmhouses—to the *homesteads,*—for it was a desolate road that he travelled; the very wagons and horses that he met were going home, or would be. It was a long road, and mile after mile was plodded over, and evening began to say there was nothing so dark it might not be darker. No Asphodel yet.

It was by the lights that he saw it at length and guessed he was near the end of his journey. It took some plodding then to reach it. Then a few inquiries brought him where he might see Mr. Glanbally.

It was a corner house, flush upon the road, bare as a poverty of boards could make it, and brown with the weather. In the twilight he could see that. Winthrop thought nothing of it; he was used to it; his own house at home was brown and bare; but alas! this looked very little like his own house at home. There wasn't penthouse enough to keep the rain from the knocker. He knocked.

"Is Mr. Glanbally at home?"

"Yes—I 'spect he is—he come in from school half an hour ago. You go in there, and I guess you'll find him."

'There,' indicated a door at right angles with the front and about a yard behind it. The woman opened the door, and left Winthrop to shut it for himself.

In a bare room, at a bare table, by an ill-to-do dip candle, sat Mr. Glanbally and his book. The book on the table, and Mr. Glanbally's face on the book, as near as possible; and both as near as possible under the candle. Reason enough for that, when the very blaze of a candle looked so little like giving light. Was that why Mr. Glanbally's eyes almost touched the letters? Winthrop wondered he could see them at all; but probably he did, for he did not look up to see anything else. He had taken the opening and shutting of the door to be by some wonted hand. Winthrop stood still a minute. There was nothing remarkable about his future preceptor, except his position. He was a little, oldish man—that was all.

Winthrop moved a step or two, and then looking hastily up, the little man pushed the candle one way and the book another and peered at his visitor.

"Ah!—Do you wish to see me, sir?"

"I wish to see Mr. Glanbally."

"That's my name, sir,—that's right."

Winthrop came a step nearer and laid a letter on the table. The old gentleman took it up, examined the outside, and then went on to scan what was within, holding the lines in the same fearful proximity to his face; so near indeed, that to Winthrop's astonishment when he got to the bottom of the page he made no scruple of turning over the leaf with his nose. The letter was folded, and then Mr. Glanbally rose to his feet.

"Well sir, and so you have come to take a place in our Academy for a spell—I am glad to see you—sit down."

Which Winthrop did; and Mr. Glanbally sat looking at him, a little business-like, a little curious, a little benevolent.

"What have you studied?"

"Very little, sir,—of anything."

"Your father says, his *second* son——What was the name of the other?"

"William, sir."

"William what?"

"Landholm."

"William Landholm—yes, I recollect—I couldn't make out exactly whether it was *Sandball* or *Lardner*—Mr. Landholm—Where is your brother now, sir?"

"He is at Little River, sir, going on with his studies."

"He made very good progress—very good indeed—he's a young man of talent, your brother. He's a smart fellow. He's going on to fit himself to enter college, ain't he?"

"Yes sir."

"He'll do well—he can do what he's a mind. Well, Mr. Landholm—what are *you* going to turn your hand to?"

"I have hardly determined, sir, yet."

"You'll see your brother—something, I don't know what, one of these days, and you'll always be his brother, you know. Now what are you going to make of yourself?—merchant or farmer?"

"Neither, sir."

"No?"—said Mr. Glanbally. He looked a little surprised, for Mr. Landholm's letter had spoken of "a few weeks."

"Well, what then?"

"I don't know what I shall like best, sir," said Winthrop.

"No, not yet; perhaps not yet. You'll be a happy man if ever you do, sir. *I* never knew what I liked best, till I couldn't have it. Well sir—what do you calculate to begin upon?—a little arithmetic, I suppose, won't be out of the way."

"I should like—Latin, if you please, sir."

"Latin! Then you're following your brother's steps? I am glad of it! It does me good to see boys studying Latin. That's right. Latin. And Algebra, perhaps."

"Yes sir."

"I'll put you into Algebra, as soon as you like."

"I shall want books, I suppose, sir. Can I get them here?"

"No; you can't get 'em, I'm afraid, this side of Deerford."

"Deerford?"

"That's six miles off, or so."

"I can't walk there to-night," said Winthrop; "but I'll go to-morrow."

"Walk there to-night! no,—but we'll see. I think you've got the stuff in you. To-night!—Maybe we can find some old books that will do to begin with; and you can walk over there some waste afternoon. How far have you come to-day?"

"About thirteen miles, sir, from home."

"On foot?"

"Yes sir."

"And you want half a dozen more to-night?"

"No sir," said Winthrop, smiling,—"not if I might choose."

"You'll find a day. Your father spoke to me about your lodgings. You can lodge here, where I do; only twelve shillings a week. I'll speak to Mrs. Nelson about it; and you can just make yourself at home. I'm very glad to see you."

'Make himself at home'! Winthrop's heart gave an emphatic answer, as he drew up a chair the opposite side of the fireplace. Make himself at home. That might only be done by a swift transport of thirteen miles. He could not do it, if he would. Would he, if he could? Nay; he had set his face up the mountain of learning, and not all the luring voices that might sound behind and beside him could tempt him to turn back. He must have the Golden Water that was at the top.

It was necessary to stuff cotton into his ears. Fancy had obstinately a mind to bring his mother's gentle tread about him, and to ring the sweet tones of home, and to shew him pictures of the summer light on the hills, and of the little snow-spread valley of winter. Nay, by the side of that cold fireplace, with Mr. Glanbally at one corner and himself at the other, she set the bright hearth of home, girdled with warm hearts and hands; a sad break in them now for his being away. Mr. Glanbally had returned to his book and was turning over the leaves of it with his nose; and Winthrop was left alone to his contemplations. How alone the turning over of those leaves did make him feel. If Mr. Glanbally would have held up his head and used his fingers, like a Christian man, it would not have been so dreary; but that nose said emphatically, "You never saw me before."

It was a help to him when somebody came in to spread that bare table with supper. Fried pork, and cheese; and bread that was not his mother's sweet baking, and tea that was very "herbaceous." It was the fare he must expect up the mountain. He did not mind that. He would have lived on bread and water. The company were not fellow-travellers either, to judge by their looks. No matter for that; he did not want company. He would sing, "My mind to me a kingdom is;" but the kingdom had to be conquered first; enough to do. He was thinking all supper-time what waste ground it was. And after supper he was taken to his very spare room. It was doubtful how the epithet could possibly have been better deserved. That mattered not; the temple of Learning should cover his head by and by; it signified little what shelter it took in the mean while. But though he cared nothing for each of these things separately, they all together told him he was a traveller; and Winthrop's heart owned itself overcome, whatever his head said to it.

His was not a head to be ashamed of his heart; and it was with no self-reproach that he let tears come, and then wiped them away. He slept at last and the sleep of a tired man should be sweet. But "as he slept he dreamed." He fell to his journeyings again. He thought himself back on the wearisome road he had come that day, and it seemed that night and darkness overtook him; such night that his way was lost. And he was sitting by the roadside, with his little bundle, stayed that he could not go on, when his mother suddenly came, with a light, and offered to lead him forward. But the way by which she would lead him was not one he had ever travelled, for the dream ended there. He awoke and knew it was a dream; yet somewhat in the sweet image, or in the thoughts and associations it brought back, touched him strangely; and he wept upon his pillow with the convulsive weeping of a little child. And prayed, that night, for the first time in his life, that in the journey before him his mother's God might be his God. He slept at last.

He awoke to new thoughts and to fresh exertion. Action, action, was the business of the day; to get up the hill of learning, the present aim of life; and to that he bent himself. Whether or not Winthrop fancied this opportunity might be a short one, it is certain he made the most of it. Mr. Glanbally had for once his heart's desire of a pupil.

It was a week or two before the walk was taken to Deerford and the books bought. At the end of those weeks the waste afternoon fell out, and Mr. Glanbally got Winthrop a ride in a wagon for one half the way. Deerford was quite a place; but to Winthrop its great attraction was—a Latin dictionary! He found the right bookstore, and his dollar was duly exchanged for a second-hand Virgil, a good deal worn, and a dictionary, which had likewise seen its best days; and that was not saying much; for it was of very bad paper and in most miserable little type. But it was a precious treasure to Winthrop. His heart yearned after some Greek books, but his hand was stayed; there was nothing more in it. He had only got the Virgil and dictionary by favour eking out his eight shillings, for the books were declared to be worth ten. So he trudged off home again with his purchases under his arm, well content. That Virgil and dictionary were a guide of the way for a good piece of the mountain. Now to get up it.

He had got home and was turning the books over with Mr. Glanbally, just in the edge of the evening, when the door opened quick and a little female figure came in. She came close up to the table with the air of one quite at home.

"Good evening, Mr. Glanbally——father told me to give you this letter."

Winthrop looked at her, and Mr. Glanbally looked at the letter. She was a slight little figure, a child, not more than thirteen or fourteen at the outside, perhaps not so much, but tall of her age. A face not like those of the Asphodel children. She did not once look towards him.

"Why I thought you were in Mannahatta, Miss Elizabeth."

"Just going there—we have just come from Little River on our way."

"This letter is for you, Winthrop," said Mr. Glanbally, handing it over. "And Mr. Haye was kind enough to bring it from Little River?"

"Yes sir—he said it was for somebody here."

"And now you are going to Mannahatta?"

"Yes sir—to-morrow. Good bye, Mr. Glanbally."

"Are you alone, Miss Elizabeth?"

"Yes sir."

"Where is Miss Cadwallader?"

"She's at home. I've just been down to see nurse."

"But it's too late for you," said Mr. Glanbally, getting up,—"it's too dark—it's too late for you to go home alone."

"O no sir, I'm not afraid."

"Stop, I'll go with you," said Mr. Glanbally,—"but I've been riding till I'm as stiff as the tongs—Winthrop, are you too tired to walk home with this young lady?—as her father has brought you a letter you might do so much."

"Certainly, sir,—I am not tired."

"I don't want anybody. I'm not in the least afraid, Mr. Glanbally," said the little lady rather impatiently, and still not glancing at her promised escort.

"But it's better, Miss Elizabeth"—

"No sir, it isn't."

"Your father will like it better, I know. This is Mr. Land holm—the brother of the Mr. Landholm you used to see last summer,—you remember."

Elizabeth looked at her guard, as if she had no mind to remember anybody of the name, and without more ado left the room. Winthrop understanding that he was to follow, did so, and with some difficulty brought himself up alongside of the little lady, for she had not tarried for him and was moving on at a smart pace. Her way led them presently out of the village and along a lonely country road. Winthrop thought he was not a needless convenience at that hour; but it was doubtful what his little charge thought. She took no manner of notice of him. Winthrop thought he would try to bring her out, for he was playing the part of a shadow too literally.

"You are a good walker, Miss Elizabeth."

A slight glance at him, and no answer.

"Do you often go out alone so late?"

"Whenever I want to."

"How do you like living in the city?"

"I?—I don't know. I have never lived there."

"Have you lived here?"

"Yes."

The tone was perfectly self-possessed and equally dry. He tried her again.

"My brother says you have a very pleasant place."

There was no answer at all this time. Winthrop gave it up as a bad business.

It had grown nearly dark. She hurried on, as much as was consistent with a pace perfectly steady. About half a mile from the village she came to a full stop, and looked towards him, almost for the first time.

"You can leave me now. I can see the light in the windows."

"Not yet," said Winthrop smiling—"Mr. Glanbally would hardly think I had done my duty."

"Mr. Glanbally needn't trouble himself about me! He has nothing to do with it. This is far enough."

"I must go a little further."

She started forward again, and a moment after hardly made her own words good. They encountered a large drove of cattle, that spread all over the road. Little independence plainly faltered here and was glad to walk behind her guard, till they had passed quite through. They came then to the iron gate of her grounds.

"You needn't come any further," she said. "Thank you."

And as she spoke she opened and shut the gate in his face. Winthrop turned about and retraced his steps homeward, to read his brother's letter. It was read by his little end of candle after he went up to bed at night.

"Little River, Nov. 1807.

"My dear Governor,

"For I expect you will be all that, one of these days, (a literal governor, I mean,) or in some other way assert your supremacy over nineteen twentieths of the rest of the human race. Methinks even now from afar I see Joseph's dream enacting, in your favour, only you will perforce lack something of his *baker's dozen* of homages in your own family. Unless—but nobody can tell what may happen. For my part I am sincerely willing to be surpassed, so it be *only by you;* and will swing my cap and hurrah for you louder than anybody, the first time you are elected. Do not think I am more than half mad. In truth I expect great things from you, and I expect without any fear of disappointment. You have an obstinacy of perseverance, under that calm face of yours, that will be more than a match for all obstacles in your way; indeed obstacles only make the rush of the stream the greater, if once it get by them; the very things which this minute threatened to check it, the next are but trophies in the foaming triumph of its onward course. You can do what you will; and you will aim high. Aim at the highest.

"*I* am aiming as hard as I can, and so fast that I can't see whether my arrows hit. Not at the capture of any pretty face,—though there are a few here that would be prizes worth capturing; but really I am not skilled in that kind of archery and on the whole am not quite ready for it. An archer needs to be better equipped, to enter those lists with any chance of success, than alas! I am at present. I am aiming hard at the dressing up of my mind, in the sincere hope that the dressing up of my person may have some place in the after-piece. In other words, I am so busy that I don't know what I am doing. Asphodel was a miserable place (though I am very glad you are in it)—my chances of success at Little River are much better. Indeed I am very much to my mind here; were I, as I said, a little better equipped outwardly, and if my aunt Landholm only had mamma's recipe for making pumpkin pies; or, as an alternative, had the pumpkin crop this season but failed. But alas! the huge number of the copper-coloured tribe that lurked among the corn forests a few weeks ago, forbid me to hope for any respite till St. Nicholas jogs my aunt L.'s elbow.

"I have left myself no room to say with how much delight I received your letter, nor with what satisfaction I think of you as having fairly started in the race. You have entered your plough, now, Governor,—quick, quick, for the other side.

"Thine in the dearest rivalry,

"WILL. RUFUS LANDHOLM.

"All manner of love to mamma, papa, and the little ones, from Will."

In another corner,—"I am sorry Mr. Haye makes so little stay at Asphodel at this time—you will not see anything of him, nor of his place."

"I can bear that," thought Winthrop.

He was much too busy to see men or places. One fortnight was given to the diligent study of Algebra; two other little fortnights to Latin; and then his father came and took him home, sooner than he expected. But he had "entered his plough."

Yet it was hard to leave it there just entered; and the ride home was rather a thoughtful one. Little his father knew what he had been about. *He* thought his son had been "getting a little schooling;" he had no notion he had begun to fit himself for College!

Just as they reached the river, at a little hamlet under the hill at the foot of the north bay, where the road branched off to skirt the face of the tableland towards the home promontory, the wagon was stopped by Mr. Underhill. He came forward and unceremoniously rested both arms upon the tire of the fore wheel.

"Mornin'. Where' you been?"

"A little way back. 'Been to Asphodel, to fetch my son Winthrop home."

"Asphodel?——that's a good way back, ain't it?"

"Well, a dozen miles or so," said Mr. Landholm laughing.

"Has he been to the 'cademy too?"

"Yes—for a little while back, he has."

"What are you going to make of your sons, neighbour Landholm?"

"Ah!—I don't know," said Mr. Landholm, touching his whip gently first on one side and then on the other side of his off horse;—"*I* can't make much of 'em—they've got to make themselves."

Neighbour Underhill gave a sharp glance at Winthrop and then came back again.

"What do you reckon's the use of all this edication, farmer?"

"O—I guess it has its uses," said Mr. Landholm, smiling a little bit.

"Well, do you s'pose these boys are goin' to be smarter men than you and I be?"

"I hope so."

"You do! Well, drive on!—" said he, taking his arms from the top of the wheel. But then replacing them before the wagon had time to move——

"Where's Will?"

"Will? he's at Little River—doing well, as I hear."

"Doing what? getting himself ready for College yet?"

"Yes—he isn't ready yet."

"I say, neighbour,—it takes a power of time to get these fellows ready to begin, don't it?"

"Yes," said Mr. Landholm with a sigh.

"After they're gone you calculate to do all the work yourself, I s'pose?"

"O I've only lost one yet," said Mr. Landholm shaking the reins; "and he'll help take care of me by and by, I expect.—Come!"

Again the other's hands slipped off the wheel, and again were put back.

"We're goin' to do without larnin' here," said he. "Lost our schoolmaster."

"That fellow Dolts gone?"

"Last week."

"What's the matter?"

"The place and him didn't fit somewheres, I s'pose; at least I don't know what 'twas if 'twa'n't that."

"What are you going to do?"

"Play marbles, I guess,—till some one comes along."

"Well, my hands 'll be too cold to play marbles, if I sit here much longer," said Mr. Landholm laughing. "Good day to ye!"

And the wheel unclogged, they drove on.

CHAPTER VI.

To be a well-favoured man is the gift of fortune ; but to write and read comes by nature.

MUCH ADO ABOUT NOTHING

LITTLE could be done in the winter. The days were short and full of employment; all the more for Will's absence. What with threshing wheat and oats, foddering cattle, and dressing flax, driving to mill, cutting wood, and clearing snow, there was no time for Virgil during the few hours of daylight; hardly time to repeat a Latin verb. The evenings were long and bright, and the kitchen cosy. But there were axe-helves to dress out, and oars, and ox-yokes; and corn to shell, and hemp to hackle; and at whichever corner of the fireplace Winthrop might set himself down, a pair of little feet would come pattering round him, and petitions, soft but strong, to cut an apple, or to play jackstraws, or to crack hickory nuts, or to roast chestnuts, were sure to be preferred; and if none of these, or if these were put off, there was still too much of that sweet companionship to suit with the rough road to learning. Winnie was rarely put off, and never rejected. And the little garret room used by Winthrop and Will when the latter was at home, and now by Winthrop alone, was too freezing cold when he went up to bed to allow him more than a snatch at his longed-for work. A few words, a line or two, were all that could be managed with safety to life; and the books had to be shut up again, with bitter mortification that it must be so soon. The winter passed and Virgil was not read. The spring brought longer days, and more to do in them.

"Father," said Winthrop one night, "they have got no one yet in Mr. Dolts' place."

"What, at Mountain Spring? I know they haven't. The foolish man thought twelve dollars a month wa'n't enough for him, I suppose."

"Why was he foolish, Mr. Landholm?"

"Because he greatly misstated his own value—which it isn't the part of a wise man to do. *I* know he wasn't worth twelve dollars."

"Do you think I am worth more than that, sir?"

"I don't know what you're worth," said his father good-humouredly. "I should be sorry to put a price upon you."

"Why, Winthrop?"—his mother said more anxiously

"Will you let me take Mr. Dolts' place, father?"

"His place? What, in the schoolhouse?"

"Yes sir. If I can get it, I mean."

"What for?"

"The twelve dollars a month would hire a man to do my work on the farm."

"Yes, and I say, what for? What do you want it for?"

"I think perhaps I might get more time to myself."

"Time?—for what?"

"Time to study, sir."

"To study!—Teach others that you may teach yourself, eh?" said Mr. Landholm, with a breath that was drawn very much like a sigh; and he was silent and looked grave.

"I am afraid you wouldn't like it, Winthrop," said his mother seriously.

"I should like the time, mamma."

"I wish I were a little richer," said Mr. Landholm, drawing his breath,—"and my sons should have a better chance. I am willing to work both *my* hands off—if that would be of any avail. You may do as you please, my dear, about the school. I'll not stand in your way."

"The twelve dollars would pay a man who would do as much work as I could, father."

"Yes, yes,—that's all straight enough."

"Is Winthrop going to teach school?" exclaimed Asahel.

"Perhaps so."

"Then I should go to school to Winthrop," said the little boy clapping his hands,—"shouldn't I, mamma? Wouldn't it be funny?"

"I too?" cried Winifred.

"Hush, hush. Hear what your father says."

"I am only sorry you should have to resort to such expedients."

"Do you think they would take me, father?"

"Take you? yes! If they don't, I'll make them."

"Thank you, sir."

Winthrop presently went with the children, who drew him out into the kitchen. Mr. Landholm sat a few moments in silent and seemingly disturbed thought.

"That boy 'll be off to College too," he said,—"after his brother."

"He'll not be likely to go after anything wrong," said Mrs. Landholm.

"No—that's pretty certain. Well, I'll do all I can for him!"

"Whatever he undertakes I think he'll succeed in," the mother went on remarking.

"I think so too. He always did, from a child. It's his character. There's a sharp edge to Rufus's metal,—but I think Winthrop's is the best stuff. Well I ain't ashamed of either one on 'em!"

Winthrop took the school. He found it numbering some thirty heads or more. That is, it would count so many, though in some instances the heads were merely nominal. There were all sorts, from boys of fifteen and sixteen that wanted to learn the Multiplication table, down to little bits of girls that did not know A, B, and C. Rough heads, with thoughts as matted as their hair; lank heads, that reminded one irresistibly of *blocks;* and one fiery red shock, all of whose ideas seemed to be standing on end and ready to fly away, so little hold had they upon either knowledge, wit, or experience. And every one of these wanted different handling, and every one called for diligent study and patient painstaking. There were often fine parts to be found under that rough and untrained state of nature; there were blocks that could be waked into life by a little skill and kind management and a good deal of time; and even the fly-away shock could be brought down to order and reason by a long course of patience and firmness. But the younger heads that had no thoughts at all,—the minds that were blank of intelligence,—the eyes that opened but to stare at the new teacher! What amount of culture, what distance of days and months, would bring something out of nothing!

It was hard, hard work. There was nobody to help the new teacher; he wrought alone; that the teacher always did. The days were days of constant, unintermitted labour; the nights were jaded and spiritless. After spelling a great deal in the course of the day, and making up an indefinite number of sums in addition and multiplication, Winthrop found his stomach was gone for Latin and Virgil. Ears and eyes and mind were sick of the din of repetitions, wearied with confusions of thought not his own; he was fain to let his own rest. The children "got on," the parents said, "first-rate;" but the poor teacher was standing still. Week passed after week, and each Saturday night found him where he was the last. He had less time than on the farm. Fresh from the plough, he could now and then snatch a half hour of study to some purpose; there was no "fresh from the school." Besides all which, he still found himself or fancied himself needed by his father, and whenever a pinch of work called for it he could not hold back his hand.

"How does it go, Winthrop?" said his mother when she saw him wearily sitting down one summer night.

"It doesn't go at all, mother."

"I was afraid that it would be so."

"How does what go?" said Asahel.

"The school."

"*How* does it go?"

"Upon my head; and I am tired of carrying it."

"Don't you like being school-teacher?"

"No."

"*I* do," said Asahel.

"I wouldn't stay in it, Winthrop," said his mother.

"I will not mamma,—only till winter. I'll manage it so long."

Eight months this experiment was tried, and then Winthrop came back to the farm. Eight months thrown away! he sadly said to himself. He was doubly needed at home now, for Mr. Landholm had again been elected to the Legislature; and one of the first uses of Winthrop's freedom was to go with his father to Vantassel and drive the wagon home again.

One thing was gained by this journey. In Vantassel, Winthrop contrived to possess himself of a Greek lexicon and a Græca Majora, and also a Greek grammar, though the only one he could get that suited his purse was the Westminster grammar, in which the alternatives of Greek were all Latin. *That* did not stagger him. He came home rich in his classical library, and very resolved to do something for himself this winter.

The day after his return from Vantassel, just as they had done supper, there was a knock at the front door. Winthrop went to open it. There he found a man, tall and personable, well-dressed though like a traveller, with a little leathern valise in his hand.

Winthrop had hardly time to think he did not look like an American, when his speech confirmed it.

"How-do-you-do?" he said, using each word with a ceremony which shewed they were not denizens of his tongue. "I am wanting to make some résèrche in dis country, and I was directet here."

Winthrop asked him in, and then when he was seated, asked him what he wanted.

"I am wishing to know if you could let me live wiz you a few days—I am wanting to be busy in your mountains, about my affairs, and I just want to know if you can let me have a bed to sleep on at night, and a little somet'ing to eat—I would be very much obliged and I would pay you whatever you please——"

"Mother," said Winthrop, "can you let this gentleman stay here a few days? he has business in the mountains, he says, and wants to stop here?"

"I do not wish to be no trouble to no person," he said blandly. "I was at a little house on de ozer side of de river, but I was told dere was no room for me, and I come to an ozer place and dey told me to come to dis place. I will not trouble no person—I only want a place to put my head while my feet are going all over."

A moment's hesitation, and Mrs. Landholm agreed to this very moderate request; and Mr. Herder, as he gave his name, and his valise, were accommodated in the 'big bedroom.' This was the best room, occupying one corner of the front of the house, while the 'keeping-room' was at the other; a tiny entry-way, of hardly two square yards, lying between, with a door in each of three sides and a steep staircase in the fourth.

Winthrop presently came to ask if the stranger had had supper.

"I have not! But I will take anysing, what you please to give me."

Mr. Herder did not belie his beginning. He made himself much liked, both by the children and the grown people; and as he said, he gave as little trouble as possible. He seemed a hearty genial nature, excessively devoted to his pursuits, which were those of a naturalist and kept him out of doors from morning till night; and in the house he shewed a particular simplicity both of politeness and kind feeling; in part springing perhaps from his German nature, and in part from the honest truthful acquaintance he was holding with the world of nature at large. "He acted like a great boy," old Karen said in wondering ridicule,—

"to be bringing in leaves, and sticks, and stones, as he was every night, and making his room such a mess she never saw!"

He had soon a marked liking and even marked respect for his young host. With his usual good-humour Winthrop helped him in his quest; now and then offered to go with him on his expeditions; tracked up the streams of brooks, shewed the paths of the mountains, rowed up the river and down the river; and often and often made his uncommon strength and agility avail for something which the more burly frame of the naturalist could not have attained. He was always ready; he was never wearied; and Mr. Herder found him an assistant as acute as he was willing.

"You do know your own woods—better than I do!"—he remarked one day when Winthrop had helped him out of a botanical difficulty.

"It's only the knowledge of the eye," Winthrop replied, with a profound feeling of the difference.

"But you do seem to love knowledge—of every kind," said the naturalist,—"and that is what I like."

"I have very little," said Winthrop. "I ought to love what I can get."

"That is goot," said Mr. Herder;—"that is de right way. Ven I hear a man say, 'I have much knowledge,'—I know he never will have much more; but ven I hear one say, 'I have a little,'—I expect great things."

Winthrop was silent, and presently Mr. Herder went on.

"What kind of learning do you love de best?"

"I don't know, sir, really."

"What have you studied?"

Winthrop hesitated.

"A little Latin, sir."

"Latin!—How much Latin have you read?"

"The Gospel of John, and nearly the first book of the Æneid. But I have very little time."

"The Evangel of St. John, and the Æneid Are you going on to study it now?"

"Yes sir,—as much as I can find time."

"Greek too?"

"No sir. I am only beginning."

"I ask, because I saw some Greek books on de table de ozer night and I wondered—excuse me—who was reading them. You do not know nothing of German?"

"No sir."

"Ah, you must learn de German—dat is *my* language."

"I don't know my own language yet," said Winthrop.

"Vat is dat?"

"English."

"English!—But how do you do, here amongst de hills—is there somebody to learn you?"

"No sir."

"And you go by yourself?—Vell, I believe you will climb anything," said Mr. Herder, with a little smile; "only it is goot to know what place to begin,—as I have found."

"I must begin where I can, sir."

"But you should get to de Université; from dere it is more easy."

"I know that, sir; that is what I am trying to fit myself for."

"You do not need so much fitting—you will fit yourself better there. I would get away to de Université. You will go up—I see it in your face—you will go up, like you go up these rocks; it is pretty steep, but you know, vere one person cannot stand, anozer will mount. And what will you do wiz yourself when you get to de top?"

"I don't know yet, sir," Winthrop said laughing.

"It is just so goot not to know," said Mr. Herder. "What thing a man may wish to make himself, no matter what, he should fit himself for some ozer thing. Or else, he may be just one thing—he might be poet, or mathématicien, or musicien maybe,—and not be a whole *man*. You understand?"

"Very well, sir."

"I did not know no more what I would be, when I first went to de Université of Halle I have been to seven Universités."

Winthrop looked at him, as if to see whether he were cased in sevenfold learning.

"I am not so very wise, neizer," he said laughing. "And now I am in de eight Université—in Mannahatta—and if you will come dere I will be very glad to see you."

"Thank you, sir;—but I am afraid Mannahatta would be too expensive for me."

"Perhaps.—But vere will you go?"

"I don't know sir, yet."

"But ven you get through, you will come to Mannahatta and let me see what you have made of yourself?"

Winthrop shook his head. "I don't know when that will be, Mr. Herder."

They were walking through a tangled woodland, along one of

the deep mountain gorges; the naturalist stopping frequently to give closer notice to something. He stood still here to examine a piece of rock.

"Will you let me give you one little direction," said he producing his little hammer,—"*two* little direction, or I should call them big direction, which may be of some goot to you?"

"I wish you would, sir."

"In de first place den, don't never go half way through nozing. If some thing you want to know is in de middle of dat rock," said he striking it, "knock de rock all to pieces but what you will have it. I mean, when you begin, finish, and do it goot."

"That is what I think, Mr. Herder."

"In de second place," continued Mr. Herder, illustrating part of his former speech by hammering off some pieces of rock from the mass,—"don't never think that no kind of knowledge is of no use to you. Dere is *nozing* dat it is not goot to know. You may say, it is no use to you to know dat colour of de outside of dis rock, and dis colour of de inside; you are wrong; you ought to learn to know it if you can; and you will find de use before you die, wizout you be a very misfortunate man. Dere is nozing little in dis world; all is truth, or it will help you find out truth; and you cannot know too much."

"I believe that, sir; and I will remember it."

"And when you have learned English and Latin and Greek, you will learn German?" said the naturalist, putting the fragments of rock in his pocket.

Winthrop laughed at his expression.

"Promise me dat you will. You will find it of use to you too."

"But all useful things are not possible," said Winthrop.

"I wish it was possible for you to bring down that bird," said the naturalist, gazing up towards a pair of huge wings above them;—"It would be very useful to me." The creature was sailing through the distant ether in majestic style, moving its wings so little that they seemed an emblem of powerful repose.

"That is a white-headed eagle," said Winthrop.

"I know him!" said the naturalist, still gazing. "I wish I had him;— but *dat* is a thing in which is no goot; as he is too far off for me to reach him. Better for him! And it will be better for us to go home, for the day is not very long."

Neither was Mr. Herder's stay in the mountains after that.

At parting he assured Winthrop "he should be very glad to do him all the goot he could do, if he would only let him know how."

This was just after the fall of the leaf. The winter was a mild one, and so fruitful in business belonging to the farm that Winthrop's own private concerns had little chance. Latin was pushed a little, and Greek entered upon; neither of them could be forwarded much, with all the stress that hope or despair could make. Snowstorm, and thaw, and frost, and sun, came after and after each other, and as surely and constantly the various calls upon Winthrop's time; and every change seemed to put itself between him and his books. Mr. Landholm was kept late in Vantassel, by a long session, and the early spring business came all upon his son's hands.

Letters were rather infrequent things in those days, waiting, as they usually did, for private carriage. It was near the end of March that the rare event of two letters in one day happened to the quiet little household.

Winthrop got one at the post-office, with the Vantassel mark; and coming home found his mother sitting before the fire with another in her hand, the matter of which she was apparently studying.

"A letter, mamma?"

"Yes—from Will."

"How did it come?"

"It came by Mr. Underhill."

"What's the matter? what does he say?"

"Not much—you can see for yourself."

"And here's one from papa."

Mrs. Landholm took it, and Winthrop took Rufus's.

"Little River, March 18, 1809.

"What does papa mean to do? Something must be done, for I cannot stay here for ever; neither in truth do I wish it. If I am ever to make anything, it is time now. I am twenty-one, and in mind and body prepared, I think, for any line of enterprise to which fortune may call me. Or if nothing can be done with me,—if what has been spent must be thrown away—it is needless to throw away any more; it would be better for me to come home and settle down to the lot for which I seemed to be born. Nothing can be gained by waiting longer, but much lost.

"I am not desponding, but seriously this transition life I am leading at present is not very enlivening. I am neither one thing nor the other; I am in a chrysalis state, which is notoriously a dull one; and I have the further aggravation, which I suppose never occurs to the nymph *bona fide*, of a miserable uncertainty whether my folded-up wings are those of a purple butterfly or of a poor drudge of a beetle. Besides, it is conceivable that the chrysalis may get weary of his case, and mine is not a silken one. I have been here long enough. My aunt Landholm is very kind; but I think she would like an increase of her household accommodations, and also that she would prefer working it by the rule of *subtraction* rather than by the more usual and obvious way of *addition*. She is a good soul, but really I believe her larder contains nothing but pork, and her pantry nothing but ——pumpkins! She has actually contrived, by some abominable mystery of the kitchen, to keep some of them over through a period of frost and oblivion, and to-day they made their appearance in *due form* on the table again; my horror at which appearance has I believe given me an indigestion, to which you may attribute whatever of gloominess there may be contained in this letter. I certainly felt very *heavy* when I sat down; but the sight of all your faces through fancy's sweet medium has greatly refreshed me.

"Nevertheless answer me speedily, for I am in earnest, although I am in jest.

"I intend to see you at all events soon.

"Love to the little ones and to dear ma and pa from

"RUFUS."

"What does father say, mother?" was all Winthrop's commentary on this epistle. She gave him the other letter, and he yielded his brother's again to her stretched-out hand.

"VANTASSEL, March 22, 1809.

"MY DEAR ORPHAH,

"I am really coming home! I never knew any months so long, it seems to me, as these three. The business will be finished I believe next week, and the Session will rise, and the first use I shall make of my recovered freedom will be—can you doubt it?—to hasten home to my family. My dear family—they are closer to me all the time than you think, and for some weeks past it seems to me they have had half of every thought. But I will be with you now, Providence willing, by the middle of the week, I hope, or as soon after as I can.

"The last fortnight has been spent in talking—we have had a very stormy discussion of that point I spoke to you of in my last.

The opposition of parties has run very high. It is gaining fearful ground in the country. I tremble for what may be the issue.

"I am quite well again. Mr. Haye has been very attentive and kind, and the Chancellor has shewn himself very friendly.

"I expect Will will be at home as soon as I am myself. I wrote to him that he had better do so. I cannot afford to keep him any longer there, and there seems nothing better for him to do at present but to come home. I hope for better days.

"Love to all till I see you, my dear wife and children,

"W. LANDHOLM.

"My son Winthrop, this word is for you. I am coming home soon I hope to relieve you of so much care. Meanwhile a word. I want Sam to go into the north hill-field with the plough, as soon as he can; I think the frost must be out of the ground with you. I intend to put wheat there and in the big border meadow. The bend meadow is in no hurry; it will take corn, I guess. You had better feed out the turnips to the old black cow and the two heifers."

The letters were read at last, and folded up, by the respective hands that held them.

"Well, Will's coming home," the mother said, with half a sigh.

Winthrop did not answer; he made over to her hand the letter he held in his own.

"The north hill-field is pretty much all ploughed already," he remarked.

"You're a good farmer, Governor," said his mother. 'But I am afraid that praise doesn't please you."

"Yes it does, mamma," he answered smiling a little.

"But it don't satisfy you?"

"No more than it does you, mamma. It helps my hope of being a good something else some day."

"I don't care much what you are, Governor, if it is only something *good*," she said.

He met her grave, wistful eyes, but this time he did not smile; and a stranger might have thought he was exceedingly unimpressible. Both were silent a bit.

"Well, it will be good to see them," Mrs. Landholm said, again with that half sighing breath; "and now we must make haste and get all ready to welcome them home."

CHAPTER VII.

Happy he
With such a mother! faith in womankind
Beats with his blood, and trust in all things high
Comes easy to him.

TENNYSON.

WHAT a coming home that was. Who could have guessed that any ungrateful cause had had anything to do with it. What kisses, what smiles, what family rejoicings at the table, what endless talks round the fire. What delight in the returned Member of Assembly; what admiration of the future Collegian. For nobody had given that up: wishes were bidden to wait awhile, that was all; and as the waiting had procured them this dear home-gathering, who could quarrel with it. Nay, there was no eye shaded, there was no voice untuned for the glad music of that time.

"Well it's worth going away, to come back again, ain't it?" said Mr. Landholm, when they were gathered round the fire that first evening.

"No," said his wife.

"Well, I didn't think so last winter," said the father of the family, drawing his broad hand over his eyes.

"I can tell you, *I* have thought so this great while," said Rufus. "It's——it's seven or eight months now since I have been home."

"Papa," said little Winifred, squeezing in and climbing up on her father's knees,—"we have wanted you every night."

"You did!" said her father, bending his face conveniently down to her golden curls;—"and what did you do by day?"

"O we wanted you; but then you know we were so busy in the day-time."

"Busy!" said her father,—"I guess *you* were busy!"

She made herself busy then, for putting both arms round his

neck she pressed and kissed his face, till feeling grew too excited with the indulgence of it, and she lay with her head quite still upon his shoulder where nobody could see her eyes. The father's eyes told tales.

"I think Winifred has forgotten me," observed Rufus.

But Winifred was in no condition to answer the charge.

"Winifred doesn't forget anybody," said her father fondly. "We're none of us given to forgetting. I am thankful that we have one thing that some richer folks want—we all love one another. Winifred,—I thought you were going to shew me that black kitten o' your'n ?"

"I haven't any kitten, papa,—it is Asahel's."

"Well let Asahel bring it then."

Which Asahel did.

"Have you looked at the cattle, Mr. Landholm ?" said his wife.

"No—not yet—this is the first specimen of live stock I've seen," said Mr. Landholm, viewing attentively a little black kitten which was sprawling very uncomfortably upon the painted floor. "I've heard of 'em though. Asahel has been giving me a detail at length of all the concerns of the farm. I think he'll make an excellent corresponding secretary by and by."

"I was only telling papa what Governor had been doing," said Asahel.

"You were afraid *he* would be forgotten. There, my dear, I would let the little cat go back to its mother."

"No papa,—Asahel wanted you should know that *Governor* didn't forget."

"Did you ever hear of the time, Asahel," said his elder brother, "that a cat was sold by the length of her tail ?"

"By the length of her tail ! " said Asahel unbelievingly.

"Yes—for as much wheat as would cover the tip of her tail when she was held so——"

And suiting the action to the word, Rufus suspended the kitten with its nose to the floor and the point of its tail at the utmost height it could reach above that level. Winifred screamed; Asahel sprang; Rufus laughed and held fast.

"It's a shame ! " said Winifred.

"You have no right to do it ! " said Asahel. "It *isn't* the law, if it was the law; and it was a very cruel law ! "

But Rufus only laughed; and there seemed some danger of a break in that kindliness of feeling which their father had vaunted, till Mrs. Landholm spoke. A word and a look of hers, to one and the other, made all smooth; and they went on again talking, of happy nothings, till it was time to separate for the night. It was only then that Mr. Landholm touched on any matter of more than slight interest.

"Well Rufus," he said when at last they rose from their chairs,—"are you all ready for College?"

"Yes sir."

A little shadow upon both faces—a very little.

"I am glad of it. Well keep ready;—you'll go yet one of these days—the time will come. You must see if you can't be contented to keep at home a spell. We'll shove you off by and by."

Neither party very well satisfied with the decision, but there was no more to be said.

To keep at home was plain enough; to be contented was another matter. Rufus joined again in the farm concerns; the well-worn Little River broadcloth was exchanged for homespun; and Winthrop's plough, and hoe, and axe, were mated again as in former time they used to be. This at least was greatly enjoyed by the brothers. There was a constant and lively correspondence between them, on all matters of interest, past, present, and future, and on all matters of speculation attainable by either mind; and though judgments and likings were often much at variance, and the issues, to the same argument, were not always the same with each; on one point, the delight of communication, they were always at one. Clearly Rufus had no love for the axe, nor for the scythe, but he could endure both while talking with Winthrop; though many a time it would happen that axe and scythe would be lost in the interest of other things; and leaning on his snathe, or flinging his axe into a cut, Rufus would stand to argue, or demonstrate, or urge, somewhat just then possessing all his faculties; till a quiet reminder of his brother's would set him to laughing and to work again; and sweetly moved the scythes through the grass, and cheerily rung the axes, for the winrows were side by side and the ringing answered from tree to tree. And the inside of home gave Rufus pleasure too. Yet there were often times,—when talk was at a standstill, and mother's "good things" were not on the table, with a string of happy faces round it, and neither axe nor scythe kept him from a present feeling of inaction,—that the shadow reappeared on Rufus's brow. He would sit in the chimney corner, looking far down into the hearth-stones, or walk moodily up and down the floor, behind the backs of the other people, with a face that seemed to belong to some waste corner of society.

"My son," said Mrs. Landholm, one evening when Mr. Landholm was out and the little ones in bed,—"what makes you wear such a sober face?"

"Nothing, mother,—only that I am doing nothing."

"Are you sure of that? Your father was saying that he never saw anybody sow broadcast with a finer hand—he said you had done a grand day's work to day."

An impatiently drawn breath was the answer.

"Rufus, nobody is doing *nothing* who is doing all that God gives him leave to do."

"No mother——and nobody ever *will* do much who does not hold that leave is given him to make of himself the utmost that he can."

"And what is that?" she said quietly.

Nobody spoke; and then Rufus said, not quietly,

"Depends on circumstances, ma'am;—some one thing and some another."

"My son Rufus,—we all have the same interest at heart with you."

"I am sorry for it, ma'am; I would rather be disappointed alone."

"I hope there will be no disappointment—I do not look for any, in the end. Cannot you bear a little present disappointment?"

"I do bear it, ma'am."

"But Winthrop has the very same things at stake as you have, and I do not see him wear such a disconsolate face,—ever."

"Winthrop—" the speaker began, and paused, every feature of his fine face working with emotion. His hearers waited, but whatever lay behind, nothing more of his meaning came out.

"Winthrop what?—" said his brother laughing.

"You are provokingly cool!" said the other, his eye changing again.

"You have a right to find fault with that," said Winthrop still laughing, "for certainly it is a quality with which *you* never provoked anybody."

Rufus seemed to be swallowing more provocation than he had expressed.

"What were you going to say of me, Rufus?" said the other seriously.

"Nothing—"

"If you meant to say that I have not the same reason to be disappointed that you have, you are quite right."

"I meant to say that; and I meant to say that you do not feel *any* disappointment as much as I do."

Winthrop did not attempt to mend this position. He only mended the fire.

"I wish you need not be disappointed!" the mother said sighing, looking at the fire with a very earnest face.

"My dear mother," said Winthrop cheerfully, "it is no use to wish that in this world."

"Yes it is—for there is a way to escape disappointments,—if you would take it."

"To escape disappointments!" said Rufus.

"Yes."

"What is it?"

"Will you promise to follow it?"

"No mother," he said, with again a singular play of light and shade over his face;—"for it will be sure to be some impossible way. I mean——that an angel's wings may get over the rough ground where poor human feet must stumble."

How much the eyes were saying that looked at each other!

"There is provision even for that," she answered. "'As an eagle stirreth up her nest, fluttereth over her young, spreadeth abroad her wings, taketh them, beareth them on her wings,' so the Lord declares he did once lead his people,—and he will again, —over rough ground or smooth."

"My dear mother," said Rufus, "you are very good, and I——am not very good."

"I don't know that that is much to the point," she said smiling a little.

'Yes it is."

"Do you mean to say you cannot go the road that others have gone, with the same help?"

"If I should say yes, I suppose you would disallow it," he replied, beginning to walk up and down again; "but my consciousness remains the same."

There was both trouble and dissatisfaction in his face.

"Will your consciousness stand this?—'Even the youths shall faint and be weary, a d the young men shall utterly fall; but they that wait upon the Lord shall renew their strength: they shall mount up with wings as eagles,'—just what you were wishing for, Rufus;—'they shall run, and not be weary; and they shall walk, and not faint.'"

He was silent a minute; and then replied, "That will always continue to be realized by some and not by others."

"If you were as easily disheartened in another line, Rufus, you would never go through College."

"My dear mother!" he said, "if you were to knock all my opinions to pieces with the Bible, it wouldn't change me."

"I know it!" she said.

There was extreme depression in voice and lip, and she bent down her face on her hand.

Two turns the length of the room Rufus took; then he came to the back of her chair and laid his hand upon her shoulder.

"But mother," he said cheerfully, "you haven't told us the way to escape disappointments yet; I didn't understand it. For aught I see, everybody has his share. Even you—and I don't know who deserves them less—even you, I am afraid, are disappointed, in me."

It was as much as he could do, evidently, to say that; his eyes were brilliant through fire and water at once. She lifted up her head, but was quite silent.

"How is it, mamma? or how can it be?"

"I must take you to the Bible again, Rufus."

"Well ma'am, I'll go with you. Where?"

She turned over the leaves till she found the place, and giving it to him bade him read.

"'Blessed is the man that walketh not in the counsel of the ungodly, nor standeth in the way of sinners, nor sitteth in the seat of the scornful; but his delight is in the law of the Lord, and in his law doth he meditate, day and night.

"'And he shall be like a tree planted by the rivers of water, that bringeth forth his fruit in due season; his leaf also shall not wither, *and whatsoever he doeth shall prosper*.'"

Rufus stopped and stood looking on the page.

"Beautiful words!" he said.

"They will bear looking at," said Mrs. Landholm.

"But my dear mother, I never heard of anybody in my life of whom this was true."

"How many people have you heard of, in your life, who answered the description?"

Rufus turned and began to walk up and down again.

"But suppose he were to undertake something not well—not right?"

"The security reaches further back," said Winthrop.

"You forget," said his mother, "he could not do that; or could not persist in it."

Rufus walked, and the others sat still and looked at the fire, till the opening of the door let in Mr. Landholm and a cold blast of air; which roused the whole party. Winthrop put more wood on the fire; Mr. Landholm sat down in the corner and made himself comfortable; and Mrs. Landholm fetched an enormous tin pan of potatoes and began paring them. Rufus presently stopped behind her chair, and said softly, "What's that for mother?"

"For your breakfast to-morrow, sir."

"Where is Karen?"

"In bed."

"Why don't you let her do them, mother?"

"She has not time, my son."

Rufus stood still and looked with a discontented face at the thin blue-veined fingers in which the coarse dirty roots were turning over and over.

"I've got a letter from my friend Haye to-day," Mr. Landholm said.

"What Haye is that?" said his wife.

"What Haye?—there's only one that I know of; my old friend Haye—you've heard me speak of him a hundred times. I used to know him long ago in Mannahatta when I lived at Pillicoddy; and we have been in the Legislature together, time and again."

"I remember now," said Mrs. Landholm paring her potatoes. "What does he want?"

"What do you guess he wants?"

"Something from the farm, I suppose."

"Not a bit of it."

"Mr. Haye of Asphodel?" said Rufus.

"Asphodel? no, of Mannahatta;—he used to be at Asphodel."

"What does he want, sir?"

"I am going to tell your mother by and by. It's her concern."

"Well tell it," said Mrs. Landholm.

"How would you like to have some company in the house this summer?"

Mrs. Landholm laid the potatoe and her knife and her hands down in the pan, and looking up asked, "What sort of company?"

"You know he has no wife this many years?"

"Yes—"

"Well—he's a couple of little girls that he wants to put

somewhere in the country this summer, for their health, I understand."

Mrs. Landholm took up her knife again and pared potatoes diligently.

"Does he want to send them here?"

"He intimates as much; and I have no doubt he would be very glad. It wouldn't be a losing concern to us, neither. He would be willing to pay well, and he can afford it."

"What has he done with his own place, at Asphodel?" said Winthrop.

"Sold it, he tells me. Didn't agree with his daughter, the air there, or something, and he says he couldn't be at the bother of two establishments without a housekeeper in nary one of 'em. And I think he's right. I don't see how he could."

Winthrop watched the quick mechanical way in which his mother's knife followed the paring round and round the potatoes, and he longed to say something. "But it is not my affair," he thought; "it is for Rufus. It is not *my* business to speak."

Nobody else spoke for a minute.

"What makes him want to send his children here?" said Mrs. Landholm without looking up from her work.

"Partly because he knows me, I suppose; and maybe he has heard of you. Partly because he knows this is just the finest country in the world, and the finest air, and he wants them to run over the hills and pick wild strawberries and drink country milk, and all that sort of thing. It's just the place for them, as I told him once, I remember."

"You told him!——"

"Yes. He was saying something about not knowing what to do with his girls last winter, and I remember I said to him that he had better send them to me; but I had no more idea of his taking it up, at the time, than I have now of going to Egypt."

Mrs. Landholm did not speak.

"You have somewhere you can put them, I suppose?"

"There's nobody in the big bedroom."

"Well, do you think you can get along with it? or will it give you too much trouble?"

"I am afraid they would never be satisfied, Mr. Landholm, with the way we live."

"Pho! I'll engage they will. Satisfied! they never saw such butter and such bread in their lives, I'll be bound, as you can give them. If they aren't satisfied it'll do 'em good."

"But bread and butter isn't all, Mr. Landholm; what will they do with our dinners, without fresh meat?"

"What will they do with them? Eat 'em, fast enough, only you have enough. I'll be bound their appetites will take care of the rest, after they have been running over the mountains all the morning. You've some chickens, hav'n't you?—and I could get a lamb now and then from neighbour Upshur; and here's Winthrop can get you birds and fish any day in the year."

"Winthrop will hardly have time."

"Yes he will; and if he don't we can call in Anderese. He's a pretty good hunter."

"I'm not a bad one," said Rufus.

"And you have Karen to help you. *I* think it will be a very fine thing, and be a good start maybe towards Rufus's going to College."

Another pause, during which nothing moved but the knife and Mrs. Landholm's fingers.

"Well—what do you say?" said her husband.

"If you think it will do—I am willing to try," she answered.

"I know it will do; and I'll go and write directly to Haye ——I suppose he'd like to know; and to-morrow my hands will have something to hold besides pens."

There was profound silence again for a little after he went out.

"How old are these children?" Mrs. Landholm said.

Neither answered promptly.

"I saw one of them when I was at Asphodel," said Winthrop; "and she was a pretty well grown girl; she must have been thirteen or fourteen."

"And that was a year and a half ago! Is her sister younger or older?"

"It isn't her sister," said Rufus; "it's her cousin, I believe; Mr. Haye is her guardian. She's older."

"How much?"

"A year or two—I don't know exactly."

Mrs. Landholm rose and took up her pan of potatoes with an air that seemed to say Miss Haye and her cousin were both in it, and carried it out into the kitchen.

Some little time had passed, and Winthrop went there to look for her. She had put her pan down on the hearth, and herself by it, and there she was sitting with her arms round her knees.

Winthrop softly came and placed himself beside her.

" Mother—"

She laid her hand upon his knee, without speaking to him or looking at him.

" Mother—I'll be your provider."

" I would a great deal rather be yours, Governor," she said, turning to him a somewhat wistful face.

" There isn't anything in the world I would rather," said he, kissing her cheek.

She gave him a look that was reward enough.

" I wonder how soon they will come," she said.

" That is what I was just asking; and pa said he supposed as soon as the weather was settled."

" That won't be yet awhile. You must see and have a good garden, Governor. Perhaps it will be all for the best."

CHAPTER VIII.

Hills questioning the heavens for light—
  Ravines too deep to scan!
As if the wild earth mimicked there
  The wilder heart of man;
Only it shall be greener far
And gladder, than hearts ever are.
E. B. BROWNING.

IT was the first of June; a fair lovely summer morning, June-like.

"I suppose Mr. Haye will come with them," said Mr. Landholm, as he pushed back his chair from the breakfast-table;—"have you anywhere you can put him?"

"There's the little bedroom, he can have," said Mrs. Landholm. "Asahel can go in the boys' room."

"Very good. Winthrop, you had better take the boat down in good time this afternoon so as to be sure and be there—I can't be spared a moment from the bend meadow. The grass there is just ready to be laid. It's a very heavy swath. I guess there's all of three tons to the acre."

"Take the boat down where?" said Asahel.

"To Cowslip's mill," said his brother. "What time will the stage be along, sir?"

"Not much before six, I expect. You'll have the tide with you to go down."

"It's well to look at the fair side of a subject," said Winthrop, as his father left the room.

"May I go with you, Governor?" said Asahel.

"No sir."

"Why?"

"Because I shall have the tide hard against me coming back."

"But I am not much, and your arms are strong," urged Asahel.

"Very true. Well—we'll see. Mother, do you want any fish to-day?"

A sort of comical taking of the whole subject somehow was expressed under these words, and set the whole family a-laughing. All but Rufus; he was impenetrable. He sat finishing his breakfast without a word, but with a certain significant air of the lip and eyebrow, and dilating nostril, which said something was wrong.

It was the fairest of summer afternoons; the sky June's deep and full-coloured blue, the sun gay as a child, the hills in their young summer dress, just put on; and the water,—well it was running down very fast, but it was running quietly, and lying under the sky and the sunshine it sparkled back their spirit of life and joy. The air was exceeding clear, and the green outlines of the hills rose sharp against the blue sky.

Winthrop stood a minute on one of the rocks at the water's edge to look, and then stepped from that to the one where his boat was moored, and began to undo the chain.

"Are you going down after those people?" said the voice of Rufus behind him. It sounded in considerable disgust.

"What do you advise?" said Winthrop without looking up.

"I would see them at the bottom of the river first!"

"Bad advice," said Winthrop. "It would be a great deal harder to go after them there."

"Do you know what effect your going now will have?"

"Upon them?"

"No, upon you."

"Well—no," said Winthrop looking at the river; "I shall have a pull up, but I shall hardly hear any news of that to-morrow."

"It will make them despise you!"

"That would be rather an effect upon them," said Winthrop, throwing the loosened chain into the boat's head and stepping in himself;—"as it strikes me."

"I wish you would take my advice," said Rufus.

"Which?" said his brother.

"Let them alone!"

"I will," said Winthrop; "I mean that."

"You are excessively provoking!"

"Are you sure?" said Winthrop smiling. "What do you propose that I should do, Rufus?"

"Send Sam Doolittle in your place."

"Willingly; but it happens that he could not fill my place You must see that."

"And are you going to bring up their baggage and all?"

"I must know the sum of two unknown quantities before I can tell whether it is just equal to a boat-load."

Rufus stood on the shore, biting his lip. The little boat was silently slipping out from between the rocks, after a light touch or two of the oars, when Asahel came bounding down the road and claimed Winthrop's promise for a place in it.

"You don't want this child with you!" said Rufus.

But Winthrop gave one or two pushes in the reverse direction and with great skill laid the skiff alongside of the rock. Asahel jumped in triumphantly, and again slowly clearing the rocks the little boat took the tide and the impulse of a strong arm at once, and shot off down the stream.

They kept the mid-channel, and with its swift current soon came abreast of the high out-jutting headland behind which the waters turned and hid themselves from the home view. Diver's Rock, it was called, from some old legend now forgotten. A few minutes more, and the whole long range of the river below was plain in sight, down to a mountain several miles off, behind which it made yet another sharp turn and was again lost. In that range the river ran a little west of south; just before rounding Diver's Rock its direction was near due east, so that the down tide at the turn carried them well over towards the eastern shore. That was what they wanted, as Cowslip's mill was on that side. So keeping just far enough from the shore to have the full benefit of the ebb, they fell softly and quick down the river; with a changing panorama of rocks and foliage at their side, the home promontory of Shahweetah lying in sight just north of them, and over it the heads of the northern mountains; while a few miles below, where the river made its last turn, the mountains on either side locked into one another and at once checked and rested the eye. The lines of ground there were beautiful; the western light sported among them, dividing hill from hill, and crowning their heads with its bright glory. It was the dynasty of the East, just then. The eastern mountains sat in stately pride; and their retainers, the woods, down to the water side, glittered in the royal green and silver; for on their fresh unsullied leaves the light played with many a sheen. The other shore was bright enough still; but the shadows were getting long and the sun was getting low, and the contrast was softly and constantly growing.

"It's pretty, aint it, Winthrop?" said Asahel.

"Yes."

"I wonder what's the reason you row so much better than Rufus—Rufus bites his lip, and works so, and makes such a splash,—and you don't seem as if you worked at all."

"Perhaps because I am stronger," said Winthrop.

"Rufus is strong enough. But that can't be the reason you do everything better than he does."

"That don't happen to be the state of the case."

"Yes it does; for you always catch the most fish, and papa said last summer he never saw any one bind and tie as fast as you did."

Again silently the boat fell down along the shore, a little dark speck amidst the glow of air and water.

"How nice you look in your white jacket and trousers," said Asahel.

"I am glad to hear it," said Winthrop laughing. "Is it such an uncommon thing?"

"It is uncommon for you to look *so* nice. You must take great care of them, Winthrop;—it took mother so long to make them."

"I have another pair, boy," said Winthrop, biting his lips, as the boat rounded to the little flight of steps at Cowslip's mill.

"Yes, but then you know, Karen——There's the stage, Governor!—and the folks are come, I guess. Do you see those heads poking out of the windows?"—

"You stay here and mind the boat, Asahel."

And Winthrop sprang ashore and went up to the crossing where the stage-coach had stopped.

At 'Cowslip's mill' there was a sloop landing; a sort of wharf was built there; and close upon the wharf the mill and storage house kept and owned by Mr. Cowslip. From this central point a road ran back over the hills into the country, and at a little distance it was cut by the high road from Vantassel. Here the stage had stopped.

By the time Winthrop got there, most of the effects he was to take charge of had been safely deposited on the ground. Two young ladies, and a gentleman seeming not far from young, stood at the end of the coach to watch the success of the driver and Mr Cowslip in disinterring sundry trunks and boxes from under the boot and a load of other trunks and boxes.

"Where's Mr. Landholm? isn't Mr. Landholm here?" said the gentleman impatiently.

"There's somebody from Mr. Landholm ahint you," remarked Mr. Cowslip in the course of tugging out one of the trunks.

The gentleman turned.

"Mr. Landholm could not be here, sir," said Winthrop; "but his boat is here, and he has sent me to take care of it."

"He has! Couldn't come himself, eh? I'm sorry for that. —The box from the top of the stage, driver—that's all.—Do you understand the management of a boat?" said he eyeing Winthrop a little anxiously.

"Certainly, sir," said Winthrop. "I am accustomed to act as Mr. Landholm's boatman. I am his son."

"His son, are you! Ah well, that makes all straight. I can trust you. Not his eldest son?"

"No sir."

"I thought it couldn't be the same. Well he's a deuced handsome pair of sons, tell him. I'm very sorry I can't stop,— I am obliged to go on now, and I must put my daughter and Miss Cadwallader in your charge, and trust you to get them safe home. I will be along and come to see you in a few days."

"The trunks is all out, sir," said the driver. "We oughtn't to stop no longer. It's a bad piece atween here and Bearfoot."

"I leave it all to you, then," said Mr. Haye. "Elizabeth, this young gentleman will see you and your baggage safe home. You won't want me. I'll see you next week."

He shook hands and was off, stage-coach and all. And Mr. Cowslip and Winthrop were left mounting guard over the baggage and the ladies. Elizabeth gave a comprehensive glance at the "young gentleman" designated by her father, and then turned it upon the black leather and boards which waited to be disposed of.

"You won't want the hull o' this for ballast, I guess, Winthrop, *this* arternoon," remarked Mr. Cowslip. "You'll have to leave some of it 'long o' me."

"Can't it all go?" said Elizabeth.

"It would be too much for the boat," said Winthrop.

"If 'twouldn't for you,"—Mr. Cowslip remarked in a kind of aside.

"Isn't there another boat?"

"There is another boat," said Mr. Cowslip—"there's mine —but she's up stream somewheres; comin' along, I guess, but she won't be here time enough for your purposes."

It was necessary to make a selection. The selection was made, and two stout trunks were successively borne down to the shore by the hands of Winthrop and Mr. Cowslip and stowed in the boat's bow. The two girls had walked down and stood looking on.

"But I haven't got any books!" said Elizabeth suddenly when she was invited to get in herself. "Won't the book-box go?"

"Is it that 'ere big board box?" inquired Mr. Cowslip. "Won't do! It's as heavy as all the nation."

"It will not do to put anything more in the boat," said Winthrop.

"I can't go without books," said Elizabeth.

"You'll have 'em in the mornin'," suggested the miller.

"O leave it, Lizzie, and come along!" said her companion. "See how late it's getting."

"I can't go without some books," said Elizabeth; "I shouldn't know what to do with myself. You are sure you can't take the box?"

"Certainly," said Winthrop smiling. "She would draw too much water, with this tide."

"Yes, you'd be on the bottom and no mistake, when you got in the bay," said Mr. Cowslip.

Elizabeth looked from one to the other.

"Then just get something and open the box if you please," she said, indicating her command to Winthrop; "and I will take out a few, till I get the rest."

"O Lizzie!" urged her companion,—"let the books wait!"

But she and her expostulation got no sort of attention. Miss Lizzie walked up the hill again to await the unpacking of the box. Miss Cadwallader straightened herself against a post. While Mr. Cowslip and Winthrop went to the store for a hammer.

"She's got spunk in her, ha'n't she, that little one?" said the miller. "She's a likely lookin' little gal, too. But I never seen any one so fierce arter books, yet."

Tools were soon found, in Mr. Cowslip's store, but the box was strongly put together and the opening of it was not a very speedy business. The little proprietor looked on patiently. When it was open, Miss Lizzie was not very easy to suit. With great coolness she stood and piled up book after book on the uncovered portion of the box, till she had got at those she wanted. She pleased herself with two or three, and then the others were carefully put back again; and she stood to watch the fastening up of the box as it was before.

"It will be safe here?" she said to the miller.

"Safe enough!" he answered. "There's nobody here'll want to pry open these here books, agin this night."

"And will the other things be safe?" said Miss Cadwallader, who had come up the hill again in despair. The miller glanced at her.

"Safe as your hair in curl-papers. You can be comfortable. Now then—"

The sun was not far from the mountain tops, when at last Miss Lizzie stood again at the water's edge with her volumes. Miss Cadwallader grumbled a little, but it met the utmost carelessness. The tide was very low; but by the help of Winthrop in the boat and Mr. Cowslip on the muddy steps, the young ladies were safely passed down and seated in the stern-sheets, not without two or three little screams on the part of Miss Cadwallader. The other, quite silent, looked a little strangely at the water coming within three or four inches of her dress, an expression of grave timidity becoming her dark eye much better than the look it had worn a few minutes before. As the boat lurched a little on pushing off, the colour started to her cheeks, and she asked "if there was any danger?"

"Not the least," Winthrop said.

Elizabeth gave another look at the very self-possessed calm face of her boatman, and then settled herself in her place with the unmistakable air of a mind at ease.

The boat had rounded the corner of the wharf and fell into its upward track, owing all its speed now to the rower's good arm; for a very strong down tide was running against them. They crept up, close under the shore, the oars almost touching the rocks; but always, as if a spirit of divination were in her, the little boat turned its head from the threatened danger, edged in and out of the mimic bays and hollows in the shores, and kept its steady onward way. The scene was a fairy-land scene now. Earth, water, and air, were sparkling with freshness and light. The sunlight lay joyously in the nest of the southern mountains, and looked over the East, and smiled on the heads of the hills in the north; while cool shadows began to walk along the western shore. Far up, a broad shoulder of the mountain stood out in bright relief under the sun's pencil; then lower down, the same pencil put a glory round the heads of the valley cedars; the valley was in shadow. Sharp and clear shewed sun-touched points of rock on the east shore, in glowing colours; and on the west the hills raised huge shadowy sides towards the sun, whom they threatened they would hide from his pensioners. And the sun stood on the mountain's brow and blinked at the world, and then dropped down; and the West had it! Not yet, but soon.

The two girls were not unmindful of all the brightness about them, for their eyes made themselves very busy with it, and little low-toned talks were held which now and then let a word escape, of "pretty!"—and "lovely!"—and "wouldn't it be lovely to have a little boat here?—I'll ask papa!"—

"'Is it hard to row?" asked the last speaker suddenly of Winthrop.

"No," he said, "not at all, wind and water quiet."

"Aren't they quiet to-night?"

"The tide is running down very strong. Asahel, trim the boat."

"How on earth can such a child do anything to the boat?' said Miss Cadwallader. "What do you want done, sir?"

"Nothing," he said. "It is done."

"*What* is done?" said the young lady, with a wondering face to her companion. "Oh aren't you hungry?" she added with a yawn. "I am, dreadfully. I hope we shall get a good supper."

"Whereabouts is Mr. Landholm's house?" said Elizabeth presently. Winthrop lay on his oars to point it out to her.

"*That?*" she said, somewhat expressively.

"Then why don't you go straight there?" inquired her companion. "You are going directly the other way."

A slight fiction; but the boat had turned into the bay, and was following the curve of its shores, which certainly led down deep into the land from the farmhouse point.

"I go here for the eddy."

"He is going right," said Asahel, who was sitting on the thwart next to the ladies.

"Eddy?" said Miss Cadwallader, with a blank look at her cousin.

"What is an eddy?" said Elizabeth.

"The return water from a point the tide strikes against."

Elizabeth eyed the water, the channel, and the *points*, and was evidently studying the matter out.

"What a lovely place!" she said.

"I wonder if the strawberries are ripe," said Miss Cadwallader. "Little boy, are there any strawberries in your woods?"

"My name is Asahel," said the 'little boy' gravely.

"Is it? I am very glad indeed to know it. Are there any strawberries in the woods here?"

"Lots of 'em," said Asahel.

"Are they ripe yet?"

"I haven't seen more than half a dozen," said Asahel.

"They are just beginning in the sunny spots," said his brother smiling.

"And do you have anything else here besides strawberries?"

The question was put to Asahel. He looked a little blank. It was a broad one.

"Any other fruit," said Elizabeth.

"Plenty," said Asahel.

"What?" said Miss Cadwallader; "tell us, will you; for I've come here to live upon wild fruit."

"Yes, ma'am," said Asahel staring a little;—"there's red raspberries, and black raspberries, and low-bush blackberries and high blackberries, and huckleberries, and bearberries, and cranberries; besides nuts, and apples. I guess that ain't all."

"Thank you," said his questioner. "That will do. I don't intend to stay till nut-time. Oh what a way it is round this bay!"

"I wish it was longer," said Elizabeth.

The sun had left all the earth and betaken himself to the clouds; and there he seemed to be disporting himself with all the colours of his palette. There were half a dozen at a time flung on his vapoury canvass, and those were changed and shaded, and mixed and deepened,—till the eye could but confess there was only one such storehouse of glory. And when the painting had faded, and the soft scattering masses were left to their natural grey, here a little silvered and there a little reddened yet,—the whole West was still lit up with a clear white radiance that shewed how hardly the sun's bright track could be forgotten.

"Are we here!" said Elizabeth with a half sigh, as the boat touched the rocks.

"Yes, to be sure," said her cousin. "Where have you been?"

"In the clouds; and I am sorry to come down again."

Mr. Landholm was standing on the rocks, and a very frank and hearty reception he gave them. With him they walked up to the house; Asahel staid behind to wait till Winthrop had made fast the boat.

"How do you like 'em, Governor?" whispered the little boy crouching upon the rocks to get nearer his brother's ear.

"How do I like 'em?" said Winthrop;—"I can't like anybody upon five minutes' notice."

"One of 'em's pretty, ain't she?—the one with the light-coloured hair?"

"I suppose so," said Winthrop, tying his chain.

"I guess they like it here pretty well," Asahel went on. "Didn't you see how they looked at everything?"

"No."

"They looked up, and they looked down, and on one side and the other side; and every now and then they looked at you."

"And what did you look at?"

"I looked at them,—some."

"Well," said Winthrop laughing, "don't look at them too much, Asahel."

"Why not?"

"Why, you wouldn't want to do anything *too* much, would you?"

"No. But what would be too much?"

"So much that they would find it out."

"Well, they didn't find it out this evening," said Asahel.

But that little speech went home, and for half the way as he walked up to the house holding Asahel's hand, there was something like bitterness in the heart of the elder brother. So long, but no longer. They had got only so far when he looked down at the little boy beside him and spoke with his usual calm clearness of tone, entire and unchanged.

"Then they aren't as clear-sighted as I am, Asahel, for I always know when you are looking at me."

"Ah, I don't believe you do!" said Asahel laughing up at him; "I very often look at you when you don't look at me."

"Don't trust to that," said Winthrop.

There was in the little boy's laugh, and in the way he wagged his brother's hand backwards and forwards, a happy and confident assurance that Winthrop could do anything, that it was good to do.

Everybody was at the supper-table; there was nothing for Winthrop then to do but to take his place; but his *countenance* to his mother, all supper-time, was worth a great deal. His cool collected face at her side heartened her constantly, though he scarcely spoke at all. Mr. Landholm played the part of host with no drawback to his cheerfulness; talked a great deal, and pressed all the good things of the table upon Miss Cadwallader; who laughing, talking, and eating, managed to do her full share of all three. She was certainly very pretty. Her 'light coloured' hair was not so light as to be uncomely, and fell in luxuriant ringlets all round the sides of her pretty head; and the head moved about enough to shake the ringlets, till they threatened to form a mazy not to catch men's eyes. The prettiest mouth in the world, set with two little rows of the most kissable teeth, if that feature ever is contemplated in a kiss; and like the ringlets, the lips seemed to be in a compact to do as much mischief as they could; to keep together and mind their own business was the last thing thought of. Yet it was wonderful how much business they managed to transact on their own account, too. The other girl sat grave and reserved, even almost with an air of shyness, eat much less, and talked none at all; and indeed her face was pale and thin, and justified what her father had said about her wanting the country. Rufus seemed to have got back his good-humour. He quite kept up the credit of his side of the table.

Immediately after supper the two girls went to their room.

"Well, how do you like 'em?" said Mr. Landholm. "Did ye ever see a prettier creature, now, than that Rose? Her face is like a rose itself."

"It is more like a peach-blossom," said Rufus.

"The little one don't look well," said Mrs. Landholm.

"I wonder who'll go strawberrying with them," said Asahel.

CHAPTER IX.

Mat. "He is of a rustical cut, I know not how; he doth not carry himself like a gentleman o. fashion.
Wel. 'Oh, Mr. Matthew, that's a grace peculiar but to a few."
EVERY MAN IN HIS HUMOUR.

THE 'big bedroom,' which belonged to the strangers by right of usage, opened from the kitchen; with another door upon the tiny entry-way once described. It had a fireplace, at present full of green pine bushes; a very clean bed covered with patchwork; the plainest of chairs and a table; and a little bit of carpet on one spot of the floor; the rest was painted. One little window looked to the south; another to the east; the woodwork, of doors and windows, exceeding homely and *un*painted. An extraordinary gay satin toilet-cushion; and over it a little looking-glass, surrounded and surmounted with more than an equal surface of dark carved wooden framing.

It was to this unwonted prospect that the early June sun opened the young ladies' eyes the next morning. Elizabeth had surveyed it quietly a few minutes, when a little rustling of the patchwork called her attention to the shaking shoulders of her companion. Miss Cadwallader's pretty face lay back on the pillow, her eyes shut tight, and her open mouth expressing all the ecstatic delight that could be expressed without sound.

"What is the matter?" said Elizabeth.

Her cousin only laughed the harder and clapped her hands over her eyes, as if quite beyond control of herself. Elizabeth did not ask again.

"Isn't this a funny place we've come to!" said Miss Cadwallader at last, relapsing.

"I don't see anything very laughable," said Elizabeth.

"But isn't it a *quizzical* place?"

"I dare say. Every place is."

"Pshaw! don't be obstinate,—when you think just as I do."

"I never did yet, about anything," said Elizabeth.

"Well, how do *you* like eating in a room with a great dresser of tin dishes on one side and the fire where your meat was cooked on the other?—in June?"

"I didn't see the tin dishes; and there wasn't any fire, of consequence."

"But did you ever see such a gallant old farmer? Isn't he comical? didn't he keep it up?"

"Not better than you did," said Elizabeth.

"But isn't he comical?"

"No; neither comical nor old. I thought you seemed to like him very well."

"O, one must do something. La! you aren't going to get up yet?"

But Elizabeth was already at the south window and had it open. Early it was; the sun not more than half an hour high, and taking his work coolly, like one who meant to do a great deal before the day was ended. A faint dewy sparkle on the grass and the sweetbriars; the song sparrows giving good-morrow to each other and tuning their throats for the day; and a few wood thrushes now and then telling of their shyer and rarer neighbourhood. The river was asleep, it seemed, it lay so still.

"Lizzie!—you ought to be in bed yet these two hours—I shall tell Mr. Haye, if you don't take care of yourself."

"Have the goodness to go to sleep, and let me and Mr. Haye take care of each other," said the girl dryly.

Her cousin looked at her a minute, and then turning her eyes from the light, obeyed her first request and went fast asleep.

A little while after the door opened and Elizabeth stood in the kitchen. It was already in beautiful order. She could see the big dresser now, but the tin and crockery and almost the wooden shelves shone, they were so clean. And they shone in the light of an opposite fire; but though the second of June, the air so early in the morning was very fresh; Elizabeth found it pleasant to take her stand on the hearth, near the warm blaze. And while she stood there, first came in Karen and put on the big iron tea-kettle; and then came Mrs. Landholm with a table-cloth and began to set the table. Elizabeth looked alternately at her and at the tea-kettle; both almost equally strange; she rather took a fancy to both. Certainly to the former. Her gown was spare, shewing that means were so, and her cap was the plainest of muslin caps, without lace or bedecking; yet in the quiet ordering of gown and cap and the neat hair, a quiet and ordered mind was almost confessed; and not many glances at the calm mouth and grave brow and thoughtful eye, would make the opinion good. It was a very comfortable home picture, Elizabeth thought, in a different line of life from that she was accustomed to,—the farmer's wife and the tea-kettle, the dresser and the breakfast table, and the wooden kitchen floor and the stone hearth. She did not know what a contrast *she* made in it; her dainty little figure, very nicely dressed, standing on the flag-stones before the fire. Mrs. Landholm felt it, and doubted.

"How do you like the place, Miss Haye?" she ventured.

To her surprise the answer was an energetic, "Very much."

"Then you are not afraid of living in a farm-house?"

"If I don't like living in it, I'll live out of it," said Elizabeth, returning a very dignified answer to Winthrop's 'good-morning' as he passed through the kitchen.

"Are you going down to Cowslip's mill, Governor?" said Mrs. Landholm.

"Yes, ma'am."

"You will lose your breakfast."

"I must take the turn of the tide. Never mind breakfast."

"Going down after my trunks?" said Elizabeth.

"Yes, ma'am."

"I'll go too. Wait a minute!"

And she was in her room before a word could be said.

"But Miss Haye," said Mrs. Landholm, as she came out with bonnet and shawl, "you won't go without your breakfast? It will be ready long before you can get back."

"Breakfast can wait."

"But you will want it."

"No—I don't care if I do."

And down she ran to the rocks, followed by Asahel.

There was a singular still sweetness in the early summer morning on the water. The air seemed to have twice the life it had the evening before; the light was fair, beyond words to tell. Here its fresh gilding was upon a mountain slope; there it stretched in a long misty beam athwart a deep valley; it touched the broken points of rock, and glanced on the river, and seemed to make merry with the birds; fresh, gladsome and pure as their song. No token of man's busy life yet in the air; the birds had it. Only over Shahweetah valley, and from Mr. Underhill's chimney on the other side of the river, and from Sam Doolittle's in the bay, thin wreaths of blue smoke slowly went up, telling that there,—and there,—and there,—man was getting ready for his day's work, and woman had begun hers! Only those, and the soft stroke of Winthrop's oars; but to Elizabeth that seemed only play. She sat perfectly still, her eye varying from their regular dip to the sunny rocks of the headland, to the coloured mountain heads, the trees, the river, the curling smoke,—and back again to the oars; with a grave, intent, deep notice-taking. The water was neither for nor against them now; and with its light load and its good oars the boat flew. Diver's Rock was passed; then they got out of the sunshine into the cool shadow of the eastern shore below the bay, and fell down the river fast to the mill. Not a word was spoken by anybody till they got there.

Nor then by Elizabeth, till she saw Mr. Cowslip and Winthrop bringing her trunks and boxes to the boat-side.

"Hollo! you've got live cargo too, Governor," said the old miller. "That aint fair,—Mornin'!—The box is safe."

"Are you going to put those things in here?" said Elizabeth.

"Sartain," said Mr. Cowslip;—"book-box and all."

"But they'll be too much for the boat?"

"Not at all," said Winthrop; "it was only because the tide was so low last night—there wasn't water enough in the bay. I am not going in the bay this morning."

"No," said Mr. Cowslip,—"tide's just settin' up along shore—you can keep along the edge of the flats."

"You have load enough without them. Don't put 'em in here, sir!" Elizabeth exclaimed;—"let them go in the other boat—your boat—you said you had a boat—it's at home now, isn't it?"

"Sartain," said Mr. Cowslip, "it's to hum, so it can start off again as soon as you like. My boy Hild can fetch up the things for you—if you think it's worth while to have it cost you a dollar."

"I don't care what it costs," said Elizabeth. "Send 'em up right away, and I'll pay for it."

So Winthrop dropped into his place again, and lightly and swiftly as before the boat went on her way back towards the blue smoke that curled up over Shahweetah; and Elizabeth's eyes again roved silently and enjoyingly from one thing to another. But they returned oftener to the oars, and rested there, and at last when they were about half way home, she said,

"I want to learn how to manage an oar—will you let me take one and try?"

Winthrop helped her to change her seat and put an oar into her hand, and gave her directions. The first attempts took effect upon nothing but Asahel's face, which gave witness to his amusement; and perhaps Winthrop's dress, which was largely splashed in the course of a few minutes. But Elizabeth did not seem to heed or care for either; she was intent upon the great problem of making her oar *feel* the water; and as gravely, if not quite so coolly, as Winthrop's instructions were delivered, she worked at her oar to follow them. A few random strokes, which did not seem to discriminate very justly between water and air, and then her oar had got hold of the water and was telling, though irregularly and fitfully, upon the boat. The difficulty was mastered; and she pulled with might and main for half the rest of the way home; Winthrop having nothing to do with his one oar but to keep the two sides of the boat together, till her arm was tired.

"Next time I'll take both oars," she said with a face of great satisfaction as she put herself back in her old seat. Asahel thought it would cure her of wearing pale cheeks, but he did not venture to make any remark.

Rose was waiting for them, sitting crouched discontentedly on the rocks.

"It's eight o'clock!"—said she,—"and I'm as hungry as a bear!"

"So am I," said Elizabeth springing ashore.

"What have you been doing?—keeping breakfast waiting this age?"

"I never saw any thing so delicious in all my life," said Elizabeth emphatically, before condescending to say what.

"I shall tell Mr. Haye you are beginning a flirtation already," whispered Miss Cadwallader laughing as they went up to the house.

But the cheek of the other at that became like a thunder-cloud. She turned her back upon her cousin and walked from her to the house, with a step as fine and firm as that of the Belvidere Apollo and a figure like a young pine tree. Rufus, who met her at the door, was astounded with a salutation such as a queen might bestow on a discarded courtier; but by the time the little lady came to the table she had got back her usual air.

"Well, how do you like boating before breakfast?" said Mr Landholm.

"*Very* much," Elizabeth said.

"I dont like it very much," said he, "for I ought to have

mowed half an acre by this time, instead of being here at my bread and butter."

"It was not my fault, sir."

"No, no; it's all right, I am glad you went. I should have taken my breakfast and been off, long ago; but I waited out of pure civility to you, to see how you did. 'Pon my word, I think you have gained half a pound of flesh already."

"She looks a great deal better," said Asahel.

Elizabeth laughed a little, but entered into no discussion of the subject.

After breakfast the trunks arrived and the young ladies were busy; and two or three days passed quietly in getting wonted.

"Mr. Landholm," said Miss Cadwallader, a few mornings after, "will you do one thing for me?"

"A great many, Miss Rose," he said, stopping with his hands on his knees as he was about to leave the table, and looking at her attentively.

"I want you to send somebody to shew me where the strawberries are."

"Strawberries! Do you want to go and pick strawberries?"

"To be sure I do. That's what I came here for."

"Strawberries, eh," said Mr. Landholm. "Well, I guess you'll have to wait a little. There aint a soul that can go with you this morning. Besides, I don't believe there are any ripe yet."

"O yes there are, papa!" said Asahel.

"I guess Bright Spot's full of them," said Mrs. Landholm.

"Bright Spot!" said the farmer. "Well, *we* must be all off to the hay-field. You see, there's some grass, Miss Rose, standing ready to be cut, that *can't* wait; so you'll have to."

"What if it wasn't cut?" said Miss Cadwallader pouting.

"What if it wasn't cut!—then the cattle would have nothing to eat next winter, and that would be worse than your wanting strawberries. No—I'll tell you,—It'll be a fine afternoon; and you keep yourself quiet, out of the sun, till it gets towards evening; and I'll contrive to spare one of the boys to go with you The strawberries will be all the riper, and you can get as many as you want in an hour or two."

So upon that the party scattered, and the house was deserted to the 'women-folks;' with the exception of little Asahel; and even he was despatched in a few hours to the field with the dinner of his father and brothers. The girls betook themselves to their room, and wore out the long day as they could.

It grew to the tempting time of the afternoon.

"Here they are!" said Rose who sat at the east window. "Now for it! That farmer is a very good man. I really didn't expect it."

"*They?*" said Elizabeth.

"Yes—both the 'boys,' as the farmer calls them."

"I should think one might have been enough," said Elizabeth.

"Well there's no harm in having two. Isn't the eldest one handsome?"

"I don't know."

"You *do* know."

"I don't! for I haven't thought about it."

"Do you have to think before you can tell whether a person is handsome?"

"Yes;—before I can tell whether I think he is."

"Well look at him,—I tell you he has the most splendid eyes."

"Rose Cadwallader!" said her cousin laying down her book, "what is it to you or me if all the farmer's sons in the land have splendid eyes?"

Elizabeth's eyebrows said it was very little to her.

"I like to look at a handsome face anywhere," said Rose pouting. "Come—will you."

Elizabeth did come, but with a very uncompromising set of the said eyebrows.

It appeared that everybody was going strawberrying, except Mrs. Landholm and Winthrop; at least the former had not her bonnet on, and the latter was not in the company at all. The children found this out and raised a cry of dismay, which was changed into a cry of entreaty as Winthrop came in. Winthrop was going after fish. But Winifred got hold of his hand, and Asahel withstood him with arguments; and at last Mrs. Landholm put in her gentle word, that strawberries would do just as well as fish, and better. So Winthrop put up his fishing-rod and shouldered the oars, and armed with baskets of all sizes the whole party trooped after him.

In the boat Elizabeth might have had a good opportunity to act upon her cousin's request; for Rufus sat in the stern with them and talked, while Winthrop handled the oars. But Rufus and her cousin had the talk all to themselves; Elizabeth held off from it, and gave her eyes to nothing but the river and the hills.

They crossed the river, going a little up, to a tiny green valley just at the water's edge. On every side but the river it was sheltered and shut in by woody walls nigh two hundred feet in height. The bottom of the valley was a fine greensward, only sprinkled with trees; while from the edge of it the virgin forest rose steeply to the first height, and then following the broken ground stretched away up to the top of the neighbouring mountains. From the valley bottom, however, nothing of these could be seen; nothing was to be seen but its own leafy walls and the blue sky above them.

"Is this the place where we are to find strawberries?" said Miss Cadwallader.

"This is the place," said Rufus; "this is Bright Spot, from time out of mind the place for strawberries; nobody ever comes here but to pick them. The vines cover the ground."

"The sun won't be on it long," said Elizabeth; "I don't see why you call it Bright Spot."

"You won't often see a brighter spot when the sun *is* on it," said Winthrop. "It gets in the shadow of Wut-a-qut-o once in a while."

"The grass is kept very fresh here," said Rufus. "But the strawberry vines are all over in it."

So it was proved. The valley was not a smooth level as it had looked from the river, but broken into little waves and hollows of ground; in parts, near the woods, a good deal strewn with loose rocks and grown with low clumpy bushes of different species of cornus, and buckthorn, and sweetbriar. In these nooks and hollows, and indeed over the whole surface of the ground the vines ran thick, and the berries, huge, rich and rare, pretended to hide themselves, while the whole air was alive with their sweetness.

The party landed and scattered with cries of delight far and near over the valley. Even Elizabeth's composure gave way. For a little while they did nothing but scatter; to sit still and pick was impossible; for the novelty and richness of the store seemed made for the eye as much as for anything else, and be the berries never so red in one place they seemed redder in another. Winthrop and Asahel, however, were soon steadily at work, and then little Winifred; and after a time Miss Cadwallader found that the berries were good for more than to look at, and Rufus had less trouble to keep in her neighbourhood. But it was a good while before Elizabeth began to pick either for lip or basket; she stood on the viney knolls, and looked, and smelled the air, and searched with her eye the openings in the luxuriant foliage that walled in the valley. At last, making a review of the living members of the picture, the young lady bethought herself, and set to work with great steadiness to cover the bottom of her basket.

In the course of this business, moving hither and thither as the bunches of red fruit tempted her, and without raising an eye beyond them, she was picking close to one of the parties before she knew whom she was near; and as they were in like ignorance she heard Asahel say,

"I wish Rufus would pick—he does nothing but eat, ever since he came; he and Miss Rose."

"You don't expect *her* to pick for you, do you?" said Winthrop.

"She might just as well as for me to pick for her," said Asahel.

"Do you think we'll get enough for mamma, Governor?" said little Winifred in a very sweet, and a little anxious, voice.

"We'll try," said her brother.

"O you've got a great parcel!—but I have only so many,—Governor?"

"There's more where those came from, Winnie."

"Here are some to help," said Elizabeth coming up and emptying her own strawberries into the little girl's basket. Winifred looked down at the fresh supply and up into the young lady's face, and then gave her an "Oh thank you!" of such frank pleasure and astonishment that Elizabeth's energies were at once nerved. But first of all she went to see what Miss Cadwallader was about.

Miss Cadwallader was squatting in a nest of strawberries, with red finger-ends.

"Rose—how many have you picked?"

"I haven't the least idea. Aren't they splendid?"

"Haven't you any in your basket?"

"Basket?—no,—where is my basket?" said she looking round. "No, to be sure I haven't. I don't want any basket."

"Why don't you help?"

"Help? I've been helping myself, till I'm tired. Come here and sit down, Bess. Aren't they splendid? Don't you want to rest?"

"No."

Miss Rose, however, quitted the strawberries and placed herself on a rock.

"Where's my helper?—O yonder,—somebody's got hold of him. Lizzie,—who'd have thought we should be so well off for beaux here in the mountains?"

The other's brow and lip changed, but she stood silent.

"They don't act like farmer's sons, do they? I never should have guessed it if I had seen them anywhere else. Look, Lizzie, —now isn't he handsome? I never saw such eyes."

Elizabeth did not look, but she spoke, and the words lacked no point that lips could give them.

"I am thankful, Rose, that *my* head does not run upon the things that yours does!"

"What does yours run upon then?" said Rose pouting. "The other one, I suppose. That's the one you were helping with your strawberries just now. I dont think it is the wisest thing Mr. Haye has ever done, to send you and me here;—it's a pity there wasn't somebody to warn him."

"Rose!"—said the other, and her eyes seemed to lighten, one to the other, as she spoke,—"you know I don't like such talk—I detest and despise it!—it is utterly beneath me. You may indulge in all the nonsense you please, and descend to what you please;—but please to understand, *I will not hear it.*"

Miss Cadwallader's eye fairly gave way under the lightning. Elizabeth's words were delivered with an intensity that kept them quiet, though with the last degree of clear utterance; and turning, as Rufus came up, she gave him a glare of her dark brown eyes that astonished him, and made off with a quick step to a part of the field where she could pick strawberries at a distance from everybody. She picked them somehow by instinct; she did not know what she was doing; her face rivalled their red bunches, and she picked with a kind of fury. That being the only way she had of venting her indignation, she threw it into her basket along with the strawberries. She hadn't worked so hard the whole afternoon. She edged away from the rest towards a wild corner, where amid rocks and bushes the strawberry vines spread rich and rank and the berries were larger and finer than any she had seen. She was determined to have a fine basketful for Winifred.

But she was unused to such stooping and steady work, and as she cooled down she grew very tired. She was in a rough grown place and she mounted on a rock and stood up to rest herself and look.

Pretty—pretty, it was. It was almost time to go home, for the sun was out of their strawberry patch and the woody walls were a few shades deeper coloured than they had been; while over the river, on the other side, the steep rocks of the home point sent back a warm glow yet. The hills beyond them stood in the sun, and in close contrast was the little deep green patch of foreground, lit up with the white or the gay dresses of the strawberry pickers. The sweet river, a bit of it, in the middle of the picture, half in sunshine, half in shade. It was like a little nest of fairy-land; so laughed the sunshine so dwelt the shade, in this spot and in that one. Elizabeth stood fast. It was bewitching to the eyes. And while she looked, the shadow of Wut-a-qut-o was creeping over the river, and now ready to take off the warm browns of the rocky point.

She was thinking it was bewitching, and drinking it in, when she felt two hands clasp her by the waist, and suddenly, swiftly, without a word of warning, she was swung off, clear to another rock about two yards distant, and there set down, "all standing." In bewildered astonishment, that only waited to become indignation, she turned to see whom she was to be angry with. Nobody was near her but Winthrop, and he had disappeared behind the rock on which she had just been standing. Elizabeth was not precisely in a mood for cool judgment; she stood like an offended brood-hen, with ruffled feathers, waiting to fly at the first likely offender. The rest of the party began to draw near.

"Come Lizzie, we're going home," said her cousin.

"I am not," said Elizabeth.

"Why?"

"Because I am not ready."

"What's the matter?"

"Nothing—only I am not ready."

"The sun's out of Bright Spot now, Miss Haye," said Rufus, with a somewhat mischievous play of feature.

Elizabeth was deaf.

"Winthrop has killed a rattlesnake!" exclaimed Asahel from the rock;—"Winthrop has killed a rattlesnake!"

And Winthrop came round the bushes bringing his trophy; a large snake that counted nine rattles. They all pressed round, as near as they dared, to look and admire; all but Elizabeth, who stood on her rock and did not stir.

"Where was it? where was it?"—

"When I first saw him, he was curled up on the rock very near to Miss Haye, but he slid down among the bushes before I could catch him. We must take care when we come here now, for the mate must be somewhere."

"*I'll* never come here again," said Miss Cadwallader. "O come!—let us go!"

"Did *you* move me?" said Elizabeth, with the air of a judge putting a query.

Winthrop looked up, and answered yes.

"Why didn't you ask me to move myself?"

"I would," said Winthrop calmly,—"if I could have got word to the snake to keep quiet."

Elizabeth did not know precisely what to say; her cousin was looking in astonishment, and she saw the corners of Rufus's mouth twitching; she shut her lips resolutely and followed the party to the boat.

The talking and laughing was general among them on the way home, with all but her; she was thinking. She even forgot her strawberries for little Winifred, which she meant to have given her in full view of her cousin. She held her basket on her lap, and looked at the water and didn't see the sunset.

The sun's proper setting was not to be seen, for he went down far behind Wut-a-qut-o. Wut-a-qut-o's shade was all over the river and had mounted near to the top of the opposite hills; but from peak to peak of them the sunlight glittered still, and overhead the sun threw down broad remembrancers of where he was and where he had been. The low hills in the distant north were all in sunlight; as the little boat pulled over the river they were lost behind the point of Shahweetah, and the last ray was gone from the last mountain ridge in view. Cool shadows and lights were over the land, a flood of beauty overhead in the sky.

It was agreed on all hands that they had been very successful; and little Winifred openly rejoiced over the quantity they had brought home for 'mother'; but still Elizabeth did not add her store, and had nothing to say. When they got to the landing-place, she would stay on the rocks to see how the boat was made fast. Winifred ran up to the house with her basket, Miss Cadwallader went to get ready for supper, Rufus followed in her steps. Asahel and Elizabeth stayed in the sunset glow to see Winthrop finish his part of the work; and then they walked up together. Elizabeth kept her position on one side of the oars, but seemed as moody as ever, till they were about half way from the rocks; then suddenly she looked up into Winthrop's face and said,

"Thank you. I ought to have said it before."

He bowed a little and smiled, in a way that set Elizabeth a thinking. It was *not* like a common farmer's boy. It spoke him as quiet in his own standing as she was in hers; and yet he certainly had come home that day in his shirt sleeves, and with his mower's jacket over his arm? It was very odd.

"What was it you said that strawberry-place was in the shadow of sometimes?"

"Wut-a-qut-o?"

"What's that?"

"The big mountain over there. *This* was in the shadow of it a little while ago."

"What a queer name! What does it mean?"

"It is Indian. I have heard that it means, the whole name, —'*He that catches the clouds.*'"

"That is beautiful!—

"You must be tremendously strong," she added presently, as if not satisfied that she had said enough,—"for you lifted me as if I had been no more than a featherweight."

"You did not seem much more," he said.

"Strong!—" said Asahel—

But Elizabeth escaped from Asahel's exposition of the subject, into her room.

She had regained her good-humour, and everybody at the table said she had improved fifty per cent. since her coming to Shahweetah. Which opinion Mr. Haye confirmed when he came a day or two afterward.

CHAPTER X.

> *Cam.* Be advised.
> *Flo.* I am; and by my fancy: if my reason
> Will thereto be obedient, I have reason;
> If not, my senses, better pleased with madness,
> Do bid it welcome. WINTER'S TALE.

THE young ladies' summering in the country had begun with good promise; there was no danger they would tire of it. Mr. Haye gave it as his judgment that his daughter had come to the right place; and he was willing to spare no pains to keep her in the same mind. He brought up a little boat with him the next time he came, and a delicate pair of oars; and Elizabeth took to boating with great zeal. She asked for very little teaching; she had used her eyes, and now she patiently exercised her arms, till her eyes were satisfied; and after that the "Merry-go-round" had very soon earned a right to its name. Her father sent her a horse; and near every morning her blue habit was fluttering along the roads, to the great admiration of the country people who had never seen a long skirt before. And every afternoon, as soon as the sun hid himself behind the great western mountain, her little white boat stole out from the rocks and coasted about under the point or lay in the bay, wandering through sunshine and shade; loitering where the north wind blew softly, or resting with poised oars when the sun was sending royal messages to earth *via* the clouds. On horseback or in the boat,—Miss Elizabeth would not take exercise in so common a way as walking,—she did honour to the nurture of the fresh air. The thin cheek rounded out; and sallow and pale gave place to the clear rich colour of health.

Asahel was her general companion in the boat. Sometimes her cousin condescended to enjoy a sail of a summer's evening, but for the most part Asahel and Elizabeth went alone. Miss

Cadwallader would neither row nor ride, and was very apt to eschew walking, unless a party were going along.

Over her books Elizabeth luxuriated all the rest of the time. Morning, noon, and night. The labour of talking she left to her cousin, who took to it kindly, and speedily made herself very popular. And there was certainly something very pleasant in her bright smile, always ready, and in her lovely face; and something pleasant too in her exceeding dainty and pretty manner of dressing. She fascinated the children's eyes, and if truth be told, more than the children. She seemed to have a universal spirit of good-humour. She never was so fast in a book but she would leave it to talk to the old or play with the young; and her politeness was unfailing. Elizabeth gave no trouble, but she seemed to have as little notion of giving pleasure; except to herself. *That* she did perfectly and without stop. For the rest, half the time she hardly seemed to know what was going on with the rest of the world.

So the summer wore on, with great comfort to most parties. Perhaps Winthrop was an exception. He had given comfort, if he had not found it. He had been his mother's secret stand-by; he had been her fishmonger, her gamekeeper, her head gardener, her man-at-need in all manner of occasions. His own darling objects meanwhile were laid upon the shelf. He did his best. But after a day's work in the harvest field, and fishing for eels off the rocks till nine o'clock at night, what time was there for Virgil or Græca Minora? Sometimes he must draw up his nets in the morning before he went to the field; and the fish must be cleaned after they were taken. Sometimes a half day must be spent in going after fruit. And whenever the farm could spare him for a longer time, he was off to the woods with his gun; to fetch home rabbits at least, if no other game was to be had. But all the while his own ground lay waste. To whomsoever the summer was good, he reckoned it a fruitless summer to him.

In the multitude of their enjoyments of out-door things, the girls took very naturally to the unwonted ways and usages of the country household. The farm living and the farm hours seemed to have no disgust for them. In the hot weather the doors often all stood open; and they sat in the keeping-room, and in the kitchen, and in their own room, and seemed to find all pleasant.

So one night Elizabeth and Mrs. Landholm were alone in the kitchen. It was a cool evening, though in midsummer, and they had gathered round the kitchen fire as being the most agreeable place. The children were long gone to bed; the rest of the family had at length followed them; Elizabeth and Mrs. Landholm alone kept their place. The one was darning some desperate-looking socks; the other, as usual, deep in a book. They had been very still and busy for a long time; and then as Elizabeth looked up for a moment and glanced at the stocking-covered hand of her neighbour, Mrs. Landholm looked up; their eyes met. Mrs. Landholm smiled.

"Do you like anything so well as reading, Miss Elizabeth?"

"Nothing in the world! What *are* you doing, Mrs. Landholm?"

"Mending——some of the boys' socks," she said cheerfully; "farmers are hard upon their feet."

"Mending——*that?*" said Elizabeth. "What an endless work!"

"No, not endless," said the mother quietly. "Thick shoes and a great deal of stepping about, make pretty hard work with stockings."

"But Mrs. Landholm!—it would be better to buy new ones, than to try to mend such holes."

Mrs. Landholm smiled again——a smile of grave and sweet life-wisdom.

"Did it ever happen to you to want anything you could not have, Miss Elizabeth?"

"No—never," said Elizabeth slowly.

"You have a lesson to learn yet."

"I hope I sha'n't learn it," said Elizabeth.

"It must be learned," said Mrs. Landholm gently. "Life would not be life without it. It is not a bad lesson either."

"It isn't a very pleasant one, Mrs. Landholm," said Elizabeth. And she went back to her reading.

"You don't read my book, Miss Elizabeth," the other remarked presently.

"What is that?"

Mrs. Landholm looked up again, and the look caught Elizabeth's eye, as she answered,

"The Bible."

"The Bible!—no, I don't read it much," said Elizabeth. "Why, Mrs. Landholm?"

"Why, my dear?—I hope you will know some day why," she answered, her voice a little changed.

"But that is not exactly an answer, Mrs. Landholm," said Elizabeth with some curiosity.

Mrs. Landholm dropped her hands and her stocking into her

lap, and looked at the face opposite her. It was an honest and intelligent face, very innocent in its ignorance of life and life-work.

"What should we do without the Bible?" she asked.

"Do without it! Why I have done without it all my days, Mrs. Landholm."

"You are mistaken even in that," she said; "but Miss Elizabeth, do you think you have lived a blameless life all your life till now?—have you never done wrong?"

"Why no, I don't think that,—of course I have," Elizabeth answered gravely, and not without a shade of displeasure at the question.

"Do you know that for every one of those wrong doings your life is forfeit?"

"Why no!"

"And that you are living and sitting there, only because Jesus Christ paid his blood for your life?—Your time is bought time;—and he has written the Bible to tell you what to do with it."

"Am I not to do what I like with my own time?" thought Elizabeth. The thought was exceeding disagreeable; but before she or anybody had spoken again, the door of the big bed-room opened gently, and Miss Cadwallader's pretty face peeped out.

"Are they all gone to bed?—are they all gone to bed?" she said;—"may I come, Mrs Landholm?—"

She was in her dressing-gown, and tripping across the floor with the prettiest little bare feet in the world, she took a chair in the corner of the fireplace.

"They got so cold," she said,—"I thought I would come out and warm them. How cosy and delightful you do look here. Dear Mrs. Landholm, do stop working. What are you talking about?"

There was a minute's hesitation, and then Elizabeth said,

"Of reading the Bible."

"The Bible! oh why should one read the Bible?" she said, huddling herself up in the corner. "It's very tiresome!"

"Do you ever read it, Miss Rose?"

"I?—no, indeed I don't. I am sorry, I dare say you will think me very wrong, Mrs. Landholm."

"Then how do you know it is tiresome?"

"O I know it is—I have read it; and one hears it read, you know; but I never want to."

Her words grated, perhaps on both her hearers; but neither of them answered.

"There was a man once," said Mrs. Landholm, "who read it a great deal; and he said that it was sweeter than honey and the honey-comb."

"Who was that?"

"You may read about him if you wish to," said Mrs. Landholm.

"But Mrs. Landholm," said Elizabeth, "do you think it is an *interesting* book?"

"Not to those who are not interested in the things, Miss Elizabeth."

"What things?"

Mrs. Landholm paused a bit.

"A friend to go with you through life's journey—a sure friend and a strong one; a home ready at the journey's end; the name and the love of forgiven children, instead of the banishment of offenders; a clean heart and a right spirit in place of this sickly and sin-stricken nature!—a Saviour and a Father instead of a Judge."

It was impossible to forget the reddening eyes and trembling lips which kept the words company. Elizabeth found her own quivering for sympathy; why, she could not imagine. But there was so much in that face,—of patience and gladness, of strength and weakness,—it was no wonder it touched her. Mrs. Landholm's eyes fell to her work and she took up her stocking again and went on darning; but there was a quick motion of her needle that told how the spirits were moving.

Elizabeth sat still and did not look at her book. Miss Cadwallader hugged herself in her wrapper and muttered under her breath something about "stupid."

"Are your feet warm?" said Elizabeth.

"Yes."

"Then come!—"

Within their own room, she shut the door and without speaking went about with a certain quick energy which she accompanied with more than her usual dignified isolation.

"Who are you angry with now?" said her cousin.

"Nobody."

"Yes you are, you are angry with me."

"It is of no sort of use to be angry with you."

"Why?"

"Because I believe you could not be wise if you were to try."

"I think it is my place to be angry now," said Miss Rose; giving no other indication of it however than a very slight pouting of her under lip. "And all because I said 'stupid!' Well I don't care—they *are* all stupid—Rufus was as stupid this afternoon as he could be; and there is no need, for he can be anything else. He was as stupid as he could be."

"What *have* you to do with Rufus?" said Elizabeth stamping slightly.

"Just what you have to do with Winthrop—amuse myself."

"You know I don't!" said Elizabeth. "How dare you say it! I do not *choose* to have such things said to me. You *know*, if that was all, that Winthrop does not amuse anybody—nobody ever sees him from meal-time to meal-time. You find Rufus very amusing, and he *can* talk very well, considering; but nobody knows whether the other one can be amusing for he never tried, so far as I know."

"I know," said her cousin; "they are a stupid set, all of them."

"They are *not* a stupid set," said Elizabeth; "there is not a stupid one of them, from the father down. They are anything but stupid."

"What does Winthrop do with himself? Rufus isn't so busy."

"I don't know," said Elizabeth; "and I am sure I don't care. He goes for eels, I think, every other night. He has been after them to-night. He is always after birds or fish or rabbits, when he isn't on the farm."

"I wonder what people find so much to do on a farm. I should think they'd grow stupid.—It is funny," said Miss Cadwallader as she got into bed, "how people in the country always think you must read the Bible."

Elizabeth lay a little while thinking about it and then fell asleep. She had slept, by the mind's unconscious measurement, a good while, when she awoke again. It startled her to see that a light came flickering through the cracks of her door from the kitchen. She slipped out of bed and softly and quickly lifted the latch. But it was not the house on fire. The light came from Mrs. Landholm's candle dying in its socket; beyond the candle, on the hearth, was the mistress of the house on her knees. Elizabeth would have doubted even then what she wás about, but for the soft whisper of words which came to her ear. She shut the door as softly and quickly again, and got into bed with a kind of awe upon her. She had certainly heard people stand up in the pulpit and make prayers, and it seemed suitable that other people should bend upon cushions and bow heads while they did so; but that in a common-roofed house, on no particular occasion, anybody should kneel down to pray when he was alone and for his own sake, was something that had never come under her knowledge; and it gave her a disagreeable sort of shock. She lay awake and watched to see how soon Mrs. Landholm's light would go away; it died, the faint moonlight stole in through the window unhindered; and still there was no stir in the next room. Elizabeth watched and wondered; till after a long half hour she heard a light step in the kitchen and then a very light fall of the latch. She sprang up to look at the moon; it had but little risen; she calculated the time of its rising for several nights back, and made up her mind that it must be long past twelve. And this a woman who was tired every day with her day's work and had been particularly tired to-night! for Elizabeth had noticed it. It made her uncomfortable. Why should *she* spend her tired minutes in praying, after the whole house was asleep? and why was it that Elizabeth could not set her down as a fool for her pains? And on the contrary there grew up in her mind, on the instant, a respect for the whole family that wrapped them about like a halo.

One morning when Elizabeth came through the kitchen to mount her horse, Mrs. Landholm was doing some fine ironing. The blue habit stopped a moment by the ironing-table.

"How dreadfully busy you are, Mrs. Landholm."

"Not so busy that I shall not come out and see you start," she answered. "I always love to do that."

"Winnie," said Elizabeth putting a bank bill into the little girl's hand, "I shall make you my messenger. Will you give that to the man who takes care of my horse, for I never see him, and tell him I say he does his work beautifully."

Winifred blushed and hesitated, and handing the note back said that she had rather not.

"Won't you give it to him!"

The little girl coloured still more. "He don't want it."

"Keep your money, my dear," said Mrs. Landholm; "there is no necessity for your giving him anything."

"But why shouldn't I give it to him if I like it?" said Elizabeth in great wonderment.

"It is a boy that works for my father, Miss Haye," said Winthrop gravely; "your money would be thrown away upon him."

"But in this he works for me."

"He don't know that."

"If he don't—Money isn't thrown away upon anybody, that ever I heard of," said Elizabeth; "and besides, what if I choose to throw it away?"

"You can. Only that it is doubtful whether it would be picked up."

"You think he wouldn't take it?"

"I think it is very likely."

"What a fool!—Then I shall send away my horse!" said Elizabeth; "for either he must be under obligation to me, or I to him; and I don't choose the latter."

"Do you expect to get through the world without being under obligation to anybody?" said Winthrop smiling.

But Elizabeth had turned, and marching out of the house did not make any reply.

"What's the objection to being under obligation, Miss Elizabeth?" said Mrs. Landholm. Elizabeth was mounting her horse, in which operation Winthrop assisted her.

"It don't suit me!"

"Fortune's suits do not always fit," said Winthrop. "But then—"

"Then what?"—

"She never alters them."

Elizabeth's eyes fired, and an answer was on her lip, but meeting the very composed face of the last speaker, as he put her foot in the stirrup, she thought better of it. She looked at him and asked,

"What if one does not choose to wear them?"

"Nothing for it but to fight Fortune," said Winthrop smiling; —"or go without any.'

"I would rather go anyhow!" said Elizabeth,—"than be obliged to anybody,—of course except to my father."

"How if you had a husband?" inquired Mrs. Landholm with a good-humoured face.

It was a turn Elizabeth did not like; she did not answer Mrs. Landholm as she would have answered her cousin. She hesitated.

"I never talk about that, Mrs. Landholm," she said a little haughtily, with a very pretty tinge upon her cheek;—"I would not be obliged to *anybody* but my father;—never."

"Why?" said Mrs. Landholm. "I don't understand."

"Don't you see, Mrs. Landholm,—the person under obligation is always the inferior."

"I never felt it so," she replied.

Her guest could not feel, what her son did, the strong contrast they made. One little head was held as if certainly the neck had never been bowed under any sort of pressure; the other, in its meek dignity, spoke the mind of too noble a level to be either raised or lowered by an accident.

"It is another meaning of the word, mother, from that you are accustomed to," Winthrop said.

Elizabeth looked at him, but nothing was to be gained from his face.

"Will you have the goodness to hand me my riding-whip," she said shortly.

"You will have to be obliged to me for that," he said as he picked it up.

"Yes," said Elizabeth; "but I pay for this obligation with a 'thank you'!"

So she did, and with a bow at once a little haughty and not a little graceful. It was the pure grace of nature, the very speaking of her mind at the moment. Turning her horse's head she trotted off, her blue habit fluttering and her little head carried very gracefully to the wind and her horse's motion. They stood and looked after her.

"Poor child!" said Mrs. Landholm,—"she has something to learn. There is good in her too."

"Ay," said her son, "and there is gold in the earth; but it wants hands."

"Yes," said Mrs. Landholm,—"if she only fell into good hands—"

It might have been tempting, to a certain class of minds, to look at that pretty little figure flying off at full trot in all the riot of self-guidance, and to know that it only wanted good hands to train her into something really fine. But Mrs. Landholm went back to her ironing, and Winthrop to drive his oxen a field.

Elizabeth trotted till she had left them out of sight; and then walked her horse slowly while she thought what had been meant by that queer speech of Winthrop's. Then she reminded herself that it was of no sort of consequence what had been meant by it, and she trotted on again.

Asahel as usual came out to hold her bridle when she returned.

"Asahel, who takes care of my horse?" she said as she was dismounting.

"Ain't it handsomely done?" said Asahel.

"Yes,—beautifully. Who does it?"

"It's somebody that always does things so," said Asahel oracularly, a little in doubt how he should answer.

"Well, who?"

"Don't you know?"

"Of course I don't! Who is it?"

"It's Winthrop."

"Winthrop!"——

"Yes. He does it."

Elizabeth's cheeks burnt.

"Where's that man of yours—why don't he do it?"

"Sam?—O he don't know—I guess he ain't up to it."

Asahel led away the horse, and Elizabeth went into the house, ready to cry with vexation. But it was not generally her fashion to vent vexation so.

"What's the matter now?" said her cousin. "What adventure have you met with this morning?"

"Nothing at all."

"Well what's the matter?"

"Nothing—only I want to lay my whip about somebody's shoulders,—if I could find the right person."

"Well 'taint me," said Rose shrinking. "Look here—I've got a delicious plan in my head—I'm going to make them take us in the boat round the bay, after huckleberries."

"Absurd!"

"What's absurd?"

"That."

"Why?"

"Who'll take you?"

"No matter—somebody, *I* don't know who;—Rufus. But you'll go?"

"Indeed I won't."

"Why?"

"The best reason in the world. I don't want to."

"But I want you to go—for my sake, Lizzie."

"I won't do it for anybody's sake. And Rose—I think you take a great deal too much of Rufus's time. I don't believe he does his duty on the farm, and he can't, if you will call upon him so much."

"He's not obliged to do what I ask him," said Rose pouting; "and I'm not going to stay here if I can't amuse myself. But come!—you'll go in the bay after huckleberries?"

"I shall not stir. You must make up your mind to go without me."

Which Rose declared was very disagreeable of her cousin, and she even shed a few tears; but a rock could not have received them with more stony indifference, and they were soon dried.

The huckleberry expedition was agreed upon at dinner, Mr. Landholm being, as he always was when he could, very agreeable. In the mean time Winthrop took the boat and went out on the bay to catch some fish.

It was near the time for him to be back again, and the whole party were gathered in the keeping-room and in the doorway; Elizabeth and Mrs. Landholm with their respective books and work, the others, children and all, rather on the expecting order and not doing much of any thing; when a quick springy footstep came round the house corner. Not Winthrop's, they all knew; his step was slower and more firm; and Winthrop's features were very little like the round good-humoured handsome face which presented itself at the front door.

"Mr. Herder!" cried the children. But Rose was first in his way.

"Miss Cadval-lader!" said the gentleman,—"I did not expect —Mrs. Landholm, how do you do?—Miss Élisabet' I did not look for this pleasure. Who would have expect' to see you here!"

"Nobody I suppose," said Elizabeth. "Isn't it pleasant, Mr. Herder?"

There was a great laughing and shaking of hands between them; and then Mr. Herder went again to Mrs. Landholm, and gave the children his cordial greeting. And was made to know Rufus.

"But where is Wint'rop?" said Mr. Herder, after they had done a great deal of talking in ten minutes.

"Winthrop is gone a fishing. We expect him home soon."

"Where is he? Tell me where he is gone and I will go after him and bring him back. I know de country. I did not come to see you, Miss Élisabet'—I have come to see my friend Wint'rop. And I do not want to stay in de house, never, while it is so pleasant wizout."

"But we are going in the bay after huckleberries," said Rose, —"won't you go with us, Mr. Herder?"

"After huckle-berry——I do not know what is that—yes, I will go wiz you, and I will go find Wint'rop and bring him home to go too."

"He is out on the bay," said Elizabeth; "I'll take you to him in my boat. Come Mr. Herder,—I don't want you, Rose; I'll take nobody but Mr. Herder;—we'll go after him."

She ran for her bonnet, seized her oars, and drew Mr. Herder with her down to the rocks.

It was a soft grey day; pleasant boating at that or at any hour, the sun was so obscured with light clouds. Elizabeth seated Mr. Herder in the stern of the 'Merry-go-round,' and pulled out lightly into the bay; he very much amused with her water-craft.

They presently caught sight of the other boat, moored a little distance out from the land, behind a point.

"There he is!"— said Mr. Herder. "But what is he doing? He is not fishing. Row your boat soft, Miss Élisabet'——hush!—do not speak wiz your—what is it you call?—We will catch him—we have the wind—unless he be like a wild duck——"

Winthrop's boat lay still upon the sleepy water,—his fishing rod dipped its end lazily in,—the cork floated at rest; and the fisher seated in his boat, was giving his whole attention seemingly to something in his boat. Very softly and pretty skilfully they stole up.

He had something of the wild duck about him; for before they could get more than near at hand, he had looked up, looked round, and risen to greet them. By his help the boats were laid close alongside of each other; and while Winthrop and Mr. Herder were shaking hands across them, Elizabeth quietly leaned over into the stern of the fishing-boat and took up one or two books which lay there. The first proved to be an ill-bound, ill printed, Greek *and Latin* dictionary; the other was a Homer! Elizabeth laid them down again greatly amazed, and wondering what kind of people she had got among.

"What brings you here now, Mr. Herder?" said Winthrop. "Have you come to look after the American Eagle?"

"Ha!—no—I have not come to look after no eagle;——and yet I do not know—I have come to see you, and I do not know what you will turn to be—the eagle flies high, you know."

Winthrop was preparing to tie the two boats together, and did not answer. Mr. Herder stepped from the one he was in and took a seat in Winthrop's. Elizabeth would not leave her own, though she permitted Winthrop to attach it to his and to do the rowing for both; she sat afar off among her cushions, alone.

"I am not very gallant, Miss Élisabet'," said the naturalist; "but if you will not come, I will not come back to you. I did not come to see you this time—I want to speak to this young American Eagle."

And he settled himself comfortably with his back to Elizabeth, and turned to talk to Winthrop, as answering to his strong arm the two boats began to fly over the water.

"You see," he said, "I have stopped here just to see you. You have not change your mind, I hope, about going to de Université?"

"No sir."

"Goot. In de Université where I am, there is a foundation —I mean by that, the College has monies, that she is in right to spend to help those students that are not quite rich enough— if they have a leetle, she gives them a leetle more, till they can get through and come out wiz their studies. This Université has a foundation; and it is full; but the President is my friend, and he knows that I have a friend; and he said to me that he would make room for one more, though we are very full, and take you in; so that it will cost you very little. I speak that, for I know that you could not wish to spend so much as some."

It was a golden chance—if it could but be given to Rufus! That was not possible; and still less was it possible that Winthrop should take it and so make his brother's case hopeless, by swallowing up all the little means that of right must go to set him forward first. There was a strong heaving of motives against each other in Winthrop's bosom. But his face did not shew it; there was no change in his cool grey eye; after a minute's hesitation he answered, lying on his oars,

"I thank you very much Mr. Herder—I would do it gladly —but I am so tied at home that it is impossible. I cannot go."

"You can not?" said the naturalist.

"I cannot—not at present—my duty keeps me at home. You will see me in Mannahatta by and by," he added with a faint smile and beginning to row again;—"but I don't know when."

"I wish it would be soon," said the naturalist. "I should like to have you there wiz me. But you must not give up for difficulties. You must come?"

"I shall come," said Winthrop.

"How would you like this?" said Mr. Herder after pondering a little. "I have a friend who is an excellent—what you call him?—bookseller—Would you like a place wiz him, to keep his books and attend to his business, for a while, and so get up by degrees? I could get you a place wiz him."

"No sir," said Winthrop smiling;—"the eagle never begins by being something else."

"Dat is true," said the naturalist. "Well—I wish I could do

you some goot, but you will not let me;—and I trust you that you are right."

"You are a good friend, sir," said Winthrop gratefully.

"Well—I mean to be," said the other, nodding his good-humoured head.

Elizabeth was too far off to hear any of this dialogue; and she was a little astonished again when they reached the land to see her boatman grasp her friend's hand and give it a very hearty shake.

"I shall never forget it, sir," she heard Winthrop say.

"I do not wish that," said the naturalist. "What for should you remember it? it is good for nozing."

"Is that boy studying Latin and Greek?" said Elizabeth as she and Mr. Herder walked up to the house together.

"That boy? That boy is a very smart boy."

"But is he studying Greek?"

"What makes you ask so?"

"Because there was a Greek book and a dictionary there in the boat with him."

"Then I suppose he is studying it," said Mr. Herder.

Elizabeth changed her mind and agreed to go with the huckleberry party; but she carried a book with her and sat in a corner with it, seldom giving her eyes to anything beside.

Yet there was enough on every hand to call them away. The soft grey sky and grey water, the deep heavy-green foliage of the banks, and the fine quiet outlines of the further mountains, set off by no brilliant points of light and shade,—made a picture rare in its kind of beauty. Its colouring was not the cold grey of the autumn, only a soft mellow chastening of summer's gorgeousness. A little ripple on the water,—a little fleckiness in the cloud,—a quiet air; it was one of summer's choice days, when she escapes from the sun's fierce watch and sits down to rest herself. But Elizabeth's eyes, if they wavered at all, were called off by some burst of the noisy sociability of the party, in which she deigned not to share. Her cousin, Mr. Herder, Rufus, Asahel, and Winifred, were in full cry after pleasure; and a cheery hunt they made of it.

"Miss Élisabet' does look grave at us," said the naturalist,—"she is the only one wise of us all; she does nothing but read. What are you reading, Miss Élisabet'?"

"Something you don't know, Mr. Herder."

"O it's only a novel," said her cousin; "she reads nothing but novels."

" That's not true, Rose Cadwallader, and you know it."

" A novel ! " said Mr. Herder. " Ah !—yes—that is what the ladies read—they do not trouble themselves wiz ugly big dictionaries—they have easy times."

He did not mean any reproof; but Elizabeth's cheek coloured exceedingly and for several minutes kept its glow; and though her eyes still held to the book, her mind had lost it.

The boat coasted along the shore, down to the head of the bay, where the huckleberry region began; and then drew as close in to the bank as possible. No more was necessary to get at the fruit, for the bushes grew down to the very water's edge and hung over, black with berries, though as Asahel remarked, a great many of them were *blue*. Everybody had baskets, and now the fun was to hold the baskets under and fill them from the overhanging bunches as fast as they could; though in the case of one or two of the party the more summary way of carrying the bushes off bodily seemed to be preferred.

" And this is huckle-berry," said Mr. Herder, with a bush in his hand and a berry in his mouth. " Well—it is sweet—a little; —it is not goot for much."

" Why Mr. Herder ! " said Rose;—" They make excellent pies, and Mrs. Landholm has promised to make us some, if we get enough."

" Pies ! " said the naturalist,—" let us get a great many huckleberry then—but I am very sorry I shall not be here to eat the pies wiz you. Pull us a little, Wint'rop—we have picked everything. Stop !—I see,—I will get you some pies !—"

He jumped from the boat and away he went up the bank, through a thick growth of young wood and undergrowth of alder and dogwood and buckthorn and maple and huckleberry bushes. He scrambled on up hill, and in a little while came down again with a load of fruity branches, which he threw into the boat. While the others were gathering them up, he stood still near the edge of the water, looking abroad over the scene. The whole little bay, with its high green border, the further river-channel with Diver's Rock setting out into it, and above, below, and over against him the high broken horizon line of the mountains; the flecked grey cloud and the ripply grey water.

" This is a pretty place ! " said the naturalist. " I have seen no such pretty place in America. I should love to live here. I should be a happy man !—But one does not live for to be happy," he said with half a sigh.

"One doesn't live to be happy, Mr. Herder!" said Elizabeth. "What does one live for, then? I am sure *I* live to be happy."

"And I am sure I do," said Rose.

"Ah, yes—you,—you may," said the naturalist good-humouredly.

"When happiness can be found so near the surface," said Rufus with a satiric glance at the cover of Elizabeth's book,—"it would be folly to go further."

"What do *you* live for, Mr. Herder?" said Elizabeth, giving Rufus's words a cool go-by.

"I?—O I live to do my work," said the naturalist.

"And what is that?"

"I live to find out the truth—to get at de truth. It is for that I spend my days and my nights. I have found out some—I will find out more."

"And what is the purpose of finding out this truth, Mr. Herder?" said Rufus;—"what is *that* for? doesn't that make you happy?"

"No," said the naturalist with a serious air,—"it does not make me happy. I must find it out—since it is there—and I could not be happy if I did not find it;—but if dere was no truth to be found, I could make myself more happy in some ozer way."

The fine corners of the young man's mouth shewed that he thought Mr. Herder was a little confused in his philosophy.

"*You* think one ought to live to be happy, don't you, Mr. Rufus?" said Miss Rose.

"No!" said Rufus, with a fire in his eye and lip, and making at the same time an energetic effort after a difficult branch of huckleberries,—"no!—not in the ordinary way!"

"In what way then?" said the young lady with her favourite pout.

"He has just shewed you, Miss Rose," said Winthrop;—"in getting the highest huckleberry bush. It don't make him happy—only he had rather have that than another."

"Let us have your sense of the matter, then," said his brother.

"But Mr. Herder," said Elizabeth, "why do you want to find out truth?—what is it for?"

"For science—for knowledge;—that is what will do goot to the world and make ozer happy. It is not to live like a man to live for himself."

"Then what *should* one live for," said Elizabeth a little impatiently,—"if it isn't to be happy?"

"I would rather not live at all," said Rose, her pretty lips black with huckleberries, which indeed was the case with the whole party.

"You yourself, Mr. Herder, that is your happiness—to find out truth, as you say—to advance science and learning and do good to other people; you find your own pleasure in it."

"Yes, Mr. Herder," chimed in Rose,—"don't you love flowers and stones and birds and fishes, and beetles, and animals—don't you love them as much as we do dogs and horses?—don't you love that little black monkey you shewed us the other day?"

"No, Miss Rose," said the naturalist,—"no, I do not love them—I do not care for them;—I love what is *back* of those things; dat is what I want."

"And that is your pleasure, Mr. Herder?"

"I do not know," said the puzzled naturalist,—"maybe it is—if I could speak German, I would tell you;—Wint'rop, you do say nozing; and you are not eating huckleberries neizer;—what do you live for?"

"I am at cross-purposes with life, just now, sir."

"Cross?"—said the naturalist.

"Winthrop is never cross," responded Asahel from behind a thick branch of huckleberry.

"Dat is to the point!" said Mr. Herder.

"Well, speak to the point," said Rufus.

"I think the point is now—or will be presently—to get home."

"But to the first point—what should a man live for?"

"It's against the law to commit suicide."

"Pish!" said Rufus.

"Come tell us what you think, Wint'rop," said Mr. Herder.

"I think, sir, I should live to be happy."

"You do!" said the naturalist.

"And I think happiness should be sought in doing all one can, first for oneself, and then for other people."

"That will do," said Mr. Herder. "I agree wiz you."

"*You* are not apt to do first for yourself," said Rufus, with a tender sort of admission-making.

"I am not sure that first for oneself," said the naturalist musing.

"Yes sir—or could one ever do much for the world?"

"Dat is true; you are right!"

"Then at any rate one is to put other people's happiness before one's own?" said Elizabeth with a mixed expression of incredulity and discontent.

"It does not seem just reason, does it?" said Mr. Herder.

"It's what nobody acts up to," said Rose.

"O Miss Cadwallader," said Asahel,—"mother does it always!"

For which he was rewarded with an inexpressible glance, which lit upon nothing, however, but the huckleberries.

"Is that your doctrine, Mr. Winthrop?" said Elizabeth.

"No," he said smiling,—"not mine. Will you sit a little more in the corner, Miss Elizabeth?—"

Elizabeth took up her book again, and gave no token of attention to anything else, good or bad, till the boat neared the rocks of the landing at Shahweetah.

CHAPTER XI.

> Thou art a dew-drop which the morn brings forth,
> Ill fitted to sustain unkindly shocks,
> Or to be trailed along the soiling earth.
>
> WORDSWORTH.

One day in September it chanced that the house was left entirely to the womenkind. Even Asahel had been taken off by his father to help in some light matter which his strength was equal to. Rufus and Winthrop were on the upland, busy with the fall ploughing; and it fell to little Winifred to carry them their dinner.

The doors stood open, as usual, for it was still warm weather, and the rest of the family were all scattered at their several occupations. Miss Cadwallader on the bed, asleep; Karen somewhere in her distant premises out of hearing; Elizabeth sat with her book in the little passage-way by the open front door, screened however by another open door from the keeping-room where Mrs. Landholm sat alone at her sewing. By and by came in Winifred, through the kitchen She came in and stood by the fireplace silent.

"Well dear," said the mother looking up from her work,—"did you find them?"

The child's answer was to spring to her side, throw her arms round her neck, and burst into convulsive tears.

"Winifred!"—said Mrs. Landholm, putting an arm round the trembling child, and dropping her work,—"what ails you, dear?—tell me."

The little girl only clung closer to her neck and shook in a passion of feeling, speechless; till the mother's tone became alarmed and imperative.

"It's nothing, mother, it's nothing," she said, clasping her hard,—"only—only—"

The words were lost again in what seemed to be uncontrollable weeping.

"Only what, dear?—what?"

"Winthrop was crying."

And having said that, scarce audibly, Winifred gave way and cried aloud.

"Winthrop crying!—Nonsense, dear,—you were mistaken."

"I wasn't—I saw him."

"What was the matter?"

"I don't know."

"What made you think he was crying?"

"I *saw* him!" cried the child, who seemed as if she could hardly bear the question and answer.

"You were mistaken, daughter;—he would not have let you see him."

"He didn't—he didn't know I was there."

"Where were you?"

"I was behind the fence—I stopped to look at him—he didn't see me."

"Where was he?"

"He was ploughing."

"What did you see, Winifred?"

"I saw him—oh mamma!—I saw him put his hand to his eyes,—and I saw the tears fall—"

Her little head was pressed against her mother's bosom, and many more tears fell for his than his had been.

Mrs. Landholm was silent a minute or two, stroking Winifred's head and kissing her.

"And when you went into the field, Winifred,—how was he then?"

"Just as always."

"Where was Rufus?"

"He was on the other side."

Again Mrs. Landholm was silent.

"Cheer up, daughter," she said tenderly;—"I think I know what was the matter with Winthrop, and it's nothing so very bad—it'll be set right by and by, I hope. Don't cry any more about it."

"What *is* the matter with him, mamma?" said the child looking up with eyes of great anxiety and intentness.

"He wants to read and to learn, and I think it troubles him that he can't do that."

"Is that it? But mamma, can't he?" said his sister with a face not at all lightened of its care.

"He can't just now very well—you know he must help papa on the farm."

"But can't he by and by, mamma?"

"I hope so;—we will try to have him," said the mother, while tears gathered now in her grave eyes as her little daughter's were dried. "But you know, dear Winnie, that God knows best what is good for dear Governor, and for us; and we must just ask him to do that, and not what we fancy."

"But mother," said the little girl, "isn't it right for me to ask him to let Winthrop go to school and learn, as he wants to?"

"Yes daughter," said the mother, bending forward till her face rested on the little brow upturned to her, and the gathered tears falling,—"let us thank God that we may ask him anything —we have that comfort—'In everything, by prayer and supplication, with thanksgiving,' we may make our requests known unto him—only we must be willing after all to have him judge and choose for us."

The child clasped her mother's neck and kissed her again and again.

"Then I won't cry any more, mamma, now that I know what the matter is."

But Elizabeth noticed when Winthrop came in at night, how his little sister attached herself to his side, and with what a loving lip and longing eye.

"Your little sister is very fond of you," she could not help saying, one moment when Winifred had run off.

"Too fond," he said.

"She has a most sensitive organization," said Rufus. "She is too fond of everything that she loves."

"She is not too fond of *you*," thought Elizabeth, as Winifred came back to her other brother, with some little matter which she thought concerned her and him. 'Sensitive organization!' What queer people these are!"

They were so queer, that Elizabeth thought she would like to see what was the farming work with which their hands were filled and which swallowed up the daily life of these people; and the next day she proposed to go with Winifred when she went the rounds again with her baskets of dinner. Miss Cadwallader was glad of any thing that promised a little variety, so she very willingly made one.

It was a pleasant September day, the great heats gone, a gentler state of the air and the light; summer was just falling gracefully into her place behind the advancing autumn. It was exceeding pleasant walking, through the still air, and Elizabeth and her cousin enjoyed it. But little Winifred was loaded down with two baskets, one in each hand. They went so for some time.

"Winnie," said Elizabeth at last, "give me one of those—I'll carry it."

"O no!" said the little girl looking up in some surprise,—"they're not very heavy—I don't want any help."

"Give it to me; you shan't carry 'em both."

"Then take the other one," said Winifred,—"thank you, Miss Elizabeth—I'm just going to take this in to father, in the field here."

"In the field where? I don't see anybody."

"O because the corn is so high. You'll see 'em directly. This is the bend-meadow lot. Father's getting in the corn."

A few more steps accordingly brought them to a cleared part of the field, where the tall and thick cornstalks were laid on the ground. There, at some distance, they saw the group of workers, picking and husking the yellow corn, the farm wagon standing by. Little Winifred crept under the fence and went to them with her basket, and her companions stood at the fence looking. There were Mr. Landholm, and Asahel, Mr. Doolittle and another man, seen here and there through the rows of corn. Asahel sat by a heap, husking; Mr. Landholm was cutting down stalks; and bushel baskets stood about, empty, or with their yellow burden shewing above the top.

"I should think farmer's work would be pleasant enough," Rose remarked, as they stood leaning over the fence.

"It looks pretty" said Elizabeth. "But I shouldn't like to pull corn from morning to night; and I don't believe you would."

"O, but men have to work, you know," said Miss Cadwallader.

Winifred came back to them and they went on their way, but Elizabeth would not let her take the basket again. It was a pretty way; past the spring where Sam Doolittle had pushed Winthrop in and Rufus had avenged him; and then up the rather steep woody road that led to the plain of the tableland. The trees stood thick, but the ascent was so rapid that they could only in places hinder the view; and as the travellers went up, the river spread itself out more broad, and Shahweetah lay below them, its boundaries traced out as on a map. A more commanding view of the opposite shore, a new sight of the southern mountains, a deeper draught from nature's free cup, they gained as they went up higher and higher. Elizabeth had seen it often before; she looked and drank in silence; though to-day September was peeping between the hills and shaking his sunny hair in the vallies;—not crowned like the receding summer with insupportable brilliants.

"I am sorry papa is coming so soon!" said Elizabeth, after she had stood awhile near the top, looking.

"Why I thought you wanted to go home," said her cousin.

"So I do;—but I don't want to go away from here."

"What do you want to stay for?"

"It is so lovely!—"

"*What* is so lovely?" asked Miss Cadwallader with a tone of mischief.

Elizabeth turned away and began to walk on, an expression of great disgust upon her face.

"I wish I was blessed with a companion who had three grains of wit!" she said.

Miss Cadwallader's light cloud of ill-humour, it seldom looked more, came on at this; and she pouted till they reached the fence of the ploughed field where the young men were at work. Here Elizabeth gave up her basket to Winifred; and creeping through the bars they all made for the nearest plough. It happened to be Winthrop's.

"What's the matter?" said he as they came up. "Am I wanted for guard or for oarsman?"

"Neither—for nothing," said Elizabeth. "Go on, won't you? I want to see what you are doing."

"Ploughing?" said he. "Have you never seen it?"

He went on and they walked beside him; Winifred laughing, while the others watched, at least Elizabeth did minutely, the process of the share in turning up the soil.

"Is it hard work?" she asked.

"No, not here; not when the business is understood."

"Like rowing, I suppose there is a sleight in it?"

"A good deal so."

"What has been growing here?"

"Corn."

"And now when you get to the fence you must just turn about and make another ridge close along by this one?"

"Yes."

"Goodness!—What's going to be sown here?"

"Wheat."

"And all this work is just to make the ground soft for the seeds!"

"Why wouldn't it do just as well to make holes in the ground and put the seeds in?" said Miss Cadwallader;—"without taking so much trouble?"

"It is not merely to make the ground soft," said Winthrop gravely, while Elizabeth's bright eye glanced at him to mark his behaviour. "The soil might be broken without being so thoroughly turned. If you see, Miss Elizabeth,—the slice taken off by the share is laid bottom upwards."

"I see—well, what is that for?"

"To give it the benefit of the air."

"The benefit of the air!—"

"The air has a sort of enriching and quickening influence upon the soil;—if the land has time and chance, it can get back from the air a great deal of what it lost in .he growing of crops."

"The soil loses, then?"

"Certainly; it loses a great deal to some crops."

"What, for instance?"

"Wheat is a great feeder," said Winthrop; "so is Indian corn."

"By its being 'a great feeder', you mean that it takes a great deal of the nourishing quality of the soil?"

"Yes."

"How many things I do not know!" said Elizabeth wistfully.

In the little pause which ensued, Winifred took her chance to say,

"Here's your dinner, Governor."

"Then when the ground is ploughed, is there anything else to be done before it is ready for the wheat?"

"Only harrowing."

Elizabeth mused a little while.

"And how much will the wheat be worth, Winthrop, from all this field?"

"Perhaps two hundred dollars; or two hundred and fifty."

"Two hundred and fifty.—And then the expenses are something."

"Less to us," said Winthrop, "because we do so much of the labour ourselves."

"Here's your dinner, Winthrop," said Winifred;—"shall I set it under the tree?"

"Yes——no, Winifred,—you may leave it here."

"Then stop and eat it now, Governor, won't you?—don't wait any longer."

He gave his little sister a look and a little smile, that told of an entirely other page of his life, folded in with the ploughing experience; a word and look very different from any he had given his questioners. Other indications Elizabeth's eye had caught under 'the tree,'—a single large beech tree which stood by the fence some distance off. Two or three books lay there.

"Do you find time for reading here in the midst of your ploughing, Mr. Winthrop?"

"Not much—sometimes a little in the noon-spell," he answered, colouring slightly.

They left him and walked on to visit Rufus. Elizabeth led near enough to the tree to make sure, what her keen eye knew pretty well already, that one of the books was the very identical old brown-covered Greek and Latin dictionary that she had seen in the boat. She passed on and stood silent by Rufus's plough.

"Well, we've come to see you, Rufus," said Miss Cadwallader.

'I thought you had come to see my brother," said he.

"I didn't come to see either one or the other," said Elizabeth "I came to see what you are doing."

"I hope you are gratified," said the young man a little tartly.

"What's the use of taking so much trouble to break up the ground?" said Rose.

"Because, unfortunately, there is no way of doing it without trouble," said Rufus, looking unspoken bright things into the furrow at his feet.

"But why couldn't you just make holes in the ground and put the seed in?"

"For a reason that you will appreciate, Miss Rose, if you will put on your bonnet the wrong way, with the front precisely where the back should be."

"I don't understand,"—said the young lady, with something of an inclination to pout, Will's face was so full of understanding.

"It isn't necessary that you should understand such a business," he said, becoming grave. "It is our fortune to do it, and it is yours to have nothing to do with it,—which is much better."

"I have the happiness to disagree with you, Mr. Rufus," said Elizabeth.

"In what?"

"In thinking that we have nothing to do with it, or that it is not necessary we should understand it."

"I don't see the happiness, Miss Elizabeth; for your disagreement imposes upon you a necessity which I should think better avoided."

"Which ploughs the best, Rufus?" said Rose;—"you or Winthrop?"

"There is one kind of ploughing," said Rufus biting his lip, "which Winthrop doesn't understand at all."

"And you understand them all, I suppose?"

He didn t answer.

"What is the kind he does not understand, Mr. Rufus?" said Elizabeth.

"Ploughing with another man's heifer."

"Why what's that, Rufus? I don't know what you mean," said Miss Cadwallader.

No more did Elizabeth, and she had no mind to engage the speaker on unequal terms. She called her cousin off and took the road home, leaving Winifred to speak to her brother and follow at her leisure.

"How different those two people are," she remarked.

"Which one do you like best?"

"Winthrop, a great deal."

"I know you like him the best," said her cousin wilfully.

"Of course you do, for I tell you."

"*I* don't. I like the other a great deal the best."

"He wasn't very glad to see us," said Elizabeth.

"Why wasn't he? Yes he was. He was as glad as the other one."

"The other one didn't care twopence about it."

"And what did this one care?"

"He cared,—" said Elizabeth.

"Well I like he should—the other one don't care about anything.'

"Yes he does," said Elizabeth.

"I shall give Mr. Haye a hint—that he had better not send you here another summer," said Rose wittily;—"there is no telling what anybody will care for. I wouldn't have thought it of you."

"Can't you be sensible about anything!" said Elizabeth, with a sort of contemptuous impatience. "If I had anybody else to talk to, I would not give you the benefit of my thoughts. I tell them to you because I have nobody else; and I really wish you could make up your mind to answer me as I deserve;—or not at all."

"You are a strange girl," said Miss Cadwallader, when they had walked in company with ill-humour as far as the brow of the hill.

"I am glad you think so."

"You are a great deal too old for your age."

"I am not!" said Elizabeth, who shading her eyes with her hand had again stopped to look over the landscape. "I should be very sorry to think that. You are two years older, Rose, in body, than I am; and ten years older in spirit, this minute."

"Does the spirit grow old faster than the body?" said Rose laughing.

"Yes—sometimes.—How pretty all that is!"

'That' meant the wide view, below and before them, of river and hill and meadow. It was said with a little breath of a sigh, and Elizabeth turned away and began to go down the road.

Winifred gave it as her opinion to her mother privately, after they got home, that Miss Haye was a very ill-behaved young lady.

CHAPTER XII.

> The thing we long for, that we are,
>   For one transcendent moment,
> Before the Present, poor and bare,
>   Can make its sneering comment.
> Still through our paltry stir and strife
>   Glows down the wished Ideal,
> And Longing moulds in clay what Life
>   Carves in the marble Real.
>
> LOWELL.

MR. HAYE came the latter part of September to fetch his daughter and his charge home; and spent a day or two in going over the farm and making himself acquainted with the river. He was a handsome man, and very comfortable in face and figure. The wave of prosperity had risen up to his very lips, and its ripples were forever breaking there in a succession of easy smiles. He made himself readily at home in the family; with a well-mannered sort of good-humour, which seemed to belong to his fine broadcloth and beautifully plaited ruffles. Mr. Landholm was not the only one who enjoyed his company. Between him and Rufus and Miss Cadwallader and Mr. Haye, the round game of society was kept up with great spirit.

One morning Mr. Haye was resting himself with a book in his daughter's room; he had had a long tramp with the farmer. Rose went out in search of something more amusing. Elizabeth sat over her book for awhile, then looked up.

"Father," she said, "I wish you could do something to help that young man."

"What young man?"

"Winthrop Landholm."

"What does he want help for?"

"He is trying to get an education—trying hard, I fancy," said Elizabeth, putting down her book and looking at her father,—"he wants to make himself something more than a farmer."

"Why should he want to make himself anything more than a farmer?" said Mr. Haye without looking off *his* book.

"Why would you, sir?"

"I would just as lief be a farmer as anything else," said Mr. Haye, "if I had happened to be born in that line. It's as good a way of life as any other."

"Why father!—You would rather be what you are now?"

"Well—I wasn't born a farmer," said Mr. Haye conclusively.

"Then you would have everybody stay where he happens to be!"

"I wouldn't have anything about it," said Mr. Haye. "That's what I want for myself—let other people do what they will."

"But some people can't do what they will."

"Well—Be thankful you're not one of 'em."

"Father, if I can have what I will, I would have you help this young man."

"I don't know how to help him, child;—he's not in my way. If he wanted to go into business, there would be something in it, but I have nothing to do with schools and Colleges."

Elizabeth's cheek lit up with one of the prettiest colours a woman's cheek ever wears,—the light of generous indignation.

"I wish *I* had the means!" she said.

"What would you do with it?"

"I would help him, somehow."

"My dear, you could not do it; they would not let you; their pride would stand in the way of everything of the kind."

"I don't believe it," said Elizabeth, the fire of her eye shining now through drops that made it brighter;—"I am sure something could be done."

"It's just as well undone," said Mr. Haye calmly.

"Why, sir?"—his daughter asked almost fiercely.

"What put this young fellow's head upon Colleges, and all that?"

"I don't know, sir!—how should I?"

"It won't last—it's just a freak to be a great man and get out of hob-nailed shoes—he'll get over it; and much better he should. It's much better he should stay here and help his father, and that's what he's made for. He'll never be anything else."

Mr. Haye threw down his book and left the room; and his daughter stood at the window with her heart swelling.

"He *will* be something else, and he'll *not* get over it," she said to herself, while her eyes were too full to let her see a single thing outside the window. "He is fit for something else, and he will have it, hard or easy, short or long; and I hope he will!—and oh, I wish father had done what would be for his honour in this thing!—"

There was a bitter taste to the last sentence, and tears would not wash it out. Elizabeth was more superb than ordinary that night at supper, and had neither smiles nor words for anybody.

A day or two after they were going away.

"Winthrop," she said at parting, (not at all by familiarity, but because she did not in common grant them a right to any title whatsoever)—"may I leave you my little Merry-go-round?—and will you let nobody have the charge of it except yourself?"

He smiled and thanked her.

"'Tisn't much thanks," she said; meaning thanks' worth. "It is I who have to thank you."

For she felt that she could not send any money to the boy who had taken care of her horse.

The family party gathered that night round the supper-table with a feeling of relief upon several of them. Mr. Landholm's face looked satisfied, as of a man who had got a difficult job well over; Mrs. Landholm's took time to be tired; Winthrop's was as usual, though remembering with some comfort that there would not be so many wantings of fish, nor so many calls upon his strength of arm for boat exercise. Rufus was serious and thoughtful; the children disposed to be congratulatory.

"It's good I can sit somewhere but on the corner," said Asahel,—"and be by ourselves."

"It's good I can have *my* old place again," said Winifred, "and sit by Governor."

Her brother rewarded her by drawing up her chair and drawing it closer.

"I am glad they are gone, for your sake, mamma," he said.

"Well, we haven't made a bad summer of it," said Mr. Landholm.

His wife thought in her secret soul it had been a busy one. Winthrop thought it had been a barren one. Rufus—was not ready to say quite that.

"Not a bad summer," repeated Mr. Landholm. "The next thing is to see what we will do with the winter."

"Or what the winter will do with us," said Rufus after a moment.

"If you like it so," said his father; "but *I* prefer the other mode of putting it. I'd keep the upper hand of time always; —I speak it reverently."

Winthrop thought how completely the summer had got the better of him.

"My friend Haye is a good fellow—a good fellow. I like him. He and I were always together in the legislature. He's a sensible man."

"He is a gentleman," said Rufus.

"Ay—Well he has money enough to be. That don't always do it, though. A man and his coat aren't always off the same piece. Those are nice girls of his, too;—pretty girls. That Rose is a pretty creature!—I don't know but I like t'other one as well in the long run though,—come to know her."

"I do—better," said Mrs. Landholm. "There is good in her."

"A sound stock, only grown a little too rank," said Winthrop.

"Yes, that's it. She's a little overtopping. Well, there will come a drought by and by that will cure that."

"Why sir?" said Rufus.

"The odds are that way," said his father. "'Taint a stand-still world, this; what's up to-day is down to-morrow. Mr. Haye may hold his own, though; and I am sure I hope he will—for his sake and her sake, both."

"He is a good business man, isn't he, sir?"

"There aint a better business man, I'll engage, than he is, in the whole city of Mannahatta; and that numbers now,—sixty odd thousand, by the last census. He knows how to take care of himself, as well as any man I ever saw."

"Then he bids fair to stand?"

"I don't believe anybody bids fairer. He was trying to make a business man of you, wa'n't he, the other day?"

"He was saying something about it."

"Would you like that?"

"Not in the first place, sir."

"No. Ah well—we'll see,—we'll see," said Mr. Landholm rising up;—"we'll try and do the best we can."

What was that? A question much mooted, by different people and in very different moods; but perhaps most anxiously and carefully by the father and mother. And the end was, that he would borrow money of somebody,—say of Mr. Haye,—and they would let both the boys go that fall to College. If this were not the best, it was the *only* thing they could do; so it seemed to them, and so they spoke of it. How the young men were to be *kept* at College, no mortal knew; the father and mother did not; but the pressure of necessity and the strength of will took and carried the whole burden. The boys must go; they should go; and go they did.

In a strong yearning that the minds of their children should not lack bread, in the self-denying love that would risk any hardship to give it them,—the father and mother found their way plain if not easy before them. If his sons were to mount to a higher scale of existence and fit themselves for nobler work in life than he had done, his shoulders must thenceforth bear a double burden; but they were willing to bear it. She must lose, not only, the nurtured joys of her hearthstone, but strain every long-strained nerve afresh to keep them where she could not see and could but dimly enjoy them; but she was willing. There were no words of regret; and thoughts of sorrow lay with thoughts of love at the bottom of their hearts, too fast-bound together and too mighty to shew themselves except in action.

The money was borrowed easily, upon a mortgage of the farm. President Tuttle was written to, and a favourable answer received. There was a foundation at Shagarack, as well as at Mannahatta; and Will and Winthrop could be admitted there on somewhat easier terms than were granted to those who could afford better. Some additions were made to their scanty wardrobe from Mr. Cowslip's store; and at home unwearied days and nights were given to making up the new, and renewing and refurbishing the old and the worn. Old socks were re-toed and re-footed; old trousers patched so that the patch could not be seen; the time-telling edges of collars and wristbands done over, so that they would last awhile yet; mittens knitted, and shirts made. It was a little wardrobe when all was done; yet how much time and care had been needed to bring it together. It was a dear one too, though it had cost little money; for it might almost be said to have been made of the heart's gold. Poor Winifred's love was less wise than her mother's, for it could not keep sorrow down. As yet she did not know that it was not better to sit at her father's board end than at either end of the highest form at Shagarack. She knitted, socks and stockings, all the day long, when her mother did not want her; but into them she dropped so many tears that the wool was sometimes wet with them; and as Karen said, half mournfully and half to hide her mourning, "they wouldn't want shrinking." Winthrop came in one day and found her crying in the chimney corner, and taking the half-knit stocking from her hand he felt her tears in it.

"My little Winnie!—" he said, in that voice with which he sometimes spoke his whole heart.

Winifred sprang to his neck and closing her arms there, wept as if she would weep her life away. And Rufus who had followed Winthrop in, stood beside them, tear after tear falling quietly on the hearth. Winthrop's tears nobody knew but Winifred, and even in the bitterness of her distress she felt and tasted them all.

The November days seemed to grow short and drear with deeper shadows than common, as the last were to see the boys go off for Shagarack. The fingers that knitted grew more tremulous, and the eyes that wrought early and late were dim with more than weariness; but neither fingers nor eyes gave themselves any holiday. The work was done at last; the boxes were packed; those poor little boxes! They were but little, and they had seen service already. Of themselves they told a story. And they held now, safely packed up, the College fit-out of the two young men.

"I wonder if Shagarack is a very smart place, mamma?" said Winifred, as she crouched beside the boxes watching the packing.

"Why?"

Winifred was silent and looked thoughtfully into the box.

"Rufus and Governor will not care if it is."

"They needn't care" said Asahel, who was also at the box side. "They can bear to be not quite so smart as other folks. Mr. Haye said he never saw such a pair of young men; and I guess he didn't."

Winifred sighed and still looked into the box, with a face that said plainly *she* would like to have them smart.

"O well, mamma," she said presently, "I guess they will look pretty nice, with all those new things; and the socks are nice, aren't they? If it was only summer—nobody can look nicer than Winthrop when he has his white clothes on."

"It will be summer by and by," said Mrs. Landholm.

The evening came at last; the supper was over; and the whole family drew together round the fire. It was not a very talkative evening. They looked at each other more than they spoke; and they looked at the fire more than they did either. At last Mr. Landholm went off, recommending to all of them to go to bed. Asahel, who had been in good spirits on the matter all along, followed his father. The mother and daughter and the two boys were left alone round the kitchen fire.

They were more silent than ever then, for a good space; and four pair of eyes were bent diligently on the rising and falling flames. Only Winifred's sometimes wandered to the face of one or the other of her brothers, but they never could abide long. It was Mrs. Landholm's gentle voice that broke the silence.

"What mark are you aiming at, boys?—what are you setting before you as the object of life?"

"What *mark*, mother?" said Rufus after an instant's pause.

"Yes."

"To make something of myself!" he said rising, and with that fire-flashing nostril and lip that spoke his whole soul at work. "I have a chance now, and it will go hard but I will accomplish it."

The mother's eye turned to her other son.

"I believe I must say the same, mother," he replied gravely. "I have perhaps some notion of *doing*, afterwards; but the first thing is to be *myself* what I can be. I am not, I feel, a tithe of that now."

"I agree with you—you are right, so far," answered the mother, turning her face again to the fire;—"but in the end, what is it you would do, and would be?"

"Profession, do you mean, mamma?" said Rufus.

"No," she said; and he needed not to ask any more.

"I mean, what is all this for?—what purpose lies behind all this?"

"To distinguish myself!" said Rufus,—"if I can,—in some way."

"I am afraid it is no better than that with me, mother," said Winthrop; "though perhaps I should rather say my desire is to *be distinguished.*"

"What's the difference?" said his brother.

"I don't know. I think I feel a difference."

"I am not going to preach to you now," said Mrs. Landholm, and yet the slight failing of her voice did it—how lastingly!—"I cannot,—and I need not. Only one word. If you sow and reap a crop that will perish in the using, what will you do when it is gone?—and remember it is said of the redeemed, that their works *do follow* them. Remember that.——One word more," she said after a pause. "Let me have it to say in that day,—'Of all which thou gavest me have I lost none'!——"

6*

Not preach to them? And what was her hidden face and bowed head?—a preaching the like of which they were never to hear from mortal voices. But not a word, not a lisp, fell from one of them. Winifred had run off; the rest hardly stirred; till Mrs. Landholm rose up, and gravely kissing one and the other prepared to leave the room.

"Where is Winifred?" said her brother suddenly missing her.

"I don't know. I am sure she is somewhere praying for you."

They said no more, even to each other, that night.

Nor much the next day. It was the time for doing, not thinking. There was not indeed much to do, except to get off; but that seemed a great deal. It was done at last. Mrs. Landholm from the window of the kitchen watched them get into the wagon and drive off; and then she sat down by the window to cry.

Asahel had gone to ride as far as the mountain's foot with his father and brothers; and Winifred knelt down beside her mother to lean her head upon her; they could not get near enough just then. It was only to help each other weep, for neither could comfort the other nor be comforted, for a time. Yet the feeling of the two, like as it seemed outwardly, was far unlike within. In the child it was the spring flood of a little brook, bringing, to be sure, momentary desolation; in the mother it was the flow of the great sea, still and mighty. And when it grew outwardly quiet, the same depth was there.

They got into each other's arms at last, and pressed cheek to cheek and kissed each other many times; but the first word was Mrs. Landholm's, saying,

"Come—we had better go and get tea—Asahel will be back directly."

Asahel came back in good spirits, having had his cry on the road, and they all took tea with what cheerfulness they might. But after tea Winifred sat in the chimney corner gazing into the fire, very still and pale and worn-looking; her sober blue eyes intently fixed on something that was not there. Very intently, so that it troubled her mother; for Winifred had not strength of frame to bear strong mind-working. She watched her.

"What, mamma?" said the little girl with a half start, as a hand was laid gently and remindingly upon her shoulder.

"I should rather ask you what," said her mother tenderly. "Rest, daughter, can't you?"

"I wasn't worrying, mamma."

"Wa'n't you?"

"I was thinking of 'They have washed their robes and made them white in the blood of the Lamb.'"

"Why, dear?"

"I am so glad I can wash mine, mother."

"Yes—Why, my dear child?"

"There are so many spots on them."

Her mother stooped down beside her and spoke cheerfully.

"What are you thinking of now, Winnie?"

"Only, mamma, I am glad to think of it," she said, nestling her sunny little head in her mother's neck. "I wanted yesterday that Will and Governor should have better clothes."

"Well Winnie, I wanted it too—I would have given them better if I had had them."

"But mamma, ought I to have wished that?"

"Why yes, dear Winnie; it is a pleasant thing to have comfortable clothes, and it is right to wish for them, provided we can be patient when we don't get them. But still I think dear Governor and Will will be pretty comfortable this winter. We will try to make them so."

"Yes mamma,—but I wanted them to be *smart*."

"It is right to be smart, Winnie, if we aren't *too* smart."

"I wish I could be always just right, mamma."

"The rightest thing will be for you to go to sleep," said her mother, kissing her eyes and cheeks. "I'll be through my work directly and then you shall sit in my lap and rest—I don't want to sew to-night. Winnie, the good Shepherd will gather my little lamb with his arm and carry her in his bosom, if she minds his voice; and then he will bring her by and by where she shall walk with him in white, and there will be no spots on the white any more."

"I know. Make haste, mother, and let us sit down together and talk."

So they did, with Asahel at their feet; but they didn't talk much. They kept each other silent and soft companionship, till Winifred's breathing told that she had lost her troubles in sleep on her mother's bosom.

"Poor little soul! she takes it hard," said Karen. "She's 'most as old as her mother now."

"You must get her to play with you, Asahel, as much as you can," Mrs. Landholm said in a whisper.

"Why mamma? aint she well?"

"I don't know—I'm afraid she wont keep so."

"She's too good to be well," said Karen.

Which was something like true. Not in the vulgar prejudice, as Karen understood it. It was not Winifred's *goodness* which threatened her well-being; but the very delicate spirits which answered too promptly and strongly every touch; too strong in their acting for a bodily frame in like manner delicate.

CHAPTER XIII.

Mess.—He hath indeed, better bettered expectation, than you must expect me to tell you how.

Leon.—He hath an uncle here in Messina will be very much glad of it.

MUCH ADO ABOUT NOTHING.

MR. LANDHOLM came back in excellent spirits from Shagarack. The boys were well entered, Will Junior and Winthrop Sophomore, and with very good credit to themselves. This had been their hope and intention, with the view of escaping the cost of one and two years of a college life. President Tuttle had received them very kindly, and everything was promising; the boys in good heart, and their father a proud man.

"Aint it queer, now," he said that evening of his return, as he sat warming his hands before the blaze, "aint it queer that those two fellows should go in like that—one Junior and t'other Sophomore, and when they've had no chance at all beforehand, you may say. Will has been a little better, to be sure; but how on earth Winthrop ever prepared himself I can't imagine. Why the fellow read off Greek there, and I didn't know he had ever seen a word of it."

"He used to learn up in his room o' nights, father," said Asahel.

"He used to carry his books to the field and study while the oxen were resting," said Winifred.

"He did!—Well, *he'll* get along. I aint afeard of him. He won't be the last man in the College, I guess."

"I guess not, father," said Asahel.

And now the months sped along with slow step, bringing toil-work for every day. It was cheerfully taken, and patiently wrought through; both at Shagarack and in the little valley at home; but those were doing for themselves, and these were truly doing love's work, for them. All was for them. The crops were grown and the sheep sheared, that Rufus and Winthrop might, not eat and be clothed,—that was a trifle,—but have the full good of a College education. The burden and the joy of the toilers was the same. There were delightful speculations round the fireside about the professions the young men would choose; what profound lawyers, what brilliant ministers, should come forth from the learned groves of Shagarack; perhaps, the father hinted,—statesmen. There were letters from both the boys, to be read and re-read, and loved and prided in, as once those of Rufus. And clothes came home to mend, and new and nice knitted socks went now and then to replace the worn ones; but that commerce was not frequent nor large; where there was so little to make, it was of necessity that there should not be too much to mend; and alas! if shirt-bosoms gave out, the boys buttoned their coats over them and studied the harder. There were wants they did not tell; those that were guessed at, they knew, cost many a strain at home; and were not all met then. But they had not gone to Shagarack to be 'smart,'—except mentally. That they were.

They were favourites, notwithstanding. Their superiors delighted in their intellectual prominence; their fellows forgave it. Quietly and irresistibly they had won to the head of their respective portions of the establishment, and stayed there; but the brilliancy and fire of Rufus and the manliness and temper of his brother gained them the general good-will, and general consent to the place from which it was impossible to dislodge them. Admiration first followed the elder brother, and liking the younger; till it was found that Winthrop was as unconquerable as he was unassuming; as sure to be ready as to be right; and a very thorough and large respect presently fell into the train of his deservings. The faculty confided in him; his mates looked up to him. There was happily no danger of any affront to Winthrop which might have called Rufus's fire disagreeably into play. And for himself, he was too universally popular. If he was always in the foreground, everybody knew it was because he *could* not be anywhere else. If Winthrop was often brought into the foreground, on great occasions, every soul of them knew it was because no other would have dignified it so well. And besides, neither Winthrop nor Rufus forgot or seemed to forget the grand business for which he was there. With all their diversity of manner and disposition, each was intent on the same thing,—to do what he had come there to do. Lasting eminence, not momentary pre-eminence, was what they sought; and that was an ambition which most of their compeers had no care to dispute with them.

"Poor fellows!" said a gay young money-purser; "they are working hard, I suppose, to get themselves a place in the eye of the world."

"Yes sir," said the President, who overheard this speech;—"and they will by and by be where you can't see them."

They came home for a few weeks in the summer, to the unspeakable rejoicing of the whole family; but it was a break of light in a cloudy day; the clouds closed again. Only now and then a stray sunbeam of a letter found its way through.

One year had gone since the boys went to College, and it was late in the fall again. Mr. Underhill, who had been on a journey back into the country, came over one morning to Mr. Landholm's.

"Good morning!" said the farmer. "Well, you've got back from your journey into the interior."

"Yes," said Mr. Underhill,—"I've got back."

"How did you find things looking, out there?"

"Middling;—their winter crops are higher up than yours and mine be."

"Ay. I suppose they've a little the start of us with the sun. Did you come through Shagarack?"

"Yes—I stopped there a night."

"Did you see my boys?"

"Yes—I see 'em."

"Well—what did they say?" said the father, with his eye alive.

"Well—not much," said Mr. Underhill.

"They were well, I suppose?"

"First-rate—only Winthrop looked to me as if he was workin' pretty hard. He's poorer, by some pounds, I guess, than he was when he was to hum last August."

"Didn't he look as usual?" said the father with a smothered anxiety.

"There wa'n't no other change in him, that I could see, of no kind. I didn't know as Rufus was going to know who I was, at first."

"He hasn't seen much of you for some time."

"No; and folks lose their memory," said Mr. Underhill. "I saw the—what do you call him?—the boss of the concern—president!—President Tuttle. I saw him and had quite a talk with him."

"The president! How came you to see him?"

"Well, 'taint much to see a man, I s'pose,—is it? I took a notion I'd see him. I wanted to ask him how Will and Winthrop was a getting along. I told him I was a friend o' yourn."

"Well did you ask him?"

"Yes I did."

"What did he say?" said Mr. Landholm, half laughing.

"I asked him how they were getting along."

"Ay, and what did he answer to that?"

"He wanted to know if Mr. Landholm had any more sons?"

"Was that all?" said the farmer, laughing quite.

"That was the hull he said, with a kind of kink of his eye that wa'n't too big a sum for me to cast up. He didn't give me no more satisfaction than that."

"And what did you tell him—to his question?"

"I?—I told him that two such plants took a mighty sight of room to grow, and that the hull county was clean used up."

"You did!" said Mr. Landholm laughing heartily. "Pretty well!—pretty good!—Have some tobacco, neighbour?"

"How is it?" said Mr. Underhill taking a bunch gravely.

"First-rate,—*I* think. Try."

Which Mr. Underhill did, with slow and careful consideration. Mr. Landholm watched him complacently.

"I've seen worse," he remarked dryly at length. "Where did you get it, squire?"

"Nowhere short of the great city, neighbour. It came from Mannahatta."

"Did, hey? Well, I reckon it might. Will you trade?"

"With what?" said Mr. Landholm.

"Some of this here."

"With you?"

"Yes."

"Well—let's hear," said the farmer.

"Don't you think the post ought to be paid?" said Mr. Underhill, diving into some far-down pockets.

"Why, are you the post?"

"Don't you think that two sealed letters, now, would be worth a leetle box o' that 'ere?"

"Have you brought letters from the boys?"

"Well I don't know who writ 'em," said Mr. Underhill;—"they guv 'em to me."

Mr. Landholm took the letters, and with a very willing face went for a 'little box,' which he filled with the Mannahatta tobacco.

"Old Cowslip don't keep anything like this," Mr. Underhill said as he received it and stowed it coolly away in his pocket. "I mean to shew it to him."

"Will you stay to dinner, neighbour?"

"No thank 'ee—I've got to get over the river; and my little woman'll have something cooked for me; and if I wa'n't there to eat it I shouldn't hear the last of my wastefulness."

"Ay? is that the way she does?" said Mr. Landholm laughing.

"Something like it. A tight grip, I tell ye!"

And with these words Mr. Underhill took himself out of the house.

"Where's your mother, Asahel? call her and tell her what's here," said Mr. Landholm, as he broke one of the seals.

"SHAGARACK, Dec. 3, 1810.

"MY DEAR PARENTS,

"I take the opportunity of friend Underhill's going home to send you a word—I can't write much more than a word, I'm so busy. I never drove my plough at home half so industriously as now I am trying to break up and sow the barren fields of mind. But oh, this is sweeter labour than that. How shall I ever repay you, my dear father and dear mother, for the efforts you are making—and enduring—to give me this blessing. I feel them to my very heart—I know them much better than from your words. And perhaps this poor return of words is all I shall ever be able to make you,—when it seems to me sometimes as if I could spill my very heart to thank you. But if success can thank you, you shall be thanked. I feel that within me which says I shall have it. Tell mother the box came safe, and was gladly received. The socks &c. are as nice as possible, and very comfortable this weather; and the mittens, tell Winnie, are like no other mittens that ever were knit; but I wish I could have hold of the dear little hands that knit them for a minute instead—she knows what would come next.

"You bid me say if I want anything—sometimes I think I want nothing but to hear from you a little oftener—or to see you!—that would be too pleasant. But I am doing very well, though I *do* want to know that ma is not working so hard. I shall relieve pa from any further charge of me after this. I consulted the President; and he has given me a form in the grammar school to take care of—I believe pa knows there is a grammar school connected with the Institution. This will pay my bills, and to my great joy relieve my father from doing so any more. This arrangement leaves me but half of the usual study hours (by day) for myself; so you see I have not much leisure to write letters, and must close.

"Your affectionate son,

"WINTHROP LANDHOLM.

"I don't forget Asahel, though I haven't said a word of him; and give my love to Karen."

Mr. and Mrs. Landholm looked up with pleasant faces at each other and exchanged letters. She took Winthrop's and her husband began upon the other, which was from Rufus. Asahel and Winifred were standing anxiously by.

"What do they say?"

"You shall hear directly."

"Does he say any thing about me?" said Winifred.

But father and mother were deep in the precious despatches, and the answer had to be waited for.

"SHAGARACK COLLEGE, Dec. 1810.

"MY DEAR FRIENDS AT HOME,

"This funny little man says he will take letters to you;—so as it is a pity not to cultivate any good disposition, Governor and I have determined to favour him. But really there is not much to write about. Our prospects are as bare as your garden in November—nothing but roots above ground or under—some thrown together, and some, alas! to be dug for; only ours are not parsnips and carrots but a particularly tasteless kind called *Greek* roots; with a variety denominated *algebraic*, of which there are *quantities*. At these roots, or at some branches from the same, Governor and I are tugging as for dear life, so it is no wonder if our very hands smell of them. I am sure I eat them every day with my dinner, and *ruminate* upon them afterwards. In the midst of all this we are as well as usual. Governor is getting along splendidly; and I am not much amiss; at least so they say. The weather is pretty stinging these few days, and I find father's old cloak very useful. I think Winthrop wants something of the sort, though he is as stiff as a pine tree, bodily and mentally, and won't own that he wants any thing. He won't want any thing long, that he can get. He is working *confoundedly* hard. I beg mamma's pardon—I wouldn't have said that if I had thought of her—and I would write over my letter now, if I were not short of time, and to tell truth, of paper. This is my last sheet, and a villainous bad one it is; but I can't get any better at the little storekeeper's here, and that at a horridly high price.

"As Governor is writing to you, he will give you all the sense, so it is less matter that there is absolutely nothing in this epistle. Only believe me, my dear father and mother and Winnie and Asahel, ever your most dutiful, grateful, and affectionate son and brother,

"WILL. RUFUS LANDHOLM.

"My dear mother, the box was most acceptable."

After being once read in private, the letters were given aloud to the children; and then studied over and again by the father and mother to themselves. Winifred was satisfied with the mention of her name; notwithstanding which, she sat with a very wistful face the rest of the afternoon. She was longing for her brother's hand and kiss.

"Have your brothers' letters made you feel sober, Winnie?" said her mother.

"I want to see him, mamma!——"

"Who?"

"Governor.—"

It was the utmost word Winifred's lips could speak.

"But dear Winnie," said her mother sorrowfully, "it is for their good and their pleasure they are away."

"I know it, mamma,—I know I am very selfish—"

"I don't think you are," said her mother. "Winnie, remember that they are getting knowledge and fitting themselves to be better and stronger men than they could be if they lived here and learnt nothing."

"Mamma," said Winifred looking up as if defining her position, "I don't think it is right, but I can't always help it."

"We have one friend never far off."

"Oh mamma, I remember that all the while."

"Then can't you look happy?"

"Not always, mamma," said the little girl covering her face quickly. The mother stooped down and put her arms round her.

"You must ask him, and he will teach you to be happy always."

"But I can't, mamma, unless I could be right always," said poor Winifred.

Mrs. Landholm was silent, but kissed her with those soft motherly kisses which had comfort and love in every touch of them. Soon answered, for Winifred lifted up her head and kissed her again.

"How much longer must they be there, mamma?" she asked more cheerfully.

"Two years," Mrs. Landholm answered, with a sigh that belonged to what was not spoken.

"Mamma," said Winifred again presently, trying not to shew from how deep her question came, "aint you afraid Winthrop wants something more to wear?"

And Mrs. Landholm did not shew how deep the question went, but she said lightly,

"We'll see about it. We'll get papa to write and make him tell us what he wants."

"Maybe he won't tell," said Winifred thoughtfully. "I wish I could write."

"Then why don't you set to and learn? Nothing would please Governor so much."

"Would it!" said Winifred with a brightened face.

"Asahel," she said, as Asahel came in a few minutes after, "mamma says Governor would like nothing so well as to have me learn to write."

"I knew that before," said Asahel coolly. "He was talking to me last summer about learning you."

"Was he! Then will you Asahel? Do you know yourself?"

"I know how to begin," said Asahel.

And after that many a sorrowful feeling was wrought into trammels and pothooks.

CHAPTER XIV.

Bard. On, on, on, on, on! to the breach, to the breach!
Nym. Pray thee, corporal, stay; the knocks are too hot; and for mine own part, I have not a case of lives: the humour of it is too hot, that is the very plain-song of it.
KING HENRY V.

"TO MR. WINTHROP LANDHOLM, SHAGARACK COLLEGE.

"Dec. 10, 1810.

"MY DEAR SON,

"We received yours of the third, per Mr. Underhill, which was very gratifying to your mother and myself, as also Will's of the same date. We cannot help wishing we could hear a little oftener, as these are the first we have had for several weeks. But we remember your occupations, and I assure you make due allowances; yet we cannot help thinking a little more time might be given to pa and ma. This is a burdensome world, and every one must bear their own burdens; yet I think it must be conceded it is right for every individual to do what may be in his power towards making the lot of others pleasanter. This I am sure you believe, for you act upon it; and you know that nothing so lightens our load as to know that Will and Governor are doing well. It is a world of uncertainties; and we cannot know this unless you will tell us.

"My dear sons, I do not mean to chide you, and I have said more on this subject than I had any intention to do. But it is very natural, when a subject lies so near the heart, that I should exceed the allotted bounds.

"Winthrop, your mother is afraid, from something in Will's letter, that you are in want of an overcoat. Tell us if you are, and we will do our best to endeavour to supply the deficiency. I thought you had one; but I suppose it must be pretty old by this time. My dear son, we have all one interest; if you want anything, let us know, and if it *can* be had you know enough of us to know you shall not want it. We have not much to spare certainly, but necessaries we will try to procure; and so long as we need not groan about the present it is not my way to grumble about the future. We shall get along, somehow, I trust.

"I shall send this by post, as I do not know of any opportunity, and do not think it best to wait for one."

"Your loving father,

"W. LANDHOLM.

"WINTHROP AND WILL."

"MY DEAR BOYS,

"It is very late to-night, and I shall not have any time in the morning, so must scratch a word as well as I can to-night—you know my fingers are not very well accustomed to handling the pen. It gives me the greatest pleasure I can have in this world when I hear that you are getting along so well—except I could hear one other thing of you,—and that would be a pleasure beyond anything in this world. Let us know everything you want—and we will try to send it to you, and if we can't we will all want it together.—We are all well—Winifred mourns for you all the while, in spite of trying not to do it. What the rest of us do is no matter. I shall send a box, if I can, before New Year, with some cakes and apples—write us before that, in time, *all you want.* YOUR MOTHER."

This double letter, being duly put in the post according to Mr. Landholm's promise, in the course of time and the post came safe to the Shagarack post-office; from whence it was drawn one evening by its owner, and carried to a little upper room where Rufus sat, or rather stood, at his books. There was not a great deal there beside Rufus and the books; a little iron stove looked as if it disdained to make anybody comfortable, and hinted that much persuasion was not tried with it; a bed was in one corner, and a deal table in the middle of the floor, at which Winthrop sat down and read his letters.

He was longer over them than was necessary to read them, by a good deal. So Rufus thought, and glanced at him sundry times, though he did not think fit to interrupt him. He lifted his head at last and passing them over coolly to Rufus, drew *his* book near and opened his dictionary. He did not look up while Rufus read, nor when after reading he began to walk with thoughtful large strides up and down the little room.

"Governor!" said Rufus suddenly and without looking at him, "sometimes I am half tempted to think I will take Mr. Haye's offer."

"Did he make you an offer?"

"He said what was near enough to it."

"What tempts you, Will?"

"Poverty. It is only, after all, taking a short road instead of a long one to the same end."

"The end of what?" said Winthrop.

"Of painstaking and struggling."

There was silence, during which Rufus continued his strides through the room, and the leaves of Winthrop's books ever and anon turned and rustled.

"What do you think of it?"

"Nothing."

"Why?"

"I don't believe in drinking of a roiled stream because it happens to be the first one you come to."

"Not if you are dry?"

"No,—not unless everything else is, too."

"But merchandise is a very honourable pursuit," said Rufus, walking and studying the floor.

"Certainly.—Twelve feet is a good growth for dogwood, isn't it?" said Winthrop gravely, looking up and meeting his cool grey eye with that of his brother.

Rufus first stared, and then answered, and then burst into a fit of laughter. Then he grew quite grave again and went on walking up and down.

"The fact is," he said a little while after,—"I don't know exactly what I am fittest for."

"You would be fit for anything if you did," answered his brother.

"Why?"

"You would be an uncommonly wise man."

"*You* might be that with very little trouble, for you are the fittest for everything of anybody I know."

Winthrop studied his books, and Rufus walked perseveringly.

"You hold to taking up law?"

"I will, when I begin it," said Winthrop.

"Where?"

"Where what?"

"Where will you take it up?"

"In Mannahatta."

"And then you will rise to the top of the tree!" said his brother half admiringly, half sadly.

"That I may catch a glimpse of you in the top of some other tree," said Winthrop.

"But this want of money is such a confounded drag!" said Rufus after a few minutes.

"Let it drag you up hill, then. A loaded arrow flies best against the wind."

"Winthrop, I wonder what you are made of!" said Rufus stopping short and looking at him and his books. "The toughest, the sturdiest——"

But Winthrop lifted up his face and gave his brother one of those smiles, which were somewhat as if the sturdy young ash to which he likened him had of a sudden put forth its flowers and made one forget its strength in its beauty. Rufus stopped, and smiled a little himself.

"My choice would be engineering," he said doubtfully.

"Stick to your choice," said Winthrop.

"That's a very good business for making money," Rufus went on, beginning to walk again;—"and there is a variety about it I should like."

"Are you in correspondence with Mr. Haye?"

"No. Why?"

"You seem to be adopting his end of life."

"I tell you, Winthrop," said Rufus stopping short again, "whatever else you may have is of very little consequence if you haven't money with it! You may raise your head like Mont Blanc, above the rest of the world; and if you have nothing to shew but your eminence, people will look at you, and go and live somewhere else."

"You don't see the snow yet, do you?" said Winthrop, so dryly that Rufus laughed again, and drawing to him his book sat down and left his brother to study in peace.

The peace was not of long lasting, for at the end of half or three quarters of an hour Winthrop had another interruption. The door opened briskly and there came in a young man,—hardly that,—a boy, but manly, well grown, fine and fresh featured, all alive in spirits and intellect. He came in with a rush, acknowledged Rufus's presence slightly, and drawing a stool close by Winthrop, bent his head in yet closer neighbourhood. The colloquy which followed was carried on half under breath, on his part, but with great eagerness.

"Governor, I want you to go home with me Christmas."

"I can't, Bob."

"Why?"

Winthrop answered with soft whistling.

"Why?"

"I must work."

"You can work there."

"No I can't."

"Why not?"

"I must work here."

"You can work afterwards."

"Yes, I expect to."

"But Governor, what have you got to keep you?"

"Some old gentlemen who lived in learned times a great while ago, are very pressing in their desires to be acquainted with me—one Plato, one Thucydides, and one Mr. Tacitus, for instance."

"You'll see enough of them, Governor;—you don't like them better than me, do you?"

"Yes, Bob,—I expect they'll do more for me than ever you will."

"I'll do a great deal for you, Governor,—I want you to come with me to Coldstream—I want you to see them all at home; we'll have a good time.—Come!"——

"How do you suppose that old heathen ever got hold of such a thought as this?"—said Winthrop composedly; and he read, without minding his auditors——

> "Τίς δ' οἶδεν, εἰ τὸ ζῆν μέν ἐστὶ κατϑανεῖν,
> Τὸ κατϑανεῖν δὲ ζῆν;"*

"*Who knows if to live is not to die, and dying but to live.*"

"I should think he had a bad time in this world," said Bob; "and maybe he thought Apollo would make interest for his verses in the land of shades."

"But Plato echoes the sentiment,—look here,—and *he* was no believer in the old system. Where do you suppose he got his light on the subject?"

"Out of a dark lantern. I say, Winthrop, I want light on *my* subject—Will you come to Coldstream?"

"I don't see any light that way, Bob;—I must stick fast by my dark lantern."

"Are you going to stay in Shagarack?"

"Yes."

* Bunyan used to say, "*The Latin I borrow.*" I must follow so illustrious an example and confess, *The Greek is lent.*

"It's a deuced shame!—"

"What do you make of this sentence, Mr. Cool?——"

But Bob declined to construe, and took himself off, with a hearty slap on Winthrop's shoulder, and a hearty shake of his hand.

"He's so strong, there's no use in trying to fight him into reason," he remarked to Rufus as he went off.

"What do you suppose Bob Cool would make of your Platonic quotation?" said Rufus.

"What do *you* make of it?" said Winthrop after a slight pause.

"Eremitical philosophy!—Do you admire it?"

"I was thinking mamma would," said Winthrop.

That year came to its end, not only the solar but the collegiate. Rufus took his degree brilliantly; was loaded with compliments; went to spend a while at home, and then went to Mannahatta; to make some preparatory arrangements for entering upon a piece of employment to which President Tuttle had kindly opened him a way. Winthrop changed his form in the grammar school for the Junior Greek class, which happened to be left without any teacher by the removal of the Greek professor to the headship of another College. To this charge he proved himself fully competent. It made the same breaches upon his time, and gave him rather more amends than his form in the grammar school. And amid his various occupations, Winthrop probably kept himself warm without a new overcoat; for he had none.

It was difficult at home, by this time, to do more than make ends meet. They hardly did that. The borrowed hundreds were of necessity yet unpaid; there was interest on them that must be kept down; and the failure of Rufus and Winthrop from the farm duty told severely upon the profits of the farm; and that after it had told upon the energies and strength of the whole little family that were left behind to do all that was done. There was never a complaint nor a regret, even to each other; much less to those for whom they toiled; but often there *was* a shadowed look, a breath of weariness and care, that spoke from husband to wife, from parent to child, and nerved—or unnerved them. Still, Rufus had graduated; he was a splendid young man; all, as well as the parents' hearts, knew that; and Winthrop,——he was never thought of, their minds and speech never went out to him, but the brows unbent, the lips relaxed, and their eyes said that their hearts sat down to rest. Winthrop? He never could do anything but well; he never had since he was a child. He would take his degree now in a few months and he would take it honourably; and then he would be off to the great city—that was said with a throe of pain and joy!—and there he would certainly rise to be the greatest of all. To their eyes could he ever be anything else? But they were as certain of it as Winthrop himself; and Winthrop was not without his share of that quality which Dr. Johnson declared to be the first requisite to great undertakings; though to do him justice the matter always lay in his mind without the use of comparatives or superlatives. And while they sat round the fire talking of him, and of Rufus, the images of their coming success quite displaced the images of weary days and careful nights with which that success had been bought.

It was not however to be quite so speedily attained as they had looked for.

The time of examination came, and Winthrop passed through it, as President Tuttle told his father, "as well as a man could;" and took honours and distinctions with a calm matter-of fact manner, that somehow rather damped the ardour of congratulation.

"He takes everything as if he had a right to it," observed a gentleman of the company who had been making some flattering speeches which seemed to hit no particular mark.

"I don't know who has a better right," said the President.

"He's not so brilliant as his brother," the gentleman went on.

"Do you think so? That can only have been because you did not understand him," said the President equivocally. "He will never flash in the pan, I promise you."

"But dang it, sir!" cried the other, "it *is* a little extraordinary to see two brothers, out of the same family, for two years running, take the first honours over the head of the whole College. What is a man to think, sir?"

"That the College has not graduated two young men with more honour to herself and them in any two years of my Presidency, sir. Allow me to introduce you to the fortunate father of these young gentlemen—Mr. Landholm."

This story Mr. Landholm used afterwards often to repeat, with infinite delight and exultation.

Rufus was not at Shagarack at this time. Instead thereof came a letter.

"MANNAHATTA, Aug. 26, 1812.

"MY DEAR GOVERNOR,

"It has cost me more than I can tell you, that I have not been able to witness your triumph. Nothing could hinder my sharing it. I shared it even before I heard a word of it. I shared it all last week, while the scenes were enacting; but when papa's letter came, it made an old boy of me—I would have thrown off my hat and hurrahed, if I had not been afraid to trust four walls with my feelings; and I finally took up with the safer indulgence of some very sweet tears. I told you it cost me a great deal to stay away from Shagarack. My sole reason for staying was, that it would have cost me more to go. The fact is, I had not the wherewithal—a most stupid reason, but for that very cause, a reason that you cannot argue with. I am just *clearing* for the North—but not, alas! your way—and I *could* not take out of my little funds what would carry me to Shagarack and back; and back I should have had to come. So I have lost what would have been one of the rare joys of my life. But I shall have another chance.—This is but your *first* degree, Governor;—your initial step towards great things; and you are not one to lag by the way.

"As for me, I am off to the regions of wildness, to see what I can do with the rocks and the hills of rude Nature—or what they will do with me, which is perhaps nearer the truth. Not very inviting, after this gay and brilliant city, where certainly the society is very bewitching. I have happened to see a good deal, and some of the best of it. Mr. Haye has been very attentive to me, and I believe would really like to renew his old offer. He lives here *en prince;* with every thing to make his house attractive *besides* the two little princesses who tenant it; and who make it I think the pleasantest house in Mannahatta. *Your* friend is amazingly improved, though she is rather more of a Queen than a princess; but the other is the most splendid little creature I ever saw. They were very gracious to your humble servant. I have seen a good deal of them and like them better and better. Herder is charming. He has introduced me to a capital set—men really worth knowing—they have also been very kind to me, and I have enjoyed them greatly:—but from all this I am obliged to break away,—and from you; for I have no more room. I will write you when I get to the N. W. L.

"P. S. When you come hither, take up your quarters with my landlord, George Inchbald—cor. Beaver and Little South Sts. He loves me and will welcome you. Inchbald is an Englishman, with a heart larger than his means, and a very kind widowed sister."

Winthrop read this letter gravely through, folded it up, and took hold of the next business in hand.

He could not go yet to the great city. The future rising steps to which Rufus looked forward so confidently, were yet far away. He owed a bill at the tailor's; and had besides one or two other little accounts unsettled, which it had been impossible to avoid, and was now impossible to leave. Therefore he must not leave Shagarack. The first thing to do was to clear these hindrances from his way. So he entered his name as law-reader at the little office of Mr. Shamminy, to save time, and took a tutorship in the College to earn money. He had the tutorship of the Junior Greek class, which his father loved to tell he carried further than ever a class had been carried before; but that was not all; he had a number of other recitations to attend which left him, with the necessary studies, scant time for reading law. That little was made the most of and the year was gained.

All the year was needed to free himself from these cobweb bindings that held him fast at Shagarack. Another Commencement over, his debts paid, he went home; to make a little pause on that landing-place of life's journey before taking his last start from it.

CHAPTER XV.

> I turn to go: my feet are set
> To leave the pleasant fields and farms:
> They mix in one another's arms
> To one pure image of regret.
>
> TENNYSON.

THAT little space of time was an exceeding sweet one. Governor was at home again,—and Governor was going away again. If anything had been needed to enhance his preciousness, those two little facts would have done it. Such an idea entered nobody's head. He was the very same Winthrop, they all said, that had left them four years ago; only taller, and stronger, and handsomer.

"He's a beautiful strong man!" said Karen, stopping in the act of rolling her cakes, to peer at him out of the kitchen window. "Aint he a handsome feller, Mis' Landholm?"

"Handsome is that handsome does, Karen."

"Don't he do handsome?" said Karen, flouring her roller. "His mother knows he does. I wish I knowed my shortcake 'd be arter the same pattern."

Winthrop pulled off his coat and went into the fields as heartily as if he had done nothing but farming all his days; and harvests that autumn came cheerily in. The corn seemed yellower and the apples redder than they had been for a long time. Asahel, now a fine boy of fifteen, was good aid in whatever was going on, without or within doors. Rufus wrote cheerfully from the North, where he still was; and there was hardly a drawback to the enjoyment of the little family at home.

There was one; and as often happens it had grown out of the family's greatest delight. Winifred was not the Winifred of former days. The rosy-cheeked, fat, laughing little roll-about of five years old, had changed by degrees into a slim, pale, very delicate-looking child of twelve. Great nervous irritability, and weakness, they feared of the spine, had displaced the jocund health and sweet spirits which never knew a cloud. It was a burden to them all, the change; and yet—so strangely things are tempered—the affections mustered round the family hearth to hide or repair the damage disease had done there, till it could scarcely be said to be poorer or worse off than before. There did come a pang to every heart but Winifred's own, when they looked upon her; but with that rose so sweet and rare charities, blessing both the giver and the receiver, that neither perhaps was less blessed than of old. Winthrop s face never shewed that there was anything at home to trouble him, unless at times when Winifred was not near; his voice never changed from its cool cheerfulness; and yet his voice had a great deal to say to her, and his face Winifred lived upon all the while he was at home. He never seemed to know that she was weaker than she used to be; but his arm was always round her, or it might be under her, whenever need was; and to be helped by his strength was more pleasant to Winifred than to have strength of her own.

She was sitting on his knee one day, and they were picking out nuts together; when she looked up and spoke, as if the words could not be kept in.

"What *shall* I do when you are gone!"

"Help mother, and keep Asahel in spirits."

Winifred could not help laughing a little at this idea.

"I wonder if anything could trouble Asahel much," she said.

"I suppose he has his weak point—like the rest of us," said Winthrop.

"*You* haven't."

"How do you know?"

"I don't *know*, but I think so,' said Winifred, touching her hand to his cheek, and then kissing him.

"What's *your* weak point?"

"They're all over," said Winifred, with a little change of voice; "I haven't a bit of strength about anything. I don't think anybody's weak but me."

"Nobody ought to be weak but you," said her brother, with no change in his.

"I oughtn't to be weak," said Winifred; "but I can't help it."

"It doesn't matter, Winnie," said her brother; "you shall have the advantage of the strength of all the rest."

"That wouldn't be enough," said Winifred, gently leaning her head upon the broad breast which she knew was hers for strength and defence.

"Not, Winnie?—What will you have?"

"I'll have the Bible," said the child, her thin intelligent face looking at him with all its intelligence.

"The Bible, Winnie?" said Winthrop cheerfully.

"Yes, because there I can get strength that isn't my own, and that is better than yours, or anybody's."

"That's true, Winnie; but what do you want so much strength for?" he said coolly.

She looked at him again, a look very hard indeed to bear.

"O I know, Winthrop," she said;—"I want it.—I want it now for your going away."

Her voice was a little checked, and again she leaned forward upon him, this time so as to hide her face.

Winthrop set down the nuts and drew her more close, and his lips kissed the little blue and white temple which was all of her face he could get at.

"It's best I should go, Winnie," he said.

"O I know you must."

"I will have a house one of these days and you shall come and keep it for me."

She sat up and shook away a tear or two, and laughed, but her speech was not as jocular as she meant it to be.

"What a funny housekeeper I should make!"

"The best in the world. You shall study, and I will knit the socks."

"O Governor! What do you know about knitting socks?"

"I know who has knit mine ever since I have been at Shagarack."

"Did mamma tell you?" said the child with a bright sharp glance.

"I found it out."

"And were they all right? Because I am going to keep on doing it, Governor."

"Till you come to be my housekeeper."

"I don't believe that'll ever be," said Winifred.

"Why not?"

"It seems so funny, to think of your ever having a house in Mannahatta!"

"Will you come, Winnie?"

"O Governor!——I dont know," she said, her face full of a world of uncertainties.

"What don't you know?"

"I don't know any thing; and you don't. O Governor"——and she flung her arms round his neck, and spoke words coined out of her heart,—"I wish you were a Christian!——"

For a minute only he did not speak; and then he said calmly in her ear,

"I shall be—I mean to be one, Winnie."

Her little head lay very still and silent a few minutes more; and when she lifted it she did not carry on the subject; unless the kisses she gave him, only too strong in their meaning, might be interpreted.

"I should feel so much better if you knew somebody in Mannahatta," she said presently.

"I do. I know Mr. Herder."

"O yes; but I mean more than that; somebody where you could stay and be nice."

"I shall not stay where I cannot be nice."

"I know that," said Winifred; "but you don't know anywhere to go, do you?"

"Yes. Uncle Forriner's."

"Uncle Forriner.——You don't know him, do you?"

"Not yet."

"Did you ever see him?"

"No."

"Maybe you won't like him."

"Then it will matter the less about his liking me."

"He can't help that," said Winifred.

"You think so?"

"But Rufus didn't stay with him?"

"No—Mr. Forriner only moved to Mannahatta about a year ago."

"Have you ever seen Aunt Forriner?

"Yes—once."

"Well—is she good?"

"I hope so."

"You don't know, Governor?"

"I don't know, Winnie."

Winifred waited a little.

"What are you going to do, Governor, when you first get there?"

"I suppose the first thing will be to go and examine Uncle Forriner and see if I like him."

Winifred laughed.

"No, no, but I mean business—what you are going to Mannahatta for—what will be the first thing?"

"To shew myself to Mr. De Wort."

"Who's he?"

"He is a lawyer in Mannahatta."

"Do you know where he lives?"

"No, Winnie; but other people do."

"What are you going to see him for, Governor?"

"To ask him if he will let me read law in his office."

"Will he want to be paid for it?"

"I don't know."

"Suppose he should, Governor?"

"Then I will pay him, Winifred."

"How can you?"

Her brother smiled a little. "My eyes are not far-sighted enough to tell you, Winnie. I can only give you the fact."

Winifred smiled too, but in her heart believed him.

"Did you ever see Mr. De Wort?"

"Never."

"Then what makes you choose him?"

"Because he is said to be the best lawyer in the city."

Winifred put her fingers thoughtfully through and through the short dark wavy brown hair which graced her brother's broad brow, and wondered with herself whether there would not be a better lawyer in the city before long. And then in a sweet kind of security laid her head down again upon his breast.

"I'll have a house for you there, by and by, Winnie," he said, as his arm drew round her.

"O I couldn't leave mother, you know," she answered.

Her mother called her at this instant, and she ran off, leaving him alone.

He had spoken to her all the while with no change on his wonted calm brow and lip; but when she left the room he left it; and wandering down to some hiding place on the rocky shore, where only the silent cedars stood witnesses, he wept there till his strong frame shook, with what he no more than the rocks would shew anywhere else. It never was shewn. He was just as he had been. Nobody guessed, unless his mother, the feeling that had wrought and was working within him; and she only from general knowledge of his nature. But the purpose of life had grown yet stronger and struck yet deeper roots instead of being shaken by this storm. The day of his setting off for Mannahatta was not once changed after it had been once fixed upon.

And it came. Almost at the end of November; a true child of the month; it was dark, chill, gloomy. The wind bore little foretokens of rain in every puff that made its way up the river, slowly, as if the sea had charged it too heavily, or as if it came through the fringe of the low grey cloud which hung upon the tops of the mountains. But nobody spoke of Winthrop's staying his journey. Perhaps everybody thought, that the day before, and the night before, and so much of the morning, it were better not to go over again.

"Hi!" sighed old Karen, as she took the coffee-pot off the hearth and wiped the ashes from it,—"it's a heavy place for our feet, just this here;—I wonder why the Lord sends 'em. *He* knows."

"Why he sends what, Karen?" said Winifred, taking the coffee-pot from her, and waiting to hear the answer.

"Oh go 'long, dear," said the old woman;—"I was quarrelling with the Lord's doings, that's all."

"*He* knows!" repeated Winnie, turning away and bending her face down till hot tears fell on the cover of the coffee-pot. She stopped at the door of the keeping-room and fought the tears with her little hand desperately, for they were too ready to come; once and again the hand was passed hard over cheeks and eyes, before it would do and she could open the door.

"Well mother," said Mr. Landholm, coming back from a look at the weather,—"let's see what comfort can be got out of breakfast!"

None that morning. It was but a sham, the biscuits and coffee. They were all feeding on the fruits of life-trials, struggles and cares, past and coming; and though some wild grown flowers of hope mingled their sweetness with the harsh things, they could not hide nor smother the taste of them. That taste was in Mr. Landholm's coffee; the way in which he set down the cup and put the spoon in, said so; it was in Winthrop's biscuit, for they were broken and not eaten; it seemed to be in the very light, to Winifred's eyes, by the wistful unmarking look she gave to everything the light shined upon.

It was over; and Mrs. Landholm had risen from the tea-board and stood by the window. There Winthrop parted from her, after some tremulous kisses, and with only the low, short, "Good bye, mother!" He turned to meet the arms of his little sister, which held him like some precious thing that they might not hold. It was hard to bear, but he bore it; till she snatched her arms away from his neck and ran out of the room. Yet she had not bid him good bye and he stood in doubt, looking after her. Then remembered Karen.

He went into the kitchen and shook the old shrivelled hand which was associated in his memory with many an old act of kindness, many a time of help in days of need.

"Good bye, Karen."

"Well—good bye,—" said the old woman slowly, and holding his hand. "I sometimes wonder what ever you were brought into the world for, Mr. Winthrop."

"Why, Karen?"

"Because I aint much better than a fool," she said, putting her other hand to her eyes. "But ye're one of the Lord's precious ones, Governor; he will have service of ye, wherever ye be."

Winthrop wrung her hand. Quitting her, he saw his sister waiting for him at the kitchen door. She let him come within it, and then holding up her Bible which had hung in one hand, she pointed with her finger to these words where she had it open;—

"God now commandeth all men everywhere to repent."

Her finger was under the word '*now.*' She added nothing, except with her eyes, which went wistfully, searchingly, beggingly, into his; till a film of tears gathered, and the book fell, and her arms went round him again and her face was hid.

"I know, dear Winnie," he said softly, stooping to her after the silent embrace had lasted a minute.—"I must go—kiss me."

There was a great deal in her kiss, of hope and despair; and then he was gone; and she stood at the window looking after him as long as a bit of him could be seen; clearing away the tears from her eyes that she might watch the little black speck of the boat, as it grew less and less, further and further off down the river. Little speck as it was, he was in it.

The world seemed to grow dark as she looked,—in two ways. The heavy rain clouds that covered the sky stooped lower down and hung their grey drapery on the mountains more thick and dark. But it did not rain yet, nor till Winifred turned wearily away from the window, saying that "they had got there;"—meaning that the little black speck on the water had reached the little white and brown spot on the shore which marked the place of Cowslip's Mill. Then the clouds began to fringe themselves off into rain, and Cowslip's Mill was soon hid, and river and hills were all grey under their thick watery veil. "But Governor will be in the stage, mamma," said Winifred. "He won't mind it."

Poor Winifred! Poor Governor!—He was not in the stage. There was no room for him. His only choice was to take a seat beside the driver, unless he would wait another day; and he never thought of waiting. He mounted up to the box, and the stage-coach went away with him; while more slowly and soberly the little boat set its head homewards and pulled up through the driving rain.

It rained steadily, and all things soon owned the domination of the watery clouds. The horses, the roads, the rocks, the stage-coach, and the two outsiders, who submitted for a long distance in like silence and quiet; though with the one it was the quiet of habit and with the other the quiet of necessity. Or it might be of abstraction; for Winthrop's mind took little heed to the condition of his body.

It was busy with many greater things. And among them the little word to which his sister's finger had pointed, lodged itself whether he would or no, and often when he would not. Now NOW,—"God NOW commandeth all men everywhere to repent." It was at the back of Winthrop's thoughts, wherever they might be; it hung over his mental landscape like the rain-cloud; he could look at nothing, as it were, but across the gentle shadows of that truth falling upon his conscience. The rain-drops dimpled it into the water, when the road lay by the river-side; and the bare tree-stems they were passing, that said so much of the past and the future, said also quietly and soberly, "NOW." The very stage-coach reminded him he was on a journey to the end of which the stage-coach could not bring him, and for the end of which he had no plans nor no preparations made. And the sweet images of home said, "*now*—make them." And yet all this, though true and real in his spirit, was so still and so softly defined, that,—like the reflection of the hills in the smooth water of the river,—he noted without noting, he saw without dwelling upon it. It was the depth of the picture, and his mind chose the stronger outlines. And then the water ruffled, and the reflection was lost.

The ride was in dull silence, till after some hours the coachman stopped to give his horses water; though he remarked, "it was contrary in them to want it." But after that his tongue seemed loosed.

"Dampish!" he remarked to his fellow-traveller, as he climbed up to his place again and took the reins.

"Can you stand it?" said Winthrop.

"Stand what?"

"Being wet through at this rate?"

"Don't signify whether a man's killed one way or another," was the somewhat unhopeful answer. "Come to the same thing in the long run, I expect."

"Might as well make as long a run as you can of it. Why don't you wear some sort of an overcoat?"

"I keep it—same way you do yourn.—No use to spoil a thing for nothing. There's no good of an overcoat but to hold so much heft of water, and a man goes lighter without it. As long as you've got to be soaked through, what's the odds?"

"I didn't lay my account with this sort of thing when I set out," said Winthrop.

"O *I* did. I have it about a third of the time, I guess. This and March is the plaguiest months in the hull year. They do use up a man."

Some thread of association brought his little sister's open book and pointed finger on the sudden before Winthrop, and for a moment he was silent.

"Yours is rather bad business this time of year," he remarked.

"Like all other business," said the man; "aint much choice. There's a wet and a dry to most things. What's yourn? if I may ask."

"Wet," said Winthrop.

"How?—" said the man.

"You need only look at me to see," said Winthrop.

"Well—I thought—" said his companion, looking at him again—"Be you a dominie?"

"No."

"Going to be?—Hum!—Get ap!—" said the driver touching up one of his horses.

"What makes you think so?" said Winthrop.

"Can't tell—took a notion. I can mostly tell folks, whether they are one thing or another."

"But you are wrong about me," said Winthrop; "I am neither one thing nor the other."

"I'll be shot if you aint, then," said his friend after taking another look at him. "Ben't you?—You're either a dominie or a lawyer—one of the six."

"I should like to know what you judge from. Are clergymen and lawyers so much alike?"

"I guess I aint fur wrong," said the man, with again a glance, a very benign one, of curiosity. "I should say, your eye was a lawyer and your mouth a clergyman."

"You can't tell what a man is when he is as wet as I am," said Winthrop.

"Can't tell what he's goin' to be, nother. Well, if the rain don't stop, we will, that's one thing."

The rain did not stop; and though the coach did, it was not till evening had set in. And that was too late. The wet and cold had wrought for more days than one; they brought on disease from which even Winthrop's strong frame and spirit could not immediately free him. He lay miserably ill all the next day and the next night, and yet another twelve hours; and then finding that his dues paid would leave him but one dollar unbroken, Winthrop dragged himself as he might out of bed and got into the stage-coach for Mannahatta which set off that same evening.

CHAPTER XVI.

I reckon this always—that a man is never undone till he be hanged; nor never welcome to a place, till some certain shot be paid, and the hostess say, welcome.

TWO GENTLEMEN OF VERONA.

WHAT a journey that was, of weariness and pain and strong will. Unfit, and almost unable to travel, empty of means and resources almost alike, he would go,—and he was going; and sheer determination stood in the place and filled the want of all things beside. It was means and resources both; for both are at the command of him who knows how to command them. But though the will stand firm, it may stand very bare of cheering or helping thoughts; and so did Winthrop's that live-long night. There was no wavering, but there was some sadness that kept him company.

The morning broke as cheerless as his mood. It had rained during the night and was still raining, or sleeting, and freezing as fast as it fell. The sky was a leaden grey; the drops that came down only went to thicken the sheet of ice that lay upon everything. No face of the outer world could be more unpromising than that which slowly greeted him, as the night withdrew her veil and the stealthy steps of the dawn said that no bright day was chasing her forward. Fast enough it lighted up the slippery way, the glistening fences, the falling sleet which sheathed fields and houses with glare ice. And the city, when they came to it, was no better. It was worse; for the dolefulness was positive here, which before in the broad open country was only negative. The icy sheath was now upon things less pure than itself. The sleet fell where cold and cheerlessness seemed to be the natural state of things. Few people ventured into the streets, and those few looked and moved as if they felt it a sad morning, which probably they did. The very horses stumbled along their way, and here and there a poor creature had lost footing entirely and gone down on the ice. Slowly and carefully picking its way along, the stage-coach drew up at last at its p.ace in Court St.

The disease had spent itself, or Winthrop's excellent constitution had made good its rights; for he got out of the coach feeling free from pain, though weak and unsteady as if he had been much longer ill. It would have been pleasant to take the refreshment of brushes and cold water, for his first step; but it must have been a pleasure paid for; so he did not go into the house. For the same reason he did not agree to the offer of the stage-driver to carry him and his baggage to the end of his journey. He looked about for some more humble way of getting his trunk thither, meaning to take the humblest of all for himself. But porters seemed all to have gone off to breakfast or to have despaired of a job. None were in sight. Only a man was shuffling along on the other side of the way, looking over at the stage-coach.

"Here, Jem—Tom—Patrick!"—cried the stage-driver,—"cant *you* take the gentleman's trunk for him?"

"Michael, at your service, and if it's all one t' ye," said the person called, coming over. "I'm the boy! Will this be the box?"

"That is it; but how will you take it?" said Winthrop.

"Sure I'll carry it—asy—some kind of a way," said Michael, handling the trunk about in an unsettled fashion and seeming to meditate a hoist of it to his shoulders. "Where will it go, sir-r?"

"Stop,—that won't do—that handle won't hold," said the trunk's master. "Haven't you a wheelbarrow here?"

"Well that's a fact," said Michael, letting the end of the trunk down into the street with a force that threatened its frail constitution;—"if the handle wouldn't hould, there'd be no hoult onto it, at all. Here!—can't you let us have a barrow, some one amongst ye?—I'll be back with it afore you'll be wanting it, I'll engage."

Winthrop seconded the application; and the wheelbarrow after a little delay came forth. The trunk was bestowed on it by the united efforts of the Irishman and the ostler.

"Now, don't let it run away from you, Pat," said the latter.

"It'll not run away from Michael, I'll engage," said that personage with a capable air, pulling up first his trowsers band and then the wheelbarrow handles, to be ready for a start. "Which way, then, sir, will I turn?"

Winthrop silently motioned him on, for in spite of weakness

of body and weariness of spirit he felt too nervously inclined to laugh, to trust his mouth with any demonstrations. Michael and the wheelbarrow went on ahead and he followed, both taking the middle of the street where the ice was somewhat broken up, for on the sidewalk there was no safety for anybody. Indeed safety anywhere needed to be cared for. And every now and then some involuntary movement of Michael and the barrow, together with some equally unlooked-for exclamation of the former, by way of comment or explanation, startled Winthrop's eye and ear, and kept up the odd contrast of the light with the heavy in his mind's musings. It had ceased to rain, but the sky was as leaden grey as ever, and still left its own dull look on all below it. Winthrop's walk along the streets was a poor emblem of his mind's travelling at the time;—a painful picking the way among difficulties, a struggle to secure a footing where foothold there was not; the uncertain touch and feeling of a cold and slippery world. All true,—not more literally than figuratively. And upon this would come, with a momentary stop and push forward of the wheelbarrow,—

"'Faith, it's asier going backwards nor for'ards!—Which way *will* I turn, yer honour? is it up or down?"

"Straight ahead."

"Och, but I'd rather the heaviest wheeling that ever was invinted, sooner nor this little slide of a place.—Here we go!—Och, stop us!—Och, but the little carriage has taken me to itself intirely. It was all I could do to run ahint and keep up wid the same. Would there be much more of the hills to go down, yer honour, the way we're going?"

"I don't know. Keep in the middle of the street."

"Sure I'm blessed if I can keep any place!" said Michael, whose movements were truly so erratic and uncertain that Winthrop's mood of thoughtfulness was more than once run down by them.—"The trunk's too weighty for me, yer honour,—it will have its own way and me after it—here we go!—Och, it wouldn't turn out if it was for an angel itself. Maybe yer honour wouldn't go ahead and stop it?"

"No chance, I'm afraid," said Winthrop, whose mouth was twitching at the trot of the Irishman's feet after the wheelbarrow.

"Och, but we'll never get down there!" he said as he paused at the top of a long slope. "Then I never knew before what a hard time the carriage has to go after the horses! We'll never get down there, yer honour?"

"Never's a great word, Michael."

"It is, sir!"—

"I think you can get down there if you try."

"Very well, sir!—I suppose I will."

But he muttered Irish blessings or cursings to himself as he took up his trowsers and wheelbarrow handles again.

"Yer honour, do ye think we'll ever keep on our feet till the bottom?"

"If you don't come down the wheelbarrow won't, I think, Michael."

"Then I suppose we'll both be to come," said the man resignedly. "Yer honour 'll consider the bad way, I expict."

'His honour' had reason to remember it. They were going down Bank St., where the fall of ground was rather rapid, and the travel of the morning had not yet been enough to break up the smooth glare of the frozen sleet. The Irishman and the barrow got upon a run, the former crying out, "Och, it *will* go, yer honour!"—and as it would go, it chose its own course, which was to run full tilt against a cart which stood quietly by the sidewalk. Neither Michael's gravity nor that of the wheelbarrow could stand the shock. Both went over, and the unlucky trunk was tumbled out into the middle of the street. But the days when the old trunk could have stood such usage were long past. The hasp and hinge gave way, the cover sprang, and many a thing they should have guarded from public eyes flew or rolled from its hiding place out upon the open street.

Winthrop from higher ground had beheld the overthrow, and knew what he must find when he got to the bottom. Two or three pair of the socks little Winnie had knitted for him had bounced out and scattered themselves far and wide, one even reaching the gutter. Some sheets of manuscript lay ingloriously upon the wheelbarrow or were getting wet on the ice. One nicely "done up" shirt was hopelessly done for; and an old coat had unfolded itself upon the pavement, and was fearlessly telling its own and its master's condition to all the passers-by. Two or three books and several clean pockethandkerchiefs lay about indifferently, and were getting no good; an old shoe on the contrary seemed to be at home. A paper of gingercakes, giving way to the suggestions of the brother shoe, had bestowed a quarter of its contents all abroad; and the open face of the trunk offered a variety of other matters to the curiosity of whom it might concern; the broken cover giving but very partial hindrance.

The Irishman had gathered himself, and himself only, out of the fallen condition in which all things were.

"Bad luck to the ould thing, then!"—was his sense of the matter.

"You needn't wish that," said Winthrop.

"Then, yer honour, I wouldn't wish anything better to meself, if I could ha' helped it. If meself had been in the box, I couldn't ha' taken it more tinder, till we began to go, and then, plase yer honour, I hadn't no hoult of anything at all at all."

"Take hold now, then," said Winthrop, "and set this up straight; and then see if you can get a sixpenny worth of rope anywhere."

The man went off, and Winthrop gathered up his stray possessions from the street and the gutter and with some difficulty got them in their places again; and then stood mounting guard over the wheelbarrow and baggage until the coming of the rope; thinking perhaps how little he had to take care of and how strange it was there should be any difficulty in his doing it.

More care, or an evener way, brought them at last, without further mishap, to Diamond St., and along Diamond St. to Mr. Forriner's house and store. Both in the same building; large and handsome enough, at least as large and handsome as its neighbours; the store taking the front of the ground floor. Mr. Forriner stood in the doorway taking a look at the day, which probably he thought promised him little custom; for his face was very much the colour of the weather.

Winthrop stopped the wheelbarrow before the house; went up and named his name.

"Winthrop Landholm!"—the touch of Mr. Forriner's hand said nothing at all unless it were in the negative;—"how d'ye do, sir. Come to make a visit in Mannahatta?"

"No, sir. I have come here to stay."

"Ah!—hum. Sister well?"

"Very well, sir."

"Left home yesterday?"

"No sir—three days ago."

Ah? where have you been?"

"In bed, sir—caught cold in the rain Tuesday."

"Tuesday!—yes, it did rain considerable all along Tuesday. Where were you?"

"By the way, sir."

"Just got here, eh?—bad time."

"I could not wait for a good one."

"What are you calculating to do here?"

"Study law, sir."

"Law!—hum. Do you expect to make money by that?"

"If I don't, I am afraid I shall not make money by anything," said Winthrop

"Hum!—I guess there aint much money made by the law," said Mr. Forriner taking a pinch of snuff. "It's a good trade to starve by. How long have you to study?"

"All the time I have to live, sir."

"Eh?—and how do you expect to live in the meantime?"

"I shall manage to live as long as I study."

"Well I hope you will—I hope you will," said Mr. Forriner. "You'll come in and take breakfast with us?"

"If you will allow me, sir."

"You haven't had breakfast yet?"

"No sir, nor supper."

"Well I guess wife's got enough for you. If that's your box you'd better get the man to help you in with it. You can set it down here behind the door."

"Is it the right place, sir?" inquired Michael as Winthrop came out to him.

"No," said Winthrop. "But you may help me in with the trunk."

Michael was satisfied that he had the right money, and departed; and Winthrop followed Mr. Forriner through a narrow entry cut off from the store, to a little back room, which was the first of the domestic premises. Here stood a table, and Mrs. Forriner; a hard-featured lady, in a muslin cap likewise hard-featured; there was a "not-give-in" look, very marked, in both, cap and lady. A look that Winthrop recognized at once, and which her husband seemed to have recognized a great while.

"Mrs. Forriner!" said that gentleman to his nephew. "My dear, this is Cousin Winthrop Landholm—Orphah's son."

"How do you do, sir?" said Mrs. Forriner's eyes and cap; her tongue moved not.

"Just come in town," pursued her husband; "and has come to take breakfast with us."

"Have you come in to stay, cousin? or are you going back again to the North?"

"I am not going back at present—I am going to stay," said Winthrop.

The lady was standing up waiting the instant arrival of breakfast, or not enough at ease in her mind to sit down. The table and room and furniture, though plain enough and even mean in their character, had notwithstanding a sufficient look of homely comfort.

"You didn't like it up there where you were?" she went on, changing the places of things on the table with a dissatisfied air.

"Up where, ma'am?"

"O this is not Rufus,—this is Winthrop, my dear," said Mr. Forriner. "Cousin Winthrop has just come down from—I forget—from home. What does brother Landholm call his place, cousin?"

"We sometimes call it after our mountain, 'Wut-a-qut-o.'"

How sweet the syllables seemed in Winthrop's lips!

"*What?*" put in the lady.

Winthrop repeated.

"I should never remember it.—Then this is another cousin?" she remarked to Mr. Forriner;—"and not the one that was here before?"

"No, my dear. It is Rufus that is in the country up North somewhere—Cousin Winthrop is coming here to be a lawyer, he tells me."

"Will you sit up, cousin?" said the lady somewhat dryly, after a minute's pause, as her handmaid set a Britannia metal tea-pot on the board. The meaning of the request being that he should move his chair up to the table, Winthrop did so; for to do the family justice he had sat *down* some time before.

"How will your mother do without you at home?" inquired Mrs. Forriner, when she had successfully apportioned the milk and sugar in the cups.

"I have not been at home for three years past."

"Has she other sons with her?"

"Not another so old as myself."

"It's pretty hard on her, aint it, to have her two eldest go off?"

"Where have you been these three years?" put in Uncle Forriner.

"At Shagarack, sir."

"Ah!—Brother Landholm is bringing up all his sons to be civilians, it seems."

Winthrop was not very clear what his questioner meant; but as it was probable Mr. Forriner himself was in the same condition of darkness, he refrained from asking.

"What's at Shagarack?" said Mrs. Forriner.

"A College, my dear."

"College!—Have you just come to the city, cousin?"

"He caught cold in the rain last Tuesday and has been lying by ever since, and only got in town this morning."

"Have you got a place to stay?"

"Not yet, ma'am. I have been but two hours here."

"Well you had better see to that the first thing, and come here and take dinner—that'll give you a chance. You'll easily find what you want."

"Not this morning, I think, unless it is to be found very near by," said Winthrop; "for my feet would hardly carry me a hundred yards."

"You see, he's weak yet," put in Mr. Forriner.

"Didn't you walk here, cousin?" said the lady.

"Unfortunately, I did, ma'am; for I have not strength to walk anywhere else."

"O well, you can go up stairs and lie down and get some rest; you'll be better by afternoon I dare say. Will you have another cup of tea?"

But Winthrop declined it.

"He don't look right smart," said Mr. Forriner. "I reckon he'll have to go to bed for a while. Cousin, if you'll come up stairs, I'll shew you a place where you can sleep."

They went up accordingly.

"Mr. Forriner—" called his wife from the bottom of the stairs when he and Winthrop had reached the top—"Mr. Forriner!—the *end room*—put him in the end room."

"Yes—it isn't very big, but you won't mind that to take a nap in," said Mr. Forriner, opening the door and ushering Winthrop in.

Where he left him; and what secrets Winthrop's pillow knew were known to none but his pillow. But the morning was not all lost in sleep; and home's fair images did come most sweet about him before sleep came at all.

He was called to dinner, but chose sleep rather, and slept well all the afternoon. Towards evening he roused himself, and though feeling very little strength to boast of, he dressed himself and went out.

The day had changed. A warmer temperature had thawed off the thin sleet, and the pavements were drying. The rain-cloud of the morning was broken up and scattering hither and thither, and through the clefts of it the sun came blinking in upon the world. The light was pleasant upon the wet streets and the long stacks of building and the rolling clouds; and the change in the air was most soothing and mild after the morning's harsh breath. Winthrop tasted and felt it as he walked up the street; but how can the outer world be enjoyed by a man to whom the world is all outer? It only quickened his sense of the necessity there was he should find another climate for his mind to live in. But his body was in no state to carry him about to make discoveries. He must care for that in the first place. After some inquiries and wandering about, he at last made his way into Bank St. and found an eating-house, very near the scene of his morning's disaster. Winthrop had very few shillings to be extravagant with; he laid down two of them in exchange for a small mutton chop and some bread; and then, somewhat heartened, set out upon his travels again, crossing over to the west side of the city. He felt glad, as he went, that his mother—and his little sister—did not know at that moment how utterly alone and foundationless he and his undertaking were standing in the place he had chosen for the scene of his labours and the home of his future life. Yet he corrected himself. Not 'foundationless,' while his strong will stood unmoved and untouched by circumstance. Let that not be conquered, it would surely be conqueror, in the long run; and he determined it should have as long a run as was necessary. He could not help the coming to his mind, as he slowly walked up Beaver St., of his mother's recipe against disappointment, and the conversation had about it years before; and the words, "Whatsoever he doeth shall prosper," as Rufus's voice had given them, came back fresh and with a moment's singular doubt and yearning touching their faithfulness. Himself, in that flash of light, he saw to be weak, and not strong. What if it should be so indeed? "*Whatsoever he doeth*—SHALL PROSPER." Upon the uncertainty of human things, upon the tumult of human difficulties and resolves, the words came like a strange breath of peace, from somewhere unknown, but felt to be a region of health and strength. Yet the qualifications to take the promise were not in Winthrop's hand; to seek them seemed to be a one side of his purpose; he left them on one side, and went on.

He was bending his steps towards the meeting of Beaver and Little South Sts., the sole point of light which he knew in the city. It seemed to him that rather less of the sun's cheer got into Diamond St. than anywhere else. Bank St. was a heartsome place in comparison. He made his way slowly up Beaver St. looking for Little South, and passing what to him were a great many streets without finding that one. As he drew near still another, his eye was taken with a man standing on the sidewalk before the corner house; a tall, personable, clean-looking man; who on his part looked first steadily at Winthrop and then came down to meet him, laughing and holding out his hand before he got near.

"How do you do?" was his first cordial salutation.—"It's Mr. Landholm!—I knew it!—I knew you, from your likeness to your brother. We've been looking for you. Come in, come in! How *is* your brother, Mr. Landholm?"

Winthrop was taken by surprise and could hardly say.

"I knew you as far off as I could see you—I said to myself, 'That's Mr. Landholm!' I am *very* glad to see you, sir. You've just got here?"

"This morning. But what right have I to be expected?"

"O we knew you were coming. Your room's ready for you —empty and waiting, and we've been waiting and lonesome too, ever since Mr. William went away. How *is* Mr. William, Mr. Landholm?"

"Well, sir, and full of kindly remembrances of you."

"Ah, he's not forgotten here," said Mr. Inchbald. "He won't be forgotten anywhere. Here's my sister, Mr. Landholm, —my sister, Mrs. Nettley.—Now, my dear sir, before we sit down, tell me,—you haven't any other place to stay?"

"I have not, Mr. Inchbald, indeed."

"Then come up and see what we have to give you, before we strike a bargain. Doll—won't you give us a cup of tea by the time we come down? Mr. Landholm will be the better of the refreshment. You have had a tiresome journey this weather, Mr. Landholm?"

As they mounted the stairs he listened to Winthrop's account of his illness, and looked at him when they got to the top, with a grave face of concern it was pleasant to meet. They had come up to the very top; the house was a small and insignificant wooden one, of two stories.

"This is your room," said Mr. Inchbald, opening the door of the front attic,—"this is the room your brother had; it's not much, and there's not much in it; but now my dear friend, *till* you find something better, will you keep possession of it? and give us the pleasure of having you?—and one thing more, will you speak of pay when you are perfectly at leisure to think of it, and not before, or never, just as it happens;—will you?"

"I'll take you at your word, sir; and you shall take me at mine, when the time comes."

"*That* I'll do," said Mr. Inchbald. "And now it's a bargain. Shake hands,—and come let's go down and have some tea. —Doll, I hope your tea is good to-night, for Mr. Landholm is far from well. Sit down—I wish your brother had the other place."

That tea was a refreshment. It was served in the little back room of the first floor, which had very much the seeming of being Mrs. Nettley's cooking room too. The appointments were on no higher scale of pretension than Mrs. Forriner's, yet they gave a far higher impression of the people that used them; why, belongs to the private mystery of cups and saucers and chairs, which have an odd obstinate way of their own of telling the truth. 'Doll' was the very contrast to the lady of the other tea-table. A little woman, rather fleshy, in a close cap and neat spare gown, with a face which seemed a compound of benevolent good-will, and anxious care lest everybody should not get the full benefit of it. It had known care of another kind too. If her brother had, his jovial, healthy, hearty face gave no sign.

After tea Winthrop went back to Diamond St.

"We didn't wait for you," said Mr. Forriner as he came in, —"for we thought you didn't intend probably to be back to tea."

"What success have you had?" inquired his better half.

"I have had tea, ma'am," said Winthrop.

"Have you found any place?"

"Or the place found me."

"You have got one!—Where is it?"

"In Beaver St.—the place where my brother used to be."

"What's the name?" said Mr. Forriner.

"Inchbald."

"What is he?" asked Mrs. Forriner.

"An Englishman—a miniature painter by profession."

"I wonder if he makes his living at that?" said Mrs. Forriner.

"What do you have to pay?" said her husband.

"A fair rent, sir. And now I will pay my thanks for storage and take away my trunk."

"To-night?" said Mr. Forriner.

"Well, cousin, we shall be glad to see you sometimes," said Mrs. Forriner.

"At what times, ma'am?" said Winthrop.

He spoke with a straightforward simplicity which a little daunted her.

"O," she said colouring, "come when you have an hour to spare—any time when you have nothing better to do."

"I will come then," he said smiling.

CHAPTER XVII.

Now he weighs time,
Even to the utmost grain.

KING HENRY V.

"MANNAHATTA, Dec. —, 1813.

"MY DEAR FRIENDS AT HOME,

"I am as well and as happy as I can be anywhere away from you. That to be sure is but a modicum of happiness and good condition—very far from the full perfection which I have known is possible; but you will all be contented, will you not, to hear that I have so much, and *that I have no more?* I don't know—I think of your dear circle at home—and though I cannot wish the heaven over your heads to be a whit less bright, I cannot help wishing that you may miss one constellation. You can't have any more than that from poor human nature—selfish in the midst of its best generosity. And yet, mother and Winifred, your faces rise up to shame me; and I must correct my speech and say *man's* nature; I do believe that some at least of your side of the world are made of better stuff than mine.

"'All are not such.'

"But you want to hear of me rather than of yourselves, and I come back to where I began.

"I went to see Mr. De Wort the day after I reached here. I like him very well. He received me politely, and very handsomely waived the customary fee ($250) and admitted me to the privileges of his office upon working terms. So I am working now, for him and for myself, as diligently as I ever worked in my life—in a fair way to be a lawyer, Winnie. By day engrossing deeds and copying long-winded papers, about the quarrels and wrongs of Mr. A. and Mr. B.—and at night digging into parchment-covered books, a dryer and barrener soil than any near Wut-a-qut-o or on the old mountain itself, and which must nevertheless be digged into for certain dry and musty fruits of knowledge to be fetched out of them. I am too busy to get the blues, but when I go out to take an exercise walk now and then at dusk or dawn, I do wish I could transport myself to the neighbourhood of that same mountain, and handle the axe till I had filled mother's fireplace, or take a turn in the barn at father's wheat or flax. I should accomplish a good deal before you were up; but I wouldn't go away without looking in at you.

"I am in the same house where Rufus lived when he was in Mannahatta, with his friend Mr. Inchbald; and a kinder friend I do not wish for. He is an Englishman—a fine-looking and fine-hearted fellow—ready to do everything for me, and putting me upon terms almost too easy for my comfort. He is a miniature painter, by profession, but I fear does not make much of a living. That does not hinder his being as generous as if he had thousands to dispose of. His heart does not take counsel with his purse, nor with anything but his heart. He lives with a widowed sister who keeps his house; and she is as kind in her way as he is in his, though the ways are different. I am as much at home here as I can be. I have Rufus's old room; it is a very pleasant one, and if there is not much furniture, neither do I want much. It holds my bed and my books; and my wardrobe at present does not require very extensive accommodations; and when I am in the middle of one of those said parchment-covered tomes, it signifies very little indeed what is outside of them or of me, at the moment. So you may think of me as having all I desire, so far as I myself am concerned; for my license and my use of it, must be worked and waited for. I shall not be a *great* lawyer, dear Winnie, under three years at least.

"For you all, I desire so much that my heart almost shuts up its store and says nothing. So much that for a long time, it may be, I can have no means of helping you to enjoy. Dear father and mother, I hope I have not on the whole lessened your means of enjoyment by striking out this path for myself. I trust it will in the end be found to be the best for us all. I have acted under the pressure of an impulse that seemed strong as life. I *could* do no other than as I have done. Yet I can hardly bear to think of you at home sometimes. Dear Winnie and Asahel, your images rise up and lie down with me. Asahel must study hard every minute of time he can get. And Winnie, you must study too every minute that it does not tire you, and when mother does not want you. And write to me. That will do you good, and it will do me good too.

"Give my love to Karen.

"Yours all, faithfully,

"WINTHROP LANDHOLM.

"P. S.—I have seen nobody yet but Mr. Herder."

When Winthrop went to put this letter in the post, he drew out the following:

"To WINTHROP LANDHOLM, ESQ.:

"At MR. GEORGE INCHBALD'S,

"Cor. Beaver and Little South Sts., Mannahatta.

"I am so tired, Governor, with the world and myself to-night, that I purpose resting myself at your expense,—in other words, to pour over all my roiled feelings from my own heart into yours, hoping benevolently to find my own thereby cleared. What will be the case with yours, I don't like to stop to think; but incline to the opinion, which I have for many years held, that *nothing can roil it.* You are infinitely better than I, Governor; you deserve to be very much happier; and I hope you are. The truth is, for I may as well come to it,—I am half sick of my work. I can see your face from here, and know just what its want of expression expresses. But stop. You are not in my place, and don't know anything about it. You are qualifying yourself for one of the first literary professions—and it is one of the greatest matters of joy to me to think that you are. You are bidding fair to stand, where no doubt you will stand, at the head of society. Nothing is beyond your powers; and your powers will stop short of nothing within their reach. I know you, and hug myself (not having you at hand) every day to think what sort of a brother I have got.

"Governor, I have something in me too, and I am just now in a place *not* calculated to develope or cultivate the finer part of a man's nature. My associates, without an exception, are boors and donkeys, not unfrequently combining the agreeable properties of both in one anomalous animal yclept a clown. With them my days, for the greater part, are spent; and my nights in a series of calculations almost equally extinguishing to any brightness of mind or spirit. The consequence is I feel my light put out!—not hid under a bushel, but absolutely quenched in its proper existence. I felt so when I began to write this letter;

but by dint of looking steadily for so long a time towards you, I perceive a reflection of light and warmth coming back upon me and beginning to take effect upon my own tinder, whereby I gather that it is capable of being ignited again. Seriously, Winthrop, I am sick of this. *This* was not what we left home for. I suppose in time, and with business enough, one might make money in this way, but money is not our object in life. It cannot satisfy me, and I trust not you. What shall I do? I must finish this piece of work—that will keep me in the wilds and fastnesses of this beautiful region (for it is a superb country, Winthrop; nature goes far here to make up for the want of all other discoursers whatever. I have sometimes felt as if she would make a poet of me, would I, nold I,) the finishing of my work here will detain me in the North at least till June or July of the coming summer; perhaps August. And then it is intimated to me my services would be acceptable out West—somewhere near Sawcusto. I have a great mind to come to Mannahatta—perhaps take a tutorship till something better offers—Herder said I would have no sort of difficulty in getting one, or at least he said what amounted to that—and perhaps, eventually, enter the political line. I am undecided, except in my disapprobation and dislike of what and where I now am. I have half an inclination to study law with you. It is hard to do anything with Fortune's wheel when one is at the very bottom; and the jade seems to act as if you were a drag upon her. And it is hard that you and I should be at opposite sides of the world while we are both tugging at said wheel. I sometimes think we could work to more advantage nearer together; we could work with somewhat more comfort. I am in exile here. Write me as soon as you can.

"My pleasantest thoughts are of you. Herder is as good as he can be, and you are his favourite; you will presently have the best literary society, through his means. You don't speak of Haye. Don't you go there? You had better, Winthrop;—you may find a short cut to the top of Fortune's wheel through the front door of his house. At any rate, there are two very pretty girls there and a number of other pleasant things, with which you will do well to make yourself acquainted, come thereafter what may. I wrote to them at home a week or two ago.

W. Landholm.

"P. S. Isn't Inchbald a good fellow?"

The next post went out with the answer.

"To WILLIAM LANDHOLM, ESQ., NORTH LYTTLETON, SASSAFRAS CO.

"MY DEAR RUFUS,

"Stick to your choice. Go West, and do *not* come here. Do not be discouraged by the fact of making money. And don't try to turn Fortune's wheel by force, for it will break your arms.

"Yours ever,

"WINTHROP LANDHOLM."

Winthrop did not tell them at home that he was giving lessons in the classics several hours daily, in order to live while he was carrying on his own studies; nor that, to keep the burden of his kind hosts, as well as his own burden, from growing any heavier, he had refused to eat with them; and was keeping himself in the most frugal manner, partly by the help of a chop-house, and partly by the countenance and support of a very humble little tin coffee-pot and saucepan in his own attic at home. Mr. Haye's front door he had never entered, and was more than indifferent where or what it led to.

"Why for do you not come to your friend, Mr. Haye, ever?" said Mr. Herder to him one day.

"I am short of time, Mr. Herder."

"Time!—But you come to see me?"

"I have time for that."

"I am glad of it," said the naturalist, "for there is no person I like to see better come into my room; but ozer people would like to see you come in too."

"I am not sure of that, Mr. Herder."

"I am sure," said his friend looking kindly at him. "You are working too much."

"I can't do that, sir."

"Come wiz me to Mr. Haye to-night!"

"No sir, thank you."

"What for do you say that?

"Because it is kind in you to ask me," said Winthrop smiling.

"You will not let nobody be of no use to you;" said the naturalist.

Winthrop replied by a question about a new specimen; and the whole world of animate nature was presently buried in the bowels of the earth, or in the depths of philosophy, which comes to about the same thing.

But it fell out that same day that Winthrop, going into the chop-house to fit himself for hard work with a somewhat better dinner than usual, planted himself just opposite a table which five minutes after was taken by Mr. Haye. It happened then that after the usual solitary and selfish wont of such places, the meals were near over before either of the gentlemen found out he had ever seen the other. But in the course of Mr. Haye's second glass of wine, his eye took a satisfied fit of roving over the company; and presently discovered something it had seen before in the figure and face opposite to him and in the eye which was somewhat carelessly running over the columns of a newspaper. Glass in hand Mr. Haye rose, and the next instant Winthrop felt a hand on his shoulder.

"Mr. Landholm—isn't it? I thought so. Why I've been on the point of coming to look after you this last fortnight past, Mr. Landholm, but business held me so tight by the button—I'm very glad to meet you—Will you join me?——"

"Thank you, sir—I must not; for business holds me by the hand at this moment."

"A glass of wine?"——

"Thank you sir, again."

"You will not?"

"No, sir. I have no acquaintance in that quarter, and do not wish to be introduced."

"But my dear Mr. Landholm!—are you serious?"

"Always, sir."

"Most extraordinary!—But can't you be persuaded? I think you are wrong."

"I must abide the consequences, I am afraid."

"Well, stay!—Will you come to my house to-night and let me give you some other introductions?"

"I cannot refuse that, sir."

"Then come up to tea. How's your father?—"

So Winthrop was in for it, and went about his afternoon business with the feeling that none would be done in the evening. Which did not make him more diligent, because it could not.

Mr. Haye's house was near the lower end of the Parade, and one of the best in the city. It was a very handsome room in which Winthrop found the family; as luxuriously fitted up as the fashion of those times permitted; and the little group gathered there did certainly look as if all the business of the world was done without them, and a good part of it *for* them; so undoubtedly easy and comfortable was the flow of their laces and the sweep of their silk gowns; so questionless of toil or endurance was the position of each little figure upon soft cushions, and the play of pretty fingers with delicate do-nothing bobbins and thread. Rose was literally playing with hers, for the true business of the hour seemed to be a gentleman who sat at her feet on an ottoman, and who was introduced to Winthrop as Mr. Satterthwaite. Elizabeth according to her fashion sat a little apart and seemed to be earnestly intent upon some sort of fine net manufacture. They three were all.

Winthrop's reception was after the former manner; from Rose extremely and sweetly free and cordial; from Elizabeth grave and matter-of-fact. She went back to her net-work; and Rose presently found Mr. Satterthwaite very interesting again, and went back to him, so far as looks and talk were concerned. Winthrop could but conclude that he was not interesting, for neither of the ladies certainly found him so. He had an excellent chance to make up his mind about the whole party; for none of them gave him any thing else to do with it.

Rose was a piece of loveliness, to the eye, such as one would not see in many a summer day; with all the sweet flush of youth and health she was not ill-named. Fresh as a rose, fresh-coloured, bright, blooming; sweet too, one would say, for a very pretty smile seemed ever at home on the lips;—to see her but once, she would be noted and remembered as a most rare picture of humanity. But Winthrop had seen her more than once. His eye passed on.

Her cousin had changed for the better; though it might be only the change which years make in a girl at that age, rather than any real difference of character. She had grown handsomer. The cheek was well rounded out now, and had a clear healthy tinge, though not at all Rose's white and red. Elizabeth's colour only came when there was a call for it and then it came promptly. And she was not very apt to smile; when she did, it was more often with a careless or scornful turn, or full and bright with a sense of the ludicrous; never a loving or benevolent smile, such as those that constantly graced Rose's pretty lip. Her mouth kept its old cut of grave independence, Winthrop saw at a glance; and her eye, when by chance she lifted it and it met his, was the very same mixture of coolness and fire that it had been of old; the fire for herself, the coolness for all the rest of the world.

She looked down again at her netting immediately, but the look had probably reminded her that nobody in her father's house was playing the hostess at the moment. A disagreeable reminder it is likely, for she worked away at her netting more vigorously than ever, and it was two or three minutes before her eyes left it again to take note of what Rose and Mr. Satterthwaite were thinking about. Her look amused Winthrop, it was so plain an expression of impatient indignation that they did not do what they left her to do. But seeing they were a hopeless case, after another minute or two of pulling at her netting, she changed her seat for one on his side of the room. Winthrop gave her no help, and she followed up her duty move with a duty commonplace.

"How do you like Mannahatta, Mr. Landholm?"

"I have hardly asked myself the question, Miss Haye."

"Does that mean you don't know?"

"I cannot say that. I like it as a place of business."

"And not as a place of pleasure?"

"No. Except in so far as the pushing on of business may be pleasure."

"You are drawing a distinction in one breath which you confound in the next," said Elizabeth.

"I didn't know that you would detect it," he said with a half smile.

"Detect what?"

"The distinction between business and pleasure."

"Do you think I don't know the difference?"

"You cannot know the difference, without knowing the things to be compared."

"The things to be compared!—" said she, with a good look at him out of her dark eyes. "And which of them do you think I don't know?"

"I supposed you were too busy to have much time for pleasure," he said quietly.

"It is possible to be busy in more ways than one," said Elizabeth, after a minute of not knowing how to take him up.

"That is just what I was thinking."

"What are *you* busy about, Mr. Landholm, in this place of business?"

"I am only learning my trade," he answered.

"A trade!—May I ask what?" she said, with another surprised and inquisitive look.

"A sort of cobbling trade, Miss Elizabeth—the trade of the law."

"What does the law cobble?"

"People's name and estate."

"*Cobble*?" said Elizabeth. "What is the meaning of cobble?'"

"I don't recollect," said Winthrop. "What meaning do you give it, Miss Haye?"

"I thought it was a poor kind of mending."

"I am afraid there is some of that work done in the profession," said Winthrop smiling. "Occasionally. But it is the profession and not the law that is chargeable, for the most part."

"I wouldn't be a lawyer if that were not so," said Elizabeth. "I wouldn't be a *cobbler* of anything."

"To be anything else might depend on a person's faculties."

"I don't care," said Elizabeth,—"I *would* not be. If I could not mend, I would let alone. I wouldn't cobble."

"What if one could neither mend nor let alone?"

"One would have less power over himself than I have, or than you have, Mr. Landholm."

"One thing at least doesn't need cobbling," he said with a smile.

"I never heard such a belittling character of the profession," she went on. "Your mother would have given it a very different one, Mr. Landholm. She would have told you, 'Open thy mouth, judge'—what is it?—'and plead the cause of the poor.'"

Whether it were the unexpected bringing up of his mother's name, or the remembrance of her spirit, something procured Miss Elizabeth a quick little bright smile of answer, very different from anything she had had from Winthrop before. So different, that her eyes went down to her work for several minutes, and she forgot everything else in a sort of wonder at the change and at the beauty of expression his face could put on.

"I didn't find those words myself," she added presently;—"a foolish man was shewing me the other day what he said was my verse in some chapter of Proverbs; and it happened to be that."

But Winthrop's answer went to something in her former speech, for it was made with a little breath of a sigh.

"I think Wut-a-qut-o is a pleasanter place than this, Miss Haye."

"O, so do I!—at least—I don't know that it signifies much to me what sort of a place I am in. If I can only have the things I want around me, I don't think I care much."

"How many things do you want to be comfortable?"

"O,—books,—and the conveniences of life; and one or two friends that one cares about."

"Cut off two of those preliminaries,—and which one would you keep for comfort, Miss Elizabeth?"

"Couldn't do without either of 'em. What's become of my Merry-go-round, Mr. Winthrop?"

"It lies in the upper loft of the barn, with all the seams open."

"Why?"

"You remember, nobody was to use it but me."

A curious recollection of the time when it was given and of the feeling, half condescending, half haughty, with which it had been given, came over Elizabeth; and for a moment or two she was a little confused. Whether Winthrop recollected it too or whether he had a mischievous mind that she should, he said presently,

"And what's become of your horse, Miss Elizabeth?"

"He's very well," she said. "At least—I don't know I am sure how he is, for he is up in the country."

Winthrop rose at the instant to greet Mr. Herder, and Elizabeth did not know whether the smile on his lips was *for* him or *at* her.

"Ah! Wint'rop," said the new-comer, "how do you do! I thought you would not come here wiz me this morning?"

"I thought not too, sir."

"How did you come? Miss Élisabet' did make you."

"Miss Elizabeth's father."

"He is a strange man, Miss Élisabet'!—he would not come for me—I could not bring him—neizer for de love of me, nor for de love of you, nor for love of himself. He does like to have his way. And now he is here—I do not know what for; but I am very glad to see him."

He walked Winthrop off.

"He *is* a strange man," thought Elizabeth;—"he don't seem to care in the least what he ever did or may do; he would just as lief remind me of it as not. It is very odd that he shouldn't want to come here, too."

She sat still and worked alone. When Mr. Haye by and by came in, he joined Winthrop and Mr. Herder, and they three formed a group which even the serving of tea and coffee did not break up. Elizabeth's eye glanced over now and then towards the interested heads of the talkers, and then at Rose and Mr. Satterthwaite, who on the other side were also enough for each other's contentment and seemed to care for no interruption. Elizabeth interrupted nobody.

But so soon as awhile after tea Mr. Satterthwaite left the company, Rose tripped across to the other group and placed her pretty person over against the naturalist and his young friend.

"Mr. Herder, you are taking up all of Mr. Landholm—I haven't seen him or spoken to him the whole evening."

"Dere he is, Miss Rose," said the naturalist. "Do what you like wiz him."

"But you don't give a chance. Mr. Landholm, are you as great a favourite with everybody as you are with Mr. Herder?"

"Everybody does not monopolize me, Miss Cadwallader."

"I wished so much you would come over our side—I wanted to make you acquainted with Mr. Satterthwaite."

Winthrop bowed, and Mr. Haye remarked that Mr. Satterthwaite was not much to be acquainted with.

"No, but still—he's very pleasant," Rose said. "And how is everything up at your lovely place, Mr. Landholm?"

"Cold, at present, Miss Cadwallader."

"O yes, of course; but then I should think it would be lovely at all times. Isn't it a beautiful place, Mr. Herder?"

"Which place, Miss Rose?"

"Why, Mr. Landholm's place, up the river, where we were that summer. And how's your mother, Mr. Landholm, and your sister?—so kind Mrs. Landholm is! And have you left them entirely, Mr. Landholm?"

"I have brought all of myself away that I could," he said with a smile.

"Don't you wish yourself back there every day?"

"No."

"Don't you! I should think you would. How's your brother, Mr. Landholm, and where is he?"

"He is well, and in the North yet."

"Is he coming back to Mannahatta soon?"

"I have no reason to think so."

"I wish he would. I want to see him again. He is such good company."

"Mr. Wint'rop will do so well, Miss Rose," said the naturalist.

"I dare say he will," said Rose with a very sweet face.

"He won't if he goes on as he has begun," said Mr. Haye. "I asked him to dine here the day after to-morrow, Rose."

"He'll come?—"

But Mr. Landholm's face said no, and said it with a cool certainty.

"Why, Mr. Landholm!—"

"He is very—you cannot do nozing wiz him, Miss Rose," said the naturalist. "Miss Élisabet'!—"

"Well, Mr. Herder?"

"I wish you would come over here and see what you can do."

"About what, Mr. Herder?"

"Wiz Mr. Wint'rop here."

"I just heard you say that nobody can do anything with him, Mr. Herder."

"Here he has refuse to come to dinner wiz all of us."

"If he can't come for his own pleasure, I don't suppose he would come for anybody else's," said Elizabeth.

She left her solitary chair however, and came up and stood behind Mr. Herder.

"He pleads business," said Mr. Haye.

"Miss Élisabet', we want your help," said Mr. Herder. "He is working too hard."

"I am not supposed to know what that means, sir."

"What?" said Mr. Haye.

"Working too hard."

"Work!" said Mr. Haye. "What do you know about work?"

"The personal experience of a life-time, sir," said Winthrop gravely. "Not much of the theory, but a good deal of the practice."

"I'll bear her witness of one thing," said Mr. Haye; "if she can't work herself, she can make work for other people."

"You've got it, Lizzie," said her cousin, clapping her hands.

"I don't take it," said Elizabeth. "For whom do I make work, father?"

"For me, or whoever has the care of you."

Elizabeth's cheek burned now, and her eye too, with a fire which she strove to keep under.

"It's not fair!" she exclaimed. "If I make work for you, I am sure it is work that nobody takes up."

"That's true," said her father laughing,—"it would be too much trouble to pretend to take it all up."

"Then you shouldn't *bring* it up!" said Elizabeth, trembling.

"It's nothing very bad to bring up," said her father. "It's only a little extra strong machinery that wants a good engineer."

"That's no fault in the machinery, sir," said Winthrop.

"And all you have to do," suggested Mr. Herder, "is to find a good engineer."

"I am my own engineer!" said Elizabeth, a little soothed by the first remark and made desperate by the second.

"So you are!" said her cousin. "There's no doubt of that."

"Are you a good one, Miss Élisabet'?" said the naturalist, smiling at her.

"You must presume not!—after what you have heard," she answered with abundant haughtiness.

"It is one mark of a good engineer to be a match for his machinery," said Winthrop quietly.

It was said so coolly and simply that Elizabeth did not take offence. She stood, rather cooled down and thoughtful, still at the back of Mr. Herder's chair. Winthrop rose to take leave, and Mr. Haye repeated his invitation.

"I will venture so far as to say I will come if I can, sir."

"I shall expect you," said the other, shaking his hand cordially.

Mr. Herder went with his friend. Mr. Haye soon himself followed, leaving the two ladies alone. Both sat down in silence at the table; Elizabeth with a book, Miss Cadwallader with her fancy work; but neither of them seemed very intent on what she was about. The work went on lazily, and the leaves of the book were not turned over.

"I wish I was Winthrop Landholm," said Rose at length.

"Why?"—said her cousin, after a sufficient time had marked her utter carelessness of what the meaning might have been.

"I should have such a good chance."

"Of what?"—said Elizabeth dryly enough.

"Of a certain lady's favour, whose favour is not very easy to gain."

"You don't care much for my favour," said Elizabeth.

"I should, if I were Winthrop Landholm."

"If you were he, you wouldn't get it, any more than you have now."

"O no. I mean, I wish I were he and not myself, you know."

"You must think well enough of him. I am sure no possible inducement could make me wish myself Mr. Satterthwaite, for a moment."

"I don't care for Mr. Satterthwaite," said Rose coolly. "But how Mr. Haye takes to him, don't he?"

"To whom?"

"Winthrop Landholm."

"I don't see how he shews it."

"Why, the way he was asking him to dinner."

"It is nothing very uncommon for Mr. Haye to ask people to dinner."

"No, but such a person."

"What 'such a person ?"

"O, a farmer's boy. Mr. Haye wouldn't have done it once But that's the way he always comes round to people when they get up in the world."

"This one hasn't got much up in the world yet."

"He is going to, you know. Mr. Herder says so; and President Darcy says there are not two such young men seen in half a century as he and his brother."

Elizabeth laid down her book and looked over at her companion, with an eye the other just met and turned away from.

"Rose,—how *dare* you talk to me so!"

"So how?" said the other, pouting and reddening, but without lifting her face from her work.

"You know,—about my father. No matter what he does, if it were the worst thing in the world, your lips have no business to mention it to my ears."

"I wasn't saying anything *bad*," said Rose.

"Your notions of bad and good, and honourable and dishonourable, are very different from mine! If he did as you say, I should be bitterly ashamed."

"I don't see why."

"I will not have such things *spoken of* to me,—Rose, do you understand? What my father does, no human being has a right to comment upon to me; and none shall!"

"You think you may talk as you like to *me*," said Rose, between pouting and crying. "I was only laughing."

"Laugh about something else."

"I wish Winthrop Landholm had been here."

"Why?"

"He'd have given you another speech about engineering."

Elizabeth took her candle and book and marched out of the room.

CHAPTER XVIII.

One man has one way of talking, and another man has another, that's all the difference between them.
GOOD-NATURED MAN.

WINTHROP found he could go. So according to his promise he dressed himself, and was looking out a pockethandkerchief from the small store in his trunk, when the door opened.

"Rufus !——"

"Ah !—you didn't expect to see me, did you ?" said that gentleman, taking off his hat and coming in and closing the door with a face of great life and glee.—"Here I am, Governor !"

"What brought you here ?" said his brother shaking his hand.

"What brought me here ?—why, the stage-coach, to be sure ; except five miles, that I rode on horseback. What should bring me ?"

"Something of the nature of a centrifugal force, I should judge."

"Centrifugal !—*You* are my centre, Governor,—don't you know that ? I tend to you as naturally as the poor earth does to the sun. That's why I am here—I couldn't keep at a distance any longer."

"My dear sir, at that rate you are running to destruction."

"No, no," said Rufus laughing,—"there's a certain degree of license in our moral planetary system——I'm going away again as soon as I am rightly refreshed with the communication of your light and warmth."

"Well," said Winthrop untying his neckcloth, "it would seem but courtesy in the sun to stand still to receive his visitor——I'm very glad to see you, Will."

"What's the matter ?"

"The sun was going out to dinner—that's all,—but you are a sufficient excuse for me."

"Going to dinner?—where?"

"No. 11, on the Parade."

"No. 11?—Mr. Haye's? were you? I'll go too. I won't hinder you."

"I am not sorry to be hindered," said Winthrop.

"But I am!—at least, I should be. We'll both go. How soon, Governor?"

"Presently."

"I'll be ready," said Rufus,—"here's my valise—but my shirt ruffles, I fear, are in a state of impoverished elegance.——I speak not in respect of one or two holes, of which they are the worse,—but solely in reference to the coercive power of narrow circumstances——which nobody knows anything of that hasn't experienced it," said Rufus, looking up from his valise to his brother with an expression half earnest, half comical.

"You are not suffering under it at this moment," said Winthrop.

"Yes I am—in the form of my frills. Look there!——I'll tell you what I'll do—I'll invoke the charities of my good friend, Mrs. Nettley. Is she down stairs?—I'll be back in a moment, Winthrop."

Down stairs, shirt in hand, went Rufus, and tapped at Mrs. Nettley's door. That is, the door of the room where she usually lived, a sort of better class kitchen, which held the place of what in houses of more pretension is called the 'back parlour.' Mrs. Nettley's own hand opened the door at his tap.

She was a strong contrast to her brother, with her rather small person and a face all the lines of which were like a cobweb set to catch every care that was flying; but woven by no malevolent spider; it was a very nest of kindliness and good-will.

"How d'ye do, Mrs. Nettley," said Rufus softly.

"Why Mr. Landholm!—are you there? Come in—how good it is to see you again! but I didn't expect it."

"Didn't expect to see me again?"

"No—O yes, of course, Mr. William," said Mrs. Nettley laughing,—"I expected to see you again; but not now—I didn't expect to see you when I opened the door."

"I had the advantage, for I did expect to see you."

"How do you do, Mr. Landholm?"

"Why, as well as a man can do, in want of a shirt," said Rufus comically.

"Mr. Landholm?——"

"You see, Mrs. Nettley," Rufus went on, "I have come all the way from North Lyttleton to dine with a friend and my brother here; and now I am come, I find that without your good offices I haven't a ruffle to ruffle myself withal; or in other words, I am afraid people would think I had packed myself bodily into my valise, and thereby conclude I was a smaller affair than they had thought me."

"Mr. Landholm!—how you do talk!—but can I do anything?"

"Why yes, ma'am,—or your irons can, if you have any hot."

"O that's it!" exclaimed Mrs. Nettley as Rufus held out the crumpled frills,—"It's to smooth them,—yes sir, my fire is all out a'most, but I can iron them in the oven. I'll do it directly Mr. Landholm."

"Well," said Rufus with a quizzical face,—"any way—if you'll ensure them against damages, Mrs. Nettley—I don't understand all the possibilities of an oven."

"We are very glad to have your brother in your room, Mr. Landholm," the good lady went on, as she placed one of her irons in the oven's mouth, where a brilliant fire was at work.

"I should think you would, ma'am; he can fill it much better than I."

"Why Mr. Landholm!—I should think——I shouldn't think, to look at you, that your brother would weigh much more than you—he's broader shouldered, something, but you're the tallest, I'm sure. But you didn't mean that."

"I won't dispute the palm of beauty with him, Mrs. Nettley, nor of ponderosity. I am willing he should exceed me in both."

"Why Mr. Landholm!—dear, I wish this iron would get hot; but there's no hurrying it;—I think it's the wood—I told George I think this wood does *not* give out the heat it ought to do. It makes it very extravagant wood. One has to burn so much more, and *then* it doesn't do the work—Why Mr. Landholm—you must have patience, sir——Your brother is excellent, every way, and he's very good looking, but you are the handsomest."

"Everybody don't think so," Rufus said, but with a play of lip and brow that was not on the whole unsatisfied. Mrs. Nettley's attention however was now fastened upon the frills. And then came in Mr. Inchbald; and they talked, a sort of whirlwind of talk, as his sister not unaptly described it; and then, the ruffles being in order Rufus put himself so, and Winthrop and he talked themselves all the way down to No. 11, on the Parade.

Their welcome was most hearty, though the company were already at table. Place was speedily made for them; and Rufus hardly waited to take his before he became the life and spirit of the party. He continued to be that through the whole entertainment, delighting everybody's eye and ear. Winthrop laughed at his brother and with him, but himself played a very quiet part; putting in now and then a word that told, but doing it rarely and carelessly; the flow and freshness of the conversation calling for no particular help from him.

Mr. Herder was there; also Mr. Satterthwaite, who sat next to Winthrop and addressed several confidential and very unimportant remarks to him, and seemed to look upon his brother as a sort of meteoric phenomenon. President Darcy, of Mr. Herder's College, was the only other guest. Elizabeth sat next to Winthrop, but after the first formal greeting vouchsafed not a single look his way; she was in a dignified mood for all the company generally, and Rose's were the only feminine words that mixed with the talk during dinner. Very feminine they were, if that word implies a want of strength; but coming from such rosy lips, set round about with such smiles of winningness, they won their way and made easy entrance into all the ears at table. With the trifling exception of a pair or two.

"What is the matter with you?" said Rose, when she and her cousin had left the gentlemen and were alone in the drawing-room.

"Nothing at all."

"You don't say a word '

"I will, when I have a word to say."

"I thought you always had words enough," said Rose.

"Not when I haven't time too."

"Time? what, for words?"

"Yes."

"What was the matter with the time?"

"It was filled up."

"Well, you might have helped fill it."

"Nothing can be more than full, very well," said Elizabeth contemptuously. "I never want *my* words to be lost on the outside of a conversation."

"You think a great deal of your words," said her cousin.

"I want other people should."

"You do! Well—I never expect them to think much of mine."

"That's not true, Rose."

"It isn't?"

"No; and your smile when you said it spoke that it wasn't."

"Well, I don't care, they *are* thought enough of," said Rose, half crying.

Elizabeth walked to the window and stood within the curtain, looking out into the street; and Rose bestowed her pouting lips and brimful eyes upon the full view of the fire.

"What's made you so cross?" she said after a quarter of an hour, when the tears were dried.

"I am not cross."

"Did you ever see anybody so amusing as Rufus Landholm?"

"Yes, he's amusing.—I don't like people that are too amusing."

"How can anybody be *too* amusing?"

"He can make it too much of his business."

"Who?—Rufus?"

"No, anybody. You asked how *anybody* could."

"Well I dont see how you can think he is too amusing."

"Why that is all you care for in a man."

"It isn't! I care for a great deal else. What do *you* care for?"

"I don't know, I am sure," said Elizabeth; "but I should say, everything else."

"Well I think people are very stupid that aren't amusing," said Rose.

Which proposition the ladies illustrated for another quarter of an hour.

The gentlemen came in then, one after another, but Elizabeth did not move from her window.

"I have something of yours in my possession, Miss Haye," said Rufus, coming to the outside of the curtain within which she stood.

"What?" said Elizabeth unceremoniously.

"Your father."

"What are you going to do with him?"

Rufus laughed a little; and Winthrop remarked there was nothing like straightforward dealing to confound a manœuvrer.

"I have a desire to put him out of my hands, into yours," said Rufus;—"but then, I have also a desire to make him fast there."

"My bracelet!" said Elizabeth.

It had a likeness of Mr. Haye in cameo.

"Where did you get it?"

"Where you left it."

"Where was that?"

"On the table, at the left hand of your plate, covered by your napkin."

Elizabeth stretched out her hand for it.

"Not so fast—I have it in my possession, as I told you, and I claim a reward for recovering it from its ignoble condition."

"I shall set my own conditions then," said Elizabeth. "I will let anybody put it on, who will do me the pleasure to explain it first."

"Explain?" said Rufus, looking in a sort of comical doubt at the cameo;—"I see the features of Mr. Haye, which never need explanation to me."

"Not in nature; but do you understand them when they look so brown on a white ground?"

"They look very natural!" said Rufus eyeing the cameo.

"That is to say, you do not understand them?"

"Pardon me, *you* are the person most difficult to understand."

"I don't ask that of you," said Elizabeth. "I want to know about this cameo, for I confess I don't."

"And I confess I don't," said Rufus. "I didn't even know it had any other name but Mr. Haye."

"What's all this?" said Rose,—"what are you talking about here?"

"We are talking about, we don't know what," said Rufus.

"What is it?"

"That's the question;—nobody knows."

"*What* is the question?"

"Who shall put on Miss Elizabeth's bracelet."

"Give it to me—I'll do it."

"Pardon me—there is said to be reason in the roasting of eggs, and there must be a good deal of reason before this bracelet goes on."

"I want somebody to tell me about the cameo," said Elizabeth.

"Well, won't somebody do it?"

"Mr. Landholm can't—I haven't asked Mr. Winthrop."

"Will you?" said Rose turning to him.

"I wasn't asked," said Winthrop.

"But I asked you."

"Do you wish to know, Miss Cadwallader?"

"No I don't. What's the use of knowing about everything?

Do leave the cameos, and come over here and sit down and talk and be comfortable!"

"It's impossible for me to be comfortable," said Rufus. "I've got Mr. Haye on my hands and I don't know what to do with him."

"Mr. Herder!"—Rose called out to him,—"do come here and tell us about cameos, that we can sit down and be comfortable."

Very good-humouredly the naturalist left Mr. Haye and came to them, and presently was deep in quartz and silica, and onyx and chalcedony, and all manner of stones that are precious. He told all that Elizabeth wanted to know, and much more than she had dreamed of knowing. Even Rose listened; and Rufus was eagerly attentive; and Elizabeth after she had asked questions as far as her knowledge allowed her to push them, sighed and wished she knew everything.

"Then you would be more wise than anybody, Miss Élisabet'—you would be too wise. The man who knows the most, knows that he knows little."

"Is that your opinion of yourself, Mr. Herder?" said Rufus.

"Certainly. I do know very little;—I will know more, I hope."

"O Mr. Herder, you know enough," said Rose. "I shouldn't think you would want to study any more."

"If I was to say, I know enough,—that would be to say that I do not know nozing at all."

"Mr. Winthrop, you don't seem as interested as the rest of us," said Elizabeth, perhaps with a little curiosity; for he had stood quietly by, letting even Mr. Satterthwaite push himself in between.

"O he," said the naturalist,—"he knows it all before."

"Then why didn't you tell me!" said Elizabeth.

"I wasn't asked," said Winthrop smiling.

"Wint'rop comes to my room the nights," Mr. Herder went on,—"and he knows pretty well all what is in it, by this time. When he is tired himself wiz work at his books and his writings, he comes and gets rested wiz my stones and my preparations. If you will come there, Miss Élisabet', I will shew you crystals of quartz, and onyx, and all the kinds of chalcedony, and ozer things."

"And I too, Mr. Herder?" said Rose.

"Wiz pleasure, Miss Rose,—if you like."

"Mr. Herder," said the young lady, "don't you love everything very much?"

"I love you very much, Miss Rose," said the naturalist, turning his good-humoured handsome face full upon her,—"I do not know about everyzing."

"No, but I mean all animals and insects, and everything that lives?"

"I do not love everyzing that lives," said the naturalist smiling. "I do not love Mr. Heinfelt."

"Who is Mr. Heinfelt?" said Rose.

"He is a man what I do not love."

"No, but Mr. Herder, I mean, don't you love other things very much—animals, and such things? You have so much to do with them."

"No—I have no love to spare for animals," he said with a grave face.

"Don't you love birds and animals, that you are always after and busy with?"

"No," said the naturalist,—"I do not love them—I love what is *back* of all that—not the animals. I keep my love for men."

"Do you think you have any more in that direction, for keeping it from the others?" said Elizabeth.

"I do not understand—"

"Do you think you love men any better because you don't give animals any love at all?"

"I do love some animals," said Mr. Herder. "I had a horse once, when I lived in Germany, that I did love. I loved him so well, that when a man did insult my horse, I made him fight me."

Rose exclaimed; Elizabeth smiled significantly; and Winthrop remarked,

"So that's the way your love for men shews itself!"

"No," said the naturalist,—"no,—I never did ask a man to meet me more than that one time. And I did not hurt him much. I only want to punish him a little."

"Why Mr. Herder!" Rose repeated. "I didn't think you would do such a thing."

"Everybody fight in Germany," said the naturalist; they all fight at the Universitées—they *must* fight. I found the only way was to make myself so good swordsman that I should be safe."

"And have you fought many duels?" said Elizabeth.

"Yes—I have fought—I have been obliged by circumstances to fight a good many.——I have seen two hundred."

"Two hundred duels, Mr. Herder!"

"Yes.—I have seen four men killed."

"Were *you* ever hurt, Mr. Herder?" said Rose.

"No—I never was wounded. I saw how it was—that the only thing to do was to excel ozers; so as in ozer things, I did in this."

"But how came you, who love men so well, to have so much to do with hurting them, Mr. Herder?"

"You cannot help it, Miss Élisabet'," said the naturalist. "They fight for *nozing*—they fight for *nozing*. I never asked one, but I have been oblige to fight a good many. The students make themselves into clubs; and the way is, when two students of different clubs, get in a quarrel, their presidents must fight it out; —so they meet people in duels that they have never spoken to, nor seen. I will give you an instance.—One of these fellows—a great fighter—he had fought perhaps forty times,—he was bragging about it, 'he had fought such one and such one,' he said; —'perhaps he ought to have fought Herder, in order to say that he was the best man with the sword of all the German students, —perhaps he ought to have met Herder, but he didn't care about it!' And a young fellow that heard him, that was by, he took it up; 'Sir,' said he, 'Herder is my friend—you must fight him —come to my room to-morrow morning at seven o'clock—he will meet you;'—'very well,' they agree upon the matter togezer. The next morning he come bouncing into my room at a quarter after seven—'Herder! Herder! come on!—Lessing is waiting to fight you in my room.'—'What is the matter?'—'O, Lessing said so and so, and I told him you would fight him at seven, and it is a quarter past'—'Well, you tell him I didn't know of this, I am not keeping him waiting; I will come directly.'—I was not up. So I got myself dressed, and in ten minutes I was there. A duel is finished when they have given twelve blows"——

"Twelve on each side, Mr. Herder?"

"Yes—when they have both of them given twelve blows apiece. Before we begun, Lessing and me, I whispered to somebody who stood there, that I would not touch him unless he touched me; and then I would give it to him in the ribs. I received ten blows on my arm, which is covered wiz a long glove; the eleven, he cut my waistcoat—I had one blow left, and I gave it to him in the ribs so long——"

Mr. Herder's words were filled out by the position of his fore fingers, which at this juncture were held some seven or eight inches apart.

"O Mr. Herder!—did you kill him!" exclaimed Rose.

"Not at all—I did not kill him—he was very good friend of mine,—he was not angry wiz me. He said, 'when I get well, Herder, you come to breakfast wiz me in my room;' and I said, 'yes!'"

"Is that kind of thing permitted in the Universities, Mr. Herder?" said Elizabeth.

"Permit?—No, it is not permitted. They would hinder it if they could."

"What would have been done to you if you had been found out?"

"Humph!—They would have shut us up!" said Mr. Herder, shrugging his shoulders.

"In your rooms?"

"No—not exactly;—in the fortress. At Munich the punishment for being found out, is eight years in the fortress;—at ozer places, four or five years;—yet they will fight."

"How many Universities have you been in, Mr. Herder?" said Rose.

"I have been in seven, of Universités in Europe."

"Fighting duels in all of them!"

"Well, yes;—no, there was one where I did fight no duel. I was not there long enough."

"Mr. Herder, I am shocked! I wouldn't have thought it of you."

"The bracelet, Mr. Herder, I believe is yours," said Rufus.

"Mine?"—said the naturalist.

"Miss Elizabeth would allow no one to put it on her hand, but a philosopher."

"That is too great an honour for me,—I am not young and gallant enough—I shall depute you,"—said Mr. Herder putting the cameo in Winthrop's hand.

But Winthrop remarked that he could not take deputed honours; and quietly laid it in the hand of its owner. Elizabeth, with a face a little blank, clasped it on for herself. Rufus looked somewhat curious and somewhat amused.

"I am afraid you will say of my brother, Miss Haye, that though certainly *young* enough, he is not very gallant," he said.

Elizabeth gave no answer to this speech, nor sign of hearing, unless it might be gathered from the cool free air with which she made her way out of the group and left them at the window. She joined herself to President Darcy, at the other side of the fire, and engaged him in talk with her about different gems and the engraving of them, so earnestly that she had no eyes nor ears for anybody else. And when any of the gentlemen brought her refreshments, she took or refused them almost without acknowledgment, and always without lifting her eyes to see to whom it might be due.

The company were all gone, and a little pause, of rest or of musing, had followed the last spoken 'good night.' It was musing on Elizabeth's part; for she broke it with,

"Father, if you can give Mr. Landholm aid in any way, I hope you will."

"My dear," said her father, "I don't know what I can do. I did offer to set him a going in business, but he don't like my line; and I have nothing to do with his, away up in the North there among the mountains."

"O I don't mean that Mr. Landholm—I mean the other."

"Winthrop," said Mr. Haye.

"Elizabeth likes him much the best," said Miss Cadwallader.

"I don't," said Mr. Haye.

"Neither do I!"

"I do," said Elizabeth. "I think he is worth at least ten of his brother."

"She likes him so well, that if you don't help him, dear Mr. Haye, there is every likelihood that somebody else will."

"I certainly would," said Elizabeth, "if there was any way that I could. But there is not."

"I don't know that he wants help," said Mr. Haye.

"Why he must, father!—he can't live upon nothing; how much means do you suppose he has?"

"I met him at the chop-house the other day," said Mr. Haye; —"he was eating a very good slice of roast beef. I dare say he paid for it."

"But he is struggling to make his way up into his profession," said Elizabeth. "He *must* be."

"What must he be?" said Rose.

"Struggling."

"Perhaps he is," said Mr. Haye, "but he don't say so. If I see him struggling, I will try what I can do."

"Oh father!——"

"Why should Winthrop Landholm be helped," said Rose, "more than all the other young men who are studying in the city?"

"Because I know him," said Elizabeth, "and don't happen to know the others. And because I like him."

"I like him too," said her father yawning, "but I don't know anything very remarkable about him. I like his brother the best."

"He is honest, and good, and *independent*," said Elizabeth; "and those are the very people that ought to be helped."

"And those are the very people that it is difficult to help," said her father. "How do you suppose he would take it, if I were to offer him a fifty dollar note to-morrow?"

"I don't suppose he would take it at all," said Elizabeth. "You couldn't help him so. But there are other ways."

"You may give him all your business, when he gets into his profession," said Mr. Haye. "I don't know what else you can do. Or you can use your influence with Mr. Satterthwaite to get his father to employ him."

"You and he may both be very glad to do it yet," said Elizabeth. "I shouldn't wonder."

"Then I don't see why you are concerned about him," said Rose.

Elizabeth was silent, with a face that might be taken to say there was nobody within hearing worthy of her words.

Rufus went back to his work in the mountains, and Winthrop struggled on; if most diligent and unsparing toil, and patient denying himself of necessary and wished-for things, were struggling. It was all his spare time could do to make clear the way for the hours given to his profession. There was little leisure for rest, and he had no means to bestow on pleasure; and that is a very favourable stating of the case as far as regards the last item. Mr. Inchbald never asked for rent, and never had it; not in those days. That the time would come, Winthrop believed; and his kind host never troubled himself to inquire.

There were pleasures, however, that Winthrop could not buy and which were very freely his. Mr. Herder's friendship introduced him to society, some of the best worth to be found, and which opened itself circle after circle to let him in. He had the freedom of President Darcy's house, and of Mr. Haye's, where he met other sets; in all, covering the whole ground of Mannahatta good society; and in all which Winthrop could not but know he was gladly seen. He had means and facilities for social enjoyment, more, by many, than he chose to avail himself of; facilities that did not lack temptation. In Mr. Herder's set, Winthrop often was found; other houses in the city saw him but rarely.

There was an exception,—he was often at Mr. Haye's; why, it did not very plainly appear. He was certainly made welcome by the family, but so he was by plenty of other families; and the house had not a more pleasant set of familiars than several other houses could boast. Mr. Haye had no sort of objection to giving him so much countenance and encouragement; and Rose kept all her coldness and doubtful speeches for other times than those when he was near. Elizabeth held very much her old manner; in general chose to have little to do with him; either haughtily or carelessly distant, it might be taken for one or the other. Though *which* it might be taken for, seemed to give no more concern to the gentleman in question than it did to herself.

CHAPTER XIX.

A man may hear this shower sing in the wind.
MERRY WIVES OF WINDSOR.

ONE summer's afternoon,—this was the first summer of Winthrop's being in Mannahatta,—he went to solace himself with a walk out of town. It was a long and grave and thoughtful walk; so that Mr. Landholm really had very little good of the bright summer light upon the grass and trees. Furthermore, he did not even find it out when this light was curtained in the west with a thick cloud, which straightway became gilt and silver-edged in a marvellous and splendid degree. The cloud of thought was thicker than that, if not quite so brilliant; and it was not until low growls of thunder began to salute his ear, that he looked up and found the silver edge fast mounting to the zenith and the curtain drawing its folds all around over the clear blue sky. His next look was earthward, for a shelter; for at the rate that chariot of the storm was travelling he knew he had not many minutes to seek one before the storm would be upon him. Happily a blacksmith's shop, that he would certainly have passed without seeing it, stood at a little distance; and Winthrop thankfully made for it. He found it deserted; and secure of a refuge, took his place at the door to watch the face of things; for though the edge of the town was near, the storm was nearer, and it would not do to run for it. The blackness covered everything now, changing to lurid light in the storm quarter, and big scattered drops began to come plashing down. This time Winthrop's mind was so much in the clouds that he did not know what was going on in the earth; for while he stood looking and gazing, two ladies almost ran over him. Winthrop's senses came back to the door of the blacksmith's shop, and the ladies recovered themselves.

"How do you do, Mr. Landholm," said the one, with a bow.

"O Mr. Winthrop!" cried the other,—"what shall we do? we can't get home, and I'm so frightened!——"

Winthrop had not time to open his lips, for either civility or consolation, when a phaeton, coming at a furious rate, suddenly pulled up before them, and Mr. Satterthwaite jumped out of it and joined himself to the group. His business was to persuade Miss Haye to take the empty place in his carriage and escape with him to the shelter of her own house or his father's. Miss Haye however preferred getting wet, and walking through the mud, and being blinded with the lightning, all of which alternatives Mr. Satterthwaite presented to her; at least no other conclusion could be drawn, for she very steadily and coolly refused to ride home with him.

"Mr. Landholm," said Mr. Satterthwaite in desperation, "don't you advise Miss Haye to agree to my proposition?"

"I never give advice, sir," said Winthrop, "after I see that people's minds are made up. Perhaps Miss Cadwallader may be less stubborn."

Mr. Satterthwaite could do no other than turn to Miss Cadwallader, who wanted very little urging.

"But Rose!" said her cousin,—"you're not going to leave me alone?"

"No, I don't," said Rose. "I'm sure you've got somebody with you; and he's got an umbrella."

"Don't, Rose!" said Elizabeth,—"stay and go home with me—the storm will be over directly."

"It won't—I can't," said Rose,—"It won't be over this hour, and I'm afraid——"

And into Mr. Satterthwaite's phaeton she jumped, and away Mr. Satterthwaite's phaeton went, with him and her in it.

"You had better step under shelter, Miss Haye," said Winthrop; "it is beginning to sprinkle pretty fast."

"No," said Elizabeth, "I'll go home—I don't mind it. I would rather go right home—I don't care for the rain."

"But you can't go without the umbrella," said Winthrop, "and that belongs to me."

"Well, won't you go with me?" said Elizabeth, with a look half doubtful and half daunted.

"Yes, as soon as it is safe. This is a poor place, but it is better than nothing. You must come in here and have patience till then."

He went in and Elizabeth followed him, and she stood there

looking very doubtful and very much annoyed; eyeing the fast falling drops as if her impatience could dry them up. The little smithy was black as such a place should be; nothing looked like a seat but the anvil, and that was hardly safe to take advantage of.

"I wish there was something here for you to sit down upon," said Winthrop peering about,—"but everything is like Vulcan's premises. It is a pity I am not Sir Walter Raleigh for your behoof; for I suppose Sir Walter didn't mind walking home without his coat, and I do."

"He only threw off his cloak," said Elizabeth.

"I never thought of wearing mine this afternoon," said Winthrop, "though I brought an umbrella. But see here, Miss Elizabeth,—here is a box, one end of which, I think, may be trusted. Will you sit down?"

Elizabeth took the box, seeming from some cause or other tongue-tied. She sat looking out through the open door at the storm in a mixture of feelings, the uppermost of which was vexation.

"I hope more than one end of this box may be trusted," she presently roused herself to say. "I have no idea of giving half trust to anything."

"Yet that is quite as much as it is safe to give to most things," said Winthrop.

"Is it?"

"I am afraid so."

"I wouldn't give a pin for anything I couldn't trust entirely," said Elizabeth.

"Which shews what a point of perfection the manufacture of pins has reached since the days of Anne Boleyn," said Winthrop.

"Of Anne Boleyn!—What of them then?"

"Only that a statute was passed in that time, entitled, 'An act for the true making of pins;' so I suppose they were then articles of some importance. But the box may be trusted, Miss Haye, for strength, if not for agreeableness. A quarter of agreeableness with a remainder of strength, is a fair proportion, as things go."

"Do you mean to compare life with this dirty box?" said Elizabeth.

"They say an image should always elevate the subject," said Winthrop smiling.

"What was the matter with the making of pins," said Elizabeth, "that an act had to be made about it?"

"Why in those days," said Winthrop, "mechanics and trades-people were in the habit occasionally of playing false, and it was necessary to look after them."

Elizabeth sat silently looking out again, wondering—what she had often wondered before—where ever her companion had got his cool self-possession; marvelling, with a little impatient wonder, how it was that he would just as lief talk to her in a blacksmith's shop in a thunder-storm, as in anybody's drawing-room with a band playing and fifty people about. She was no match for him, for she felt a little awkward. She, Miss Haye, the heiress in her own right, who had lived in good company ever since she had lived in company at all. Yet there he stood, more easily, she felt, than she sat. She sat looking straight out at the rain and thinking of it.

The open doorway and her vision were crossed a moment after by a figure which put these thoughts out of her head. It was the figure of a little black girl, going by through the rain, with an old basket at her back which probably held food or firing that she had been picking up along the streets of the city. She wore a wretched old garment which only half covered her, and that was already half wet; her feet and ancles were naked; and the rain came down on her thick curly head. No doubt she was accustomed to it; the road-worn feet must have cared little for wet or dry, and the round shock of wool perhaps never had a covering; yet it was bowed to the rain, and the little blackey went by with lagging step and a sort of slow crying. It touched Elizabeth with a disagreeable feeling of pain. The thought had hardly crossed her mind, that she was sorry for her, when to her great surprise she saw her companion go to the door and ask the little object of her pity to come in under the shed. The child stopped her slow step and her crying and looked up at him.

"Come in here till the rain's over," he repeated.

She gave her head a sort of matter-of-course shake, without moving a pair of intelligent black eyes which had fixed on his face.

"Come in," said Winthrop.

The child shook her head again, and said,

"Can't!"

"Why not?" said Winthrop.

"Mustn't!"

"Why mustn't you?"

"'Cause."

"Come in," said Winthrop,—and to Elizabeth's exceeding

astonishment he laid hold of the little black shoulder and drew the girl into the shop,—"it is going to storm hard;—why mustn't you?"

The little blackey immediately squatted herself down on the ground against the wall, and looking up at him repeated,

"'Cause."

"It's going to be a bad storm;—you'll be better under here."

The child's eyes went out of the door for a moment, and then came back to his face, as if with a sort of fascination.

"How far have you to go?"

"Home."

"How far is that?"

"It's six miles, I guess," said the owner of the eyes.

"That's too far for you to go in the storm. The lightning might kill you."

"Kill me!"

"Yes. It might."

"I guess I'd be glad if it did," she said, with another glance at the storm.

"Glad if it did!—why?"

"'Cause."

"'Cause what?" said Winthrop, entering more into the child's interests, Elizabeth thought, than he had done into hers.

"'Cause," repeated the blackey.—"I don't want to get home."

"Who do you live with?"

"I live with my mother, when I'm to home."

"Where do you live when you are not at home?"

"Nowheres."

The gathered storm came down at this point with great fury. The rain fell, whole water; little streams even made their way under the walls of the shanty and ran across the floor. The darkness asked no help from black walls and smoky roof.

"Isn't this better than to be out?" said Winthrop, after his eyes had been for a moment drawn without by the tremendous pouring of the rain. But the little black girl looked at it and said doggedly,

"I don't care."

"Where have you been with that basket?"

"Down yonder—where all the folks goes," she said with a slight motion of her head towards the built-up quarter of the country.

"Do you bring wood all the way from there on your back?"

"When I get some."

"Aren't you tired?"

The child looked at him steadily, and then in a strange somewhat softened manner which belied her words, answered,

"No."

"You don't bring that big basket full, do you?"

She kept her bright eyes on him and nodded.

"I should think it would break your back."

"If I don't break my back I get a lickin'."

"Was that what you were crying for as you went by?"

"I wa'n't a cryin'!" said the girl. "Nobody never see me a cryin' for nothin'!"

"You haven't filled your basket to-day."

She gave an askant look into it, and was silent.

"How came that?"

"'Cause!—I was tired, and I hadn't had no dinner and I don't care! That's why I wished the thunder would kill me. I can't live without eatin'."

"Have you had nothing since morning?"

"I don't get no mornin'—I have to get my dinner."

"And you could get none to-day?"

"No. Everything was eat up."

"Everything isn't quite eaten up," said Winthrop, rummaging in his coat pocket; and he brought forth thence a paper of figs which he gave the girl. "He isn't so short of means as I feared, after all," thought Elizabeth, "since he can afford to carry figs about in his pocket." But she did not know that the young gentleman had made his own dinner off that paper of figs; and she could not guess it, even when from his other coat pocket he produced some biscuits which were likewise given to eke out the figs in the little black girl's dinner. She was presently roused to very great marvelling again by seeing him apply his foot to another box, one without a clean side, and roll it over half the length of the shed for the child to sit upon.

"What do you think of life now, Miss Elizabeth?" he said, leaving his charge to eat her figs and coming again to the young lady's side.

"*That* isn't life," said Elizabeth.

"It seems without the one quarter of agreeableness," he said.

"But it's horrible, Mr. Winthrop!—"

He was silent, and looked at the girl, who sitting on her coal box was eating figs and biscuits with intense satisfaction.

"She is not a bad-looking child," said Elizabeth.

"She is a very good-looking child," said Winthrop; "at least her face has a great deal of intelligence; and I think, something more."

"What more?"

"Feeling, or capacity of feeling."

"I wish you had a seat, Mr. Landholm," said Elizabeth, looking round.

"Thank you—I don't wish for one."

"It was very vexatious in Rose to go and leave me!"

"There isn't another box for her if she had stayed," said Winthrop.

"She would have me go out with her this afternoon to see her dressmaker, who lives just beyond here a little; and father had the horses. It was so pleasant an afternoon, I had no notion of a storm."

"There's a pretty good notion of a storm now," said Winthrop.

So there was, beyond a doubt; the rain was falling in floods, and the lightning and thunder, though not very near, were very unceasing. Elizabeth still felt awkward and uneasy, and did not know what to talk about. She never had talked much to Mr. Landholm; and his cool matter-of-fact way of answering her remarks, puzzled or baffled her.

"That child sitting there makes me very uncomfortable," she said presently.

"Why, Miss Elizabeth?"

Elizabeth hesitated, and then said she did not know.

"You don't like the verification of my setting forth of life," he said smiling.

"But *that* is not life, Mr. Winthrop."

"What is it?"

"It is the experience of one here and there—not of people in general."

"What do you take to be the experience of people in general?"

"Not mine, to be sure," said Elizabeth after a little thought, —"nor hers."

"Hers is a light shade of what rests upon many."

"Why Mr. Winthrop! do you think so?"

"Look at her," he said in a low voice;—"she has forgotten her empty basket in a sweet fig."

"But she must take it up again."

"She won't lessen her burden, but she will her power of forgetting."

Elizabeth sat still, looking at her vis-à-vis of life, and feeling very uneasily what she had never felt before. She began therewith to ponder sundry extraordinary propositions about the inequalities of social condition and the relative duties of man to man.

"What right have I," she said suddenly, "to so much more than she has?"

"Very much the sort of right that I have to be an American, while somebody else is a Chinese."

"Chance," said Elizabeth.

"No, there is no such thing as chance,' he said seriously.

"What then?"

"The fruit of industry, talent, and circumstance."

"Not mine."

"No, but your father's, who gives it to you."

"But why ought I to enjoy more than she does?—in the abstract, I mean."

"I don't know," said Winthrop.—"I guess we had better walk on now, Miss Elizabeth."

"Walk on!—it rains too hard."

"But we are in the shed, while other people are out?"

"No but,—suppose that by going out I could bring them in?"

"Then I would certainly act as your messenger," he said smiling. "But you can't reach *all* the people who are so careless as to go out without umbrellas."

Elizabeth was betrayed into a laugh—a genuine hearty laugh of surprise, in which her awkwardness was for a moment forgotten.

"How came you to bring one, such a day?"

"I thought the sun was going to shine."

"But seriously, Mr. Landholm, my question,"—said Elizabeth

"What was it?"

"How ought I to enjoy so much more than she has?"

"Modestly, I should think."

"What do you mean?"

"If you were to give the half of your fortune to one such, for instance," he said with a slight smile, "do you fancy you would have adjusted two scales of the social balance to hang even?"

"No," said Elizabeth,—"I suppose not."

"You would have given away what she could not keep; you would have put out of your power what would not be in hers;

and on the whole, she would be scantly a gainer and the world would be a loser."

"Yet surely," said Elizabeth, "something is due from my hand to hers."

Her companion was quite silent, rather oddly, she thought; and her meditations came back for a moment from social to individual distinctions and differences. Then, really in a puzzle as to the former matter, she repeated her question.

"But what can one do to them, then, Mr. Winthrop?—or what should be one's aim?"

"Put them in the way of exercising the talent and industry and circumstance which have done such great things for us."

"So that by the time they have the means they will be ready for them?——But dear me! that is a difficult matter!" said Elizabeth.

Her companion smiled a little.

"But they haven't any talent, Mr. Landholm,—nor industry nor circumstance either. To be sure those latter wants might be made up."

"Most people have talent, of one sort or another," said Winthrop. "There's a little specimen pretty well stocked."

"Do you think so?"

"Try her."

"I don't know how to try her!" said Elizabeth. "I wish you would."

"I don't know how, either," said Winthrop. "Circumstances have been doing it this some time."

"I wish she hadn't come in," said Elizabeth. "She has unsettled all my ideas."

"They will rest the better for being unsettled."

Elizabeth looked at him, but he did not acknowledge the look. Presently, whether to try how benevolence worked, or to run away from her feeling of awkwardness, she got up and moved a few steps towards the place where the little blackey sat.

"Have you had dinner enough?" she said, standing and looking down upon her as a very disagreeable social curiosity.

"There aint no more, if I hain't," said the curiosity, with very dauntless eyes.

"Where do you get your dinner every day?"

"'Long street," said the girl, turning her eyes away from Elizabeth and looking out into the storm.

"Do you often go without any?"

"When the folks don't give me none."

"Does that happen often?"

"They didn't give me none to-day."

"What do you do then?"

The eyes came back from the door to Elizabeth, and then went to Winthrop.

"What do you do then?" Elizabeth repeated.

"I gets 'em."

"You didn't get any to-day?" said Winthrop.

She shook her head.

"You mustn't any more."

"Nobody ha'n't no business to let me starve," said the blackey stoutly.

"No, but I'll tell you where to go the next time you can't get a dinner, and you shall have it without stealing."

"I ha'n't stole it—nobody never see me steal—I only tuk it,"—said the girl with a little lowering of her voice and air.

"What's your name?"

"Clam."

"Clam!" said Elizabeth,—"where did you get such an odd name?"

"'Long street," said the girl, her black eyes twinkling.

"Where did you get it?" said Winthrop gravely.

"I didn't get it nowheres—it was guv to me."

"What's your other name?"

"I ha'n't got no more names—my name's Clam."

"What's your mother's name?"

"She's Sukey Beckinson."

"Is she kind to you?" asked Elizabeth.

"*I* don' know!"

"Did you have dinner enough?" said Winthrop with a smile.

Clam jumped up, and crossing her hands on her breast dropped a brisk little courtsey to her benefactor. She made no other answer, and then sat down again.

"Are you afraid to go home with your empty basket when the storm's over?" said he kindly.

"No," she said; but it was with a singular expression of cold and careless necessity.

"The rest of the basketful wouldn't be worth more than that, would it?" said he giving her a sixpence.

Clam took it and clasped it very tight in her fist, for other place of security she had none; and looked at him, but made no more answer than that.

"You won't forget where to come the next time you can't get an honest dinner," said he. "The corner of Beaver and Little South Streets. You know where it is? That is where I live. Ask for Mr. Landholm."

Clam nodded and said, "I know!"

"I hope you'll get some supper to-night," said he.

"I will!" said Clam determinately.

"How will you?" said Elizabeth.

"I'll make mammy give me some," said the girl flourishing her clasped fist.

"Wouldn't you like to leave picking things out of the street, and go to live with somebody who would take care of you and teach you to be a good girl?" said Elizabeth.

Clam tossed her sixpence up and down in her hand, and finally brought her eyes to bear upon Elizabeth and said,

"I don't want nobody to take care of me."

"If she could be taught, and would, I'd take care of her afterwards," said Elizabeth to Winthrop.

"If *he'd* say so, I would," said Clam.

"Look here," said Winthrop. "Would you like to come into some kind house—if I can find you one—and learn to do clean work?"

"It don't make no odds," said Clam looking at her basket.

"What do you say?"

"I guess no one don't want me."

"Perhaps not; but if somebody would have you, would you be a good girl?"

"I s'pose I'd get dinner reglar," said the little black girl, still fingering the edge of her basket.

"Certainly!—and something better than figs."

"Be them figs?" said Clam, suddenly looking up at him.

"Yes—the sweet ones."

"Goody!—I didn't know that before."

"Well—you haven't answered me yet."

"I don't care much,"—said Clam. "Is it your house?"

"Maybe."

"I'll come!" said she clapping her hands. "I'll clear out, and mother won't never give it to me no more.—Nor nobody else sha'n't?" said she looking up at Winthrop.

"If you behave yourself."

"I'll go now right off!" said Clam, jumping up in great spirits. Then with a changing and doubtful tone she added, looking to Winthrop, "Will you take me?"

"Yes," he said smiling, "but not this evening. You must go home now, when the storm is over, for to-night; and I'll come and see your mother about it."

"What for?" was the very earnest and prompt answer.

"If you agree to come, I must get her to bind you out."

"I aint goin' to be bound," said Clam shaking her head;—'if you bind me, I'll run."

"Run as fast as you please," said Winthrop;—"run whenever you want to;—but I can't take you unless you be bound, for I won't have your mother coming after you."

"Can't she do nothin' to me if I'm bound?" said Clam.

"Nothing at all, till you grow up to be a woman; and then you can take care of yourself."

"I'll take care of myself all along," said Clam. "Nobody else aint a goin' to."

"But somebody must give you clothes to wear, and a bed to sleep in, and your dinner, you know; and you must do work for somebody, to pay for it."

"To pay for my dinner?"

"Yes."

"Very good!" said Clam. "I guess I'll stand it. Will it be for you?"

"No, I think not."

"Won't you?" said Clam wishingly. "I'll do work for you."

"Thank you. Maybe you shall."

"I'm goin' home now," said Clam, getting up and shouldering her basket.

"The storm's too bad yet," said Winthrop.

"Crackey! what do you think I care for that! The rain won't wet *me* much."

"Come to my house to-morrow, if you want to see me again," said Winthrop,—"about dinner-time."

Clam nodded, and fixing her bright eyes very intently first on one and then on the other of the friends she was leaving, she ended with a long parting look at Winthrop which lasted till she had passed from sight out of the door of the shed.

The violence of the storm was gone over; but though the thunder sounded now in the distance and the lightning played fainter, the rain fell yet all around them, in a gentle and very full shower.

"Do you suppose she has six miles to go?" said Elizabeth.

"No."

"I thought you answered as if you believed her when she said so."

"It isn't best to tell all one's thoughts," said Winthrop smiling.

Elizabeth went back to her box seat.

"I wish the rain would let us go home too," she said.

"Your wishes are so accustomed to smooth travelling, they don't know what to make of a hindrance," said her companion.

Elizabeth knew it was true, and it vexed her. It seemed to imply that she had not been tried by life, and that nobody knew what she would be till she was tried. That was a very disagreeable thought. There again he had the advantage of her. Nothing is reliable that is not tried. "And yet," she said to herself, "I *am* reliable. I know I am."

"What can anybody's wish make of a hindrance?" was her reply.

"Graff it in well, and anybody can make a pretty large thorn of it."

"Why Mr. Winthrop!—but I mean, in the way of dealing with it pleasantly?"

"Pleasantly?—I don't know," said he; "unless they could get my mother's recipe."

"What does *her* wish do with a hindrance?"

'It lies down and dies," he said, with a change of tone which shewed whither his thoughts had gone.

"I think I never wish mine to do that," said Elizabeth.

"What then? Remember you are speaking of hindrances absolute—that cannot be removed."

"But Mr. Winthrop, do you think it is possible for one's wish to lie down and die so?"

"If I had not seen it, I might say that it was not."

"I don't understand it—I don't know what to make of it," said Elizabeth. "I don't think it is possible for mine."

Winthrop's thoughts went back a moment to the sweet calm brow, the rested face, that told of its truth and possibility in one instance. He too did not understand it, but he guessed where the secret might lie.

"It must be a very happy faculty," said Elizabeth;—"but it seems to me—of course it is not so in that instance,—but in the abstract, it seems to me rather tame;—I don't like it. I have no idea of giving up!"

"There is no need of your giving up, in this case," said Winthrop. "Do you see that sunshine?"

"And the rainbow!" said Elizabeth.

She sprang to the door; and they both stood looking, while

the parting gifts of the clouds were gently reaching the ground, and the sun taking a cleared place in the western heaven, painted over against them, broad and bright, the promissory token that the earth should be overwhelmed with the waters no more. The rain-drops glittered as they fell; the grass looked up in refreshed green where the sun touched it; the clouds were driving over from the west, leaving broken fragments behind them upon the blue; and the bright and sweet colours of the rainbow swept their circle in the east and almost finished it in the grass at the door of the blacksmith's shop. It was a lovely show of beauty that is as fresh the hundredth time as the first. But though Elizabeth looked at it and admired it, she was thinking of something else.

"You have no overshoes," said Winthrop, when they had set out on their way;—"I am afraid you are not countrywoman enough to bear this."

"O yes I am," said Elizabeth,—"I don't mind it—I don't care for it. But Mr. Winthrop—"

"What were you going to say?" he asked, when he had waited half a minute to find out.

"You understood that I did not mean to speak of your mother, when I said that, about thinking it seemed tame to let one's wishes die out?—I excepted her entirely in my thought—I was speaking quite in the abstract."

"I know that, Miss Elizabeth."

She was quite satisfied with the smile with which he said it.

"How much better that odd little black child liked you than she did me," she went on with a change of subject and tone together.

"You were a little further off," said Winthrop.

"Further off?" said Elizabeth.

"I suppose she thought so."

"Then one must come near people in order to do them good?"

"One mustn't be *too* far off," said Winthrop, "to have one's words reach them."

"But I didn't mean to be far off," said Elizabeth.

"I didn't mean to be near."

Elizabeth looked at him, but he was grave; and then she smiled, and then laughed.

"You've hit it!" she exclaimed. "I shall remember that."

"Take care, Miss Elizabeth," said Winthrop, as her foot

slipped in the muddy way,—" or you will have more to remember than would be convenient. You had better take my arm."

So she did; musing a little curiously at herself and that arm, which she had seen in a shirt-sleeve, carrying a pickaxe on shoulder; and making up her mind in spite of it all that she didn't care! So the walk home was not otherwise than comfortable. Indeed the beauty of it was more than once remarked on by both parties.

"Well!" said Rose, when at last Elizabeth came into the room where she was sitting,—" have you got home?"

"Yes."

"What have you been doing all this while?"

"Getting very angry at you in the first place; and then cooling down as usual into the reflection that it was not worth while."

"Well, I hope Winthrop made good use of his opportunity?'

"Yes, he did," said Elizabeth coolly, taking off her things.

"And you have engaged him at last as your admirer?"

"Not at all;—I have only engaged a little black girl to be my servant."

"A servant! What?"

"What do you mean by 'what'?" said Elizabeth contemptuously.

"I mean, what sort of a servant?"

"I am sure I don't know—a black servant."

"But what for?"

"To do my bidding."

"But what is she? and where did you pick her up?"

"She is an odd little fish called Clam; and I didn't pick her up at all;—Mr. Landholm did that."

"O ho!" said Rose,—"it's a joint concern!—that's it. But I think you are beginning to make up your household very early."

Elizabeth flung down her shoe and lifted her head, and Miss Cadwallader shrunk; even before her companion said with imperious emphasis, "Rose, how dare you!!—"

Rose did not dare, against the flushed face and eye of fire which confronted her. She fell back into her chair and her book and was dumb.

CHAPTER XX.

Ford. They do say, if money go before, all ways do lie open.
Fal. Money is a good soldier, sir, and will on.
MERRY WIVES OF WINDSOR.

SOMEWHAT to Winthrop's surprise, Clam came the next day to remind him of his promise; very much in earnest to wear a clean frock and have her dinner regular. She was duly bound, and entered into clean service accordingly. The indentures were made out to Miss Haye; but for the present Clam was put to learn her business under somebody that knew it; and for that end was finally sent to Mrs. Landholm. A week or two with Mrs. Nettley proved to the satisfaction of both parties that neither would much advantage the other. At Shahweetah, Clam, as Mrs. Landholm expressed it, "took a new start," and got on admirably. What much favoured this, was the fact that she speedily became very much attached to the whole family; with the single exception of Karen, between whom and herself there was an unallayed state of friction; a friction that probably served only to better Clam's relish of her dinner, while poor Karen declared "she didn't leave her no rest day nor night."

"She's not a bad child, Karen," said her mistress.

"Which part of her's good?" said Karen. "'Taint her eyes, nor her fingers; and if the Bible didn't say there wa'n't no such a fountain, I should think her tongue was one o' them fountains that sent out at the same place both salt water and fresh."

"Her fingers are pretty good, Karen."

"There's a two-sided will in 'em, Mrs. Landholm."

There was no two-sided will in Clam's first friend, nor in the energies which were steadily bearing him on towards his aim. Steadily and surely, as he knew. But his life in those days had almost as little to tell of, as it had much to do. From early morning till——almost till early morning again, or till a new day had begun to count the hours,—every minute had its work; yet the record of the whole could be given in very few words, and those would not be interesting. How should the record be, when the reality was not, even to himself. It was all preparatory work; it must be done; but the interest of the matter lay beyond, at that point whither all these efforts tended. Meanwhile work and have patience, and work,—was the epitome of his life.

There were some breaks, but not many. Now and then a swift and sweet run home, to *live* for a moment in the midst of all this preparing to live; to rest among the home hearts; to breathe a few breaths in absolute freedom; to exchange Mr. De Wort's dusty office for the bright little keeping-room of the farm-house, and forget the business of the hard brick and stone city under the shadow or the sunshine that rested on Wut-a-qut-o. Then Winthrop threw off his broadcloth coat and was a farmer again. Then Mrs. Landholm's brow laid down its care, and shewed to her son only her happy face. Then poor Winifred was strong and well and joyous, in the spite of sickness and weakness and nervous ail. And then also, Clam sprang round with great energy, and was as Karen averred, "fifty times worse and better than ever."

But all faded and died away, save the sweet memory and refreshment; that staid yet a little while. Winthrop went back to his musty parchments and lonely attic; and the little family at home gathered itself together for a new season of duty-doing, and hope, and looking forward. The sunshine and the shadow slept upon Wut-a-qut-o, as it did a little while ago; but neither sunshine nor shadow was the same thing now, for Winthrop was away.

He had lost perhaps less than they; though the balance was struck pretty fair. But he was actively bending every energy to the accomplishment of a great object. The intensity of effort might swallow up some other things, and the consciousness of sure and growing success might make amends for them. Besides, he had been long fighting the battle of life away from home, and was accustomed to it; they never got accustomed to it. Every fresh coming home was the pledge of a fresh parting, the pleasure of the one not more sure than the pain of the other. If Winthrop had changed, in all these years and goings and comings, it might have been different; if they could have found that their lost treasure was less true or strong or fair, than when they first let it go. But he was so exactly the same Winthrop that they had been sorry for that first time, that they could only be sorry again with the same sorrow;—the same, but for the lost novelty of that first time, and the added habit of patience, and the nearer hope of his and their reward.

So through the first winter and the first summer, and the second winter and the second summer, of his city apprenticeship, Winthrop wrought on; now with a cold room and little fire in his chimney, and now with the sun beating upon the roof, and the only hope of night's sea-breeze. But the farmer's boy had known cold and heat a great while ago, and he could bear both. He could partly forget both, sometimes in literary unbending with Mr. Herder and his friends; and at other times in a solitary walk on the Green overlooking the bay, to catch the sea-breeze more fresh and soon, and look up the river channel towards where the shadows lay upon Wut-a-qut-o. And sometimes in a visit at Mr. Haye's.

Of late, in the second summer, this last sort of pleasure-taking grew to be more frequent. Mr. Herder was less visited, and Mr. Haye more. Winthrop was always welcome, but there was no change in the manner of his being received. Unless perhaps a little more graciousness on Elizabeth's part, and a trifle less on Rose's, might be quoted.

So the sea-breezes blew through the dog-days; and September ushered in and ushered out its storms; and October came, clear and fair, with strength and health for body and mind. With October came Rufus, having just made an end of his work in the North country. He came but for a few days' stay in passing from one scene of labours to another. For those few days he abode with his brother, sharing his room and bed.

"Well, Winthrop, I've stuck to my choice," he remarked, the second evening of his being there. The tone indicated the opening of a great budget of thoughts. Winthrop was bending over a parchment-coloured volume, and Rufus pacing up and down the longest stretch of the little room.

"I am glad of it," said Winthrop, without looking up.

"I am not sure that I am."

"What's the matter?"

"I don't see that I gain much by it, and I certainly lose."

"What do you expect to gain?"

"Nothing but money,—and I don't get that."

"It's safe, isn't it?"

"Yes, and so are winter's snows, in their treasury;—and I could as soon get it by asking for it."

"Let us hope it will come with the snows," said Winthrop, his head still bent down over his book.

"You may talk;—it is easy waiting for you."

"Query, how that would give me a right to talk," said Winthrop turning over a leaf;—"supposing it to be a fact; of which I have some doubts."

"What have you been doing all to-day?"

"The usual routine—which after all is but preparing to do."

"What has been the routine to-day?"

"You saw my breakfast and saw me get it.—Then I went out.—Then I read, according to custom."

"What?"

"Classics."

"Do you!"

"For awhile. The rest of the morning between engrossing deeds and the Record Office. First half of the afternoon, or rather a larger proportion, ditto; the rest to meet my friends Messrs. Jones and Satterthwaite."

"Satterthwaite!—what does *he* want?"

"To read Greek with me."

"Greek! What has put that into his head? Bob. Satterthwaite!"—and Rufus threw back his head and laughed in a great state of amusement. "What has put *that* into his head?—eh, Winthrop?"

"I don't inquire. It puts money in my pocket."

"Not much," said Rufus.

"No, not much."

"What's the reason, do you think? What moves *him* to woo the Muses?—I'm afraid it's because he thinks it is a preliminary wooing he must go through before he can be successful in another quarter."

And again Rufus laughed, in high delight.

"I have no business with that," said Winthrop.

"What are you doing now?"

"Studying law."

"Stop."

"What for?"

"To talk to me."

"It seems to me I have been doing that for some time," said Winthrop, without looking off his book.

"But I haven't begun. Winthrop,—I have a great mind to give up this engineering business."

"To do what instead?"

"Why—you know I shall have some money coming to me—quite a little sum;—Mr. Haye has very kindly offered to put me in the way of laying it out to good advantage, and eventually of getting into another line of occupation which would at the same time be more lucrative, less laborious, and would keep me in the regions of civilization.—And perhaps—Winthrop—something might follow thereupon,——"

"What?" said his brother looking up.

"Something——"

"More definite in your purpose than in your speech."

"Not my purpose, exactly," said Rufus,—"but in possibility."

"There is no peg in possibility for a wise man to hang his cap on."

"Perhaps I am not a wise man," said Rufus, with a very queer face, as if his mind were giving an askance look at the subject.

"That's a supposititious case I shall leave you to deal with."

"Why it's the very sort of case it's your business to deal with," said Rufus. "If the world was full of wise men you'd stand a pretty fair chance of starving, Governor. But seriously,—do you think it is unbecoming a wise man to take any lawful means of keeping out of the way of that same devil of starvation?"

"Do you mean to say that you are in any danger of it?" said Winthrop looking up again.

"Why no,—not exactly; taking the words literally. But one may starve and yet have enough to eat."

"If one refuses one's food."

"If one don't! I tell you, I have been starving for these two years past. It is not living, to make to-day only feed to-morrow. Besides—I don't see any harm in purchasing, if one can, an exemption from the universal doom of eating one's bread in the sweat of one's brow."

"I think it depends entirely on what one pays for the purchase," said Winthrop.

"Suppose one pays nothing."

"One executes a most unaccountable business transaction."

Rufus stopped and looked at him, and then took up his walk, and half laughing went on.

"Suppose we leave talking in the dark, and understand one another. Do you know what I am driving at?"

"Have you set off?" said Winthrop, with again a glance which seemed to add to Rufus's amusement.

"No," he said,—"I am just waiting for you to give me leave."

"The reins are not in my hands."

"Yes they are. Seriously, Winthrop, do you know what we are talking about?—What do you think of my making suit to one of these ladies?"

"I do not think about it."

"You do not conceive it would be any disfavour to either of them to induce her to accept me, I suppose.—What do you say?"

"You are indifferent towards which of them the suit should incline?" said Winthrop.

"Why, that's as it may be—I haven't thought enough about it to know. They're a pretty fair pair to choose from—"

"Supposing that you have the choice," said Winthrop.

"Do you know anything to the contrary?—Has anybody else a fairer entrance than myself?"

"I am not on sufficiently near terms with the family to be able to inform you."

"Do *you* think of entering *your* plough, Governor?"

"Not in your field."

"What do you mean?"

"I mean that I am not in your way."

"Shall I be in yours?"

"No," said his brother coolly.

"In whose way then?"

"I am afraid in your own, Will."

"How do you mean?" asked the other a little fiercely.

"If you are so intent upon marrying money-bags, you may chance to get a wife that will not suit you."

"You must explain yourself!" said Rufus haughtily. "In what respect would either of these two not suit me?"

"Of two so different, it may safely be affirmed that if one would the other would not."

"Two so different!" said Rufus. "What's the matter with either of them?"

"There is this the matter with both—that you do not know them."

"I *do* know them!"

"From the rest of the world; but not from each other."

"Why not from each other?"

"Not enough for your liking or your judgment to tell which would suit you."

"Why would not either suit?" said Rufus.

"I think—if you ask me—that one would not make you

happy, in the long run; and the other, with your present views and aims, you could not make happy."

"Which is which?" said Rufus, laughing and drawing up a chair opposite his brother.

"Either of them is which," said Winthrop. "Such being the case, I don't know that it is material to inquire."

"It is very material! for I cannot be satisfied without the answer. I am in earnest in the whole matter, Winthrop."

"So am I, very much in earnest."

"Which of them should I not make happy?"—Rufus went on.—"Rose?—She is easily made happy."

"So easily, that you would be much more than enough for it."

"Then it is the other one whose happiness you are afraid for?"

"I don't think it is in much danger from you."

"Why?—what then?" said Rufus quickly.

"I doubt whether any one could succeed with her whose first object was something else."

Rufus drew his fingers through his hair, in silence, for about a minute and a half; with a face of thoughtful and somewhat disagreeable consideration.

"And with the other one you think he could?"

"What?"

"Succeed?—one whose first object, as you say, was something else?"

"With the other I think anybody could."

"I don't know but I like that," said Rufus;—"it is amiable. She has more simplicity. She is a lovely creature!"

"If you ask your eye."

"If I ask yours!"—

"Every man must see with his own eyes," said Winthrop.

"Don't yours see her lovely?"

"They might, if they had not an inward counsellor that taught them better."

"She is very sweet-tempered and sweet-mannered," said Rufus.

"Very."

"Don't you think so?"

"Certainly—when it suits her."

"When it suits her!"

"Yes. She is naturally rude, and politically polite."

"And how's the other one? isn't she naturally rude too?"

"Not politically anything."

"And you think she wouldn't have me?"

"I am sure she would not, if she knew your motive."

"My motive!—but my motive might change," said Rufus, pushing back his chair and beginning to walk the floor again. "It isn't necessary that my regards should be *confined* to her gracious adjunctive recommendations.—"

He walked for some time without reply, and again the leaves of Winthrop's book said softly now and then that Winthrop's head was busy with them.

"Governor, you are very unsatisfactory!" said his brother at length, standing now in front of him.

Winthrop looked up and smiled and said, "What would you have?"

"Your approbation!"—was the strong and somewhat bitter thought in Rufus's mind. He paused before he spoke.

"But Governor, really I am tired of this life— it isn't what I am fit for;—and why not escape from it, if I can, by some agreeable road that will do nobody any harm?"

"With all my heart," said Winthrop. "I'll help you."

"Well?—"

"Well—"

"You think this is not such a one?"

"The first step in it being a stumble."

"To whom would it bring harm, Governor?"

"The head must lower when the foot stumbles," said Winthrop. "That is one harm."

"But you are begging the question!" said Rufus a little impatiently.

"And you have granted it."

"I haven't!" said Rufus. "I don't see it. I don't see the stumbling or the lowering. I should not feel myself lowered by marrying a fine woman, and I hope she would not feel her own self-respect injured by marrying me."

"You will not stand so high upon her money-bags as upon your own feet."

"Why not have the advantage of both?"

"You cannot. People always sit down upon money-bags. The only exception is in the case of money-bags they have filled themselves."

Rufus looked at Winthrop's book for three minutes in silence.

"Well, why not then take at once the ease, for which the alternative is a long striving?"

"If you can. But the long striving is not the whole of the alternative; with that you lose the fruits of the striving—all that makes ease worth having."

"But I should not relinquish them," said Rufus. "I shall not sit down upon my money-bags."

"They are not *your* money-bags."

"They will be—if I prove successful."

"And how will you prove successful?"

"Why!"—said Rufus,—"what a question!—"

"I wish you would answer it nevertheless—not to me, but to yourself."

Whether Rufus did or not, the answer never came out. He paced the floor again; several times made ready to speak, and then checked himself.

"So you are entirely against me,—" he said at length.

"I am not against you, Will;—I am *for* you."

"You don't approve of my plan."

"No—I do not."

"I wish you would say why."

"I hardly need," said Winthrop with a smile. "You have said it all to yourself."

"Notwithstanding which assumption, I should like to hear you say it."

"For the greater ease of attack and defence?

"If you please. For anything."

"What do you want me to do, Will?" said Winthrop looking up.

"To tell me why I should not marry Miss Haye or Miss Cadwallader."

"You not knowing, yourself."

"Yes—I don't," said Rufus.

Winthrop turned over a few leaves of his book and then spoke.

"You are stronger, not to lean on somebody else's strength. You are more independent, not to lean at all. You are honester, not to gain anything under false pretences. And you are better to be yourself, Will Landholm, than the husband of any heiress the sun shines upon, at such terms."

"What terms?"

"False pretences."

"What false pretences?"

"Asking the hand, when you only want the key that is in it. Professing to give yourself, when in truth your purpose is to give nothing that is not bought and paid for."

Rufus looked very grave and somewhat disturbed.

"That's a very hard characterizing of the matter, Governor," said he. "I don't think I deserve it."

"I hope you don't," said his brother.

Rufus began again to measure the little apartment with his long steps.

"But this kind of thing is done every day, Winthrop."

"By whom?" said Winthrop.

"Why!—by very good men;—by everybody."

"Not by everybody."

"By what sort of people is it not done?"

"By you and me," said Winthrop smiling.

"You think then that a poor man should never marry a rich woman?"

"Never,—unless he can forget that she is rich and he poor."

Rufus walked for some time in silence.

"Well," he said, in a tone between dry and injured,—"I am going off to the West again, luckily; and I shall have no opportunity for the present to disturb you by making false pretences, of any sort."

"Is opportunity all that you lack?" said Winthrop looking up, and with so simple an expression that Rufus quitted his walk and his look together.

"Why did you never make trial for yourself, Winthrop?" he said. "You have a remarkably fine chance; and fine opening too, I should think. You are evidently very well received down yonder."

"I have a theory of my own too, on the subject," said Winthrop,—"somewhat different from yours, but still enough to work by."

"What's that?"

"I have no mind to marry any woman who is unwilling to be obliged to me."

Rufus looked at his brother and at the fireplace awhile in gravity.

"You are proud," he said at length.

"I must have come to it by living so high in the world," said Winthrop.

"So high?"—said Rufus.

"As near the sun as I can get. I thought it was very near, some time in August last."

Winthrop laid by his book; and the two young men stood

several minutes, quite silent, on opposite sides of the hearth, with folded hands and meditative countenances; but the face of the one looked like the muddy waters of the Shatemuc tossed and tumbled under a fierce wind; the other's was calm and steady as Wut-a-qut-o's brow.

"So you won't have any woman that you don't *oblige* to marry you!" Rufus burst out. "Ha, ha, ha!—ho, ho, ho!—"

Winthrop's mouth gave the slightest good-humoured token of understanding him,—it could not be called a smile. Rufus had his laugh out, and cooled down into deeper gravity than before.

"Well!"—said he,—"I'll go off to my fate, at the limitless wild of the West. It seems a rough sort of fate."

"Make your fate for yourself," said Winthrop.

"*You* will," said his brother. "And it will be what you will, and that's a fair one. And you will oblige anybody you have a mind to. And marry an heiress."

"Don't look much like it—things at present," said Winthrop. "I don't see the way very clear."

"As for me, I don't know what ever I shall come to," Rufus added.

"Come to bed at present," said Winthrop. "That is one step."

"One step towards what?"

"Sleep in the first place; and after that, anything."

"What a strange creature you are, Governor! and how doubtlessly and dauntlessly you pursue your way," Rufus said sighing.

"Sighs never filled anybody's sails yet," said Winthrop. "They are the very airs of a calm."

"Calm!" said Rufus.

"A dead calm," said his brother laughing.

"I wish I had *your* calm," said Rufus. And with that the evening ended.

CHAPTER XXI.

O what men dare do! what men may do! what men daily do! not knowing what they do!

MUCH ADO ABOUT NOTHING.

ONE morning, about these days, Mr. and Miss Haye were seated at the opposite ends of the breakfast-table. They had been there for some time, silently buttering rolls and sipping coffee, in a leisurely way on Mr. Haye's part, and an ungratified one on the part of his daughter. He was considering, also in a leisurely sort of way, the columns of the morning paper; she considering him and the paper, and at intervals knocking with her knife against the edge of her plate,—a meditative and discontented knife, and an impassive and unimpressed plate. So breakfast went on till Elizabeth's cup was nearly emptied.

"Father," said she, "it is very unsociable and stupid for you to read the paper, and me to eat my breakfast alone. You might read aloud, if you must read."

Mr. Haye brought his head round from the paper long enough to swallow half a cupful of coffee.

"Where's Rose?"

"In bed, for aught I know. There is no moving her till she has a mind."

"'Seems to me, it is quite as difficult to move you," said her father.

"Ay, but then I *have a mind*—which makes all the difference."

Mr. Haye went back to his paper and considered it till the rest of his cup of coffee was thoroughly cold. Elizabeth finished her breakfast, and sat, drawn back into herself, with arms folded, looking into the fireplace. Finding his coffee cold, Mr. Haye's attention came at length back upon his daughter.

"What do you want me to talk about?" he said.

"It don't signify, your talking about anything now," said Elizabeth. "Everything is cold—mind and matter together. I don't know how you'll find the coffee, father."

Mr. Haye stirred it, with a discontented look.

"Rose is late," he remarked again.

"*That's* nothing new," said Elizabeth. "Late is her time."

Mr. Haye drunk his cold cupful.

"You're very fond of her, Lizzie, aren't you?"

"No," said Elizabeth. "I don't think I am."

"Not fond of her!" said Mr. Haye in a very surprised tone.

"No," said Elizabeth,—"I don't think I am."

"I thought you were," said her father, in a voice that spoke both chagrin and displeasure.

"What made you think so?"

"You always seemed fond of her," said Mr. Haye.

"I can't have seemed so, for I never was so. There isn't enough of her to be fond of. I talk to her, and like her after a fashion, because she is the only person near me that I *can* talk to—that's all."

"*I* am fond of her," said Mr. Haye.

"It takes more to make me fond of anybody," said his daughter. "I know *you* are."

"What does Rose want, to have the honour of your good opinion?"

"O don't talk in that tone!" said Elizabeth. "I had rather you would not talk at all. You have chosen an unhappy subject. It takes a good deal to make me like anybody much, father."

"What does Rose want?"

"As near as possible, everything," said Elizabeth,—"if you *will* have the answer."

"What?"

"Why father, she has nothing in the world but a very pretty face."

"You grant her that," said Mr. Haye.

"Yes, I grant her that, though it is a great while since *I* saw it pretty. Father, I care nothing at all for any face which has nothing beneath the outside. It's a barren prospect to me, however fair the outside may be—I don't care to let my eye dwell on it."

"How do you like the prospect of your own, in the glass?"

"I should be very sorry if I didn't think it had infinitely

more in it than the face we have been speaking of. It is not so beautifully tinted, nor so regularly cut; but *I* like it better."

"I am afraid few people will agree with you," said her father dryly.

"There's one thing," said Elizabeth,—"I sha'n't know it if they don't. But then I see my face at a disadvantage, looking stupidly at itself in the glass—I hope it does better to other people."

"I didn't know you thought quite so much of yourself," said Mr. Haye.

"I haven't told you the half," said Elizabeth, looking at him. "I am afraid I think more of myself than anybody else does, or ever will."

"If you do it so well for yourself, I'm afraid other people won't save you the trouble," said her father.

"I'm afraid *you* will not, by the tone in which you speak, father."

"What has set you against Rose?"

"Nothing in the world! I am not set against her. Nothing in the world but her own emptiness and impossibility of being anything like a companion to me."

"Elizabeth!—"

"Father!—What's the matter?"

"How dare you talk in that manner?"

"Why father," said Elizabeth, her tone somewhat quieting as his was roused,—"I never saw the thing yet I didn't dare say, if I thought it. Why shouldn't I?"

"Because it is not true—a word of it."

"I'm sure I wish it wasn't true," said Elizabeth. "What I said was true. It's a sorrowful truth to me, too, for I haven't a soul to talk to that can understand me—not even you, father, it seems."

"I wish I didn't understand you," said Mr. Haye.

"It's nothing very dreadful to understand," said Elizabeth, —"what I have been saying now. I wonder how you can think so much of it. I know you love Rose better than I do."

"I love her so well—" said Mr. Haye, and stopped.

"So well that what?"

"That I can hardly talk to you with temper."

"Then don't let us talk about it at all," said Elizabeth, whose own heightened colour shewed that her temper was moving.

"Unhappily it is necessary," said Mr. Haye dryly.

"Why in the world is it necessary? You can't alter the matter, father, by talking;—it must stand so."

"Stand how?"

"Why, as it does stand—Rose and I as near as possible nothing to each other."

"Things can hardly stand so," said Mr. Haye. "You must be either less or more."

Elizabeth sat silent and looked at him. He looked at nothing but what was on his plate.

"How would you like to have Rose take your place?"

"My place?" said Elizabeth.

"Yes," said Mr. Haye laconically.

"No place that I fill, *could* be filled by Rose" said Elizabeth, with the slightest perceptible lifting of her head and raising of her brow.

"We will try that," said Mr. Haye bitterly; "for I will put her over your head, and we will see."

"Put her *where?*" said Elizabeth.

"Over this house—over my establishment—at this table—in your place as the head of this family."

"You will take *her* for your daughter, and discard me?" said Elizabeth.

"No—I will not,—" said Mr. Haye, cutting a piece of beefsteak in a way that shewed him indifferent to its fate. "I will not!—I will make her my wife!—"

Elizabeth had risen from the table and now she stood on the rug before the fire, with her arms behind her, looking down at the breakfast-table and her father. Literally, looking down *upon* them. Her cheeks were very pale, but fires that were not heaven-lit were burning somewhere within her, shining out at her eye and now and then colouring her face with a sudden flare. There was a pause. Mr. Haye tried what he could do with his beefsteak; and his daughter's countenance shewed the cloud and the flame of the volcano by turns. For awhile the father and daughter held off from each other. But Mr. Haye's breakfast gave symptoms of coming to an end.

"Father," said Elizabeth, bringing her hands in front of her and clasping them,—"say you did not mean that!"

"Ha!—" said Mr. Haye without looking at her, and brushing the crumbs from his pantaloons.

Elizabeth waited.

"What did you mean?"

"I spoke plain enough," said he.

"Do you mean to say that you *meant* that?" said Elizabeth, the volcanic fires leaping up bright.

"Meant it?" said Mr. Haye, looking at her. "Yes, I meant it."

"Father, you did not!—"

Mr. Haye looked again at her hands and her face, and answered coolly,

"Ask Rose whether I meant it,—"

And left the room.

Elizabeth neither saw nor heard, for some minutes; they might have been many or few. Then she became aware that the servant was asking her if he should leave the breakfast-table still for Miss Cadwallader; and her answer, "No—take it away!"—was given with startling decision. The man had known his young mistress before to speak with lips that were supreme in their expression. He only obeyed, without even wondering. Elizabeth in a whirl of feeling that like the smoke of the volcano hid everything but itself, went and stood in the window; present to nothing but herself; seeing neither the street without nor the house within. Wrapped in that smoke, she did not know when the servant went out, nor whether anybody else came in. She stood there pale, with lips set, her hands folded against her waist, and pressing there with a force the muscles never relaxed. How long she did not know. Something aroused her, and she discerned, through the smoke, another figure in the room and coming towards her. Elizabeth stepped out from the window, without altering anything but her place, and stood opposite to Winthrop Landholm. If it had been Queen Elizabeth of old and one of her courtiers, it would have been all one; the young man's respectful greeting could not have been met with more superb regality of head and brow.

"I have a letter for Mr. Haye," said Winthrop, "which my brother left in my charge. That brought me here this morning, and I ventured to make business an excuse for pleasure."

"It may lie on the table till he comes," said Elizabeth with the slightest bend of her stately little head. She might have meant the letter or the pleasure or the business, or all three.

"You are well, Miss Haye?" said Winthrop doubtfully.

"No—I am well enough," said Elizabeth. A revulsion of feeling had very nearly brought down her head in a flood of tears; but she kept that back carefully and perfectly; and the next instant she started with another change, for Rose came in. *She* gave Winthrop a very smiling and bright salutation; which he acknowledged silently, gravely, and even distantly.

"Aren't you well, Mr. Landholm?" was Rose's next instant question, most sweetly given.

"Very well," he said with another bow.

"What have you been talking about, to get so melancholy? Lizzie—"

But Rose caught sight of the gathered blackness of that face, and stopped short. Elizabeth bestowed one glance upon her; and as she then turned to the other person of the party the revulsion came over her again, so strong that it was overcoming. For a minute her hands went to her face, and it was with extreme difficulty that the rising heart was kept down. Will had the mastery, however, and her face looked up again more dark than ever.

"We have talked of nothing at all," she said. "Mr. Landholm only came to bring a letter."

Mr. Landholm could not stay after that, for anything. He bowed himself out; and left Elizabeth standing in the middle of the floor, looking as if the crust of the earth had given way under her and 'chaos was come again.' She stood there as she had stood in the window, still and cold; and Rose afar off by the chimney corner stood watching her, as one would a wild beast or a venomous creature in the room, not a little fear mingled with a shadow of something else in her face.

Elizabeth's first movement was to walk a few steps up and down, swinging one clenched hand, but half the breadth of the room was all she went. She sunk down there beside a chair and hid her face, exclaiming or rather groaning out, one after the other,—"Oh!—oh!"—in such tones as are dragged from very far down in the heart; careless of Rose's hearing her.

"What is the matter, Lizzie?"—her companion ventured timidly. But Elizabeth gave no answer; and neither of them stirred for many minutes, an occasional uneasy flutter of Rose's being the exception. The question at last was asked over again, and responded to.

"That my father has disgraced himself, and that you are the cause!"

"There's no disgrace," said Rose.

"Don't say he has not!" said Elizabeth, looking up with an eye that glared upon her adversary. "And before he had done it, I wish you had never been born,—or I."

"It's no harm,—" said Rose confusedly.

"Harm!—harm,—" repeated Elizabeth; then putting her face down again; "Oh!—what's the use of living, in such a world!"

"I don't see what harm it does to you," said Rose, muttering her words.

"Harm?" repeated Elizabeth. "If it was right to wish it, —which I believe it isn't,—I could wish that I was dead. It almost seems to me I wish I were!"

"You're not sure about it," said Rose.

"No, I am not," said Elizabeth looking up at her again with eyes of fire and a face from which pain and passion had driven all but livid colour,—but looking at her steadily,—"because there is something after death; and I am not sure that I am ready for it. I *dare* not say I wish I was dead, Rose Cadwallader, or you would drive me to it!"

"I'm sure, I've done nothing,"—said Rose whimpering.

"Done nothing!" said Elizabeth with a concentrated power of expression. "Oh I wish you had done anything, before my father had lowered himself in my eyes and you had been the cause!—"

"I'm not the cause of anything," said Rose.

Elizabeth did not answer; she was crouching by the side of the chair in an uneasy position that said how far from ease the spirit was.

"And he hasn't lowered himself," Rose went on pouting.

"It is done!"—said Elizabeth, getting up from the floor and standing, not unlike a lightning-struck tree.—"I wonder what will become of me!—"

"What are you going to do?"

"I would find a way out of this house, if I knew how."

"That's easy enough," said Rose with a slight sneer. "There are plenty of ways."

"Easy enough,—if one could find the right one."

"Why you've had me in the house a great while, already," said Rose.

"I *have had*—" said Elizabeth.—"I wonder if I shall ever have anything again!"

"Why what have you lost?"

"Everything—except myself."

"You have a great respect for Mr. Haye," said Rose.

"I had."

Rose at this point thought fit to burst into a great fit of tears. Elizabeth stood by the table, taking up and putting down one book after another, as if the touch of them gave her fingers pain; and looking as if, as she said, she had lost everything. Then stood with folded arms eyeing something that was not before her; and then slowly walked out of the room.

"Lizzie—" said Rose.

"What?" said Elizabeth stopping at the door.

"What's the use of taking things so?"

"The use of necessity."

"But we can be just as we were before."

Elizabeth went on and gained her own room; and there she and pain had a fight that lasted the rest of the day.

The fight was not over, and weary traces of it were upon her face, when late in the afternoon she went out to try the change of a walk. The walk made no change whatever. As she was coming up the Parade, she was met by Winthrop going down. If he had seen only the gravity and reserve of the morning, it is probable he would not have stopped to speak to her; but though those were in her face still, there was beside a weary set of the brow and sorrowful line of the lips, very unwonted there, and the cheeks were pale; and instead of passing with a mere bow he came up and offered his hand. Elizabeth took it, but without the least brightening of face.

"Are you out for a walk?" said he.

"No—I am for home—I have had a walk."

"It is a very fine afternoon," said he, turning and beginning to walk along slowly with her.

"Is it?"

"Haven't you found out that it is?"

"No."

"Where have you been, not to know it?"

"Hum—" said Elizabeth,—"if you mean where my *mind* has been, that is one question; as for my bodily self, I have been on the Castle Green."

"You have lost your walk," said he. "Don't you feel inclined to turn about with me and try to pick up what you came out for?"

"Better there than at home," thought Elizabeth, and she turned about accordingly.

"People come out for a variety of things," she remarked however.

"That is true," said Winthrop smiling. "I am afraid I was hasty in presuming I could help you to find your object. I was thinking only of mine."

"I don't know but you could, as well as anybody," said

Elizabeth. "If you could give me your mother's secret for not minding disagreeable things."

"I am afraid I cannot say she does not mind them," he answered.

"What then?—I thought you said so."

"I do not remember what I said. I might have said that she does not struggle with them—those at least which cannot be removed by struggling."

"Not struggle with them?" said Elizabeth. "Sit down quietly with them!"

"Yes," he said gravely. "Not at first, but at last."

"I don't believe in it," said Elizabeth. "That is, I don't believe in it as a general thing. It may be possible for her. I am sure it never could be for me."

Winthrop was silent, and they walked so for the space of half a block.

"Would she say that it is possible for everybody?" inquired Elizabeth then.

"I believe she would say that it is not temperament, nor circumstance, nor stoical philosophy."

"What then?"

"A drop of some pacifying oil out of a heaven-wrought chalice."

"I don't think figures are the easiest mode of getting at things, Mr. Landholm. You don't make this clear."

He smiled a little, as he pushed open the little wicket gate of the Green, and without saying anything more they sauntered in, along the broad gravel walk sweeping round the enclosure; slowly, till they had passed the fortifications and stood looking upon the bay over towards Blue Point. The sun was almost on the low ruddied horizon; a stirring north breeze came down from the up country, roughening the bay, and the sunbeams leapt across from the opposite western shore giving a touch of light to every wave. The air was very fine; the sky without a cloud, except some waiting flecks of vapour around the sun. The two friends stood still some little time, to look or to think; looking especially at the fair glowing western heaven, and the tossing water between, every roll of which was with a dance and a sparkle.

"Does *this* make anything clear?" asked Winthrop, when some time had gone by without speech or movement from either of them.

He spoke lightly enough; but the answer was given in a tone that bespoke its truth.

"Oh no!—"

And Elizabeth's face was turned away so that he could see nothing but her bonnet, beside the tremulous swell of the throat; that he *did* see.

"It has very often such an effect for me,"—he went on in the same tone. "And I often come here for the very purpose of trying it; when my head gets thick over law-papers."

"That may do for some things," said Elizabeth. "It won't for others."

"This would work well along with my mother's recipe" he said.

"What is that?" said Elizabeth harshly. "You didn't tell me."

"I am hardly fit to tell you," he answered, "for I do not thoroughly know it myself. But I know she would send you to the Bible,—and tell you of a hand that she trusts to do everything for her, and that she knows will do all things well, and kindly."

"But does that hinder disagreeables from being disagreeables?" said Elizabeth with some impatience of tone. "Does that hinder aches from being pain?"

"Hardly. But I believe it stops or soothes the aching. I believe it, because I have seen it."

Elizabeth stood still, her bosom swelling, and that fluttering of her throat growing more fluttering. It got beyond her command. The mixed passions and vexations, and with them a certain softer and more undefined regret, reached a point where she had no control over them. The tears would come, and once arrived at that, they took their own way; with such a rush of passionate indulgence, that a thought of the time and the place and the witness, made nothing, or came in only to swell the rush. The flood poured over the barrier with such joy at being set free, that it carried all before it. Elizabeth was just conscious of being placed on a seat, near to which it happened that she was standing; and she knew nothing more. She did not even know how completely she was left to herself. Not till the fever of passion was brought a little down, and recollection and shame began to take their turn, and she checked her tears and stole a secret glance around to see what part of the gravel walk supported a certain pair of feet, for higher than the ground she dared not look. Her surprise was a good deal to find that her glance must take quite a wide range to meet with them; and then venturing a single upward look, she saw that her companion standing at a little distance was not watching her, nor apparently had been; his attitude bespoke him quietly fixed upon something else and awaiting her leisure. Elizabeth brought her eyes home again.

"What a strange young man!" was her quick thought;—"to have been brought up a farmer's boy, and to know enough and to dare enough to put me on this seat, and then to have the wit to go off and stand there in that manner!"

But this tribute of respect to Winthrop was instantly followed by an endeavour to do herself honour, in the way of gaining self-possession and her ordinary looks as speedily as possible. She commanded herself well after once she got the reins in hand; yet however it was with a grave consciousness of swollen eyes and flushed cheeks that she presently rose from her place and went forward to the side of the quiet figure that stood there with folded arms watching the rolling waters of the bay. Elizabeth stood at his elbow a minute in hesitation.

"I am ready now, Mr. Landholm. I am sorry I have kept you by my ridiculousness."

"I have not been kept beyond my pleasure," he said.

"I lost command of myself," Elizabeth went on. "That happens to me once in a while."

"You will feel better for it," he said, as they turned and began to walk homewards.

"He takes things coolly!" thought Elizabeth.

"Do you men ever lose command of yourselves?"

"Sometimes—I am afraid," he said with a smile.

"I suppose your greater power of nerve and of guarding appearances, is one secret of the triumphant sort of pride you wear upon occasion. There—I see it in your face now."

"I hope not," said Winthrop laughing. "The best instance of self-control that I ever saw, was most unaccompanied with any arrogance of merit or power."

"He means his mother again," thought Elizabeth.

"Was that instance in a man or a woman, Mr. Landholm?"

"It was in a woman——unfortunately for your ground."

"Not at all," said Elizabeth. "Exceptions prove nothing."

Winthrop said nothing, for his thoughts were busy with that image of sweet self-guidance which he had never known to be unsteady or fail; and which, he knew, referred all its strength and all its stableness to the keeping of another hand. Most feminine, most humble, and most sure.

"Mr. Winthrop, your mother puzzles me," said Elizabeth. "I wish I knew some of her secrets."

"I wish I did," he answered with half a sigh.

"Why, don't you!"

"No."

"I thought you did."

"No; for she says they can only be arrived at through a certain initiation which I have not had——after certain preliminary steps, which I have not yet taken."

Elizabeth looked at him, both surprised and curious.

"What are they?"

Winthrop's face was graver than usual, as he said,

"I wish my mother were here to answer you."

"Why, cannot you?"

"No."

"Don't you know the preliminary steps, Mr. Landholm?"

He looked very grave again.

"Not clearly enough to tell you. In general, I know she would say there is a narrow way to be passed through before the treasures of truth, or its fair prospects, can be arrived at; but I have never gone that way myself and I cannot point out the way-marks."

"Are you referring to the narrow gate spoken of in the Bible?"

"To the same."

"Then you are getting upon what *I* do not understand," said Elizabeth.

They had mounted the steps of No. 11, and were waiting for the door to be opened. They waited silently till it was done, and then parted with only a 'good night.' Elizabeth did not ask him in, and it hardly occurred to Winthrop to wonder that she did not.

Mr. Landholm read no classics that night. Neither law. Neither, which may seem more strange, did he consult his Book of books at all. He busied himself, not exactly with the study of the human mind, but of *two* human minds,—which, though at first sight it may seem an enlargement of the subject, is in fact rather a contracted view of the same.

CHAPTER XXII.

Sir Toby. Do not our lives consist of the four elements?
Sir And. 'Faith, so they say, but, I think, it rather consists of eating and drinking.
TWELFTH NIGHT.

"DEAR, Mr. Winthrop,——what makes all this smoke here?" exclaimed Mrs. Nettley one morning, as she opened the door of his attic.

"I suppose, the wind, Mrs. Nettley," said Winthrop looking up from the book he was studying.

"O dear!—how do you manage?"

"I can't manage the smoke, Mrs. Nettley——Its resources exceed mine."

"It's that chimney!" exclaimed the good lady, standing and eyeing it in a sort of desperate concern, as if she would willingly have gone up the flue herself, so that only she could thereby have secured the smoke's doing the same. "I always knew that chimney was bad—I had it once a while myself—I'm sorry you've got it now. What *do* you do, Mr. Winthrop?"

"The smoke and I take turns in going out, Mrs. Nettley."

"Eh?—Does it often come in so? Can't you help it?"

"It generally takes advice with the wind, not with me ma'am."

"But the chimney might have better advice. I'll get George to fetch a doctor—I had forgotten it was so bad, I had quite forgotten it, and you never say a word—Mr. Landholm you never come to see us."

"I have so much else to see," he said, glancing at his book.

"Yes, and that reminds me—Have you heard the news?"

"I have heard none to-day."

"Then you heard it yesterday,—of course you did; but I hear so little, when anything comes to me that's new I always think it must be new to everybody else. But of course *you* must know it, as it is about friends of yours; I dare say you knew it long ago;—though such things *are* kept close sometimes, even from friends; and I somehow was surprised to hear this, though I had no right to be, for I suppose I had no reason for my fancy. I think a good many things I have no reason for, George thinks. Maybe I do. I cant help it."

"But what is the thing in this case, Mrs. Nettley?" said Winthrop smiling.

"Why George told me—don't you know? I was a little disappointed, Mr. Winthrop."

"Why?"

"Why, I had a fancy things were going another way."

"I don't know what you are talking about."

"That's because I talk so ill—It's this piece of news George brought home yesterday—he was dining out, for a wonder, with this gentleman who is going to sit to him; I forget his name,—Mr.——I don't know what it is!—but I am foolish to talk about it. Won't you come down and take a cup of tea with us to-night, Mr. Landholm? that's what I came up to ask, and not to stand interrupting you. But you've quite forgotten us lately."

"Thank you, Mrs. Nettley, I'll come with great pleasure—on condition that you tell me your news."

"The news? O it's no news to you—it's only this about Miss Haye."

"What about Miss Haye?"

"They say that she is going to get married, to a Mr. Cadwallader, George said. Her cousin I suppose; there is a cousinship of that name, isn't there, Mr. Landholm?"

Mr. Landholm bowed.

"And had you heard of it before?"

"No, I had not."

"And is it a good match? She is a fine girl, isn't she?"

"I know really nothing of the matter, Mrs. Nettley—I have never seen the gentleman."

"Really! Haven't you?—then it *was* news," said the lady. "I thought you were accustomed to see them so often—I didn't think I was telling you anything. George and I—you must forgive us, Mr. Winthrop, people will have such thoughts; they will come in, and you cannot help it—I don't know what's to keep 'em out, unless one could put bars and gates upon one's minds, and you can't well do that;—but George and I used to have suspicions of you, Mr. Landholm. Well, I have interrupted you long enough. Dear! what windows! I'm ashamed. I'll send the girl up, the first chance you are out of the house. I told her to come up too; but she is heedless. I haven't been to see 'em myself in I don't know how many days; but you're always so terribly busy—and now I've staid twice too long!"——

And away she hurried, softly closing the door after her.

Mr. Landholm's quiet study was remarkably quiet for a good while after she went out. No leaf of his book rustled over; not a foot of his chair grated on the floor,—for though the floor did boast a bit of carpet, it lay not where he sat, by the window; and the coals and firebrands fell noiselessly down into the ashes and nobody was reminded that the fire would burn itself out in time if it was let alone. The morning light grew stronger, and the sunbeams that never got there till between nine and ten o'clock, walked into the room; and they found Winthrop Landholm with his elbow on the table and his head in his hand, where they often were; but with his eyes where they *not* often were—on the floor. The sunbeams said very softly that it was time to be at the office, but they said it very softly, and Winthrop did not hear them.

He heard however presently a footstep on the stair, in the next story at first, and then mounting the uppermost flight that led to the attic. A heavy brisk energetic footstep,—not Mrs. Nettley's soft and slow tread, nor the more deliberate one of her brother. Winthrop listened a moment, and then as the last impatient creak of the boot stopped at his threshold he knew who would open the door. It was Rufus.

"*Here* you are. Why I expected to find you at the office!" was the first cheery exclamation, after the brothers had clasped hands.

"What did you come here to find, then?" said Winthrop.

"Room for my carpet-bag, in the first place; and a pair of slippers, and comfort. It's stinging weather, Governor!"

"I know it. I came down the river the night before last."

"I shouldn't think you knew it, for you've let your fire go down confoundedly. Why Winthrop! there's hardly a spark here! What have you been thinking about?"

"I was kindling the fire, mentally," said Winthrop.

"Mentally!—where's your kindling?—I can tell you!—if you had been out in this air you'd want some breath of material flame, before you could set any other agoing. And I am afraid *this* isn't enough—or won't be,—I want some fuel for another sort of internal combustion—some of my Scotchman's haggis."

And Rufus stopped to laugh, with a very funny face, in the midst of his piling chips and brands together.

"Haggis?" said Winthrop.

"Yes.—There was a good fellow of a Scotchman in the stage with me last night—he had the seat just behind me—and he and a brother Scotchman were discoursing valiantly of old world things; warming themselves up with the recollection.—Winthrop, have you got a bit of paper here?—And I heard the word 'haggis' over and over again,—'haggis' and 'parritch.' At last I turned round gravely—'Pray sir,' said I, 'what *is* a haggis?' 'Weel, sir,' said he good-humouredly,—'I don't just know the ingredients—it's made of meal,—and onions, I believe,—and other combustibles!!'—Winthrop, have you got any breakfast in the house?"

"Not much in the combustible line, I am afraid," said Winthrop, putting up his books and going to the closet.

"Well if you can enact Mother Hubbard and 'give a poor dog a bone,' I shall be thankful,—for anything."

"I am afraid hunger has perverted your memory," said Winthrop.

"How?"

"If the cupboard should play its part now, the dog would go without any."

"O you'll do better for me than that, I hope," said Rufus; "for I couldn't go on enacting the dog's part long; he took to laughing, if I remember, and I should be beyond that directly."

"Does that ever happen?" said Winthrop, as he brought out of the cupboard his bits of stores; a plate with the end of a loaf of bread, a little pitcher of milk, and another plate with some remains of cold beefsteak. For all reply, Rufus seized upon a piece of bread, to begin with, and thrusting a fork into the beefsteak, he held it in front of the just-burning firebrands. Winthrop stood looking on, while Rufus, the beefsteak, and the smoke, seemed mutually intent upon each other. It was a question of time, and patience; not to speak of fortitude.

"Winthrop," said Rufus changing hands with his fork,—"have you any coffee?"

"No sir."

"Tea?"

"No."

"Out of both?"

"For some time."

"Do you live without it?"

"I live without it."

"Without either of them?"

"Without either of them."

"Then how in the world *do* you live?" said Rufus turning his beefsteak in a very gingerly manner and not daring to take his eyes from it.

"Without combustibles—as I told you."

"I should think so!" exclaimed his brother. "You are the coolest, toughest, most stubborn and unimpressible piece of sensibility, that ever lived in a garret and deserved to live—somewhere else."

"Doubtful strain of commendation," said Winthrop. "What has brought you to Mannahatta?"

"But Winthrop, this is a new fancy of yours?"

"No, not very."

"How long since?"

"Since what?"

"Since you gave up all the good things of this life?"

"A man can only give up what he has," said Winthrop. "Those I delivered into your hands some ten minutes ago."

"But tea and coffee—You used to drink them?"

"Yes."

"Why don't you?"

"For a variety of reasons, satisfactory to my own mind."

"And have you abjured butter too?"

"I am sorry, Will," said Winthrop smiling a little,—"I will try to have some butter for you to-morrow."

"Don't you eat it in ordinary?"

"Always, when I can get it. What has brought you to Mannahatta?"

"What do you think?"

"Some rash scheme or resolution."

"Why?"

"From my judgment of your character, which might be stated as the converse of that just now so happily applied to me."

"And do natures the opposite of that never act otherwise than rashly?"

"I hope so; for as the coolest are sometimes excited, so the hot may be sometimes cool."

"And don't I look cool?"

"You did when you came in," said Winthrop.

"I should think living on bread and milk might help that, in ordinary," said Rufus. "Just in my present condition it has rather a different effect. Well Governor, I've come to Mannahatta—"

"I see that," said Winthrop.

"I'll thank you not to interrupt me. I've come to Mannahatta—on a piece of business."

Winthrop waited, and Rufus after another cut of the bread and meat, went on.

"Governor, I'm going to quit engineering and take to another mode of making money."

"Have you done with your last piece of work at the West?"

"No—I'm going back there to finish it. O I'm going back there—I've only come here now to sign some papers and make some arrangements; I shall come finally, I suppose, about May, or April. I've been corresponding with Haye lately."

"About what?"

"About this! What should I correspond with him about? By the way, what an infernal piece of folly this marriage is!"

"Not mixed up with your business, is it?"

"No, of course; how should it? but I am tremendously surprised. Aren't you?"

"People of my temperament never are, you know."

"People of your temperament—have a corner for their thoughts," said Rufus. "Well, there's one chance gone for you, Governor."

"Which it does not appear that I ever had."

"No indeed, that's very true. Well, about my business.—Haye has advocated my leaving the country and coming here. And he knows what he is about, Winthrop; he is a capital man of business. He says he can put me in a way of doing well for myself in a very short time here, and he recommended my coming."

"What's his object?" said Winthrop.

"What's his object?"

"Yes."

"How should I know! He wants to serve me, I suppose; and I believe he has kindliness enough for me, to be not unwilling to get me in the same place of business with himself."

"What will he do for you?"

"This, to begin with. He has a quantity of cotton lying in his stores, which he offers to make over to me, upon a certain valuation. And I shall ship it to Liverpool, as he recommends."

"Have you got your money from the North Lyttleton company?"

"No, nor from anybody else;—not yet; but it's coming."

"Is this purchase of cotton to be executed immediately?"

"Immediately. That's what I have come down for."

"How are you to pay Mr. Haye?"

"By bills upon the consignees."

"Does the purchase swallow up all your means?"

"None of them," said Rufus impatiently. "I tell you, it is to be consummated by drawing bills in Haye's favour upon the consignees—Fleet, Norton & Co."

"Suppose the consignment don't pay?"

"It *will* pay, of course! Don't you suppose Haye knows what he is about?"

"Yes; but that don't satisfy me, unless I know it too."

"*I* do," said Rufus. "He takes an interest in me for my father's sake; and I think I may say without vanity, for my own; and he is willing to do me a kindness, which he can do without hurting himself. That is all; and very simple."

"Too simple," said Winthrop.

"What do you mean?"

"What are you going to do when you come here?"

"Look after my in-comings; and I shall probably go into Haye's office and rub up my arithmetic in the earlier branches. What are *you* going to do?"

"I am going to the office,—Mr. De Wort's."

"What to do there, Governor?"

"Read, write, and record, law and lawpapers."

"Always at the same thing!"

"Always."

"Seems a slow way of getting ahead."

"It's sure," said Winthrop.

"*You* are sure, I believe, of whatever you undertake. By the way—have you undertaken the other adventure yet?"

"I don't know what you mean."

"The adventure we were talking about.—The heiress."

"I can adventure nothing upon speculation," said Winthrop.

"Then you have not had a chance to carry out your favourite idea of obligation. Do you know, I never should have suspected you of having such an idea."

"Shews how much we go upon speculation even with our nearest friends," said Winthrop.

"And how speculation fails there as elsewhere. What a fool Haye has made of himself!"

"In what?"

"Why, in this match."

"What has he done?"

"Done! why he has done *it*. Enough, I should think. I wish his folly stood alone."

"How do you know he has done it?"

"He told me so himself. I met him as I came along just now; and he told me he was to be married to-morrow and would attend to my business next day."

"Told you *who* would?"

"He. Himself. Haye."

"Told you *he* was to be married?"

"Yes. Who else?"

"To whom?"

"Why!—to his niece—ward—what *is* she? Rose Cadwallader."

"*Mr.* Haye and Miss Cadwallader!" said Winthrop.

"To be sure. What are you thinking of? What have we been talking about?"

"You know best," said Winthrop. "My informant had brought another person upon the stage."

"Who?"

"A Mr. Cadwallader."

"There's no such thing as a Mr. Cadwallader. It's Haye himself; and it only shews how all a man's wisdom may be located in one quarter of his brain and leave the other empty."

"To-morrow?" said Winthrop.

"Yes; and you and I are invited to pay our respects at eleven. Haven't you had an invitation?"

"I don't know—I have been out of town—and for the present I must pay my respects in another direction. I must leave you, Will."

"Look here. What's the matter with you, Winthrop?"

"Nothing at all," said Winthrop facing round upon his brother.

"Well I believe there isn't," said Rufus, taking a prolonged look at him,—"but somehow I was thinking—You're a fine-looking fellow, Winthrop!"

"You'll find wood in the further end of the closet," said Winthrop smiling. "I am afraid Mother Hubbard's shelves are in classical order—that is, with nothing on them."

"I sha'n't want anything more till dinner," said Rufus. "Where do you dine?"

"At the chop-house to-day."

"I'll meet you there. Won't you be home till night?"

"I never am."

"Well—till dinner," said Rufus waving his hand. And his brother left him.

Turning away from the table and his emptied dishes and fragmentary beef-bone, Rufus sat before the little fireplace, gazing into it at the red coals, and taking casual and then wistful note of various things about his brother's apartment that told of the man that lived there.

"Spare!"—said Rufus to himself, as his eye marked the scanty carpet, the unpainted few wooden chairs, the curtainless bed, the rough deal shelves of the closet which shewed at the open door, and the very economical chimney place, which now, the wind having gone down, did no longer smoke;—"Spare!—but he'll have a better place to live in, one of these days, and will furnish it."—And visions of mahogany and of mirrors glanced across Rufus's imagination, how unlike the images around him and before his bodily eye.—"Spare!—poor fellow!—he's working hard just now; but pay-time will come. And orderly,—just like him; his books piled in order on the window-sill—his papers held down by one on the table, the clean floor,—yes,"—and rising Rufus even went and looked into the closet. There was the little stack of wood and parcel of kindling, like wise in order; there stood Winthrop's broom in a corner; and there hung Winthrop's few clothes that were not folded away in his trunk. Mother Hubbard's department was in the same spare and thoroughly kept style; and Rufus came back thoughtfully to his seat before the fire.

"Like him, every bit of it, from the books to the broom. Like him;—his own mind is just as free from dust or confusion; rather more richly furnished. What a mind it is! and what wealth he'll make out of it, for pocket and for name both. And I——"

Here Rufus's lucubrations left his brother and went off upon a sea of calculations, landing at Fleet, Norton & Co. and then coming back to Mannahatta and Mr. Haye's counting-room. He had plenty of time for them, as no business obviously could be done till the day after to-morrow.

CHAPTER XXIII.

Touch. All your writers do consent that *ipse* is he ; now you are not *ipse*, for I am he.
Well. Which he, sir ?

As You Like It.

In due course of time the morrow brought round eleven o'clock; and the two brothers took their way, whither all the world severally were taking theirs, to Mr. Haye's house. The wedding was over and the guests were pouring in.

For some reason or other the walk was taken in grave silence, by both parties, till they were mounting the steps to the hall door.

"How do you suppose Elizabeth will like this ?" Rufus whispered.

Winthrop did not say, nor indeed answer at all; and his brother's attention was caught the next minute by Mr. Herder whom they encountered in the hall.

"How do you do ?" said the naturalist grasping both his young friends' hands,—"when did you come ? and how is all wiz you ? I hope you are not going to be married !"

"Why, Mr. Herder ?" said Rufus laughing.

"It is very perplexing, and does not satisfy nobody," said the naturalist. "So quick as a man thinks of somebody else a leetle too hard, he forgets himself altogezer; and then, he does not be sure what he is doing. Now—dis man—"

"Isn't he sure what he has done ?" said Rufus much amused.

"No, he does not know," said Mr. Herder.

"What does his daughter think of it ?"

"She looks black at it. I do not know what she is thinking. I do not want to know."

"Ha! What does she say?"

"She says nozing at all; she looks black," said the naturalist shrugging his shoulders. "Don't you go to get married. You will not satisfy nobody."

"Except myself," said Rufus.

"Maybe. I do not know," said the naturalist. "A man has not no right to satisfy himself wizout he can satisfy ozer people too. I am sorry for poor Miss Elisabet'."

"I wonder how many matches would be made upon that rule!" said Rufus, as they parted and Mr. Herder joined the company within.

"They would be all matches made by other people," said Winthrop.

"And on the principle that 'to-morrow never comes'—the world would come to an end."

So they entered the drawing-rooms.

There were many people there, and certainly for the present there were few unsatisfied faces; for the bride was lovely enough and the bridegroom of consequence enough, to make compliments to them a matter of pleasure to the giver. The room was blooming with beauty and brightness. But Miss Haye was not there; and as soon as they could withdraw from the principal group the two brothers made their way to an inner room, where she stood, holding as it were a court of her own; and an unpropitious monarch she would have looked to her courtiers had they been real ones. Her face was as lowering as Mr. Herder had described it; settled in pain and pride; though now and then a quick change would pass over it, very like the play of lightning on a distant cloud;—fitful, sharp, and traceless. Just as Rufus and Winthrop had made their bow, and before they had time to speak, another bow claimed Elizabeth's return, and the tongue that went therewith was beforehand with theirs. The speaker was a well dressed and easy mannered man of the world; but with a very javelin of an eye, as ready for a throw as a knight's lance of old, and as careless what it met in its passage through humanity.

"You have wandered out of your sphere, Miss Elizabeth."

"What do you mean, sir?"—was given with sufficient keenness.

"The bright constellation of beauty and happiness is in the other room. Stars set off one another."

"I shine best alone," said Élizabeth.

"You disdain the effect of commingled and reflected light?"

"Yes I do, heartily, in this case. I wish for no glory that does not belong to me."

"But does not the glory of your father and mother belong to you?" said the gentleman. He spoke with the most smooth deference of manner, that all but covered his intent; but the flush and fire started into Elizabeth's face reminding one of the volcano again. Her eye watered with pain too, and she hesitated; she was evidently not ready with an answer. Perhaps for that reason it was given with added haughtiness.

"You need not trouble yourself to reckon what does or what does not belong to me. I know my belongings, and will take care of them."

"You are satisfied with them," said the gentleman, "and willing they should stand alone?"

"I am willing they should take their chance, sir."

"I know no one who can better say that," remarked Rufus.

"With better confidence, or better grounds do you mean?"

"I hope you do not need to be told!" said Rufus, his eye sparkling half with fun and half with admiration at the face and manner with which Elizabeth turned upon him.

"Which leaves the lady at liberty to suppose what she pleases," said the first speaker.

"It leaves her at liberty to suppose nothing of the kind!" Rufus rejoined, with a little dilating of the nostril.

"Nothing can constrain my liberty in that respect," said the lady in question.

"Except your knowledge of human nature?" said Rufus.

"I have no hindrance in that," said Elizabeth.

"To supposing what you please?"

"Or what pleases you, perhaps," said the first speaker.

"Anything but that, Mr Archibald!"

"Then it was no surprise to you that your father should set a young and lovely Mrs. Haye at the head of his establishment, even though he found her in the person of your playmate?"

Elizabeth hesitated; she drew in her under lip, and her eye darkened and lightened; but she hesitated. Then she spoke, looking down.

"I was surprised."

"Not a pleasant surprise?" said Mr. Archibald.

The girl's face literally flashed at him; from her two eyes the fire flew, as if the one would confound the other.

"How dare you ask me the question, sir!"

"Pardon me—I had no idea there was any harm in it," said the person at whom the fire flew.

"Your ideas want correcting, sir, sadly!—and your tongue."

"I will never offend again!" said Mr. Archibald bowing, and smiling a little.

"You never shall, with my good leave."

Mr. Archibald bowed again.

"Good morning! You will forgive me; and when I think time enough has elapsed, and I may with safety, I will come again."

"To visit my father, sir!——"

Not Queen Elizabeth, with ruff and farthingale, could have said it with more consciousness of her own dignity, or more superb dismission of that of another. But probably Queen Elizabeth would not have cast upon her courtiers the look, half asking for sympathy and half for approval, with which Elizabeth Haye turned to her companions. Her eye fell first upon Winthrop. But his did not meet her, and the expression of his face was very grave. Elizabeth's look went from it to Rufus. His was beaming.

"Capital!" he said. "That was admirable!"

"No," said Elizabeth after a slight hesitation,—"it was not."

"I thought it was," said Rufus,—"admirably done. Why was it not, Miss Haye?—if I am not as impertinent as another?—I thought he richly deserved his punishment."

"Yes," said Elizabeth in a dissatisfied kind of way,—"enough of that,—but I deserved better of myself than to give it to him."

"You are too hard upon yourself."

"Circumstances are sometimes."

"Will it do to say that?" said Winthrop looking up.

"Why not?"

"Will it do to confess oneself—one's freedom of mind—under the power of *circumstance*, and so not one's own?"

"I must confess it," said Elizabeth, "for it's true, of *me*. I suppose, not of every one."

"Then you cannot depend upon yourself."

"Well,—I can't."

He smiled.

"On whom then?"

"On no one!—"

And the blood sprung to her cheeks and the water to her eyes, with a sudden rush. It seemed that circumstance was not the only thing too hard for her; feeling had so far the mastery, for the minute, that her head bent down and she could not at once raise it up. Rufus walked off to the window, where he gave his attention to some greenhouse plants; Winthrop stood still.

"I would give anything in the world," said Elizabeth, lifting her head and at first humbly and then proudly wiping her tears away,—"if I could learn self-control—to command myself. Can one do it, Mr. Landholm?—one with whom it is not born?"

"I believe so."

"After all, you can't tell much about it," said Elizabeth, "for it belongs to your nature."

"No credit to him," said Rufus returning;—"it comes of the stock. An inch of self-control in one not accustomed to it, is worth more honour than all Governor's, which he can't help."

"I wouldn't give a pin for self-control in one not accustomed to it!" said Elizabeth; "it is the *habitual* command over oneself, that I value."

"No let-up to it?" said Rufus.

"No;—or only so much as to shew in what strength it exists. I am glad, for instance, that Washington for once forgot himself—or no, he didn't *forget* himself; but I am glad that passion got the better of him once. I respect the rest of his life infinitely more."

"Than that instance?"

"No, no!—*for* that instance."

"I am afraid you have a little tendency to hero-worship, Miss Elizabeth."

"A very safe tendency," said the young lady. "There aren't many heroes to call it out."

"Living heroes?"

"No, nor dead ones,——if one could get at more than the great facts of their lives, which don't shew us the men."

"Then you are of opinion that 'trifles make the sum of human things?'"

"I don't know what are trifles," said Elizabeth.

"Dere is nozing is no trifle," said Mr. Herder, coming in from the other room. "Dere is no such thing as trifle. Miss Élisabet' hang her head a little one side and go softly,—and people say, 'Miss Élisabet' is sad in her spirit—what is the matter?'—and you hold up your head straight and look bright out of your eyes, and they say, 'Miss Élisabet' is fière—she feels herself goot; she do not fear nozing, she do not care for nozing."

"I am sure it is a trifle whether I look one way or another, Mr. Herder," said Elizabeth, laughing a little.

"Ozer people do not think so," said the naturalist.

"Besides, it is not true, that I fear nothing and care for nothing."

"But then you do not want to tell everybody what you do think," said the naturalist.

"I don't care much about it!" said Elizabeth. "I think *that* is a trifle, Mr. Herder."

"Which is?"—said the naturalist.

"What people think about me."

"You do not think so?"

"I do."

"I am sorry," said the naturalist.

"Why?"

"It is not goot, for people to not care what ozer people thinks about them."

"Why isn't it good? I think it is. I am sure it is comfortable."

"It shews they have a mind to do something what ozer people will not like."

"Very well!——"

"Dat is not goot."

"Maybe it is good, Mr. Herder. People are not always right in their expectations."

"It is better to go smooth wiz people," said the naturalist shaking his head a little.

"Or without them," said Elizabeth.

"Question, can you do that?" said Rufus.

"What?" said his brother.

"Live smoothly, or live at all, without regard to other people."

"It is of the world at large I was speaking," said Elizabeth. "Of course there are some few, a very few, whose word—and whose thought—one would care for and strive for,—that is not what I mean."

"And who are those few fine persons?" said Mr. Herder significantly.

"He is unhappy that doesn't know one or two," Elizabeth answered with infinite gravity.

"And the opinions of the rest of men you would despise?" said Rufus.

"Utterly!—so far as they trenched upon my freedom of action."

"You can't live so," said Rufus shaking his head.

"I *will* live so, if I live at all."

"Wint'rop, you do not say nozing," said the naturalist.

"What need, sir?"

"Dere is always need for everybody to say what he thinks," said Mr. Herder. "Here we have all got ourselves in a puzzle, and we don't know which way we stand."

"I am afraid every man must get out of that puzzle for himself, sir."

"Is it a puzzle at all?" said Elizabeth facing round upon him.

"Not when you have got out of it."

"Well, what's the right road out of it?"

"Break through everything in the way," said Rufus. "That seems to be the method in favour.'

"What do you think is the *right* way?" Elizabeth repeated without looking at the last speaker.

"If you set your face in the right quarter, there is always a straight road out in that direction," Winthrop answered with a little bit of a smile.

"Doesn't that come pretty near my rule?" said Elizabeth with a smile much broader.

"I think not. If I understood, your rule was to make a straight road out for yourself in *any* direction."

Elizabeth laughed and coloured a little, with no displeased expression. The laugh subsided and her face became very grave again as the gentlemen made their parting bows.

The brothers walked home in silence, till they had near reached their own door.

"How easily you make a straight way for yourself anywhere!" Rufus said suddenly and with half a breath of a sigh.

"What do you mean?" said Winthrop starting.

"You always did."

"What?"

"What you pleased."

"Well?" said Winthrop smiling.

"You may do it now. And will to the end of your life."

"Which seems to afford you somehow a gloomy prospect of contemplation," said his brother.

"Well—it does——and it should."

"I should like to hear you state your premises and draw your conclusion."

Rufus was silent and very sober for a little while. At last he said,

"Your success and mine have always been very different, in everything we undertook."

"Not in everything," said Winthrop.

"Well—in almost everything."

"You say I do whatever I please. The difficulty with you sometimes, Will, is that you do not 'please' hard enough."

"It would be difficult for anybody to rival you in that," Rufus said with a mingling of expression, half ironical and half bitter. "You please so 'hard' that nobody else has a chance."

To which Winthrop made no answer.

"I am not sorry for it, Governor," Rufus said just as they reached their door, and with a very changed and quiet tone.

To which also Winthrop made no answer except by a look.

CHAPTER XXIV.

> I watch thee from the quiet shore;
> Thy spirit up to mine can reach;
> But in dear words of human speech
> We two communicate no more.
>
> TENNYSON.

MRS. NETTLEY was putting the finishing touches to her breakfast—that is, to her breakfast in prospect. A dish of fish and the coffee-pot stood keeping each other cheerful on one side the hearth; and Mrs. Nettley was just, with some trouble, hanging a large round griddle over the blazing fire. Her brother stood by, with his hands on his sides, and a rather complacent face.

"What's that flap-jack going on for?"

"For something I like, if you don't," said his sister. "George—"

Mrs Nettley stopped while her iron ladle was carefully bestowing large spoonfuls of batter all round the griddle.

"What?" said Mr. Inchbald, when it was done.

"Somebody up-stairs likes 'em. Don't you suppose you could get Mr. Landholm to come down. He likes 'em, and he don't get 'em now-a-days—nor too much of anything that's good. I don't know what he *does* live on, up there."

"Anything is better than those things," said her brother.

"Other people are more wise than you. Do go up and ask him, will you, George? I hope he gets good dinners somewhere, for it's very little of anything he cooks at that smoky little fireplace of his. Do you ever see him bring anything in?"

"Nothing. I don't see him bring himself in, you know. But he'll do. He'll have enough by and by, Dame Nettley. I know what stuff he's of."

"Yes, but no stuff 'll last without help," said Mrs. Nettley taking her cakes off the griddle and piling them up carefully. "Now I'm all ready, George, and you're standing there—it's always the way—and before you can mount those three pair of stairs and down again, these 'll be cold. Do go, George; Mr. Landholm likes his cakes hot—I'll have another plateful ready before you'll be here; and then they're good for nothing but to throw away."

"That's what I think," said Mr. Inchbald; "but I'll bring him down if I can, to do what you like with 'em—only I must see first what this knocking wants at the front door."

"And left this one open too!"—said Mrs. Nettley,—"and now the whole house 'll be full of smoke and everything—Well!—I might as well not ha' put this griddleful on."—

But the door having refused to latch, gave Mrs. Nettley a chance to hear what was going on. She stood, slice in hand, listening. Some unaccustomed tones came to her ear—then Mr. Inchbald's round hearty voice, saying,

"Yes sir—he is here—he is at home."

"I'd like to see him——"

And then the sounds of scraping feet entering the house.

"I'd like to go somewheres that I could see a fire, too," said the strange voice. "Ben ridin' all night, and got to set off again, you see, directly."

And Mrs. Nettley turned her cakes in a great hurry, as her brother pushed open the door and let the intruder in.

He took off his hat as he came, shewing a head that had seen some sixty winters, thinly dressed with yellow hair but not at all grey. The face was strong and Yankee-marked with shrewdness and reserve. His hat was wet and his shoulders, which had no protection of an overcoat.

"Do you wish to see Mr. Landholm in his room?" said Mr. Inchbald. "He's just coming down to breakfast."

"That'll do as well," said the stranger nodding. "And stop—you may give him this—maybe he'd as lieve have it up there."

Mr. Inchbald looked at the letter handed him, the outside of which at least told no tales; but his sister with a woman's quick instinct had already asked,

"Is anything the matter?"

"Matter?"—said the stranger,—"well, yes.—He's wanted to hum."

Both brother and sister stood now forgetting everything, both saying in a breath,

"Wanted, what for?"

"Well—there's sickness—"

"His father?"

"No, his mother."

Mrs. Nettley threw down her slice and ran out of the room. Mr. Inchbald turned away slowly in the other direction. The stranger, left alone, took a knife from the table and dished the neglected cakes, and sat down to dry himself between them and the coffee.

Mr. Inchbald slowly mounted the stairs to Winthrop's door, met the pleasant face that met him there, and gave the letter.

"I was coming to ask you down to breakfast with us, Mr. Landholm; but somebody has just come with that for you, and wishes you to have it at once."

The pleasant face grew grave, and the seal was broken, and the letter unfolded. It was a folio half sheet, of coarse yellowish paper, near the upper end of which a very few lines were irregularly written.

"My dear Son,

"It is with great pain I write to tell you that you must leave all and hasten home if you would see your mother. Friend Underhill will take this to you, and your shortest way will be, probably, to hire a horse in M. and travel night and day; as the time of the boat is uncertain and the stage does not make very good time—Her illness has been so short that we did not know it was necessary to alarm you before. My dear son, come without delay—

"Your father,

"W. Landholm."

Mr. Inchbald watched the face and manner of his friend as he read, and after he read, these few words,—but the one expressed only gravity, the other, action. Mr. Inchbald felt he could do nothing, and slowly went down stairs again to Mr. Underhill. He found him still over the fire between the cakes and the coffee. But Mr. Inchbald totally forgot to be hospitable, and not a word was said till Winthrop came in and he and the letter-bringer had wrung each other's hand, with a brief 'how d' ye do.'

"How did you leave them, Mr. Underhill?"

"Well—they were wantin' you pretty bad—"

"Did *she* send for me?"

"Well—no—I guess not," said the other with something of hesitancy, or of consideration, in his speech. Winthrop stood silent a moment.

"I shall take horse immediately. You will go—how?"

"May as well ride along with you," said Mr. Underhill, settling his coat. "I'm wet—a trifle—but may as well ride it off as any way. Start now?"

"Have you breakfasted?"

"Well—no, I hain't had time, you see—I come straight to you."

"Mr. Inchbald, I must go to the office a few minutes—will you give my friend a mouthful?"

"But yourself, Mr. Landholm?"

"I have had breakfast."

Mr. Inchbald did his duty as host then; but though his guest used despatch, the 'mouthful' was hardly a hungry man's breakfast when Winthrop was back again. In a few minutes more the two were mounted and on their way up the right bank of the river.

They rode silently. At least if Mr. Underhill's wonted talkativeness found vent at all, it was more than Winthrop was able ever to recollect. He could remember nothing of the ride but his own thoughts; and it seemed to him afterwards that they must have been stunning as well as deafening; so vague and so blended was the impression of them mixed up with the impression of everything else. It was what Mr. Underhill called 'falling weather'; the rain dropped lightly, or by turns changing to mist hung over the river and wreathed itself about the hills, and often stood across his path; as if to bid the eye turn inward, for space to range without it might not have. And passing all the other journeys he had made up and down that road, some of them on horseback as he was now, Winthrop's thoughts went back to that first one, when through ill weather and discouragement he had left the home he was now seeking, to enter upon his great-world career. Why did they so? He had been that road in the rain since; he had been there in all weathers; he had been there often with as desponding a heart as brought him down that first time; which indeed did not despond at all then, though it felt the weight of life's undertakings and drawbacks. And the warm rain, and yellow, sun-coloured mist of this April day, had no likeness to the cold, pitiless, pelting December storm. Yet passing all the times between, his mind went back constantly to that first one. He felt over again, though as in a dream, its steps of loneliness and heart-sinking—its misty looking forward—and most especially that Bible word '*Now*'—which his little sister's finger had pointed out to him. He remembered how constantly that day it came back to him in everything he looked at,—from the hills, from the river, from the beat of the horses' hoofs, from the falling rain. 'Now'—'now'—he remembered how he had felt it that day; he had almost forgotten it since; but now it came up again to his mind as if that day had been but yesterday. What brought it there? Was it the unrecognized, unallowed sense, that the one of all the world who most longed to have him obey that word, might be to-day beyond seeing him obey it—for ever? Was it possibly, that passing over the bridge of Mirza's vision he suddenly saw himself by the side of one of the open trap-doors, and felt that some stay, some security he needed, before his own foot should open one for itself? He did not ask; he did not try to order the confused sweep of feeling which for the time passed over him; one dread idea for the time held mastery of all others, and kept that day's ride all on the edge of that open trap-door. Whose foot had gone down there?——And under that thought,—woven in with the various tapestry of shower and sunshine, meadow and hillside, that clothed his day's journey to the sense,—were the images of that day in December—that final leaving of home and his mother, that rainy cold ride on the stage-coach, Winnie's open Bible, and the 'Now,' to which her finger, his mother's prayers, and his own conscience, had pointed all the day long.

It made no difference, that as they went on, this April day changed from rain and mist to the most brilliant sunshine. The mists rolled away, down the river and along the gulleys of the mountains; the clouds scattered from off the blue sky, which looked down clear, fair, and soft, as if Mirza's bridge were never under it. The little puddles of water sparkled in the sunshine and reflected the blue; the roads made haste to dry; the softest of spring airs wafted down from the hill-sides a spicy remembrance of budding shoots and the drawn-out sweetness of pine and fir and hemlock and cedar. The day grew sultrily warm. But though sunlight and spring winds carried their tokens to memory's gates and left them there, they were taken no note of at the time, by one traveller, and the other had no mental apparatus fine enough to gather them up.

He had feeling or delicacy enough of another kind, however, to keep him quiet. He sometimes looked at Winthrop; never spoke to him. Almost never; if he spoke at all, it was in some aside or counsel-taking with himself about the weather, the way or the prospect and management of the farming along the river. They stopped only to bait or to rest their horses; even at those times Mr. Underhill restrained himself not only from talking to Winthrop but from talking before him; and except when his companion was at a distance, kept as quiet as he. Winthrop asked no questions.

The road grew hilly, and in some places rough, trying to the horses; and by the time they were fairly among the mountain land that stood down far south from Wut-a-qut-o, the sun was nearing the fair broken horizon line of the western shore. The miles were long now, when they were no longer many; the road was more and more steep and difficult; the horses weary. The sun travelled faster than they did. A gentler sunlight never lay in spring-time upon those hills and river; it made the bitter turmoil and dread of the way seem the more harsh and ungentle. Their last stopping-place was at Cowslip's Mill—on the spot where seven years before, Winthrop had met the stage-coach and its consignment of ladies.

" The horses must have a minute here—and a bite," said Mr. Underhill letting himself slowly down from his beast;—" lose no time by it."

For a change of posture Winthrop threw himself off, and stood leaning on the saddle, while his travelling companion and Mr. Cowslip came up the rise bringing water and food to the horses. No more than a grave nod was exchanged between Winthrop and his old neighbour; neither said one word; and as soon as the buckets were empty the travellers were on their way again.

It was but a little way now. The sun had gone behind the mountain, the wind had died, the perfect stillness and loveliness of evening light was over hill and river and the home land, as the riders came out from the woods upon the foot of the bay and saw it all before them. A cloudless sky,—the white clear western light where the sun had been,—the bright sleeping water,—the sweet lights and shades on Wut-a-qut-o and its neighbour hills, the lower and darker promontory throwing itself across the landscape; and from one spot, that half-seen centre of the picture, the little brown speck on Shah-wee-tah,—a thin, thin wreath of smoke slowly went up. Winthrop for one moment looked, and then rode on sharply and Mr. Underhill was fain to bear him company. They had rounded the bay—they had ridden over the promontory neck—they were within a little of home,—when Winthrop suddenly drew bridle. Mr. Underhill stopped. Winthrop turned towards him, and asked the question not asked till then.

"How is it at home, Mr. Underhill?"

And Mr. Underhill without looking at him, answered in the same tones, a moment of pause between,

"She's gone."

Winthrop's horse carried him slowly forward; Mr. Underhill's was seen no more that night—unless by Mr. Cowslip and his son.

Slowly Winthrop's horse carried him forward—but little time then was needed to bring him round to the back of the house, at the kitchen door, whither the horse-path led. It was twilight now; the air was full of the perfume of cedars and pines, —the clear white light shone in the west yet. Winthrop did not see it. He only saw that there was no light in the windows. And that curl of thin smoke was the only thing he had seen stirring about the house. He got off his horse and went into the kitchen.

There was light enough to see who met him there. It was his father. There was hardly light to see faces; but Mr. Landholm laid both hands on his son's shoulders, saying,

"My dear boy!—it's all over!——"

And Winthrop laid his face on his father's breast, and for a few breaths, sobbed, as he had not done since——since his childish eyes had found hiding-place on that other breast that could rest them no more.

It was but a few minutes;—and manly sorrow had given way and taken again its quiet self-control; once and for ever. The father and son wrung each other's hands, the mute speech of hand to hand telling of mutual suffering and endurance, and affection, —all that could be told; and then after the pause of a minute, Winthrop moved on towards the family room, asking softly, "Is she here?"——But his father led him through, to the seldom-used east-room.

Asahel was there; but he neither spoke nor stirred. And old Karen was there, moving about on some trifling errand of duty; but her quick nature was under less government; it did not bear the sight of Winthrop. Dropping or forgetting what she was about, she came towards him with a bursting cry of feeling, half for herself, half sympathetic; and with the freedom of old acquaintance and affection and common grief, laid her shrivelled black hand on his shoulder and looked up into his face, saying, almost as his father had done, but with streaming eyes and quivering lips,

"My dear son!—she has gone!——"

Winthrop took the hand in his and gave it a moment's pressure, and then saying very gently but in a way that was obeyed, "Be quiet Karen,"—he passed her and stood at his mother's bedside.

She was there—lying quietly in her last sleep. Herself and not another. All of her that *could* write and leave its character on features of clay, was shewn there still—in its beauty. The brow yet spoke the calm good sense which had always reigned beneath it; the lines of toil were on the cheek; the mouth had its old mingling of patience and hope and firm dignity—the dignity of meek assurance which looked both to the present and the future. It was there now, unchanged, unlessened; Winthrop read it; that as she had lived, so she had died, in sure expectation of 'the rest that remaineth.' Herself and no other!—ay! that came home too in another sense, with its hard stern reality, pressing home upon the heart and brain, till it would have seemed that nature could not bear it and must give way. But it did not. Winthrop stood and looked, fixedly and long, so fixedly that no one cared to interrupt him, but so calmly in his deep gravity that the standers-by were rather awed than distressed. And at last when he turned away and Asahel threw himself forward upon his neck, Winthrop's manner was as firm as it was kind; though he left them all then and forbade Asahel to follow him.

"The Lord bless him!" said Karen, loosing her tongue then and giving her tears leave at the same time. "And surely the Lord has blessed him, or he wouldn't ha' borne up so. She won't lose that one of her childr'n—she won't, no she won't!—I know she won't!—"

"Where is Winnie, Karen?" said Asahel suddenly.

"Poor soul!—I dun know," said Karen;—"she was afeard to see the Governor come home, and dursn't stop nowheres—I dun know where she's hid.—The Lord bless him! nobody needn't ha' feared him. He's her own boy—aint he her own boy!——"

Asahel went out to seek for his little sister, but his search was in vain. She was not to be seen nor heard of. Neither did Winthrop come to the sorrowful gathering which the remnant of the family made round the supper-table. *In* the house he was not; and wherever he was out of the house, he was beyond reach.

"Could they have gone away together?" said Asahel.

"No!" said his father.

"They didn't," said Clam. "I see him go off by himself."

"Which way?"

" Off among the trees," said Clam.

"Which way?" said Mr. Landholm.

"His back was to the house, and he was goin' off towards the river some place—I guess he didn't want no one to foller him."

" There aint no wet nor cold to hurt him," said Karen.

There was not; but they missed him.

And the house had been quiet, very quiet, for long after supper-time, when softly and cautiously one of the missing ones opened the door of the east-room and half came in. Only Karen sat there at the foot of the bed. Winnie came in and came up to her.

"He's not here, darlin'," said the old woman,—"and ye needn't ha' started from him.—O cold face, and white face!—what ha' you done with yourself, Winnie, to run away from him so? Ye needn't ha' feared him. Poor lamb!—poor white lamb!—"

The girl sat down on the floor and laid her face on Karen's lap, where the still tears ran very fast.

" Poor white lamb!" said the old woman, tenderly laying her wrinkled hand on Winnie's fair hair,—" Ye haven't eat a crumb —Karen'll fetch you a bit?—ye'll faint by the way—"

Winnie shook her head. " No—no."

"What did you run away for?" Karen went on. " Ye run away from your best comfort—but the Lord's help, Winnie;—he's the strongest of us all."

But something in that speech, Karen could not divine what, made Winnie sob convulsively; and she thought best to give up her attempts at counsel or comforting.

The wearied and weakened child must have needed both, for she wept unceasingly on Karen's knees till late in the night; and then in sheer weariness the heavy eyelids closed upon the tears that were yet ready to come. She slumbered, with her head still on Karen's lap.

"Poor lamb!" said Karen when she found it out, bending over to look at her,—"poor lamb!—she'll die of this if the Governor can't help her,—and she the Lord's child too.—Maybe best, poor child!—maybe best!—'Little traveller Zion-ward' ——I wish we were all up at those gates, O Lord!——"

The last words were spoken with a heavy sigh, and then the old woman changed her tone.

" Winnie!—Winnie!—go to bed—go to bed! Your mother 'd say it if she was here."

Winnie raised her head and opened her eyes, and Karen repeating her admonition in the same key, the child got up and went mechanically out of the room, as if to obey it.

It was by this time very late in the night; the rest of the inmates of the house had long been asleep. No lights were burning except in the room she had left. But opening the door of the kitchen, through which her way lay to her own room, Winnie found there was a glimmer from the fire, which usually was covered up close; and coming further into the room, she saw some one stretched at full length upon the floor at the fireside. Another step, and Winnie knew it was Winthrop. He was asleep, his head resting on a rolled-up cloak against the jamb. Winnie's tears sprang forth again, but she would not waken him. She kneeled down by his side, to look at him, as well as the faint fire-glow would let her, and to weep over him; but her strength was worn out. It refused even weeping; and after a few minutes, nestling down as close to him as she could get, she laid one arm and her head upon his breast and went to sleep too. More peacefully and quietly than she had slept for several nights.

The glimmer from the fire-light died quite away, and only the bright stars kept watch over them. The moon was not where she could look in at those north or east kitchen windows. But by degrees the fair April night changed. Clouds gathered themselves up from all quarters of the horizon, till they covered the sky; the faces of the stars were hid; thunder began to roll along among the hills, and bright incessant flashes of white lightning kept the room in a glare. The violence of the storm did not come over Shah-wee-tah, but it was more than enough to rouse Winthrop, whose sleep was not so deep as his little sister's. And when Winnie did come to her consciousness she found herself lifted from the floor and on her brother's lap; he half sitting up; his arms round her, and her head still on his breast. Her first movement of awakening was to change her position and throw her arms around his neck.

"Winnie——" he said gently.

The flood-gates burst then, and her heart poured itself out, her head alternately nestling in his neck and raised up to kiss his face, and her arms straining him with nervous eagerness.

"O Winthrop!—O Winthrop!—O dear Winthrop!—" was the cry, as fast as sobs and kisses would let her.

"Winnie—" said her brother again.

"O Winthrop!—why didn't you come!"

He did not answer that, except by the heaving breast which poor Winnie could not feel.

"I am here now, dear Winnie."

"O Winthrop!—" Winnie hesitated, and the burden of her heart would burst forth,——"why aren't you a Christian!—"

It was said with a most bitter rush of tears, as if she felt that the most precious thing she had, lacked of preciousness; that her most sure support needed a foundation. But when a minute had stilled the tears, and she could hear, she heard him say, very calmly,

"I am one, Winnie."

Her tears ceased absolutely on his shoulder, and Winnie was for a moment motionless. Then as he did not speak again, she unclasped her arms and drew back her head to look at him. The constant flashes of light gave her chance enough.

"You heard me right," he said.

"Are you?"—she said wistfully.

"By God's help——this night and for ever."

Winnie brought her hands together, half clapping, half clasping them, and then threw them to their former position around his neck, exclaiming,—

"Oh if *she* had known it before—!"

There was no answer to that, of words; and Winnie could not see the sudden paleness which witnessed to the answer within. But it came, keen as those lightning flashes, home-thrust as the thunderbolts they witnessed to, that his 'now' had come too late for her.

The lightnings grew fainter, and failed—the thunder muttered off in the distance, and ceased to be heard—the clouds rolled down the river and scattered away, just as the dawn was breaking on Wut-a-qut-o. There had been nothing spoken in the farmhouse kitchen since Winnie's last words. Winthrop was busy with his own thoughts, which he did not tell; and Winnie had been giving hers all the expression they could bear, in tears and kisses and the strong clasp of her weak arm, and the envious resting, trusting, lay of her head upon Winthrop's shoulder and breast. When the glare of the lightning had all gone, and the grey light was beginning to walk in at the windows, her brother spoke to her.

"Winnie,—you would be better in bed."

"Oh no,—I wouldn't.—Do you want me to go, Governor?" she added presently.

"Not if you could rest as well here, but you want rest, Winnie."

"I couldn't rest so well *anywhere!*"—said Winifred energetically.

"Then let me take the big chair and give you a chance."

He took it, and took her in his arms again, where she nestled herself down as if she had been a child; with an action that touchingly told him anew that she could rest so well nowhere else.

"Governor—" she said, when her head had found its place—"you haven't kissed me."

"I did, Winnie,—it must have been before you were awake."

But he kissed her again; and drawing one or two long breaths, of heart-weariness and heart-rest, Winnie went to sleep.

The grey dawn brightened rapidly; and a while after, Karen came in. It was fair morning then. She stood by the hearth, opposite the two, looking at them.

"Has she been here all night?" she whispered.

Winthrop nodded.

"Poor lamb!—Ye're come in good time, Master Winthrop."

She turned and began to address herself to the long gone-out fire in the chimney.

"What are you going to do, Karen?" he said softly.

She looked back at him, with her hand in the ashes.

"Haven't you watched to-night?"

"I've watched a many nights," she said shaking her head and beginning again to rake for coals in the cold fireplace,—"this aint the first. *That* aint nothin'. I'll watch now, dear, 'till the day dawn and the shadows flee away';—what else should Karen do? 'Taint much longer, and I'll be where there's no night again. O come, sweet day!—" said the old woman clasping her hands together as she crouched in the fireplace, and the tears beginning to trickle down,—"when the mother and the childr'n'll all be together, and Karen somewheres—and our home won't be broken up no more!—"

She raked away among the ashes with an eager trembling hand.

"Karen,—" said Winthrop softly,—"Leave that."

"What, dear?"—she said.

"Leave that."

"Who'll do it, dear?"

"I will."

She obeyed him, as perhaps she would have done for no one else. Rising up, Winthrop carried his sleeping sister without wakening her, and laid her on the bed in her own little room, which opened out of the kitchen; then he came back and went to work in the fireplace. Karen yielded it to him with equal admiration and unwillingness; remarking to herself as her relieved hands went about other business, that, "for sure, nobody could build a fire handsomer than Mr. Winthrop";—and that "he was his mother's own son, and deserved to be!"

CHAPTER XXV.

> That thee is sent receive in buxomness;
> The wrestling of this worlde askith a fall;
> Here is no home, here is but wildernesse,
> Forthe, pilgrim, forthe, o best out of thy stall,
> Loke up on high, and thanke thy God of all.
>
> CHAUCER.

As soon as she was awake Winnie sought her brother's side again; and from that moment never left it when it was possible to be there. In his arms, if she could; close by his side, if nearer might not be; she seemed to have no freedom of life but in his shadow. Her very grief was quieted there; either taking its tone from his calm strength, or binding itself with her own love for him. Her brother was the sturdy tree round which this poor little vine threw its tendrils, and climbed and flourished, all it could.

He had but a few days to spend at Shahweetah now. Towards the end of them, she was one evening sitting, as usual, on his knee; silent and quiet. They were alone.

"Winnie," said her brother, "what shall I do with you?"

She put her arms round his neck and kissed him,—a very frequent caress; but she made no answer.

"Shall I take you to Mannahatta with me?"

"Oh yes, Winthrop!"

It was said with breathless eagerness.

"I am almost afraid to do it."

"Why, Winthrop?"

"Hush—" he said gently; for her words came out with a sort of impatient hastiness;——"You don't know what kind of a place it is, Winnie. It isn't much like what home used to be."

"Nor this aint, neither," she murmured, nestling her head in his bosom.

"But you wouldn't have the free air and country—I am afraid it wouldn't be so good for you."

"Yes it would—it would be better for me.—I can't hardly be good at all, Governor, except where you are. I get cross now-a-days—it seems I can't help it—and I didn't use to do so——"

How gently the hand that was not round her was laid upon her cheek, as if at once forbidding and soothing her sorrow. For it was true,—Winnie's disease had wrought to make her irritable and fretful, very different from her former self. And it was true that Winthrop's presence governed it, as no other thing could.

"Would you rather go with me, Winnie?"

"Oh yes, Governor!—oh yes!"

"Then you shall."

He went himself first to make arrangements, which he well knew were very necessary. That one little attic room of his and that closet which was at once Mother Hubbard's cupboard and his clothes press, could never do anything for the comfort of his little sister. He went home and electrified Mrs. Nettley with the intelligence that he must leave her and seek larger quarters, which he knew her house could not give.

"To be sure," said Mrs. Nettley in a brown study,——"the kitchen's the kitchen,—and there must be a parlour,—and George's painting room,—and the other's my bedroom,—and George sleeps in that other little back attic.—Well, Mr. Landholm, let's think about it. We'll see what *can* be done. We can't let you go away—George would rather sleep on the roof."

"He would do what is possible, Mrs. Nettley; and so would I."

It was found to be possible that 'the other little back attic' should be given up. Winthrop never knew how, and was not allowed to know. But it was so given that he could not help taking. It was plain that they would have been worse straitened than in their accommodations, if he had refused their kindness and gone somewhere else.

Mrs. Nettley would gladly have done what she could towards furnishing the same little back attic for Winnie's use; but on this point Winthrop was firm. He gathered himself the few little plain things the room wanted, from the cheapest sources whence they could be obtained; even that was a serious drain upon his purse. He laid in a further supply of fuel, for Winnie's health, he knew, would not stand the old order of things,—a fire at meal-times and an old cloak at other times when it was not very cold. Happily it was late in the season and much more fire would not be needed; a small stock of wood he bought, and carried up and bestowed in the closet; he could put his clothes in Winnie's room now and the closet need no longer act as a wardrobe. A few very simple stores to add to Mother Hubbard's shelves, and Winthrop had stretched his limited resources pretty well, and had not much more left than would take him to Wut-a-qut-o, and bring him back again.

"I don't see but I shall have to sell the farm," said Mr. Landholm on this next visit of his son's.

"Why, sir?"

"To pay off the mortgage—that mortgage to Mr. Haye."

Winthrop was silent.

"I can't meet the interest on it;—I haven't been able to pay any these five years," said Mr. Landholm with a sigh. "If he don't foreclose, I must.——I guess I'll take Asahel and go to the West."

"Don't do it hastily, father."

"No," said Mr. Landholm with another sigh;—"but it'll come to that."

Winthrop had no power to help it. And the money had been borrowed for him and Rufus. Most for Rufus. But it had been for them; and with this added thought of sorrowful care, he reached Mannahatta with his little sister.

It was early of a cold spring day, the ground white with a flurry of snow, the air raw, when he brought Winnie from the steamboat and led her, half frightened, half glad, through the streets to her new home. Winnie's tongue was very still, her eyes very busy. Her brother left the eyes to make their own notes and comments, at least he made none, till they had reached the corner of Little South St. He made none then; the door was opened softly, and he brought her up the stairs and into his room without disturbing or falling in with anybody. Putting her on a calico-covered settee, Winthrop pulled off his coat and set about making a fire.

Winnie had cried all the day before and as much of the night as her poor eyelids could keep awake; and now in a kind of lull, sat watching him.

"Governor, you'll catch cold——"

"Not if I can make the fire catch," said he quietly

"But you wanted me to keep on *my* things."

"Did you want to take them off?"

Winnie sat silent again, shrugging her shoulders to the chill air. But presently the fire caught, and the premonitory snapping and crackling of the kindling wood gave notice of a sudden change of temperature. Winnie's feelings took the cheery influence of the promise and she began to talk in a more hearty strain.

"Is this your room, Winthrop?"

"This is my room, Winnie. Yours is there, next to it."

"Through that door?"

"No—through the entry;—that is the door of my storehouse."

Winnie got up to look at it.

"'Tisn't a very large storehouse," was her conclusion.

"And not much in it. But the large storehouses are not far off, Winnie. Shall I leave you here for five minutes, while I go to get something from one of them?"

"Do you mean out of doors?—from the shops?"

"Yes. Shall I leave you five minutes?"

"Oh yes!"

He had come before her and was holding both her hands. Before he let them go he stooped down and kissed her.

It was not a very common thing for Winthrop to kiss her; and Winnie sat quieted under the power and the pleasure of it till the five minutes were run out and he had got back again. His going and coming was without seeing any one of the house; a fact owing to Mrs. Nettley's being away to market and Mr. Inchbald out on another errand.

Winthrop came in with his hands full of brown papers. Winnie watched him silently again while he put his stores in the closet and brought out plates and knives and forks.

"Where do you sleep, Governor?"

"In a pleasanter place than I slept in last night," said her brother.

"Yes, but where? I don't see any bed."

"You don't see it by day. It only shews itself at night."

"But where is it, Governor?"

"You're sitting on it, Winnie."

"This!—"

"What is the matter with it?"

"Why,—" said Winnie, looking dismayfully at the couch

with which Winthrop had filled the place of his bed, transferred to her room,—"it's too narrow!"

"I don't fall out of it," said her brother quietly.

"It isn't comfortable!"

"I am, when I am on it."

"But it's hard!"

"Not if I don't think it is hard."

"I don't see how that makes any difference," said Winnie discontentedly. "It's hard to me."

"But it's not your bed, Winnie."

"I don't like it to be yours, Winthrop."

He was busy laying a slice of ham on the coals and putting a skillet of water over the fire; and then coming to her side he began, without speaking, and with a pleasant face, to untie the strings of her bonnet and to take off that and her other coverings, with a gentle sort of kindness that made itself felt and not heard. Winnie bore it with difficulty; her features moved and trembled.

"It's too much for you to have to take care of me," she said in a voice changed from its former expression.

"Too much?" said Winthrop.

"Yes."

"Why?"

"It's too much. Can you do it?"

"I think I can take care of you, Winnie. You forget who has promised to take care of us both."

She threw her arms round his neck exclaiming, "I forget everything!—"

"No, not quite," said he.

"I do!—except that I love you. I wish I could be good, Winthrop!—even as good as I used to be."

"That wouldn't content me,' said her brother;—"I want you to be better."

She clasped her arms in an earnest clasp about his neck, very close, but said nothing.

"Now sit down, Winnie," said he presently, gently disengaging her arms and putting her into a chair,—"or something else will not be good enough."

She watched him again, while he turned the ham and put eggs in the skillet, and fetched out an odd little salt-cellar and more spoons and cups for the eggs.

"But Winthrop!"—she said starting,—"where's your tea-kettle?"

"I don't know. *I* have never had it yet, Winnie."

"Never had a tea-kettle?"

"No."

"Then how do you do, Winthrop?"

"I do without," he said lightly. "Can't you?"

"Do without a tea-kettle!"

"Yes."

"But how do you make tea and coffee?"

"I don't make them."

"Don't you have tea and coffee?"

"No, except when somebody else makes it for me."

"I'll make it for you, Winthrop!"

"No, Winnie—I don't want you to have it any more than myself."

"But Winthrop—I can't drink water!"

"I think you can—if I want you to."

"*I won't*," was in Winnie's heart to say; it did not get to her lips. With a very disturbed and unsettled face, she saw her brother quietly and carefully supply her plate—the ham and the eggs and the bread and the butter,—and then Winnie jumped up and came to his arms to cry; the other turn of feeling had come again. He let it have its way, till she had wept out her penitence and kissed her acknowledgment of it, and then she went back to her seat and her plate and betook herself to her breakfast. Before much was done with it, however, Mrs. Nettley and Mr. Inchbald came to the door; and being let in, overwhelmed them with kind reproaches and welcomes. Winnie was taken down stairs to finish her breakfast *with* tea and coffee; and Winthrop leaving her in hands that he knew would not forget their care of her, was free to go about his other cares, with what diligence they might require.

That same morning, before she had left her own room, Miss Haye was informed that a black girl wished to speak with her. Being accordingly ordered up, said black girl presented herself. A comely wench, dressed in the last point of neatness, though not by any means so as to set off her good accidents of nature. Nevertheless they could not be quite hid; no more than a certain air of abundant capacity, for both her own business and other people's. She came in and dropped a curtsey.

"Who are you?" said Elizabeth.

"I am Clam, ma'am."

"Clam!" said Elizabeth. "O, are you Clam? Where have you come from?"

"From the boat, last place, ma'am."

"Boat! what boat?"

"The boat what goes with wheels and comes down the river," said Clam lucidly.

"Oh!—And have you just come down?"

"We was comin' down all yesterday and last night, ma'am."

"*Who* were coming?"

"Mr. Winthrop Landholm, and Winifred, and me."

"Winifred and you," said Elizabeth. "And did he send you to me?"

Clam nodded. "He said he would ha' writ somethin', if he'd ha' had a piece of paper or card or anything, but he hadn't nothing."

"He would have written what?"

"Don't know—didn't say."

"Do you know who I am?"

Clam nodded again and shewed her teeth. "The lady Mr. Winthrop sent me to."

"Do you remember ever seeing me before?"

"When he was out walkin' with you in the rain," said Clam, her head first giving significant assent.

"Look here," said Elizabeth a little shortly,—"when I speak to you, speak, and don't nod your head."

To which Clam gave the prohibited answer.

"What are you sent here for now?"

"I dun' know, ma'am."

"What did Mr. Winthrop say you were to do?"

"Said I was to come here, and behave."

"Why have you come away from Mrs. Landholm?"

"Didn't," said Clam. "She went away first. She's gone to heaven."

"Mrs. Landholm! Is she dead?"

Clam nodded.

"When?—and what was the matter?"

"'Twa'n't much of anything the matter with her," said Clam;——"she took sick for two or three days and then died. It's more'n a fortnight ago."

"And they sent for Mr. Winthrop?"

"Job Underhill rode down after him as hard as he could and fetched him up on horseback."

"In time?" said Elizabeth.

"He was in time for everything but himself. It was too late for him. But all the rest of the folks had the good of his coming."

"Why what was there for him to do?" said Elizabeth.

"He finds enough to do—or he's pretty apt to—whenever he comes to a place," said Clam. "There was everybody to put in order, about. There was Mr. Landholm hardly fit to live, he was so willin' to die; and Winifred was crazy. She went and crawled under one of the beds to hide when she thought he was a comin'."

"When who was coming?"

"He—Mr. Winthrop. And Karen was takin' airs—*that* aint out o' the common—but I'd a little liever have him master than her mistress—she wa'n't mine, neither."

"And where was Mr. Asahel?"

"He was there——and good enough what there was of him; but he won't never stand in other folks' shoes."

"Do you say Winifred was *crazy?*"

"She was so feared to see her brother come home."

"Her brother Winthrop?"

"There wa'n't no other coming," said Clam.

"Poor thing!" said Elizabeth. "And you say he has brought her down to Mannahatta?"

Clam nodded. "She don't think she's alive when he aint near her; so he's took her down to live with him. I guess it's good living with him," said Clam sagaciously. "I wish I did it."

"I must go and see her. Where is she?"

"She's wherever he's took her to."

"But where's that?—don't you know?"

"It's to his house—if you know where that is."

"Do you know what you've come here to do?" said Elizabeth after a slight pause

Clam shook her head.

"One thing I can tell you, first of all," said Elizabeth,—"it is to mind what I say to you."

"Mr. Winthrop said I was to behave," said Clam with another glimpse of her white teeth.

"Then don't shake your head any more when I speak to you. What have you been doing at Wut-a-qut-o?"

"At Wuttle-quttle?" said Clam.

"At Wut-a-qut-o. What did you do there?"

"'Tain't the name of the place," said Clam. "They call it Shah-wee-tah."

"Wut-a-qut-o is the name of the mountain—it's all one. What have you been used to do there?"

"Set tables—" said Clam considerately.

"What did Mrs. Landholm teach you?"

"She learned me 'most everything," said Clam. "What she learned me most of all, was to have me read the Bible every day, and do nothin' wrong o' Sundays, and never say nothin' that wa'n't."

"That wasn't what?"

"That wa'n't *it*," said Clam. "Never to say nothin' that wa'n't the thing."

"Why, did you ever do that?" said Elizabeth.

"Maybe I did," said Clam, considering her new mistress's dressing-table. "Mis' Landholm was afeard on't."

"Well you must be just as careful about that here," said Elizabeth. "I love truth as well as she did."

"All kinds?" said the girl.

Elizabeth looked at her, with a mouthful of answer which she did not dare to bring out. Nothing was to be made of Clam's face, except that infallible air of capacity. There was no sign of impertinent meaning.

"You look as if you could learn," she said.

"Been learnin' ever since I was big enough," said the black girl. And she looked so.

"Are you willing to learn?"

"Like nothin' better."

"Provided it's the right kind, I suppose," said Elizabeth, wholly unable to prevent her features giving way a little at the unshakable coolness and spirit she had to do with. Clam's face relaxed in answer, after a different manner from any it had taken during the interview; and she said,

"Well I'll try. Mr. Winthrop said I was to be good; and I ain't a goin' to do nothin' to displease him, anyhow!"

"But the matter is rather to please *me*, here," said Elizabeth.

"Well," said Clam with her former wide-awake smile, "I guess what'll please him'll please you, won't it?"

"Go down stairs, and come to me after breakfast," said her mistress. "I'll let you make some new dresses for yourself the first thing. And look here,——" said she pulling a bright-coloured silk handkerchief out of a drawer,—"put that into a turban before you come up and let me see what you're up to."

Clam departed without an answer; but when she made her appearance again, the orange and crimson folds were twisted about her head in a style that convinced Elizabeth her new waiting-maid's capacity was equal to all the new demands she would be likely to make upon it.

CHAPTER XXVI.

> Never his worldly lot, or worldly state torments him:
> Less he would like, if less his God had sent him.
>
> FLETCHER.

WINTHROP had taken no little charge upon himself in the charge of his little sister. In many ways. He had a scanty purse, and it better bore the demands of one than of two; but that was only a single item. Winnie was not a charge upon his purse alone, but upon his heart and his head and his time. The demands were all met, to the full.

As much as it was possible, in the nature of Winthrop's business, his sister had him with her; and when he could not be there, his influence and power. It was trying enough for the poor child to be left alone as much as she was, for she could not always find solace in Mrs. Nettley, and sometimes could not endure her presence. Against this evil Winthrop provided as far as he might by giving Winnie little jobs to do for him while he was gone, and by setting her about what courses of self-improvement her delicate system of mind and body was able to bear. He managed it so that all was for him; not more the patching and knitting and bits of writing which were strictly in his line, than the pages of history, the sums in arithmetic, and the little lesson of Latin, which were for Winnie's own self. He knew that affection, in every one of them, would steady the nerves and fortify the will to go patiently on to the end. And the variety of occupation he left her was so great that without tiring herself in any one thing, Winnie generally found the lonely hours of her day pretty well filled up. Mrs. Nettley was a great help, when Winnie was in the mood for her company; that was not always.

His little sister's bodily and mental health was another care upon Winthrop's mind, and on his time. Disease now constantly ruffled the sweet flow of spirits which once was habitual with her Nothing ruffled his; and his soothing hand could always quiet her, could almost always make her happy, when it was practicable for him to spare time. Very often when he had no time to give beyond what a word or a look would take from his business. But those times were comparatively few. He was apt to give her what she needed, and make up for it afterwards at the cost of rest and sleep when Winnie was abed. Through the warm summer days he took her daily and twice daily walks, down to the Green where the sea air could blow in her face fresh from its own quarter, where she and he too could turn their backs upon brickwork and pavement and look on at least one face of nature unspotted and unspoiled. At home he read to her, and with her, the times when he used to read the classics; and many other times; he talked to her and he played with her, having bought a second-hand backgammon board for the very purpose; he heard her and set her her lessons; and he amused her with all the details of his daily business and experience that he could make amusing.

If these things were a charge, it was one for which he was abundantly rewarded, every night and every morning, and knew it. But the other part of the burden, the drain upon his purse, was not so easily to be met withal. There was no helping it. Winnie's state of health made her simple wants, simple as they were, far more costly than his own had been; and he would and did supply them. He could bear to starve himself and lie hard; but Winnie would very soon starve to death; and the time when she could sleep softly on a hard bed had once been, but would never be again, literally or figuratively. Winthrop never shewed her how it was with him; not the less it was almost the ebb; and whence the flow was to come, was a point he saw not. He was not yet admitted to practise law; his slender means were almost all gathered from teaching; and he could not teach any more than he did. And this consciousness he carried about with him, to the office, to market, and to his little sister's presence. For her his face was always the same; and while she had it Winnie thought little was wanting to her life.

One morning when she had it not, she was lying wearily stretched out on the couch which was hers by day and Winthrop's by night. It was early June; the sun was paying his first instalment of summer heat, and doing it as if he were behind-hand with pay-day. Winnie's attic roof gave her a full share of his benefits.

The hours of the morning had worn away, when towards noon a slow step was heard ascending the stairs. It was her hostess, come up to look after her.

"All alone?" said Mrs. Nettley.

"Oh yes!—" came with most fervent breath from Winnie. Her head uneasily turned the other cheek to the pillow.

"Poor child!" said Mrs. Nettley; and every line of her careful and sympathetic face said it over again. "Poor child!—And Mr. Winthrop's been away all the morning!"

"I don't know why you call me *poor*," said Winnie, whose nerves could not bear even that slight touch 'f it happened to touch the wrong way;—"Of course he's been away all the morning—he always is."

"And you're tired. I didn't mean *poor*, dear, in the way that I am poor myself;—not that poor,—I only meant, because you were so much here all alone without your brother."

"I know what you meant," said Winnie.

"It's hot up here, isn't it," said Mrs. Nettley going to the window. "Dreadful. It's hot down stairs too. Can't we let a little air in?"——

"Don't! It's hotter with it."

Mrs. Nettley left the window and came and stood by Winnie's couch, her face again saying what her voice did not dare to say, —"Poor child!"—

"Mrs. Nettley——"

"What, my love?"

"I'm very cross——"

"No you aren't, my love! you're only tired."

"I'm very cross—I don't know what makes me so—but sometimes I feel so it seems as if I couldn't help it. I'm cross even to Winthrop. I'm very much obliged to you, but you must think I aint."

"I don't think the least thing of the kind, dearest—I know it's miserable and suffocating up here, and you *can't* feel—I wish I could make it better for you!"

"O it'll be better by and by—when Governor gets home and it grows cool."

"Come down and take a bit of dinner with me."

"O no, thank you, Mrs. Nettley," said Winnie brightening up,——"I don't want anything; and Governor 'll be home by and by and then we'll have our dinner. I'm going to broil the chicken and get everything ready."

"Well, that 'll be sweeter than anything I've got," said the good lady.—"Why, who's there?——"

Somebody there was, knocking at the door; and when the door was opened, who was there shewed herself in the shape of a young lady, very bright looking and well dressed. She glanced at Mrs. Nettley with a slight word of inquiry and passing her made her way on up to the couch.

"Is this Winifred?" she said, looking, it might be, a little shocked and a little sorrowful at the pale and mind-worn face that used to be so round and rosy; and about which the soft fair hair still clustered as abundantly as ever.

"Yes ma'am," Winifred said, half rising.

"Don't get up,—don't you know me?"

Winnie's eye keenly scanned the bright fresh face that bent over her, but she shook her head and said 'no'.

"Can't you remember my being at your house—some time ago?—me and"——she stopped. "Don't you remember? We spent a good while there—one summer—it was when you were a little girl."

"O!"—said Winnie,—"are you——"

"Yes."

"I remember. But you were not so large then, either."

"I am not very large now," said her visiter, taking a chair beside Winnie's couch.

"No. But I didn't know you."

"How do you do, dear?"

"I don't know," said Winnie. "I am not very well now-a-days."

"And Mannahatta is hot and dusty and disagreeable—more than any place you ever were in before in your life, isn't it?"

"I don't care," said Winnie. "I'd rather be with Winthrop."

"And can he make up for dust and heat and bad air and all?"

The smile that broke upon Winnie's face Elizabeth remembered was like that of old time; there was a sparkle in the eyes that looked up at her, the lips had their childish play, and the thin cheek even shewed its dimple again. As she met the look, Elizabeth's own face grew grave and her brow fell; and it was half a minute before she spoke.

"But he cannot be with you a great deal of the time."

"O yes he is," said Winnie;—"he is here in the morning, and at breakfast and dinner and tea, and all the evening. And all Sundays."

"That's the best day of the week then, I suppose."

"It's always that," said Winnie. "And he takes a great many walks with me—every day almost, when it gets cool—we go down on the Green and stay there as long as it's pleasant."

Elizabeth was silent again.

"But doesn't he have studying or writing to do in the evenings? I thought he had."

"O yes," said Winnie, "but then it don't hinder him from talking to me."

"And is he good enough to make you like this place better than your beautiful country home?"

"I would rather be here," said Winnie. But she turned her face a little from her questioner, and though it remained perfectly calm, the eyes filled to overflowing. Elizabeth again paused, and then bending over her where she still lay on her couch, she pressed her own full red lips to Winnie's forehead. The salute was instantly returned upon one of her little kid gloves which Winnie laid hold of.

"You don't know how rich you are, Winifred, to have such a good brother."

"Yes I do," said Winifred. "*You* don't."

If there was not a rush to Elizabeth's eyes, it was because she fought for it.

"Perhaps I don't," she said quietly;—"for I never had any one. Will you go and ride with me to-morrow, Winifred?"

"Ride?" said Winifred.

"Yes. In my carriage. We'll go out of town."

"O yes! O thank you! I should like it very much."

"You don't look very strong," said Elizabeth. "How is it that you can take such long walks?"

"O Winthrop don't let me get tired you know."

"But how does he manage to help it?" said Elizabeth smiling. "Can he do everything?"

"I don't know," said Winnie. "He don't let me stand too long, and he doesn't let me walk too fast; and his arm is strong, you know;—he can almost hold me up if I do get tired."

"I have—or my father has,"—said Elizabeth, "some very old, very good wine.—I shall send you some. Will you try it? I think it would make you stronger."

"I don't know whether Winthrop would let me drink it."

"Why not?"

"O he don't like me to drink anything but water and milk

—he don't let me have tea or coffee—and I don't know whether he'd like wine;—but I'll ask him."

"Don't let you have tea or coffee!"

"No; we drink milk, and water."

"But don't he let you do whatever you have a mind?"

"No," said Winnie; "and I don't want to, either."

"Don't want to do what?"

"Why——anything that he don't like."

"Do you love him well enough for that——not to *wish* to do what he don't like, Winifred?"

"Yes!" said Winifred. "I think I do. I may wish it at first, of course; but I don't want to do it if he wishes me not."

"How did he ever get such power over you!"

"Power!" said Winnie, raising herself up on her elbow,—"why I don't know what you mean! I should think everybody would do what Winthrop likes—it isn't *power*."

"I wonder what is, then!" said Elizabeth significantly.

"Why it's——it's——goodness!" said Winnie, shutting her eyes, but not before they had filled again. Elizabeth bit her lips to keep her own from following company; not with much success.

"That's what it is," said Winnie, without opening her eyes; —"he always was just so. No he wasn't either,—though it almost seems as if he was,—but now he's a Christian."

If outward signs had kept inward feelings company, Elizabeth would have started. She sat still; but the lines of her face wore a look of something very like startled gravity. There was a silence of more than one minute. Winnie opened her eyes and directed them upon her still companion.

"Is he any better than he used to be?" she forced herself to say.

"Why yes," said Winnie,—"of course—he must be. He used to be as good as he could be, except that;—and now he's that too."

"What difference does 'that' make, Winifred?"

Winnie looked keenly once more at the face of her questioner.

"Don't you know what it is to be a Christian, Miss Haye?"

Elizabeth shook her head.

"You must ask Winthrop," said Winnie. "He can tell you better than I can."

"I want you to tell me. What difference, for instance, has it made in your brother?"

Winnie looked grave and somewhat puzzled.

"He don't seem much different to *me*," she said,—"and yet

he *is* different.—The difference is, Miss Haye, that before, he loved *us*—and now he loves God and keeps his commandments."

"Don't he love you now?"

"Better than ever!" said Winnie with her eyes opening;—"why what makes you ask that?"

"Didn't he keep the commandments of the Bible before?"

"No,—not as he does now. Some of them he did, because he never was bad as some people are;—but he didn't keep them as he does now. He didn't keep the first commandment of all."

"Which is that?" said Elizabeth.

Winnie gave her another earnest look before she answered.

"Don't you know?"

"No."

"'Thou shalt love the Lord thy God with all thy heart, and with all thy mind, and with all thy soul, and with all thy strength.'"

If Winifred's face was grave, Elizabeth's took a double shade of gravity—it was even dark for a minute, as if with some thought that troubled her. Winnie's eyes seemed to take note of it, and Elizabeth roused herself. Yet at first it was not to speak.

"When—How long ago, do you suppose," she said, "your brother was changed in this way?"

"Since—since the time I came here;—since mother died," Winnie said softly.

There was again a few minutes of absolute silence; and then Elizabeth rose to go.

"Shall I send you the wine?" she said smiling.

"I don't believe Winthrop will let me take it," Winifred said.

"Because he is good, are you bound not to get strong?" Elizabeth said with an air of slight vexation.

"No,"—said Winnie, "but because he is good I must do what he says."

"I wish I liked anybody so well as that!" said Elizabeth kissing her. "Good bye, dear,—I'll come for you to-morrow. There's no objection to that, I suppose?"

"No," Winnie said laughing; and they parted.

Five minutes Winnie was alone, thinking over her visit and visiter. They were a great novelty, and very interesting. Winnie's thoughts roved with an odd mixture of admiration and pity over the beautiful dress, and fine face, and elastic step; they were bewitching; but Winnie had seen a shadow on the face, and she knew that the best brightness had never lighted it. Five minutes were all she had to think about it; then she heard a very different step on the stairs.

"I heard her go," said Mrs. Nettley, coming in, "and I had a little more time to spare; so I thought I would spend it with you;—unless you've got enough with such a gay visiter and don't want me."

"O no indeed, Mrs. Nettley, I want you just as much. Have you done dinner?"

"George isn't ready yet;" and Mrs. Nettley took Miss Haye's chair and set her knitting-needles a going. "Has she tired you with talking?"

"No—talking doesn't tire me,—and she wasn't a gay visiter, either, Mrs. Nettley—what do you mean by 'gay'?"

"O, she was handsome, and young, and 'fine feathers make fine birds' I'm sure," said Mrs. Nettley;—"wasn't she smartly dressed?"

"Yes," said Winnie, "she had handsome things on; but that didn't make her *gay*."

"Well that was what I meant. How do you like that young lady?"

"I don't know," said Winnie. "I think I like her."

"This isn't the first of your seeing her, dear!"

"O no—she was at our house once. I've seen her before, but that was a great while ago. I didn't know her again at first."

"Then she remembered you best."

"O—" said Winnie, considering,—"she has seen Rufus and Winthrop since then."

"She's a handsome young lady, don't you think so?

"I don't know—" said Winnie.

"Ask your brother if he don't think so.'

"Why?"

"See if he don't think so."

"Which brother?"

"Your brother that's here—your brother Winthrop."

"Does he think she is?"

"Ask him," repeated Mrs. Nettley.

"I don't know why I should ask him," said Winnie turning over uneasily on her couch;—"I don't care if she is or no."

"Ay, but you might care."

"I don't know why," said Winnie.

"How would you like to have a new sister one of these days?—by and by?"

"A sister?"

Mrs. Nettley nodded.

"A sister!" said Winnie. "How should I have a sister?"

"Why such a thing might be," said Mrs. Nettley. "Did you never think of one of your brothers getting married?"

"Winthrop won't!" said Winnie,—"and I don't care what Rufus does."

"What makes you think Winthrop won't?"

"He won't!" said Winnie with flushing cheeks.

"Wouldn't you be glad? You would like anything that would make him happy."

"Happy!" said Winnie.—"Glad!—I do wish, Mrs. Nettley, you would go down stairs and leave me alone!"

Mrs. Nettley went away, in some astonishment. And before her astonishment had cooled off in her own kitchen, down came Winnie, with flushed cheeks still, and watery eyes, and a distressed face, to beg Mrs. Nettley's forgiveness. It was granted with her whole heart, and a burden of apologies besides; but Winnie's face remained a distressed face still. The chicken, broiled on Mrs. Nettley's fire, was salted with some tears; and all the simple and careful preparations for Winthrop's dinner were made more carefully than usual; but when Winthrop came home, his little sister was as far from being herself as ever.

It happened that Winthrop was very busy that day and had no time to talk, except the disjointed bits of talk that could come between the joints of the chicken; and pleasant as those bits were, they could not reach the want of poor Winnie's heart. Immediately after dinner Winthrop went out again; and she was left to get through the afternoon without help of anybody.

It had worn on, and the long summer day was drawing to its close, when Winthrop was at last set free from his business engagements and turned his face and his footsteps towards home. The day had been sultry and his toil very engrossing; but that was not the reason his footsteps flagged. They flagged rarely, but they did it now. It needed not that he should have noticed his little sister's face at dinner; his ordinary burdens of care were quite enough and one of them just now pressing. In a sort of brown study he was slowly pacing up one of the emptying business streets, when his hand was seized by some one, and Winthrop's startled look up met the round jocund well-to-do face of the German professor.

"Wint'rop!—Where are you going?"

"Home, sir,"—said Winthrop returning the grasp of his friend's hand.

"How is all wiz you?"

"As usual, sir."

"Wint'rop—what is de matter wiz you?"

"Nothing!—" said Winthrop.

"I know better!" said the naturalist,—"and I know what it is, too. Here—I will give you some work to do one of these days and then I will pay you the rest."

And shaking Winthrop's hand again, the philosopher dashed on. But Winthrop's hand was not empty when his friend's had quitted it; to his astonishment he found a roll of bills left in it, and to his unbounded astonishment found they were bills to the amount of three hundred dollars.

If he was in any sort of a study as he paced the rest of his way home, it was not a brown study; and if his steps were slow, it was not that they flagged any more. It had come in time; it was just what was needed; and it was enough to keep him on, till he should be admitted to the bar and might edge off his craft from her moorings to feel the wind and tide 'that lead on to fortune.' Winthrop never doubted of catching both; as little did he doubt now of being able some time to pay back principal and interest to his kind friend. He went home with a lighter heart. But he had never let Winnie know of his troubles, and could not for the same reason talk to her of this strange relief.

Thinking so, he went up the stairs and opened the door of his and her sitting-room. The sun was down by that time, and the evening light was failing. The table stood ready for tea; Winnie had all the windows open to let in the freshening air from the sea, which was beginning to make head against the heats and steams of the city; herself sat on the couch, away from the windows, and perhaps her attitude might say, away from everything pleasant. Winthrop came silently up and put a little basket in her hand.

"Oh!—" Winnie sprang forward with an accent of joy,—"Strawberries!—Beautiful!—and so sweet! O Winthrop, aren't they sweet!—how good they will be."

"I hope so," said he. "How are you?"

"O—I'm well," said Winnie. "How big they are—and fresh. They do smell so sweet, don't they, Governor?"

Winthrop thought they were not so fresh nor so sweet as those which grew in the Bright Spot under Wut-a-qut-o; but he didn't remind Winnie of that. He smiled at her, as she was picking over her basket of strawberries with an eager hand. Yet when Winnie had got to the bottom of the basket and looked up at him his face was very grave indeed.

"There's plenty for you and me, Governor," she said.

"No," said her brother.

"There is plenty, Winthrop!"

"There is only just enough for you, and you must prove that by eating them all."

"Why didn't you get some for yourself, Governor!"

He answered that by spreading for her a particularly nice piece of bread and butter and laying it on her plate alongside of the strawberries. Winnie took it in the same pleasant mood and began upon both with great zeal; but before she had got half through the strawberries something seemed to come over her recollection; and the latter part of the meal her face grew more shadowy than the growing evening. When it was over, Winthrop placed her gently on the couch, and himself put away the dishes and glasses and eatables from the table. Then he came and sat down beside her and drew her head to lean upon him. It was darkening by that time, and the air coming in more and more fresh at the windows.

"Have you been very tired to-day?"

"No—I don't know—" said Winnie doubtfully.

"We couldn't have our walk this evening—I am sorry for that—but I was kept so long with Bob Satterthwaite. He is in a great feaze about some property that he thinks is owing to him somewhere, and he has been giving me a long detail of matters and things connected with the business.—I believe that if I were in practice he would commission me to get his rights for him. And an old classmate and friend of mine, Bob Cool, was in town to-day and came to see me. *He* was expressing a very earnest wish that I were working on my own hook."

"Oh I wish you were!"—said Winnie.

"Patience. I shall be in a little while more, if all goes well. Mr. Cool promises I shall have all his business."

"Is that much?"

"I don't know. It seems so."

"But isn't Mr. Satterthwaite rich?"

"Yes—very."

"Then what is he in a feaze about money for?"

"He is not so rich he mightn't be richer, I suppose, Winnie. And besides, nobody likes to be cheated."

"Is Mr. Haye rich?"

"Yes! What made you think of him?"

Winnie hesitated. "She was here to-day."

"She! Who?——Clam?"

"No, not Clam."

"Who then?"

"Why—Miss Haye."

"Was *she* here?"

"Yes."

"When?"

"This morning. She staid a good while with me."

"It was kind of her," said Winthrop after a little pause.

There was a pause then of some length.

"Has Miss Haye's being here and talking to you, tired you, Winnie?" said her brother, the arm that was round her drawing her more near.

"No—" Winnie said; but by no means as if Miss Haye's visit had had a sprightly effect.

"Staid here a good while talking? What did she talk about?"

"O—I don't know,—" said Winnie,—"about my drinking wine, and going to ride with her."

"She is very kind. And what did you tell her?"

"I said I didn't know whether you would let me drink it. I said I would go to ride."

"I am very much obliged to Miss Haye, and very glad for you, Winnie. It will do you good."

"Would you let me drink wine, if she should send it to me?"

"Did she speak of doing that?"

"Yes."

There was a little silence.

"Would you let me take it, Winthrop?"

"I suppose I should."

"I hope she won't send it," said Winnie; "and I wish I wasn't going to ride, either."

"Why?"

"O—I'd rather stay here."

They sat a little while without speaking another word; and then Winthrop withdrawing his arm proposed to have 'some light on the subject.' Winifred sprang to get it, but he held her back, and himself got the candle and lit it and placed it on the table. The light shewed Winnie's face flushed and unresting, and of doubtful signification about the eyes. Winthrop came and took his former place and position by her side.

"How has the day been with you, Winnie?"

The tone was most gentle and kindly. Winnie hesitated and then said,

"It hasn't been good."

"What's the matter?"

"*I* haven't been good."

"That isn't such a new thing that you need be surprised at it,—is it?" he said gently.

"No"—under breath.

"And it isn't so strange a thing that I love you a bit the less for it."

"But it's very uncomfortable," said poor Winnie, whose voice bore her witness.

"I find it so often."

"You, Governor!—you *never* do!" said Winnie energetically.

"Never do what?"

"Never feel like me."

"No, Winnie—I am strong and you are weak——you are sick and I am well. I have no excuse—you have, a little."

"It don't make it a bit better," said poor Winnie. "I don't want to make any excuse. I got *so* cross with Mrs. Nettley today."

"What about?"

"O I couldn't bear to hear her talk, and I almost told her so."

"I dare say you did what you could to mend it afterwards, Winnie."

"O yes;—and she didn't think anything of it at all; but I am always doing so, Winthrop."

"You never do it to me," said her brother soothingly.

"To you!—But O Winthrop!—if I loved God enough, I never should do anything to displease him!"

She had thrown herself further into her brother's arms and at this was weeping with all her heart.

"He said once himself," said Winthrop, "'Blessed are they that mourn now, for they shall be comforted.'"

Winnie clung faster to him, with a grateful clasp, and her tears came more gently.

"We sha'n't be quit of it till we get to heaven, Winnie;—and 'the people that dwell therein,' you know, 'shall be forgiven their iniquity.' And more than that, 'white robes are given unto every one of them.' 'And they shall see the King's face, and his name shall be in their foreheads."

"I wish it was in mine now!" said Winnie.

"Stop, Winnie.—I hope it is there,—only not so bright as it will be by and by."

"But it ought to be bright now," said Winnie raising herself.

"Let it be brighter every day then," said her brother.

"I do try, Governor," said poor Winnie,—"but sometimes I think I don't get ahead at all!"

It was with great tenderness that again he put his arm round her, and drew down her head upon him, and pressed her close to his side.

"Rest!—" said he,—"and trust what is written, that 'they shall praise the Lord that seek him.' 'Wait on the Lord; be of good courage, and he shall strengthen thine heart; wait, I say, on the Lord.'"

"How much better I feel already," said poor Winnie presently.

There was a long silence. Winnie lay there still, and Winthrop was softly playing with one of her hands and striking it and stroking it against his own. The air came in fresh and cool from the sea and put the candle flame out of all propriety of behaviour; it flared and smoked, and melted the candle sideways, and threatened every now and then to go out entirely; but Winnie lay looking at Winthrop's hand which the moonlight shone upon, and Winthrop—nobody knows what he was looking at; but neither of them saw the candle. Winnie was the one to break the silence.

"What sort of a person is she, Winthrop?"

"Who?" said her brother.

"What?—O, I mean—I meant—I meant, who was here today,—Miss Haye."

"You have seen her, Winnie," he said after a moment's hesitation.

"Yes, but you know her. Do you think she is a person I would like?"

"I do not know."

"You don't know!—"

"But *you* know her, Winthrop," said Winnie a little timidly when she found he added nothing to his former words.

"Yes."

"Don't *you* like her?"

"Yes."

"Then why don't you know?"

"You don't like everything that I like," said her brother.

"Why yes I do!— Don't I?"

"Not everything."

"What don't I?"

"Euripides—and Plato."

"Ah but I don't understand those," said Winnie.

Winthrop was silent. Was that what he meant?—was Winnie's instant thought. Very disagreeable. And his 'yes's' were so quiet—they told nothing. Winnie looked at her brother's hand again, or rather at Miss Haye in her brother's hand; and Winthrop pursued his own meditations.

"Governor," said Winnie after a while, "is Miss Haye a Christian?"

"No."

Winnie asked no more; partly because she did not dare, and partly because the last answer had given her so much to think of. She did not know why, either, and she would have given a great deal to hear it over again. In that little word and the manner of it, there had been so much to quiet and to disquiet her. Undoubtedly Winnie would have done anything in the world, that she could, to make Miss Haye a Christian; and yet, there was a strange sort of relief in hearing Winthrop say that word; and at the same time a something in the way he said it that told her her relief had uncertain foundation. The 'no' had not been spoken like the 'yes'—it came out half under breath; what meaning lurked about it Winnie could not make out; she puzzled herself to think; but though she could not wish it had been a willing 'no,' she wished it had been any other than it had. She could not ask any more; and Winthrop's face when he went to his reading was precisely what it was other evenings. But Winnie's was not; and she went to bed and got up with a sore spot in her heart, and a resolution that *she* would not like Miss Haye, for she would not know her well enough to make sure that she could.

CHAPTER XXVII.

Ha, ha! what a fool honesty is! and trust, his sworn brother, a very simple gentleman
WINTER'S TALE.

POOR Winnie held to her resolution, though half unconsciously and quite involuntarily. She did not enjoy her ride, and therefore did not seem to enjoy it; for it was not in her nature to seem other than she was. Neither did she take or shew any but a very qualified pleasure in Miss Haye's company; and for this reason or for others Miss Haye made her visits few.

But this did not a bit help the main question; and in the want of data and the absence of all opportunity for making observations, Winnie had full chance to weary herself with fancies and fears. She could not get courage enough to say anything about Miss Haye again to her brother; and he never spoke of her. There was no change in him; he was always as careful of his little sister; always bestowed his time upon her in the same way; was always at home in the evenings. Unless when, very rarely, he made an arrangement that she should spend one with Mrs. Nettley and Mr. Inchbald. These times were seldom; and Winnie generally knew where he was going and that it was not to Mr. Haye's. But she was not sure of the integrity of her possession of him; and that want of security opened the sluice-gates to a flood-tide of wearisome possibilities; and Winnie's nervous and morbid sensibilities made the most of them. It was intolerable, to think that Winthrop should love anybody as he did her; that he should love anybody *better*, happily for Winnie, never entered her imaginings. She could not endure to think that those lips, which were to her the sweetest of earthly things, should touch any other cheek or mouth but her own. They were *hers*. It was bitter as wormwood to think that his strong arm could ever hold and guide another as it held and guided his little sister. "But *guide?*——*she'd* never let him guide her!"—said Winnie in a great fit of sisterly indignation. And her thoughts would tumble and toss the matter about, till her cheek was in a flush; she was generally too eager to cry. It wore upon her; she grew thinner and more haggard; but nobody knew the cause and no one could reach the remedy.

With all this the end of summer came, and Rufus. He came to establish himself under Mr. Haye's direction. 'For the time,'—as Winthrop told Winnie, when she asked him if Rufus was going to turn merchant. And when she asked him further 'what for?'——he answered that Rufus was a spice merchant and dealt in variety. With the end of autumn came Winthrop's admission to the bar.

And Winnie drew a mental long breath. Winthrop was a lawyer himself, and no longer in a lawyer's office. Winthrop had an office of his own. The bark was shoved from the shore, with her sails set; and Winnie, no more than her brother, doubted not that the gales of prosperity would soon fill them. Rufus was greatly amused with her.

"*You* think it's a great thing to be a lawyer, don't you?" said he one night.

"I think it's a great thing to be such a lawyer as Governor will be," said Winnie.

At which Rufus laughed prodigiously.

"*I* think it's a great thing to be such a governor as this lawyer will be," he said when he had recovered himself. "Nothing less, Governor! You have your title beforehand."

"'Once a judge always a judge,'" said Winthrop. "I am afraid if you reverse the terms, so you will the conclusion."

"Terms!" said Rufus. "You will be governor of this state, and I shall be your financial secretary—on any terms you please. By the way—what keeps you from Haye's now-a-days? Not this girl?"

"No," said Winthrop.

It was that same 'no' over again. Winnie knew it, and her heart throbbed.

"What then? I haven't seen you there since I've been in town."

"How often are you there yourself?"

"O!—every evening almost. What keeps you?"

"Duty—" said Winthrop.

"But what sort of duty! What on earth can hinder your

coming there as you used to do, to spend a rational hour now and then?"

"My dear sir, it is enough for any man to know his own duty; it is not always possible for him to know that of another man."

"And therefore I ask you!" said Rufus.

"What?"

"Why ——what's your reason for keeping away."

"In brief—my engagements."

"You've nothing to do with briefs yet," said Rufus; "have the goodness to enlarge a little. You've not been more busy lately than you were a while ago."

"Yes I have."

"Yes, I suppose you have,"—said Rufus meditatively. "But not so much more as to make that a reason?"

"If my reasons were not only 'as plenty' but as precious, as blackberries," said his brother, "you could not shew more eagerness for them."

"I am afraid the blackberries would be the more savoury,' said Rufus laughing a little. "But you didn't use to make such a hermit of yourself, Winthrop."

"I don't intend to be a hermit always. But as I told you, duty and inclination have combined to make me one lately."

Winnie could not make much of this conversation. The words might seem to mean something, but Winthrop's manner had been so perfectly cool and at ease that she was at a loss to know whether they meant anything.

Winthrop's first cause was not a very dignified one—it was something about a man's horse. Winnie did not think much of it; except that it was his first cause, and it was gained; but that she was sure beforehand it would be. However, more dignified pieces of business did follow, and came fast; and at every new one Winnie's eyes sparkled and glistened, and her nervous troubles for the moment laid themselves down beneath joy, and pride in her brother, and thankfulness for his success. Before many months had passed away, something offered that in better measure answered her wishes for his opportunity.

Their attic room had one evening a very unwonted visiter in the shape of Mr. Herder. Beside Mr. Inchbald and his sister, Rufus was the sole one that ever made a third in the little company. Winthrop's friends, for many reasons, had not the entrance there. But this evening, near the beginning of the new year, there came a knock at the door, and Mr. Herder's round face walked in rounder than ever.

"Good evening!—How is all wiz you, Wint'rop?—and you?—I would not let no one come up wiz me—I knew I should find you."

"How did you know that, Mr. Herder?"

"O!——I have not looked so long for strange things on the earth—and *in* the earth—that I cannot find a friend—de most strange thing of all."

"Is that your conclusion, Mr. Herder? I didn't know you had quite so desperate an opinion of mankind."

"It is not despairate," said the naturalist;—"I do not despair of nobody. Dere is much good among de world——dere might be more—a good deal. I hope all will be good one day—it will be—then we shall have no more trouble. How is it wiz you, Wint'rop?"

"Nothing to complain of, Mr. Herder."

"Does he never have nozing to complain of?" said the naturalist turning to Winnie.

"He never thinks he has," said Winnie. She had answered the naturalist's quick eye with a quick smile, and then turned on Winthrop a look that spoke of many a thing he must have passed over to make her words good. Mr. Herder's eye followed hers.

"How is everything with *you*, Mr. Herder?"

"It is well enough," said the naturalist,—"like the common. I do not complain, neizer. I never have found time to complain. Wint'rop, I am come to give you some work."

"What do you want me to do, sir?"

"I do not know," said the naturalist;—"I do not know nozing about what is to be done; but I want you to do something."

"I hope you will give me something more to go to work upon, sir. What is the matter?"

"It is not my matter," said the naturalist;—"I did never get in such a quarrel but one, and I will never again in anozer—it is my brother, or the man who married my sister—his name is Jean Lansing."

"What is the matter with him?"

"Dere is too many things the matter wiz him," said Mr. Herder, "for he is sick abed—that is why I am here. I am come to tell you his business and to get you to do it."

"I shall think I am working for you, Mr. Herder," Winthrop said, as he tied up a bundle of papers which had been lying loose about the table.

"Have you got plenty to do?" said the naturalist, giving them a good-humoured eye.

"Can't have too much, sir. Now what is your brother's affair?"

"I do not know as I can tell you," said the other, his bright jovial face looking uncommonly mystified,—"it seems to me he does not know very well himself. He does not know that anybody has done nozing, but he is not *satisfied.*"

"And my business is to satisfy him?"

"If you can do that——you shall be satisfied too!" said the naturalist. "He does not know that any one has wronged him, but he thinks one has."

"Who?"

"Ryle——John Ryle. He was Mr. Lansing's partner in business for years—I do not know how many."

"Here?"

"In Manna-hatta—here—they were partners; and Ryle had brothers in England, and he was the foreign partner and Lansing was here, for the American part of the business. Well they were working togezer for years;—and at the end of them, when they break up the business, it is found that Ryle has made himself money, and that my brother has not made none! So he is poor, and my sister, and Ryle is rich."

"How is that?"

"It is that way as I tell you; and Ryle has plenty, and Lansing and Therésa they have not."

"But has Mr. Lansing no notion how this may have come about?"

'He knows nozing!" said the naturalist,—"no more than you know—except he knows he is left wizout nozing, and Ryle has not left himself so. Dat is all he knows."

"Can I see Mr. Lansing?"

"He is too sick. And he could tell you nozing. But he is not satisfied."

"Is John Ryle of this city?"

"He is of this city. He is not doing business no more, but he lives here."

"Well we can try, Mr. Herder," said Winthrop, tapping his bundle of papers on the table, in a quiet wise that was a strong contrast to the ardent face and gestures of the philosopher. It was the action, too, of a man who knew how to try and was in no doubt as to his own power. The naturalist felt it.

"What will you do, Wint'rop?"

"You wish me to set about it?"

"I do. I put it in your hands."

"I will try, Mr. Herder, what can be done."

"What will you do first?" said the naturalist.

"File a bill in equity," said Winthrop smiling.

"A bill?—what is that?"

"A paper setting forth certain charges, made on supposition and suspicion only, to which charges they must answer on oath"

"*Who* will answer?"

"Ryle and his brothers."

"Dere is but one of them alive."

"Well, Ryle and his brother, then."

"But what charges will you make? We do not know nozing to charge."

"Our charges will be merely on supposition and suspicion—it's not needful to swear to them."

"And they must swear how it is?"

"They must swear to their answers."

"That will do!" said the naturalist, looking 'satisfied' already. "That will do. We will see what they will say.—Do you do nozing but write bills all night, every night, and tie up papers?—you do not come to my room no more since a long time."

"Not for want of will, Mr. Herder. I have not been able to go."

"Bring your little sister and let her look at my things some time—while you and me we look at each other. It is good to look at one's friend sometime."

"I have often found it so, Mr. Herder. I will certainly bring Winnie if I can."

"Do you not go nowhere?" said the naturalist as if a thought had struck him. "What is de reason that I do not meet you at Mr. Haye's no more?"

"I go almost nowhere, sir."

"You are wrong," said the naturalist. "You are not right. Dere is more will miss you than me; and there is somebody there who wants you to take care of her."

"I hope you are mistaken, sir."

"She wants somebody to take care of her," said Mr. Herder; "and I do not know nobody so good as you. I am serious. She is just as afraid as ever one should take care of her, and poor thing she wants it all the more. She will not let your brother do it neizer."

"Do you think he is trying, Mr. Herder?" Winthrop said coolly.

"I believe he would be too glad! he looks at her so hard as he can; but she will not look at the tops of his fingers. She does not know what she shall do wiz herself, she is so mad wiz her father's new wife."

"What has she been doing?" Winthrop asked.

"Who, Rose?—she has not done nozing, but to marry Élisabet's father, and for that she never will forgive her. I am sorry—he was foolish man.—Wint'rop, you must not shut yourself up here—you will be directly rich—you must find yourself a wife next thing."

"Why should a lawyer have a wife any more than a philosopher?" said Winthrop.

"A philosopher," said Mr. Herder, with the slightest comical expression upon his broad face,—"has enough for him to do tc take care of truth—he has not time to take care of his wife too. While I was hunting after de truth, my wife would forget me."

"Does it take you so long for a hunt?"

"I am doing it all de time," said the naturalist; "it is what I spend my life for. I live for that."

The last words were spoken with a quiet deliberation which told their truth. And if the grave mouth of the other might have said 'I live for truth' too, it would not have belied his thoughts. But it was truth of another kind.

Winnie watched the course of this piece of business of Mr. Herder's with the most eager anxiety. That is, what there was to watch; for proceedings were slow. The very folio pages of that 'Bill,' that she saw Winthrop writing, were scrolls of interest and mysterious charm to Winnie's eyes, like nothing surely that other eyes could find in them. Certainly not the eyes of Mr. Ryle and his lawyer. Winnie watched the bill folded up and superscribed, standing over her brother with her hand on his shoulder.

"What is that about, now, Governor?—what is it to do?"

"It charges Mr. Ryle and his brother with malpractices, Winnie—with dealing unfairly by Mr. Lansing."

"But you don't know that they have done anything?"

"They can shew it, in that case; and the object of this bill is to make them shew one thing or the other, by their answer."

"And, dear Governor, how soon will they answer?"

"In forty days, Winnie, they must."

Winnie drew a breath of patience and impatience, and went back to her seat.

But before the forty days were gone by, Winthrop came home one night and told Winnie he had got the answer; and smiled at her face of eagerness and pleasure. Winnie thought his smiles were not very often, and welcomed every one.

"But it is not likely this answer will settle the question, Winnie," he remarked.

"O no, I suppose not; but I want to know what they say."

So they had supper; and after supper she watched while he sat reading it; as leaf after leaf was turned over, from the close-written and close-lying package in Winthrop's hand to the array of pages that had already been turned back and lay loose piled on the table; while Winthrop's pencil now and then made an admonitory note in the margin. How his sister admired him!—and at last forgot the bill in studying the face of the bill-reader. It was very little changed from its old wont; and what difference there might be, was not the effect of a business life. The cool and invariable self-possession and self-command of the character had kept and promised to keep him *himself*, in the midst of these and any other concerns, however entangling or engrossing. The change, if any, was traceable to somewhat else; or to somewhat else Winnie laid it,—though she would not have called it a change, but only an added touch of perfection. She could not tell, as she looked, what that touch had done; if told, perhaps it might be, that it had added sweetness to the gravity and gravity to the sweetness that was there before. How Winnie loved that broad brow, and the very hand it rested on! All the well-known lines of calmness and strength about the face her eye went over and over again; she had quite forgotten Mr. Ryle; and she saw Winthrop folding up the voluminous 'answer,' and she hardly cared to ask what was in it. She watched the hands that were doing it. *They* seemed to speak his character, too; she thought they did; calmness and decision were in the very fingers. Before her curiosity had recovered itself enough to speak, Mr. Herder came in.

They talked for awhile about other things; and then Winthrop told him of the answer.

"You have it!" cried the naturalist. "And what do they say?"

"Nothing, fully and honestly."

"Ah ha!—And do they grant—do they allow anything of your charges, that you made in your bill?"

"Yes—in a vague and unsatisfactory way, they do."

"Vague—?" said the naturalist.

"Not open and clear. But the other day in the street I was stopped by Mr. Brick——"

"Who is Brick?" said Mr. Herder.

"He is Ryle's lawyer. He stopped me a few days ago and told me there was one matter in the answer with which perhaps I would not be satisfied—which perhaps I should not think sufficiently full; but he said, he, who had drawn the answer, *knew*, personally, all about it; and he assured me that the answer in this matter granted all, and more, than I could gain in any other way; and that if I carried the proceedings further, in hopes to gain more for my client, the effect would only be an endless delay."

"Do they offer to give him *something?*" said the naturalist.

"The answer does make disclosures, which though, as I said, vague and imperfect, still promise to give him something."

"And you think it might be more?"

"Brick assures me, on his own knowledge, that by going on with the matter we shall only gain an endless lawsuit."

"What do you think, Wint'rop?"

"I want you to give this paper to Mr. Lansing, and ask him what *he* thinks. Ask him to read it, and tell him what Brick says; and then let him make up his mind whether we had better go on or not."

"I do not care for nobody's mind but yours," said the naturalist.

"Let us have Mr. Lansing's first."

So Mr. Herder carried away the answer to Mr. Lansing, and in a few days came back to report progress.

"He has read it," said Mr. Herder, "and he says he do not make anything of it at all. He leaves the whole thing wiz you."

"Does he understand what is hinted at by these half disclosures?"

"He says he does not understand nozing of it—he knows not what they mean—he does not know whether to go on, whether to stop here. He says, and I say, you judge and do what you please."

"I confess, Mr. Herder, that Mr. Brick's kind warning has made me suspicious of his and his principal's good faith; and my will would be to go on."

"Go on, then!" said the naturalist—"I say so too—go on! I do not trust that Brick no more than you do; and Mr. Ryle, *him* I do not trust. Now what will you do next?"

"Take exceptions to the answer, where it seems to be insufficient, and make them answer again."

"Exception—?" said the naturalist.

In answer to which Winthrop went into explanations at some length; from which at least this much was clearly made out by Mr. Herder and Winnie,—that the cause would come to a hearing probably in May, before Chancellor Justice; when Winthrop and Mr. Brick would stand openly pitted against each other and have an opportunity of trying their mutual strength, or the strength of their principles; when also it would, according to the issue of said conflict, be decided whether the Ryles must or not reply to Winthrop's further demands upon them.

"And this Chancellor Justice—is he good man?" said Mr. Herder.

"As good a man as I want to argue before,' said Winthrop. "I ask no better. All is safe in that quarter."

That all was safe in another quarter, both Mr. Herder and Winnie felt sure; and both looked eagerly forward to May; both too with very much the same feeling of pride and interest in their champion.

Winnie's heart jumped again at hearing a few days after, that Mr. Satterthwaite had put his affairs into Winthrop's hands; partly, Winthrop said he supposed, out of friendship for him, and partly out of confidence in him. It was rather a mark of the former, that he insisted upon paying a handsome retaining fee.

"Now where's Mr. Cool and his affairs?" said Winnie.

"I suppose Mr. Cool is at Coldstream, where he keeps 'cool' all the year round, I understand."

"But he promised to put *his* affairs into your hands."

"Then he'll do it. Perhaps they keep cool too."

"I wish May would be here," said Winnie.

Winthrop was at the table one evening,—while it still wanted some weeks of the May term,—writing, as usual, with heaps of folio papers scattered all about him; writing fast; and Winnie was either reading or looking at him, who was the book she loved best to study; when Rufus came in. Both looked up and welcomed him smilingly; but then Winthrop went on with his writing; while Winnie's book was laid down. She had enough else now to do. Rufus took a seat by the fire and did as she often did,—looked at Winthrop.

"Are you always writing?" said he somewhat gloomily.

"Not always," said Winthrop. "I sometimes read for variety."

"Law papers?"

'Law papers—when I can't read anything else."

"That's pretty much all the time, isn't it?"

"O no," said Winnie;—"he reads a great deal to me—we were reading a while ago, before you came in—we read every evening."

Rufus brought his attention round upon her, not, as it seemed, with perfect complacency.

"What time does this girl go to bed?"

How Winnie's face changed. Winthrop answered without stopping his pen.——

"When she is tired of sitting up—not until then."

"She ought to have a regular hour—and an early one."

"You are an adviser upon theory, you see," said Winthrop going on with his writing;—"I have the advantage of practice."

"I fancy any adviser would tell you the same in this case,' said the elder brother somewhat stiffly.

"I can go now," Winifred said rising, and speaking with a trembling lip and a tremulous voice,—"if you want to talk about anything."

She lit a candle and had got to the door, when her other brother said,

"Winnie!—"

Winnie stopped and turned with the door in her hand. Winthrop was busy clearing some books and papers from a chair by his side. He did not speak again; when he had done he looked up and towards her; and obeying the wish of his face, as she would have done had it been any other conceivable thing, Winnie shut the door, set her candle down, and came and took the chair beside him. But then, when she felt his arm put round her, she threw her head down upon him and burst into a fit of nervously passionate tears. *That* was not his wish, she knew, but she could not help it.

"Mr. Landholm," said Winthrop, "may I trouble you to put out that candle. We are not so extravagant here as to burn bed-lights till we want them.—Hush, Winnie,—" softly said his voice in her ear and his arm at the same time.

"Absurd!" said Rufus, getting up to do as he was bid.

"What?" said his brother.

"Why I really want to talk to you."

"I am really very willing to listen."

"But I do not want to talk to anybody beside you."

"Winnie hears everything that is said here, Will," said the younger brother gravely, at the same time restraining with his arm the motion he felt Winnie made to go.

"It don't signify!" said Rufus, getting up and beginning to walk up and down the room gloomily.

"What doesn't signify?"

"Anything!—"

The steps were quicker and heavier, with concealed feeling. Winthrop looked at him and was silent; while Rufus seemed to be combating some unseen grievance, by the set of his lip and nostril.

"What do you think Haye has done?"—he broke out, like a horse that is champing the bit.

"What?" said Winthrop.

"He has sued me."

"Sued you!" exclaimed Winthrop, while even Winnie forgot her tears and started up. Rufus walked.

"What do you mean, Will?"

"I mean he has sued me!"—said Rufus stopping short and facing them with eyes that for the moment had established a natural pyrotechny of their own.

"How, and what for?"

"How?—by the usual means! What for?—I will tell you!"

Which he sat down to do; Winthrop and Winnie both his most earnest auditors.

"You know it was Haye's own proposition, urged by himself, that I should go into business with him. Nobody asked him—it was his own doing; it was his declared purpose and wish, unsolicited by me or my father or by anybody, to set me forward in his own line and put me in the way of making my fortune!—as he said."

Winthrop knew it, and had never liked it. He did not tell Rufus so now; he gave him nothing but the attention of his calm face; into which Rufus looked while he talked, as if it were the safe, due, and appointed treasury in which to bestow all his grievances and passionate sense of them.

"Well!—you know he offered, a year ago or more, that by way of making a beginning, I should take off his hands some cotton which he had lying in storage, and ship it to Liverpool on my own account; and as I had no money, I was to pay him by drawing bills in his favour upon the consignees."

"I remember very well," said Winthrop.

"Well sir!—the cotton reached Liverpool and was found good for nothing!"

"Literally?"

"Literally, sir!—wasn't worth near the amount of my bills, which of course were returned—and Haye has sued me for the rest!"

Rufus's face looked as if a spark from it might easily have burnt up the whole consignment of cotton, if it had happened to be in the neighbourhood.

"How was the cotton?—damaged?"

"Damaged?—of course!—kept in vaults here till it was spoiled; and he knew it!"

"For what amount has he sued you?" said Winthrop when Rufus had fed his fire silently for a couple of minutes.

"For more than I can pay—or will!—"

"How much does that stand for, in present circumstances?"

"How much? A matter of several hundreds!"

"How many?"

"So many, as I should leave myself penniless to pay, and then not pay. You know I lost money down there."

"I know," said his brother.

Winifred brought her eyes round to Winthrop; and Winthrop looked grave; and Rufus, as before, fiery; and there was a silence this time of more than two minutes.

"My dependence is on you, Governor," Rufus said at last.

"I wish I could help you, Will."

"How can I get out of this scrape?"

"You have no defence in law."

"But there must be a defence somewhere!" said Rufus drawing himself up, with the whole spirit of the common law apparently within him, energizing the movement.

"The only hope of relief would be in the equity courts."

"How there?" said Rufus.

Winthrop hesitated.

"A plea of fraud—alleging that Mr. Haye has overreached you, putting off upon you goods which he *knew* to be worthless."

"To be sure he did!" said Rufus. "Knew it as well as he does now. It was nothing but a fraud. An outrageous fraud!"

Winthrop made no answer, and the brothers paused again, each in his meditations. Winnie, passing her eyes from one to the other, thought Winthrop looked as if his were very grave.

"I depend upon you, Governor," the elder brother said more quietly.

"To do what?"

"Why!—" said Rufus firing again,—"to do whatever is necessary to relieve me! Who should do it?"

"I wish you could get somebody else, Will," said the other.

"I am sorry I cannot!" said Rufus. "If I had the money I would pay it and submit to be trodden upon—I would rather take it some ways than some others—but unhappily necessity is laid upon me. I *cannot* pay, and I am unwilling to go to jail, and I *must* ask you to help me, painful as it is."

Winthrop was silent, grave and calm as usual; but Winnie's heart ached to see *how* grave his eye was. Did she read it right? He was silent still; and so was Rufus, though watching for him to speak.

"Well!" said Rufus at last getting up with a start, "I will relieve you! I am sorry I troubled you needlessly—I shall know better than to do it again!—"

He was rushing off, but before he reached the door Winthrop had planted himself in front of it.

"Stand out of my way."

"I am not in it. Go back, Will."

"I won't, if you please.——I'll thank you to let me open the door."

"I will not. Go back to your seat, Rufus—I want to speak to you."

"I was under the impression you did *not*," said Rufus, standing still. "I waited for you to speak."

"It is safe to conclude that when a man makes you wait, he has something to say."

"You are more certain of it when he lets you know what it is," said Rufus.

"Provided he knows first himself."

"How long does it take *you* to find out what you have to say?" said Rufus, returning to his ordinary manner and his seat at once. The fire seemed to have thrown itself off in that last jet of flame.

"I sometimes find I have too much; and then there is apt to be a little delay of choice."

"A delay to choose?—or a choice of delay?" said Rufus.

"Sometimes one and sometimes the other."

One or the other seemed still in force with Winthrop's present matter of speech, for he came before the fire and stood mending it, and said nothing.

"Winthrop," said Rufus gravely, "have you any *particular* reason to decline doing this business for me?"

Winthrop hesitated slightly, and then came forth one of those same 'no's,' that Winnie knew by heart.

"Have you any particular reason to dislike it?"

"Yes. They were my friends once."

"But is your friendship for them stronger than for anybody else?"

"It does not stand in the way of my duty to you, Will."

"Your *duty* to me,——" said the other.

"Yes. I cannot in this instance call it pleasure."

It was the turn of Rufus to hesitate; for the face of his brother expressed an absence of pleasure that to him, in the circumstances, was remarkable.

"Then you do not refuse to undertake this job for me?"

"I will do what I can," said Winthrop, working at a large forestick on the fire. How Winnie wished he would let it alone, and place himself so that she could see him.

"And don't you think there is good prospect of our succeeding?"

"If Chancery don't give it you, I'll take it to the Court of Errors," said Winthrop, arranging the log to his satisfaction, and then putting the rest of the fire in order.

"I'm sorry to give you trouble, Governor," his brother said thoughtfully.

"I'm sorry you've got it to give, Will."

But Rufus went on looking into the fire, and seeming to get deeper into the depths of something less bright as he looked.

"After all I am much the most to be pitied," he began. "I thought to-day, Governor——I did not know what would become of me!"

"I can tell you that beforehand," said his brother. "You will become, exactly, what you choose to make yourself."

"That is what you always say," returned Rufus a little cynically.

"That is what I have found in my own practice," said Winthrop. He put up the tongs and took his old seat by Winnie. Rufus looked still into the fire.

"I am thrown out of this employment now," he said;—"I am disgusted with it——and if I were not, there is no way for me to follow it with advantage."

"I am not sorry for that, Will. I never liked it for you, nor you for it."

"I have nothing to do.—I am a loose pin in the Mosaic of society—the pattern is all made up without me."

"What pin has got your place?" said Winthrop.

"What do you mean?"

"Simply, that as in the nature of things there cannot be too many pins, a pin that is out of place must be such by a derelict of duty."

"What is my place?"

"If my word would set you in it, I would tell you."

"Tell me, and perhaps it will."

"I should bid you return to your engineer's work and serve God in it."

"Very poor chance for serving God or man, in that work," said Rufus. "Or myself."

"And no chance at all so long as you are doing nothing."

"I cannot bear to compare myself with you,"—Rufus went on moodily.

"Compare yourself with yourself, Will,——the actual with the possible,——and then go forward."

"What is possible in an engineer's life!" said Rufus.

"Everything is possible, in any place where Providence has put you, for the future at least. And the firm purpose of serving God in it, will dignify for the present any life.

"'A man that looks on glass
"'On it may stay his eye;
"'Or, if he pleaseth, through it pass,
"'And then the heaven espy!'"

Rufus met the grave slight smile on his brother's face, and his eye watered.

"You are better than I am," he said with one of very different meaning.

"If that be true to-day, Will, don't let it be true to-morrow."

They wrung each other's hands, and the elder brother went soberly away.

CHAPTER XXVIII.

An't be any way, it must be with valour; for Policy I hate: I had as lief be a Brownist as a politician.

TWELFTH NIGHT.

THE family at No. 11 on the Parade, were seated at breakfast one morning towards the latter end of May; the old trio, only with Elizabeth and Rose in each other's places.

"What is the reason Winthrop Landholm don't come here any more?" said the latter lady.

"I don't know," said Mr. Haye, when the silence had threatened the failure of any answer at all.

"What's the reason, Lizzie?"

"I don't know!—how should I?"

"I am sure I can't tell," said Rose, "but I didn't know but you did. I wish you'd ask him to come again, Mr. Haye—do you know how he is getting up in the world?"

"I know how cotton is falling," said Mr. Haye, swallowing his tea and the newspaper apparently both at the same time.

"Cotton!—" said Rose. "Now Mr. Haye, just put down that paper and listen to me;—do you know how Winthrop Landholm is holding his head up?"

"No," said Mr. Haye, looking at the pretty little head which was holding itself up, over against him.

"Well he is. You didn't hear what Mr. Satterthwaite was saying about him last night, did you?"

"I didn't hear Mr. Satterthwaite say anything."

"Well he says he's had quite a great cause come on, now, just a few days ago——"

"Who has? Mr. Satterthwaite?"

"Why no, Mr. Haye!—of course!—I mean Mr. Landholm has—a cause that he was to argue, you know—that's what I mean—before Chancellor Justice—and Mr. Satterthwaite says he did it splendidly!—he said everybody stood and looked;—and the Chancellor gave him everything he asked for—made all his exceptions, he said, whatever that means"—

"*Allowed* his exceptions," said Elizabeth.

"O you could listen when Mr. Satterthwaite was speaking of Winthrop Landholm!"

"Mr. Satterthwaite don't often have so good a subject. I listened certainly, and was very much interested;—the only time I ever remember Mr. Satterthwaite's saying anything I cared to hear."

"Well now, Mr. Haye, why isn't it just as well to say '*made* an exception,' as '*allowed* an exception'? I don't think '*allowed* an exception' is good English."

"It is good law English, I suppose, Rose."

"Well I don't care—at any rate, he said the Chancellor allowed every one of Mr. Landholm's exceptions,—I suppose *you* understand it,—and wouldn't allow a single thing to Mr. Brick; and Mr. Brick was the lawyer on the other side; and Mr. Satterthwaite said it was a great triumph for Mr. Landholm."

"Dustus O. Brick?" said Mr. Haye.

"Yes," said Elizabeth.

"I don't know," said Rose; "he said Mr. Brick,—or the noted Mr. Brick—I suppose that's the man."

"Dustus O. Brick!" said Mr. Haye—"he's one of the best men in the bar, and a very clever man too; a distinguished lawyer; there's no one more thought of."

"That's what Mr. Satterthwaite said,—he said so,—he said it was a great triumph for Mr. Landholm;—and now Mr. Haye, *won't* you ask him to come here again as he used to?"

"Who?"

"Winthrop Landholm."

"What for?"

"Why I want to *see* him—and so do you, Mr. Haye. Now Mr. Haye, won't you?—Though I don't know but Elizabeth would be the best one to ask him."

"Why?" dryly said the master of the house.

"I guess he'd be more likely to come."

"If I thought so, and it were my part to do it, I certainly should ask him," said Elizabeth. "There isn't any person so pleasant as he to take his place, among all that come here."

"You were glad of what Mr. Satterthwaite told us last night weren't you?" said Rose with a sinister smile.

"Very glad!"

"Did you ever hear Mr. Satterthwaite go on so about anybody? One would have thought Mr. Landholm was his own brother. I wonder if that was for your sake, Lizzie?"

"I presume it was for his own sake," said Elizabeth. "I should think anybody who had the privilege of being Mr. Landholm's friend, would know how to value it."

"*You* would value it, for instance, I suppose?"

"I have no doubt I should."

"It seems to me you are a little too sure of valuing it," said Mr. Haye,—"for a young lady who has *not* that privilege."

Elizabeth's cheeks burned on the instant, but her eye was steady, and it looked full on her father while she asked him,

"Why, sir?"

"It is not worth while for you to like other people faster than they like you?"

"Why not?"—said Elizabeth, her cheek and eye both deepening in their fire, but her look as steady and full,—"Why not?—if it should happen that I am less likeable than they?"

"Pshaw!" said Mr. Haye.

"If I were to gauge the respect and esteem I give others, by the respect and esteem they might be able to give me,—I should cut off maybe the best pleasures of my life."

"Are respect and esteem the best pleasures of your life?" said Rose satirically.

"I have never known any superior to them," said Elizabeth. But she brought, as she spoke, her eye of fire to bear upon her cousin, who gave way before it and was mum.

"And what may respect and esteem lead to?" said Mr. Haye.

"I don't know," said Elizabeth. "And I don't care—even to ask."

"Suppose they are not returned?"

"I have supposed that in the first place," she answered.

"At that rate you might be over head and ears in your regard for several people at once, none of whom cared a straw for you," said Mr. Haye.

"When I find *several*, men or women, that deserve the sort of respect and esteem I am talking of," said Elizabeth—"I am not talking of a common kind, that you can give common people—I shall be in a new world!"

"And have you this sort of 'respect and esteem' for Mr. Winthrop Landholm?" said her father.

"That's another question," said Elizabeth, for the first time dropping her eye and speaking more quietly;—"I was talking of the general principle."

"And I am asking of the particular instance. Have you this respect and esteem for this particular person of your acquaintance?"

"I never gave it to many people in my life," said Elizabeth, colouring again somewhat. "He has as fair a share of it as most have."

"A little more?" said Mr. Haye smiling.

This time the answer she flashed at him was of proud and indignant bar to any further questioning—with her eyes only; her lips did not move.

"Does he know it, Elizabeth?"

"Know what, sir?"

"This favour you have expressed for him."

"I have expressed nothing but what I would express for any one to whom I thought it due."

"But I ask, does he know it?"

"I feel injured, father, by your asking me such questions!—I presume he does not know, since he has not had the honour of being told!"

The air with which this was given was regal.

"I wouldn't tell him, Lizzie," said her father quietly.

But at the insinuation conveyed in these words, Elizabeth's mood took another turn.

"I will tell whomsoever it may concern to know, at any time when I see occasion," she answered. "It is not a thing to be ashamed of; and I will neither do nor think anything I am unwilling to own."

"You had better reform public opinion in the first place," said Mr. Haye dryly.

"Why?" she said with startling quickness.

"It is apt to hold rather light of young ladies who tell their minds without being asked."

"How can you speak so, father!—I said, *when I saw occasion*—it seems I have very much misjudged in the present instance."

"And as that might happen again," said Mr. Haye, "it is just as safe, on the whole, that the person in question does not come here any more. I am glad that I have advertised his place for sale."

"*What!*" exclaimed Elizabeth and Rose both at once.

"Hush—don't fire at a man in that way. His father's place, I should say."

"*What* have you done to it?" said Elizabeth.

"Advertised it for sale. You don't hear me as well as you do Mr. Satterthwaite, it seems."

"How come you to have it to sell?"

"Because it was mortgaged to me—years ago—and I can't get either principal or interest; so I am taking the best way I can to secure my rights."

"But Mr. Landholm was your friend?"

"Certainly—but I am a better friend to myself. Can't do business with your friends on different principles from those you go upon with other people, Lizzie."

Elizabeth looked at him, with eyes that would have annihilated a large portion of Mr. Haye's principles, if they had been sentient things. Rose began a running fire of entreaties that *he* would have nothing to do with Shahweetah, for that she could not bear the place. Elizabeth brought her eyes back to her plate, but probably she still saw Mr. Haye there, for the expression of them did not change.

"*I'm* not going to have anything to do with the place, Rose," said Mr. Haye—"further than to get it off my hands. I don't want to live there any more than you do. All I want to do is to pay myself."

"Father," said Elizabeth looking up quietly, "*I'll* buy it of you."

"*You!*" said Mr. Haye,—while Rose went off into a succession of soft laughs.

"Do you care who does it, so that you get the money?"

"No,—but what will you do with it?"

"Find a way, in time, of conveying it back to its right owners," said Rose. "Don't you see, Mr. Haye?"

Elizabeth favoured her with a look which effectually spiked that little gun, for the time, and turned her attention again to her father.

"Do you care who buys it of you, so that you get the money?"

"Why no—but you don't want such a piece of property, Lizzie."

"I want just such a piece of property."

"But my child, you can't manage it. It would be an absurd spending of *your* money. There's a farm of two or three hundred acres—more,—besides woodland. What could you do with it?"

"Trust me to take care of my own. May I have it, father?"

"Mr. Haye!—" Rose put in, pouting and whimpering,—"I wish you'd tell Lizzie she's not to look at me so!—"

"Will you sell it to me?" pursued Elizabeth.

"If you'll promise it shall not go back to the original owners in any such way as Rose hinted."

"Are those your terms of sale?" said Elizabeth. "Because, though I may not choose to submit myself to them, I can find you another purchaser."

"What do you want of a great piece of land like that?"

"Nothing; I want the land itself."

"You can't do anything with it."

"It don't signify, if it all grows up to nettles!" said Elizabeth. "Will you take the money of me and let me take the land of you?"

"Hum—" said Mr. Haye,—"I think you have enlightened me too much this morning. No—I'll find a more disinterested purchaser; and let it teach you to take care of your eyes as well as your tongue."

Rose bridled. Mr. Haye got up leisurely from the breakfast-table and was proceeding slowly to the door, when his path was crossed by his daughter. She stood still before him.

He might well tell her to take care of her eyes. They glowed in their sockets as she confronted him, while her cheek was as blanched as a fire at the heart could leave it. Mr. Haye was absolutely startled and stood as still as she.

"Father," she said, "take care how you drive me too far! You have had some place in my heart, but I warn you it is in danger.—If you care for it, I warn you!—"

She was gone, like a flash; and Mr. Haye after casting a sort of scared look behind him at his wife, went off too; probably thinking he had got enough for one morning.

No doubt Elizabeth felt so for her part. She had gone to her own room, where she put herself on a low seat by the window and sat with labouring breath and heaving bosom, and the fire in her heart and in her eyes glowing still, though she looked now as if it were more likely to consume herself than anybody else. If herself was not present to her thoughts, they were busy with nothing then present; but the fire burned.

While she sat there, Clam came in, now one of the smartest of gay-turbaned handmaidens, and began an elaborate dusting of the apartment. She began at the door, and by the time she had worked round to Elizabeth at the window, she had made by many times a more careful survey of her mistress than of any piece of furniture in the room. Elizabeth's head had drooped; and her eyes were looking, not vacantly, but with no object in view, out of the window.

"I guess you want my friend here just now, Miss 'Lizabeth," said Clam, her lips parting just enough to show the line of white between them.

"Whom do you mean by your friend?"

"O—Governor Landholm, to be sure—he used to fix everybody straight whenever he come home to Wuttle Quttle."

Elizabeth passed over the implication that she wanted 'fixing,' and asked, "How?—"

"*I* don' know. He used to put 'em all in order, in less'n no time," said Clam, going over and over the dressing-table with her duster, as that piece of furniture kept her near her mistress. "Mis' Landholm used to get her face straight the minute his two feet sounded outside the house, and she'd keep it up as long as he stayed; and Winifred stopped to be queer and behaved like a Christian; and nobody else in the house hadn't a chance to take airs but himself."

"What sort of airs did *he* take?" said Elizabeth.

"O I don' know," said Clam;—"*his* sort;—they wa'n't like nobody else's sort."

"But what do you mean by airs?

"Can't tell," said Clam,—"nothin' like yours, Miss 'Lizabeth,—I take a notion to wish he was here, once in a while—it wouldn't do some folks no harm."

"Didn't his coming put you in order too?"

Clam gave a little toss of her head, infinitely knowing and satisfied at the same time, and once more and more broadly shewed the white ivory between her not unpretty parted teeth.

"I think you want putting in order now," said her mistress.

"Always did," said Clam with a slight arch of her eyebrows,—"always shall. Best get him to manage it, Miss 'Lizabeth—he can do it quicker 'n anybody else—for me,—and I dare say he would for you."

"I don't believe you ever were put in order," said Elizabeth,—"to stay."

"I didn't use to do a wrong thing as long as he was in the house!" said Clam. "Didn't want to.—You wouldn't neither, if you was in the house with him."

"What do you mean by Mrs. Landholm's getting her face straight when he came?—was'nt it always so?"

"'Twa'n't always *so*," said Clam,—"for when he come, half the wrinkles went away, and the grey hairs all turned black again."

There came such a pang to Elizabeth's heart, such a gush to

her eyes, that she hid her face on her knees and heard nothing of what her handmaid said for a long time after. If Clam talked, she had the talk all to herself; and when Elizabeth at last raised her head, her handmaiden was standing on the other side of the fireplace looking at her, and probably making up her mind that she wanted 'fixing' very much. There was no further discussion of the subject, however; for Miss Haye immediately called for her bonnet and veil, wrapped herself in a light scarf and went out. The door had hardly closed upon her when the bell rang again, and she came running up-stairs to her room.

"Clam, get me the newspaper."

"What news, Miss 'Lizabeth?"

"All the newspapers—every one you can find;—yesterday's and to-day's, or the day before."

Much wondering, Clam hunted the house and brought the fruits of her search; and much more wondering, she saw her mistress spend one hour in closely poring over the columns of page after page; she who never took five minutes a day to read the papers. At last a little bit was carefully cut from one of those Clam had brought up, and Elizabeth again prepared herself to go forth.

"If it had been Mr. Winthrop, now, who was doing that," said Clam, "he'd have took off his hat most likely, and sat down to it. How you do look, Miss 'Lizabeth!"

"Mr. Winthrop and I are two different people," said Elizabeth, hurriedly putting on the one glove she had drawn off.

"Must grow a little more like before you'll be one and the same," observed Clam.

Elizabeth let down her veil over her face and went out again.

With a quick nervous step she went, though the day was warm, making no delay and suffering no interruption; till she reached the University where Professor Herder made his daily and nightly abode. The professor was attending one of his classes. Elizabeth asked to be shewn to his room.

She felt as if she was on a queer errand, as she followed her conductor up the wide stone stairs and along the broad corridors, where the marks were evidently of only man's use and habitation, and now and then a man's whistle or footstep echoed from the distance through the halls. But she went on swiftly, from one corridor to another, till the guide opened a door and she stepped out from the public haunts of life to a bit of quite seclusion.

It was a pleasant enough place that Mr. Herder called home. A large, airy, light, high-ceiled apartment, where plainly even tc a stranger's eye, the naturalist had grouped and bestowed around him all the things he best liked to live among. Enormous glass cases, filled with the illustrations of science, and not less of the philosopher's investigating patience, lined all the room; except where dark-filled shelves of books ran up between them from the floor to the ceiling. A pleasant cloth-covered table, with books and philosophical instruments, stood towards one side of the room, a little table with a lamp at the other; and scattered about, all over, were big stout comfortable well-worn leather arm-chairs, that said study and learning sat easy there and often received visits of pleasure in that room. Elizabeth felt herself as little akin to pleasure as to learning or study, just then. She put herself in one of the great leather chairs, with a sense of being out of her element—a little piece of busy, bustling, practical life, within the very palings of science and wisdom.

She sat and waited. But that pulse of busy life beat never the cooler for all the cool aspect of the place and the grave shade of wisdom that lingered there; nay, it throbbed faster and more flutteringly. She got up to try the power of distraction the glass cases might hold; but her eye roved restlessly and carelessly over object and object of interest that withheld its interest from her; and weariedly she went báck to her arm-chair and covered her face with her hands, that her mind might be at least uninterruptedly busy in its own way.

It must have been very busy, or the quick little step of the German professor must have been very soft withal; for he had come within a few feet of her before he knew who she was or she knew that he was there.

"Miss Élisabet'!" he exclaimed with a most good-humoured face of wonderment,—"I never was so honoured before! How did you get in my arm-chair?"

Elizabeth jumped up and shook hands with him, laughing in very relief to see him come.

"How did I get here?—I came up through the sun, Mr. Herder."

"I have asked you to come in better time," said the naturalist,—"that is, better for you—dis is very good time for me. I have nozing to do, and I will give you lesson in whatever you want."

"No sir,—I am come to give *you* a lesson, Mr. Herder."

"*Me?* Well, I will take it," said the naturalist, who began at the same time to run about his room and open closet doors and jingle glasses together, apparently on his own business,—" I like always to take lessons,—it is not often that I have such a teacher. I will learn the best I can—after I have got you some lemonade. I have two lemons here,—somevere,—ah !—"

" I don't want it, Mr. Herder."

" I cannot learn nozing till you have had it," said Mr. Herder bringing his lemons and glasses to the table ;—" that sun is beating my head what was beating yours, and it cannot think of nozing till I have had something to cool him off.—"

Elizabeth sat still, and looked, and thought, with her heart beating.

" I did not know what was in my room when I see you in my chair wiz your head down—you must be study more hard than me, Miss Élisabet'—I never put my head down, for nozing."

" Nor your heart either, I wonder ? " thought Elizabeth.

" I *was* studying, Mr. Herder,—pretty hard."

" Is that what you are going to give me to study ? " said the naturalist.

" Not exactly—it was something about it. I want you to do something for me, Mr. Herder,—if I may ask you,—and if you will be so very kind as to take some trouble for me."

" I do not like trouble," said the naturalist shaking his head good-humouredly over a squeeze of his lemon ;—" dere is no use in having trouble—I get out of it so soon as I can—but I will get in it wiz pleasure for you, Miss Élisabet'—what you tell me —if you will tell me if that is too much sucker."

" To take trouble, and to be *in* trouble, are not quite the same thing, Mr. Herder," said Elizabeth, having at the moment a vivid realization of the difference.

" I thought trouble was trouble," said the naturalist, finishing the preparing his own glass of lemonade. " If you will lesson me to find trouble is no trouble—Miss Élisabet'—I will thank you much for that."

Elizabeth heartily wished anybody could teach her that particular lesson. She sipped her lemonade, slowly and abstractedly, busy yet with the study which Mr. Herder had broken off; while he talked benignly and kindly, to ears that did not hear. But the last of Elizabeth's glass was swallowed hastily and the glass set down.

" Mr. Herder, I have come to ask you to do something for me."

" I am honoured, Miss Élisabet'," said the philosopher bowing.

"Will you not speak of it to anybody?"

"Not speak of it!" said the naturalist. "Then it is a secret?"

The quick energetic little bend of Elizabeth's head said before her lips spoke the word, "Yes!"

"It is more honour yet," he said. "What am I to do, Miss Élisabet'?"

"Nothing, if it will be any real trouble to you, Mr. Herder. Promise me that first."

"Promise?—what shall I promise?"—said Mr. Herder.

"Promise me that if what I am going to ask would be any real trouble to you or to your business, you will tell me so."

"I do not love to be troubled," said the naturalist. "It shall not be no trouble to me."

"But promise me that you will tell me, Mr. Herder."

"Suppose you was to tell me first. I cannot tell nozing till I know."

"You will not speak of it to anybody, Mr. Herder?"

"I will not speak of nozing, Miss Élisabet'."

"Mr. Herder, there is a piece of land which I want to buy; and I have come to ask you, if you can, and if you will, to buy it for me."

"Miss Élisabet'," said the naturalist looking a little surprised at his fair questioner,—"I will tell you the truth—I have no money."

"I have, Mr. Herder. But I cannot go into the market and buy for myself."

"Cer-tain-ly, you cannot do that," said Mr. Herder. "But what is it you wish to buy?"

"It is a farm,—" said Elizabeth, feeling glad that her back was to the light;—"it is a piece of land in the country—up on the Shatemuc river. I think you have been there, Mr. Herder,—it is the place where the Landholms' father lives. Wut-a-qut-o, they call it—or Shahweetah;—Wut-a-qut-o is the mountain opposite."

"Landholm!" cried the naturalist. "Is it Winthrop's place?"

Elizabeth bowed her head and answered, "His father's."

"Winthrop's place! Is *that* what you want, Miss Élisabet?"

Elizabeth bowed her head again, this time without answering.

"Suppose they might not want to sell it?" said the naturalist.

"They do not—but they can't help themselves. It must be sold—they can't pay money that is owing upon it."

"Money!"—said the naturalist;—"that is de trouble of all that is in the world. I wish there was no such thing as money! It makes all the mischief."

"Or the want of it," said Elizabeth.

"No!" said the naturalist,—"it is not that! I have want money all my life, Miss Élisabet', and I have never got into no trouble at all."

"Except when you fought the duels, Mr. Herder."

"*Dat* was not no trouble!" said the philosopher. "There was nozing about money there; and it was not no trouble,—neizer before, neizer after."

"I have had money all my life; and it never made me any trouble."

"Ah you have not come to the time," said Mr. Herder. "Wait, you will find it. Now you are in trouble because you want to buy this ground, and you could not do it wizout money."

"I can't do it with, unless you will help me, Mr. Herder—you or somebody."

"I could get somebody," said Mr. Herder;—"I know somebody what I could get."

"I don't know anybody who would be as good as you, sir."

"I do," said the naturalist. "Where is Mr. Haye?—is he sick?"

"No sir,—I don't wish him to know anything about it, Mr. Herder.—He is the person making the sale."

"Your father?—do you mean that Mr. Haye is the man what is selling the ground of Mr. Landholm?"

"Yes sir. And I wish to buy it."

"Then Miss Élisabet', what for do you not ask my friend Winthrop to buy it for you? He knows all business. He will do it."

"I cannot—I have not the liberty—He is not enough a friend of mine, for me to ask him such a favour."

"But Miss Élisabet', what will you do wiz all that large ground and water?"

"Buy it,—first, sir; and then I will see. I want it."

"I see you do," said the naturalist. "Well, then I shall get it for you—if I can—I hope your money will not get *me* in trouble."

"If you are at all afraid of that, Mr. Herder, I will find some other way——"

"I never was afraid of nozing in my life, Miss Élisabet'—

only I do not know neizer how to get money, neizer how to spend it—in this way. What will Mr. Haye say to me when I go to buy all this great land of him? He will say——"

"You're not to buy it of *him*, Mr. Herder."

"No?" said the naturalist. "Of who, then? I thought you said he was going to sell it."

"Yes, he is—but he has somebody else to do it for him. Here, Mr. Herder,—here is the advertisement;—see—don't read the first part,—all *that* has nothing to do with it,—here is the place. 'At the Merchant's Exchange, in the city of Mannahatta, on the first day of September, 1821, at 12 o'clock noon of that day' —and then comes the description of the place. It is to be sold at public auction."

"Auc-sion?—" said the naturalist.

"It's to be sold in public, to whoever offers to give most for it."

"O, I know that," said Mr. Herder.

"And dear Mr. Herder, all I ask of you is to be there, at 12 o'clock the first of September, and buy it for me; and let nobody know. Can you do it?"

"I can do so much," said the naturalist. "I think I can. But suppose somebody will give more than you."

"Do not suppose that, sir. I will give more than anybody."

"Are you sure you will?" said the naturalist. "Maybe you do not know."

"I do know, sir, and am sure."

"Well," said the naturalist, shaking his head,—"I do not know much about buying grounds—I do know a leetle of some things—but I do not know what sort of a lesson is this, Miss Élisabet'. But I will see if I can do it. Who is going to live up there wiz you?"

"Don't you suppose I can live alone, Mr. Herder."

"No, not there," said the naturalist. "You want some one to take care of you—de engineer, Miss Élisabet'," said he smiling.

Elizabeth made no answer; she had risen up to go; and he guided her through the halls and down the staircases, till she was in the open street again. Then, after a farewell squeeze of his hand and nod of her little head, she pulled her veil down and went homeward, more slowly than she had come.

"*Do* I want somebody to take care of me?" she thought. "I believe I do! An engineer?—I do not think the engine *is* under very good guidance— it *is* too strong for me—How could he know that? Oh what earthly thing would I give, for a hand wise and strong enough to lead me, and good enough that I could submit myself to!"

The wish was so deep drawn that her breast heaved with it, and starting tears made her draw her veil thicker before them. She bit her lip, and once more quickened her steps towards home.

CHAPTER XXIX.

Then think I of deep shadows on the grass,—
Of meadows where in sun the cattle graze,
Where, as the breezes pass,
The gleaming rushes lean a thousand ways,—
Of leaves that slumber in a cloudy mass,
Or whiten in the wind,—of waters blue
That from the distance sparkle through
Some woodland gap,—and of a sky above,
Where one white cloud like a stray lamb doth move.

LOWELL.

FINDING that the old farm must pass out of his hands, Mr. Landholm made up his mind not to spend another summer of labour and of life upon it; but at once with his son Asahel to move off to the West. He stayed but to reap the standing crops of winter grain, dispose of stock, and gather up all the loose ends of business; and left the hills of the Shatemuc, to seek better fortunes on a Western level.

They passed through Mannahatta on their way, that they might have a short sight of Winthrop and Winifred and say good-bye to them. It was not so joyful a visit that anybody wished it to be a long one.

"It's pretty hard," said the farmer, "to start life anew again at my time of day;——but these arms are not worn out yet; I guess they'll do something—more or less—on a new field."

"Asahel's got strong arms, father," said Winifred, who was fain to put in a word of comfort when she could.

"Ay, and a strong heart too," said his father. "He's a fine fellow. He'll do, I guess, in the long run,—at the West or somewhere; and at the West *if* anywhere, they say. I'm not concerned much about him."

"There's no need, I think," said Winthrop.

"Where's Will?—and what's he doing?"

"Will has just set off for Charleston—on some agency business."

"Charleston in South Carolina?"

"Yes."

"Then he is not engineering now?"

"No."

"How long does he expect to be gone?"

"Some months—more or less;—I don't know."

"Is it a good business for him?"

"He has chosen it,—not I."

"I would sooner trust your choice," said the father. "There's one thing Rufus wants; and that is, judgment."

"He'll do yet," said Winthrop. "And I shall not leave you long at the West, father. You will come when I send for you?"

"No, my boy," said the farmer looking gratified;—"I'll live by my own hands as long as I have hands to live by; and as I said, mine haven't given out yet! No—if the Lord prospers us, we'll have a visit from you and Winnie out there, I expect——by and by, when we get things in order;——you and Winnie, and anybody else you've a mind to bring along!"

It was spoken heartily, but with a tear in the eye; and nobody answered; unless it were answer, the long breath which Winnie drew at the very idea of such a visit.

Winthrop heard it; but through the long weeks of summer he could give her nothing more of country refreshment than the old walks on the Green and an occasional ride or walk on the opposite shore of one or the other of the rivers that bordered the city. Business held him fast, with a grip that he must not loosen; though he saw and knew that his little sister's face grew daily more thin and pale, and that her slight frame was slighter and slighter. His arm had less and less to do, even though her need called for more. He felt as if she was slipping away from him. August came.

"Winnie," said he one evening, when he came home and found her lying on her couch as usual,—"how would you like to go up and pay Karen a visit?"

"Karen?"——said Winnie,—"where?"

"At home.—At Wut-a-qut-o."

"Wut-a-qut-o!" said Winnie;—"is Karen there? I thought Shahweetah was sold."

"It isn't sold yet—it won't be till September—and Karen is there yet, keeping house with her brother Anderese."

"Anderese!—is old Anderese there?" said Winnie. "O I

should like to go, Governor!" she said raising herself on her elbow. "Can we?"

"Yes, if you like. Hildebrand Cowslip is down here with his father's sloop——how would you like to go up in her?"

"In the sloop?—O how good!" said Winnie bringing her thin hands together. "Can we? But dear Governor, you can't be away?"

"Yes—just as well as not. There isn't much doing in August—everybody takes a resting time; and so you and I will, Winnie," said he, bending down to kiss her.

Winnie looked up at him gratefully and lovingly with her wistful large eyes, the more expressive from the setting of illness and weakness in the face.

"I'd like you to have a rest, dear Governor."

He stood stroking back the ringlets from the thin blue-veined temple.

"Wouldn't it do you good to see Wut-a-qut-o again?"

"O I am sure it would!—And you too, wouldn't it?"

"I am good enough already," said Winthrop looking down at her.

"Too good," said Winnie looking up at him. "I guess you want pulling down!"

She had learned to read his face so well, that it was with a pang she saw the look with which he turned off to his work. A stranger could not have seen in it possibly anything but his common grave look; to Winnie there was the slight shadow of something which seemed to say the 'pulling down' had not to be waited for. So slight that she could hardly tell it was there, yet so shadowy she was sure it had come from something. It was not in the look merely—it was in the air,—it was, she did not know what, but she felt it and it made her miserable. She could not see it after the first minute; his face and shoulders, as he sat reading his papers, had their usual calm stability; Winnie lay looking at him, outwardly calm too, but mentally tossing and turning.

She could not bear it. She crawled off her couch and came and sat down at his feet, throwing her arms around his knee and looking up at him.

"Dear Governor!—I wish you had whatever would do you good!—"

"The skill of decyphering would do me a little good just now," said her brother. She could detect nothing peculiar in look or word, though Winnie's eyes did their best.

"But somehow I don't feel as if you had," she went on to say.

"Where is your faith?"—he said quietly, as he made a note in the margin of the paper he was reading. Winnie could make nothing of him.

"Governor, when shall we go?"

"Hildebrand moves his sloop off to-morrow afternoon."

"And shall we go to-morrow?"

"If you don't object."

Winnie left the floor, clapping her hands together, and went back to her couch to think over at large the various preparations which she must make. Which pleasant business held her all the evening.

They were not large preparations, however; longer to think of than to do; especially as Winthrop took upon himself the most of what was done. One or two nick-nackeries of preparation, in the shape of a new basket, a new book, and a new shawl, seemed delightful to Winnie; though she did not immediately see what she might want of the latter in August.

"We shall find it cooler when we get under the shadow of Wut-a-qut-o, Winnie," said her brother; and Winnie was only too glad of a pretext to take the pretty warm wrapper of grey and blue worsted along.

She did not want it when they set out, the next afternoon. It was very warm in the streets, very warm on the quays; and even when the sloop pushed her way slowly out and left the quays at her back, there was little air stirring and the August sun beat down steadily on river and shore.

"This don't look much like gettin' up to Cowslip's Mill *this* night," said the skipper. "Ain't it powerful!"

"The wind is coming off from the South," said Winthrop.

"Yes, I felt some little puffs on my cheek," said Winnie.

"Glad to hear it," said the sloop master, a tall, bony, ill-set-together specimen of a shore and water man;—"there ain't enough now to send an egg-shell along, and I'd like to shew you a good run, Mr. Landholm, since you're goin' along with me. She looks smart, don't she?"

"If she'll only work as well," said Winthrop. "Hild', you haven't got much cargo aboard."

"Only as much as'll keep her steady," answered the skipper. "'Seems to me nobody ain't a wantin' nothin' up our ways. I guess you're the heaviest article on board, Winthrop;—she never carried a lawyer before."

"Are lawyers heavy articles?" said Winnie laughing.

"'Cordin' to what I've heern, I should say they be; ain't

they, squire?—considerable,—especially when they get on folks's hands. I hope you're a better sort, Winthrop,—or ain't there much choice in 'em?"

"You shall try me when you get into trouble," said Winthrop.

"Is this Mr. Cowslip's old sloop?" said Winnie.

"She don't look old, does she?" inquired Mr. Hildebrand.

"But I mean, is it the same he used to have?—No, she looks very handsome indeed."

"She's the old one though," said the skipper, "the same old Julia Ann. What's the use o' askin' ladies' ages?—she's just as good as when she was young; and better dressed. I've had the cabin fixed up for you, Mr. Landholm,—I guess it'll be pretty comfortable in there."

"It's a great deal pleasanter here," said Winnie. "There comes the wind!—that was a puff!—"

"Well we're ready for it," said the skipper.

And stronger puffs came after, and soon a steady fair southerly breeze set up the river and sent the Julia Ann on before it. Straight up the river their course lay, without veering a point for miles. The sun was lowering towards the horizon and the heat was lessening momently, even without the south breeze which bade it be forgotten; and the blue waters of the river, so sluggish a little while ago, were briskly curling and rippling, and heading like themselves for Wut-a-qut-o.

Winnie sat still and silent in the shadow of the huge sail. Winthrop was standing close beside her, talking with the skipper; but he knew that his little sister had hold of his hand and had laid her unbonneted head against his arm; and when the skipper left him he stooped down to her.

"What do you think of it, Winnie?"

"O Winthrop!—how delicious!—Aren't you glad it is such beautiful world?"

"What are you thinking of in particular?"

"O everything. It isn't down here like Wut-a-qut-o, but everything is so delicious——the water and the shore and the sunshine and the wind!——"

"Poor Winnie," said her brother stroking her hair,—"you haven't seen it in a good while."

She looked up at him, a glance which touchingly told him that where he was she wanted nothing; and then turned her eyes again towards the river.

"I was thinking, Governor, that maybe I shall never go up here again."——

"Well Winnie?—"

"I am very glad I can go this time. I am so much obliged to you for bringing me."

"Obliged to me, Winnie!"

He had placed himself behind his little sister, with one hand holding her lightly by each shoulder; and calm as his tone was, perhaps there came a sudden thought of words that he knew very well——

"There fairer flowers than Eden's bloom,
"Nor sin nor sorrow know;
"Blest seats! through rude and stormy seas
"I onward press to you."——

For he was silent, though his face wore no more than its ordinary gravity.

"Governor," said Winnie half turning her head round to him, "I wish these people were not all round here within hearing, so that we could sing.——I feel just like it."

"By and by, Winnie, I dare say we can."

"How soon do you think we shall get to Wut-a-qut-o."

"Before morning, if the wind holds."

The wind held fair and rather strengthened than lost, as the evening went on. Under fine headway the Julia Ann swept up the river, past promontory and bay, nearing and nearing her goal. Do her best, however, the Julia Ann could not bring them that night to any better sleeping advantages than her own little cabin afforded; and for those Winthrop and Winnie were in no hurry to leave the deck. After the skipper's hospitality had been doubtfully enjoyed at supper, and after they had refreshed themselves with seeing the sun set and watching the many-coloured clouds he left behind him, the moon rose in the other quarter and threw her 'silver light' across the deck, just as duskiness was beginning to steal on. The duskiness went on and shrouded the hills and the distant reaches of the river in soft gloom; but on board the Julia Ann, on her white sails and deck floor where the brother and sister were sitting, and on a broad pathway of water between them and the moon, her silver light threw itself with brightening and broadening power. By and by Mr. Hildebrand's two or three helpers disposed of themselves below deck, and nobody was left but Mr. Hildebrand himself at the helm.

"Now we can sing!" exclaimed Winnie, when one or two turns of her head had made her sure of this; and to Winthrop's surprise she struck up the very words part of which had been in his own remembrance.

"'Jerusalem! my happy home—
"'Name ever dear to me—
"'When shall my labours have an end,
"'In joy and peace in thee!'"

Winnie's voice was as sweet and clear as a bird's, if weakness left it not much stronger; that of her brother was deep, mellow, and exceeding fine; it was no wonder that the skipper turned his head and forgot his tiller to catch the fulness of every note. When the last had sounded, there was nothing to be heard but the rippling of water under the sloop's prow; the sails were steady and full, the moonlight not more noiseless; the wind swept on with them softly, just giving a silent breath to their cheeks; the skipper held his tiller with a moveless hand.

"What next, Winnie?" her brother whispered. The soft gurgle of the water had been heard for several minutes.

"How fond Karen is of that hymn," said Winifred. "Governor, do you think I shall live long in this world?"

She was leaning, half lying, upon Winthrop, with his arm round her. Her voice had put the question in precisely the same tone that it had given the remark.

"Why do you ask me that, Winnie?"

"Because—sometimes I think I sha'n't,—and I want to know what you think."

"You will live, I am sure, dear Winnie, till God has done for you all he means to do;—till he has fitted his child for heaven;—and then he will take her."

"I know that," said Winifred with a grateful half look up at him;—"but I mean—you know I am not well quite, and weak, and I don't think I get any better;—don't you think that it won't take a very great while, very likely?"

"How would you feel, Winnie, if you thought that was so?"

"I *do* think it sometimes—pretty often,"— said Winnie, "and it don't make me feel sorry, Governor."

"You think heaven is better than earth."

"Yes,—and then—that's one good thing of my sickness—it don't seem as if I ever could do much if I lived, so it matters the less."

"Nobody knows how much he does, who does his duty," said Winthrop.

"Why I can't do anything at all!" said Winnie.

"Every talent that isn't buried brings something into the treasury," said Winthrop.

"Yes—that's pleasant," said Winnie;—"but I don't know what mine is."

"The good that people do unconsciously is often more than that they intend."

"Unconsciously!—But then they don't know whether they do it or not?"

"It don't hurt them, not to know," said her brother smiling.

"But what sort of good-doing is that, Winthrop?"

"It only happens in the case of those persons whose eye is very single;—with their eye full of the light they are reflecting, they cannot see the reflection. But it is said of those that 'their works do follow them.'"

Winnie was tearfully silent, thinking of the ingathering of joy there would be for one that she knew; and if Winthrop's arm was drawn a little closer round her little figure perhaps it was with a like thought for her. How bright the moonlight shone!

"That's pleasant to think, Governor,—both parts of it," said Winifred softly, beating his hand slightly with one of her own. He was silent.

"Now won't you sing something else?—for I'm tired," she said, nestling her head more heavily on his breast.

And he sang again.——

"'Vain are all terrestrial pleasures,
"'Mixed with dross the purest gold;
"'Seek we then for heavenly treasures,
"'Treasures never growing old.
"'Let our best affections centre
"'On the things around the throne;
"'There no thief can ever enter,—
"'Moth and rust are there unknown.

"'Earthly joys no longer please us,
"'Here would we renounce them all,
"'Seek our only rest in Jesus,
"'Him our Lord and Master call.
"'Faith, our languid spirits cheering,
"'Points to brighter worlds above;
"'Bids us look for his appearing,
"'Bids us triumph in his love.

"'Let our lights be always burning,
"'And our loins be girded round,
"'Waiting for our Lord's returning,
"'Longing for the joyful sound.
"'Thus the christian life adorning,
"'Never need we be afraid,
"'Should he come at night or morning,
"'Early dawn, or evening shade.'"

The air was slow, tender, and plaintive, and borne by the deep voice over all the breadth of the moon-lit river. Winnie's breath was fuller drawn; the skipper held his, and forgot his helm; and in every pause of the song, the sweet interlude was played by the water under the sloop's prow.

"Governor——" said Winnie, when the bubbling water had been listened to alone for a while.

"What?"

"Do you think those words are quite true?"

"Those words of the hymn?"

"Yes—some of them. I think you like that hymn better than I do. 'Earthly joys no longer please us';—do you think that is right?—They please me."

"It is only by comparison that they can be true, Winnie, certainly;—except in the case of those persons whose power of enjoyment is by some reason or other taken away."

"But you like that hymn very much?"

"Yes. Don't you?"

"I like part of it very much, and I like the tune; but I like to be able to say all the words of a hymn. How sweet that was!—Governor, don't you think it would be pleasant to stay here all night?"

"Singing?"

"No—but talking, and sleeping."

"I am afraid it would sadly hinder to-morrow's talk, and oblige you to sleep instead."

"Then I'll go right away. Do you think we shall be at Wut-a-qut-o in the morning?"

"If the wind holds."

By Winthrop's care and management the little cabin was made not absolutely uncomfortable, and Winnie's bed was laid on the floor between door and window so that she could sleep without being smothered. He himself mounted guard outside, and sleeping or waking kept the deck for the whole night.

"Governor," said Winnie cautiously putting her head out at the door, just as the summer dawn was growing into day,—"Governor!—are we there?"

"We are *here*."

"Where?"

"Lying at Cowslip's Mill."

"Oh!——"

The rest of Winnie's joyous thought was worked into her shoes and dress and bonnet-strings, and put away in her bag with her night-cap. How fast it was all done! and she pushed open her cabin door and stood on the deck with Winthrop.

Yes—there was the green wooded shore—how fresh to her eyes!—There was Mr. Cowslip's brown old house and mill; there was the old stage road; and turning, there two miles off lay Shahweetah, and there rose up Wut-a-qut-o's green head. And with a sob, Winnie hid her face in Winthrop's arms. But then in another minute she raised it again, and clearing away the mute witnesses of joy and sorrow, though it was no use for they gathered again, she looked steadily. The river lay at her feet and stretched away off up to Shahweetah, its soft gray surface unbroken by a ripple or an eddy, smooth and bright and still. Diver's Rock stood out in its old rough outline, till it cut off the west end of Shahweetah and seemed to shut up the channel of the river. A little tiny thread of a north wind came down to them from Home, over the river, with sweet promise. And as they looked, the morning light was catching Wut-a-qut-o's grave head, and then hill-top after hill-top, and ridge after ridge of the high mountain land, till all of them were alight with the day's warm hues, while all beneath slept yet in the greys of the dawn. The brother and sister stood side by side, perfectly silent; only Winnie's tears ran, sometimes with such a gush that it brought her head down, and sobs that could be heard came to Winthrop's ears. They stood till they were hailed by the old miller.

"Ha! Winthrop—glad to see ye! how do you do? Haven't seen your face this great while. Winnie? is it?—Glad to see ye! She's growed a bit. Come right along into the house—we'll have something for breakfast by and by, I expect. I didn't know you was here till five minutes ago—I was late out myself—ain't as spry as I used to be;—Come!"—

"Oh Governor, let's go straight home!" said Winnie.

"There's time enough yet, Mr. Cowslip, for your purposes. What o'clock do you suppose it is?"

"Well, I s'pose it's somewhere goin' on to six, ain't it?"

"It has left five. We can breakfast with Karen yet, Winnie."

"Oh do, Governor!"

"If you'll give us a boat instead of a breakfast, Mr. Cowslip, we will thank you just as much, and maybe take your hospitality another time."

"But won't you stop and take just a mouthful first? you'd better."

"No thank you. We shall have to take it up there; and two breakfasts a day don't agree with me."

With some sorrow on Mr. Cowslip's part, this was submitted to. The boat was got out; Hildebrand dropped into it and took the oars, "guessing he wouldn't mind going himself;" and Winthrop and Winnie sat close together in the stern. Not to steer; for Hildebrand was much too accustomed an oarsman to need any such help in coasting the river for miles up and down.

CHAPTER XXX.

> Away, away, from men and towns,
> To the wild wood and the downs—
> To the silent wilderness
> Where the soul need not repress
> Its music, lest it should not find
> An echo in another's mind.
>
> SHELLEY.

WINNIE drew a breath of gratification, as the oars began to dimple the still water and the little boat rounded out from behind the wharf and headed up the river; the very same way by which Winthrop had taken Mr. Haye's two young ladies once long before. The tide was just at the turn, and Hildebrand made a straight run for the rocks.

"How pleasant it is to hear the oars again!" Winnie said. Winthrop said nothing.

Swiftly they pulled up, dappling the smooth grey water with falling drops from the oar-blades, and leaving behind them two lines of spreading wavelets that tracked the boat's way. Cowslip's Mill fell into the distance, and all that shore, as they pulled out into the middle of the river; then they drew near the old granite ridge of Diver's Rock on the other side. The sun had got so low down as that now, and the light of years ago was on the same grey bluffs and patches of wood. It was just like years ago; the trees stood where they did, ay, and the sunlight; the same shadows fell; and the river washed the broken foot of the point with, it might be, the very same little waves and eddies. And there, a mile further on, Wut-a-qut-o's high green side rose up from the water. Winnie had taken off her bonnet and sat with her head resting upon Winthrop's side or arm, her common position whenever she could get it. And she sat and looked, first at one thing and then at another, with quiet tears running and sometimes streaming down her face. Then the boat struck off from Diver's Rock and pushed straight over for the rocks of Shahweetah. As it neared them, the dear old trees stood forth more plainly to view, each one for itself; and the wonted footholds, on turf and stone, could be told and could be seen, apart one from the other. Poor Winnie could not look at them then, but she put her head down and sobbed her greeting to them all.

"Winnie,"—said Winthrop softly, and she felt his arm closer drawn around her,——"you must not do that."

It mattered little what Winthrop asked Winnie to do; she never failed to obey him. She stopped crying now, and in another moment was smiling to him her delight, through the drops that held their place yet in her eyes and on her cheeks.

The little boat was shoved in to the usual place among the rocks and the passengers got out.

"What's the fare, Hild'?—sloop and all?"

The skipper stood on the rocks and looked into the water.

"Will you let me come to you to clear me out, the first time I get into trouble?"

"Yes."

"Then we're square!" he said, preparing to jump back into his boat.

"*Then* hasn't come," said Winthrop; "let's keep things square as we go along."

"All right," said the skipper. "Couldn't take nothin' from you the first time, Governor."

And Hildebrand after giving Winthrop's hand a shake, into which there went a sort of grateful respect which he would never have yielded to one who had laid any manner of claim to it, dropped into his seat again and pushed off. Winthrop and Winnie turned their steps slowly towards the house.

Very slowly; for each step now was what they had come for. How untravelled the road was!

"How it looks as if we didn't live here, Governor," Winnie said with half a sigh.

"Old Karen and Anderese don't come this way very often," replied her brother.

"Governor, I am very sorry it has got to be sold!"

They walked a few more steps up the rocky path in silence.

"O Governor, look at that great limb of that cedar tree——all dragging! What a pity."

"Broken by the wind," said Winthrop.

"How beautifully the ivy hangs from that cedar—just as it

did. Dear Governor, won't you get a saw while you're here, and take off the branch and make it look nice again?—as nice as it can;——and there's the top of that little white pine!"——

"Winter-killed," said Winthrop.

"Won't you put it in order, as you used to do, this one time more?"

"If I can get a saw, I will, Winnie,—or a hatchet."

"I'm sorry we can't do it but this one time more," said Winnie, with a second and a better defined sigh, as they reached the house level. "O how funny it looks, Governor! how the grass has run up! and how brown it is! But the cedars don't change, do they?"

"It is August, Winnie," was all Winthrop's remark.

The front of the house was shut up; they went round. Old Anderese was cutting wood at the back of the house; but without stopping to enlighten him, Winthrop passed on and led Winnie into the kitchen. There the kitchen fire was burning as of yore, and on the hearth before it stood Karen, stooping down to oversee her cooking breakfast. At Winthrop's voice she started and turned. She looked at them; and then came a long and prolonged "Oh!——" of most mingled and varied tone and expression; hands and eyes keeping it company.

"Karen, we have come to see you."

In perfect silence she shook the hand of each, and then sat down and threw her apron over her face. Winnie stood still and sobbed; Winthrop walked off.

"Oh, dear," said the old woman presently rising and coming up to Winine,——"what's made ye come to see me again? What did you come for, dear?"

The tone was wondering and caressing, and rejoicing, all in a breath. Winnie dried her eyes and answered as well as she could.

"Why we wanted to see the old place again, Karen, and to see you; and Governor thought it would do me good to be in the country a little while; and he couldn't come before, and so we have come up now to stay a few days. And we've brought things to eat, so you needn't be troubled about that."

"Ye needn't," said old Karen. "Anderese and me'd find something for you to eat, in all the wide country—do ye think we wouldn't? And how are you, dear," said she scanning Winnie's pale face;—"are ye ever yet any stronger?"

Winnie shook her head smiling and answered, "Not much."

"I see ye ain't. Well—ye're the Lord's child. He'll do what he will with his own. Where did ye come from, dear?"

"Up from Mr. Cowslip's mill," said Winnie. "We came in his sloop last night."

"The sloop!" said Karen. "Why then ye haven't had anything to eat!—and what was I thinking of! Sit down, dear——take your own chair, till I get the other room fit for ye; and you shall have breakfast jus' so soon I can make it. Where's the Governor gone to?"

He came in; and Karen's face grew bright at the sight of him. All the while she was getting the breakfast he stood talking with her; and all the while, her old face kept the broad gleam of delight that had come into it with his entering the kitchen. With what zeal that breakfast was cooked for him; with what pleasure it was served. And while they were eating it, Karen sat in the chimney corner and looked at them, and talked.

"And isn't the place sold then, Governor?"

"Not yet, Karen——in a few weeks it will be."

"And who's goin' to buy it?"

"I don't know."

"And ye ain't goin' fur to buy it yourself?"

"No Karen—I am not rich enough to keep a country house."

"You had ought to have it," said Karen. "It don't belong to nobody else but you. And you don't know who's a goin' to have it, Governor?"

"I don't know."

"'Tain't likely they'll let the old woman stay in her corner, whoever they'll be," said Karen. "Well—'tain't fur now to the end,—and then I'll get a better place where they won't turn me out. I wish I was there, Governor."

"'There' will be better at the end of your way, Karen, than at any other time."

"Ay—O I know it, dear; but I get so impatient, days,——I want to be gone. It's better waiting."

"Perhaps you'll have something yet to do for us, Karen," said Winnie.

"Ye're too fur off," said the old woman. "Karen's done all she can for ye when she's took care of ye this time. But I'll find what I have to do—and I'll do it—and then I'll go!"——she said, with a curious modulation of the tones of her voice that came near some of the Methodist airs in which she delighted. "Governor 'll take care o' you, Winnie; and the Lord 'll take care o' him!"

Both brother and sister smiled a little at Karen's arrangement of things; but neither contradicted her.

"And how do you manage here, Karen, all alone ?—do you keep comfortable ? "

"I'm comfortable, Mr. Winthrop," she said with half a smile; —"I have lived comfortable all my life. I seem to see Mis' Landholm round now, times, jus' like she used to be; and I know we'll be soon all together again. I think o' that when I'm dreary."

She was a singular old figure, as she sat in the corner there with her head a little on one side, leaning her cheek on her finger, and with the quick change of energetic life and subdued patience in her manner.

"Don't get any dinner for us, Karen," said Winthrop as they rose from table. "We have enough for dinner in our basket."

"Ye must take it back again to Mannahatta," said Karen. "Ye'r dinner 'll be ready—roast chickens and new potatoes and huckleberry pie—the chickens are just fat, and ye never see nicer potatoes this time o' year; and Anderese don't pick very fast, but he'll have huckleberries enough home for you to eat all the ways ye like. And milk I know ye like 'm with, Governor."

"Give me the basket then, Karen, and I'll furnish the huckleberries."

"He'll do it—Anderese 'll get 'em, Mr. Winthrop,—not you."

"Give me the basket!——I would rather do it, Karen. Anderese has got to dig the potatoes."

"O yes, and we'll go out and spend the morning in the woods, won't we, Governor ? " said his sister.

The basket and Winnie were ready together and the brother and sister struck off into the woods to the north of the house. They had to cross but a little piece of level ground and sunshine and they were under the shade of the evergreens which skirted all the home valley. The ground as soon became uneven and rocky, broken into little heights and hollows, and strewn all over with a bedding of stones, large and small; except where narrow foot-tracks or cowpaths wound along the mimic ravines or gently climbed the hilly ridges. Among these stones and sharing the soil with them, uprose the cedars, pines, hemlocks, and a pretty intermingling of deciduous trees; not of very tall or vigorous growth, for the land favoured them not, but elegant and picturesque in varied and sweet degree. That it pleased those eyes to which it had been long familiar, and long strange, was in no measure.

Leaving the beaten paths, the brother and sister turned to the right of the first little ravine they had entered, just where a large boulder crowned with a tuft of ferns marked the spot, and toiled up a very rough and steep rising. Winthrop's help was needed here to enable Winnie to keep footing at all, much more to make her way to the top. There were steep descents of ground, spread with dead pine leaves, a pretty red-brown carpeting most dainty to the eyes but very unsure to the foot;—there were sharp turns in the rocky way, with huge granitic obstacles before and around them;—Winnie could not keep on her feet without Winthrop's strong arm; although in many a rough pitch and steep rise of the way, young hickories and oaks lent their aid to her hand that was free. Mosses and lichens, brown and black with the summer's heat, clothed the rocks and dressed out their barrenness; green tufts of fern nodded in many a nook, and kept their greenness still; and huckleberry bushes were on every hand, in every spare place, and standing full of the unreaped black and blue harvest. And in the very path, under their feet, sprang many an unassuming little green plant, that in the Spring had lifted its head in glorious beauty with some delicate crown of a flower. A stranger would have made nothing of them; but Winnie and Winthrop knew them all, crowned or uncrowned.

"It's pretty hard getting up here, Governor—I guess I haven't grown strong since I was here last; and these old yellow pines are so rotten I am afraid to take hold of anything—but your hand. It's good you are sure-footed. O look at the Solomon's Seal—don't you wish it was in flower!"

"If it was, we shouldn't have any huckleberries," said her brother.

"There's a fine parcel of them, isn't there, Winthrop? O let's stop and pick these—there are nice ones—and let me rest."

Winnie sat down to breathe, with her arm round the trunk of a pine tree, drinking in everything with her eyes, while that cluster of bushes was stripped of its most promising berries; and then a few steps more brought Winthrop and Winnie to the top of the height.

Greater barrenness of soil, or greater exposure to storms, or both causes together, had left this hill-top comparatively bare; and a few cedars that had lived and died there had been cut away by the axe, for firewood; making a still further clearance. But the shallow soil everywhere supported a covering of short grass or more luxuriant mosses; and enough cedars yet made good their hold of life and standing to overshadow pretty well the whole ground;

leaving the eye unchecked in its upward or downward rovings. The height was about two hundred feet above the level of the river, and seemed to stand in mid-channel, Shahweetah thrusting itself out between the north and southerly courses of the stream, and obliging it to bend for a little space at a sharp angle to the West. The north and south reaches, and the bend were all commanded by the height, together with the whole western shore and southern and southeastern hills. To the northwest was Wut-a-qut-o, seen almost from the water's edge to the top; but the outjutting woods of Shahweetah impinged upon the mountain's base, and cut the line of the river there to the eye. But north there was no obstruction. The low foreground of woods over which the hill-top looked, served but as a base to the picture, a setting on the hither side. Beyond it the Shatemuc rolled down from the north in uninterrupted view, the guardian hills, Wut-a-qut-o and its companions, standing on either side; and beyond them, far beyond, was the low western shore of the river sweeping round to the right, where the river made another angle, shewing its soft tints; and some faint and clear blue mountains still further off, the extreme distance of all. But what varied colouring,—— what fresh lights and shades,——what sweet contrast of fair blue sky and fair blue river,—the one, earth's motion; the other heaven's rest; what deep and bright greens in the foreground, and what shadowy, faint, cloud-like, tints of those far off mountains. The soft north wind that had greeted the travellers in the early morning, was blowing yet, soft and warm; it flickered the leaves of the oaks and chestnuts with a lazy summer stir; white sails spotted the broad bosom of the Shatemuc and came down with summer gentleness from the upper reaches of the river. And here and there a cloud floated over; and now and then a locust sang his monotone; and another soft breath of the North wind said that it was August; and the grasshoppers down in the dell said yes, it was.

Winnie sat or lay down under the trees, and there Winthrop left her for a while; when he came back it was with flushed face and crisped hair and a basket full of berries. He threw himself down on the ground beside Winnie, threw his hat off on the other side, and gave her the basket. Winnie set it down again, after a word of comment, and her head took its wonted place of rest with a little smothered sigh.

"How do you feel, Winnie?" said her brother, passing his hand gently over her cheek.

"O I feel very well," said Winnie. "But Governor, I wish you could keep all this!—"

"I couldn't live here and in Mannahatta too, Winnie."

"But Governor, you don't mean always to live in Mannahatta, do you?—and nowhere else?"

"My work is there, Winnie."

"Yes, but you can't play there, Governor."

"I don't want to play," he said gently and lightly.

"But why, Governor?"—said Winnie, whom the remark made uneasy, she couldn't tell why;—"why don't you want to play? why shouldn't you?"

"I feel more appetite for work."

"But you didn't use to be so," said Winnie, raising her head to look at him. "You used to like play as well as anybody, Winthrop?"

"Perhaps I do yet, Winnie, if I had a chance."

"But then what do you mean by your having more appetite for work? and not wanting to play?"

"I suppose it means no more but that the chance is wanting."

"But *why* is it wanting, Governor?"

"Why are your Solomon's Seals not in flower?"

Winnie turned her head to look at them, and then brought it round again with the uneasiness in full force.

"But Governor!—you don't mean to say that your life is like that?"

"Like what, Winnie?" said he with a pleasant look at her.

"Why, anything so dismal—like the Solomon's Seals with the flower gone?"

"Are they dismal?"

"Why, no,—but you would be, if you were like anything of that kind."

"Do I look like anything of that kind?"

"No," said Winnie, "indeed you don't,—you never *look* the least bit dismal in the world."

"I am not the least bit in the world, Winnie."

"I wish you had everything in the world that would give you pleasure!" she said, looking at him wistfully, with a vague unselfish consciousness that it might not all be for hers.

"That would be too much for any man's share, Winnie. You would make a Prince in a fairy tale of me."

"Well, what if I would?" said Winnie, half smiling, half sighing, and paying him all sort of leal homage in her heart's core.

"That is not commonly the lot of those who are to reign hereafter in a better kingdom."

Winnie rose up a little so that she could put both hands on his shoulders, and kissed him on forehead and cheeks; most loving kisses.

"But dear Governor, it isn't wrong for me to wish you to have both things, is it?"

"I hope not, dear Winnie. I don't think your wishes will do any mischief. But I am content to be here to-day."

"Are you? do you enjoy it?" she asked eagerly

"Very much."

"I am so glad! I was afraid somehow you didn't—as much as I did. But I am sorry you can't keep it, Governor. Isn't it all beautiful? I didn't know it was so delightful as it is."

And Winnie sighed her wish over again.

"You can't have your possessions in both worlds, Winnie."

"No,—and I don't want to."

"You only wish that I could," he said smiling.

"Well, Winthrop,——I can't help that."

"I am in better hands than yours, Winnie. Look at that shadow creeping down the mountain."

"It's from that little white cloud up there," said Winnie. "O how beautiful!——"

"You see how something that is bright enough in itself may cast a shadow," he said.

"Was that what you thought of when you told me to look at it?"

"No,—not at that minute."

"But then we can see the cloud and we know that it is bright."

"And in the other case we *don't* see the cloud and we know that it is bright. 'We *know* that all things shall work together for good to them that love God, to them who are the called according to his purpose!'"

"But Governor, what are you talking of?"

"That little cloud which is rolling away from Wut-a-qut-o."

"But what cloud is over you, or rolling away from you?"

"I thought the whole land was in shadow to you, Winnie, because I cannot buy it."

"Why no it isn't," said Winnie. "It never looked so bright to me. It never seemed near so beautiful when it was ours."

'The other land never seemed so bright and never will seem

so beautiful, as when it *is* ours. 'Thine eyes shall see the King in his beauty; they shall behold the land that is very far off.'"

Winnie smiled a most rested, pleased, gratified smile at him; and turned to another subject.

"I wonder what's become of your old little boat, Governor—the Merry-go-round?"

"I suppose it is lying in the barn-loft yet," he replied rather gravely.

"I wonder if it is all gone to pieces."

"I should think not. Why?"

"I was looking at the river and thinking how pleasant it would be to go out on it, if we could."

"If we can get home, Winnie, I'll see how the matter stands."

"I don't want to go home," said Winnie.

"But I want to have you. And Karen will want the huckleberries."

"Well—I'll go," said Winnie. "But we'll come again, Governor—won't we?"

"As often as you please. Now shall I carry you?"

"O no!"

But Winthrop presently judged of that also for himself, and taking his little sister on one arm, made his way steadily and swiftly down to the level ground.

"*You're* a good climber," was Winnie's remark when he set her on her feet again. "And I don't know but I was once. I've almost forgotten. But it's as good to have you carry me, and to see you do it."

The Merry-go-round was found in good condition, only with her seams a little, or not a little, opened. That trouble however was got over by the help of a little caulking and submersion and time; and she floated again as lightly as ever. Some days still passed, owing to weather or other causes, before the first evening came when they went out to try her.

That evening,—it was the seventeenth of August, and very fair,—they went down to the rocks, just when the afternoon had grown cool in the edge of the evening. Winnie put herself in the stern of the little white boat, and Winthrop took his old place and the oars. Winnie's eyes were sparkling.

"It will be harder work to pull than it used to be," she remarked joyously,—"you're so out of the habit of it."

Winthrop only replied by pushing the little skiff off.

"However," continued Winnie, "I guess it isn't much to pull *me* anywhere."

"Which way shall we go?" said Winthrop, one or two slow strokes of his oar sending the little boat forward in a way that made Winnie smile.

"I don't know—I want to go everywhere—Let's go up, Winthrop, and see how it looks—Let's go over under Wut-a-qut-o. O how beautiful it is, Winthrop!—"

Winthrop said nothing, but a repetition of those leisurely strokes brought the boat swiftly past the cedars and rocks of Shahweetah's shore and then out to the middle of the river, gradually drawing nearer to the other side. But when the mid-river was gained, high enough up to be clear of the obstructing point of Shahweetah, Winnie's ecstatic cry of delight brought Winthrop's head round; and with that he lay upon his oars and looked too. He might. The mountains and the northern sky and clouds were all floating as it were in a warm flush of light—it was upon the clouds, and through the air, and upon the mountains' sides,—so fair, so clear, but beyond that, so rich in its glowing suffusion of beauty, that eyes and tongue were stayed,—the one from leaving the subject, the other from touching it. Winthrop's oars lay still, the drops falling more and more slowly from the wet blades. The first word was a half awed whisper from Winnie—

"O Winthrop,—did you ever see it look so?"

The oars dipped again, and again lay still.

"O Winthrop, this isn't much like Mannahatta!" Winnie said next, under breath.

The oars dipped again, and this time to purpose. The boat began to move slowly onward.

"But Winthrop you don't say anything?" Winnie said uneasily.

"I don't know how."

"I wish I could keep a picture of that," she went on with regretful accent as her eyes turned again to the wonderful scene before them in the north, floating as it seemed in that living soft glow.

"I shall keep a picture of it," said Winthrop.

Winnie sighed her regrets again, and then resigned herself to looking with her present eyes, while the little boat moved steadily on and the view was constantly changing; till they were close under the shadow of Wut-a-qut-o, and from beneath its high green and grey precipice rising just above them, only the long sunny reach of the eastern shore remained in view. They looked at it, till the sunset began to make a change.

"O Winthrop, there is Bright Spot," said Winnie, as her head came round to the less highly coloured western shore.

"Yes,"—said Winthrop, letting the boat drop a little down from under the mountain.

"How it has grown up!—and what are all those bushes at the water's edge?"

"Alders. Look at those clouds in the south."

There lay, crossing the whole breadth of the river, a spread of close-folded masses of cloud, the under edges of which the sun touched, making a long network of salmon or flame-coloured lines. And then above the near bright-leaved horizon of foliage that rose over Bright Spot, the western sky was brilliantly clear; flecked with little reaches of cloud stretching upwards and coloured with fairy sunlight colours, gold, purple, and rose, in a very witchery of mingling.

Winthrop pushed the boat gently out a little further from the shore, and they sat looking, hardly bearing to take their eyes from the cloud kaleidoscope above them, or to speak, the mind had so much to do at the eyes. Only a glance now and then for contrast of beauty, at the south, and to the north where two or three little masses of grey hung in the clear sky. Gently Winthrop's oars dipped from time to time, bringing them a little further from the western shore and within fuller view of the opening in the mountains. As they went, a purplish shade came upon the grey masses in the north;—the sunlight colours over Bright Spot took richer and deeper hues of purple and red; the salmon network in the south changed for rose. And then, before they had got far, the moon's crescent, two or three days old, a glittering silver thread, hung itself out amid the bright rosy flecks of cloud in the west just hard by the mountain's brow. Winnie had to look sharp to find it.

"And there is Venus too," said Winthrop;—"look at her."

"Where?"

"In the blue—a little lower down than the moon; and further to the south—do you see?—"

"That white bright star?—O how beautiful!—in that clear blue sky. O how bright!—how much brighter than the moon, Winthrop?"

"Yes,—she has a way of looking bright."

"How did you know it was Venus, or how *do* you know?"

"Very much in the same way that I know it is Winnie. I have seen her before. I never saw those clouds before."

"Did you ever see *such* clouds before! And how long they stay, Winthrop. O what a place!"

Slowly the little boat pulled over the river, getting further and further from Bright Spot and its bright bit of sky scenery, which faded and changed very slowly as they sailed away. They neared the high rocky point of Shahweetah, and then instead of turning down the river, kept an easterly course along the low woody shore which stretched back from the point. As they went on, and as the clouds lost their glory, the sky in the west over Wut-a-qut-o's head tinged itself with violet and grew to an opal light, the white flushing up liquidly into rosy violet, which in the northeast quarter of the horizon melted away to a clear grave blue.

"It's more beautiful than the clouds," said Winnie.

"It is a wonderful evening," said Winthrop, as he set his oars more earnestly in the water and the little boat skimmed along.

"But dear Governor, where are you going?"

"Going to land, somewhere."

"To land! But it'll be time to go home, won't it? We're a great way from there."

"We'll take a short cut home," said Winthrop, looking round for a place to execute his purpose.

"How can you?"

"Through the woods. Wouldn't you like it? You've had no exercise to-day."

"O I'd like it. But what will you do with the boat? leave her here?—O in the Ægean sea, Winthrop!"

"That is what I am steering for," said her brother. "But I want to see the after-glow come out first."

The 'Ægean Sea' was a little bay-like cove on the north side of Shahweetah; to which a number of little rock-heads rising out of the water, or some freak of play, had long ago given its classic name. Winthrop pushed his boat to the shore there, and made her fast; and then he and Winnie waited for the after-glow. But it was long coming and the twilight grew on; and at last they left the bay and plunged into the woods. A few steps brought them to a path, which rough and untravelled as it was, their knowledge of the land enabled them easily to follow. Easily for all but their feet. Winnie's would have faltered utterly, so rough, stony, and broken it was, without her brother's strong arm; but helped and led and lifted by him, she went on joyously through the gathering gloom and under the leafy canopy that shut out all the sky and all knowledge of the after-glow, if it came. But when they had got free of the woods, and had come out upon the little open cedar field that was on the river side of Shahweetah, near home,—there it was! Over Wut-a-qut-o's head lay a solid little long mass of cloud with its under edges close-lined with fine deep beautiful red. The opal light was all gone; the face of the heavens was all clear blue, in the gravity of twilight. Venus and the moon were there yet, almost down—bright as ever; the moon more brilliant and bright; for now the contrast of her sharp crescent was with Wut-a-qut-o's dark shadowy side.

That was the beginning of that August boating. And often again as in old times the little skiff flew over the water, in the shadow of the mountain and the sunlight of the bay, coasting the shores, making acquaintance with the evergreens and oaks that skirted them and looked over into the water's edge. Where once Elizabeth had gone, Winthrop and Winnie with swifter and surer progress went; many an hour, in the early and the late sunbeams. For those weeks that they stayed, they lived in the beauties of the land, rather than according to old Karen's wish, on the fatness of it.

But she did her best; and when at last Winthrop must return to his business, and they bid her good bye and left her and Wut-a-qut-o once more, the old woman declared even while she was wiping the eyes that would not be dry, that their coming had "done both of 'em real good—a power of it—and her too."

"He hasn't his beat in *this* country," she said to old Anderese her brother, as she was trying to take up again her wonted walk through the house.—"And she, dear thing! ain't long for this world; but she's ready for a better."

CHAPTER XXXI.

It is not growing like a tree
In bulk, doth make man better be,
Or standing long an oak, three hundred year,
To fall at last a log, dry, bald, and sear.
A lily of a day
Is fairer far, in May

BEN JONSON.

"WHAT has become of the Landholms?" said Mr. Haye's young wife, one evening in the end of December.

"Confound the Landholms!"——was Mr. Haye's answering ejaculation, as he kicked his bootjack out of the way of his just-slippered foot.

"Why Mr. Haye!" said Rose, bridling over her netting-work. "What have the Landholms done?"

"Done!"

"Well, what have they?"

"One of them won't pay me his dues, and the other is fighting me for trying to get them," said Mr. Haye, looking at the evening paper with infinite disgust.

"What dues?"

and "What fighting, Mr. Haye?" said Elizabeth and Rose in a breath.

"I can't answer you if you both speak at once."

"Well what do you mean by fighting, Mr. Haye?"

"Fighting."

"Well, but what sort?" said Rose laughing, while the other lady laid down her book and waited.

"With his own cursed weapons."

"And what are those, Mr. Haye? you haven't told us which of the Landholms you mean, yet."

"One of 'em hasn't any weapons but his fists and his tongue," said Mr. Haye. "He hasn't tried the first on me——I have some small knowledge of the last."

"What has the other done?" said Elizabeth.

"He is doing what he can, to hinder my getting my rights of his brother."

"What does his brother owe you?"

"Money,——" said Mr. Haye shortly.

"I suppose so. But what for?"

"Business! What does it signify what for?"

"I should like to know, father. It must be something which can be told."

"He bought cotton of me."

"Can he pay for it?"

"I suppose so. I'll try."

"But what is his brother doing?"

"Trying to hinder, as I told you."

"But how? How can he?"

"Don't ask me what lawyers can or can't do. They can put their fingers into any dirty job that offers!"

Elizabeth sat silent a minute with a very disturbed look. Rose had gone back to her netting, only glancing up once in a while at the faces of the other two.

"Upon what plea does he pretend to hinder it, father?"

"A plea he won't be able to bear out, I fancy," said Mr. Haye, turning round in his chair so as to bring his other side to the fire, and not ceasing to look at the paper all this while.

"But what?"

"What does it signify *what!* Something you can't understand."

"I can understand it, father; and I want to know."

"A plea of *fraud*, on my part, in selling the cotton. I suppose you would like to cultivate his acquaintance after that."

Elizabeth sat back in her seat with a little start, and did not speak again during the conversation. Rose looked up from her mesh-stick and poured out a flood of indignant and somewhat incoherent words; to which Mr. Haye responded briefly, as a man who was not fond of the subject, and finally put an end to them by taking the paper and walking off. Elizabeth changed her position then for a low seat, and resting her chin on her hand sat looking into the fire with eyes in which there burned a dark glow that rivalled it.

"Lizzie," said her companion, "did you ever *hear* of such a thing!"

"Not 'such a thing,'" she answered.

"Aren't you as provoked as you can be?"

"'Provoked' is not exactly the word," Elizabeth replied.

"Well you know what to think of Winthrop Landholm now, don't you?"

"Yes."

"Aren't you surprised?"

"I wish I could never be surprised again," she answered, laying her head down for an instant on her lap; but then giving it the position it held before.

"You take it coolly!" said Rose, jerking away at her netting.

"Do I? *You* don't."

"No, and I shouldn't think you would. Don't you *hate* those Landholms?"

"No."

"Don't you! You ought. What *are* you looking at in the fire?"

"Winthrop Landholm,—just at that minute."

"I do believe," said Rose indignantly, "you like Winthrop Landholm better than you do Mr. Haye!"

Elizabeth's eyes glared at her, but though there seemed a moment's readiness to speak, she did not speak, but presently rose up and quitted the room. She went to her own; locked the door, and sat down. There was a moment's quiver of the lip and drawing of the brow, while the eyes in their fire seemed to throw off sparks from the volcano below; and then the head bent, with a cry of pain, and the flood of sorrow broke; so bitter, that she sometimes pressed both hands to her head, as if it were in danger of parting in two. The proud forehead was stooped to the knees, and the shoulders convulsed in her agony. And it lasted long. Half hour and half hour passed before the struggle was over and Elizabeth had quieted herself enough to go to bed. When at last she rose to begin the business of undressing, she startled not a little to see her handmaid Clam present herself.

"When did you come in?" said Elizabeth after a moment's hesitation.

"When the door opened," said Clam collectedly.

"How long ago?"

"How long have you been here, do you s'pose, Miss 'Lizabeth?"

"That's not an answer to my question."

"Not ezackly," said Clam; "but if you'd tell, I could give a better guess."

Elizabeth kept a vexed silence for a little while.

"Well Clam," she said when she had made up her mind, "I have just one word to say to you—keep your tongue between your teeth about all *my* concerns. You are quite wise enough, and I hope, good enough for that."

"I ain't so bad I mightn't be better," said Clam picking up her mistress's scattered things. "Mr. Winthrop didn't give up all hopes of me. I 'spect he'll bring us all right some of these days."

With which sentence, delivered in a most oracular and encouraging tone, Clam departed; for Elizabeth made no answer thereto.

The next morning, after having securely locked herself into her room for an hour or more, Elizabeth summoned her handmaid.

"I want you to put on your bonnet, Clam, and take this note for me up to Mr. Landholm's; and give it with your own hand to him or to his sister."

Clam rather looked her intelligence than gave any other sign of it.

"If he's out, shall I wait till I see him?"

"No,—give it to his sister."

"I may put on more than my bonnet, mayn't I, Miss 'Lizabeth? *This* won't keep me warm, with the snow on the ground."

But Elizabeth did not choose to hear; and Clam went off with the note.

Much against her expectations, she found Mr. Winthrop at home and in his room, and his sister not there.

"Mornin', Mr. Winthrop!" said Clam, with more of a courtesy than she ever vouchsafed to her mistress or to any one else whomsoever. He came forward and shook her hand very kindly and made her sit down by the fire. The black girl's eyes followed him, as if, though she didn't say it, it was good to see him again.

"What's the word with you, Clam?"

"'Tain't with me—the word's with you, Mr. Winthrop."

"What is it?"

"I don' know, sir. I've nothin' to do but to bring it."

"How do you do this cold day?"

"*I* ain't cold," said Clam. "I bethought me to put my cloak on my shoulders. Miss 'Lizabeth wanted me to come off with only my bonnet."

And she produced the note, which Winthrop looked at and laid on the table.

"How is Miss Elizabeth?"

"She's sort o'," said Clam. "She has her ups and downs like other folks. She was down last night and she's up this mornin' —part way."

"I hope she is pleased with you, Clam."

"She ain't pleased with anything, much," said Clam; "so it can't be expected. I believe she's pleased with me as much as with anything else in our house. Last night she was cryin' as if her head would split—by the hour long."

"That is not part of your word to me, is it?"

"Not just," said Clam. "Mr. Winthrop, will you have me come back for an answer?"

"Did Miss Elizabeth desire it?"

"I guess so," said Clam. "But she didn't tell me to come but once."

"Then don't come again."

Clam rose to go and settled her cloak as she moved towards the door.

"If she sends me I may come again, mayn't I, Mr. Winthrop?" she said pausing.

"Yes," he said with a smile; but it was a very little bit of one.

"How is Winifred?" said Clam.

"She is not well."

The smile had entirely passed away; his face was more grave than ever.

"Is she more than common unwell?"

"Yes. Very much."

"Can I go in and see her, Mr. Winthrop?"

"Yes, if you please."

Clam went; and Winthrop took up Elizabeth's note.

"No 11 Parade, Dec. 20, 1821.

"I have just heard, briefly and vaguely, of the difficulties be tween my father and your brother, and of the remedies you, Mr. Landholm, ar employing. I do not know the truth nor the details of anything beyond the bare outlines. Those are enough, and more than I know how to bear. I don't wish to have anything explained to me. But Mr. Landholm, grant me one favour—you *must* grant it, if you please—do not let it be explained any further to anybody. All you want, I suppose, is to see your brother righted. I will pay the utmost of what is due to him. I do not understand how the business lies—but I will furnish all the money that is wanting to set it right and put an end to these proceedings, if you will only let me know what it is. Please let me know it, and let me do this, Mr. Landholm; it is *my right;* and I need not ask you, keep my knowledge of it secret from everybody. I am sure you must see that what I ask is my right.

"ELIZABETH HAYE."

Winthrop had hardly more than time to read this when Clam put herself within his door again, shutting it at her back.

"If the Governor 'll let me," she said, "I'll come and take care of her;—or I'll run up and down stairs, from the bottom to the top,—whichever's useful."

"It is very kind of you, Clam. Winnie and I thank you very much. But your mistress will want you."

"She won't. She'll want me here. Let me come, Governor. I shan't do nothin' for Miss 'Lizabeth if I stay with her."

"Go and do all she wants you to do. No, I can't let you come. My sister is taken care of."

"She'd be that where you are," muttered Clam as she went out and went down the stairs,—"and so would anybody else. I wish some of the rest of us had a chance. Well—maybe we'll get it yet!—"

She found Elizabeth at her desk where she had left her, waiting.

"Did you find him?"

"Yes, miss."

"And you gave him the note?"

'No, miss—I mean, yes, miss."

"Don't say 'miss' in tnat kind of way. Put a name to it."

"What name?" said Clam.

"Any one you like. Did you see anybody else?"

"I see the brother and the sister," said Clam. "The brother was never lookin' better, and the sister was never lookin' worse;—she ain't lookin' bad, neither."

"Is she ill?"

"She's lyin' abed, and so far from bein' well that she'll never be well again."

"She hasn't been well this great while, Clam; *that's* nothing new."

"*This* is," said Clam.

"Does her brother think she is very ill?"

"He knows more about it than I do," said Clam. "I said I would go to take care of her, and he said I wouldn't, for you'd be a wantin' me."

"I don't want you at all!" said Elizabeth,—"if you could be of any use. Are you quiet and careful enough for a nurse?"

"Firstrate!"—said Clam;—"no, I guess I'm not ezackly, here; but I were, up to Wutsey-Qutsey."

"Up where?" said Elizabeth.

"Yes, miss."

"I told you not to speak to me so."

Clam stood and gave no sign.

"Do you think you could be of any use up there, Clam?"

"Mr. Winthrop says everybody can be of use."

"Then go and try; I don't want you; and stay as long as they would like to have you."

"When will I go, Mis' Landholm?"

"What?"

"I asked Mis' Landholm, when will I go."

"What do you mean, Clam!"

"You said call you any name I liked—and I like that 'bout as well as any one," said Clam sturdily.

"But it isn't my name."

"I wish 'twas," said Clam;—"no, I don' know as I do, neither; but it comes kind o' handy."

"Make some other serve your turn," said Elizabeth gravely. "Go up this afternoon, and say I don't want you and shall be most happy if you can be of any service to Miss Winifred."

"Or Mr. Winthrop—" said Clam. "I'll do all I can for both of 'em, Miss 'Lizabeth."

She was not permitted to do much. She went and stayed a night and a day, and served well; but Winifred did not like her company, and at last confessed to Winthrop that she could not bear to have her about. It was of no use to reason the matter; and Clam was sent home. The answer to Elizabeth's note came just before her handmaiden, by some other conveyance.

"Little South St. Dec. 21, 1821.

"Your note, Miss Haye, has put me in some difficulty, but after a good deal of consideration I have made up my mind to allow the 'right' you claim. It is your right, and I have no right to deprive you of it. Yet the difficulty reaches further still; for without details, which you waive, the result which you wish to know must stand upon my word alone. I dislike exceedingly it should so stand; but I am constrained here also to admit, that if you choose to trust me rather than have the trouble of the accounts, it is just that you should have your choice.

"My brother's owing to Mr. Haye, for which he is held responsible, is in the sum of eleven hundred and forty-one dollars.

"I have the honour to be, with great respect,

"WINTHROP LANDHOLM."

Elizabeth read and re-read.

"It is very polite—it is very hanasome—nothing could be clearer from any shadow of implications or insinuations—no, nor of anything but 'great respect' either," she said to herself. "It's very good of him to trust and understand me and give me just what I want, without any palaver. *That* isn't like common people, any more. Well, my note wasn't, either. But he hasn't said a word but *just* what was necessary.—Well, why should he?——"

She looked up and saw Clam.

"What's brought you back again?"

"I don' know," said Clam. "My two feet ha' brought me, but I don' know what sent me."

"Why did you come then?"

"'Cause I had to," said Clam. "Nothin' else wouldn't ha' made me. I told you it was good livin' with him. I'd stay as long as I got a chance, if I was anybody!"

"Then what made you come home?"

"I don' know," said Clam. "He wouldn't let me stay. He don't stop to make everything clear; he thinks it's good enough for him to say so; and so it is, I suppose; and he told me to come."

"I am afraid you didn't do your duty well."

"I'd like to see who wouldn't," said Clam. "I did mine as well as he did his'n."

"How is Winifred?"

"She's pretty bad. I guess he don't think he'll have much more of her, and he means to have all he can these last days. And she thinks she's almost in Paradise when he's alongside of her."

Elizabeth laid her face down and asked no more questions.

But she concerned herself greatly to know how much and what she might do in the premises, to shew her kind feeling and remembrance, without doing too much. She sent Clam once with jellies; then she would not do that again. Should she go to see Winifred herself? Inclination said yes; and backed its consent with sundry arguments. It was polite and kind; and everybody likes kindness; she had known Winifred, and her brother, long ago, and had received kindness in the family, yes, even just now from Winthrop himself; and though his visiting had so long been at an end, this late intercourse of notes and business gave her an opening. And probably Winifred had very few friends in the city to look after her. And again inclination said 'Go.' But then came in another feeling that said 'Go not. You have *not* opening enough. Mr. Landholm's long and utter cessation of visits, from whatever cause, says plainly enough that he does not desire the pleasure of your society; don't do anything that even looks like forcing it upon him. People will give it a name that will not please you.' 'But then,' said inclination on the other hand, 'my going *could* not have that air, to him, for he knows and I know that in the existing state of affairs it is perfectly impossible that he should ever enter the doors of my father's house—let me do what I will.' 'People don't know as much,' said the other feeling; 'err on the safe side if at all, and stay at home.' 'And I don't care much for people,'—said Elizabeth.

It was so uncommon a thing for her to find any self-imposed check upon what she wished to do, that Miss Haye was very much puzzled; and tried and annoyed out of all proportion by her self-consultations. She was in a fidget of uneasiness all day long; and the next was no better.

"What *is* the matter, Lizzie?" said Rose, as she busily threaded her netting-needle through mesh after mesh, and Elizabeth was patiently or impatiently measuring the length of the parlour with her steps. "You look as if you had lost all your friends."

"Do I?"

"Yes. Why do you look so?"

"What is the difference between losing all one's friends, and having none to lose?"

"Why——haven't you any?"

"Whom have I?"

"Well, you might have. I am sure *I* have a great many."

"Friends!" said Elizabeth.

"Well—I don't know who you call friends," said Rose, breaking her silk with an impatient tug at a knot,——"There!—dear! how *shall* I tie it again?——I should think you needn't look so glum."

"Why shouldn't I?"

"Why—because. You have everything in the world."

"Have I?" said Elizabeth bitterly. "I am alone as I can be."

"Alone!" said Rose.

"Yes. I am alone. My father is buried in his business; I have nothing of him, even what I might have, or used to have—— *you* never were anything to me. There is not a face in the world that my heart jumps to see."

"Except that one?" said Rose.

"'That one,' as you elegantly express it, I do not see, as it happens."

"It's a pity he didn't know what effect his coming and looking in at our windows might have," said Rose. "I am sure he would be good enough to do it."

But Elizabeth thought a retort unworthy of the subject; or else her mind was full of other things; for after a dignified silence of a few minutes she left Rose and went to her own quarters. Perhaps the slight antagonistic spirit which was raised by Rose's talk came in aid of her wavering inclinations, or brought back her mind to its old tone of wilfulness; for she decided at once that she would go and see Winifred. She had a further reason for going, she said to herself, in the matter of the money which she wished to convey to Winthrop's hands. She did not want to send Clam with it; she did not like to commit it to the post; there was no other way but to give it to him herself; and that, she said, she would do; or to Winifred's hands for him.

She left home accordingly, when the morning was about half gone, and set out for Little South Street; with a quick but less firm step than usual, speaking both doubt and decision. Decision enough to carry her soon and without stopping to her place of destination, and doubt enough to make her tremble when she got there. But without pausing she went in, mounted the stairs, with the same quick footstep, and tapped at the door, as she had been accustomed to do on her former visits to Winifred.

No gentle voice said 'come in,' however, and the step which Elizabeth heard withinside after her knock, was not Winifred's. She had not expected that it would be; she had no reason to suppose that Winifred was well enough to be moving about as usual, and she was not surprised to see Winthrop open the door. The shadow of a surprise crossed his face for an instant,——then bowing, he stepped back and opened the door wide for her to enter; but there was not the shadow of a smile.

"Well, you *do* look wonderfully grave!" was Elizabeth's thought as her foot crossed the threshold,——"I wonder if I am doing something dreadful——"

And the instant impulse was to account for her being there,

by presenting her business—not the business she had intended to mention first.

She came in and stood by the table and began to speak; then he placed a chair for her, and after a second of hesitation she sat down. She was embarrassed for a minute, then she looked up and looked him full in the face.

"Mr. Landholm, I am exceedingly obliged to you for your kindness in this late business,——you were very good to me."

"It was not kindness——I felt you had a right to ask what I could not refuse, Miss Elizabeth."

"I have come to bring you the money which I did not like to get to you by any other means."

She handed it to him, and he took it and counted it over. Elizabeth sat looking on, musing how tremulous her own hand had been, and how very cool and firm his was; and thinking that whatever were said by some people, there certainly was character in some hands.

"This will be handed to Mr. Haye," he said, as he finished the counting,——"and all the proceedings will fall to the ground at once."

"Thank you."

"I cannot receive any thanks, Miss Elizabeth. I am merely an agent, doing what I have been obliged to conclude was my duty."

"I must thank you, though," said Elizabeth. "I feel so much relieved. You are not obliged to disclose my name to Mr. Rufus Landholm?"

"Not at all. To no one."

"That is all my excuse for being here," said Elizabeth with a slight hesitation,—"except I thought I might take the privilege of old friendship to come and see your sister."

"Thank you," he said in his turn, but without raising his eyes. Yet it was not coldly spoken. Elizabeth did not know what to think of him.

"Can I see her, Mr. Landholm? Is she well enough to see me?"

He looked up then; and there was, hardly a smile, but a singular light upon his whole face, that made Elizabeth feel exceedingly grave.

"She is well, but she will not see you again, Miss Elizabeth. Winnie has left me."

"Left!——" said Elizabeth bewildered.

"Yes. She has gone to her home. Winnie died yesterday morning, Miss Haye."

Elizabeth met the clear intent eye which, she did not know why, fixed hers while he spoke; and then dropping her own, trembled greatly with constrained feeling. She could not tell in the least how to answer, either words or look; but it would have been impossible for her to stir an inch from the spot where she stood.

"Does it seem terrible to you?" he said. "It need not. Will you see her?"

Elizabeth wished very strongly not; but as she hesitated how to speak, he had gently taken her hand and was leading her forward out of the room; and Elizabeth could not draw away her hand nor hinder the action of his; she let him lead her whither he would.

"Are you afraid?" he said, as he paused with his hand upon the door of the other room. Elizabeth uttered an incomprehensible 'no,' and they went in.

"There is no need," he said again in a gentle grave tone as he led her to the side of the bed and then let go her hand. Elizabeth stood where he had placed her, like a person under a spell.

'There was no need' indeed, she confessed to herself, half unconsciously, for all her thoughts were in a terrible whirl. Winnie's face looked as though it might have been the prison of a released angel. Nothing but its sweetness and purity was left, of all that disease and weariness had ever wrought there; the very fair and delicate skin and the clustering sunny locks seemed like angel trappings left behind. Innocence and rest were the two prevailing expressions of the face,—entire, both seemed. Elizabeth stood looking, at first awe-stricken; but presently thoughts and feelings, many and different ones, began to rise and crowd upon one another with struggling force. She stood still and motionless, all the more.

"There is no pain in looking there?" said her companion softly. Elizabeth's lips formed the same unintelligible 'no,' which her voice failed to bring out.

"Little sleeper!" said Winthrop, combing back with his fingers the golden curls, which returned instantly to their former position,—" she has done her work. She has begun upon her rest. I have reason to thank God that ever she lived.—I shall see the day when I can quietly thank him that she has died."

Elizabeth trembled, and in her heart prayed Winthrop not to say another word.

"Does not this face look, Miss Haye, as if its once owner had 'entered into peace?'"

If worlds had depended on Elizabeth's answering, she could not have spoken. She could not look at the eye which, she knew, as this question was put, sought hers; her own rested only on the hand that was moving back those golden locks, and on the white brow it touched; she dared not stir. The contact of those two, and the signification of them, was as much as she could bear, without any help. She knew his eye was upon her.

"Isn't it worth while," he said, "to have such a sure foothold in that other world, that the signal for removing thither shall be a signal of *peace?*"

Elizabeth bowed her head low in answer.

"Have you it?" was his next question. He had left the bed's side and stood by hers.

Elizabeth wrung her hands and threw them apart with almost a cry,—"Oh I would give uncounted worlds if I had!—"

And the channel being once opened, the seal of silence and reserve taken off, her passion of feeling burst forth into wild weeping that shook her from head to foot. Involuntarily she took hold of the bedpost to stay herself, and clung to it, bending her head there like a broken reed.

She felt even at the time, and remembered better afterwards, how gently and kindly she was drawn away from there and taken back into the other room and made to sit down. She could do nothing at the moment but yield to the tempest of feeling, in which it seemed as if every wind of heaven shook her by turns. When at last it had passed over, the violence of it, and she took command of herself again, it was even then with a very sobered and sad mind. As if, she thought afterwards, as if that storm had been, like some storms in the natural world, the forerunner and usher of a permanent change of weather. She looked up at Winthrop, when she was quieted and he brought her a glass of water, not like the person that had looked at him when she first came in. He waited till she had drunk the water and was to appearance quite mistress of herself again.

"You must not go yet," he said, as she was making some movement towards it;—"you are cold. You must wait till you are warmed."

He mended the fire and placed a chair for her, and handed her to it. Elizabeth did as she was bade, like a child; and sat there before the fire a little while, unable to keep quiet tears from coming and coming again.

"I don't know what you must think of me, Mr. Winthrop," she said at last, when she was about ready to go. "I could not help myself.—I have never seen death before."

"You must see it again, Miss Elizabeth;—you must meet it face to face."

She looked up at him as he said it, with eager eyes, from which tears ran yet, and that were very expressive in the intensity of their gaze. His were not less intent, but as gentle and calm as hers were troubled.

"Are you ready?" he added.

She shook her head, still looking at him, and her lips formed that voiceless 'no.' She never forgot the face with which he turned away,—the face of grave gentleness, of sweet gravity,—all the volume of reproof, of counsel, of truth, that was in that look. But it was truth that, as it was known to him, he seemed to assume to be known to her; he did not open his lips.

Elizabeth rose; she must go; she would have given a world to have him say something more. But he stood and saw her put on her gloves and arrange her cloak for going out, and he said nothing. Elizabeth longed to ask him the question, "What must I do?"—she longed and almost lingered to ask it;—but something, she did not know what, stopped her and choked her, and she did not ask it. He saw her down to the street, in silence on both sides, and they parted there, with a single grasp of the hand. *That* said something again; and Elizabeth cried all the way home, and was well nigh sick by the time she got there.

CHAPTER XXXII.

How now?
Even so quickly may one catch the plague?
TWELFTH NIGHT.

MISS HAYE came down to breakfast the next morning; but after little more than a nominal presentation of herself there, she escaped from Rose's looks and words of comment and inuendo and regained her own room. And there she sat down in the window to muse, having carefully locked out Clam. She had reason. Clam would certainly have decided that her mistress 'wanted fixing,' if she could have watched the glowing intent eyes with which Elizabeth was going deep into some subject—it might be herself, or some other. Herself it was.

"Well,"—she thought, very unconscious how clearly one of the houses on the opposite side of the street was defined on the retina of either eye,—"I have learned two things by my precious yesterday's expedition, that I didn't know before—or that if I did, it was in a sort of latent, unrecognized way;—two pretty important things!—That I wish I was a Christian,—yes, I do,—and that there is a person in the world who don't care a pin for me, whom I would lay down my life for!—How people would laugh at me if they knew it—and just because themselves they are not capable of it, and cannot understand it.—Why shouldn't I like what is worthy to be liked?—why shouldn't I *love* it? It is to my honour that I do!—Because he don't like *me*, people would say;—and why should he like me? or what difference does it make? It is not a fine face or a fair manner that has taken me—if it were, I should be only a fool like a great many others;—it is those things which will be as beautiful in heaven as they are here—the beauty of goodness—of truth—and fine character.—Why should I not love it when I see it? I shall not see it often in my life-time. And what has his liking of me to do with it? How *should* he like me! The very reasons for which I look at him would hinder his ever looking at me—and ought. I am not good,—not good enough for him to look at me; there are good things in me, but all run wild, or other things running wild over them. I am not worthy to be spoken of in the day that his name is mentioned. I wish I was good!—I wish I was a Christian!—but I know one half of that wish is because he is a Christian.—That's the sort of power that human beings have over each other! The beauty of religion, in him, has drawn me more, unspeakably, than all the sermons I ever heard in my life. What a beautiful thing such a Christian is!—what living preaching!—and without a word said. Without a word said,—it is in the eye, the brow, the lips,—the very carriage has the dignity of one who isn't a piece of this world. Why aren't there more such!—and this is the only one that ever I knew!—of all I have seen that called themselves Christians.—Would any possible combination ever make *me* such a person?—Never!—never. I shall be a rough piece of Christianity if ever I am one at all. But I don't even know what it is to be one. Oh, why couldn't he say three words more yesterday! But he acted—and looked—as if I could do without them. What did he mean!——"

When she had got to this point, Elizabeth left her seat by the window and crossed the room to a large wardrobe closet, on a high shelf of which sundry unused articles of lumber had found a hiding-place. And having fetched a chair in, she mounted upon the top of it and rummaged, till there came to her hand a certain old bible which had belonged once to her mother or her grandmother. Elizabeth hardly knew which, but had kept a vague recollection of the book's being in existence and of its having been thrust away up on that shelf. She brought it down and dusted off the tokens of many a month's forgetfulness and dishonour; and with an odd sense of the hands to which it had once been familiar and precious, and of the distant influence under the power of which it was now in her own hands, she laid it on the bed, and half curiously, half fearfully, opened it. The book had once been in hands that loved it, for it was ready of itself to lie open at several places. Elizabeth turned the leaves aimlessly, and finally left it spread at one of these open places; and with both elbows resting on the bed and both hands supporting her head, looked to see what she was to find there. It chanced to be the beginning of the 119th psalm.

"BLESSED ARE THE UNDEFILED IN THE WAY, WHO WALK IN THE LAW OF THE LORD."

By what thread of association was it, that the water rushed to her eyes when they read this, and for some minutes hindered her seeing another word, except through a veil of tears.

"Am I becoming a Christian?" she said to herself. "But something more must be wanting than merely to be sorry that I am not what he is. How every upright look and word bear witness that this description belongs to him. And I——I am out of 'the way' altogether."

"BLESSED ARE THEY THAT KEEP HIS TESTIMONIES, AND THAT SEEK HIM WITH THE WHOLE HEART."

"'Keep his testimonies,'" said Elizabeth,—"and 'seek him with the whole heart.'—I never did, or began to do, the one or the other. '*With the whole heart*'—and I never gave one bit of my heart to it—and how is he to be *sought?*——"

"THEY ALSO DO NO INIQUITY; THEY WALK IN HIS WAYS."

The water stood in Elizabeth's eyes again.

"How far from me!—how very far I am from it! 'Do no iniquity,'—and I suppose I am always doing it—'They walk in his ways,' and I don't even so much as know what they are.—I wish Mr. Winthrop had said a little more yesterday!"—

She pondered this verse a little, feeling if she did not recognize its high and purified atmosphere; but at the next she sprang up and went back to her window.

"THOU HAST COMMANDED US TO KEEP THY PRECEPTS DILIGENTLY."

Elizabeth and the Bible were at issue.

She could heartily wish that her character were that fair and sweet one the first three verses had lined out; but the *command* met a denial; or at the least a putting off of its claim. She acknowledged all that went before, even in its application to herself; but she was not willing, or certainly she was not ready, to take the pains and bear the restraint that should make her and it at one. She did not put the case so fairly before herself. She kept that fourth verse at arm's length, as it were, conscious that it held something she could not get over; unconscious what was the precise why. She rushed back to her conclusion that the Bible teaching was unsatisfactory, and that she wanted other; and so travelling round in a circle she came to the point from which she had begun. With a more saddened and sorrowful feeling, she stood looking at Winthrop's character and at her own; more certified, if that had been wanting, that she herself was astray; and well she resolved that if ever she got another chance she would ask him to tell her more about her duty, and how she should manage to do it.

But how was she to get another chance? Winthrop never came, nor could come, to Mr. Haye's; all that was at an end; she never could go again to his rooms. That singular visit of yesterday had once happened, but could never happen again by any possibility. She knew it; she must wait. And weeks went on, and still her two wishes lived in her heart; and still she waited. There was nobody else of whom she chose to ask her questions; either from want of knowledge, or from want of trust, or from want of attraction. And there were few indeed that came to the house whom she could suppose capable of answering them.

One evening it happened that Mr. Satterthwaite came in. He often did that; he had never lost the habit of finding it a pleasant place. This time he threw himself down at the tea-table, in tired fashion, just as the lady of the house asked him for the news.

"No news, Mrs. Haye—sorry I haven't any. Been all day attending court, till I presume I'm not fit for general society. I hope a cup of tea 'll do something for me."

"What's taken you into court?" said Rose, as she gave the asked-for tea.

"A large dish of my own affairs,—that is to say, my uncle's and father's and grandfather's—which is in precious confusion."

"I hope, getting on well?" said Rose sweetly.

"Don't know," said Mr. Satterthwaite contentedly. "Don't know till we get out of the confusion. But I have the satisfaction of knowing it's getting on as well as it *can* get on,—from the hands it is in."

"Whose hands are they?" Elizabeth asked.

"In Mr. Landholm's.—He'll set it right, if anybody can. I know he will. Never saw such a fellow. Mrs. Haye—thank you—this bread and butter is all sufficient. Uncommon to have a friend for one's lawyer, and to know he is both a friend *and* a lawyer."

"Rather uncommon," said Elizabeth.

"Is Winthrop Landholm your friend?" said Rose dryly.

"Yes! The best friend I've got. I'd do anything in the world for that fellow. He deserves it."

"Mr. Satterthwaite," said Elizabeth, "that bread and butter isn't so good as these biscuits—try one."

"He don't deserve it from everybody!" said Rose, as Mr. Satterthwaite gratefully took a biscuit.

"Why not?"

"He don't deserve it from *me*. I've known him to do unhandsome things. Mean!"

"Winthrop Landholm!—My dear Mrs. Haye, you are under some misapprehension. I'll stake my reputation he *never* did an unhandsome or a mean thing. He *couldn't*."

"He did," said Rose.

"Will you favour me with the particulars you have heard?"

"I haven't *heard*," said Rose,—"I *know*."

"You *have* heard!" said Elizabeth sternly,—"and only heard. You forget. You may not have understood anything right."

The gentleman looked in a little astonishment from the bright-coloured cheeks of one lady to the cloudy brow of the other; but as neither added anything further, he took up the matter.

"I am almost certain Miss Elizabeth is right. I am sure Mr. Landholm would not do what you suspect him of. He *could* not do it."

"He is mortal, I suppose," said Rose sourly, "and so he *could* do what other mortals do."

"He is better than some other mortals," said Mr. Satterthwaite. "I am not a religious man myself; but if anything would make me believe in it, it would be that man."

"Don't you 'believe in it,' Mr. Satterthwaite?" asked Elizabeth.

"In a sort of way, yes, I do;—I suppose it's a thing one must come to at last."

"If you want to come to it at last, I should think you would at first," said Elizabeth. "*I* would. I shouldn't think it was a very safe way to put it off."

Mr. Satterthwaite mused over his tea and made no answer; clearly the conversation had got upon the wrong tack.

"Are you going to be in court to-morrow again, Mr. Satterthwaite?" asked the lady of the house.

"I don't know—not for my own affairs—I don't know but I shall go in to hear Winthrop's cause come on against Mr. Ryle."

"I never was in court in my life," said Elizabeth.

"Suppose you go, Miss Elizabeth—If you'll allow me to have the honour of taking care of you, I shall be very happy. There'll be something to hear, between Chancellor Justice and my friend Winthrop and Mr. Brick."

"Is Mr. Brick going to speak to-morrow?" said Rose.

"Yes—he is on the other side."

"Let's go, Lizzie," said her cousin. "Will you take me too, Mr. Brick?—Mr. Satterthwaite, I mean."

Mr. Satterthwaite declared himself honoured, prospectively; Elizabeth put no objection of her own in the way; and the scheme was agreed on.

The morrow came, and at the proper hour the trio repaired to the City Hall and mounted its high white steps.

"Don't you feel afraid, Lizzie, to be coming here?" said her cousin. "I do."

"Afraid of what, Mrs. Haye?" inquired their attendant.

"O I don't know,—it looks so;—it makes me think of prisoners and judges and all such awful things!"

Mr. Satterthwaite laughed, and stole a glance beyond Mrs. Haye to see what the other lady was thinking of. But Elizabeth said nothing and looked nothing; she marched on like an automaton beside her two companions, through the great halls, one after another, till the room was reached and they had secured their seats. Then certainly no one who had looked at her face would have taken it for an automaton. Though she was as still as a piece of machine-work, except the face. Rose was in a fidget of business, and the tip of her bonnet's white feather executed all manner of arcs and curves in the air, within imminent distance of Mr. Satterthwaite's face.

"Who's who?—and where's anybody, Mr. Satterthwaite," she inquired.

"That's the Chancellor, sitting up there at the end, do you see?—Sitting alone, and leaning back in his chair."

"*That?*" said Rose. "I see. Is that Chancellor Justice? A fine-looking man, very, isn't he?"

"Well—I suppose he is," said Mr. Satterthwaite. "He's a *strong* man."

"Strong?" said Rose;—"is he? Lizzie!—isn't Chancellor Justice a fine-looking man?"

"Fine-looking?"—said Elizabeth, bringing her eyes in the Chancellor's direction. "No, I should think not."

"Is there *anybody* that is fine-looking here?" whispered Rose in Elizabeth's bonnet.

"Our tastes are so different, it is impossible for one to tell what will please the other," replied Elizabeth coolly.

"Where's Mr. Landholm, Mr. Satterthwaite?"

"Winthrop?—He is down there—don't you see him?"

"'Down there?'" said Rose,—"There are a great many people down there——"

"There's Mr. Herder shaking hands with him now—"

"Mr. Herder?—Lizzie, do you see them?"

"Who?"

"Winthrop Landholm and Mr. Herder."

"Yes."

"Where are they?"

"Hush—"

For just then proceedings began, and Rose's tongue for a few minutes gave way in favour of her ears. And by the time she had found out that she could not make anything of what was going on, Mr. Herder had found his way to their side.

"Miss Élisabet'!" he said,—"and Mistress Haye! what has made you to come here to-day?"

"Mr. Satterthwaite wanted us to hear your favourite Mr. Landholm," said Rose,—"so I came. Lizzie didn't come for that."

Elizabeth shook hands with her friend smilingly, but said never a word as to why she was there.

"Winthrop is good to hear," said Mr. Herder, "when you can understand him. He knows how to speak. I can understand *him*—but I cannot understand Mr. Brick—I cannot make nozing of him when he speaks."

"What are they doing to-day, Mr. Herder?" said Elizabeth.

"It is the cause of my brother-in-law, Jean Lansing, against Mr. Ryle,—he thinks that Mr. Ryle has got some of his money, and I think so too, and so Winthrop thinks; but nobody *knows*, except Mr. Ryle—he knows all of it. Winthrop has been asking some questions about it, to Mr. Ryle and Mr. Brick"—

"When?"

"O a little while ago—a few weeks;—and they say no,—they do not choose to make answer to his questions. Now Winthrop is going to see if the Chancellor will not make that they must tell what he wants to know; and Mr. Brick will fight so hard as he can not to tell. But Winthrop will get what he wants."

"How do you know, Mr. Herder?"

"He does, always."

"What does he want, Mr. Herder?" said Rose.

"It is my brother-in-law's business," said the naturalist. "He wants to know if Mr. Ryle have not got a good deal of his money someveres; and Mr. Ryle, he does not want to say nozing about it; and Winthrop and Mr. Brick, they fight; and the

Chancellor he says, 'Mr. Landholm, you have the right; Mr Brick, you do what he tell you.'"

"Then why isn't the cause ended?" said Elizabeth.

"Because we have not found out all yet; we are pushing them, Mr. Ryle and Mr. Brick, leetle by leetle, into the corner; and when we get 'em into the corner, then they will have to pay us to get out."

"You seem very sure about it, Mr. Herder," said Rose.

"I do not know," said the naturalist. "I am not much afraid. My friend Winthrop—he knows what he is doing."

And to that gentleman the party presently gave their attention; as also did the sturdy strong face of Mr. Justice the Chancellor, and the extremely different physiognomy of Mr. Dustus Brick.

Winthrop and Mr. Brick spoke alternately; and as this was the case on each point, or question,—as Mr. Herder called them,—and as one at least of the speakers was particularly clear and happy in setting forth his meaning, the listeners were kept from weariness and rewarded, those of them that had minds for it, with some intellectual pleasure. It was pretty much on this occasion as Mr. Herder had given the general course of the suit to be; after every opening of a matter on Winthrop's part, the Chancellor would say, very curtly,

"I allow that exception! Mr. Brick, what have you got to say?"—

Mr. Brick generally had a good deal to say. He seemed to multiply his defences in proportion to the little he had to defend; in strong contrast to his antagonist's short, nervous, home-thrust arguments. The Court generally seemed tired with Mr. Brick.

"Oh that man!—I wish he would stop!" said Rose.

Elizabeth, who for the most part was as still as a mouse, glanced round at these words, one of her few and rare secondings of anything said by her cousin. She did not know that her glance shewed cheeks of fire, and eyes all the power of which seemed to be in full life.

"Can you understand that man?" said the naturalist.

"He don't understand himself," said Elizabeth.

"I don't understand anybody," said Rose. "But I like to hear the Chancellor speak—he's so funny,—only I'm getting tired. I wish he would stop that man. Oh that Mr. Brick!—Now see the Chancellor!—"

"I've decided that point, Mr. Brick!"

Mr. Brick could not think it decided. At least it seemed so, for he went on.

"What a stupid man!" said Rose.

"He will have the last word," said Mr. Herder.

"Miss Haye, are *you* tired?" asked Mr. Satterthwaite, leaning past the white feather.

"I?—No."

"I am," said Rose. "And so is the Chancellor. Now look at him——"

"Mr. Brick—I have decided that point!" came from the lips of Mr. Justice, a little more curtly than before.

"Now he will stop,—" said Rose.

No—Mr. Brick was unmoveable.

"Very well!" said the Chancellor, throwing himself half way round on his chair with a jerk——"you may go on, and I'll read the newspaper!—"

Which he did, amid a general titter that went round the court-room, till the discomfited Mr. Brick came to a stand. And Winthrop rose for his next point.

"Are you going to wait till it's all done, Mr. Herder?" said Rose. "I'm tired to death. Lizzie—Lizzie!"—she urged, pulling her cousin's shoulder.

"What!" said Elizabeth, giving her another sight of the same face that had flashed upon her half an hour before.

"My goodness!" said Rose. "What's the matter with you?"

"What do you want?—" said Elizabeth with a sort of fiery impatience, into which not a little disdain found its way.

"You are not interested, are you?" said Rose with a satirical smile.

"Of course I am!"——

"In that man, Lizzie?"

"What do you want!" said Elizabeth, answering the whisper in a plain voice.

"I want to go home."

"I'm not ready to go yet."

And her head went round to its former position.

"Lizzie—Lizzie!" urged Rose in a whisper,—"How can you listen to that man!—you oughtn't to.—Lizzie!—"

"Hush, Rose! be quiet!—I *will* listen. Let me alone."

Nor could Rose move her again by words, whispers, or pulls of her shoulder. "I am not ready,"—she would coolly reply. Mrs. Haye was in despair, but constrained to keep it to herself for fear she should be obliged to accept an escort home, and because of an undefined unwillingness to leave Elizabeth there alone. She had to wait, and play the agreeable to Mr. Satterthwaite, for both her other companions were busy listening; until Winthrop had finished his argument, and the Chancellor had nodded,

"I allow that exception, Mr. Landholm—it is well taken—Mr. Brick, what have you to say?"——

Mr. Brick rose to respond. Elizabeth rose too then, and faced about upon her companions, giving them this silent notice, for she deigned no word, that she was willing Rose's pleasure should take its course. Mr. Satterthwaite was quite ready, and they went home; Elizabeth changed to an automaton again.

But when she got into her own room she sat down, without taking off her bonnet, to think.

"This is that farmer's boy that father wouldn't help—and that he has managed to separate from himself—and from me! What did I go there for to-day? Not for my own happiness—And now perhaps I shall never see him again. But I am glad I did go;—if that is the last."

And spring months and summer months succeeded each other; and she did not see him again.

CHAPTER XXXIII.

> Since he doth lack
> Of going back
> Little, whose will
> Doth urge him to run wrong, or to stand still.
>
> BEN JONSON.

ONE of the warm evenings in that summer, when the windows were all open of Winthrop's attic and the candles flared in the soft breeze from the sea, Rufus came in. Winthrop only gave him a look and a smile from his papers as he appeared; and Rufus flung himself, or rather dropped down, upon the empty couch where Winnie used to lie. Perhaps the thought of her came to him, for he looked exceedingly sober; only he had done that ever since he shewed his face at the door. For some minutes he sat in absorbed contemplation of Winthrop, or of somewhat else; he was certainly looking at him. Winthrop looked at nothing but his papers; and the rustling of them was all that was heard, beside the soft rush of the wind.

"Always at work?" said Rufus, in a dismal tone, half desponding and wholly disconsolate.

"Try to be.——"

"Why don't you snuff those candles?" was the next question, given with a good deal more life.

"I didn't know you wanted more light," said Winthrop, stopping to put in order the unruly wicks his brother referred to.

"What are you at there?"

"A long answer in chancery."

"Ryle's?"

"No—Mr. Eversham's case."

"How does Ryle's business get on?"

"Very satisfactorily. I've got light upon that now."

"What's the last thing done?"

"The last thing I did was to file a replication, bringing the cause to an issue for proofs; and proofs are now taking before an Examiner."

"You have succeeded in every step in that cause?"

"In every step."

"The steps must have been well taken."

Winthrop was silent, going on with his 'answer.'

"How much do you expect you'll get from them?"

"Can't tell yet. I somewhat expect to recover a very large sum."

"Winthrop—I wish I was a lawyer—" Rufus said presently with a sigh.

"Why?" said his brother calmly.

"I should—or at least I might—be doing something."

"Then you think all the work of the world rests upon the shoulders of lawyers? I knew they had a good deal to do, but not so much as that."

"I don't see anything for me to do," Rufus said despondingly.

"Is it not possible you might, if you looked in some other direction than my papers?"

Rufus got off his couch and began gloomily to walk up and down.

"How easily those who are doing well themselves can bear the ill haps of their friends!" he said.

Winthrop went back to his papers and studied them, with his usual calm face and in silence, for some time. Rufus walked and cogitated for half an hour.

"I ought not to have said that, Winthrop," were his first words. "But now look at me!"

"With pleasure," said Winthrop laying down his 'answer'—'I have looked at many a worse man."

"Can't you be serious?" said Rufus, a provoked smile forcing itself upon him.

"I thought I was rarely anything else," said Winthrop. "But now I look at you, I don't see anything in the world the matter."

"Yet look at our different positions—yours and mine."

"I'd as lieve be excused," said Winthrop. "You always made the best show, in any position."

"Other people don't think so," said Rufus, turning with a curious struggle of feeling in his face, and turning to hide it in his walk up and down.

"What ails you, Will?—I don't know what you mean."

"You deserve it!" said Rufus, swallowing something in his mind apparently, that cost him some trouble.

"I don't know what I deserve," said Winthrop gravely. "I am afraid I have not got it."

"How oddly and rightly we were nicknamed in childhood!' Rufus went on bitterly, half communing with himself.—"I for fiery impulse, and you for calm rule."

"I don't want to rule," said Winthrop half laughing. "And I assure you I make no effort after it."

"You do it, and always will. You have the love and respect and admiration of everybody that knows you—in a very high degree; and there is not a soul in the world that cares for me, except yourself."

"I do not think that is true, Will," said Winthrop after a little pause. "But even suppose it were—those are not the things one lives for."

"What *does* one live for then!" Rufus said almost fiercely.

"At least they are not what I live for," said Winthrop correcting himself.

"What do *you* live for?"

His brother hesitated.

"For another sort of approbation—That I may hear 'Well done,' from the lips of my King,—by and by."

Rufus bit his lip and for several turns walked the room in silence—evidently because he could not speak. Perhaps the words, 'Them that honour me, I will honour,'—might have come to his mind. But when at last he began to talk, it was not upon that theme.

"Governor,"—he said in a quieter tone,—"I wish you would help me."

"I will—if I can."

"Tell me what I shall do."

"Tell me your own thoughts first, Will."

"I have hardly any. The world at large seems a wretched and utter blank to me."

"Make your mark on it, then."

"Ah!—that is what we used to say.—I don't see how it is to be done."

"It is to be done in many ways, Rufus; in many courses of action; and there is hardly one you can set your hand to, in which it may not be done."

Rufus again struggled with some feeling that was too much for him.

"Your notions have changed a little from the old ones,—and I have kept mine," he said.

"I spoke of *making your mark*,—not of being seen to do it," his brother returned.

Again Rufus was silent.

"Well but the question is not of that now," he said, "but of doing *something*;—to escape from the dishonour and the misery of doing nothing."

"Still you have not told me your thoughts, Will. You are not fit for a merchant."

"I'll never enter a counting-house again!—for anything!" was Rufus's reply.

"If I were in your place, I should take up my old trade of engineering again, just where I left it off."

Rufus walked, and walked.

"But I am fit for better things,"—he said at length.

"Then you are fit for that."

"I suppose that follows," said Rufus with some disdainful expression.

"There is no more respectable profession."

"It gives a man small chance to distinguish himself," said Rufus,—"and it takes one out of the world."

"Distinction may be attained almost anywhere," said Winthrop.

"'Who sweeps a room as for thy laws,
"'Makes that and th' action fine.'"

"I should like to see *you* do it!" was Rufus's scornful rejoinder.

"What?"

"Sweep rooms by way of distinction."

"I don't know about the distinction," said Winthrop; "but the *thing* you may see me do any morning, if you come at the right hour."

"Sweep these rooms?"

"With a broomstick."

"Why Winthrop, that's beneath you!"

"I have been thinking so lately," said Winthrop. "It wasn't, in the days when I couldn't afford to pay any one for doing it; and those days reached down to a very late point."

"Afford!" said Rufus, standing still in his walk;—"Why you have made money enough ever since you began practice, to afford such a thing as that."

"Ay—if I could have put it all on the floor."

"Where had you to put it?"

"I had Mr. Inchbald to reward for his long trust in me, and Mr. Herder to reimburse for his kindness,—and some other sources of expenditure to meet."

"Mr. Herder could have been paid out of the costs of this lawsuit."

"No, he couldn't."

"And thereupon, you would recommend the profession of a street-sweeper to me!" said Rufus, beginning his walk with renewed energy.

"On the whole, I think I would not," said Winthrop gravely. 'I am of opinion you can do something better."

"I don't like engineering!" said Rufus presently.

"What *do* you like?"

Rufus stopped and stood looking thoughtfully on the table where Winthrop's papers lay.

"I consider that to be as honourable, as useful, and I should think quite as pleasant a way of life, as the one I follow."

"Do you?—" said Rufus, looking at the long 'answer in Chancery.'

"I would as lieve go into it to-morrow, and make over my inkstand to you, if I were only fit for that and you for this."

"Would you!" said Rufus, mentally conceding that his brother was 'fit' for anything.

"Just as lieve."

Rufus's brow lightened considerably, and he took up his walk again.

"What would you like better, Will?"

"I don't know—' said Rufus meditatively—" I believe I'll take your advice. There was an offer made to me a week or two ago—at least I was spoken to, in reference to a Southern piece of business——"

"Not another agency?"

"No—no, engineering;—but I threw it off, not thinking then, or not knowing, that I would have anything more to do with the matter—I dare say it's not too late yet."

"But Will," said his brother, "whatever choice you make now, it is your last choice."

"How do you know it is my last choice?" said Rufus.

"Because it ought to be."

Rufus took to silence and meditating again.

"Any profession rightly managed, will carry you to the goal of honour; but no two will, ridden alternately.

"It seems so," said Rufus bitterly.

And he walked and meditated, back and forth through the room; while Winthrop lost himself in his 'answer.' The silence lasted this time till Rufus came up to the table and extending his hand bid his brother 'good night.'

"Are you going?" said Winthrop starting up.

"Yes—going; and going South, and going to be an engineer, and if possible to reach the goal of honour on the back of that calling, by some mysterious road which as yet I see not."

"Stay here to-night, Will."

"No, I can't—I've got to see somebody."

"All night?"

"Why, no," said Rufus smiling. "I suppose I could come back; more especially as I am going bona fide away. By the way, Winthrop, do you know they say the yellow fever is here?"

"I know they say so."

"What will you do?"

"Nothing."

"I mean, of course, if the report is true."

"So I mean."

"But you will not stay here?"

"I think I will."

"But it would be much better to go out of town."

"If I think so, I'll go."

"I'll make you think so," said Rufus putting on his hat,—"or else I won't go engineering! I'll be back in an hour."

CHAPTER XXXIV.

Yea, men may wonder, while they scan
A living, thinking, feeling man,
In such a rest his heart to keep;
But angels say,—and through the word
I ween their blessed smile is heard,—
"He giveth his beloved sleep!"

ELIZABETH BARRETT BROWNING.

NOTWITHSTANDING however Rufus's assurance, he did go off to his engineering and he did not succeed in changing his brother's mind. Winthrop abode in his place, to meet whatever the summer had in store for him.

It brought the city's old plague, though not with such fearful presence as in years past. Still the name and the dread of it were abroad, and enough of its power to justify them. Many that could, ran away from the city; and business, if it was not absolutely checked, moved sluggishly. There was much less than usual done.

There was little in Winthrop's line, certainly. Yet in the days of vacant courts and laid-by court business, the tenant of Mr. Inchbald's attic went out and came in as often as formerly. What he did with his time was best known to himself.

"I wonder how he does, now, all alone," said Mrs. Nettley to her brother.

"I've a notion he isn't so much of the time alone," said Mr. Inchbald. "He's not at home any more than he used to be, nor so much. I hear him going up or down the stairs—night and day."

"Surely there are no courts now?" said Mrs. Nettley.

"Never are in August—and especially not now, of course."

"I'm afraid he's lonesome, poor fellow!"

"Never saw a fellow look less like it," said Mr. Inchbald.

"He's a strong man, he is, in his heart and mind. I should expect to see one of the pyramids of Egypt come down as soon as either of 'em. Lonesome? I *never* saw him look lonesome."

"He has a trick of not shewing what he feels then," said his sister. "I've seen him times when I know he *felt* lonesome,—though as you say, I can't say he shewed it. He's a strong build of a man, too, George."

"Like body, like mind," said her brother. "Yes. I like to see a man all of a piece. But his brother has a finer figure."

"Do you think so?" said Mrs. Nettley. "That's for a painter. Now I like Winthrop's the best."

"That's for a woman," said Mr. Inchbald laughing. "You always like what you love."

"Well what do you suppose he finds to keep him out so much of the time?"

"I don't know," said Mr. Inchbald,—"and I daren't ask him. I doubt some poor friends of his know."

"Why do you?"

"I can't tell you why;—something—the least trifle, once or twice, has given me the idea."

"He's a Christian to look at!" said Mrs. Nettley, busying herself round her stove and speaking in rather an undertone. "He's worse than a sermon to me, many times."

Her brother turned slowly and went out, thereby confessing, his sister thought, that Winthrop had been as bad as a sermon to him.

As he went out he saw a girl just mounting the stairs.

"Is Mr. Landholm in?" she said putting her head over the balusters.

"I don't know, my girl—I think he may be."

"I'll know before long," she rejoined, taking the stairs at a rate that shewed she meant what she said. Like no client at law that ever sought his lawyer's chambers, on any errand. Before Mr. Inchbald had reached the first landing, she was posted before the desired door, and had tapped there with very alert fingers. Winthrop opened the door.

"Clam!"—said he.—"Come in."

"Mr. Winthrop," said Clam, coming in as slowly as she had mounted the stairs fast, and speaking with unusual deliberation, and not in the least out of breath,—"don't you want to help the distressed?"

"What's the matter, Clam?"

"Why Mr. Haye's took, and Miss 'Lizabeth's all alone with

him; and she's a little too good to be let die of fright and worry, if she ain't perfect. Few people are."

"All alone!"

"She's keeping house with him all alone this minute."

"What do you mean by all alone?"

"When there ain't but two people in the house and one o' them's deathly sick."

"Where are the servants? and Mrs. Haye?"

"They was all afraid they'd be took—she and them both; so they all run—the first one the best feller. I stayed, 'cause I thought the yaller fever wouldn't do much with one o' my skin; and anyhow it was as good to die in the house as in the street—I'd rather."

"When did they go?" said Winthrop beginning to put up books and papers.

"Cleared out this mornin'—as soon as they knowed what was the matter with Mr. Haye."

"His wife too?" said Winthrop.

"Not she! *she* went off for fear she'd be scared—years ago."

"Has Miss Haye sent for no friends?"

"She says there ain't none to send to; and I guess there ain't."

"Run home to your mistress, Clam, as fast as you can.—When was Mr. Haye taken sick?"

"Some time yesterday. Then you're comin', Mr. Winthrop?"

"Yes. Run."

Clam ran home. But quick as her speed had been, when she got the handle of the door in her hand she saw a figure that she knew, coming down the street; and waited for him to come up. Winthrop and she passed into the house together.

The gentleman turned into one of the deserted parlours; and Clam with a quick and soft step ran up stairs and into the sick room. Mr. Haye lay there unconscious. Elizabeth was sitting by the side of the bed, with a face of stern and concentrated anxiety.

"Here's the stuff," said Clam, setting some medicine on the table;—"and there's a gentleman down stairs that wants to see you, Miss 'Lizabeth—on business."

"Business!" said Elizabeth,—"Did you tell him what was in the house?"

"I told him," said Clam, "and *he* don't care. He wants to see you."

Elizabeth had no words to waste, nor heart to speak them.

She got up and went down stairs and in at the open parlour door, like a person who walks in a dream through a dreadful labyrinth of pain, made up of what used to be familiar objects of pleasure. So she went in. But so soon as her eye caught the figure standing before the fireplace, though she did not know what he had come there for, only that he was there, her heart sprang as to a pillar of hope. She stopped short and her two hands were brought together with an indescribable expression, telling of relief.

"Oh Mr. Landholm! what brought you here!"

He came forward to where she stood and took one of her hands; and felt that she was trembling like a shaking leaf.

"How is your father?" was his question.

"I don't know!" said Elizabeth bending down her head while tears began to run fast,—"I don't know anything about sickness—I never was with anybody before——"

She had felt one other time the gentle kind hands which, while her own eyes were blinded with tears, led her and placed her on the sofa. Elizabeth took the sofa cushion in both arms and laid her head upon it, turning her face from her companion; and her whole frame was racked and shaken with terrible agitation.

In a few minutes this violent expression of feeling came to an end. She took her arms from the pillow and sat up and spoke again to the friend at her side; who meanwhile had been perfectly quiet, offering neither to check nor to comfort her. Elizabeth went back to a repetition of her last remark, as if for an excuse.

"I never even tried to nurse anybody before—and the doctor couldn't stay with me this morning——"

"I will do both now," said Winthrop.

"What?"—said Elizabeth looking at him bewilderedly.

"Stay with you, and take care of Mr. Haye."

"Oh no! you must not!" she said with a sort of eager seriousness;—"I shouldn't like to have you."

"I have seen something of the disease," he said smiling slightly, "and I am not afraid of it.—Are you?"

"Oh yes!—oh yes!!"

How much was confessed in the tone of those words!—and she hid her face again. But her companion made no remark.

"Is there no friend you would like to have sent for?"

"No," said Elizabeth,—"not one! not one here——and not anywhere, that I should care to have with me."

"May I go up and see Mr. Haye now?" he said presently. "Which is the room?"

Elizabeth rose up to shew him.

"No," he said, gently motioning her back,—"I am going alone. You must stay here."

"But I must go too, Mr. Landholm!——"

"Not if I go," he said.

"But I am his daughter,—I must."

"I am not his daughter—so as far as that goes we are even. And by your own confession you know nothing of the matter; and I do. No—you must not go above this floor."

"Until when, Mr. Landholm?" said Elizabeth looking terrified.

"Until new rules are made," he said quietly. "While you can do nothing in your father's room, both for him and for you it is much better that you should not be there."

"And can't I do anything?" said Elizabeth.

"If I think you are wanted, I will let you know. Meanwhile there is one thing that can be done everywhere."

He spoke, looking at her with a face of steady kind gravity. Elizabeth could not meet it; she trembled with the effort she made to control herself.

"It is the thing of all others that I cannot do, Mr. Landholm."

"Learn it now, then. Which is the room?"

Elizabeth told him, without raising her eyes; and stood motionless on the floor where he left her, without stirring a finger, as long as she could hear the sound of his footsteps. They went first to the front door, and she heard him turn the key; then they went up the stairs.

The locking of that door went to her heart, with a sense of comfort, of dependence, of unbounded trust in the hand, the heart, the head, that had done it. It roused, or the taking off of restraint roused again, all the tumult of passions that had raged after her first coming in. She dropped on her knees by the sofa and wrapping her arms round the cushion as she had done before, she laid her head down on it, and to all feeling laid her heart down too; such bitter and deep and long sobs shook and racked her breast.

She was alive to nothing but feeling and the indulgence of it, and careless how much time the indulgence of it might take. It was passion's time. She was startled when two hands took hold of her and a grave voice said,

"If you do in this way, I shall have two patients instead of one, Miss Elizabeth."

Elizabeth suffered herself to be lifted up and placed on the sofa, and sat down like a child. Even at the instant came a flash of recollection bringing back the time, long past, when Winthrop had lifted her out of the rattlesnake's way. She felt ashamed and rebuked.

"This is not the lesson I set you," he said gently.

Elizabeth's head drooped lower. She felt that he *had* two patients—if he had only known it!

"You might set me a great many lessons that I should be slow to learn, Mr. Landholm," she said sadly.

"I hope not," he said in his usual tone. "There is no present occasion for this distress. I cannot see that Mr. Haye's symptoms are particularly unfavourable."

Elizabeth could have answered a great deal to that; but she only said, tearfully,

"How good you are to take care of him!"

"I will be as good as I can," said he smiling a little. "I should like to have you promise to do as much."

"That would be to promise a great deal, Mr. Landholm," said Elizabeth looking up earnestly.

"What then?"

Elizabeth looked down and was silent, but musing much to herself.

"Is it too much of a promise to make?" said he gravely.

"No—" said Elizabeth slowly,—"but more than I am ready to make."

"Why is that?"

"Because, Mr. Landholm," said she looking up again at him, "I don't believe I should keep it if I made it."

"You expect me to say, in that case you are quite right not to make it. No,—you are quite wrong."

He waited a little; but said no more, and Elizabeth could not. Then he left the room and she heard him going *down stairs!* Her first thought was to spring up and go after to help him to whatever he wanted; then she remembered that he and Clam could manage it without her, and that he would certainly choose to have it so. She curled herself up on her sofa and laying her head on the cushion in more quiet wise, she went off into a long fit of musing; for Winthrop's steps, when they came from down stairs went straight up stairs again, without turning into the parlour. She mused, on her duty, her danger, her sorrow and her joy. There was something akin to joy in the enormous comfort, rest, and pleasure she felt in Winthrop's presence. But it was very grave musing after all; for her duty, or the image of it, she shrank from; her danger she shrank from more unequivocally; and joy and sorrow could but hold a mixed and miserable reign. The loss of her father could not be to Elizabeth what the loss of his mother had been to Winthrop. Mr. Haye had never made himself a part of his daughter's daily inner life; to her his death could be only the breaking of the old name and tie and associations, which of late years had become far less dear than they used to be. Yet to Elizabeth, who had nothing else, they were very much; and she looked to the possible loss of them as to a wild and dreary setting adrift upon the sea of life without harbour or shore to make anywhere. And then rose the shadowy image of a fair port and land of safety, which conscience whispered she could gain if she would. But sailing was necessary for that; and chart-studying; and watchful care of the ship, and many an observation taken by heavenly lights; and Elizabeth had not even begun to be a sailor. She turned these things over and over in her mind a hundred times, one after another, like the visions of a dream, while the hours of the day stole away noiselessly.

The afternoon waned; the doctor came. Elizabeth sprang out to meet him, referred him to her coadjutor up stairs, and then waited for his coming down again. But the doctor when he came could tell her nothing; there was no declarative symptom as yet; he knew no more than she did; she must wait. She went back to her sofa and her musing.

The windows were open, but with the sultry breath of August little din of business came into the room; the place was very quiet. The house was empty and still; seldom a footfall could be heard overhead. Clam was busy, up stairs and down, but she went with a light step when she pleased, and she pleased it now. It was a relief to have the change of falling night; and then the breeze from the sea began to come in at the windows and freshen the hot rooms; and twilight deepened. Elizabeth wished for a light then, but for once in her life hesitated about ringing the bell; for she had heard Clam going up and down and feared she might be busied for some one else. And she thought, with a heart full, how dismal this coming on of night would have been, but for the friend up stairs. Elizabeth wished bitterly she could follow his advice.

She sat looking out of the open window into the duskiness, and at the yellow lights of the street lamps which by this time spotted it; thinking so, and feeling very miserable. By and by Clam came in with a candle and began to let down the blinds.

"What are you going to do?" said her mistress. "You needn't pull those down."

"Folks 'll see in," said Clam.

"No they won't—there's no light here."

"There's goin' to be, though," said Clam. "Things is goin' straight in this house, as two folks can make 'em."

"I don't want anything—you may let the lamps alone, Clam."

"I dursn't," said Clam, going on leisurely to light the two large burners of the mantle lamps,—' Mr. Winthrop told me to get tea for you and do everything just as it was every night; so I knowed these had to be flarin' up—You ain't goin' to be allowed to sit in the shades no longer."

"I don't want anything!" said Elizabeth. "Don't bring any tea here."

"Then I'll go up and tell him his orders is contradickied," said Clam.

"Stop!" said her mistress when she had reached the door walking off,—"don't carry any foolish speech up stairs at such a time as this;—fetch what you like and do what you like,—I don't care."

The room was brilliantly lighted now; and Clam set the salver on the table and brought in the tea-urn; and miserable as she felt, Elizabeth half confessed to herself that her coadjutor up stairs was right. Better this pain than the other. If the body was nothing a gainer, the mind perhaps might be, for keeping up the wonted habits and appearances.

"Ask Mr. Landholm to come down, Clam."

"I did ask him," said the handmaiden, "and he don't want nothin' but biscuits, and he's got lots o' them."

"Won't he have a cup of tea?"

"He knows his own mind mostly," said Clam; "and he says he won't."

"What arrangements can you make for his sleeping up there to-night, Clam?"

"Him and me 'll see to it," responded Clam confidently. "I know pretty much what's in the house; and the best of it ain't too good for him."

So Elizabeth drank her cup of tea alone; and sat alone through the long evening and mused. For still it was rather musing than thinking; going over things past and things present; things future she cared not much to meddle with. It was not a good time, she said for taking up her religious wants and duties; and in part that was true, severely as she felt them; for her mind was in such a slow fever that none of its pulses were healthful. Fear, and foreboding, for her father and for herself,—hope springing along with the fear; a strong sense that her character was different from what it ought to be, and a strong wish that it were not,—and a yet mightier leaning in another direction;—all of these, meeting and modifying each other and struggling together, seemed to run in her veins and to tell in each beat of the tiny timekeeper at her wrist. How could she disentangle one from the other, or give a quiet mind to anything, when she had it not to give?

She was just bitterly asking herself this question, when Winthrop came in at the open parlour door; and the immediate bitter thought which arose next was, did he ever have any *but* a quiet mind to give to anything? The two bitters were so strong upon her tongue that they kept it still; till he had walked up to the neighbourhood of her sofa.

"How is my father, Mr. Landholm?" she said rising and meeting him.

"As you mean the question I cannot answer it—There is nothing declarative, Miss Elizabeth. Yes," he said kindly, meeting and answering her face,—"you must wait yet awhile longer."

Elizabeth sat down again, and looked down.

"Are you troubled with fears for yourself?" he said gently, taking a chair near her.

"No—" Elizabeth said, and said truly. She could have told him, what indeed she could *not*, that since his coming into the house another feeling had overmastered that fear, and kept it under.

"At least," she added,—"I suppose I have it, but it doesn't trouble me now."

"I came down on principle," said he,—"to exchange the office of nurse for that of physician;—thinking it probably better that you should see me for a few minutes, than see nobody at all."

"I am sure you were right," said Elizabeth. "I felt awhile ago as if my head would go crazy with too many thoughts."

"Must be unruly thoughts," said Winthrop.

"They were," said she looking up.

"Can't you manage unruly thoughts?"

"No!—never could."

"Do you know what happens in that case?—They manage you."

"But how can I help it, Mr. Landholm? There they are, and here am I;—they are strong and I am weak."

"If they are the strongest, they will rule."

Elizabeth sat silent, thinking her counsellor was very unsatisfactory.

"Are you going to sit up all night, Miss Elizabeth?"

"No—I suppose not—"

"I shall; so you may feel easy about being alone down here. There could be no disturbance, I think, without my knowing it. Let Clam be here to keep you company; and take the best rest you can."

It was impossible for Elizabeth to say a word of thanks, or of his kindness; the words choked her; she was mute.

"Can I do anything, Mr. Landholm?"

"Nothing in the world—but manage your thoughts," he said smiling.

Elizabeth was almost choked again, with the rising of tears this time.

"But Mr. Landholm—about that—what is wrong cannot be necessary; there must be some way of managing them?"

"You know it," he said simply.

But it finished Elizabeth's power of speech. She did not even attempt to look up; she sat pressing her chin with her hand, endeavouring to keep down her heart and to keep steady her quivering lips. Her companion, who in the midst of all her troubles she many times that evening thought was unlike any other person that ever walked, presently went out into the hall and called to Clam over the balusters.

"Is he going to give her directions about taking care of me?" thought Elizabeth in a great maze, as Winthrop came back into the parlour and sat down again. When Clam appeared however he only bade her take a seat; and then bringing forth a bible from his pocket he opened it and read the ninety-first psalm. Hardly till then it dawned upon Elizabeth what he was thinking to do; and then the words that he read went through and through her heart like drawn daggers. One after another, one after another. Little he imagined, who read, what strength her estimate of the reader's character gave them; nor how that same estimate made every word of his prayer tell, and go home to her spirit with the sharpness as well as the gentleness of Ithuriel's spear. When Elizabeth rose from her knees, it was with a bowed head which she could in no wise lift up; and after Winthrop had left the room, Clam stood looking at her mistress and thinking her own thoughts, as long as she pleased unrebuked.

"One feels sort o' good after that, now, don't they?" was her opening remark, when Elizabeth's head was at last raised from her hands. "Do you think the roof of any house would ever fall in over *his* head? He's better'n a regiment o' soldiers."

"Is everything attended to down stairs, Clam?"

"All's straight where the Governor is," said Clam with a sweeping bend of her head, and going about to set the room in order;—"there ain't two straws laid the wrong way."

"Where he is!" repeated Elizabeth—"He isn't in the kitchen, I suppose, Clam."

"Whenever he's in the house, always seems to me he's all over," said Clam. "It's about that. He's a governor, you know. Now Miss 'Lizabeth, how am I goin' to fix you for the night?"

"No way," said Elizabeth. "I shall just sleep here, as I am. Let the lamps burn, and shut down the blinds."

"And then will I go off to the second story and leave you?"

"No, indeed—Fetch something that you can lay on the floor, and stay here with me."

Which Clam presently did; nothing more than a blanket however; and remarked as she curled herself down with her head upon her arm,

"Ain't he a handsome man, Miss 'Lizabeth?"

"Who?—" ungraciously enough.

"Why, the Governor."

"Yes, for aught I know. Lie still and go to sleep, Clam, if you can; and let me."

Very promptly Clam obeyed this command; but her less happy mistress, as soon as the deep drawn breaths told her she was alone again, sat up on her sofa to get in a change of posture a change from pain.

How alone!—In the parlour after midnight, with the lamps burning as if the room were gay with company; herself, in her morning dress, on the sofa for a night's rest, and there on her blanket on the carpet, Clam already taking it. How it told the story, of illness and watching and desertion and danger; how it put life and death in near and strong contrast; and the summer wind blew in through the blinds and pushed the blinds themselves gently out into the room, just as Elizabeth had seen and felt in many a bright and happy hour not so long past. The same summer breath, and the summer so different! Elizabeth could hardly bear it. She longed to rush up stairs where there was somebody; but then she must not; and then the remembrance that somebody was there quieted her again. That thought stirred another train, the old contrast between him and herself, the contrast between his condition and hers, now brought more painfully than ever home. "He is ready to meet anything," she thought, —"nothing can come amiss to him;—he is as ready for that world as for this—and more!"—

The impression of the words he had read that evening came back to her afresh, and the recollection of the face with which he had read them,—calm, happy, and at rest;—and Elizabeth threw herself off the sofa and kneeled down to lay her head and arms upon it, in mere agony of wish to change something, or rather of the felt want that something should be changed. O that she were at peace like him! O that she had like him a sure home and possession beyond the reach of sickness and death! O that she were that rectified, self-contained, pure, strong spirit, that he was!—The utmost of passionate wish was in the tears that wept out these yearnings of heart—petitions they half were,—for her mind in giving them form, had a half look to the only possible power that could give them fruition. But it was with only the refreshment of tears and exhaustion that she laid herself on her couch and went to sleep.

Clam had carried away her blanket bed and put out the lamps, before Elizabeth awoke the next morning. It was a question whether the room looked drearier by night or by day. She got up and went to the window. Clam had pulled up the blinds. The light of the summer morning was rising again, but it shone only without; all was darkness inside. Except that light-surrounded watcher up stairs. How Elizabeth's heart blessed him.

The next thing was, to get ready to receive his report. That morning's toilet was soon made, and Elizabeth sat waiting. He might come soon, or he might not; for it was early, and he might not know whether she was awake and risen yet. She was unaccustomed, poor child, to a waiting of pain; and her heart felt tired and sore already from the last forty-eight hours of fears and hopes. Fears and hopes were in strong life now, but a life that had become very tender to every touch. Clam was setting the breakfast-table—Could breakfast be eaten or not? The very cups and saucers made Elizabeth's heart ache. She was glad when Clam had done her work and was gone and she sat waiting alone. But the breaths came painfully now, and her heart was weary with its own aching.

The little knock at the door came at last. Elizabeth ran to

open it, and exchanged a silent grasp of the hand with the news-bearer; her eyes looked her question. He came in just as he came last night; calm and grave.

"I can tell you nothing new, Miss Elizabeth," he said. "I cannot see that Mr. Haye is any better—I do not know that he is any worse."

But Elizabeth was weak to bear longer suspense; she burst into tears and sat down hiding her face. Her companion stood near, but said nothing further.

"May I call Clam?" he asked after a few minutes.

Elizabeth gave eager assent; and the act of last night was repeated, to her unspeakable gratification. She drank in every word, and not only because she drank in the voice with them.

"Breakfast's just ready, Mr. Winthrop," said Clam when she was leaving the room;—"so you needn't go up stairs."

The breakfast was a very silent one on Elizabeth's part. Winthrop talked on indifferent subjects; but she was too full-hearted and too sick-hearted to answer him with many words. And when the short meal was ended and he was about quitting the parlour she jumped up and followed him a step or two.

"Mr. Winthrop—won't you say a word of comfort to me before you go?——"

He saw she needed it exceedingly; and came back and sat down on the sofa with her.

"I don't know what to say to you better than this, Miss Elizabeth," he said, turning over again the leaves of his little bible;—"I came to it in the course of my reading this morning; and it comforted me."

He put the book in her hands, but Elizabeth had to clear her eyes more than once from hot tears, before she could read the words to which he directed her.

"And there shall be a tabernacle for a shadow in the day-time from the heat, and for a place of refuge, and for a covert from storm and from rain."

Elizabeth looked at it.

"But I don't understand it, Mr. Landholm?" she said, raising her eyes to his face.

He said nothing; he took the book from her and turning a few leaves over, put it again in her hands. Elizabeth read;—

"And a man shall be as an hiding-place from the wind, and a covert from the tempest; as rivers of water in a dry place; as the shadow of a great rock in a thirsty land."

"Is that plainer?" he asked.

"It means the Saviour?" said Elizabeth.

"Certainly it does! To whom else should we go?"

"But Mr. Landholm," said Elizabeth after a minute's struggle, "why do you shew me this, when you know *I* can do nothing with it?"

"*Will* you do nothing?" he said.

The words implied that she could; an implication she would not deny; but her answer was another burst of tears. And with the book in her hand he left her.

The words were well studied that day! by a heart feeling the blast of the tempest and bitterly wanting to hide itself from the wind. But the fact of her want and of a sure remedy, was all she made clear; how to match the one with the other she did not know. The book itself she turned over with the curiosity and the interest of fresh insight into character. It was well worn, and had been carefully handled; it lay open easily anywhere, and in many places various marks of pencilling shewed that not only the eyes but the mind of its owner had been all over it. It was almost an awful book to Elizabeth's handling. It seemed a thing too good to be in her hold. It bore witness to its owner's truth of character, and to her own consequent being far astray; it gave her an opening such as she never had before to look into his mind and life and guess at the secret spring and strength of them. Of many of the marks of his pencil she could make nothing at all; she could not divine why they had been made, nor what could possibly be the notable thing in the passage pointed out; and longing to get at more of his mind than she could in one morning's hurried work, she found another bible in the house and took off a number of his notes, for future and more leisurely study.

It was a happy occupation for her that day. No other could have so softened its exceeding weariness and sadness. The doctor gave her no comfort. He said he could tell nothing *yet;* and Elizabeth could not fancy that this delay of amendment gave any encouragement to hope for it. She did not see Winthrop at dinner. She spent the most of the day over his bible. Sickness of heart sometimes made her throw it aside, but so surely sickness of heart made her take it up again.

The thought of Winthrop himself getting sick, did once or twice look in through the window of Elizabeth's mind; but her mind could not take it in. She had so much already to bear, that this tremendous possibility she could not bear so much as to look at; she left it a one side; and it can hardly be numbered among her recognized causes of trouble.

The day wore to an end. The evening and the sea-breeze came again. The lamps were lit and the table dressed with the salver and tea-urn. And Elizabeth was thankful the day was over; and waited impatiently for her friend to make his appearance.

She thought he looked thoughtfuller than ever when he came. That might have been fancy.

"I don't know, Miss Elizabeth," he said, taking her hand as he had done in the morning, and answering her face. "We must wait yet.—How have you borne the day?"

"I have borne it by the help of your book," she said looking down at it and trembling.

"You could have no better help," he said with a little sigh, as he turned away to the table,—"except that of the Author of it."

The tea was very silent, for even Winthrop did not talk much; and very sad, for Elizabeth could hardly hold her head up.

"Mr. Winthrop," she said when he rose,—"can you give me a minute or two before you go?—I want to ask you a question."

"Certainly,"—he said; and waited, both standing, while she opened his bible and found the place he had shewed her in the morning. She shewed it to him now.

"This—I don't quite understand it.—I see what is spoken of, and the need of it,—but—how can I make it my own?"

She looked up as she put the question, with most earnest eyes, and lips that only extreme determination kept from giving way. He looked at her, and at his book.

"By giving your trust to the Maker of the promise."

"How?—"

"The same unquestioning faith and dependence that you would give to any sure and undoubted refuge of human strength."

Elizabeth looked down and pressed her hands close together upon her breast. She knew so well how to give that!—so little how to give the other.

"Do you understand what Christ requires of those who would follow him?"

"No," she said looking up again,—"not clearly—hardly at all."

"One is—that you give up everything, even in thought, that is contrary to his authority."

He was still, and so was she, both looking at each other.

"That is what is meant by repentance. The other thing is, —that you trust yourself for all your wants—from the forgiveness of sin, to the supply of this moment's need,—to the strength and love of Jesus Christ;—and that because he has paid your price and bought you with his own blood."

"You mean," said Elizabeth slowly, "that his life was given in place of mine."

Winthrop was silent. Elizabeth stood apparently considering.

"'Everything that is contrary to his authority'"—she added after a minute,—"how can I know exactly all that?"

He still said nothing, but touched with his finger once or twice the book in his hand.

Elizabeth looked, and the tears came to her eyes.

"You know,—" she said, hesitating a little,—"what physicians say of involuntary muscular resistance, that the physical frame makes sometimes?"

He answered her with an instant's light of intelligence, and then with the darkened look of sorrow. But he took his bible away with him and said no more.

Elizabeth sat down and struggled with herself and with the different passions which had been at work in her mind, till she was wearied out; and then she slept.

She waked up in the middle of the night, to find the lamps burning bright and Clam asleep on the floor by her side; she herself was sitting yet where she had been sitting in the evening, on a low seat with her head on the sofa cushion. She got up and with a sort of new spring of hope and cheer, whence come she knew not, laid herself on the sofa and slept till the morning.

"You'd best be up, Miss 'Lizabeth," were Clam's first words.

"Why?" said Elizabeth springing up.

"It's time," said her handmaiden.

Elizabeth rose from her sofa and put her face and dress in such order as a few minutes could do. She had but come back from doing this, and was standing before the table, when Winthrop came in. It was much earlier than usual. Elizabeth looked, but he did not answer, the wonted question. He led her gently to the window and placed himself opposite to her.

"You must leave here, Miss Elizabeth," he said.

"Must I?"—said Elizabeth looking up at him and trembling

"You must—" he answered very gently.

"Why, Mr. Landholm?" Elizabeth dared to say.

"Because there is no longer any reason why you should stay here."

She trembled exceedingly, but though her very lips trembled, she did not cry. He would have placed her on a chair, but she resisted that and stood still.

"Where do you want me to go, Mr. Winthrop?" she said presently, like a child.

"I will take you wherever you say—to some friend's house?"

She caught at his arm and her breath at once, with a kind of sob; then releasing his arm, she said,

"There isn't anywhere."

"No house in the city?"

She shook her head.

"If you will let me, I will take you to a safe and quiet place; and as soon as possible away from the city."

"When?"

"When from here?—Now,—as soon as you can be ready."

Elizabeth's eye wandered vaguely towards the table like a person in a maze.

"Mayn't I go up stairs again?" she said, her eye coming back to his.

"I would rather you did not."

She gave way then and sat down covering her face with her hands. And sobs as violent as her tremblings had been, held her for a little while. The moment she could, she rose up and looked up again, throwing off her tears as it were, though a sob now and then even while she was speaking interrupted her breath.

"But Mr. Winthrop—the house,—how can I go and leave it with everything in it?"

"I will take care, if you will trust me"

"I will trust you," she said with running tears. "But you?——"

"I will take care of it and you too.—I will try to."

"That was not what I meant——"

"I am safe," he said.

He gently seated her; and then going off to Clam at the other side of the room he bade her fetch her mistress's bonnet and shawl. He himself put them on, and taking her arm in his, they went forth of the house.

CHAPTER XXXV.

> The One remains, the many change and pass;
> Heaven's light forever shines, Earth's shadows flee;
> Life, like a dome of many- coloured glass
> Stains the clear radiance of Eternity,
> Until Death shiver it to atoms.
>
> SHELLEY.

THE dawn of the summer morning was just flushing up over the city, when Winthrop and his trembling companion came out of the house. The flush came up upon a fair blue sky, into which little curls of smoke were here and there stealing; and a fresh air in the streets as yet held place of the sun's hot breath. One person felt the refreshment of it, as he descended the steps of the house and began a rather swift walk up the Parade. But those were very trembling feet that he had to guide during that early walk; though his charge was perfectly quiet. She did not weep at all; she did not speak, nor question any of his movements. Neither did he speak. He kept a steady and swift course till they reached Mr. Inchbald's house in Little South Street, and then only paused to open the door. He led Elizabeth up-stairs to his own room, and there and not before took her hand from his arm and placed her on a chair. Himself quietly went round the room, opening the windows and altering the disposition of one or two things. Then he came back to her where she sat like a statue, and in kind fashion again took one of her hands.

"I will see that you are waited upon," he said gently; "and I will send Clam to you by and by for your orders. Will you stay here for a little while?—and then I will take care of you."

How she wished his words meant more than she knew they did. She bowed her head, thinking so.

"Can I give you anything?"

She managed to say a smothered 'no,' and he went; first pulling out of his pocket his little bible which he laid upon the table.

Was that by way of answering his own question? It might be, or he might not have wanted it in his pocket. Whether or no, Elizabeth seized it and drew it towards her, and as if it had contained the secret charm and panacea for all her troubles, she laid her hands and her head upon it, and poured out there her new and her old sorrows; wishing even then that Winthrop could have given her the foundation of strength on which his own strong spirit rested.

After a long while, or what seemed such, she heard the door softly open and some one come in. The slow careful step was none that she knew, and Elizabeth did not look up till it had gone out and the door had closed again. It was Mrs. Nettley, and Mrs. Nettley had softly left on the table a waiter of breakfast. Elizabeth looked at it, and laid her head down again.

The next interruption came an hour later and was a smarter one. Elizabeth had wearied herself with weeping, and lay comparatively quiet on the couch.

"Miss 'Lizabeth," said the new-comer, in more gentle wise than it was her fashion to look or speak,—"Mr. Winthrop said I was to come and get your orders about what you wanted."

"I can't give orders—Do what you like," said Elizabeth keeping her face hid.

"If I knowed what 'twas,"—said Clam, sending her eye round the room for information or suggestion. "Mr. Winthrop said I was to come.—Why you haven't took no breakfast?"

"I didn't want any."

"You can't go out o' town that way," said Clam. "The Governor desired you would take some breakfast, and his orders must be follered. You can't drink cold coffee neither—"

And away went Clam, coffee-pot in hand.

In so short a space of time that it shewed Clam's business faculties, she was back again with the coffee smoking hot. She made a cup carefully and brought it to her mistress.

"You can't do nothin' without it," said Clam. "Mr. Winthrop would say, 'Drink it' if he was here—"

Which Elizabeth knew, and perhaps considered in swallowing the coffee. Before she had done, Clam stood at her couch again with a plate of more substantial supports.

"He would say 'Eat,' if he was here—" she remarked.

"Attend a little to what *I* have to say," said her mistress.

"While you're eatin'," said Clam. "I wasn't to stop to get breakfast."

A few words of directions were despatched, and Clam was off

again; and Elizabeth lay still and looked at the strange room and thought over the strange meaning and significance of her being there. A moment's harbour, with a moment's friend. She was shiveringly alone in the world; she felt very much at a loss what to do, or what would become of her. She felt it, but she could not think about it. Tears came again for a long uninterrupted time.

The day had reached the afternoon, when Clam returned, and coming into Mrs. Nettley's kitchen inquired if her mistress had had any refreshment. Mrs. Nettley declared that she dursn't take it up and that she had waited for Clam. Upon which that damsel set about getting ready a cup of tea, with a sort of impatient promptitude.

"Have you got all through?" Mrs. Nettley asked in the course of this preparation.

"What?" said Clam.

"Your work."

"No," said Clam. "Never expect to. My work don't get done."

"But has Mr. Landholm got through his work, down at the house?"

"Don't know," said Clam. "He don't tell *me*. But if we was to work on, at the rate we've been a goin' to-day—we'd do up all Mannahatta in a week or so."

"What's been so much to do?—the funeral, I know."

"The funeral," said Clam, "and everything else. That was only one thing. There was everything to be locked up, and everything to be put up, and the rest to be packed; and the silver sent off to the Bank; and everybody to be seen to. I did all I could, and Mr. Winthrop he did the rest."

"He'll be worn out!" said Mrs. Nettley.

"No he won't," said Clam. "He ain't one o' them that have to try hard to make things go—works like oiled 'chinery—powerful too, I can tell you."

"What's going to be done?" said Mrs. Nettley meditatively.

"Can't say," said Clam. "I wish my wishes was goin' to be done—but I s'pose they ain't. People's ain't mostly, in this world."

She went off with her dish of tea and what not, to her mistress up-stairs. But Elizabeth this time would endure neither her presence nor her proposal. Clam was obliged to go down again leaving her mistress as she had found her. Alone with herself.

Then, when the sun was long past the meridian, Elizabeth

heard upon the stair another step, of the only friend, as it seemed to her, that she had. She raised her head and listened to it. The step went past her door, and into the other room, and she sat waiting. "How little he knows," she thought, "how much of a friend he is! how little he guesses it. How far he is from thinking that when he shall have bid me good bye—somewhere—he will have taken away all of help and comfort I have.—"

But clear and well defined as this thought was in her mind at the moment, it did not prevent her meeting her benefactor with as much outward calmness as if it had not been there. Yet the quiet meeting of hands had much that was hard to bear. Elizabeth did not dare let her thoughts take hold of it.

"Have you had what you wanted?" he said, in the way in which one asks a question of no moment when important ones are behind.

"I have had all I could have," Elizabeth answered.

There was a pause; and then he asked,

"What are your plans, Miss Elizabeth?"

"I haven't formed any.—I couldn't, yet."

"Do you wish to stay in the city, or to go out of it?"

"Oh to go out of it!" said Elizabeth,—"if I could—if I knew where."

"Where is your cousin?"

"She was at Vantassel; but she left it for some friend's house in the country, I believe. I don't want to be where she is."

Elizabeth's tears came again.

"It seems very strange—" she said presently, trying to put a stop to them, but her words stopped.

"What?" said Winthrop.

"It seems very strange,—but I hardly know where to go. I have no friends near—no *near* friends, in any sense; there are some, hundreds of miles off, in distance, and further than that in kind regard. I know plenty of people, but I have no friends.—I would go up to Wut-a-qut-o, if there was anybody there," she added after a minute or two.

"Shahweetah has passed into other hands," said Winthrop.

"I know it," said Elizabeth;—"it passed into mine."

Winthrop started a little, and then after another moment's pause said quietly,

"Are you serious in wishing to go there now?"

"Very serious!" said Elizabeth, "if I had anybody to take care of me. I couldn't be there with only Clam and Karen."

"You would find things very rough and uncomfortable."

"What do you suppose I care about how rough?" said Elizabeth. "I would rather be there than in any other place I can think of."

"I am afraid you would still be much alone there—your own household would be all."

"I must be that anywhere," said Elizabeth bitterly. "I wish I could be there."

"Then I will see what I can do," said he rising.

"About what?" said Elizabeth.

"I will tell you if I succeed."

Mr. Landholm walked down stairs into Mrs. Nettley's sanctum, where the good lady was diligently at work in kitchen affairs.

"Mrs. Nettley, will you leave your brother and me to keep things together here, and go into the country with this bereaved friend of mine?"

Mrs. Nettley stood still with her hands in the dough of her bread and looked at the maker of this extraordinary proposition.

"Into the country, Mr. Landholm!—When?"

"Perhaps this afternoon—in two or three hours."

"Dear Mr. Landholm!—"

"Dear Mrs. Nettley."

"But it's impossible."

"Is it?"

"Why—What does she want me for, Mr. Landholm?"

"She is alone, and without friends at hand. She wishes to leave the city and take refuge in her own house in the country, but it is uninhabited except by servants. She does not know of my application to you, which I make believing it to be a case of charity."

Mrs. Nettley began to knead her dough with a haste and vigour which told of other matters on hand.

"Will *you* go, Mr. Landholm?"

"Certainly—to see you safe there—and then I will come back and take care of Mr. Inchbald."

"How far is it, sir?"

"So far as my old home, which Miss Haye has bought."

"What, Wut——that place of yours?" said Mrs. Nettley.

"Yes," Winthrop said gravely.

"And how long shall I be wanted, Mr. Landholm?"

"I do not know, Mrs. Nettley."

Mrs. Nettley hastily cut her dough into loaves and threw it into the pans.

"You are going, Mrs. Nettley?"

"Why sir—in two hours, you say?"

"Perhaps in so little as that—I am going to see."

"But Mr. Landholm," said the good lady, facing round upon him after bestowing her pans in their place, and looking somewhat concerned,—"Mr. Landholm, do you think she will like me?—Miss Haye?"

Winthrop smiled a little.

"I think she will be very thankful to you, Mrs. Nettley—I can answer no further."

"I suppose it's right to risk that," Mrs. Nettley concluded. "I'll do what you say, Mr. Landholm."

Without more words Mr. Landholm went out and left the house.

"Are Miss Haye's things all ready?" asked Mrs. Nettley of Clam, while she nervously untied her apron.

"All's ready that *he* has to do with," Clam answered a little curtly.

"But has he to do with your mistress's things."

"He has to do with everything, just now," said Clam. "I wish the now 'd last for ever!"

"How can we go to-night?—the boats and the stages and all don't set off so late."

"Boats don't stop near Wutsey Qutsey," said Clam.

Mrs. Nettley went off to make her own preparations.

When Mr. Landholm came again, after an interval of some length, he came with a carriage.

"Are you ready, Mrs. Nettley?" he said looking into that lady's quarters.

"In a little bit, Mr. Landholm!—"

Whereupon he went up-stairs.

"If you wish to go to Wut-a-qut-o, Miss Elizabeth," he said, "my friend Mrs. Nettley will go with you and stay with you, till you have made other arrangements. I can answer for her kindness of heart, and unobtrusive manners, and good sense. Would you like her for a companion?"

"I would like anybody—that you can recommend."

"My friend Cowslip's little sloop sets sail for the neighbourhood of Wut-a-qut-o this evening."

"Oh thank you!—Will she take us?"

"If you wish it."

"Oh thank you!——"

"Would you not be better to wait till to-morrow?—I can make the sloop wait."

"Oh no, let us go," said Elizabeth rising. "But your friend is very good—your friend who is going with me, I mean."

"Mrs. Nettley. But you need not move yet—rest while you can."

"Rest!"—said Elizabeth. And tears said what words did not.

"There is only one rest," said Winthrop gravely; "and it is in Christ's hand. 'Come unto me, all ye that labour and are heavy laden, AND I WILL GIVE YOU REST.'"——

Elizabeth's sobs were bitter. Her counsellor added no more however; he left the room after a little while, and soon returned to tell her that all was ready. She was ready too by that time.

"But Mr. Winthrop," she said looking at him earnestly, "is everything here so that you can leave it?"

She dared not put the whole of her meaning into words. But Winthrop understood, and answered a quiet "yes;" and Elizabeth lowered her veil and her head together and let him lead her to the carriage.

A few minutes brought them to the pier at the end of which the Julia Ann lay.

"You're sharp upon the time, Mr. Landholm," said her master;—"we're just goin' to cast off. But we shouldn't have done it, nother, till you come. All right!"

"Is all right in the cabin?" said Winthrop as they came on board.

"Well it's slicked up all it could be on such short notice," said the skipper. "I guess you wont have to live in it long; the wind's coming up pretty smart ahind us. Haul away there!—"

It was past six o'clock, and the August sun had much lessened of its heat, when, as once before with Mr. Landholm for a passenger, the Julia Ann stood out into the middle of the river with her head set for the North.

Mrs. Nettley and Clam hid themselves straightway in the precincts of the cabin. Elizabeth stood still where she had first placed herself on the deck, in a cold abstracted sort of carelessness, conscious only that her protector was standing by her side, and that she was not willing to lose sight of him. The vessel, and her crew, and their work before her very eyes, she could hardly be said to see. The sloop got clear of the wharf and edged out into the mid-channel, where she stood bravely along before the fair wind. Slowly the trees and houses along shore were dropped behind, and fresher the wind and fairer the green river-side seemed to become. Elizabeth's senses hardly knew it, or only in a kind of underhand way; not recognized.

"Will you go into the cabin? or will you have a seat here?" she heard Winthrop say.

Mechanically she looked about for one. He brought a chair and placed her in it, and she sat down; choosing rather the open air and free sky than any shut-up place, and his neighbourhood rather than where he was not; but with a dulled and impassive state of feeling that refused to take up anything, past, present or future. It was not rest, it was not relief, though there was a seeming of rest about it. She knew then it would not last. It was only a little lull between storms; the enforced quiet of wearied and worn-out powers. She sat mazily taking in the sunlight, and the view of the sunlighted earth and water, the breath of the sweeping fresh air, the creaking of the sloop's cordage, in the one consciousness that Winthrop kept his place at her side all this time. How she thanked him for that! though she could not ask him to sit down, nor make any sort of a speech about it.

Down went the sun, and the shadows and the sunlight were swept away together; and yet fresher came the sweet wind. It was a sort of consolation to Elizabeth, that her distress gave Winthrop a right and a reason to attend upon her; she had had all along a vague feeling of it, and the feeling was very present now. It was all of comfort she could lay hold of; and she clutched at it with even then a foreboding sense of the desolation there would be when that comfort was gone. She had it now; she had it, and she held it; and she sat there in her chair on the deck in a curious half stupor, half quiet, her mind clinging to that one single point where it could lean.

There came a break-up however. Supper was declared to be ready; and though nobody but Winthrop attended the skipper's table, Elizabeth was obliged to take some refreshments of her own, along with a cup of the sloop's tea, which most certainly she would have taken from no hand but the one that presented it to her. And after it, Elizabeth was so strongly advised to go to the cabin and take some rest, that she could not help going; resting, she had no thought of. Her companions were of easier mind; for they soon addressed themselves to such sleeping conveniencies as the little cabin could boast. Miss Haye watched them begin and end their preparations and bestow themselves in resting positions to sleep; and then drawing a breath of comparative rest herself, she placed herself just within the cabin threshold, on the floor, where she could look out and have a good view of the deck through the partly open door.

It was this night as on the former occasion, a brilliant moonlight; and the vessel had no lamps up to hinder its power. The mast and sails and lines stood out in sharp light and shadow. The man at the helm Elizabeth could not see; the moonlight poured down upon Winthrop, walking slowly back and forth on the deck, his face and figure at every turn given fully and clearly to view. Elizabeth herself was in shadow; he could not look within the cabin door and see her; she could look out and see him right well, and she did. He was pacing slowly up and down, with a thoughtful face, but so calm in its thoughtfulness that it was a grievous contrast to Elizabeth's own troubled and tossed nature. It was all the more fascinating to her gaze; while it was bitter to her admiration. The firm quiet tread,—the manly grave repose of the face,—spoke of somewhat in the character and life so unlike what she knew in her own, and so beautiful to her sense of just and right, that she looked in a maze of admiration and self-condemning; rating herself lower and lower and Winthrop higher and higher, at every fair view the moonlight gave, at every turn that brought him near or took him further from her. And tears —curious tears—that came from some very deep wells of her nature, blinded her eyes, and rolled hot down her cheeks, and were wiped away that she might look. "What shall I do when he gets tired of that walk and goes somewhere else?"—she thought; and with the thought, as instantly, Elizabeth gathered herself up from off the floor, wiped her cheeks from the tears, and stepped out into the moonlight. "I can't say anything, but I suppose he will," was her meditation. "Nobody knows when I shall have another chance."—

"They could not make it comfortable for you in there?" said Winthrop coming up to her.

"I don't know—yes,—I have not tried."

"Are you very much fatigued?"

"I suppose so.—I don't feel it."

"Can I do anything for you?"

The real answer nearly burst Elizabeth's bounds of self-control, but nevertheless her words were quietly given.

"Yes,—if you will only let me stay out here a little while."

He put a chair for her instantly, and himself remained standing near, as he had done before.

"Walk on, if you wish," said Elizabeth. "Don't mind me."

But instead of that he drew up another chair, and sat down.

There was silence then that might be felt. The moonlight poured down noiselessly on the water, and over the low dusky distant shore; the ripples murmured under the sloop's prow; the wind breathed gently through the sails. Now and then the creak of the rudder sounded, but the very stars were not more calmly peaceful than everything else.

"There is quiet and soothing in the speech of such a scene as this," Winthrop said after a time.

"Quiet!" said Elizabeth. Her voice choked, and it was a little while before she could go on.—"Nothing is quiet to a mind in utter confusion."

"Is yours so?"

"Yes."

The sobs were at her very lips, but the word got out first.

"It is no wonder," he observed gently.

"Yes it is wonder," said Elizabeth;—"or at least it is what needn't be. Yours wouldn't be so in any circumstances."

"What makes the confusion?"—he asked, in a gentle considerate tone that did not press for an answer.

"The want of a single fixed thing that my thoughts can cling to."

He was silent a good while after that.

"There is nothing fixed in this world," he said at length.

"Yes there is," said Elizabeth bitterly. "There are friends—and there is a self-reliant spirit—and there is a settled mind."

"Settled—about what?"

"What it will and what it ought to do."

"Is yours not settled on the latter point?" he asked.

"If it were," said Elizabeth with a little hesitation and struggling,—"that don't make it settled."

"It shews where the settling point is."

"Which leaves it as far as ever from being settled," said Elizabeth, almost impatiently.

"A self-reliant spirit, if it be not poised on another foundation than its own, hath no fixedness that is worth anything, Miss Elizabeth;—and friends are not safe things to trust to."

"Some of them are," said Elizabeth.

"No, for they are not sure. There is but one friend that cannot be taken away from us."

"But to know that, and to know everything else about him, does not make him our friend," said Elizabeth in a voice that trembled.

"To agree to everything about him, does."

"To agree?—How?—I do agree to it," said Elizabeth.

"Do you? Are you willing to have him for a King to reign over you?—as well as a Saviour to make you and keep you safe?"

She did not answer.

"You do not know everything about him, neither."

"What don't I know?"

"Almost all. You cannot, till you begin to obey him; for till then he will not shew himself to you. The epitome of all beauty is in those two words—Jesus Christ.

She made no answer yet, with her head bowed, and striving to check the straining sobs with which her breast was heaving. She had a feeling that he was looking on compassionately; but it was a good while before she could restrain herself into calmness; and during that time he added nothing more. When she could look up, she found he was not looking at her; his eyes were turned upon the river, where the moon made a broad and broadening streak of wavy brightness. But Elizabeth looked at the quiet of his brow, and it smote her; though there was now somewhat of thoughtful care upon the face. The tears that she thought she had driven back, rushed fresh to her eyes again.

"Do you believe what I last said, Miss Elizabeth?" he said turning round to her.

"About the epitome of all beauty?"

"Yes. Do you believe it?"

"You say so—I don't understand it," she said sadly and somewhat perplexed.

"I told you so," he answered, looking round to the moonlight again.

"But Mr. Landholm," said Elizabeth in evident distress, "won't you tell me something more?"

"I cannot."

"Oh yes you can,—a great deal more," she said weeping.

"I could," he said gravely,—"yet I should tell you nothing—you would not understand me. You must find it out for yourself."

"How in the world can I?"

"There is a promise,—'If any man will do his will, he shall know of the doctrine.'"

"I don't know how to begin, nor anything about it," said Elizabeth, weeping still.

"Begin anywhere."

"How? What do you mean?"

"Open the Bible at the first chapter of Matthew, and read.

Ask honestly, of your own conscience and of God, at each step, what obligation upon you grows out of what you are reading. If you follow his leading he will lead you on,—to himself."

Elizabeth sobbed in silence for some little time; then she said, "I will do it, Mr. Landholm."

"If you do," said he, "you will find you can do nothing."

"Nothing!" said Elizabeth.

"You will find you are dependent upon the good pleasure of God for power to take the smallest step."

"His good pleasure!—Suppose it should not be given me."

"There is no 'suppose' about that," Winthrop answered, with a slight smile, which seen as it was through a veil of tears, Elizabeth never forgot, and to which she often looked back in after time;—"'Whosoever *will*, let him take the water of life freely.' But he does not always get a draught at the first asking. The water of life was not bought so cheap as that. However, 'to him that knocketh, it shall be opened.'"

Elizabeth hearkened to him, with a curious mixture of yielding and rebellion at once in her mind. She felt them both there. But the rebellion was against the words; her yielding was for the voice that brought the words to her ear. She paused awhile.

"At that rate, people might be discouraged before they got what they wanted," she observed, when the silence had lasted some little time.

"They might," said Winthrop quietly.

"I should think many might."

"Many have been," he answered.

"What then?" she asked a little abruptly.

"They *did not get what they wanted.*"

Elizabeth started a little, and shivered, and tears began to come again.

"What's to hinder their being discouraged, Mr. Landholm?" she asked in a tone that was a little querulous.

"Believing God's word."

So sweet the words came, her tears ceased at that; the power of the truth sank for a moment with calming effect upon her rebellious feeling; but with this came also as truly the thought, "You have a marvellous beautiful way of saying things quietly!" —However for the time her objections were silenced; and she sat still, looking out upon the water, and thinking that with the first quiet opportunity she would begin the first chapter of Matthew.

For a little while they both were motionless and silent; and then rising, Winthrop began his walk up and down the deck again. Elizabeth was left to her meditations; which sometimes roved hither and thither, and sometimes concentred themselves upon the beat of his feet, which indeed formed a sort of background of cadence to them all. It was such a soothing reminder of one strong and sure stay that she might for the present lean upon; and the knowledge that she might soon lose it, made the reminder only the more precious. She was weeping most bitter tears during some of that time; but those footsteps behind her were like quiet music through all. She listened to them sometimes, and felt them always, with a secret gratification of knowing they would not quit the deck till she did. Then she had some qualms about his getting tired; and then she said to herself that she could not put a stop to what was so much to her and which she was not to have again. So she sat and listened to them, weary and half bewildered with the changes and pain of the last few days and hours; hardly recognizing the reality of her own situation, or that the sloop, Winthrop's walk behind her, the moonlight, her lonely seat on the deck, and her truly lonely place in the world, were not all parts of a curious phantasm. Or if realizing them, with senses so tried and blunted with recent wear and tear, that they refused to act and left her to realize it quietly and almost it seemed stupidly. She called it so to herself, but she could not help it; and she was in a manner thankful for that. She would wake up again. She would have liked to sit there all night under that moonlight and with the regular fall of Winthrop's step to and fro on the vessel.

"How long can you stand this?" said he, pausing beside her.

"What?" said Elizabeth looking up.

"How long can you do without resting?"

"I am resting.—I couldn't rest so well anywhere else."

"Couldn't you?"

"No!—" she said earnestly.

He turned away and went on walking. Elizabeth blessed him for it.

The moon shone, and the wind blew, and steadily the vessel sailed on; till higher grounds began to rise on either side of her, and hills stood back of hills, ambitious of each other's standing, and threw their deep shadows all along the margin of the river. As the sloop entered between these narrowing and lifting walls of the river channel, the draught of air became gentler, often hindered by some outstanding high point she had left behind; more slowly she made her way past hill and hill-embayed curves of the river, less stoutly her sails were filled, more gently her prow rippled over the smoother water. Sometimes she passed within the shadow of a lofty hill-side; and then slipped out again into the clear fair sparkling water where the moon shone.

"Are we near there?" said Elizabeth suddenly, turning her head to arrest her walking companion. He came to the back of the chair.

"Near Wut-a-qut-o?"

"Yes."

"No. Nearing it, but not near it yet."

"How soon shall we be?"

"If the wind holds, I should think in two hours."

"Where do we stop?"

"At the sloop's quarters—the old mill—about two miles down the river from Shahweetah."

"Why wouldn't she carry us straight up to the place?"

"It would be inconvenient landing there, and would very much delay the sloop's getting to her moorings."

"I'll pay for that!—"

"We can get home as well in another way."

"But then we shall have to stay here all night."

"Here, on the sloop, you mean? The night is far gone already."

"Not half!" said Elizabeth. "It's only a little past twelve."

"Aren't you tired?"

"I suppose so, but I don't feel it."

"Don't you want to take some sleep before morning?"

"No, I can't. But you needn't walk there to take care of me, Mr. Winthrop. I shall be quite safe alone."

"No, you will not," he said; and going to some of the sloop's receptacles, he drew out an old sail and laying it on the deck by her side he placed himself upon it, in a half sitting, half reclining posture, which told of some need of rest on his part.

"*You* are tired," she said earnestly. "Please don't stay here for me!"

"It pleases me to stay," he said lightly. "It is no hardship, under ordinary circumstances, to pass such a night as this out of doors."

"What is it in these circumstances?" said Elizabeth quickly.

"Not a hardship."

"You don't say much more than you are obliged to," thought Elizabeth bitterly. "It is 'not a hardship' to stay there to take care of me;—and there is not in the world another person left to me who could say even as much."—

"There is a silent peace-speaking in such a scene as this," presently said Winthrop, lying on his sail and looking at the river.

"I dare say there is," Elizabeth answered sadly.

"You cannot feel it, perhaps?"

"Not a particle. I can just see that it might be."

"The Bible makes such constant use of natural imagery, that to one familiar with it, the objects of nature bring back as constantly its teachings—its warnings—its consolations."

"What now?" said Elizabeth.

"Many things. Look at those deep and overlapping shadows. 'As the mountains are round about Jerusalem, so the Lord is round about his people, from henceforth"——

"Stop, Mr. Winthrop!" Elizabeth exclaimed;—"Stop! I can't bear it."

"Why?"

"I can't bear it," she repeated, in a passion of tears.

"Why?" said he again in the same tone, when a minute had gone by.

"Those words don't belong to me—I've nothing to do with them," she said, raising her head and dashing her tears right and left.

But Winthrop made no sort of answer to that, and a dead silence fell between the parties. Again the prow of the sloop was heard rippling against the waves; and slowly she glided past mountain and shadow, and other hills rose and other deep shadows lay before them. Elizabeth, between other thoughts, was tempted to think that her companion was as impassive and cold as the moonlight, and as moveless as the dark mountain lines that stood against the sky. And yet she knew and trusted him better than that. It was but the working of passing impatience and bitter feeling; it was only the chafing of passion against what seemed so self-contained and so calm. And yet that very self-continence and calmness was what passion liked, and what passion involuntarily bent down before.

She had not got over yet the stunned effect of the past days and nights. She sat feeling coldly miserable and forlorn and solitary; conscious that one interest was living at her heart yet, but also conscious that it was to live and die by its own strength as it might; and that in all the world she had nothing else; no, nor never should have anything else. She could not have a father again; and even he had been nothing for the companionship of such a spirit as hers, not what she wanted to make her either good or happy. But little as he had done of late to make her either, the name, and even the nominal guardianship, and what the old childish affection had clung to, were gone—and never could come back; and Elizabeth wept sometimes with a very bowed head and heart, and sometimes sat stiff and quiet, gazing at the varying mountain outline, and the fathomless shadows that repeated it upon the water.

The night drew on, as the hills closed in more and more upon the narrowing river channel, and the mountain heads lifted themselves more high, and the shadows spread out broader upon the river. Every light along shore had long been out; but now one glimmered down at them faintly from under a high thick wooded bluff, on the east shore; and the Julia Ann as she came up towards it, edged down a little constantly to that side of the river.

"Where are we going?" said Elizabeth presently. "We're getting out of the channel."

But she saw immediately that Winthrop was asleep. It made her feel more utterly alone and forlorn than she had done before. With a sort of additional chill at her heart, she looked round for some one else of whom to ask her question, and saw the skipper just come on deck. Elizabeth got up to speak to him.

"Aren t we getting out of our course?"

"Eg-zackly," said Mr. Hildebrand. "'Most out of it. That light's the Mill, marm."

"The Mill! Cowslip's Mill?"

"Well it's called along o' my father, 'cause he's lived there, I s'pose,—and made it,—and owns to it, too, as far as that goes;—I s'pose it's as good a right to have his name as any one's."

Elizabeth sat down and looked at the light, which now had a particularly cheerless and hopeless look for her. It was the token of somebody's home, shining upon one who had none; it was a signal of the near ending of a guardianship and society which for the moment had taken home's place; a reminder that presently she must be thrown upon her own guidance; left to take care of herself alone in the world, as best she might. The journey, with all its pain, had been a sort of little set-off from the rest of her life, where the contrasts of the past and the future did not meet. They were coming back now. She felt their shadows lying cold upon her. It was one of the times in her life of greatest desolation, the while the sloop was drawing down to her berth under the home light, and making fast in her moorings.

The moon was riding high, and dimly shewed Elizabeth the but half-remembered points and outlines;—and there was a contrast! She did not cry; she looked, with a cold chilled feeling of eye and mind that would have been almost despair, if it had not been for the one friend asleep at her side. And he was nothing to her. Nothing. He was nothing to her. Elizabeth said it to herself; but for all that he was there, and it was a comfort to see him there.

The sails rattled down to the deck; and with wind and headway the sloop gently swung up to her appointed place. Another light came out of the house, in a lantern; and another hand on shore aided the sloop's crew in making her fast.

"How can he sleep through it all!" thought Elizabeth. "I wonder if anything ever could shake him out of his settled composure—asleep or awake, it's all the same."

"Ain't you goin' ashore?" said the skipper at her side.

"No—not now."

"They'll slick up a better place for you than we could fix up in this here little hulk. Though she ain't a small sloop neither, by no means."

"What have you got aboard there, Hild'?" called out a voice that came from somewhere in the neighbourhood of the lantern. "Gals?"

"Governor Landholm and some company," said the skipper in a more moderate tone. The other voice took no hint of moderation.

"Governor Landholm?—is *he* along? Well—glad to see him. Run from the yallow fever, eh?"

"Is mother up, father?"

"Up?—no!—What on arth!"

"Tell her to get up, and make some beds for folks that couldn't sleep aboard sloop; and have been navigatin' all night."

"Go, and I'll look after the sloop till morning, Captain," said Winthrop sitting up on his sail.

"Won't you come ashore and be comfortable?" said father and son at once.

"I am comfortable."

"But you'll be better off there, Governor."

"Don't think I could, Hild'. I'm bound to stay by the ship."

"Won't you come, Miss?" said the skipper addressing Elizabeth. "You'll be better ashore."

"Oh yes—come along—all of you," said the old sloop-master on the land.

"I'm in charge of the passengers, Captain," said Winthrop; "and I don't think it is safe for any of them to go off before morning."

The request was urged to Elizabeth. But Winthrop quietly negatived it every time it was made; and the sloop's masters at last withdrew. Elizabeth had not spoken at all.

"How do you do?" said Winthrop gravely, when the Cowslips, father and son, had turned their backs upon the vessel.

"Thank you——" said Elizabeth,—and stopped there.

"You are worn out."

"No,"—Elizabeth answered under her breath; and then gathering it, went on,—"I am afraid you are."

"I am perfectly well," he said. "But you ought to rest."

"I will,—by and by," said Elizabeth desperately. "I will stay here till the daylight comes. It will not be long, will it?"

He made no answer. The sloop's deck was in parts blockaded with a load of shingles. Winthrop went to these, and taking down bundle after bundle, disposed them so as to make a resting-place of greater capabilities than the armless wooden chair in which Elizabeth had been sitting all night. Over this, seat, back, sides and all, he spread the sail on which he had been lying.

"Is there nothing in the shape of a pillow or cushion that you could get out of the cabin now?" said he.

"But you have given me your sail," said Elizabeth.

"I'm master of the sloop now. Can't you get a pillow?"

Since so much had been done for her, Elizabeth consented to do this for herself. She fetched a pillow from the cabin; and Winthrop himself bestowed it in the proper position; and with a choking feeling of gratitude and pleasure that did not permit her to utter one word, Elizabeth placed herself in the box seat made for her, took off her bonnet and laid her head down. She knew that Winthrop laid her light shawl over her head; but she did not stir. Her thanks reached only her pillow, in the shape of two or three hot tears; then she slept.

CHAPTER XXXVI.

Beneath my palm-trees, by the river side,
I sat a weeping; in the whole world wide
There was no one to ask me why I wept,—
And so I kept
Brimming the water-lily cups with tears
Cold as my fears.

SHELLEY.

THE dawn had fairly broken, but that was all, when Winthrop and old Mr. Cowslip met on the little wharf landing which served instead of courtyard to the house. The hands clasped each other cordially.

"How do you do? Glad to see you in these parts!" was the hearty salutation of the old man to the young.

"Thank you, Mr. Cowslip," said Winthrop, returning the grasp of the hand.

"I don't see but you keep your own," the old man went on, looking at him wistfully. "Why don't you come up our way oftener? It wouldn't hurt you."

"I don't know about that," said Winthrop. "My business lies that way, you know."

"Ah!—'tain't as good business as our'n, now," said Mr. Cowslip. "You'd better by half be up there on the old place, with your wife and half a dozen children about you. Ain't married yet, Governor, be you?"

"No sir."

"Goin' to be?"

"I don't know what I am going to be, sir."

"Ah!—" said the old miller with a sly smile. "Is that what you've got here in the sloop with you now? I guessed it, and Hild' said it wa'n't—not as he knowed on—but I told him he didn't know everything."

"Hild' is quite right. But there are two ladies here who are going up to Shahweetah. Can you give us a boat, Mr. Cowslip?"

"A boat?—How many of you?"

"Four—and baggage. Your boat is large enough—used to be when I went in her."

"Used to be when *I* went in her," said the old skipper; "but there it is! She won't hold nobody now."

"What's the matter?"

"She took too many passengers the other day,—that is, she took one too many. Shipped a cargo of fresh meat, sir, and it wa'n't stowed in right, and the 'Bessie Bell' broke her heart about it. Like to ha' gone to the bottom."

"What do you mean?"

"Why, I was comin' home from Diver's Rock the other day—just a week ago last Saturday—I had been round there up the shore after fish;—you know the rock where the horse mackerel comes?—me and little Archie; lucky enough we had no more along. By the by, I hope you'll go fishing, Winthrop—the mackerel's fine this year. How long you're goin' to stay?"

"Only a day or two, sir."

"Ah!—Well—we were comin' home with a good mess o' fine fish, and when we were just about in the middle of the river, comin' over,—the fish had been jumping all along the afternoon, shewing their heads and tails more than common; and I'd been sayin' to Archie it was a sign o' rain—'tis, you know,—and just as we were in the deepest of the river, about half way over, one of 'em came up and put himself aboard of us."

"A sturgeon?"

"Just that, sir; as sound a fellow as ever you saw in your life—just the length of one of my little oars—longer than I be—eight feet wanting one inch, he measured, for the blade of that oar has been broken off a bit—several inches,—and what do you think he weighed?—Two hundred and forty pound."

"So it seems you got him safe to land, where you could weigh him."

"And measure him. I forgot I was talkin' to a lawyer," said the old man laughing. "Yes, I didn't think much how long he was at the time, I guess! He came in as handsome as ever you saw anything done—just slipped himself over the gunwale so—and duv under one of the th'arts and druv his nose through the bottom of the boat."

"Kept it there, I hope?"

"Ha, ha! Not so fast but there came in a'most water enough to float him again by the time we got to land. He was a power of a fellow!"

"And the 'Bessie' don't float?"

"No; she's laid up with three broken ribs."

"No other boat on hand?"

"There's a little punt out there, that Hild' goes a fishin' in—that'd carry two or three people. But it wouldn't take the hull on ye."

"There's the sloop's boat."

"She leaks," said the miller. "She wants to be laid up as bad as the 'Bessie.'"

"Have you any sort of a team, Mr. Cowslip?"

"Yes!—there's my little wagon—it'll hold two. But you ain't wanting it yet, be you?"

"As soon as it can go—if it *can* go. Is there a horse to the wagon?"

"Sartain! But won't you stop and take a bit?"

"No sir. If you will let some of the boys take up the punt with her load, I'll drive the wagon myself, and as soon as you can let me have it."

"Jock!—tackle up the wagon!—that 'ere little red one in the barn," shouted the miller. "Hild' 'll see to the boat-load—or I will,—and send it right along. I'm sorry you won't stop."

Winthrop turned back to the sloop. Elizabeth met him there with the question, "if she might not go now?"

"As soon as you please. I am going to drive you up to Shahweetah. The boat will carry the rest, but it is too small to take all of us."

"I'm very glad!"—Elizabeth could not help saying.

She granted half a word of explanation to Mrs. Nettley, her bonnet was hastily thrown on, and she stood with Winthrop on the wharf before the little wagon was fairly ready. But Jock was not tardy neither; and a very few minutes saw them seated and the horse's head turned from the Mill.

The dawn was fresh and fair yet, hardly yielding to day. In utter silence they drove swiftly along the road, through the woods and out upon the crest of tableland overlooking the bay; just above the shore where the huckleberry party had coasted along, that afternoon years before. By the time they got there, the day had begun to assert itself. Little clouds over Wut-a-qut-o's head were flushing into loveliness, and casting down rosy tints on the water; the mountain slopes were growing bright, and a soft warm colouring flung through all the air from the coming rays of the coming sun. The cat-birds were wide awake and very busy; the song sparrows full of gladness; and now and then, further off, a wood-thrush, less worldly than the one and less unchastened than the other, told of hidden and higher sweets, in tones further removed from Earth than his companions knew. The wild, pure, ethereal notes thrilled like a voice from some clear region where earthly defilement had been overcome, and earthly sorrows had lost their power. Between whiles, the little song sparrows strained their throats with rejoicing; but that was the joy of hilarious nature that sorrows and defilement had never touched. The cat-birds spoke of business, and sung over it, ambitious and self-gratulatory, and proud. And then by turns came the strange thrush's note, saying, as if they knew it and had proved it,

"WHEN HE GIVETH QUIETNESS, THEN WHO CAN MAKE TROUBLE?"

The travellers had ridden so far without speaking a word. If Elizabeth was sometimes weeping, she kept herself very quiet, and perfectly still. The sights and sounds that were abroad entered her mind by a side door, if they entered at all. Winthrop might have taken the benefit of them; but up to the bend of the bay he had driven fast and attentively. Here he suffered the horse to slacken his pace and come even to a walk, while his eye took note of the flushing morning, and perhaps the song of the birds reached his ear. It was not of them he spoke.

"Do you mean to begin upon the first chapter of Matthew?" he said, when the horse had walked the length of some two or three minutes.

"Yes!—I do"—said Elizabeth, turning her face towards him.

"According to the rules?"

The answer was spoken more hesitatingly, but again it was 'yes.'

"I am glad of that," he said.

"Mr. Winthrop," said Elizabeth presently, speaking it seemed with some effort,—"if I get into any difficulty—if I cannot understand,—I mean, if I am in any real trouble,—may I write to you to ask about it?"

"With great pleasure. I mean, it would give me great pleasure to have you do so."

"I should be very much obliged to you," she said humbly.

She did not see, for she did not look to see, a tiny show of a smile which spread itself over her companion's face. They drove on fast, till the bottom of the bay was left and they descended from the tableland, by Sam Doolittle's, to the road which skirted the south side of Shahweetah. Winthrop looked keenly as he passed at the old fields and hillsides. They were uncultivated now; fallow lands and unmown grass pastures held the place of the waving harvests of grain and new-reaped stubblefields that used to be there in the old time. The pastures grew rank, for there were even no cattle to feed them; and the fallows were grown with thistles and weeds. But over what might have been desolate lay the soft warmth of the summer morning; and rank pasture and uncared fallow ground took varied rich and bright hues under the early sun's rays. Those rays had now waked the hilltops and sky and river, and were just tipping the woods and slopes of the lower ground. By the bend meadow Winthrop drew in his horse again and looked fixedly.

"Does it seem pleasant to you?" he asked.

"How should it, Mr. Winthrop?" Elizabeth said coldly.

"Do you change your mind about wishing to be here?"

"No, not at all. I might as well be here as anywhere. I would rather—I have nowhere else to go."

He made no comment, but drove on fast again, till he drew up once more at the old back door of the old house. It seemed a part of the solitude, for nothing was stirring. Elizabeth sat and watched Winthrop tie the horse; then he came and helped her out of the wagon.

"Lean on me," said he. "You are trembling all over."

He put her arm within his, and led her up to the door and knocked.

"Karen is up—unless she has forgotten her old ways," said Winthrop. He knocked again.

A minute after, the door slowly opened its upper half, and Karen's wrinkled face and white cap and red shortgown were before them. Winthrop did not speak. Karen looked in bewilderment; then her bewilderment changed into joy.

"Mr. Winthrop!—Governor!"—

And her hand was stretched out, and clasped his in a long mute stringent clasp, which her eyes at least said was all she could do.

"How do you do, Karen?"

"I'm well—the Lord has kept me. But you——"

"I am well," said Winthrop. "Will you let us come in, Karen?—This lady has been up all night, and wants rest and refreshment."

Karen looked suspiciously at 'this lady,' as she unbolted the lower half of the door and let them in; and again when Winthrop carefully placed her in a chair and then went off into the inner room for one which he knew was more easy, and made her change the first for it.

"And what have ye come up for now, Governor?" she said, when she had watched them both, with an unsatisfied look upon her face and a tone of deep satisfaction coming out in her words.

"Breakfast, Karen. What's to be had?"

"Breakfast? La!"—said the old woman,—"if you had told me you's coming—What do you expect I'll have in the house for my breakfast, Governor?"

"Something ——," said Winthrop, taking the tongs and settling the sticks of wood in the chimney to burn better. Karen stood and looked at him.

"What have you got, Karen?" said Winthrop, setting up the tongs.

"I ha'n't got nothing for company," said Karen, grinning.

"That'll do very well," said Winthrop. "Give me the coffee and I'll make it; and you see to the bread, Karen. You have milk and cream, haven't you?"

"Yes, Governor."

"And eggs?"

"La! yes."

"Where are they?"

"Mr. Landholm, don't trouble yourself, pray!" said Elizabeth. "I am in no hurry for anything. Pray don't!"

"I don't intend it," said he. "Don't trouble *your* self. Would you rather go into another room?"

Elizabeth would not; and therefore and thereafter kept herself quiet, watching the motions of Karen and her temporary master. Karen seemed in a maze; but a few practical advices from Winthrop at last brought her back to the usual possession of her senses and faculties.

"Who is she?" Elizabeth heard her whisper as she began to bustle about. And Winthrop's answer, not whispered,

"How long ago do you suppose this coffee was parched?"

"No longer ago than yesterday. La sakes! Governor,—I'll do some fresh for you if you want it."

"No time for that, Karen. You get on with those cakes."

Elizabeth watched Winthrop with odd admiration and curiosity, mixed for the moment with not a little of gratified feeling; but the sense of desolation sitting back of all. He seemed to have come out in a new character, or rather to have taken up an old one; for no one could suppose it worn for the first time.

Karen had been set to making cakes with all speed. Winthrop seemed to have taken the rest of the breakfast upon himself. He had found the whereabout of the eggs, and ground some coffee, and made it and set it to boil in Karen's tin coffeepot.

"What are you after now, Mr. Winthrop?" said Karen, looking round from her pan and moulding board. "These'll be in the spider before your coffee's boiled."

"They'll have to be quick, then," said Winthrop, going on with his rummaging.

"What are you after, Governor?—there's nothin' there but the pots and kittles."

One of which, however, Winthrop brought out as if it was the thing wanted, and put upon the fire with water in it. Going back to the receptacle of 'pots and kittles,' he next came forth with the article Karen had designated as the 'spider,' and set that in order due upon its appropriate bed of coals.

"La sakes! Governor!" said Karen, in a sort of fond admiration,—"ha'n't you forgot nothin'?"

"Now Karen," said Winthrop, when she had covered the bottom of the hot iron with her thin cakes,"—you set the table and I'll take care of 'em."

"There's the knife, then," said Karen. "Will ye know when to turn them? There ain't fire enough to bake 'em by the blaze."

"I've not forgotten so much," said Winthrop. "Let's have a cup and saucer and plate, Karen."

"Ye sha'n't have *one*," said Karen, casting another inquisitive and doubtful glance towards the silent, pale, fixed figure sitting in the middle of her kitchen. He did have one, however, before she had got the two ready; despatched Karen from the table for sugar and cream; and then poured out himself a cup of his own preparation, and set it on Karen's half-spread table, and came to Elizabeth. He did not ask her if she would have it, nor say anything in fact; but gently raising her with one hand, he brought forward her chair with the other, and placed both where he wanted them to be, in the close neighbourhood of the steaming coffee. Once before, Elizabeth had known him take the same sort of superintending care of her, when she was in no condition to take care of herself. It was inexpressibly soothing; and yet she felt as if she could have knelt down on the floor, and given forth her very life in tears. She looked at the coffee with a motionless face, till his hand held it out to her. Not to drink it was impossible, though she was scarcely conscious of swallowing anything but tears. When she took the cup from her lips, she found an egg, hot out of the water, on her plate, which was already supplied also with butter. Her provider was just adding one of the cakes he had been baking.

"I can't eat!" said Elizabeth, looking up.

"You must,—" Winthrop answered.

In the same tone in which he had been acting. Elizabeth obeyed it as involuntarily.

"Who is the lady, Governor?" Karen ventured, when she had possessed herself of the cake-knife, and had got Winthrop fairly seated at *his* breakfast.

"This lady is the mistress of the place, Karen."

"The mistress! Ain't you the master?"—Karen inquired instantly.

"No. I have no right here any longer, Karen."

"I heered it was selled, but I didn't rightly believe it," the old woman said sadly. "And the mistress 'll be turning *me* away now?"

"Tell her no," whispered Elizabeth.

"I believe not, Karen, unless you wish it."

"What should I wish it for? I've been here ever since I come with Mis' Landholm, when she come first, and she left me here; and I want to stay here, in her old place, till I'm called to be with her again. D'ye think it'll be long, Governor?"

"Are you in haste, Karen?"

"I don't want fur to stay" said the old woman. "She's gone, and I can't take care o' you no longer, nor no one. I'd like to be gone, too—yes, I would."

"You have work to do yet, Karen. You may take as good care as you can of this lady."

Again Karen looked curiously and suspiciously at her, for a minute in silence.

"Is she one of the Lord's people?" she asked suddenly.

Elizabeth looked up on the instant, in utter astonishment at the question; first at Karen and then at Winthrop. The next thing was a back-sweeping tide of feeling, which made her drop her bread and her cup from her hands, and hide her face in them with a bitter burst of tears. Winthrop looked concerned, and Karen confounded. But she presently repeated her question in a half whisper at Winthrop.

"Is she?—"

"There is more company coming, Karen, for you to take care of," he said quietly "I hope you have cakes enough. Miss

Haye—I see the boat-load has arrived—will you go into the other room?"

She rose, and not seeing where she went, let him lead her. The front part of the house was unfurnished; but to the little square passage-way where the open door let in the breeze from the river, Winthrop brought a chair, and there she sat down. He left her there and went back to see to the other members of the party, and as she guessed to keep them from intruding upon her. She was long alone.

The fresh sweet air blew in upon her hot face and hands, reminding her what sort of a world it came from; and after the first few violent bursts of pain, Elizabeth presently raised her head to look out and see, in a sort of dogged willingness to take the contrast which she knew was there. The soft fair hilly outlines she remembered, in the same August light;—the bright bend of the river—a sloop sail or two pushing lazily up;—the same blue of a summer morning overhead;—the little green lawn immediately at her feet, and the everlasting cedars, with their pointed tops and their hues of patient sobriety—all stood nearly as she had left them, how many years before. And herself—Elizabeth felt as if she could have laid herself down on the doorstep and died, for mere heart-heaviness. In this bright sunny world, what had she to do? The sun had gone out of her heart. What was to become of her? What miserable part should she play, all alone by herself? She despised herself for having eaten breakfast that morning. What business had she to eat, or to have any appetite to eat, when she felt so? But Winthrop had made her do it. What for? Why should he? It was mere aggravation, to take care of her for a day, and then throw her off for ever to take care of herself. How soon would he do that?—

She was musing, her eyes on the ground; and had quite forgotten the sunny landscape before her with all its gentle suggestions; when Winthrop's voice sounded pleasantly in her ear, asking if she felt better. Elizabeth looked up.

"I was thinking," she said, "that if there were nothing better to be had in another world, I could almost find it in my heart to wish I had never been born into this!"

She expected that he would make some answer to her, but he did not. He was quite silent; and Elizabeth presently began to question with herself whether she had said something dreadful. She was busily taking up her own words, since he had not saved her the trouble. She found herself growing very much ashamed of them.

"I suppose that was a foolish speech," she said, after a few moments of perfect silence,—"a speech of impatience."

But Winthrop neither endorsed nor denied her opinion; he said nothing about it; and Elizabeth was exceedingly mortified.

"If you wanted to rebuke me," she thought, "you could not have done it better. I suppose there is no rebuke so sharp as that one is obliged to administer to oneself. And your cool keeping silence is about as effectual a way of telling me that you have no interest in my concerns as even you could have devised."

Elizabeth's eyes must have swallowed the landscape whole, for they certainly took in no distinct part of it.

"How are you going to make yourself comfortable here?" said Winthrop presently;—"these rooms are unfurnished."

She might have said that she did not expect to be comfortable anywhere; but she swallowed that too.

"I will go and see what I can do in the way of getting some furniture together," he went on. "I hope you will be able to find some way of taking rest in the mean time—though I confess I do not see how."

"Pray do not!" said Elizabeth starting up, and her whole manner and expression changing. "I am sure you are tired to death now."

"Not at all. I slept last night."

"How much? Pray do not go looking after anything! You will trouble me very much."

"I should be sorry to do that."

"I can get all the rest I want."

"Where?"

"On the rocks—on the grass."

"Might do for a little while," said Winthrop;—"I hope it will; but I must try for something better."

"Where can you find anything—in this region?"

"I don't know," said he; "but it must be found. If not in this region, in some other."

"To-morrow, Mr. Landholm."

"To-morrow—has its own work" said he; and went.

"Will he go to-morrow?" thought Elizabeth, with a pang at her heart. "Oh, I wish—no, I dare not wish—that I had never been born! What am I to do with myself?—"

Conscience suggested very quietly that something might be done; but Elizabeth bade conscience wait for another time, though granting all it advanced. She put that by, as she did Mrs. Nettley and Clam who both presently came where Winthrop had been standing, to make advances of a different nature.

"What'll I do, Miss 'Lizabeth?" said the latter, in a tone that argued a somewhat dismal view of affairs.

"Anything you can find to do."

"Can't find nothin,—" said Clam," 'cept Karen. One corner of the house is filled enough with her; and the rest ha'n't got nothin' in it."

"Let Karen alone, and take care of your own business, Clam."

"If I knowed what 'twas," said the persevering damsel. "I can't make the beds, for there ain't none; nor set the furnitur to rights, for the rooms is 'stressed empty."

"You can let me alone, at all events. The rooms will have something in them before long. You know what to do as well as any one;—if you don't, ask Mr. Landholm."

"Guess I will!" said Clam; "when I want to feel foolisher than I do. Did the furnitur come by the sloop?"

"No. Mr. Landholm will send some. I don't care anything about it."

"Ha! then if *he's* goin' to send it," said Clam turning away, "the place 'll have to be ready for it, I s'pose."

Mrs. Nettley appeared in Clam's place. Elizabeth was still sitting on the door-step, and though she knew by a side view that one had given place to the other, she did not seem to know it and sat looking straight before her at the sunny landscape.

"It's a beautiful place," said Mrs. Nettley after a little pause of doubt.

"Very beautiful," said Elizabeth coldly.

"I did not know it was so beautiful. And a healthy place, I should suppose."

Elizabeth left the supposition unquestioned.

"You are sadly fatigued, Miss Haye," said Mrs. Nettley after a longer pause than before.

"I suppose I am," said Elizabeth rising, for patience had drawn her last breath;—"I am going down by the water to rest. Don't let any one follow me or call me—I want nothing—only to rest by myself."

And drawing her scarf round her, she strode through the rank grass to the foot of the lawn, and then between scattered rocks and sweetbriars and wild rose-bushes, to the fringe of cedar trees which there clothed the rocks down to the water. Between and beneath them, just where she came out upon the river, an outlooking mass of granite spread itself smooth and wide enough to seat two or three people. The sun's rays could not reach there, except through thick cedar boughs. Cedar trees and the fall of ground hid it from the house; and in front a clear opening gave her a view of the river and opposite shore, and of a cedar-covered point of her own land, outjutting a little distance further on. Solitude, silence, and beauty invited her gently; and Elizabeth threw herself down on the grey lichen-grown stone; but rest was not there.

"Rest!"—she said to herself in great bitterness;—"rest! How can I rest?—or where can there be rest for me?——"

And then passionate nature took its will, and poured out to itself and drank all the deep draughts of pain that passion alone can fill and refill for its own food. Elizabeth's proud head bowed there, to the very rock she sat on. Yet the proud heart would not lay itself down as well; *that* stood up to breast pain and wrestle with it, and take the full fierce power of the blast that came. Till nature was tired out,—till the frame subsided from convulsions that racked it, into weary repose,—so long the struggle lasted; and then the struggle was not ended, but only the forces on either side had lost the power of carrying it on. And then she sat, leaning against a cedar trunk that gave her its welcome support, which every member and muscle craved; not relieved, but with that curious respite from pain which the dulled senses take when they have borne suffering as long and as sharply as they can.

It was hot in the sun; but only a warm breath of summer air played about Elizabeth where she sat. The little waves of the river glittered and shone and rolled lazily down upon the channel, or curled up in rippling eddies towards the shore. The sunlight was growing ardent upon the hills and the river; but over Elizbeth's head the shade was still unbroken. A soft aromatic smell came from the cedars, now and then broken in upon by a faint puff of fresher air from the surface of the water. Hardly any sound, but the murmur of the ripple at the water's edge and the cherup-ing of busy grasshoppers upon the lawn. Now and then a locust did sing out; he only said it was August and that the sun was shining hot and sleepily everywhere but under the cedar trees. His song was irresistible. Elizabeth closed her eyes and listened to it, in a queer kind of luxurious rest-taking which was had because mind and body would have it. Pain was put away, in a sort; for the senses of pain were blurred. The aromatic smell of the evergreens was wafted about her; and then came a touch, a most gentle touch, of the south river-breeze upon her face; and then the long dreamy cry of the locust; and the soft plashing sound of the water at her feet. All Elizabeth's faculties were crying for sleep; and sleep came, handed in by the locust and the summer air, and laid its kind touch of forgetfulness upon mind and body. At first she lost herself leaning against the cedar tree, waking up by turns to place herself better; and at last yielding to the overpowering influences without and within, she curled her head down upon a thick bed of moss at her side and gave herself up to such rest as she might.

What sort of rest? Only the rest of the body, which had made a truce with the mind for the purpose. A quiet which knew that storms were not over, but which would be quiet nevertheless. Elizabeth felt that, in her intervals of half-consciousness. But all the closer she clung to her pillow of dry moss. She had a dispensation from sorrow there. When her head left it, it would be to ache again. It should not ache now. Sweet moss! —sweet summer air!—sweet sound of plashing water!—sweet dreamy lullaby of the locust!—Oh if they could put her to sleep for ever!——sing pain out and joy in!——

A vague, half-realized notion of the fight that must be gone through before rest 'for ever' could in any wise be hoped for—of the things that must be gained and the things that must be lost before that 'for ever' rest could in any sort be looked forward to,——and dismissing the thought, Elizabeth blessed her fragrant moss pillow of Lethe and went to sleep again.

How she dreaded getting rested; how she longed for that overpowering fatigue and exhaustion of mind and body to prolong itself! And as the hours went on, she knew that she was getting rested, and that she would have to wake up to everything again by and by. It should not be at anybody's bidding.

"Miss 'Lizabeth!—" sounded Clam's voice in the midst of her slumbers.

"Go away, Clam!" said the sleeper, without opening her eyes.

"Miss 'Lizabeth, ain't ye goin' to eat nothin'?"

"No—Go away."

"Miss 'Lizabeth!—dinner's ready."

"Well!—"

"You're a goin' to kill yourself."

"Don't *you* kill me!" said Elizabeth impatiently. "Go off."

"To be sure," said Clam as she turned away,—"there ain't much company."

It was very vexing to be disturbed. But just as she was

getting quiet again, came the tread of Mrs. Nettley's foot behind her, and Elizabeth knew another colloquy was at hand.

"Are you asleep, Miss Haye?" said the good lady a little timidly.

"No," said Elizabeth lifting her head wearily,—"I wish I were."

"There's dinner got ready for you in the house."

"Let anybody eat it that can.—I can't."

"Wouldn't you be better for taking a little something? I'm afraid you'll give way if you do not."

"I don't care," said Elizabeth. "Let me give way—only let me alone!"

She curled her head down determinately again.

"I am afraid, Miss Haye, you will be ill," said poor Mrs. Nettley.

"I am willing,"—said Elizabeth. "I don't care about anything, but to be quiet!—"

Mrs. Nettley went off in despair; and Elizabeth in despair also, found that vexation had effectually driven away sleep. In vain the locust sang and the moss smelled sweet; the tide of feeling had made head again, and back came a rush of disagreeable things, worse after worse; till Elizabeth's brow quitted the moss pillow to be buried in her hands, and her half-quieted spirit shook anew with the fresh-raised tempest. Exhaustion came back again; and thankfully she once more laid herself down to sleep and forgetfulness.

Her sleep was sound this time. The body asserted its rights; and long, long she lay still upon her moss pillow, while the regular deep-drawn breath came and went, fetching slow supplies of strength and refreshment. The sun quitted its overhead position and dipped towards Wut-a-qut-o, behind the high brow of which, in summer-time, it used to hide itself. A slant ray found an opening in the thick tree-tops, and shone full upon Elizabeth's face; but it failed to rouse her; and it soon went up higher and touched a little song sparrow that was twittering in a cedar tree close by. Then the shadows of the trees fell long over the grass towards the rocks on the east.

Elizabeth was awakened at last by a familiar adjuration.

"Miss 'Lizabeth!—you'll catch a Typhus, or an agur, or somethin' dreadful, down there! Don't ye want to live no more in the world?"

Elizabeth sat up, and rested her face on her knees, feeling giddy and sick.

"Don't ye feel bad?"

"Hush, Clam!——"

"I'm sent after ye," said Clam,—"I dursn't hush. Folks thinks it is time you was back in the house."

"Hush!—I don't care what folks think."

"Not what *nobody* thinks?" said Clam.

"What do you mean!" said Elizabeth flashing round upon her. "Go back into the house.—I will come when I am ready."

"You're ready now," said Clam. "Miss 'Lizabeth, ye ain't fit for anything, for want of eatin'. Come!—they want ye."

"Not much,"—thought Elizabeth bitterly,—"if they left it to her to bring me in."

"Are you sick, Miss 'Lizabeth?"

"No."

"He's come home," Clam went on;—"and you never saw the things he has brought! Him and me's been puttin' 'em up and down. Lots o' things. Ain't he a man!"

"'Up and down!'" repeated Elizabeth.

"Egg-zackly,"—said Clam;—"Floor-spreads—what-d'ye-call-ems?—and bedsteads—and chairs. He said if he'd know'd the house was all stripped, he'd never have fetched you up here."

"Yes he would," said Elizabeth. "What do I care for a stripped house!"—"with a stripped heart," her thought finished it.

"Well don't you care for supper neither?—for that old thing is a fixin' it," said Clam.

"You must not call her names to me."

"Ain't she old?" said Clam.

"She is a very good old woman, I believe."

"Ain't you comin' Miss 'Lizabeth? They won't sit down without you."

"Who sent you out here?"

"Karen axed where you was; and Mrs. Nettley said she dursn't go look for you; and Mr. Landholm said I was to come and bring you in."

"He didn't, Clam!——"

"As likely as your head's been in the moss there, he did, Miss 'Lizabeth."

"Go yourself back into the house. I'll come when I am ready, and I am not ready yet."

"He ha'n't had nothin' to eat to-day, I don't believe," said Clam, by way of a parting argument. But Elizabeth let her go without seeming to hear her.

She sat with her hands clasped round her knees, looking down upon the water; her eyes slowly filling with proud and bitter tears. Yet she saw and felt how coolly the lowering sunbeams were touching the river now; that evening's sweet breath was beginning to freshen up among the hills; that the daintiest, lightest, cheeriest gilding was upon every mountain top, and wavelet, and pebble, and stem of a tree. "Peace be to thee, fair nature, and thy scenes!"—and peace from them seems to come too. But oh how to have it! Elizabeth clasped her hands tight together and then wrung them mutely. "O mountains—O river —O birds!"—she thought,—"If I could but be as senseless as you—or as good for something!——"

CHAPTER XXXVII.

When cockleshells turn silver bells,
  When wine dreips red frae ilka tree,
When frost and snaw will warm us a',
  Then I'll come doun an' dine wi' thee.
JEANNIE DOUGLASS.

THE sun was low, near Wut-a-qut-o's brow, when at last slowly and lingeringly, and with feet that, as it were, spurned each step they made, Elizabeth took her way to the house. But no sooner did her feet touch the doorstep than her listless and sullen mood gave place to a fit of lively curiosity—to see what Winthrop had done. She turned to the left into the old keeping-room.

It had been very bare in the morning. Now, it was stocked with neat cane-bottomed chairs, of bird's-eye maple. In the middle of the floor rested an ambitious little mahogany table with claw feet. A stack of green window-blinds stood against the pier between the windows, and at the bottom on the floor lay a paper of screws and hinges. The floor was still bare, to be sure, and so was the room, but yet it looked hopeful compared with the morning's condition. Elizabeth stood opening her eyes in a sort of mazed bewilderment; then hearing a little noise of hammering in the other part of the house, she turned and crossed over to the east room—her sleeping-room of old and now. She went within the door and stood fast.

Her feet were upon a green carpet which covered the room. Round about were more of the maple chairs, looking quite handsome on their green footing. There was a decent dressing-table and chest of drawers of the same wood, in their places; and a round mahogany stand which seemed to be meant for no particular place but to do duty anywhere. And in the corner of the room was Winthrop, with Mrs. Nettley and Clam for assistants, busy putting up a bedstead. He looked up slightly from his work when Elizabeth shewed herself, but gave her no further attention. Clam grinned. Mrs. Nettley was far too intent upon holding her leg of the bedstead true and steady, to notice or know anything else whatever.

Elizabeth looked for a moment, without being able to utter a word; and then turned about and went and stood at the open door, her breast heaving thick and her eyes too full to see a thing before her. Then she heard Winthrop pass behind her and go into the other room. Elizabeth followed quickly. He had stooped to the paper of screws, but stood up when she came in, to speak to her.

"I am ashamed of myself for having so carelessly brought you to a dismantled house. I had entirely forgotten that it was so, in this degree,—though I suppose I must at some time have heard it."

"It would have made no difference,—" said Elizabeth, and said no more.

"I will return to the city to-morrow, and send you up immediately whatever you will give order for. It can be here in a very few days."

Elizabeth looked at the maple chairs and the mahogany table, and she could not speak, for her words choked her. Winthrop stooped again to his paper of screws and hinges and began turning them over.

"What are you going to do?" said Elizabeth, coming a step nearer.

"I am going to see if I can put up these blinds?"

"Blinds!" said Elizabeth.

"Yes.—I was fortunate enough to find some that were not very far from the breadth of the windows. They were too long; and I made the man shorten them. I think they will do."

"What *did* you take all that trouble for?"

"It was no trouble."

"Where did all these things come from?"

"From Starlings—I hadn't to go any further than that for them."

"How far is it?"

"Twelve miles."

"Twelve miles there and back!"

"Makes twenty-four."

"In this hot day!—I am very sorry, Mr. Landholm!"

"For what?" said he, shouldering one of the green blinds.

"You are not going to put those on yourself?"

"I am going to try—as I said."

"You have done enough day's work," said Elizabeth. "Pray don't, at least to-night. It's quite late. Please don't! — "

"If I don't to-night, I can't to-morrow," said Winthrop, marching out. "I must go home to-morrow."

Home! It shook Elizabeth's heart to hear him speak the old word. But she only caught her breath a little, and then spoke, following him out to the front of the house.

"I would rather they were not put up, Mr. Landholm. I can get somebody to do it."

"Not unless I fail."

"It troubles me very much that you should have such a day."

"I have nad just such a day——as I wanted," said Winthrop, measuring with his eye and rule the blind and the window-frame respectively.

"Miss 'Lizabeth, Karen's got the tea all ready, she says," Clam announced from the door; "and she hopes everybody's tired of waitin'."

"You've not had tea!—" exclaimed Elizabeth. "Come then, Mr. Winthrop."

"Not now," said he, driving in his gimlet,—"I must finish this first. 'The night cometh wherein no man can work.'"

Elizabeth shrank inwardly, and struggled with herself.

"But the morning comes also," she said.

Winthrop's eye went up to the top hinge of the blind, and down to the lower one, and up to the top again; busy and cool, it seemed to consider nothing but the hinges. Elizabeth struggled with herself again. She was mortified. But she could not let go the matter.

"Pray leave those things!" she said in another minute. "Come in, and take what is more necessary."

"When my work is done," said he. "Go in, Miss Elizabeth. Karen will give me something by and by."

Elizabeth turned; she could do nothing more in the way of persuasion. As she set her foot heavily on the door-step, she saw Clam standing in the little passage, her lips slightly parted in a satisfied bit of a smile. Elizabeth was vexed, proud, and vexed again, in as many successive quarter seconds. Her foot was heavy no longer.

"Have you nothing to do, Clam?"

"Lots," said the damsel.

"Why aren't you about it, then?"

"I was waitin' till you was about your'n, Miss 'Lizabeth. I like folks to be out o' my way."

"Do you! Take care and keep out of mine," said her mistress. "What are you going to do now?"

"Settle your bed, Miss 'Lizabeth. It's good we've got linen enough, anyhow."

"Linen,—" said Elizabeth,—"and a bedstead,—have you got a bed to put on it?"

"There's been care took for that," said Clam, with the same satisfied expression and a little turn of her head.

Half angry and half sick, Elizabeth left her, and went in through her new-furnished keeping-room, to Karen's apartment where the table was bountifully spread and Mrs. Nettley and Karen awaited her coming. Elizabeth silently sat down.

"Ain't he comin'?" said Karen.

"No—I am very sorry—Mr. Landholm thinks he must finish what he is about first."

"He has lots o' *thoughts*," said Karen discontentedly,—"he'd think just as well after eatin'.—Well, Miss—Karen's done her best—There's been worse chickens than those be—Mis' Landholm used to cook 'em that way, and she didn't cook 'em no better. I s'pose he'll eat some by'm by—when he's done thinkin'."

She went off, and Elizabeth was punctually and silently taken care of by Mrs. Nettley. The meal over, she did not go back to her own premises; but took a stand in the open kitchen door, for a variety of reasons, and stood there, looking alternately out and in. The sun had set, the darkness was slowly gathering; soft purple clouds floated up from the west, over Wut-a-qut-o's head, which however the nearer heads of pines and cedars prevented her seeing. A delicate fringe of evergreen foliage edged upon the clear white sky. The fresher evening air breathed through the pine and cedar branches, hardly stirred their stiff leaves, but brought from them tokens of rare sweetness; brought them to Elizabeth's sorrowful face, and passed on. Elizabeth turned her face from the wind and looked into the house. Karen had made her appearance again, and was diligently taking away broken meats and soiled dishes and refreshing the look of the table; setting some things to warm and some things to cool; giving the spare plate and knife and fork the advantage of the best place at table; brushing away crumbs, and smoothing down the salt-cellar. "You *are* over particular!" thought Elizabeth;—"it would do him no harm to come after me in handling the salt-spoon!—that even that trace of me should be removed." She looked out again.

Her friend the locust now and then was reminding her of the long hot day they had passed through together; and the intervals between were filled up by a chorus of grasshoppers and crickets and katydids. Soft and sweet blew the west wind again; *that* spoke not of the bygone day, with its burden and heat; but of rest, and repose, and the change that cometh even to sorrowful things. The day was passed and gone. "But if one day is passed, another is coming,"—thought Elizabeth; and tears, hot and bitter tears, sprang to her eyes. How could those clouds float so softly!—how could the light and shadow rest so lovely on them!—how could the blue ether look so still and clear! "Can one be like that?"—thought Elizabeth. "Can I?—with this boiling depth of passion and will in my nature?—*One* can—" and she again turned her eyes within. But nothing was there, save the table, the supper, and Karen. The question arose, what she herself was standing there for? but passion and will said they did not care! she would stand there; and she did. It was pleasant to stand there; for passion and will, though they had their way, seemed to her feeling to be quieted down under nature's influences. Perhaps the most prominent thought now was of a great discord between nature and her, between her and right,—which was to be made up. But still, while her face was towards the western sky and soft wind, and her mind thought this, her ear listened for a step on the kitchen floor. The colours of the western sky had grown graver and cooler before it came.

It came, and there was the scrape of a chair on the wooden floor. He had sat down, and Karen had got up; but Elizabeth would not look in.

"Are ye hungry enough now, Governor?"

"I hope so, Karen,—for your sake."

"Ye don't care much for your own," said Karen discontentedly.

Perhaps Winthrop—perhaps Elizabeth, thought that she made up his lack of it. Elizabeth watched, stealthily, to see how the old woman waited upon him—hovered about him—supplied his wants, actual and possible, and stood looking at him when she could do nothing else. She could not understand the low word or two with which Winthrop now and then rewarded her. Bitter feeling overcame her at last; she turned away, too much out of tune with nature to notice any more, unless by way of contrast, what nature had spread about her and over her. She went round the house again to the front and sat down in the doorway. The stars were out, the moonlight lay soft on the water, the dews fell heavily.

"Miss Lizzie!—you'll catch seven deaths out there!—the day's bad enough, but the night's five times worse,"—Clam exclaimed.

"I shan't catch but one," Elizabeth said gloomily.

"Your muslin's all wet, drinchin'!"

"It will dry."

"I can hang it up, I s'pose; but what 'll I do with you if you get sick?"

"Nothing whatever! Let me alone, Clam."

"Mis' Nettles!—" said Clam going in towards the kitchen, —"Mis' Nettles!—where's Mr. Landholm?—Governor Winthrop —here's Miss 'Lizabeth unhookin' all them blinds you've been a hookin' up."

"What do you mean, Clam?"

"I don't mean no harm," said Clam lowering her tone,— "but Miss 'Lizabeth does. I wish you would go and see what she *is* doing, Mr. Winthrop; she's makin' work for somebody; and if it ain't nobody else, it's the doctor."

Winthrop however sat still, and Clam departed in ignorance how he had received her information. Presently however his supper was finished, and he sauntered round to the front of the house. He paused before the doorway where its mistress sat.

"It is too damp for you there."

"I don't feel it."

"I do."

"I am not afraid of it."

"If the fact were according to your fears, that would be a sufficient answer."

"It will do me no harm."

"It must not; and that it may not, you must go in," he said gravely.

"But you are out in it," said Elizabeth, who was possessed with an uncompromising spirit just then.

"I am out in it. Well?"

"Only—that I may venture—" she did not like to finish her sentence.

"What right have you to venture anything?"

"The same right that other people have."

"I risk nothing," said he gravely.

"I haven't much to risk."

"You may risk your life."

"My life!" said Elizabeth. "What does it signify!—" But she jumped up and ran into the house.

The next morning there was an early breakfast, for which Elizabeth was ready. Then Winthrop took her directions for things to be forwarded from Mannahatta. Then there was a quiet leave-taking; on his part kind and cool, on hers too full of impassioned feeling to be guarded or constrained. But there was reason and excuse enough for that, as she knew, or guard and restraint would both have been there. When she quitted his hand, it was to hide herself in her room and have one struggle with the feeling of desolation. It was a long one.

Elizabeth came out at last, book in hand.

"Dear Miss Haye!" Mrs. Nettley exclaimed—"you're dreadful worn with this hot weather and being out of doors all day yesterday!"

"I am going out again," said Elizabeth. "Clam will know where to find me."

"If you had wings, I'd know where to find you," said Clam; "but on your feet 'taint so certain."

"You needn't try, unless it is necessary," said Elizabeth dryly.

"But dear Miss Haye!" pleaded Mrs. Nettley,—"you're not surely going out to try the sun again to-day?"

Elizabeth's lip quivered.

"It's the pleasantest place, Mrs. Nettley—I am quite in the shade—I can't be better than I am there, thank you."

"Don't she look dreadful!" said the good lady, as Elizabeth went from the house. "Oh, I never have seen anybody so changed!"

"She's pulled down a bit since she come," said Karen, who gave Elizabeth but a moderate share of her good will at any time. "She's got her mind up high enough, anyway, for all she's gone through."

"Who hain't?" said Clam. "Hain't the Governor *his* mind up high enough? And you can't pull him down, but you can her."

"His don't never need," said Karen.

"Well—I don' know,—" said Clam, picking up several things about the floor—"but them high minds is a trial."

"Hain't you got one yourself, girl?" said old Karen.

"Hope so, ma'am. I take after my admirers. That's all the way I live,—keeping my head up—always did."

Karen deigned no reply, but went off.

"Mis' Nettles," said Clam, "do *you* think Miss Haye 'll ever stand it up here all alone in this here place?"

"Why not?" said Mrs. Nettley innocently.

"I guess your head ain't high enough up for to see her'n," said Clam, in scornful impatience. And she too quitted the conversation in disgust.

CHAPTER XXXVIII.

'Resolve,' the haughty moralist would say,
'The single act is all that we demand.'
Alas! such wisdom bids a creature fly
Whose very sorrow is, that time hath shorn
His natural wings. WORDSWORTH.

THE book in Elizabeth's hand was her bible. It was the next thing, and the only thing to be done after Winthrop's going away, that she could think of, to begin upon the first chapter of Matthew. It was action, and she craved action. It was an undertaking; for her mind remembered and laid hold of Winthrop's words—"Ask honestly, of your own conscience and of God, at each step, what obligation upon you grows out of what you read." And it was an undertaking that Winthrop had set her upon. So she sought out her yesterday's couch of moss with its cedar canopy, and sat down in very different mood from yesterday's mood, and put her bible on her lap. It was a feeling of dull passive pain now; a mood that did not want to sleep.

The day itself was very like yesterday. Elizabeth listened a minute to the sparrow and the locust and the summer wind, but presently she felt that they were overcoming her; and she opened her book to the first chapter of Matthew. She was very curious to find her first *obligation*. Not that she was unconscious of many resting upon her already; but those were vague, old, dimly recognized obligations; she meant to take them up now definitely, in the order in which they might come.

She half paused at the name in the first verse,—was there not a shadow of obligation hanging around that? But if there were, she would find it more clearly set forth and in detail as she went on. She passed it for the present.

From that she went on smoothly as far as the twenty-first verse. That stopped her.

"And she shall bring forth a son; and thou shalt call his name Jesus; for he shall save his people from their sins."

"'*His people,*'—" thought Elizabeth. "I am not one of his people. Ought I not to be?"

The words of the passage did not say; but an imperative whisper at her heart said "Ay!"

"*His people!*—but how can I be one of his people?" she thought again. And impatience bade her turn over the leaf, and find something more or something else; but conscience said, "Stop—and deal with this obligation first."

"What obligation?—'*He shall save his people from their sins.*' Then certainly I ought to let him save me from mine—that is the least I can do. But what is the first thing—the first step to be taken? I wish Mr. Landholm was here to tell me.—"

She allowed herself to read on to the end of the page, but that gave her not much additional light. She would not turn over the leaf; she had no business with the second obligation till the first was mastered; she sat looking at the words in a sort of impatient puzzle; and not permitting herself to look forward, she turned back a leaf. That gave her but the titlepage of the New Testament. She turned back another, to the last chapter of the Old. Its opening words caught her eye.

"For behold, the day cometh that shall burn as an oven; and all the proud, yea, and all that do wickedly, shall be stubble; and the day that cometh shall burn them up, saith the Lord of Hosts, that it shall leave them neither root nor branch."

"*The proud, and they that do wickedly*—that is my character and name truly," thought Elizabeth. "I am of them.—And it is from this, and this fate, that 'his people' shall be delivered. But how shall I get to be of them?" Her eye glanced restlessly up to the next words above—

"Then shall ye return and discern between the righteous and the wicked, between him that serveth God and him that serveth him not."

"'*Then,*'—in that day,"—thought Elizabeth, "I can discern between them now, without waiting for that.—Winthrop Landholm is one that serveth God—I am one that serve him not. There is difference enough, I can see now—but this speaks of the difference at that day; another sort of difference.—Then I ought to be a servant of God——"

The obligation was pretty plain.

"Well, I will, when I find out how,"—she began. But conscience checked her.

"This is not the first chapter of Matthew," she said then. "I will go back to that."

Her eye fell lower, to the words.

"But unto you that fear my name shall the Sun of Righteousness arise with healing in his wings."

The tears started to Elizabeth's eyes. "This is that same who will save his people from their sins,—is it?—and that is his healing? Oh, I want it!—There is too much difference between me and them. He shall save his people from their sins,—I have plenty,—plenty. But how?—and what shall I do? It don't tell me here."

It did not; yet Elizabeth could not pass on. She was honest; she felt an obligation, arising from these words, which yet she did not at once recognize. It stayed her. She must do something—what could she do? It was a most unwelcome answer that at last slid itself into her mind. *Ask* to be made one of 'his people'—or to be taught how to become one? Her very soul started. *Ask?*—but now the obligation stood full and strong before her, and she could cease to see it no more. *Ask?*—why she never did such a thing in her whole life as ask God to do anything for her. Not of her own mind, at her own choice, and in simplicity; her thoughts and feelings had perhaps at some time joined in prayers made by another, and in church, and in solemn time. But *here?* with the blue sky over her, in broad day, and in open air? It did not seem like praying time. Elizabeth shut her book. Her heart beat. Duty and she were at a struggle now; she knew which must give way, but she was not ready yet. It never entered her head to question the power or the will to which she must apply herself, no more than if she had been a child. Herself she doubted; she doubted not him. Elizabeth knew very little of his works or word, beyond a vague general outline, got from sermons; but she knew one servant of God. That servant glorified him; and in the light which she saw and loved, Elizabeth could do no other but, in her measure, to glorify him too. She did not doubt, but she hesitated, and trembled. The song of the birds and the flow of the water mocked her hesitancy and difficulty. But Elizabeth was honest; and though she trembled she would not and could not disobey the voice of conscience which set before her one clear, plain duty. She was in great doubt whether to stand or to kneel; she was afraid of being seen if she knelt; she would not be so irreverent as to pray sitting; she rose to her feet, and clasping a cedar tree with her arms, she leaned her head beside the trunk, and whispered her prayer, to him who saves his people from their sins, that he would make her one of them, she did not know how, she confessed; she prayed that he would teach her.

She kept her position and did not move her bended head, till the tears which had gathered were fallen or dried; then she sat down and took up her book again and looked down into the water. What had she done? Entered a pledge, she felt, to be what she had prayed to be; else her prayer would be but a mockery, and Elizabeth was in earnest. "What a full-grown fair specimen he is of his class," she thought, her mind recurring again to her adviser and exemplar; "and I—a poor ignorant thing in the dark, groping for a bit of light to begin!"—The tears gathered again; she opened the second chapter of Matthew.

She looked off again to feel glad. Was a pledge entered only on her side?—was there not an assurance given somewhere, by lips that cannot lie, that prayer earnestly offered should not be in vain? She could not recal the words, but she was sure of the thing; and there was more than one throb of pleasure, and a tiny shoot of grateful feeling in her heart, before Elizabeth went back to her book. What was the next 'obligation'? She was all ready for it.

Nothing stopped her much in the second chapter. The 'next obligation' did not start up till the words of John the Baptist in the beginning of the third—

"Repent ye, for the kingdom of heaven is at hand."

"What is repentance?—and what is the kingdom of heaven?" pondered Elizabeth. "I wish somebody was here to tell me. Repent?—I know what it is to repent—it is to change one's mind about something, and to will just against what one willed before. —And what ought I to repent about?—Everything wrong! *Everything wrong!*—That is, to turn about and set my face just the other way from what it has been all my life!—I might as good take hold of this moving earth with my two fingers and give it a twist to go westwards.——"

Elizabeth shut up her book, and laid it on the moss beside her.

"Repent?—yes, it's an obligation. Oh what shall I do with it!—"

She would have liked to do with it as she did with her head—lay it down.

"These wrong things are iron-strong in me—how can I unscrew them from their fastenings, and change all the out-goings and in-comings of my mind?—when the very hands that must do the work have a bent the wrong way. How can I ?—I am strong for evil—I am weak as a child for good."

"I will try!" she said the next instant, lifting her head up—"I will *try* to do what I can.—But that is not changing my whole inner way of feeling—that is not *repenting*. Perhaps it will come. Or is this determination of mine to *try*, the beginning of it? I do not know that it is—I cannot be sure that it is. No—one might wish to be a good lawyer, without at all being willing to go through all the labour and pains for it which Winthrop Landholm has taken.—No, *this* is not, or it may not be, repentance—I cannot be sure that it is anything. But will it not come? or how can I get it? How alone I am from all counsel and help!—Still it must be my duty to try—to try to do particular things right, as they come up, even though I cannot feel right all at once. And if I try, won't the help come, and the knowledge?—What a confusion it is! In the midst of it all it is my duty to repent, and I haven't the least idea how to set about it, and I can't do it! O I wish Winthrop Landholm was here!——"

Elizabeth pondered the matter a good deal; and the more she thought about it, the worse the confusion grew. The duty seemed more imminent, the difficulty more obstinate. She was driven at last, unwillingly again, to her former resource—what she could not give herself, to ask to have given her. She did it, with tears again, that were wrung from breaking pride and weary wishing. More quietly then she resolved to lay off perplexing care, and to strive to meet the moment's duty, as it arose. And by this time with a very humbled and quieted brow, she went on with her chapter. The words of the next verse caught her eye and her mind at once.

"For this is he that was spoken of by the prophet Esaias, saying, The voice of one crying in the wilderness, prepare ye the way of the Lord, make his paths straight."

"Is not this it?" cried Elizabeth. "If I do my part—all I can—is not that *preparing the way* for him to do what I cannot do?"

She thought so, at any rate, and it comforted her.

"Miss 'Lizabeth," said Clam, just behind her, "Karen wants to know what time you'll have dinner?"

"I don't care."

"That's 'zackly Karen's time o' day," said Clam discontentedly.

"I don't care at all, Clam."

"And she says, *what* 'll you have?"

"Nothing—or anything. Don't talk to me about it."

"Ain't much good in choosing," said Clam, "when there ain't three things to choose from. How long can you live on pork, Miss 'Lizabeth?"

Elizabeth looked up impatiently.

"Longer than you can. Clam!—"

"Ma'am?"

"Let me alone. I don't care about anything."

Clam went off; but ten minutes had not gone when she was back again.

"Miss Lizzie,—Anderese wants to know if he'll go on cuttin' wood just as he's a mind to?"

"Anderese?—who's he?"

"Karen and him used to be brother and sister when they was little."

"What does he want?"

"Wants to know if he shall go on cuttin' wood just as ever."

"Cutting wood!—what wood?"

"I s'pect it's your trees."

"Mine! What trees?"

"Why the trees in the woods, Miss Lizzie. As long as they was nobody's, Anderese used to cut 'em for the fire; now they're yourn, he wants to know what he shall do with 'em."

"Let 'em alone, certainly! Don't let him cut any more."

"Then the next question is, where'll he go for something to make a fire?"

"To make a fire!"

"Yes, Miss Lizzie—unless no time 'll do for dinner as well as any time. Can't cook pork without a fire. And *then* you'd want the kettle boiled for tea, I reckon."

"Can't he get wood anywhere, Clam? without cutting down trees.'

"There ain't none to sell anywheres—*he* says."

"What trees has he been cutting?" said Elizabeth, rousing herself in despair.

"Any that come handy, I s'pose, Miss Lizzie—they'll all burn, once get 'em in the chimney."

"He mustn't do that. Tell him—but you can't tell him—and *I* can't.——"

She hesitated, between the intense desire to bid him cut whatever he had a mind, and the notion of attending to all her duties, which was strong upon her.

"Tell him to cut anything he pleases, for to-day—I'll see about it myself the next time."

Two minutes' peace; and then Clam was at her back again.

"Miss Lizzie, he don't know nothin' and he wants to know a heap. Do you want him to cut down a cedar, he says, or an oak, or somethin' else. There's the most cedars, he says; but Karen says they snap all to pieces."

Elizabeth rose to her feet.

"I suppose I can find a tree in a minute that he can cut without doing any harm.—Bring me a parasol, Clam,—and come along with me."

Clam and the parasol came out at one door, and Anderese and his axe at another, as Elizabeth slowly paced towards the house. The three joined company. Anderese was an old grey-haired negro, many years younger however than his sister. Elizabeth asked him, "Which way?"

"Which way the young lady pleases."

"I don't please about it," said Elizabeth,—"I don't know anything about it—lead to the nearest place—where a tree can be soonest found."

The old man shouldered his axe and went before, presently entering a little wood path; of which many struck off into the leafy wilderness which bordered the house. Leaves overhead, rock and moss under foot; a winding, jagged, up and down, stony, and soft green way, sometimes the one, sometimes the other. Elizabeth's bible was still in her hand, her finger still kept it open at the second chapter of Matthew; she went musingly along over grey lichens and sunny green beds of moss, thinking of many things. How she was wandering in Winthrop's old haunts, where the trees had once upon a time been cut by him, she now to order the cutting of the fellow trees. Strange it was! How she was desolate and alone, nobody but herself there to do it; her father gone; and she without another protector or friend to care for the trees or her either. There were times when the weight of pain, like the pressure of the atmosphere, seemed so equally distributed that it was distinctly felt nowhere,—or else so mighty that the nerves of feeling were benumbed. Elizabeth wandered along in a kind of maze, half wondering half indignant at herself that she could walk and think at all. She did not execute much thinking, to do her justice; she passed through the sweet broken sunlight and still shadows, among the rough trunks of the cedars, as if it had been the scenery of dreamland. On every hand were up-shooting young pines, struggling oaks that were caught in thickets of cedar, and ashes and elms that were humbly asking leave to spread and see the light and reach their heads up to freedom and free air. They asked in vain. Elizabeth was only conscious of the struggling hopes and wishes that seemed crushed for ever, her own.

"She don't see nothin'," whispered Clam to Anderese, whom she had joined in front. "She's lookin' into vacancy. If you don't stop, our axe and parasol 'll walk all round the place, and one 'll do as much work as the other. I can't put up my awning till you cut down something to let the sun in."

The old man glanced back over his shoulder at his young lady.

"What be I goin' to do?" he whispered, with a sidelong glance at Clam.

"Fling your axe into something," said Clam. "That'll bring her up."

The old man presently stepped aside to a young sapling oak, which having outgrown its strength bent its slim altitude in a beautiful parabolic curve athwart the sturdy stems of cedars and yellow pines which lined the path. Anderese stopped there and looked at Elizabeth. She had stopped too, without noticing him, and stood sending an intent, fixed, far-going look into the pretty wilderness of rock and wood on the other side of the way. All three stood silently.

"Will this do to come down, young lady?" inquired Anderese, with his axe on his shoulder. Elizabeth faced about.

"'Twon't grow up to make a good tree—it's slantin' off so among the others." He brought his axe down.

"*That?*" said Elizabeth,—"that reaching-over one? O no · you mustn't touch that. What is it?"

"It's an oak, miss; it's good wood."

"It's a better tree. No indeed—leave that. Never cut such trees. Won't some of those old things do?"

"Them?—them are cedars, young lady."

"Well, won't they do?"

"They'd fly all over and burn the house up," said Clam.

"What do you want?"

"Some o' the best there is, I guess," said Clam.

"Hard wood is the best, young lady."

"What's that?"

"Oak—maple—hickory—and there's ash, and birch—'tain't very good."

Elizabeth sighed, and led the way on again, while the old negro shouldered his axe and followed with Clam; probably sighing on his own part, if habitual gentleness of spirit did not prevent. Nobody ever knew Clam do such a thing.

"Look at her!" muttered the damsel;—"going with her head down,—when'll she see a tree? Ain't we on a march! Miss 'Lizabeth!—the tree won't walk home after it's cut."

"What?" said her mistress.

"How'll it get there?"

"What?"

"The tree, Miss Lizzie—when Anderese has cut it."

"Can't he carry some home?"

"He'll be a good while about it—if he takes one stick at a time—and we ain't nigh home, neither."

Elizabeth came to a stand, and finally turned in another direction, homewards. But she broke from the path then, and took up the quest in earnest, leading her panting followers over rocks and moss-beds and fallen cedars and tangled vines and undergrowth, which in many places hindered their way. She found trees enough at last, and near enough home; but both she and her companions had had tree-hunting to their satisfaction. Elizabeth commissioned Anderese to find fuel in another way; and herself in some disgust at her new charge, returned to her rock and her bible. She tried to go through with the third chapter of Matthew; and her eye did go over it, though often swimming in tears. But that was the end of her studies at that time. Sorrow claimed the rest of the day for its own, and held the whole ground. Her household and its perplexities—her bible and its teachings—her ignorance and her necessities,—faded away from view; and instead thereof rose up the lost father, the lost home, and the lost friend yet dearer than all.

"What's become of Miss Haye?" whispered Mrs. Nettley late in the evening.

"Don' know," answered Clam. "Melted away—all that can melt, and shaken down—all that can shake, of her. That ain't all, so I s'pose there's somethin' left."

"Poor thing!—no wonder she takes it hard," said the good lady.

"No," said Clam,—"she never did take nothin' easy."

"Has she been crying all the afternoon?"

"Don' know," said Clam; "the eye of curiosity ain't invited; but she don't take *that* easy neither, when she's about it. I've seen her cry—once; she'd do a year o' *your* crying in half an hour."

CHAPTER XXXIX.

O Land of Quiet! to thy shore the surf
Of the perturbed Present rolls and sleeps
Our storms breathe soft as June upon thy turf,
And lure out blossoms.

LOWELL.

THEY were days of violent grief which for a little while followed each other. Elizabeth spent them out of doors; in the woods, on the rocks, by the water's edge. She would take her bible out with her, and sometimes try to read a little; but a very few words would generally touch some spring which set her off upon a torrent of sorrow. Pleasant things past or out of her reach, the present time a blank, the future worse than a blank,—she knew nothing else. She did often in her distress repeat the prayer she had made over the first chapter of Matthew; but that was rather the fruit of past thought; she did not think in those days; she gave up to feeling; and the hours were a change from bitter and violent sorrow to dull and listless quiet. Conscience sometimes spoke of duties resolved upon; impatient pain always answered that their time was not now.

The first thing that roused her was a little letter from Winthrop, which came with the pieces of furniture and stores he sent up to her order. It was but a word,—or two words; one of business, to say what he had done for her; and one of kindness, to say what he hoped she was doing for herself. Both words were brief, and cool; but with them, with the very handwriting of them, came a waft of that atmosphere of influence—that silent breath of truth which every character breathes—which in this instance was sweetened with airs from heaven. The image of the writer rose before her brightly, in its truth and uprightness and high and fixed principle; and though Elizabeth wept bitter tears at the miserable contrast of her own, they were more healing tears than she had shed all those days. When she dried them, it was with a new mind, to live no more hours like those she had been living. Something less distantly unlike him she could be, and would be. She rose and went into the house, while her eyes were yet red, and gave her patient and unwearied attention, for hours, to details of household arrangements that needed it. Her wits were not wandering, nor her eyes; nor did they suffer others to wander. Then, when it was all done, she took her bonnet and went back to her old wood-place and her bible, with an humbler and quieter spirit than she had ever brought to it before. It was the fifth chapter of Matthew now.

The first beatitude puzzled her. She did not know what was meant by 'poor in spirit,' and she could not satisfy herself. She passed it as something to be made out by and by, and went on to the others. There were obligations enough.

"'Meek?'" said Elizabeth,—"I suppose if there is anything in the world I am *not*, it is meek. I am the very, very opposite. What can I do with this? It is like a fire in my veins. Can *I* cool it? And if I could control the outward seeming of it, that would not be the change of the thing itself. Besides, I couldn't, I must *be* meek, if I am ever to seem so."

She went on sorrowfully to the next.

"'Hunger and thirst after righteousness'—I do desire it—I do not '*hunger and thirst*.' I don't think I do—and it is those and those only to whom the promise is given. I am so miserable that I cannot even wish enough for what I need most. O God, help me to know what I am seeking, and to seek it more earnestly!—"

"'Merciful?'" she went on with tears in her eyes—"I think I am merciful.—I haven't been tried, but I am pretty sure I am merciful. But there it is—one must have all the marks, I suppose, to be a Christian. Some people may be merciful by nature—I suppose I am.—"

"Blessed are the *pure in heart*."

She stopped there, and even shut up her book, in utter sorrow and shame, that if 'pure in heart' meant pure to the All-seeing eye, hers was so very, very far from it. There was not a little scrap of her heart fit for looking into. And what could she do with it? The words of Job recurred to her,—"Who can bring a clean thing out of an unclean? not one."

Elizabeth was growing 'poor in spirit' before she knew what the words meant. She went on carefully, sorrowfully, earnestly.

—till she came to the twenty-fourth verse of the sixth chapter. It startled her.

"No man can serve two masters: for either he will hate the one and love the other; or else he will hold to the one and despise the other. Ye cannot serve God and Mammon."

"That is to say then," said Elizabeth, "that I must devote myself *entirely* to God—or not at all. All my life and possessions and aims. It means all that!—"

And for 'all that' she felt she was not ready. One corner for self-will and doing her own pleasure she wanted somewhere; and wanted so obstinately, that she felt, as it were, a mountain of strong unwillingness rise up between God's requirements and her; an iron lock upon the door of her heart, the key of which she could not turn, shutting and barring it fast against his entrance and rule. And she sat down before the strong mountain and the locked door, as before something which must, and could not, give way; with a desperate feeling that it *must*—with another desperate feeling that it would not.

Now was Elizabeth very uncomfortable, and she hated discomfort. She would have given a great deal to make herself right; if a movement of her hand could have changed her and cleared away the hindrance, it would have been made on the instant; her judgment and her wish were clear; but her will was not. Unconditional submission she thought she was ready for; unconditional obedience was a stumbling-block before which she stopped short. She *knew* there would come up occasions when her own will would take its way—she could not promise for it that it would not; and she was afraid to give up her freedom utterly and engage to serve God in *everything*. An enormous engagement, she felt! How was she to meet with ten thousand the enemy that came against her with twenty thousand?—Ay, how? But if he were not met—if she were to be the servant of *sin* for ever—all was lost then! And she was not going to be lost; therefore she *was* going to be the unconditional servant of God. When?—

The tears came, but they did not flow; they could not, for the fever of doubt and questioning. She dashed them away as impertinent asides. What were they to the matter in hand. Elizabeth was in distress. But at the same time it was distress that she was resolved to get out of. She did not know just what to do; but neither would she go into the house till something was done.

"If Mr. Landholm were here!—"

"What could he do?" answered conscience; "there is the question before you, for you to deal with. You must deal with it. It's a plain question."

"I cannot"—and "Who will undertake for me?"—were Elizabeth's answering cry.

Her heart involuntarily turned to the great helper, but what could or would he do for her?—it was his will she was thwarting. Nevertheless, "*to whom should she go?*"—the shaken needle of her mind's compass turned more and more steadily to its great centre. There was light in no other quarter but on that 'wicket-gate' towards which Bunyan's Pilgrim first long ago set off to run. With some such sorrowful blind looking, she opened to her chapter of Matthew again, and carelessly and sadly turned over a leaf or two; till she saw a word which though printed in the ordinary type of the rest, stood out to her eyes like the lettering on a sign-board. "Ask."—

"Ask, and it shall be given you; seek, and ye shall find; knock, and it shall be opened unto you."

The tears came then with a gush.

"Ask what?—it doesn't say,—but it must be whatever my difficulty needs—there is no restriction. 'Knock'!—I will—till it is opened to me—as it will be!—"

The difficulty was not gone—the mountain had not suddenly sunk to a level; but she had got a clue to get over the one, and daylight had broken through the other. Elizabeth felt not changed at all; no better, and no tenderer; but she laid hold of those words as one who has but uncertain footing puts his arms round a strong tree,—she clung as one clings there; and clasped them with assurance of life. Ask?—did she not ask, with tears that streamed now; she knocked, clasping that stronghold with more glad and sure clasp; she *knew* then that everything would be 'made plain' in the rough places of her heart.

She did not sit still long then for meditation or to rest; her mood was action. She took her bible from the moss, and with a strong beating sense both of the hopeful and of the forlorn in her condition, she walked slowly through the grass to the steps of her house door. As she mounted them a new thought suddenly struck her, and instead of turning to the right she turned to the left.

"Mrs. Nettley," said Elizabeth as she entered the sitting-room, "isn't it very inconvenient for you to be staying here with me?"

Good Mrs. Nettley was sitting quietly at her work, and looked up at this quite startled.

"Isn't it inconvenient for you?" Elizabeth repeated.

"Miss Haye!—it isn't inconvenient;—I am very glad to do it—if I can be of any service——"

"It is very kind of you, and very pleasant to me; but aren't you wanted at home?"

"I don't think I am wanted, Miss Haye,—at least I am sure my brother is very glad to have me do anything for Mr. Landholm, or for you, I am sure;—if I can."

Elizabeth's eye flashed; but then in an instant she called herself a fool, and in the same breath wondered why it should be, that Winthrop's benevolence must put him in the way of giving her so much pain.

"Who fills your place at home, while you are taking care of me here, Mrs. Nettley?"

"I don't suppose any of 'em can just do that," said the good lady with a little bit of a laugh at the idea.

"Well, is there any one to take care of your house and your brother?"

"Mr. Landholm—he said he'd see to it."

"Mr. Landholm!—"

"He promised he'd take care of George and the house as well.—I dare say they don't manage much amiss."

"But who takes care of Mr. Landholm?"

"Nobody does, if he don't himself," said Mrs. Nettley with a shake of her head. "He don't give that pleasure to any other living person."

"Not when you are at home?"

"It makes no difference, Miss Haye," said Mrs. Nettley going on with her sewing. "He never will. He never did."

"But surely he boards somewhere, don't he? He don't live entirely by himself in that room?"

"That's what he always used," said Mrs. Nettley; "he *does* take his dinners somewhere now, I believe. But nothing else. He makes his own tea and breakfast,—that is!—for he don't drink anything. If it was any one else, one would be apt to say one would grow unsociable, living in such a way; but it don't make any change in him, no more than in the sun, what sort of a place he lives in."

Elizabeth stood for a minute very still; and then said gently, "Mrs. Nettley, I mustn't let you stay here with me."

"Why not, Miss Haye?—I am sure they don't want me. I can just as well stay as not. I am very glad to stay."

"You are wanted more there than here. I must learn to get along alone.—It don't matter how soon I begin."

"Dear Miss Haye, not yet. Never mind now—we'll talk about it by and by," said Mrs. Nettley hurriedly and somewhat anxiously. She was a little afraid of Elizabeth.

"How could you get home from this place?"

"O by and by—there'll be ways—when the time comes."

"The time must come, Mrs. Nettley. You are very good—I'm very much obliged to you for coming and staying with me,—but in conscience I cannot let you stay any longer. It don't make any difference, a little sooner or later."

"Later is better, Miss Elizabeth."

"No—I shall feel more comfortable to think you are at home, than to think I am keeping you here. I would rather you should make your arrangements and choose what day you will go; and I will find some way for you to go."

"I am very sorry, Miss Elizabeth," said Mrs. Nettley most unaffectedly. "I am sure Mr. Landholm would a great deal rather I should stay."

It was the last word Elizabeth could stand. Her lip trembled, as she crossed the passage to her own room and bolted the door; and then she threw herself on her knees by the bedside and hid the quivering face in her hands.

Why should it, that kind care of his, pierce her like thorns and arrows? why give her that when he could give her no more? "But it will all be over," she thought to herself,—"this struggle like all other struggles will come to an end; meanwhile I have it to bear and my work to do. Perhaps I shall get over this feeling in time—time wears out so much.—But I should despise myself if I did. No, when I have taken up a liking on so good and solid grounds, I hope I am of good enough stuff to keep it to the end of my days."

Then came over her the feeling of forlornness, of loneliness, well and thoroughly realized; with the single gleam of better things that sprung from the promise her heart had embraced that day. True and strong it was, and her soul clung to it. But yet its real brightness, to her apprehension, shone upon a "land that is very far off;" and left all the way thereunto with but a twilight earnest of good things to come; and Elizabeth did not like looking forward; she wanted some sweetness in hand. Yet she clung to that, her one stand-by. She had a vague notion that its gleam might lead to more brightness even this side of heaven; that there might be a sort of comfort growing out of doing one's duty, and the favour of him whose service duty is. Winthrop Landholm was always bright,—and what else had he to make him so? She would try what virtue there might be in it; she would essay those paths of wisdom which are said to be 'pleasantness;' but again came the longing for help; she felt that she knew so little. Again the word '*ask*'—came back to her; and at last, half comforted, wholly wearied, she rose from her long meditation by the bedside and went towards the window.

There was such a sparkling beauty on everything outside, under the clear evening sun, that its brilliancy half rebuked her. The very shadows seemed bright, so bright were the lines of light between them, where the tall pointed cedars were casting their mantle on the grass. Elizabeth stood by the open window, wondering. She looked back to the time when she had been there before, when she was as bright, though not as pure, as all things else; and now—father and friend were away from her, and she was alone. Yet still the sun shone—might it not again some time for her? Poor child, as she stóod there the tears dropped fast, at that meeting of hope and sorrow; hope as intangible as the light, sorrow a thicker mantle than that of the cedar trees. And now the sunlight seemed to say '*Ask*'—and the green glittering earth responded—"and ye shall receive." Elizabeth looked;—she heard them say it constantly. She did not question the one word or the other. It seemed very sweet to her, the thought of doing her duty; and yet,—the tears which had stayed, ran fast again when she thought of Mrs. Nettley's going away and how utterly alone she should be.

She had sat down and was resting her arm on the window-sill; and Miss Haye's face was in a state of humbled and saddened gravity which no one ever saw it in before these days. As she sat there, Karen's voice reached her from the back of the house somewhere; and it suddenly occurred to Elizabeth that it might be as well for her to acquaint herself somewhat better with one of her few remaining inmates, since their number was to be so lessened. She dried her eyes, and went out with quick step through the kitchen till she neared the door of the little back porch where Karen was at work. There she paused.

The old woman was singing one of her Methodist songs, in a voice that had once very likely been sweet and strong. It was trembling and cracked now. Yet none of the fire and spirit of old was wanting; as was shewn, not indeed by the power of the notes, but by the loving flow or cadence the singer gave them. Elizabeth lingered just within the door to listen. The melody was as wild and sweet as suited the words. The first of the song she had lost; it went on—

"till Jesus shall come,
"Protect and defend me until I'm called home;
"Though worms my poor body may claim as their prey,
"'Twill outshine, when rising, the sun at noon-day.

"The sun shall be darkened, the moon turned to blood,
"The mountains all melt at the presence of God;
"Red lightnings may flash, and loud thunders may roar,
"All this cannot daunt me on Canaan's blest shore.

"A glimpse of bright glory surprises my soul,
"I sink in sweet visions to view the bright goal;
"My soul, while I'm singing, is leaping to go,
"This moment for heaven I'd leave all below

"Farewell, my dear brethren—my Lord bids me come;
"Farewell, my dear sisters—I'm now going home;
"Bright angels are whispering so sweet in my ear,—
"Away to my Saviour my spirit they'll bear.

"I am going—I'm going—but what do I see!—"

She was interrupted.

"Do you mean all that, Karen?" said Elizabeth, stepping without the door.

Karen stopped her song and looked round.

"Do you mean all that you are singing, Karen?"

"What I'm singing?—"

"Yes. I've been listening to you.—Do you feel and mean all those words of your hymn?"

"I don't say no words I don't mean," said Karen, going on with her work;—"anyhow, I don't mean to."

"But those words you have been singing—do you mean that you feel them all?"

Karen stood up and faced her as she answered,

"Yes!"

"Do you mean that you would rather die than live?"

"If 'twas the Lord's will, I would," said Karen, without moving her face.

"Why?"

Karen looked at her still, but her face unbent in a little bit of a smile.

"You ain't one of the Lord's people, be you, young lady?"

"I don't know—" said Elizabeth, blushing and hesitating,—"I mean to be."

"Do you mean to be one of 'em?" said Karen.

"I wish to be—yes, I mean to be,—if I can."

The old woman dried her hand which had been busy in water, and coming up took one of Elizabeth's,—looked at its delicate tints in her own wrinkled and black fingers, and then lifting a moistened eye to Elizabeth's face, she answered expressively,

"*Then* you'll know."

"But I want to know something about it now," said the young lady as Karen went back to her work. "Tell me. How can you wish to 'leave all for heaven,' as you were singing a moment ago?"

"I'd ha' done that plenty o' years ago," said Karen. "I'd got enough of this world by that time."

"Is that the reason?"

"What reason?" said Karen.

"Is that the reason you would like to go to heaven?"

"It's the reason why I'm willing to leave the earth," said Karen. "It hain't nothin' to do with heaven."

"Anybody might be willing to go to heaven at that rate," said Elizabeth.

"That ain't all, young lady," said Karen, working away while she spoke. "I'm not only willin' to go—I'm willin' to *be* there when I get there—and I'm ready too, thank the Lord!"

"How can one be 'ready' for it, Karen?—It seems such a change."

"It'll be a good change," said Karen. "Mis' Landholm thinks it is."

Elizabeth stood silent, the tears swelling; she got little light from Karen.

"You wa'n't one of the Lord's people when you come?—be you?—" said Karen suddenly, looking round at her.

"I hardly know whether I am one now, Karen,—but I mean to try."

"Tryin' ain't no use," said Karen. "If you want to be one of the Lord's people, you've only to knock, and it shall be opened to you."

"Did you never know that fail?"

"I never tried it but once—it didn't fail me then," said the old woman. "The Lord keeps his promises.—I tried it a good while—it don't do to stop knockin'."

"But I must—one must try to do something—I must try to do my duty," said Elizabeth.

"Surely!" said Karen, facing round upon her again, "but you

can't help that. Do you s'pose you can love Jesus Christ, and *not* love to please him? 'Tain't in natur'—you can't help it."

"But suppose I don't love him, Karen?" said Elizabeth, her voice choking as she said it. "I don't know him yet—I don't know him enough to love him."

There was a little pause; and then without looking at her, Karen said in her trembling voice, a little more trembling than it was,

"I don't know, Miss 'Lizabeth—'To them gave he power to become the sons of God, even to them that believe on his name!' —I heard a man preach that once."

The tears rushed in full measure to Elizabeth's eyes. She stood, not heeding Karen nor anything else, and the thick veil of tears hiding everything from her sight. It was a moment of strong joy; for she knew she believed in him! She was, or she would be, one of 'his people.' Her strong pillar of assurance she clasped again, and leaned her heart upon, with unspeakable rest.

She stood, till the water had cleared itself from her eyes; and then she was turning into the house, but turned back again, and went close up to the old black woman.

"Thank you, Karen," said she. "You have given me comfort."

"You hain't got it all," said Karen without looking at her.

"What do you mean?"

"Did you ever read a book called the 'Pilgrim's Progress,' young lady?"

"No."

"I ain't much like the people there," said Karen, "but they was always glad to hear of one more that was going to be a pilgrim; and clapped their hands, they did."

"Did *you* ever read it, Karen?"

"I hearn Mis' Landholm read it—and the Governor."

Elizabeth turned away, and she had not half crossed the kitchen when she heard Karen strike up, in a sweet refrain,

"I'll march to Canaan's land,
"I'll land on Canaan's shore,"—

Then something stopped the song, and Elizabeth came back to her room. She sat down by the window. The light was changed. There seemed a strange clear brightness on all things without that they had not a little while ago, and that they never had before. And her bread was sweet to her that night.

CHAPTER XL.

> Heaven doth with us as we with torches do;
> Not light them for themselves: for if our virtues
> Did not go forth of us, 'twere all alike
> As if we had them not.
>
> SHAKSPEARE.

MUCH against Mrs. Nettley's will, she was despatched on her journey homewards within a few days after. She begged to be allowed to stay yet a week or two, or three; but Elizabeth was unmoveable. "It would make no difference," she said, "or at least I would rather you should go. You ought to be there—and I may as well learn at once to get used to it."

"But it will be very bad for you, Miss Elizabeth."

"I think it is right, Mrs. Nettley."

So Mrs. Nettley went; and how their young lady passed her days and bore the quietude and the sorrow of them, the rest of the household marvelled together.

"She'd die, if there was dyin' stuff in her," said Clam; "but there ain't."

"What for should she die?" said Karen.

"I'm as near dead as I can be, myself," was Clam's conclusive reply.

"What ails you, girl?"

"I can't catch my breath good among all these mountains," said Clam. "I guess the hills spiles the air hereabouts."

"Your young lady don't think so."

"No," said Clam,—"she looks at the mountains as if she'd swaller them whole—them and her Bible;—only she looks into that as if it would swaller her."

"Poor bird! she's beat down;—it's too lonesome up here for her!" said Karen more tenderly than her wont was.

"That ain't no sign she'll go," said Clam. "She's as notional as the Governor himself, when she takes a notion; only there's some sense in his, and you never know where the sense of hers is till it comes out."

"The house is so still, it's pitiful to hear it," said Karen. "I never minded it when there wa'n't nobody in it—I knowed the old family was all gone—but now I hear it, seems to me, the whole day long. You can't hear a foot, when you ain't in there."

"That'll last awhile, maybe," said Clam; "and then you'll have a row. 'Tain't in her to keep still more'n a certain length o' time; and when she comes out, there'll be a firing up, I tell ye."

"The Lord 'll keep his own," said Karen rising from the table. Which sentence Clam made nothing of.

Spite of her anticipations, the days, and the weeks, sped on smoothly and noiselessly. Indeed *more* quietness, and not less, seemed to be the order of them. Probably too much for Elizabeth's good, if such a state of mere mind-life had been of long lasting. It would not long have been healthy. The stir of passion, at first, was fresh enough to keep her thoughts fresh; but as time went on there were fewer tears and a more settled borne-down look of sorrow. Even her Bible, constantly studied, —even prayer, constantly made over it, did not hinder this. Her active nature was in an unnatural state; it could not be well so. And it sometimes burst the bounds she had set to it, and indulged in a passionate wrestling with the image of joys lost and longed for. Meanwhile, the hot days of August were passed, the first heats of September were slowly gone; and days and nights began to cool off in earnest towards the frosty weather.

"If there ain't some way found to keep Miss Haye's eyes from cryin', she won't have 'em to do anything else with. And she'll want 'em, some day."

Clam, like Elizabeth of old, having nobody else to speak to, was sometimes driven to speak to the nearest at hand.

"Is she cryin', now?" said Karen.

"I don' know what *you* 'd call it," said Clam. "'Tain't much like other folks' cryin'."

"Well there's a letter Anderese fetched—you 'd better take it to her as soon as it 'll do. Maybe it 'll do her good."

"Where from?" said Clam seizing it.

"Anderese fetched it from Mountain Spring."

"Now I wish 'twas—but it ain't!—" said Clam. "I'll take it to her anyhow."

Elizabeth knew that *it wasn't*, as soon as she took it. The letter was from the gentleman who had been her father's lawyer in the city.

Mannahatta, Sept. 26, 1817.

"Dear Madam,

Upon arrangement of Mr. Haye's affairs, I regret to say, we find it will take nearly all his effects to meet the standing liabilities and cover the failure of two or three large operations in which Mr. Haye had ventured more upon uncertain contingencies than was his general habit in business matters. So little indeed will be left, at the best issue we can hope for, that Mrs. Haye's interest, whose whole property, I suppose you are aware, was involved, I grieve to say will amount to little or nothing. It were greatly to be wished that some settlement had in time been made for her benefit; but nothing of the kind was done, nor I suppose in the circumstances latterly was possible. The will makes ample provision, but I am deeply pained to say, is, as matters stand, but a nullity. I enclose a copy.

"I have thought it right to advertise you of these painful tidings, and am,

"Dear madam, with great respect,

"Your obedient servant,

"Dustus O. Brick."

Elizabeth had read this letter, and pondered over it by turns half the day, when a startling thought for the first time flashed into her mind. Rose's desolate condition! Less desolate than her own indeed, in so far that Rose had less strength to feel; but more desolate by far, because being as friendless she was much more helpless than herself. "What will she do, without money and friends?—for she never had any near and dear friends but father and me. Where can she live?——"

Elizabeth jumped up and ran into the house to get away from the inference. But when she had sat down in her chair the inference stood before her.

"Bring her here!—I cannot. I cannot. It would ruin my life." Then, clear and fair, stood the words she had been reading—'Whatsoever ye would that men should do unto you——'

"But there is no bed-room for her but this—or else there will be no sitting-room for either of us;—and then we must eat in the kitchen!——"

"*She* has neither house, nor home, nor friend, nor money. What wouldst thou, in her place?——"

Elizabeth put her face in her hands and almost groaned. She

took it up and looked out, but in all bright nature she could find nothing which did not side against her. She got up and walked the room; then she sat down and began to consider what arrangements would be necessary, and what would be possible. Then confessed to herself that it would not be *all* bad to have somebody to break her solitude, even anybody; then got over another qualm of repugnance, and drew the table near her and opened her desk.

Shahweetah, Sept. 26, 1817.

"Dear Rose,

"I am all alone, like you. Will you come here and let us do the best we can together? I am at a place you don't like, but I shall not stay here all the time, and I think you can bear it with me for a while. I shall have things arranged so as to make you as comfortable as you can be in such straitened quarters, and expect you will come as soon as you can get a good opportunity. Whether you come by boat or not, part of the way, you will have to take the stage-coach from Pimpernel here; and you must stop at the little village of Mountain Spring, opposite Wut-a-qut-o. From there you can get here by wagon or boat. I can't send for you, for I have neither one nor the other.

"Yours truly, dear Rose,

"Elizabeth Haye."

With the letter in her hand, Elizabeth went forth to the kitchen.

"Karen, is there any sort of a cabinet-maker at Mountain Spring?"

"What's that?" said Karen.

"Is there any sort of a cabinet-maker at the village?—a cabinet-maker,—somebody that makes tables and bedsteads, and that sort of thing?"

"A furnitur' shop?" said Karen.

"Yes—something of that kind. Is there such a thing in Mountain Spring?"

Karen shook her head.

"They don't make nothin' at Mountain Spring."

"Where do the people get their tables and chairs? where do they go for them?"

"They go 'most any place," said Karen;—"sometimes they goes to Pimpernel,—and maybe to Starlings, or to Deerford; they don't go much nowheres."

"Can I get such things at Pimpernel?"

"If you was there, you could, I s'pose," said Karen.

"Could Anderese get a horse and cart at the village, to go for me?"

"I guess he can find a wagon round somewheres," said Karen. "You couldn't go in a cart handy."

"I!—no, but I want to send him, to fetch home a load of things."

"How'll he know what to get?"

"I will tell him. Couldn't he do it?"

"If he knowed what was wanted, he could," said Karen. "Me and him'll go, Miss Lizzie, and we'll do it."

"You, Karen! I don't want to send you."

"Guess I'll do the best," said the old woman. "Anderese mightn't know what to fetch. What you want, Miss Lizzie?"

Elizabeth thought a moment whether she should ask Winthrop to send up the things for her; but she could not bear to do it.

"I want a bedstead, Karen, in the first place."

"What sort'll a one?"

"The best you can find."

"That'll be what'll spend the most money," said Karen musingly.

"I don't care about that, but the nicest sort you can meet with. And a bureau——"

"What's that?" said Karen. "I dun' know what that means."

"To hold clothes—with drawers—like that in my room."

"A cupboard?" said Karen;—"some sort like that?"

"No, no; I'll shew you what I mean, in my room; it is called a bureau. And a washstand—a large one, if you can find it. And a rocking-chair—the handsomest one that can be had."

"I know them two," said Karen. "That'll be a load, Miss Lizzie. I don't b'lieve the wagon 'll hold no more."

"The first fine day, Karen, I want you to go."

"The days is all fine, I speck, hereabouts," said Karen. "We'll start as quick as Anderese gets a wagon."

"Who's comin', Miss 'Lizabeth?" said Clam as she met her young lady coming out of the kitchen.

"I don't know—possibly Mrs. Haye. I wish all things to be in readiness for her."

20

"Where'll she sleep, Miss 'Lizabeth," said Clam with opening eyes.

"Here."

"Will she have this for her bedroom?—And what'll you do, Miss 'Lizabeth?"

"If she comes, we will eat in the kitchen." And with the thought the young lady stepped back.

"I forgot—Karen, do you think the wagon will hold no more? Anderese must get a large one. I want a few neat chairs—plain ones—cane-bottomed, or rush-bottomed will do; I want them for this room; for if this lady comes we shall have to take this for our eating-room. I don't want a table; we can make this do;—or we can take the one I use now; but we want the chairs."

"Well, Miss Lizzie, you'll have to have 'em—we'll manage to pile 'em on someways."

And Miss Haye withdrew.

"Ain't this a start now?" said Clam after she had rubbed her knives in silence for several minutes. "Didn't I tell you so?"

"Tell what?" said Karen.

"Why! that Miss 'Lizabeth couldn't keep quiet more'n long enough to get her spunk up. What in the name of variety is she at work at now!"

"What's the matter with you?" grumbled Karen.

"Why I tell you," said Clam facing round, "them two love each other like pison!"

"That's a queer way to love," said Karen.

"They hate each other then—do you understand me? they hate so, one wouldn't thaw a piece of ice off the other's head if it was freezin' her!"

"Maybe 'tain't jus' so," said Karen.

"What do you know about it!" said Clam contemptuously.

"What do you, perhaps?" suggested Karen.

"I know *my* young lady," said Clam rubbing her knives, "and I know t'other one. There ain't but one person in *this* world that can make Miss 'Lizabeth keep her fire down—but she does have an idee of mindin' him."

"Who's that?" said Karen.

"Somebody you don't know, I guess," said Clam.

"If 'twas all true, she wouldn't want her here," said Karen.

"It's all true," said Clam,—"'cept the last. *You* don't know nothin', Karen. We'll see what a time there'll be when she comes. Eat in here!——"

"She's eat in here afore now—and I guess she can again," said old Karen, in a tone of voice which spoke her by no means so discomposed as Clam's words would seem to justify.

Perhaps Elizabeth herself had a thought or two on the close quarters which would be the infallible result of Mrs. Haye's seizure of the old 'keeping-room.'

The twenty-seventh, spite of Karen's understanding of the weather, was a rainy day. The twenty-eighth, Karen and Anderese went to Pimpernel on their furniture hunting, and came back at night with the articles, selected somewhat in accordance with a limited experience of the usual contents of a cabinet-maker's warehouse. The very next day, Elizabeth set Anderese to foisting out and putting together her little old boat, the Merry-go-round. Putting together, literally; she was dropping to pieces from the effects of years and confinement. Anderese was hardly equal to the business; Elizabeth sent for better help from Mountain Spring, and watched rather eagerly the restoring of her favourite to strength and beauty. Watched and pressed the work, as if she was in a hurry. But after tightening and caulking, the boat must be repainted. Elizabeth watched the doing of that; and bargained for a pair of light oars with her friend the workman. He was an old, respectable-looking man, of no particular calling, that appeared.

"Where was this here boat built?" he inquired one day as he was at work and Elizabeth looking on.

"It was built in Mannahatta."

"A good while ago, likely?"

"Yes, it was."

"Did this here belong to old Squire Landholm?"

"No."

"'Twa'n't fetched here lately, I guess, was it?"

"No—it has lain here a long time."

"Who *did* it belong to, then?"

"It belonged to me."

"Is it your'n now?" said the man looking up at her

"No," said Elizabeth colouring,—"it is not; but it belongs to a friend of mine."

"Was you ever in these parts before?"

"Some time ago."

"Then you knew the old family, likely?"

"Yes, I did."

"There was fine stuff in them Landholms," said the old man, perhaps supplied with the figure by the timber he was nailing,—

"real what I call good stuff—parents and children. There was a great deal of good in all of 'em; only the boys took notions they wouldn't be nothin' but ministers or lawyers or some sort o' people that wears black coats and don't have to roll up their trowsers for nothin'. They were clever lads, too. I don't mean to say nothin' agin 'em."

"Do you know how they're gettin' on?" he asked after a pause on his part and on Elizabeth's.

"I believe Asahel is with his father,—gone West."

"Ay, ay; but I mean the others—them two that went to College. I ha'n't seen Rufus for a great spell—I went down and fetched up Winthrop when his mother died."

"Will you have paint enough to finish that gunwale?"

"Guess so," said the old man looking into his paint-pot. "There's more oil in the bottle. What be them two doing now? Winthrop's a lawyer, ain't he?"

"Yes."

"Well he's made a smart one, ha'n't he?—ain't he about as smart as ary one they've got in Mannahatta?"

"I'm not a judge," said Elizabeth, who could not quite keep her countenance. "I dare say he is."

"He was my favourite, always, Winthrop was,—the Governor, as they called him. Well—I'd vote for him if he was sot up for that office—or any other office—if they'd do it while I'm above ground. Where is he now?—in Mannahatta?"

"Yes."

"Where's t'other one—the oldest—Rufus—where's he?"

"I don't know where he is. How soon will this do to be put in the water, Mr. Underhill?"

"Well—I guess it'll want somethin' of a dryin' fust. You can get along without it till next week, can't you?"

"Next week! and this is Tuesday!——"

"Yes—will you want it afore that? It hadn't ought to be put in the water one day afore Monday—if you want it to look handsome—or to wear worth speakin' of."

Miss Haye was silent, and the old man's brush made long sweeps back and forward over the shining gunwale.

"You see," Mr. Underhill went on, "it'll be all of night afore I get the bottom of this here done.—What's Rufus doin'? is he got to be a minister yet?"

"No."

"Another lawyer?"

"No"

"What is he then?"

"I don't know—I believe he was an engineer."

"An engineer?" said the old man standing up and looking at her. "Do you mean he's one o' them fellers that sees to the ingines on the boats?—*that* ain't much gettin' up in the world. I see one o' them once—I went to Mannahatta in the boat, just to see what 'twas—is Rufus one o' them smutty fellers standing over the fires there?"

"Not at all; it's a very different business, and as respectable as that of a clergyman or lawyer."

"There ain't anything more respectable than what his father was," said Mr. Underhill. "But Rufus was too handsome—he wanted to wear shiny boots always."

Elizabeth walked off.

So it was not till the early part of October that the little boat was painted and dried and in the water; and very nice she looked. Painted in the old colours; Elizabeth had been particular about that. Rose in the meantime had been heard from. She was coming, very soon, only staying for something, it wasn't very clearly made out what, that would however let her go in a few days. Elizabeth threw the letter down, with the mental conclusion that it was "just like Rose;" and resolved that her arms should be in a good state of training before the 'few days' were over.

"Who's goin' in this little concern?" said Mr. Underhill as he pushed it into the water. "Looks kind o' handsome, don't it?"

"Very nice!" said Elizabeth.

"That old black feller ain't up to rowin' you anywhere, is he? I don't believe he is."

"I'll find a way to get about in her, somehow."

"You must come over and see our folks—over the other side. My old mother's a great notion to see you—" said he, pulling the boat round into place,—"and I like she should have what she's a fancy for."

"Thank you," said Elizabeth; with about as much heed to his words as if a coney had requested her to take a look into his burrow. But a few minutes after, some thought made her speak again.

"Have you a mother living, sir?"

"Ay," he said with a little laugh, "she ain't a great deal older than I be. She's as spry in her mind, as she was when she was sixteen. Now—will you get into this?"

"Not now. Whereabouts do you live?"

"Just over," he said, pointing with his thumb over his shoulder and across the river,—"the only house you can see, under the mountain there—just under Wut-a-qut-o. 'Tain't a very sociable place and we are glad to see visiters."

He went; and Elizabeth only waited to have him out of sight, when she took gloves and oars and planted herself in the little 'Merry-go-round.'

"My arms won't carry me far to-day," she thought, as she pushed away from the rocks and slowly skimmed out over the smooth water. But how sweet to be dappling it again with her oar-blades,—how gracefully they rose and fell—how refreshing already that slight movement of her arms—how deliciously independent and alone she felt in her light carriage. Even the thrill of recollection could not overcome the instant's pleasure. Slowly and lovingly Elizabeth's oars dipped into the water; slowly and stealthily the little boat glided along. She presently was far enough out to see Mr. Underhill's bit of a farmhouse, sitting brown and lone at the foot of the hill, close by the water's edge. Elizabeth lay on her oars and stopped and looked at it.

"Go over there! Ridiculous! Why should I?——"

"And why shouldn't I?" came in another whisper. "Do me no harm—give them some pleasure. It is doing as I would be done by."

"But I can't give pleasure to all the old women in the land," she went on with excessive disgust at the idea.

"And this is only *one* old woman," went on the other quiet whisper,—"and kindness is kindness, especially to the old and lonesome.——"

It was very disagreeable to think of; Elizabeth rebelled at it strongly; but she could not get rid of the idea that Winthrop in her place would go, and would make himself exceedingly acceptable; she knew he would; and in the light of that idea, more than of any other argument that could be brought to bear, Elizabeth's conscience troubled her. She lay still on her oars now and then to think about it; she could not go on and get rid of the matter. She pondered Winthrop's fancied doing in the circumstances; she *knew* how he would comport himself among these poor people; she felt it; and then it suddenly flashed across her mind, "Even Christ pleased not himself;"—and she knew then why Winthrop did not. Elizabeth's head drooped for a minute. "I'll go,"—she said to herself.

Her head was raised again then, and with a good will the

oars made the little boat go over the water. She was elated to find her arms so strong, stronger now than they had been five minutes ago; and she took her way down towards the bottom of the bay, where once she had gone huckleberrying, and where a rich growth of wood covered the banks and shewed in one or two of its members here and there already a touch of frost. Here and there an orange or reddish branch of maple leaves—a yellow-headed butternut, partly bare—a ruddying dogwood or dogwood's family connection,—a hickory shewing suspicions of tawny among its green. A fresh and rich wall-side of beauty the woody bank was. Elizabeth pulled slowly along, coasting the green wilderness, exulting in her freedom and escape from all possible forms of home annoyance and intrusion; but that exulting, only a very sad break in a train of weary and painful thoughts and remembrances. It was the only break to them; for just then sorrowful things had got the upper hand; and even the Bible promises to which she had clung, and the faith that laid hold of them, and the hopes that grew out of them, could not make her be other than downcast and desponding. Even a Christian life, all alone in the world, with nobody and for nobody, seemed desolate and uncheering. Winthrop Landholm led such a life, and was not desolate, nor uncheered.—"But he is very different from me; he has been long a traveller on the road where my unsteady feet have but just set themselves; he is a man and I am a woman!" —And once Elizabeth even laid down her oars, and her head upon the hands that had held them, to shed the tears that would have their own peculiar way of comfort and relief. The bay, and the boat, and the woody shore, and the light, and the time of year, all had too much to say about her causes of sorrow. But tears wrought their own relief; and again able to bear the burden of life, Elizabeth pulled slowly and quietly homewards.

Looking behind her as she neared the rocks, to make sure that she was approaching them in a right direction, she was startled to see a man's figure standing there. Startled, because it was not the bent-shouldered form of Mr. Underhill, nor the slouching habit of Anderese; but tall, stately and well put on. It was too far to see the face; and in her one startled look Elizabeth did not distinctly recognize anything. Her heart gave a pang of a leap at the possibility of its being Winthrop; but she could not tell whether it were he or no; she could not be sure that it was, yet who else should come there with that habit of a gentleman? Could Mr. Brick?—No, he had never such an air, even at a distance. It was not Mr. Brick. Neither was it Mr.

Herder; Mr. Herder was too short. Every nerve now trembled, and her arms pulled nervously and weakly her boat to the shore. When might she look again? She did not till she must; then her look went first to the rocks, with a vivid impression of that dark figure standing above them, seen and not seen—she guided her boat in carefully—then just grazing the rocks she looked up. The pang and the start came again, for though not Winthrop it was Winthrop's brother. It was Rufus.

The nervousness and the flutter quieted themselves, almost; but probably Elizabeth could not have told then by the impulse of what feeling or feelings it was, that she coolly looked down again and gave her attention so steadily and minutely to the careful bestowment of her skiff, before she would set foot on the rocks and give her hand and eye to the person who had been waiting to claim them. By what impulse also she left it to him entirely to say what he was there for, and gave him no help whatever in her capacity of hostess.

"You are surprised to see me," said Rufus after he had shaken the lady's hand and helped her on shore.

"Rather. I could not imagine at first who it might be."

"I am glad to find you looking so well," said the gentleman gravely. "Very well indeed."

"It is the flush of exercise," said Elizabeth. "I was not looking well, a little while ago; and shall not be, in a little time to come."

"Rowing is good for you," said Rufus.

"It is pleasant," said Elizabeth. "I do it for the pleasantness, not for the goodness."

"Rather severe exercise, isn't it?"

"Not at all!" said Elizabeth a little scornfully. "I am not strong-armed just now—but it is nothing to move a boat like that."

"Some ladies would not think so."

They had been slowly moving up the path towards the house. As they reached the level of the grassy garden ground, where the path took a turn, Rufus stopped and faced about upon the river. The fair October evening air and light were there, over the water and over the land.

"It is beautiful!" he said somewhat abstractedly.

"You are not so fond of it as your brother, Mr. Landholm," said Elizabeth.

"What makes you think so?"

There was quick annoyance in his tone, but Miss Haye was not careful

"Am I wrong? Are you as fond of it?"

"I don't know," said Rufus. "His life has been as steadily given to his pursuits as mine has to mine."

"Perhaps more. But what then? I always thought you loved the city."

"Yes," Rufus said thoughtfully,—"I did;—but I love this too. It would be a very cold head and heart that did not."

Elizabeth made no reply; and the two enjoyed it in silence for a minute or two longer.

"For what do you suppose I have intruded upon you at this time, Miss Haye?"

"For some particular purpose—what, I don't know. I have been trying to think."

"I did not venture to presume upon making an ordinary call of civility."

What *less* are you going to do?—thought Elizabeth, looking at him with her eyes a little opened.

"I have been—for a few months past—constantly engaged in business at the South; and it is but a chance which permitted me to come here lately—I mean, to Mannahatta—on a visit to my brother. I am not willing to let slip any such opportunity."

"I should think you would not," said Elizabeth, wondering.

"There I heard of you.—Shall we walk down again?"

"If you please. I don't care whether up or down."

"I could not go home without turning a little out of my way to pay this visit to you. I hope I shall be forgiven."

"I don't know what I have to forgive, yet," said Elizabeth.

He was silent, and bit his lip nervously.

"Will you permit me to say—that I look back with great pleasure to former times passed in your society—in Mannahatta;—that in those days I once ventured to entertain a thought which I abandoned as hopeless,—I had no right to hope,—but that since I have heard of the misfortunes which have befallen you, it has come back to me again with a power I have not had the strength to resist— along with my sympathy for those misfortunes. Dear Miss Haye, I hope for your forgiveness and noble interpretation, when I say that I have dared to confess this to you from the impulse of the very circumstances which make it seem most daring."

"The misfortunes you allude to, are but one," said Elizabeth.

"One—yes,—but not one in the consequences it involved."

"At that rate of reckoning," said Elizabeth, "there would be no such a thing as *one* misfortune in the world."

"I was not thinking of one," said Rufus quietly. "The actual loss you have suffered is one shared by many—pardon me, it does not always imply equal deprivation, nor the same need of a strong and helping friendly hand."

Elizabeth answered with as much quietness,—

"It is probably good for me that I have care on my hands—it would be a weak wish, however natural, to wish that I could throw off on some agent the charge of my affairs."

"The charge I should better like," said Rufus looking at her, —"the only charge I should care for,—would be the charge of their mistress."

An involuntary quick movement of Elizabeth put several feet between them; then after half a minute, with a flushed face and somewhat excited breathing, she said, not knowing precisely what she said,

"I would rather give you the charge of my property, sir. The other is, you don't very well know what."

"My brother would be the better person to perform the first duty, probably," Rufus returned, with a little of his old-fashioned haughtiness of style.

Elizabeth's lips parted and her eye flashed, but as she was not looking at him, it only flashed into the water. Both stood proudly silent and still. Elizabeth was the first to speak, and her tone was gentle, whatever the words might be.

"You cannot have your wish in this matter, Mr. Landholm, and it would be no blessing to you if you could. I trust it will be no great grief to you that you cannot."

"My grief is my own," said Rufus with a mixture of expressions. "How should that be no blessing to me, which it is the greatest desire of my life to obtain, Miss Haye?"

"I don't think it is," said Elizabeth. "At least it will not be. You will find that it is not. It is not the desire of mine, Mr. Landholm."

There was silence again, a mortified silence on one part,—for a little space.

"You will do justice to my motives?" he said. "I have a right to ask that, for I deserve so much of you. If my suit had been an ungenerous one, it might better have been pressed years ago than now."

"Why was it not?" said Elizabeth.

It was the turn of Rufus's eyes to flash, and his lips and teeth saluted each other vexedly.

"It would probably have been as unavailing then as now,"

he replied. "I bid you good evening, Miss Haye. I ask nothing from you. I beg pardon for my unfortunate and inopportune intrusion just now. I shall annoy you no more."

Elizabeth returned his parting bow, and then stood quite still where he left her while he walked up the path they had just come down. She did not move, except her head, till he had passed out of sight and was quite gone; then she seated herself on one of the rocks near which her boat was moored, and clasping her hands round her knees, looked down into the water. What to find there?—the grounds of the disturbance in which her whole nature was working? it lay deeper than that. It wrought and wrought, whatever it was—the colour flushed and the lips moved tremulously,—her brow knit,—till at last the hands came to her eyes and her face sunk down, and passionate tears, passionate sobbing, told what Elizabeth could tell in no other way. Tears proud and humble—rebelling and submitting.

"It is good for me, I suppose," she said as she at last rose to her feet, fearing that her handmaid might come to seek her,—"my proud heart needed to be brought down in some such way—needed to be mortified even to this. Even to this last point of humiliation. To have my desire come and mock me so and as it were shake my wish in my face! But how could *he* think of me?—he could not—he is too good—and I am a poor thing, that may be made good, I suppose——"

Tears flowed again, hot and unbidden; for she was walking up to the house and did not want anybody to see them. And in truth before she was near the house Clam came out and met her half way down the path.

"Miss 'Lizabeth,—I don' know as you want to see nobody—"

"Who is there for me to see?"

"Well—there's an arrival—I s'pect we'll have to have supper in the kitchen to-night."

CHAPTER XLI.

> With weary steps I loiter on,
>   Though always under altered skies
>   The purple from the distance dies,
> My prospect and horizon gone.
>
> TENNYSON.

WHETHER or not Elizabeth wanted to see anybody she did not say—except to herself. She walked into the house, fortified with all the muniments of her spirit for the meeting. It was a quiet one on the whole. Rose cried a good deal, but Elizabeth bore it without any giving way; saving once or twice a slight twinkling of lip and eye, instantly commanded back. Rose had all the demonstration to herself, of whatever kind. Elizabeth sat still, silent and pale; and when she could get free went and ordered supper.

The supper was in Mrs. Landholm's old kitchen; they two alone at the table. Perhaps Elizabeth thought of the old time, perhaps her thoughts had enough to do with the present; she was silent, grave and stern, not wanting in any kind care nevertheless. Rose took tears and bread and butter by turns; and then sat with her face in her handkerchief all the evening. It seemed a very, very long evening to her hostess, whose face bespoke her more tired, weary, and grave, with every succeeding half hour. Why was this companion, whose company of all others she least loved, to be yet her sole and only companion, of all the world? Elizabeth by turns fretted and by turns scolded herself for being ungrateful, since she confessed that even Rose was better for her than to be utterly alone. Yet Rose was a blessing that greatly irritated her composure and peace of mind. So the evening literally wore away. But when at last Rose was kissing her hostess for good night, between sobs she stammered, " I am very glad to be here Lizzie,—it seems like being at home again."

Elizabeth gave her no answer besides the answering kiss; but her eyes filled full at that, and as soon as she reached her own room the tears came in long and swift flow, but sweeter and gentler and softer than they had flowed lately. And very thankful that she had done right, very soothed and refreshed that her right doing had promised to work good, she laid herself down to sleep.

But her eyes had hardly closed when the click of her door-latch made them open again. Rose's pretty night-cap was presenting itself.

" Lizzie!—aren't you afraid without a man in the house?"

" There *is* a man in the house."

" Is there?"

" Yes. Anderese—Karen's brother."

" But he is old."

" He's a man."

" But aren't you ever afraid?"

" It's no use to be afraid," said Elizabeth. " I am accustomed to it. I don't often think of it."

" I heard such queer noises," said Rose whispering. " I didn't think of anything before, either. May I come in here?"

" It's of no use, Rose," said Elizabeth. " You would be just as much afraid to-morrow night. There is nothing in the world tc be afraid of."

Rose slowly took her night-cap away and Elizabeth's head went down on her pillow. But her closing eyes opened again at the click of the latch of the other door.

" Miss 'Lizabeth!——"

" Well, Clam?——"

" Karen's all alive, and says she ain't goin' to live no longer."

" What!—"

" Karen."

" What's the matter?"

" Maybe she's goin', as she says she is; but I think maybe she ain't."

" Where is she?" said Elizabeth jumping up.

" In here," said Clam. " She won't die out of the kitchen."

Elizabeth threw on her dressing-gown and hurried out; thinking by the way that she had got into a thorn forest of difficulties, and wishing the daylight would look through. Karen was sitting before the fire, wrapped up in shawls, in the rocking chair.

"What's the matter, Karen?"

Karen's reply was to break forth into a tremulous scrap of her old song,—

"'I'm going,—I'm going,—I'm going,——'"

"Stop," said Elizabeth. "Don't sing. Tell me what's the matter."

"It's nothin' else, Miss Lizzie," said the old woman. "I'm goin'—I think I be."

"Why do you think so? How do you feel?"

"I don't feel no ways, somehow;—it's a kinder givin' away. I think I'm just goin', ma'am."

"But what *ails* you, Karen?"

"It's time," said Karen, jerking herself backwards and forwards in her rocking-chair. "I'm seventy years and more old. I hain't got no more work to do. I'm goin'; and I'm ready, praise the Lord! They're most all gone;—and the rest is comin' after;—it's time old Karen was there."

"But that's no sign you mayn't live longer," said Elizabeth. "Seventy years is nothing. How do you feel sick?"

"It's all over, Miss Lizzie," said the old woman. "Its givin' away. I'm goin'—I know I be. The time's come."

"I will send Anderese for a doctor—where is there one?"

Karen shivered and put her head in her hands, before she spoke.

"There ain't none—I don't want none—there was Doctor Kipp to Mountain Spring, but he ain't no 'count; and he's gone away."

"Clam, do speak to Anderese and ask him about it, and tell him to go directly, if there is any one he can go for.—What can I do for you, Karen?"

"I guess nothin', Miss Lizzie.—If the Governor was here, he'd pray for me; but it ain't no matter—I've been prayin' all my life—It's no matter if I can't pray good just right now. The Lord knows all."

Elizabeth stood silent and still.

"Shall I—would you like to have me read for you?" she asked somewhat timidly.

"No," said Karen—"not now—I couldn't hear. Read for yourself, Miss Lizzie. I wish the Governor was here."

What a throbbing wish to the same effect was in Elizabeth's heart! She stood, silent, sorrowful, dismayed, watching Karen, wondering at herself in her changed circumstances and life and occupation; and wondering if she were only going down into the valley of humiliation, or if she had got to the bottom. And almost thinking Karen to be envied if she were, as she said, 'going.'

"What's the matter?" said Rose and her night-cap at the other door.

"Karen don't feel very well. Don't come here, Rose."

"What are you there for?"

"I want to be here. You go to bed and keep quiet—I'll tell you another time."

"Is she sick?"

"Yes—I don't know—Go in, Rose, and be quiet!"

Which Rose did. Clam came back and reported that there was no doctor to be sent for, short of a great many miles. Elizabeth's heart sunk fearfully. What could she and her companions do with a dying woman?—if she were really that. Karen crept nearer the fire, and Clam built it up and made it blaze. Then she stood on one side, and her young mistress on the other.

"Go to bed, Miss 'Lizabeth," said Clam. "I'll see to her."

But Elizabeth did not move so much as an eyelid.

"I don't want nothin'," said Karen presently. "Miss Lizzie, if you see the Governor—tell him—"

"Tell him what?"

"Tell him to hold on,—will you?—the way his mother went and the way he's a goin'. Tell him to hold on till he gets there. Will you tell him?"

"Certainly! I will tell him anything you please."

Karen was silent for a little space, and then began again.

"Is't *your* way?"

Elizabeth's lips moved a little, but they closed and she made no answer.

"Mis' Landholm went that way, and Governor's goin', and I'm goin' too.

"'I'm going,—I'm going,—I'm——'"

"Do you feel better, Karen?" said Elizabeth interrupting her.

"I'm goin'—I don' know how soon axactly, Miss Lizzie—but I feel it. I am all givin' away. It's time. I've seen my life all through, and I'm ready. I'm ready—praise the Lord.

I was ready a great while ago, but it wa'n't the Lord's time; and now if he pleases, I'm ready."

"Wouldn't you feel better if you were to go to your own room and lie down?"

Karen made no answer for some time and then only was half understood to say that "this was the best place." Elizabeth did not move. Clam fetched a thick coarse coverlid and wrapping herself in it, lay down at full length on the floor.

"Go to bed, Miss 'Lizabeth,—I'm settled. I'll see to her. I guess she ain't goin' afore mornin'."

"You will go to sleep, Clam, and then she will have nobody to do anything for her."

"I'll wake up once in a while, Miss 'Lizabeth, to see she don't do nothin' to me."

Elizabeth stood another minute, thinking bitterly how invaluable Winthrop would be, in the very place where she knew herself so valueless. Another sharp contrast of their two selves; and then she drew up a chair to the fire and sat down too; determined at least to do the little she could do, give her eyes and her presence. Clam's entreaties and representations were of no avail. Karen made none.

They watched by her, or at least Elizabeth did, through hour after hour. She watched alone, for Clam slept and snored most comfortably; and Karen's poor head much of the time rested in her hands. Whether conscious or unconscious, she was very quiet; and her watcher trimmed the fire and mused with no interruption. At first with much fear and trembling; for she did not know how soon Karen's prophecy might come true; but as the night wore on and no change was to be seen or felt, this feeling quieted down and changed into a very sober and sad review of all the things of her own life, in the past and in the future. The present was but a point, she did not dwell on it; yet in that point was the sweetest and fairest thing her mind had in possession; her beginning of a new life and her hold of the promise which assured her that strength should not be wanting to live it until the end. She did look over her several present duties and made up her mind to the self-denying and faithful performance of them; but then her longing came back, for a human hand to hold her and help her on the journey's way. And her head bowed to the chair-back; and it was a good while before she recollected again to look at the fire or at her charge in front of it.

Karen's attitude was more easy; and Elizabeth excessively fatigued, with pain as well as weariness, felt inclined to steal off to bed and leave her door open, that she might readily hear if she was wanted. But it occurred to her that Winthrop for his own ease never would have deserted his post. She dismissed the thought of sleep and rest; and disposed herself to wear out the remnant of the night as she had begun it; in attendance on what she was not sure needed her attendance.

A longer night Elizabeth never knew, and with fear in the first part and watching in the last part of it, the morning found her really haggard and ill. But Karen was no worse; and not knowing what to think about her, but comforting herself with the hope that at least her danger was not imminent, Elizabeth went to bed, coveting sleep inexpressibly, for its forgetfulness as well as its rest. But sleep was not to be had so promptly.

"Miss 'Lizabeth !—" And there stood Clam before her opening eyes, as fresh and as black as ever, with a clean turban in the last state of smartness.

"What *is* the matter ? "

"Where will you have breakfast ? Karen ain't goin' at all at present. Where will you have it ? "

"Nowhere."

"Will I clear her out of the kitchen ? "

"No !—let her alone. Mrs. Haye's woman may see to breakfast in her mistress's room—I don't want anything—but sleep. Let Karen have and do just what she wants."

"Won't Clam do as much ! "—said the toss of the clean turban as its owner went out of the room. And the issue was, a very nice little breakfast brought to Miss Haye's bed-side in the space of half an hour. Elizabeth was waked up and looked dubious.

"You want it," said her handmaid. "The Governor said you was to take it."

"Is he here ! " exclaimed Elizabeth, with an amount of fire in eye and action that, as Clam declared afterwards, "had like to have made her upset everything." But she answered demurely,

"He ain't here just yet. I guess he's comin', though."

Elizabeth's eye went down, and an eye as observant if not so brilliant as her own, watched how the pink tinge rose and mounted in the cheeks as she betook herself to the bread and coffee. "Ain't she eatin' her breakfast like a good child ! " said Clam to herself. "*That* put her down."

And with a "Now you'll sleep—" Clam carried off the breakfast tray, and took care her mistress should have no second disturbance from anybody else. Elizabeth only heard once or twice in the course of the day that nothing was wanted from her; so slept her sleep out.

It was slept out at last, and Elizabeth got up and began to dress. Or rather, took her dressing-comb in hand and planted herself in front of the window, and there forgot what she had to do. It was a fine afternoon of October, late in the day. It was very fair outside. The hills touched here and there in their green with a frost-spot—yellow, or tawny, or red; the river water lying very calm; and a calm sky over-head; the air as pure as though vapours and mists were refined away for ever. The distant trees of the woodland shewed in round distinct masses of foliage, through such an atmosphere; the rocky shore edge cut sharp against the water; the nearer cedars around the home valley seemed to tell their individual leaves. Here and there in some one of them a Virginia creeper's luxuriant wreaths were colouring with suspicious tokens of crimson. Not in their full brilliancy yet, the trees and the vine-leaves were in fair preparation; and fancy could not imagine them more fair than they looked that afternoon.

"So bright without!—and so dark within!"—Elizabeth thought. "When will it end—or is it only beginning? Such a flood of brightness was over me a little while ago,—and now, there is one burden in one room, and another in another room, and I myself am the greatest burden of all. Because my life has nothing to look forward to—in this world—and heaven is not enough; I want something in this world.—Yes, I do.—Yet Winthrop Landholm has nothing more than I have, in this world's things, and he don't feel like me. What is the reason? Why is his face *always* so at rest,—so bright—so strong? Ah, it must be that he is so much better than I!—he *has* more, not of this world's things; religion is something to him that it is not to me; he must love his Master far better than I do.—Then religion might be more to me.—It shall be—I will try;—but oh! if I had never seen another Christian in all my life, how well his single example would make me know that religion is a strong reality. What a reward his will be! I wonder how many besides me he will have drawn to heaven—he does not dream that he has ever done me any good. Yet it is pleasant to owe so much to him—and it's bitter!——"

"You'll tire yourself with lookin', Miss 'Lizabeth," said Clam behind her. "Mannahatta ain't so far off as that."

Elizabeth started a little from her fixed attitude and began to handle her dressing-comb.

"'Taint so far folks can't get here, I guess."

"Clam!"—said her mistress facing about.

"Well, Miss Lizzie——"

"Go and take care of Karen. I don't want you."

"*She* don't want me," said Clam. "And you've had no dinner."

"Do as I tell you. I shall not have any."

With this spur, Elizabeth was soon dressed, and then walked into Mrs. Haye's room. Rose apparently had had leisure for meditation and had made up her mind upon several things; but her brow changed as her cousin came in.

"Lizzie!—Why you've been up all night, Emma says."

"That's nothing. I have been down all day."

"But what's the matter with this old woman?"

"I don't know. She don't know herself."

"But Emma said she thought she was dying?"

"So she did. I don't know whether she is right or not."

"Dying!—is she!" said Rose with a little scream.

"I don't know. I hope not, so soon as she thinks. She is no worse to-night."

"But what are you going to do?"

"Nothing—more than I have done."

"But are you going to stay here?"

"Stay here, Rose!—"

'Yes—I mean—who's going to take care of her? And isn't she your cook?"

A curious quick gleam of a laugh passed over Elizabeth's face; it settled graver than before.

"Clam can cook all you and I want."

"But who's going to take care of her?"

"I have sent for help, and for a doctor."

"Haven't you sent for a doctor before! Why Lizzie!"

"I sent early this morning. The messenger had to go a number of miles."

"And isn't there anybody about the house but Clam and Emma?"

"Anderese is here. I sent somebody else."

"What use is an old thing like that about a place?"

Elizabeth was silent. The cloud gathered on Rose's face, and as if that it might not cast its shadow on her cousin, she looked out of the window. Then Clam came in.

"Where'll supper be, Miss 'Lizabeth?"

"Is Karen in the kitchen?"

"Oh!—I won't have tea in there!" said Rose with one of her old little screams.

"Let it be here, Clam."

"What'll it be, Miss 'Lizabeth?"

"Anything you please."

"There's nothing in the house to be pleased with," said Clam; "and you've had no dinner."

"Bread and butter and tea—and boil an egg."

"That would be pleasant," said Clam, capacity and fun shining out of every feature;—"but Karen's hens don't lay no eggs when she ain't round."

"Bread and butter and tea, then."

"Butter's gone," said Clam.

"Bread and cold meat, then."

"Fresh meat was all eat up days ago; and you and Mis' Haye don't make no 'count of ham."

Elizabeth got up and went out to Anderese and despatched him to Mountain Spring after what forage he could find. Then from a sense of duty went back to her cousin. Rose was looking out of the window again when she came in, and kept silence for a little space; but silence was never Rose's forte.

"Lizzie—what makes you live in such a place?"

"It was the pleasantest place I could find," said her cousin, with a tone of suppressed feeling.

"It's so lonely!" said Rose.

"It suited me."

"But it isn't safe," said Rose. "What if something happened to you, with nobody about,—what would you do?"

"It has not been a subject of fear with me," said Elizabeth. "I haven't thought about it."

"Who comes to see you here? anybody?"

"No. Who should come?" said Elizabeth sternly. "Whom should I want to see?"

"Don't you want to see anybody, ever? I do. I don't like to be in a desert so."

Elizabeth was silent, with a set of the lips that told of thoughts at work.

"Doesn't Winthrop Landholm come here?"

"No!"

"I'm not used to it," said Rose whimpering,—"I can't live so. It makes me feel dreadfully."

"Whom do *you* want to see, Rose?" said Elizabeth, with an expression that ought to have reminded her companion whom she was dealing with.

"I don't care who—any one. It's dreadful to live so, and see nothing but the leaves shaking and the river rolling and this great empty place."

"Empty!" said Elizabeth, with again a quick glancing laugh. "Well!—you are yourself yet! But at any rate the leaves don't shake much to-day."

"They did last night," said Rose. "I was so frightened I didn't know what to do, and with no man in the house either, good for anything—I didn't sleep a wink till after one o'clock."

"Was your sleep ever disturbed by anything of more importance than the wind?"

"I don't know what you mean," said Rose in tears. "I think you're very unkind!——"

"What would you like me to do, Rose?"

"Let's go away from here."

"Where?"

"I don't care—to Mannahatta."

"What do you want to do in Mannahatta?"

"Why, nothing,—what everybody does—live like other people. I shall die here."

"Is the memory of the best friend you ever had, so little worth, Rose, that you are in a hurry to banish it your company already?"

"I don't know what you mean," said Rose, with one of her old pouts and then bursting into fresh weeping. "I don't know why one should be miserable any more than one can help. I have been miserable enough, I am sure. Oh Lizzie!—I think you're very unkind!—"

Elizabeth's face was a study; for the fire in her eyes shone through water, and every feature was alive. But her lips only moved to tremble.

"I won't stay here!" said Rose. "I'll go away and do something. I don't care what I do. I dare say there's enough left for me to live upon; and I can do without Emma. I can live somehow, if not quite as well as you do."

"Hush, Rose, and keep a little sense along with you," said Elizabeth.

"There *must* be enough left for me somehow," Rose went on, sobbing. "Nobody had any right to take my money. It was mine. Nobody else had a right to it. It is mine. I ought to have it."

"Rose!——"

Rose involuntarily looked up at the speaker who was standing before her, fire flashing from eye and lip, like the relations of Queen Gulnare in the fairy story.

"Rose!—do not dare speak to me in that way!—ever again! —whatever else you do. I will leave you to get back your senses."

With very prompt and decided action, Miss Haye sought her rowing gloves in her own room, put them on, and went down to the rocks where the Merry-go-round lay. She stopped not to look at anything; she loosened the boat and pushed out into the water. And quick and smartly the oars were pulled, till the skiff was half way over the river towards Mr. Underhill's house. Suddenly there they stopped. Elizabeth's eyes were bent on the water about two yards from the stern of the boat; while the paddles hung dripping, dripping more and more slowly, at the sides, and the little skiff floated gently up with the tide. But if Elizabeth's eyes were looking into nature, it was her own; her face grew more settled and grave and then sorrowful every minute; and at last the paddle-handles were thrown across the boat and her arms and her head rested upon them. And the little skiff floated gently up stream.

It had got some distance above Mr. Underhill's, when its mistress lifted her head and looked about, with wet eyelashes, to see where she was. Then the boat's head was turned, and some steady pulling brought her to the gravelly beach in front of Mr. Underhill's house. Its owner was luckily there to help her out.

"Well, I declare that's clever of you," said he, as he grasped the bow of the little vessel to draw it further up. "I didn't much expect you'd come when I asked you. Why you can row, real smart."

"I don't see how I am going to get out, Mr. Underhill."

"Step up on there, can't you—I'll hold her,—can you jump?"—

"But Mr. Underhill, that's going to do no good to my boat.——"

"What aint?——"

"That gravel—grating and grinding on it, as the tide makes."

"'Twon't do nothin'—it'll just stay still so. Well, you go in and speak to mother, and I'll see to her. I didn't know you could row so smart,—real handsome!"

"I learnt a good while ago," said Elizabeth. "I'll not be gone long, Mr. Underhill."

Up the neglected green slope she ran, wondering at herself the while. What new steps were these, which Miss Haye was not taking for her own pleasure. What a strange visit was this, which her heart shrank from more and more as she neared the house door.

The house was tenanted by sundry younger fry of the feminine gender, of various ages, who met Elizabeth with wonder equal to her own, and a sort of mixed politeness and curiosity to which her experience had no parallel. By the fireside sat the old grandam, very old, and blind, as Elizabeth now perceived she was. Miss Haye drew near with the most utter want of knowledge what to do or say to such a person,—how to give the pleasure she had come to give. She hoped the mere fact of her coming and presence would do it, for to anything further she felt herself unequal. The old lady looked up curiously, hearing the noise of entering feet and a stranger's among them.

"Will you tell your grandmother who I am," Elizabeth asked, with a shy ignorance how to address her, and an exceeding reluctance to it.

"Grand'ma," said the eldest girl, "here is Miss Haye,—the young lady from Shahweetah—she's here."

The old woman turned her sightless eyes towards her visiter, got up and curtseyed.

"Don't do that," said Elizabeth, taking a seat near her. "Mr. Underhill asked me some time ago to come and see his mother."

"I've heerd of ye," said the old woman. "'Siah was over to your place, makin' of a boat, or mendin', or somethin', he telled me. I'm glad to see ye. How did ye come across?"

"In a boat—in the boat he mended for me."

"Have you got somebody to row ye over?

"I rowed myself over."

"Why did ye?—ain't ye afeard? I wouldn't ha' thought! 'Siah said she was a slim handsome girl, as one would see in the country."

"Well I can row," said Elizabeth colouring; for she had an instant sense that several pairs of eyes *not* blind were comparing the report with the reality.

"Be you the owner of Shahweetah now?"

"Yes."

"I heerd it was so. And what's become of the old family?"

"They are scattered. Mr. Landholm is gone West, with one of his sons; the others are in different places."

"And the girl is dead, ain't she?"

"Winnie?—yes."

Elizabeth knew that!

"The mother was gone first—to a better place. She had a fine lot o' children. Will was a pictur;—the farmer, he was a fine man too;—but there was one—the second boy—Winthrop, —he was the flower of the flock, to my thinkin'. I ha'n't seen him this great while. He's been here since I lost my sight, but I thought I could see him when I heerd him speak."

There was silence. Elizabeth did not feel inclined to break it.

"Do you know him, maybe?" the old woman said presently. Winthrop *had* made himself pleasant there!——

"Yes."

"Is he lookin' as well as he used to?"

"Quite as well, I believe."

"Is he gettin' along well?"

"Yes—I believe so—very well."

"Whatever he does 'll prosper, *I* believe," said Mrs. Underhill; "for the Lord knoweth the way of the righteous. Is that a way you have any knowledge of, young lady?"

"Not much—" said Elizabeth hesitating.

"'Siah says he 'spects you're rich."

"What makes him think so?"

"He says that's what he 'spects. Does the hull Shahweetah farm belong to you?"

"Yes."

"It's a good farm. Who's goin' to take care of it for you?"

"I don't know, yet."

"I 'spose you'll be gettin' married, one of these days, and then there 'll be some one to do it for you. Be you handsome, particular, as 'Siah says?"

Elizabeth coloured exceedingly, and a tittering laugh, somewhat boisterous, ran round the group of spectators and listeners, with a murmured "Oh Grand'ma!—"

"Whisht!"—said the old woman;—"I'm not talkin' like you. I'm old and blind. I can't see for myself, and I want to know. She can tell me."

"Father telled ye already," said the eldest girl.

"I can tell better from what *she* says," said Mrs. Underhill, turning her face towards her visiter. "What does she say? Be you uncommon fair and handsome?—or not more than the common?"

The red deepened on Elizabeth's cheek and brow, but she answered, not without some hesitation,

"I believe—more than the common."

A little glimpse of a smile stole over the old woman's face.

"Handsome, and rich. Well—Be you happy too, young lady, above the common?"

"I have learned, ma'am, that that depends upon right-doing;—so I am not always happy."

"Have you learned that lesson?" said the old woman. "It's a good one. Let me see your hand?"

Elizabeth drew near and gave it.

"It's a pretty hand,"—said the old woman. "It's soft—it hain't done much work. It feels rich and handsome. Don't you give it to no one who will help you to forget that the blessing of God is better than silver and gold."

"Thank you. I will not."

"Be you a servant of the Lord, young lady?"

"I hope I am, Mrs. Underhill," Elizabeth answered with some hesitation. "Not a good one."

The old woman dropped her hand and fell back in her chair, only saying, for Elizabeth had risen,

"Come and see me again—I'll be pleased to see ye."

"If I do!—" thought Elizabeth as she ran down to her boat. The free air seemed doubly free. But then came the instant thought,—"Winthrop Landholm would not have said that. How far I am—how far!—from where he stands!"—

She walked slowly down to the water's edge.

"Mr. Underhill," she said as she prepared to spring into the boat which he held for her,—"I have forgotten, while I was at the house, what I partly came for to-night. We are out of provisions—have you any eggs, or anything of any kind, to spare?"

"Eggs?"—said Mr. Underhill, holding the boat,—"what else would you like along of eggs?"

"Almost anything, that is not salt meat."

"Chickens?—we've got some o' them."

"Very glad of them indeed,—or fresh meat."

"Ha'n't got any of that just to-day," said the old farmer shaking his head. "I'll see. The boat won't stir—tide's makin' yet. You'll have a pull home, I expect."

He went back to the house, and Elizabeth stood waiting, alone with her boat.

There was refreshment and strength to be had from nature's pure and calm face; so very pure and calm the mountains looked down upon her and the river smiled up. The opposite hill-tops shone in the warm clear light of the October setting sun, the more warm and bright for the occasional red and yellow leaves that chequered their green, and many tawny and half turned trees that mellowed the whole mountain side. Such clear light as shone upon them! such unearthly blue as rose above them! such a soft and fair water face that gave back the blue! What could eyes do but look; what could the mind do but wonder, and be thankful; and wonder again, at the beauty, and grow bright in the sunlight, and grow pure in that shadowless atmosphere. The sharp cedar tops on Shahweetah were so many illuminated points, and further down the river the sunlight caught just the deep bend of the water in the bay; the rest was under shadow of the western hills. All was under a still and hush,—nothing sounded or moved but here and there a cricket; the tide was near flood and crept up noiselessly; the wind blew somewhere else, but not in October. Softly the sun went down and the shadows stole up.

Elizabeth stood with her hands pressed upon her breast, drinking in all the sights and sounds, and many of their soft whisperings that only the spirit catches; when her ear was caught by very dissimilar and discordant notes behind her,—the screaming of discomposed chickens and the grating of Mr. Underhill's boots on the gravel.

"Here's chickens for ye," said the farmer, who held the legs of two pair in his single hand, the heads of the same depending and screaming in company,—"and here's three dozen of fresh eggs—if you want more you can send for 'em. Will you take these along in the Merry-go-round?"

"If you please—there is no other way," said Elizabeth. "Wait—let me get in first, Mr. Underhill—Are they tied so they can't get loose?"

"La! yes," said the old man putting them into the bow of the boat,—"they can't do nothin'! I'll engage they won't hurt ye. Do you good, if you eat 'em right. Good bye!—it's pretty nigh slack water, I guess—you'll go home easy. Come again!—and you shall have some more fowls to take home with ye!"—

Elizabeth bowed her acknowledgments, and pulled away towards home, over the bright water, wondering again very much at herself and her chickens. The dark barrier of the western hills rose up now before her, darkening and growing more distant—as she went all the way over the river home. Elizabeth admired them and admired at herself by turns.

Near the landing, however, the boat paused again, and one oar splashed discontentedly in the water and then lay still, while the face of its owner betrayed a struggle of some sort going on.

The displeased brow, and the firm-set lips, said respectively, 'I would not,' and 'I must;' and it was five minutes good before the brow cleared up and the lips unbent to their usual full free outline; and the oars were in play once more, and the Merry-go-round brought in and made fast.

"Well, Miss 'Lizabeth!" said Clam who met her at the door,—"where *have* you been! Here's Mis' Haye been cryin' and the tea-kettle singing an hour and a half, if it isn't two hours."

"Has Anderese come home?"

"Yes, and supper's ready, and 'taint bad, for Mis' Landholm learned me how to do fresh mutton and cream; and it's all ready. You look as if you wanted it, Miss 'Lizabeth. My!——"

"There are some eggs and chickens down in the boat, Clam"

"In what boat, Miss 'Lizabeth?"

"In mine—down at the rocks."

"Who fetched 'em?"

"I did, from Mr. Underhill's. You may bring them up to the house."

Leaving her handmaid in an excess of astonishment unusual with her, Elizabeth walked into her guest's room, where the table was laid. Rose sat yet by the window, her head in her handkerchief on the window-sill. Elizabeth went up to her.

"Rose——"

"What?"—said Rose without moving.

"Rose—look up at me——"

The pretty face was lifted at her bidding, but it was sullen, and the response was a sullen "Well——"

"I am very sorry I spoke to you so—I was very wrong. I am very sorry. Forgive me and forget it—will you?"

"It was very unkind!"—said Rose, her head going down again in fresh tears.

"It was very unkind and unhandsome. What can I say more, but that I am sorry? Won't you forget it?"

"Of course," said Rose wiping her eyes,—"I don't want to remember it if you want to forget it. I dare say I was foolish——"

"Then come to supper," said Elizabeth. "Here's the tea—I'm very hungry."

CHAPTER XLII.

> And Phant'sie, I tell you, has dreams that have wings,
> And dreams that have honey, and dreams that have stings,
> Dreams of the maker, and dreams of the teller,
> Dreams of the kitchen, and dreams of the cellar.
>
> BEN JONSON.

A FEW days more passed; days of sameness in the house, while Autumn's beautiful work was going on without, and the woods were changing from day to day with added glories. It seemed as if the sun had broken one or two of his beams across the hills, and left fragments of coloured splendour all over. The elm trees reared heads of straw-colour among their forest brethren; the maples shewed yellow and red and flame-colour; the birches were in bright orange. Sad purple ashes stood the moderators of the Assembly; and hickories of gold made sunny slopes down the mountain sides. All softened together in the distance to a mellow, ruddy, glowing hue over the whole wood country.

The two cousins sat by the two windows watching the fading light, in what used once to be the 'keeping-room'—Mrs. Haye's now. Elizabeth had been long looking out of the window, with a fixed, thoughtful, sorrowful, gaze. Rose's look was never fixed long upon anything and never betrayed her thoughts to be so. It wavered now uneasily between her cousin and the broad and bright hills and river—which probably Mrs. Haye did not see.

"How long are you going to stay here, Lizzie?"

"I don't know."

"How is that old woman?"

"I don't know. There don't seem to be much difference from one day to another."

"What ails her?"

"I don't know. I suppose it is as the doctor says,—that there is a general breaking up of nature."

"Is she going to live long?"

"I don't know. He said probably not."

"Well, who's going to take care of her?"

"She is taken care of. There is a woman here from Mountain Spring, to do all that is necessary."

"Why must *we* stay here, Lizzie?—it's so dismal."

"*We* mustn't—*I* must."

"Why?"

"I would rather—and I think it is right."

"To take care of that old woman?"

"No—I can't do much for her—but I can see that she is taken care of."

"But how would she have done if you had never come here?"

"I don't know. I don't know what that has to do with it, seeing that I am here."

"You wouldn't stay for her now, if she wasn't somebody's old nurse."

Elizabeth did not answer.

"But how long *do* you mean to stay here, Lizzie?—anyhow?"

"Till I must go—till it is less pleasant here than somewhere else."

"And when will you think that?"

"Not for a good while."

"But *when*, Lizzie?"

"I don't know. I suppose when the cold weather comes in earnest."

"I'm sure it has come now!" said Rose shrugging her shoulders. "I'm shivering every morning after the fire goes out. What sort of cold weather do you mean?"

"I mean snow and ice."

"Snow and ice!—And then you will go—where will you go?" said Rose discontentedly.

"I suppose, to Mannahatta."

"Will you go the first snow?"

"I cannot tell yet, Rose."

There was a pause. Elizabeth had not stirred from her position. Her head rested yet on her hand, her eyes looked steadily out of the window.

"It will seem so lonely there!" said Rose whimpering.

"Yes!— more lonely than here."

"I meant in the house. But there one can get out and see some one."

"There isn't a soul in Mannahatta I care to see."

"Lizzie!—"

"Not that I know of."

"Lizzie!—Mr. Landholm?"

"I mean, not one that I am like to see."

"What do you go to Mannahatta for, then?" said Rose unbelievingly.

"One must be somewhere, to do something in the world."

"To do what?"

"I don't know—I suppose I shall find my work."

"Work?—what work?"—said Rose wonderingly.

"I don't know yet, Rose. But everybody has something to do in the world—so I have,—and you have."

"I haven't anything. What have we to do, except what we like to do?"

"I hope I shall like my work," said Elizabeth. "I must like it, if I am to do it well."

"What do you mean?—what are you talking of, Lizzie?"

"Listen to me, Rose. Do you think that you and I have been put in this world with so many means of usefulness, of one sort and another, and that it was never meant we should do anything but trifle away them and life till the end of it came? Do you think God has given us nothing to do for him?"

"*I* haven't much means of doing anything," said Rose, half pouting, half sobbing. "Have you taken up your friend Winthrop Landholm's notions?"

There was a rush to Elizabeth's heart, that his name and hers, in such a connection, should be named in the same day; but the colour started and the eyes flushed with tears, and she said nothing.

"What sort of 'work' do you suppose you are going to do?"

"I don't know. I shall find out, Rose, I hope, in time."

"I guess he can tell you,—if you were to ask him," said Rose meaningly.

Elizabeth sat a minute silent, with quickened breath.

"Rose," she said, leaning back into the room that she might see and be seen,—"look at me and listen to me."

Rose obeyed.

"Don't say that kind of thing to me again."

"One may say what one has a mind to, in a free land," said Rose pouting,—"and one needn't be commanded like a child or a servant. Don't I know you would never plague yourself with that old woman if she wasn't Winthrop's old nurse?"

Elizabeth rose and came near to her.

"I will not have this thing said to me!" she repeated. "My motives, in any deed of charity, are no man's or woman's to meddle with. Mr. Landholm is most absolutely nothing to me, nor I to him; except in the respect and regard he has from me, which he has more or less, I presume, from everybody that has the happiness of knowing him. Do you understand me, Rose? clearly?"

Another answer was upon Rose's tongue, but she was cowed, and only responded a meek 'yes.' Elizabeth turned and walked off in stately fashion to the door of the kitchen. The latch was raised, and then she let it fall again, came back, and stood again with a very different face and voice before her guest.

"Rose," she said gravely, "I didn't speak just in the best way to you; but I do not always recollect myself quickly enough. You mustn't say that sort of thing to me—I can't bear it. I am sorry for anything in my manner that was disagreeable to you just now."

And before Rose had in the least made up her mind how to answer her, Elizabeth had quitted the room.

"She ain't goin' never!" said Clam, meeting and passing her mistress as she entered the kitchen. "*I* don't believe! She's a goin' to stay."

Karen sat in her wonted rocking-chair before the fire, rocking a very little jog on her rockers. Elizabeth came up to the side of the fireplace and stood there, silent and probably meditative. She had at any rate forgotten Karen, when the old woman spoke, in a feebler voice than usual.

"Is the Governor comin'?"

"What, Karen?" said Elizabeth, knowing very well what she had asked, but not knowing so well the drift and intent of it.

"Is the Governor comin'? will he be along directly?"

"No—I suppose not. Do you want to see him, Karen?"

"I'd like to see him," said the old woman covering her eyes with her withered hand. "I thought he was comin'."

"Perhaps something may bring him, some day. I dare say you will see him by and by— I don't know how soon."

"I'll see him *there*," said the old woman. "I can't stay here long."

"Why you don't seem any worse, Karen, do you? Aren't you going to be well again?"

"Not here," said the old woman. "I'm all goin' to pieces. I'll go to bed to-night, and I won't get up again."

"Don't say that, Karen; because I think you will."

"I'll go to bed," she repeated in a rather plaintive manner "I thought he'd be here."

It touched Elizabeth acutely; perhaps because she had so near a fellow feeling that answered Karen's, and allowed her to comprehend how exceedingly the desire for his presence might grow strong in one who had a right to wish for it. And she knew that he would reckon old Karen his friend, whatever other people would do.

"What can I do for you, Karen?" she said gently. "Let me be the best substitute I can. What can I do for you, that he could do better?"

"There can't nobody do just the Governor's work," said his old nurse. "I thought he'd ha' been here. This 'll be my last night, and I'd like to spend it hearin' good things."

"Would you like me to send for anybody," said Elizabeth.

"Could ye send for *him?*" said Karen earnestly.

"Not in time. No, Karen,—there'd be no time to send a message from here to Mannahatta and get him here to-night."

She jogged herself back and forward a little while on her rocking-chair; and then said she would go to bed. Elizabeth helped her into the little room, formerly Asahel's, opening out of the kitchen, which she had insisted Karen should take during her illness; and after she was put to bed, came again and asked her what she should do for her. Karen requested to have the Bible read.

Elizabeth set open the kitchen door, took a low seat by Karen's bedside, and established herself with her book. It was strange work to her, to read the Bible to a person who thought herself dying. She, who so lately had to do with everything else but the Bible, now seated by the bedside of an old black woman, and the Bible the only matter in hand between the two. Karen's manner made it more strange. She was every now and then breaking in upon the reading, or accompanying it, with remarks and interjections. Sometimes it was "Hallelujah!"—sometimes, "That's true, that's true!"—sometimes, and very often, "Praise the Lord!" Not loud, nor boisterous; they were most of the time little underbreath words said to herself, words seemingly that she could not help, the good of which she took and meant for nobody else's edification. They were however very disagreeable and troublesome to Elizabeth's ears and thoughts; she had half a mind to ask Karen to stop them; but the next sighing "That's true!"—checked her; if it was such a comfort to the old woman to hold counsel with herself, and Elizabeth could offer nothing better, the least she could do was to let her alone. And then Elizabeth grew accustomed to it; and at last thoughts wandered a little by turns to take up their new trade of wondering at herself and at the new, unwonted life she seemed beginning to lead. There was a singular pleasantness in what she was doing; she found a grave sweet consciousness of being about the right work; but presently to her roving spirit the question arose whether *this*,—this new and certainly very substantial pleasure,—were perhaps the chief kind she was hereafter to look forward to, or find in this life;—and Elizabeth's heart confessed to a longing desire for something else. And then her attention suddenly came back to poor Karen at her side saying, softly, "Bless the Lord, O my soul!"—Elizabeth stopped short; she was choked.

At this juncture Clam noiselessly presented herself

"He's come, Miss 'Lizabeth."

The start that Miss Haye's inward spirits gave at this, was not to be seen at all on the outside. She looked at Clam, but she gave no sign that her words had been understood. Yet Elizabeth had understood them so well, that she did not even think at first to ask the question, and when she did, it was for form's sake, *who* had come? Probably Clam knew as much, for she only repeated her words.

"He's come. What 'll I do with him, Miss 'Lizabeth?"

"Where is he?"

"He ain't come yet—he's comin'."

"Coming when? And what do you mean by saying he is come?"

"I don't mean nothin' bad," said Clam. "He's just a comin' up the walk from the boat—I see him by the moon."

"See who it is, first, before you do anything with him; and then you can bring me word."

Elizabeth closed her book however, in some little doubt what she should do with herself. She knew,—it darted into her mind,—that it would please Winthrop to find her there; that it would meet his approbation; and then with the stern determination that motives of self-praise, if they came into her head should not come into her life, she hurried out and across the kitchen and hid her book in her own room. Then came out into the kitchen and stood waiting for the steps outside and for the opening of the door.

"You are come in good time," she said, as she met and answered Winthrop's offered hand.

"I am glad I am in time," he said.

"Karen has been wishing for you particularly to-night—but I don't know that that is any sign, except to the superstitious, that she is in particular danger."

"I shall be all the more welcome, at any rate."

"I don't know whether that is possible, in Karen's case. But did you know she wanted you?—did you know she was ill?"

"Do you suppose nothing but an errand of mercy could bring me?" he answered slightly, though with a little opening of the eyes which Elizabeth afterwards remembered and speculated upon. But for the present she was content with the pleasant implication of his words. Clam was ordered to bring refreshments. These Winthrop declined; he had had all he wanted. Then Elizabeth asked if he would like to see Karen.

She opened the door, which she had taken care to shut, and went in with him.

"Karen—here is the Governor, that you were wishing for."

The old woman turned her face towards them; then stretched out her hand, and spoke with an accent of satisfied longing that went at least to one heart.

"I thought he'd come," she said. "Governor!—"

Winthrop leaned over to speak to her and take her hand. Elizabeth longed to hear what he would say, but she had no business there; she went out, softly closing the door.

She was alone then; and she stood on the hearth before the fire in a little tumult of pleasure, thinking how she should dispose of her guest and what she might do for him.

"Once more I have a chance," she thought; "and I may never in the world have another—He will not come here again before I go back to Mannahatta, he cannot stay in my house there, —and another summer is very far off, and very uncertain. He'll not be very likely to come here—he may be married—and I am very sure I shall not want to see his wife here—I shall not do it.—Though I might ask her for his sake—No! I should better break with him at once and have no more to do with him; it would be only misery." "And what is it now?" said something else. And "Not misery"—was the answer.

"Where will I put him, Miss 'Lizabeth?" said the voice of Clam softly at her elbow. Elizabeth started.

"You must take my room. I will sleep with Mrs. Haye. Clam—what have we got in the house? and what can you do in the way of cooking?"

"I can do some things—for some folks," said Clam. "Wa'n't my cream gravy good the other day?"

"Cream gravy!—with what?"

"Fresh lamb,—mutton, I would say."

"But you have got no fresh mutton now, have you?"

"Maybe Mr. Underhill has," said Clam with a twinkle of her bright eye.

"Mr. Underhill's fresh mutton is on the other side of the river. What have we got on this side?"

"Pretty much of nothing," said Clam, "this side o' Mountain Spring. Anderese ain't no good but to make the fire—it takes mor'n him to find somethin' to put over it."

"Then you'll have to go to Mountain Spring before breakfast, Clam."

"Well, m'm. Who'll take care of the house while I'm gone, Miss 'Lizabeth?"

"Mrs. Cives—can't she?"

"Mis' Cives is gone off home."

"Gone home!—what, to Mountain Spring?"

"That's where her home is, she says."

"What for? and without asking?"

"She wanted to spend to-night at home, she said; and she asked no questions and went."

"To night of all nights! when Karen seems so much worse!"

"It's good we've got the Governor," said Clam.

"But he can't sit up all night with her."

"Guess he will," said Clam. "Pretty much like him. You can sleep in your bed, Miss 'Lizabeth."

"You go and get the room ready—he must not sit up all night—and we'll see in the morning about Mountain Spring. Somebody must go."

"He'll go if you ask him," said Clam. "He'd do the marketing best, now, of all of us. He knows just where everything is. 'Fact is, we want him in the family pretty much all the time."

"Let him know when his room is ready, and offer him refreshments,—and call me if I am wanted."

Clam departed; but Elizabeth, instead of doing the same, took a chair on the kitchen hearth and sat down to await any possible demands upon her. She could hear a quiet sound of talking in Karen's room; now and then the old woman's less regulated voice, more low or more shrill, broke in upon the subdued tones of the other. Elizabeth thought she would have given *anything* to be a hearer of what was said and listened to there; but the door was shut; it was all for Karen and not for her; and she gave up at last in despair and retreated to her cousin's room.

"So he's come?" said Rose.

"Yes!—he's come, Did you know he was coming?"

"I!—No,—I didn't know he was coming. How should I?"

"Did you *think* he was coming, Rose?"

"I didn't know but he'd come," said Rose a little awkwardly, "I didn't know anything about it."

Elizabeth chose to ask no further question. Somewhat mortified already, she would not give herself any more certain ground of mortification, not at that time. She would talk no more with Rose. She went to bed; and long after her companion was asleep, she listened for Winthrop's coming out or Clam's colloquy with him, and for any possible enquiry after herself. She heard Clam tap at the door—she heard the undistinguished sound of words, and only gathered that Winthrop probably was declining all proffered comforts and luxuries and choosing to spend the night by Karen's pillow. And weary and sorry and sick of everything in the world, Elizabeth went to sleep.

She waked up in the morning to hear the twittering of the birds around the house. They were singing busily of the coming day, but the day had not come yet; at least it was some time before sunrise. Elizabeth softly got up, softly dressed herself, and went out into the kitchen. That messenger must be despatched for something for breakfast.

She was met by Clam coming in from another door.

"Well, Clam," said her mistress, "where is everybody this morning?"

"I don't know where I am yet," said Clam. "Everybody's abed and asleep, I 'spose. Where be you, Miss 'Lizabeth?"

"Did Mr. Landholm sit up all night?"

"'Most. He said 'twas near upon two o'clock."

"When?"

"When he had done sittin' up, and went to bed."

"How was Karen?"

"I 'spose she was *goin'*, but she ain't in no hurry—she ain't gone yet."

"Then she was no worse?"

"She was better. She was slicked up wonderful after seein' the Governor, she telled me. I wonder who ain't."

"He has not come out of his room yet, I suppose?"

"I hope he haint," said Clam, "or I don' know when we'll get breakfast—'less he turns to and helps us."

"He will want a good one, after last night, and yesterday's journey. Where's Anderese?"

"He took some bread and milk," said Clam.

"Well—where's Anderese? we must send him to Mountain Spring."

"He's got to go after wood, Miss 'Lizabeth—there ain't three sticks more 'n 'll set the fire agoing."

'Must he! Then you must go, Clam."

"Very good. Who'll set the table, Miss 'Lizabeth?"

"Emma can. Or you can, after you get back."

"And there's the fire to make, and the floor to sweep, and the knives to clean, and the bread to make—"

"Bread!—" said Miss Haye.

"Or cakes," said Clam. "One or t'other 'll be wanted. I don't care which."

"Don't Emma know how?"

"She don't know a thing, but how to put Mrs. Haye's curls over a stick—when she ain't doin' her own."

"Then give me a basket—I'll go to Mountain Spring myself."

"Who'll bring the meat and things home?"

"I will;—or fish, or eggs,—something, whatever I can get."

"It 'll tire you, Miss 'Lizabeth—I guess, before you get back."

"You find me a basket—while I put on my bonnet," said Clam's mistress. And the one thing was done as soon as the other.

"I 'spect I'll wake up some morning and find myself playing on the pianny-forty," said Clam, as she watched her young mistress walking off with the basket.

CHAPTER XLIII.

When was old Sherwood's head more quaintly curled?
Or looked the earth more green upon the world?
Or nature's cradle more enchased and purled?
When did the air so smile, the wind so chime,
As quiristers of season, and the prime?

BEN JONSON.

MISS HAYE, however, had never sent her fingers over the keys with more energy, than now her feet tripped over the dry leaves and stones in the path to Mountain Spring. She took a very rough way, through the woods. There was another, much plainer, round by the wagon road; but Elizabeth chose the more solitary and prettier way, roundabout and hard to the foot though it was.

For some little distance there was a rude wagon-track, very rough, probably made for the convenience of getting wood. It stood thick with pretty large stones or heads of rock; but it was softly grass-grown between the stones and gave at least a clear way through the woods, upon which the morning light if not the morning sun beamed fairly. A light touch of white frost lay upon the grass and covered the rocks with bloom, the promise of a mild day. After a little, the roadway descended into a bit of smooth meadow, well walled in with trees, and lost itself there. In the tree-tops the morning sun was glittering; it could not get to the bottom yet; but up there among the leaves it gave a bright shimmering prophecy of what it would do; it was a sparkle of heavenly light touching the earth. Elizabeth had never seen it before; she had never in her life been in the woods at so early an hour. She stood still to look. It was impossible to help feeling the light of that glittering promise; its play upon the leaves was too joyous, too pure, too fresh. She felt her heart grow stronger and her breath come freer. What was the speech of those light-touched leaves, she might not have told; something her spirit took knowledge of while her reason did not. Or had not leisure to do; for if she did not get to Mountain Spring in good season she would not be home for breakfast. Yet she had plenty of time, but she did not wish to run short. So she went on her way.

From the valley meadow for half a mile, it was not much more or much better than a cow-path, beaten a little by the feet of the herdsman seeking his cattle or of an occasional foot-traveller to Mountain Spring. It was very rough indeed. Often Elizabeth must make quite a circuit among cat-briars and huckleberry bushes and young underwood, or keep the path at the expense of stepping up and stepping down again over a great stone or rock blocking up the whole way. Sometimes the track was only marked over the grey lichens of an immense head of granite that refused moss and vegetation of every other kind; sometimes it wound among thick alder bushes by the edge of wet ground; and at all times its course was among a wilderness of uncared-for woodland, overgrown with creepers and vines tangled with underbrush, and thickly strewn with larger and smaller fragments and boulders of granite rock. But how beautiful it was! The alders, reddish and soft-tinted, looked when the sun struck through them as if they were exotics out of witch-land; the Cornus family, from beautiful dogwood a dozen feet high stretching over Elizabeth's head, to little humble nameless plants at her feet, had edged and parted their green leaves with most dainty clear hues of madder lake; white birches and hickories glimmered in the sunlight like trees of gold, the first with stems of silver; sear leaves strewed the way; and fresh pines and hemlocks stretched out their arms amidst the changing foliage, with their evergreen promise and performance. The morning air and the morning walk no doubt had something to do with the effect of the whole; but Elizabeth thought, with all the beauty her eyes had ever seen they had never been more bewitched than they were that day.

With such a mood upon her, it was no wonder that on arriving at Mountain Spring she speedily made out her errand. She found whom and what she had come for; she filled her basket with no loss of time or pleasure; and very proud of her success set out again through the wood-path homeward.

Half way back to the bit of tree-enclosed meadow-ground, the path and the north shore of Shahweetah approached each other, where a little bay curve, no other than the *Ægean Sea*, swept in among the rocks. Through the stems of the trees Elizabeth could see the blue water with the brightness of the hour upon it. Its sparkle tempted her. She had plenty of time, or she resolved that she had, and she wanted to look at the fair broad view she knew the shore edge would give her. She hesitated, and turned. A few bounding and plunging steps amid rocks and huckleberry bushes brought her where she wished to be. She stood on the border, where no trees came in the way of the northern view. The mountains were full before her, and the wide Shatemuc rolled down between them, ruffled with little waves, every one sparkling cool in the sunlight. Elizabeth looked at the water a minute, and turned to the west. Wut-a-qut-o's head had caught more of the frosts than Shahweetah had felt yet; there were broad belts of buff and yellow along the mountain, even changing into sear where its sides felt the north wind. On all that shore the full sunlight lay. The opposite hills, on the east, were in dainty sunshine and shadow, every undulation, every ridge and hollow, softly marked out. With what wonderful sharp outline the mountain edges rose against the bright sky; how wonderful soft the changes of shade and colour adown their sloping sides: what brilliant little ripples of water rolled up to the pebbles at Elizabeth's feet. She stood and looked at it all, at one thing and the other, half dazzled with the beauty; until she recollected herself, and with a deep sighful expression of thoughts and wishes unknown, turned away to find her path again.

But she could not find it. Whereabouts it was, she was sure; but the *where* was an unfindable thing. And she dared not strike forward without the track; she might get further and further from it, and never get home to breakfast at all!—There was nothing for it but to grope about seeking for indications; and Miss Haye's eyes were untrained to wood-work. The woodland was a mazy wilderness now indeed. Points of stone, beds of moss, cat-briar vines and huckleberry bushes, in every direction; and between which of them lay that little invisible track of a foot-path? The more she looked the more she got perplexed. She could remember no waymarks. The way was all cat-briars, moss, bushes, and rocks; and rocks, bushes, moss and cat-briars were in every variety all around her. She turned her face towards the quarter from which she had come and tried to recognize some tree or waymark she could remember having passed. One part of the wood looked just like another; but for the mountains and the river she could not have told where lay Mountain Spring.

Then a little sound of rustling leaves and crackling twigs reached her ear from behind her.

"There is a cow!" thought Elizabeth;—"now I can find the path by her. But then!—cows don't always—"

Her eye had been sweeping round the woody skirts of her position, in search of her expected four-footed guide, when her thoughts were suddenly brought to a point by seeing a two-footed creature approaching, and one whom she instantly knew.

"It is Winthrop Landholm!—he is going to Mountain Spring to take an early coach, without his breakfast!—Well, you fool, what is it to you?" was the next thought. "What does it signify whether he goes sooner or later, when it would be better for you not to see him at all, if your heart is going to start in that fashion at every time.—"

Meanwhile she was making her way as well as she could, over rocks and briars, towards the new-comer; and did not look up till she answered his greeting—

"Good morning!—"

It was very cheerfully spoken.

"Good morning," said Elizabeth, entangled in a cat-briar, from which with a desperate effort she broke free before any help could be given her.

"Those are naughty things."

"No," said Elizabeth, "they look beautiful now when they are growing tawny, as a contrast with the other creepers and the deep green cedars. And they are a beautiful green at other times."

"Make the best of them. What were you looking at, a minute ago?"

"Looking for my way. I had lost it."

"You don't know it very well, I guess."

"Yes.—No, not very well, but I could follow it, and did, till coming home I thought I had time to look at the view; and then I couldn't find it again. I got turned about."

"You were completely turned about when I saw you."

"O I was not going that way—I knew better than that. I was trying to discover some waymark."

"How did you get out of the way?"

"I went to look at the view—from the water's edge there."

"Have you a mind to go back to the river edge again? I have not seen that view in a long while. *I* shall not lose the path."

"Then you cannot be intending to go by an early coach," thought Elizabeth, as she picked her way back over rocks and moss to the water's edge. But Winthrop knew the ground, and brought her a few steps further to a broad standing-place of rock where the look-out was freer. There was again before her the sparkling river, the frost-touched mountain, the sharp outlines, the varying shadows, that she had looked at a few minutes back. Elizabeth looked at them again, thinking now not of them but of something different at every turn.

"The rock is too wet," said Winthrop, "or I should propose your sitting down."

"You certainly must have had your breakfast," thought Elizabeth, "and not know that I haven't had mine."

"I don't want to sit down," she said quietly. A pang of fear again came to her heart, that in another minute or two he would be off to Mountain Spring. But his next movement negatived that. It was to take her basket, which she had till then tried to carry so that it would not be noticed. She was thankful he did not know what was in it.

"Do you often take such early walks as this?"

"No, not often," said Elizabeth guiltily. "I row more."

"So early?"

"No, not generally. Though there is no time more pleasant."

"You are looking well," he said gravely. "Better than I ever saw you look."

"It's very odd," thought Elizabeth,—"it must be the flush of my walk—I didn't look so this morning in the glass—nor last night.—" But she looked up and said boldly, laughing,

"I thought you came here to see the prospect, Mr. Landholm."

"I have been looking at it," he said quietly. "I need not say anything about that—it never changes."

"Do you mean that I do?" said Elizabeth.

"Everybody ought to change for the better, always," he said with a little smile,—"so I hope you are capable of that."

Elizabeth thought in her heart, though she was no better, yet that she had truly changed for the better, since former times; she half wanted to tell him so, the friend who had had most to do with changing her. But a consciousness of many things and an honest fear of speaking good of herself, kept her lips shut; though her heart beat with the wish and the doubt. Winthrop's next words in a few minutes decided it.

"What is the fact, Miss Elizabeth?"

Elizabeth hesitated,—and hesitated. He looked at her.

"I hope I am changed, a little, Mr. Landholm; but there is a great deal more to change!"

Her face was very ingenuous and somewhat sorrowful, as she turned it towards him; but his looked so much brighter than she had ever seen it, that the meeting of the two tides was just more than her spirits could bear. The power of commanding herself, which for the last few minutes had been growing less and less, gave way. Her look shrank from his. Winthrop had come nearer to her, and had clasped the hand that was nearest him and held it in his own. It was a further expression of the pleasure she had seen in his smile. Elizabeth was glad that her own face was hidden by her sunbonnet. She would not have either its pain or its pleasure to be seen. Both were sharp enough just then. But strong necessity made her keep outwardly quiet.

"What does the change date from?"

"As to time, do you mean?" said Elizabeth struggling.

"As to time, and motive."

"The time is but lately," she said with a tremulous voice,—"though I have thought about it, more or less, for a good while."

"Thought what?"

"Felt that you were right and I was wrong, Mr. Landholm."

"What made you think you were wrong?"

"I felt that I was—I knew it."

"What makes you think you are changed now?"

"I hardly dare speak of it—it is so little."

"You may, I hope,—to me."

"It is hardly *I* that am changed, so much as my motives and views."

"And they—how?" he said after waiting a moment.

"It seems to me," she said slowly, "lately, that I am willing to go by a new rule of life from that I used to follow."

"What is the new rule?"

"Well—Not my own will, Mr. Landholm."

He stood silent a little while. Her hand was still held in his. Elizabeth would have thought he had forgotten it, but that it was held in a free clasp which did not seem to imply forgetfulness. It was enough to forbid it on her part.

"How does the new rule work?" was his next question.

"It works hard, Mr. Landholm!" said Elizabeth, turning her face suddenly upon him for an instant. His look was bright, but she felt that her own eyes were swimming.

"Do you know that I am very glad to hear all this?" he said after another little pause.

"Yes," said Elizabeth under breath,—"I supposed you would be.—I knew you would."

"I hope you like being catechized," he said in a lighter tone.

"Yes—I do—by anybody that has a right to do it."

"I have taken the right."

"Certainly!—You have the best in the world."

"I am glad you think so, though I don't exactly see how you make it out."

"Why!—it's not necessary to explain how I make it out," said Elizabeth.

"No,—especially as I am going to ask you to give it to me for the future."

"What?"—said she looking at him.

He became grave.

"Miss Haye, I have a great boon to ask of you."

"Well?"—said Elizabeth eagerly. "I am very glad you nave!"

"Why?"

"Why?—why, because it's pleasant."

"You don't know what it is, yet."

"No," said Elizabeth,—"but my words are safe."

"I want you to give me something."

"You preface it as if it were some great thing, and you look as if it was nothing," thought Elizabeth a little in wonderment. But she said only,

"You may have it. What is it?"

"Guess."

"I can't possibly."

"You are incautious. You don't know what you are giving away."

"What is it?" said Elizabeth a little impatiently.

"Yourself."

Elizabeth looked quick away, not to see anything, with the mind's eye or any other, for a blur came over both. She was no fainter; she was strong of mind and body; but the one and the other were shaken; and for that bit of time, and it was several minutes, her senses performed no office at all. And when consciousness of distinct things began to come back, there came among all her other feelings an odd perverse fear of shewing the uppermost one or two, and a sort of mortified unreadiness to strike her colours and yield at once without having made a bit of fight for it. Yet these were not the uppermost feelings, but they were there, among them and struggling with them. She stood quite still, her face hidden by her sunbonnet, and her companion was quite still too with her hand still in his, held in the same free light clasp; and she had a vexed consciousness of his being far the cooler of the two. While she was thus silent, however, Elizabeth's head, and her very figure, was bowed lower and lower with intensity of feeling.

"What is the matter?" Winthrop said; and the tone of those words conquered her. The proud Miss Haye made a very humble answer.

"I am very glad, Mr. Landholm—but I am not good enough."

"For what?"

But Elizabeth did not answer.

"I will take my risk of that," said he kindly. Besides, you have confessed the power of changing."

The risk, or something else, seemed to lie upon Elizabeth's mind, from the efforts she was making to overcome emotion. Winthrop observed her for a moment.

"But you have not spoken, yet," said he. "I want a confirmation of my grant."

She knew from his tone that his mood was the very reverse of hers; and it roused the struggle again. "Provoking man!" she thought, "why couldn't he ask me in any other way!—And why need he smile when I am crying!—" She commanded herself to raise her head, however, though she did not dare look.

"Am I to have it?"

"To have what?"

"An answer."

"I don't know what it's to be, Mr. Landholm," Elizabeth stammered. "What do you want?"

"Will you give me what I asked you for?"

"I thought you knew you had it already," she said, not a little vexed to have the words drawn from her.

"It is mine, then?"

"Yes—"

"Then," said he, coming in full view of her blushing face and taking the other hand,—"what are you troubled for?"

Elizabeth could not have borne it one instant, to meet his eye, without breaking into a flood of tears she had no hands to cover. As her only way of escape, she sprang to one side freeing one of her hands on the sudden, and jumped down the rock, muttering something very unintelligibly about 'breakfast.' But her other hand was fast still, and so was she at the foot of the rock.

"Stop," said Winthrop,—"we must take this basket along.—I don't know if there is anything very precious in it."—

He reached after it as he spoke, and then they went on; and by the help of his hand her backward journey over rocks, stones, and trunks of trees in the path, was easily and lightly made; till they reached the little bit of meadow. Which backward journey Elizabeth accomplished in about two minutes and a quarter. There Winthrop transferred to his arm the hand that had rested in his, and walked more leisurely.

"Are you in such a hurry for your breakfast?" said he. "I have had mine."

"Had it!—before you came out?"

"No,"—said he smiling,—"since."

"Are you laughing at me?—or have you had it?" said Elizabeth looking puzzled.

"Both," said Winthrop. "What are you trembling so for?"

It hushed Elizabeth again, till they got quit of the meadow, and began more slowly still, the ascent of the rough half-made wheel-road.

"Miss Haye—" said Winthrop gently.

She paused in her walk, looking at him.

"What are you thinking of?"

"Thinking of!—"

"Yes. You don't look as happy as I feel."

"I am,"— she said.

"How do you know?"

What a colour spread over Elizabeth's face! But she laughed too, so perhaps his end was gained.

"I was thinking," she said, with the desperate need of saying something,—"a little while ago, when you were helping me through the woods,—how a very few minutes before, I had been so quite alone in the world."

"Don't forget there is one arm that never can fail you," he replied gravely. "Mine may."

Elizabeth looked at him rather timidly, and his face changed.

"There was no harm in that," he said, with so bright an expression as she had never before seen given to her. "What will you say, if I tell you that I myself at that same time was thinking over in my mind very much the same thing—with relation to myself, I mean."

Elizabeth's heart beat and her breath came short. That was what she had never thought of. Like many another woman, what *he* was to her, she knew well; what *she* might be to him, it had never entered her head to think. It seemed almost a new and superfluous addition to her joy, yet not superfluous from that time forth for ever. Once known, it was too precious a thought to be again untasted. She hung her head over it; she stepped all unwittingly on rocks and short grass and wet places and dry, wherever she was led. It made her heart beat thick to think *she* could be so valued. How was it possible! How she wished—how keenly—that she could have been of the solid purity of silver or gold, to answer the value put upon her. But instead of that—what a far-off difference! Winthrop could not know how great, or he would never have said that, or felt it; nor could he? What about her could possibly have attracted it?

She had not much leisure to ponder the question, for her attention was called off to answer present demands. And there was another subject for pondering—Winthrop did not seem like the same person she had known under the same name, he was so much more free and pleasant and bright to talk than he had ever been to her before, or in her observation, to anybody. He talked to a very silent listener, albeit she lost never a word nor a tone. She wondered at him and at everything, and stepped along wondering, with a heart too full to speak, almost too full to hide its agitation.

They were nearing home, they had got quit of the woodway road, and were in a cleared field, grown with tall cedars, which skirted the river. Half way across it, Elizabeth's foot paused, and came to a full stop. What was the matter?

Elizabeth faced round a little, as if addressing her judge, though she spoke without lifting her eyes.

"Mr. Landholm—do you know that I am *full* of faults?"

"Yes."

"And aren't you afraid of them?"

"No,—not at all," he said, smiling, Elizabeth knew. But she answered very gravely,

"I am."

"Which is the best reason in the world why I should not be. It is written 'Blessed is the man that feareth always.'"

"I am afraid—you don't know me."

"I don't know," said he smiling. "You haven't told me anything new yet."

"I am afraid you think of me, somehow, better than I deserve."

"What is the remedy for that?"

Elizabeth hesitated, with an instant's vexed consciousness of his provoking coolness; then looking up met his eye for a second, laughed, and went on perfectly contented. But she wondered with a little secret mortification, that Winthrop was as perfectly at home and at his ease in the newly established relations between them as if they had subsisted for six months. "Is it nothing new to him?" she said to herself. "Did he know that it only depended on him to speak?—or is it his way with all the world?" It was not that she was undervalued, or slightly regarded, but valued and regarded with such unchanged self-possession. Meanwhile they reached the edge of the woodland, from which the house and garden were to be seen close at hand.

"Stay here," said Winthrop;—"I will carry this basket in and let them know you may be expected to breakfast."

"But if you do that,—" said Elizabeth colouring—

"What then?"

"I don't know what they will think."

"They may think what they have a mind," said he with a little bit of a smile again. "I want to speak to you."

Elizabeth winced a bit. He was gone, and she stood thinking, among other things, that he might have asked what *she* would like. And how did he know but breakfast was ready then? Or did he know everything? And how quietly and unqualifiedly, to be sure, he had taken her consignment that morning. She did not know whether to like it or not like it,—till she saw him coming again from the house.

"After all," said he, "I think we had better go in and take breakfast, and talk afterwards. It seems to be in a good state of forwardness."

CHAPTER XLIV.

From eastern quarters now
  The sun's up-wandering,
His rays on the rock's brow
  And hill-side squandering;
Be glad my soul! and sing amidst thy pleasure,
  Fly from the house of dust,
  Up with thy thanks and trust
To heaven's azure!

THOMAS KINGO.

IT was sufficiently proven at that breakfast, to Elizabeth's satisfaction, that it is possible for one to be at the same time both very happy and a little uncomfortable. She had a degree of consciousness upon her that amounted to that, more especially as she had a vexed knowledge that it was shared by at least one person in the room. The line of Clam's white teeth had never glimmered more mischievously. Elizabeth dared not look at her. And she dared not look at Winthrop, and she dared not look at Rose. But Rose, to do her justice, seemed to be troubled with no consciousness beyond what was usual with her, and which generally concerned only herself; and she and Winthrop kept up the spirit of talk with great ease all breakfast time.

"Now how in the world are we going to get away?" thought Elizabeth when breakfast was finishing;—"without saying flat and bald why we do it. Rose will want to go too, for she likes Winthrop quite well enough for that."—

And with the consciousness that she could not make the slightest manœuvre, Elizabeth rose from table.

"How soon must you go, Mr. Landholm?" said Rose winningly.

"Presently, ma'am."

"I am sorry you must go so soon! But we haven't a room to ask you to sit down in, if you were to stay."

"I am afraid I shouldn't wait to be asked, if I stayed," said Winthrop. "But as I am not to sit down again—Miss Haye—if you will put on your bonnet and give me your company a little part of my way, I will keep my promise."

"What promise?" said Rose.

"I will do better than my promise, for I mean to shew Miss Haye a point of her property which perhaps she has not looked at lately."

"Oh will you shew it to me too?" said Rose.

"I will if there is time enough after I have brought Miss Haye back—I can't take both at once."

Rose looked mystified, and Elizabeth very glad to put on her bonnet, was the first out of the house; half laughing, and half trembling with the excitement of getting off.

"There is no need to be in such a hurry," said Winthrop as he came up,—"now that breakfast is over."

Elizabeth was silent, troubled with that consciousness still, though now alone with the subject of it. He turned off from the road, and led her back into the woods a little way, in the same path by which she had once gone hunting for a tree to cut down.

"It isn't as pretty a time of day as when I went out this morning," she said, forcing herself to say something.

But Winthrop seemed in a state of pre-occupation too; till they reached a boulder capped with green ferns.

"Now give me your hand," said he. "Can you climb?"

They turned short by the boulder and began to mount the steep rugged hill-path, down which he had once carried his little sister. Elizabeth could make better footing than poor Winifred; and very soon they stood on the old height from which they could see the fair Shatemuc coming down between the hills and sweeping round their own little woody Shahweetah and off to the South Bend. The sun was bright on all the land now, though the cedars shielded the bit of hill-top well; and Wut-a-qut-o looked down upon them in all his gay Autumn attire. The sun was bright, but the air was clear and soft and free from mist and cloud and obscurity, as no sky is but October's.

"Sit down," said Winthrop, throwing himself on the bank which was carpeted with very short green grass.

"I would just as lieve stand," said Elizabeth.

"I wouldn't as lieve have you. You've been on your feet long enough to-day. Come!——"

She yielded to the gentle pulling of her hand, and sat down

on the grass; half amused and half fretted; wondering what he was going to say next. Winthrop was silent for a little space; and Elizabeth sat looking straight before her, or rather with her head a little turned to the right, from her companion, towards Wut-a-qut-o; the deep sides of her sun-bonnet shutting out all but a little framed picture of the gay woody foreground, a bit of the blue river, and the mountain's yellow side.

"How beautiful it was all down there, three or four hours ago," said Elizabeth.

"I didn't know you had so much romance in your disposition—to go there this morning to meet me."

"I didn't go there to meet you."

"Yes you did."

"I didn't!" said Elizabeth. "I never thought of such a thing as meeting you."

"Nevertheless, in the regular chain and sequence of events, you went there to meet me—if you hadn't gone you wouldn't have met me."

"O, if you put it in that way," said Elizabeth,—"there's no harm in that."

"There is no harm in it at all. Quite the contrary."

"I think it was the prettiest walk I ever took in my life," said Elizabeth,—"before that, I mean," she added blushing.

"My experience would say, after it," said Winthrop, in an amused tone.

"It was rather a confused walk after that," said Elizabeth. "I never was quite so much surprised."

"You see I had not that disadvantage. I was only—gratified."

"Why," said Elizabeth, her jealous fear instantly starting again, "you didn't know what my answer would be before you asked me?"

She waited for Winthrop's answer, but none came. Elizabeth could not bear it.

"Did you?" she said, looking round in her eagerness.

He hesitated an instant, and then answered,

"Did *you?*"

Elizabeth had no words. Her face sought the shelter of her sunbonnet again, and she almost felt as if she would have liked to seek the shelter of the earth bodily, by diving down into it. Her brain was swimming. There was a rush of thoughts and ideas, a train of scattered causes and consequences, which then she had no power to set in order; but the rush almost overwhelmed her, and what was wanting, shame added. She was vexed with herself for her jealousy in divining and her impatience in asking foolish questions; and in her vexation was ready to be vexed with Winthrop,—if she only knew how. She longed to lay her head down in her hands, but pride kept it up. She rested her chin on one hand and wondered when Winthrop would speak again,—*she* could not,—and what he would say; gazing at the blue bit of water and gay mountain-side, and thinking that she was not giving him a particularly favourable specimen of herself that morning, and vexed out of measure to think it.

Then upon this, a very quietly spoken "Elizabeth!"—came to her ear. It was the first time Winthrop had called her so; but that was not all. Quietly spoken as it was, there was not only a little inquiry, there was a little amusement and a little admonition, in the tone. It stirred Elizabeth to her spirit's depths, but with several feelings; and for the life of her she could not have spoken.

"What is the reason you should hide your face so carefully from me?" he went on presently, much in the same tone. "Mine is open to you—it isn't fair play."

Elizabeth could have laughed if she had not been afraid of crying. She kept herself hid in her sunbonnet and made no reply.

"Suppose you take that thing off, and let me look at you."

"It shades my face from the sun."

"The cedar trees will do that for you."

"No—they wouldn't."

And she kept her face steadily fixed upon the opposite shore, only brought straight before her now; thinking to herself that she would carry this point at any rate. But in another minute she was somewhat astounded to find Winthrop's left hand, he was supporting himself carelessly on his right, quietly, very quietly, untying her sunbonnet strings; and then rousing himself, with the other hand he lifted the bonnet from her head. It gave a full view then of hair in very nice order and a face not quite so; for the colour had now flushed to her very temples with more feelings than one, and her eye was downcast, not caring to shew its revelations. She knew that Winthrop took an observation of all, to his heart's content; but she could not look at him for an instant. Then without saying anything, he got up and went off to a little distance where he made himself busy among some of the bushes and vines which were gay with the fall colouring Elizabeth sat drooping her head on her knees, for she could not absolutely hold it up. She looked at her sunbonnet lying on the bank beside her; but it is not an improper use of language to say that she dared not put it on.

"I have met my master now," she thought, and her eyes sparkled,—"once for all—if I never did before.—What a fool I am!"

For she knew, she acknowledged to herself at the same moment, that she did not like him the less for it—she liked him exceedingly the more; in spite of a twinge of deep mortification about it, and though there was bitter shame that he should know or guess any of her feeling. If her eyes sparkled, they sparkled through tears.

The tears were got rid of, for Winthrop came back and threw himself down again. Then with that he began to put wreaths of the orange and red winterberries and sprays of wych hazel and bits of exquisite ivy, one after the other, into her hands. Her hands took them mechanically, one after the other. Her eyes buried themselves in them. She wished for her sunbonnet shield again.

"What do you bring these to me for?" she said rather abruptly.

"Don't you like to have them?" said he, putting into her fingers another magnificent piece of Virginia creeper.

"Yes indeed—very much—but—"

"It will be some time before I see you again," said he as he added the last piece of his bunch. "These will be all gone."

"Some time!" said Elizabeth.

"Yes. There is work on my hands down yonder that admits of no delay. I could but just snatch time enough to come up here."

"I am very much obliged to you for these!" said Elizabeth, returning to her bunch of brilliant vine branches.

"You can pay me for them in any way you please."

The colour started again, but it was a very gentle, humble, and frank look which she turned round upon him. His was bright enough.

"How soon do you think of coming to Mannahatta?"

"I don't know,—" said Elizabeth, not choosing to say exactly the words that came to her tongue.

"If I could be here too, I should say this is the best place."

"Can't you come often enough?"

"How often would be often *enough?*" said he with an amused look.

"Leave definitions on one side, and please answer me."

"Willingly. I leave the definition on your side. I don't like to speak in the dark."

"Well, can't you come *tolerably* often?" said Elizabeth colouring.

He smiled.

"Not for some time. My hands are very full just now."

"You contrive to have them so always, don't you?"

"I like to have them so. It is not always my contrivance."

"What has become of that suit—I don't know the names now—in which you were engaged two or three years ago—in which you took so many objections, and the Chancellor allowed them all,—against Mr. Brick?"

"Ryle?"

"Yes!—I believe that's the name."

"For a man called Jean Lessing?"

"I don't know anything about Lessing—I think Ryle was the other name—You were against Ryle."

"Lessing was Mr. Herder's brother-in-law."

"I don't remember Mr. Herder's brother-in-law—though I believe Mr. Herder *did* have something to do with the case, or some interest in it."

"How did you know anything about it?"

"You haven't answered me," said Elizabeth, laughing and colouring brightly.

"One question is as good as another," said Winthrop smiling.

"But one answer is much better than another," said Elizabeth in a little confusion.

"The suit against Ryle was very successful. I recovered for him some ninety thousand dollars."

"Ninety thousand dollars!"—Her thoughts took somewhat of a wide circle and came back.

"The amount recovered is hardly a fair criterion of the skill employed, in every instance. I must correct your judgment."

"I know more about it than that," said Elizabeth. "How far your education has gone!—and mine is only just beginning."

"I should be sorry to think mine was much more than beginning. Now do you know we must go down?—for I must be at Mountain Spring to meet the stage-coach."

"How soon?" said Elizabeth springing up.

"There is time enough, but I want not to hurry you down the hill."

He had put her sunbonnet on her head again and was re-tying it.

"Mr. Landholm—"

"You must not call me that," he said.

"Let me, till I can get courage to call you something else."

"How much courage does it want?"

"If you don't stop," said Elizabeth, her eyes filling with tears, "I shall not be able to say one word of what I want to say."

He stood still, holding the strings of her sunbonnet in either hand. Elizabeth gathered breath, or courage, and went on.

"A little while ago I was grieving myself to think that you did not know me—now, I am very much ashamed to think that you do."—

He did not move, nor she.

"I know I am not worthy to have you look at me. My only hope is, that you will make me better."

The bonnet did not hide her face this time. He looked at it a little, at the simplicity of ingenuous trouble which was working in it,—and then pushing the bonnet a little back, kissed first one cheek and then the lips, which by that time were bent down almost out of reach. But he reached them; and Elizabeth was obliged to take her answer, in which there was as much of gentle forgiveness and promise as of affection.

"You see what you have to expect, if you talk to me in this strain," said he lightly. "I think I shall not be troubled with much more of it. I don't like to leave you in this frame of mind. I would take you to Mountain Spring in the boat—if I could bring you back again."

"I could bring myself back," said Elizabeth. They were going down the hill; in the course of which, it may be remarked, Winthrop had no reason to suppose that she once saw anything but the ground.

"I am afraid you are too tired."

"No indeed I am not. I should like it—if there is time."

"Go in less time that way than the other."

So they presently reached the lower ground.

"Do you want anything from the house?" said Winthrop as they came near it.

"Only the oars—If you will get those, I will untie the boat."

"Then I'll *not* get the oars. I'll get them on condition that you stand still here."

So they went down together to the rocks, and Elizabeth put herself in the stern of the little boat and they pushed off.

To any people who could think of anything but each other, October offered enough to fill eyes, ears, and understanding; that is, if ears can be filled with silence, which perhaps is predicable. Absolute silence on this occasion was wanting, as there was a good deal of talking; but for eyes and understanding, perhaps it may safely be said that those of the two people in the Merry-go-round took the benefit of *everything* they passed on their way; with a reduplication of pleasure which arose from the throwing and catching of that ball of conversation, in which, like the herb-stuffed ball of the Arabian physician of old,—lay perdu certain hidden virtues, of sympathy. But Shahweetah's low rocky shore never offered more beauty to any eyes, than to theirs that day, as they coasted slowly round it. Colours, colours! If October had been a dyer, he could not have shewn a greater variety of samples.

There were some locust trees in the open cedar-grown field by the river; trees that Mr. Landholm had planted long ago. They were slow to turn, yet they were changing. One soft feathery head was in yellowish green, another of more neutral colour; and blending with them were the tints of a few reddish soft-tinted alders below. That group was not gay. Further on were a thicket of dull coloured alders at the edge of some flags, and above them blazed a giant huckleberry bush in bright flame colour; close by that were the purple red tufts of some common sumachs—the one beautifully rich, the other beautifully striking. A little way from them stood a tulip tree, its green changing with yellow. Beyond came cedars, in groups, wreathed with bright tawny grape vines and splendid Virginia creepers, now in full glory. Above their tops, on the higher ground, was a rich green belt of pines—above *them*, the changing trees of the forest again.

Here shewed an elm its straw-coloured head—there stood an ash in beautiful grey-purple; very stately. The cornus family in rich crimson—others crimson purple; maples shewing yellow and flame-colour and red all at once; one beauty still in green was *orange-tipped* with rich orange. The birches were a darker hue of the same colour; hickories bright as gold.

Then came the rocks, and rocky precipitous point of Shahweetah; and the echo of the row-locks from the wall. Then the point was turned, and the little boat sought the bottom of the bay, nearing Mountain Spring all the while. The water was glassy smooth; the boat went—too fast.

Down in the bay the character of the woodland was a little different. It was of fuller growth, and with many fewer evergreens, and some addition to the variety of the changing deciduous leaves. When they got quite to the bottom of the bay and were coasting along close under the shore, there was perhaps a more striking display of Autumn's glories at their side, than the rocks of Shahweetah could shew them. They coasted slowly along, looking and talking. The combinations were beautiful.

There was the dark fine bright red of some pepperidges shewing behind the green of an unchanged maple; near by stood another maple the leaves of which were all seemingly withered, a plain reddish light wood-colour; while below its withered foliage a thrifty poison sumach wreathing round its trunk and lower branches, was in a beautiful confusion of fresh green and the orange and red changes, yet but just begun. Then another slight maple with the same dead wood-coloured leaves, into which to the very top a Virginia creeper had twined itself, and that was now brilliantly scarlet, magnificent in the last degree. Another like it a few trees off—both reflected gorgeously in the still water. Rock oaks were part green and part sear; at the edge of the shore below them a quantity of reddish low shrubbery; the cornus, dark crimson and red brown, with its white berries shewing underneath, and more pepperidges in very bright red. One maple stood with its leaves parti-coloured reddish and green—another with beautiful orange-coloured foliage. Ashes in superb very dark purple; they were all changed. Then alders, oaks, and chestnuts still green. A kaleidoscope view, on water and land, as the little boat glided along sending rainbow ripples in towards the shore.

In the bottom of the bay Winthrop brought the boat to land, under a great red oak which stood in its fair dark green beauty yet at the very edge of the water. Mountain Spring was a little way off, hidden by an outsetting point of woods. As the boat touched the tree-roots, Winthrop laid in the oars and came and took a seat by the boat's mistress.

"Are you going to walk to Mountain Spring the rest of the way?" she said.

"No."

"Will the stage-coach take you up here?"

"If it comes, it will. What are you going to do with yourself now, till I see you again?"

"There's enough to do," said Elizabeth sighing. "I am going to try to behave myself. How soon will the coach be here now?"

"I think, not until I have seen you about half way over the bay on your way home."

"O you will not see me," said Elizabeth. "I am not going before the coach does."

"Yes you are."

"What makes you think so?"

"Because it will not come till I have seen you at least, I should judge, half across the bay."

"But I don't *want* to go."

"You are so unaccustomed to doing things you don't want to do, that it is good discipline for you."

"Do you mean that seriously?" said Elizabeth, looking a little disturbed.

"I mean it half seriously," said he laughing, getting up to push the boat to shore, which had swung a little off.

"But nobody likes, or wants, self-imposed discipline," said Elizabeth.

"This isn't self-imposed—I impose it," said he throwing the rope round a branch of the tree. "I don't mean anything that need make you look *so*," he added as he came back to his place.

Elizabeth looked up and her brow cleared.

"I dare say you are right," she said. "I will do just as you please."

"Stop a minute," said he gently taking her hand—"What do you 'dare say' I am right about?"

"This—or anything," Elizabeth said, her eye wavering between the water and the shore.

"I don't want you to think that."

"But how am I going to help it?"

He smiled a little and looked grave too.

"I am going to give you a lesson to study."

"Well?—" said Elizabeth with quick pleasure; and she watched, very like a child, while Winthrop sought in his pocket and brought out an old letter, tore off a piece of the back and wrote on his knee with a pencil.

Then he gave it to her.

But it was the precept,—

'Little children, keep yourselves from idols.'

Elizabeth's face changed, and her eyes lifted themselves not up again. The colour rose, and spread, and deepened, and her head only bent lower down over the paper. That thrust was with a barbed weapon. And there was a profound hush, and a bended head and a pained brow, till a hand came gently between her eyes and the paper and occupied the fingers that held it. It was the same hand that her fancy had once seen full of character —she saw it again now; her thoughts made a spring back to that time and then to this. She looked up.

It was a look to see. There was a witching mingling of the frank, the childlike, and the womanly, in her troubled face; frankness that would not deny the truth that her monitor seemed to have read, a childlike simplicity of shame that he should have divined it, and a womanly self-respect that owned it had nothing to be ashamed of. These were not all the feelings that were at work, nor that shewed their working; and it was a face of brilliant expression that Elizabeth lifted to her companion. In the cheeks the blood spoke brightly; in the eyes, fire; there was more than one tear there, too; and the curve of the lips was unbent with a little tremulous play. Winthrop must have been a man of self-command to have stood it; but he looked apparently no more concerned than if old Karen had lifted up her face at him.

"Do you know," she said, and the moved line of the lips might plainly be seen,—"you are making it the more hard for me to learn your lesson, even in the very giving it me?"

"What shall I do?"

Elizabeth hesitated, and conquered herself.

"I guess you needn't do anything," she said half laughing. "I'll try and do my part."

There was a little answer of the face then, that sent Elizabeth's eyes to the ground.

"What do you mean by these words?" she said looking at them again.

"I don't mean anything. I simply give them to you."

"Yes, and I might see an old musket standing round the house; but if you take it up and present it at me, it is fair to ask, what you mean?"

"It is not an old musket, to begin with," said Winthrop laughing; "and if it goes off, it will shoot you *through the heart.*"

"You have the advantage of me entirely, this morning!" said Elizabeth. "I give up. I hope the next time you have the pleasure of seeing me, I shall be myself."

"I hope so. I intend to keep *my* identity. Now as that stage-coach will not come till you get half over the bay——"

And a few minutes thereafter, the little boat was skimming back for the point of Shahweetah, though not quite so swiftly as it had come. But Elizabeth was not a mean oarsman; and in good time she got home, and moored the Merry-go-round in its place.

She was walking up to the house then, in very happy mood, one hand depending musingly at either string of her sunbonnet, when she was met by her cousin.

"Well," said Rose,—"have you been out in the woods all this while?"

"No."

"I suppose it's all settled between you and Mr. Landholm?"

Elizabeth stood an instant, with hands depending as aforesaid, and then with a little inclination of her person, somewhat stately and more graceful, gave Rose to understand, that she had no contradiction to make to this insinuation.

"Is it!" said Rose. "Did he come up for that?"

"I suppose you know what he came for better than I do."

"Did you know I wrote a letter to him?"

"I guessed it afterwards. Rose!"—said Elizabeth suddenly, "there was nothing but about Karen in it?"

"Nothing in the world!" said Rose quickly. "What should there be?"

"What did you write for?"

"I was frightened to death, and I wanted to see somebody; and I knew *you* wouldn't send for him. Wasn't it good I did!—"

Rose clapped her hands. The colour in Elizabeth's face was gradually getting brilliant. She passed on.

"And now you'll live in Mannahatta?"

Elizabeth did not answer.

"And will you send for old Mr. Landholm to come back and take care of this place again?"

"Hush, Rose!—Mr. Landholm will do what he pleases."

"*You* don't please about it, I suppose?"

"Yes I do, Rose,—not to talk at all on the subject!"

THE END.

A LIST

OF

NEW WORKS

IN GENERAL LITERATURE,

PUBLISHED BY

D. APPLETON & COMPANY,

346 & 348 Broadway.

**** Complete Catalogues, containing full descriptions, to be had on application to the Publishers.*

Agriculture and Rural Affairs.

Title	Price
Boussingault's Rural Economy,	1 25
The Poultry Book, illustrated,	5 00
Waring's Elements of Agriculture,	75

Arts, Manufactures, and Architecture.

Title	Price
Appleton's Dictionary of Mechanics. 2 vols.	12 00
" Mechanics' Magazine. 3 vols. each,	3 50
Allen's Philosophy of Mechanics,	3 50
Arnot's Gothic Architecture,	4 00
Bassnett's Theory of Storms,	1 00
Bourne on the Steam Engine,	75
Byrne on Logarithms,	1 00
Chapman on the American Rifle,	1 25
Coming's Preservation of Health,	75
Cullum on Military Bridges,	2 00
Downing's Country Houses,	4 00
Field's City Architecture,	2 00
Griffith's Marine Architecture,	10 00
Gillespie's Treatise on Surveying,	
Haupt's Theory of Bridge Construction,	3 00
Henck's Field-Book for R. Road Engineers,	1 75
Hoblyn's Dictionary of Scientific Terms,	1 50
Huff's Manual of Electro-Physiology,	1 25
Jeffers' Practice of Naval Gunnery,	2 50
Knapen's Mechanics' Assistant,	1 00
Lafever's Modern Architecture,	4 0
Lyell's Manual of Geology,	1 75
" Principles of Geology,	2 25
Reynold's Treatise on Handrailing,	2 00
Templeton's Mechanic's Companion,	1 00
Ure's Dict'ry of Arts, Manufactures, & c. 2 vols.	5 00
Youmans' Class-Book of Chemistry,	75
" Atlas of Chemistry, cloth,	2 00
" Alcohol,	50

Biography.

Title	Price
Arnold's Life and Correspondence,	2 00
Capt. Canot, or Twenty Years of a Slaver,	1 25
Cousin's De Longueville,	1 00
Croswell's Memoirs,	2 00
Evelyn's Life of Godolphin,	50
Garland's Life of Randolph,	1 50
Gilfillan's Gallery of Portraits. 2d Series,	1 00
Hernan Cortez's Life,	38
Hull's Civil and Military Life,	2 00
Life and Adventures of Daniel Boone,	38
Life of Henry Hudson,	38
Life of Capt. John Smith,	38
Moore's Life of George Castriot,	1 00
Napoleon's Memoirs. By Duchess D'Abrantes,	4 00
Napoleon By Laurent L'Ardèche,	3 00
Pinkney (W.) Life. By his Nephew,	2 00
Party Leaders: Lives of Jefferson, &c.	1 00
Southey's Life of Oliver Cromwell,	38
Wynne's Lives of Eminent Men,	1 00
Webster's Life and Memorials. 2 vols.	1 00

Books of General Utility.

Title	Price
Appletons' Southern and Western Guide,	1 00
" Northern and Eastern Guide,	1 25
Appletons' Complete U. S. Guide,	2 63
" Map of N. Y. City,	26
American Practical Cook Book,	
A Treatise on Artificial Fish-Breeding,	75
Chemistry of Common Life. 2 vols. 12mo.	
Cooley's Book of Useful Knowledge,	1 25
Cust's Invalid's Own Book,	50
Delisser's Interest Tables,	4 00
The English Cyclopaedia, per vol.	2 50
Miles on the Horse's Foot,	25
The Nursery Basket. A Book for Young Mothers,	38
Pell's Guide for the Young,	38
Reid's New English Dictionary,	1 00
Stewart's Stable Economy,	1 00
Spalding's Hist. of English Literature,	1 00
Soyer's Modern Cookery,	1 00
The Successful Merchant,	1 00
Thomson on Food of Animals,	50

Commerce and Mercantile Affairs.

Title	Price
Anderson's Mercantile Correspondence,	1 00
Delisser's Interest Tables,	4 00
Merchants' Reference Book,	4 00
Oates' (Geo.) Interest Tables at 6 Per Cent. per Annum. 8vo.	2 00
" " Do. do. Abridged edition,	1 25
" " 7 Per Cent. Interest Tables,	2 00
" " Abridged,	1 25
Smith's Mercantile Law,	4 00

Geography and Atlases.

Title	Price
Appleton's Modern Atlas. 34 Maps,	3 50
" Complete Atlas. 61 Maps,	9 00
Atlas of the Middle Ages. By Kœppen,	4 50
Black's General Atlas. 71 Maps,	12 00
Cornell's Primary Geography,	50
" Intermediate Geography,	
" High School Geography,	

History.

Title	Price
Arnold's History of Rome,	3 00
" Later Commonwealth,	2 50
" Lectures on Modern History,	1 25
Dew's Ancient and Modern History,	2 00
Koeppen's History of the Middle Ages. 2 vols.	2 50
" The same, folio, with Maps,	4 50
Kohlrausch's History of Germany,	1 50
Mahon's (Lord) History of England, 2 vols.	4 00
Michelet's History of France, 2 vols.	3 50
" History of the Roman Republic,	1 00
Rowan's History of the French Revolution,	63
Sprague's History of the Florida War,	2 50
Taylor's Manual of Ancient History,	1 25
" Manual of Modern History,	1 50
" Manual of History. 1 vol. complete,	2 50
Thiers' French Revolution. 4 vols. Illustrated,	5 00

Illustrated Works for Presents.

Title	Price
Bryant's Poems. 16 Illustrations. 8vo. cloth,	3 50
" " cloth, gilt,	4 50
" " " mor. antique,	6 00

Gems of British Art. 30 Engravings. 1 vol. 4to. morocco, 18 00
Gray's Elegy. Illustrated. 8vo. 1 50
Goldsmith's Deserted Village, 1 50
The Homes of American Authors. With Illustrations, cloth, 4 00
" " " cloth, gilt, 5 00
" " " mor. antqe. 7 00
The Holy Gospels. With 40 Designs by Overbeck. 1 vol. folio. Antique mor. 20 00
The Land of Bondage. By J. M. Wainwright, D. D. Morocco, 6 00
The Queens of England. By Agnes Strickland. With 29 Portraits. Antique mor. 10 00
The Ornaments of Memory. With 18 Illustrations. 4to. cloth, gilt, 6 00
" " Morocco, 10 00
Royal Gems from the Galleries of Europe. 40 Engravings, 25 00
The Republican Court; or, American Society in the Days of Washington. 21 Portraits. Antique mor. 12 00
The Vernon Gallery. 67 Engrav'gs. 4to. Ant. 25 00
The Women of the Bible. With 18 Engravings. Mor. antique, 10 00
Wilkie Gallery. Containing 60 Splendid Engravings. 4to. Antique mor. 25 00
A Winter Wreath of Summer Flowers. By S. G. Goodrich. Illustrated. Cloth, gilt, 3 00

Juvenile Books.

A Poetry Book for Children, 75
Aunt Fanny's Christmas Stories, 50
American Historical Tales, 75

UNCLE AMEREL'S STORY BOOKS.

The Little Gift Book. 18mo. cloth, 25
The Child's Story Book. Illust. 18mo. cloth, 25
Summer Holidays. 18mo. cloth, 25
Winter Holidays. Illustrated. 18mo. cloth, 25
George's Adventures in the Country. Illustrated. 18mo. cloth, 25
Christmas Stories. Illustrated. 18mo. cloth, 25

Book of Trades, 50
Boys at Home By the Author of Edgar Clifton, 75
Child's Cheerful Companion, 50
Child's Picture and Verse Book. 100 Engs 50

COUSIN ALICE'S WORKS.

All's Not Gold that Glitters, 75
Contentment Better than Wealth, 63
Nothing Venture, Nothing Have, 63
No such Word as Fail, 63
Patient Waiting No Loss, 63

Dashwood Priory. By the Author of Edgar Clifton, 75
Edgar Clifton; or Right and Wrong 75
Fireside Fairies. By Susan Pindar, 63
Good in Every Thing. By Mrs. Barwell, 50
Leisure Moments Improved, 75
Life of Punchinello, 75

LIBRARY FOR MY YOUNG COUNTRYMEN.

Adventures of Capt. John Smith. By the Author of Uncle Philip, 38
Adventures of Daniel Boone. By do. 38
Dawnings of Genius. By Anne Pratt, 38
Life and Adventures of Henry Hudson. By the Author of Uncle Philip, 38
Life and Adventures of Hernan Cortez. By do. 38
Philip Randolph. A Tale of Virginia. By Mary Gertrude, 38
Rowan's History of the French Revolution. 2 vols. 75
Southey's Life of Oliver Cromwell, 38

Louis' School-Days. By E. J. May, 75
Louise; or, The Beauty of Integrity, 25
Maryatt's Settlers in Canada, 62
" Masterman Ready, 63
" Scenes in Africa, 63
Midsummer Fays By Susan Pindar, 65

MISS McINTOSH'S WORKS.

Aunt Kitty's Tales, 12mo. 75
Blind Alice; A Tale for Good Children, 38
Ella Leslie; or, The Reward of Self-Control, 38
Florence Arnott; or, Is She Generous? 38
Grace and Clara; or, Be Just as well as Generous, 38
Jessie Graham; or, Friends Dear, but Truth Dearer, 38
Emily Herbert; or, The Happy Home, 37
Rose and Lillie Stanhope, 37

Mamma's Story Book, 75
Pebbles from the Sea-Shore, 37
Puss in Boots. Illustrated. By Otto Specter, 25

PETER PARLEY'S WORKS.

Faggots for the Fireside, 1 13
Parley's Present for all Seasons, 1 00
Wanderers by Sea and Land, 1 13
Winter Wreath of Summer Flowers, 3 00

TALES FOR THE PEOPLE AND THEIR CHILDREN.

Alice Franklin. By Mary Howitt, 38
Crofton Boys (The). By Harriet Martineau, 38
Dangers of Dining Out. By Mrs. Ellis, 38
Domestic Tales. By Hannah More. 2 vols. 75
Early Friendship. By Mrs. Copley, 38
Farmer's Daughter (The). By Mrs. Cameron, 38
First Impressions. By Mrs. Ellis, 38
Hope On, Hope Ever! By Mary Howitt, 38
Little Coin, Much Care. By do. 38
Looking-Glass for the Mind. Many plates, 38
Love and Money. By Mary Howitt, 38
Minister's Family. By Mrs. Ellis, 38
My Own Story. By Mary Howitt, 38
My Uncle, the Clockmaker. By do. 38
No Sense Like Common Sense. By do. 38
Peasant and the Prince. By H. Martineau, 38
Poplar Grove. By Mrs. Copley, 38
Somerville Hall. By Mrs. Ellis, 38
Sowing and Reaping. By Mary Howitt, 38
Story of a Genius. 38
Strive and Thrive. By do. 38
The Two Apprentices. By do. 38
Tired of Housekeeping. By T. S. Arthur, 38
Twin Sisters (The). By Mrs. Sandham, 38
Which is the Wiser? By Mary Howitt, 38
Who Shall be Greatest? By do. 38
Work and Wages. By do. 38

SECOND SERIES.

Chances and Changes. By Charles Burdett, 38
Goldmaker's Village. By H. Zschokke, 38
Never Too Late. By Charles Burdett, 38
Ocean Work, Ancient and Modern. By J. H. Wright, 38

Picture Pleasure Book, 1st Series, 1 25
" " " 2d Series, 1 25
Robinson Crusoe. 300 Plates, 1 50
Susan Pindar's Story Book, 75
Sunshine of Greystone, 75
Travels of Bob the Squirrel, 37
Wonderful Story Book, 50
Willy's First Present, 75
Week's Delight; or, Games and Stories for the Parlor, 75
William Tell, the Hero of Switzerland, 50
Young Student. By Madame Guizot, 75

Miscellaneous and General Literature.

An Attic Philosopher in Paris, ... 25
Appletons' Library Manual, ... 1 25
Agnell's Book of Chess, ... 1 25
Arnold's Miscellaneous Works, ... 2 00
Arthur. The Successful Merchant, . . . 75
A Book for Summer Time in the Country, . 50
Baldwin's Flush Times in Alabama, . . . 1 25
Calhoun (J. C.), Works of. 4 vols. publ., each, 2 00
Clark's (W. G.) Knick Knacks, . . . 1 25
Cornwall's Music as it Was, and as it Is, . 63
Essays from the London Times. 1st & 2d Series, each, ... 50
Ewbanks' World in a Workshop, ... 75
Ellis' Women of England, ... 50
" Hearts and Homes, ... 1 50
" Prevention Better than Cure, . . . 75
Foster's Essays on Christian Morals, . . . 50
Goldsmith's Vicar of Wakefield, ... 75
Grant's Memoirs of an American Lady, . . 75
Gaieties and Gravities. By Horace Smith, . 50
Guizot's History of Civilization, ... 1 00
Hearth-Stone. By Rev. S. Osgood, ... 1 00
Hobson. My Uncle and I, ... 75
Ingoldsby Legends, ... 50
Isham's Mud Cabin, ... 1 00
Johnson's Meaning of Words, ... 1 00
Kavanagh's Women of Christianity, . . . 75
Leger's Animal Magnetism, ... 1 00
Life's Discipline. A Tale of Hungary, . . 63
Letters from Rome. A. D. 138, ... 1 90
Margaret Maitland, ... 75
Maiden and Married Life of Mary Powell, . 50
Morton Montague; or a Young Christian's Choice, ... 75
Macaulay's Miscellanies. 5 vols. 5 00
Maxims of Washington. By J. F. Schroeder, 1 00
Mile Stones in our Life Journey, ... 1 00

MINIATURE CLASSICAL LIBRARY.

Poetic Lacon; or, Aphorisms from the Poets, 38
Bond's Golden Maxims, ... 31
Clarke's Scripture Promises. Complete, . 38
Elizabeth; or, The Exiles of Siberia, . . 31
Goldsmith's Vicar of Wakefield, ... 38
" Essays, ... 38
Gems from American Poets, ... 38
Hannah More's Private Devotions, . . . 31
" " Practical Piety. 2 vols. . 75
Hemans' Domestic Affections, ... 31
Hoffman's Lays of the Hudson, &c. . . . 38
Johnson's History of Rasselas, ... 38
Manual of Matrimony, ... 31
Moore's Lalla Rookh, ... 38
" Melodies. Complete, ... 38
Paul and Virginia, ... 31
Pollok's Course of Time, ... 38
Pure Gold from the Rivers of Wisdom, . . 38
Thomson's Seasons, ... 38
Token of the Heart. Do. of Affection. Do. of Remembrance. Do. of Friendship. Do. of Love. Each, ... 31
Useful Letter-Writer, ... 38
Wilson's Sacra Privata, ... 31
Young's Night Thoughts, ... 38

Little Pedlington and the Pedlingtonians, . 50
Prismatics. Tales and Poems, . . . 1 25
Papers from the Quarterly Review, . . . 50
Republic of the United States. Its Duties, &c. 1 00
Preservation of Health and Prevention of Disease, ... 75
School for Politics. By Chas. Gayerre, . . 75
Select Italian Comedies. Translated, . . 75
Shakespeare's Scholar. By R. G. White, . 2 50
Spectator (The). New ed. 6 vols. cloth, . 9 00
Swett's Treatise on Diseases of the Chest, . 3 00
Stories from Blackwood, ... 50

THACKERAY'S WORKS.

The Book of Snobs, ... 50
Mr. Browne's Letters, ... 50
The Confessions of Fitzboodle, ... 50
The Fat Contributor, ... 50
Jeames' Diary. A Legend of the Rhine . 50
The Luck of Barry Lyndon, ... 1 00
Men's Wives, ... 50
The Paris Sketch Book. 2 vols. . . . 1 00
The Shabby Genteel Story, ... 50
The Yellowplush Papers. 1 vol. 16mo. . . 50
Thackeray's Works. 6 vols. bound in cloth, . 5 00

Trescott's Diplomacy of the Revolution, . 75
Tuckerman's Artist Life, ... 75
Up Country Letters, ... 75
Ward's Letters from Three Continents, . . 1 00
" English Items, ... 1 00
Warner's Rudimental Lessons in Music . 50
Woman's Worth, ... 38

Philosophical Works.

Cousin's Course of Modern Philosophy, . . 3 00
" Philosophy of the Beautiful, . . 62
" on the True, Beautiful, and Good, 1 50
Comte's Positive Philosophy. 2 vols. . . 4 00
Hamilton's Philosophy. 1 vol. 8vo. . . 1 50

Poetry and the Drama.

Amelia's Poems. 1 vol. 12mo. 1 25
Brownell's Poems. 12mo. 75
Bryant's Poems. 1 vol. 8vo. Illustrated, . 3 50
" " Antique mor. 6 00
" " 2 vols 12mo. cloth, . . 2 00
" " 1 vol. 18mo. 63
Byron's Poetical Works. 1 vol. cloth, . . 3 00
" " " Antique mor. . 6 00
Burns' Poetical Works. Cloth, ... 1 00
Butler's Hudibras. Cloth, ... 1 00
Campbell's Poetical Works. Cloth, . . . 1 00
Coleridge's Poetical Works. Cloth, . . . 1 25
Cowper's Poetical Works, ... 1 00
Chaucer's Canterbury Tales, ... 1 00
Dante's Poems. Cloth, ... 1 00
Dryden's Poetical Works. Cloth, ... 1 00
Fay (J. S.), Ulric; or, The Voices, . . . 75
Goethe's Iphigenia in Tauris. Translated, . 75
Gilfillan's Edition of the British Poets. 12 vols. published. Price per vol. cloth, . . . 1 00
Do. do. Calf, per vol. 2 50
Griffith's (Mattie) Poems, ... 75
Hemans' Poetical Works. 2 vols. 16mo. . 2 00
Herbert's Poetical Works. 16mo. cloth, . 1 00
Keats' Poetical Works. Cloth, 12mo. . . 1 25
Kirke White's Poetical Works. Cloth, . . 1 00
Lord's Poems. 1 vol. 12mo. 75
" Christ in Hades. 12mo. 75
Milton's Paradise Lost. 18mo. 38
" Complete Poetical Works, . . . 1 00
Moore's Poetical Works. 8vo. Illustrated, . 3 00
" " " Mor. extra, . . . 6 00
Montgomery's Sacred Poems. 1 vol. 12mo. . 75
Pope's Poetical Works. 1 vol. 16mo. . . 1 00
Southey's Poetical Works. 1 vol. 3 00
Spenser's Faerie Queene. 1 vol. cloth, . . 1 00
Scott's Poetical Works. 1 vol. 1 00
" Lady of the Lake. 16mo. 38
" Marmion, ... 37
" Lay of the Last Minstrel, ... 25
Shakspeare's Dramatic Works, ... 2 00
Tasso's Jerusalem Delivered. 1 vol. 16mo. . 1 00
Wordsworth (W.). The Prelude, ... 1 00

Religious Works.

Arnold's Rugby School Sermons, . . . 50
Anthon's Catechism on the Homilies, . . 06
" Early Catechism for Children, . 06
Burnet's History of the Reformation. 3 vols. . 2 50
" Thirty-Nine Articles, ... 2 [illegible]

Bradley's Family and Parish Sermons, 2 00
Cotter's Mass and Rubrics, 38
Coit's Puritanism, 1 00
Evans' Rectory of Valehead, 50
Grayson's True Theory of Christianity, 1 00
Gresley on Preaching, 1 25
Griffin's Gospel its Own Advocate, 1 00
Hecker's Book of the Soul,
Hooker's Complete Works. 2 vols. 4 00
James' Happiness, 25
James on the Nature of Evil, 1 00
Jarvis' Reply to Milner, 75
Kingsley's Sacred Choir, 75
Keble's Christian Year, 37
Layman's Letters to a Bishop, 25
Logan's Sermons and Expository Lectures, 1 13
Lyra Apostolica, 50
Marshall's Notes on Episcopacy, 1 00
Newman's Sermons and Subjects of the Day, 1 00
" Essay on Christian Doctrine, 75
Ogilby on Lay Baptism, 50
Pearson on the Creed, 2 00
Pulpit Cyclopædia and Ministers' Companion, 2 50
Sewell's Reading Preparatory to Confirmation, 75
Southard's Mystery of Godliness, 75
Sketches and Skeletons of Sermons, 2 50
Spencer's Christian Instructed, 1 00
Sherlock's Practical Christian, 75
Sutton's Disce Vivere--Learn to Live, 75
Swartz's Letters to my Godchild, 38
Trench's Notes on the Parables, 1 75
" Notes on the Miracles. 1 75
Taylor's Holy Living and Dying, 1 00
" Episcopacy Asserted and Maintained, 75
Tyng's Family Commentary, 2 00
Walker's Sermons on Practical Subjects, 2 00
Watson on Confirmation, 06
Wilberforce's Manual for Communicants, 38
Wilson's Lectures on Colossians, 75
Wyatt's Christian Altar, 38

Voyages and Travels.

Africa and the American Flag, 1 25
Appletons' Southern and Western Guide, 1 00
" Northern and Eastern Guide, 1 25
" Complete U. S. Guide Book, 2 00
" N. Y. City Map, 25
Bartlett's New Mexico, &c. 2 vols. Illustrated, 5 00
Burnet's N. Western Territory, 2 00
Bryant's What I Saw in California, 1 25
Coggeshall's Voyages. 2 vols. 2 50
Dix's Winter in Madeira, 1 00
Huc's Travels in Tartary and Thibet. 2 vols. 1 00
Layard's Nineveh. 1 vol. 8vo. 1 25
Notes of a Theological Student. 12mo. 1 00
Oliphant's Journey to Katmundu, 50
Parkyns' Abyssinia. 2 vols. 2 50
Russia as it Is. By Gurowski, 1 00
" By Count de Custine, 1 25
Squier's Nicaragua. 2 vols. 5 00
Tappan's Step from the New World to the Old, 1 75
Wanderings and Fortunes of Germ. Emigrants, 75
Williams' Isthmus of Tehuantepec. 2 vols. 8vo. 3 50

Works of Fiction.

GRACE AGUILAR'S WORKS.

The Days of Bruce. 2 vols. 12mo. 1 50
Home Scenes and Heart Studies. 12mo. 75
The Mother's Recompense. 12mo. 75
Woman's Friendship. 12mo. 75
Women of Israel. 2 vols. 12mo. 1 50

Basil. A Story of Modern Life. 12mo. 75
Brace's Fawn of the Pale Faces. 12mo. 75
Busy Moments of an Idle Woman 75
Chestnut Wood. A Tale 2 vols. 1 75
Don Quixotte, Translated. Illustrated, 1 25
Drury (A. H.). Light and Shade, 75
Dupuy (A. E.). The Conspirator, 75

MRS. ELLIS' WORKS.

Hearts and Homes; or, Social Distinctions, 1 50
Prevention Better than Cure, 75
Women of England, 50

Emmanuel Phillibert. By Dumas, 1 25
Farmingdale. By Caroline Thomas, 1 00
Fullerton (Lady G.). Ellen Middleton, 75
" " Grantley Manor. 1 vol. 12mo. 75
" " Lady Bird. 1 vol. 12mo. 75
The Foresters. By Alex. Dumas, 75
Gore (Mrs.). The Dean's Daughter. 1 vol. 12mo. 75
Goldsmith's Vicar of Wakefield. 12mo. 75
Gil Blas. With 500 Engravings. Cloth, gt. edg. 2 50
Harry Muir. A Tale of Scottish Life, 75
Hearts Unveiled; or, I Knew You Would Like Him, 75
Heartsease; or, My Brother's Wife. 2 vols. 1 50
Heir of Redclyffe. 2 vols. cloth, 1 50
Heloise; or, The Unrevealed Secret. 12mo. 75
Hobson. My Uncle and I. 12mo. 75
Holmes' Tempest and Sunshine. 12mo. 1 00
Home is Home. A Domestic Story, 75
Howitt (Mary). The Heir of West Wayland, 50
Io. A Tale of the Ancient Fane. 12mo. 75
The Iron Cousin. By Mary Cowden Clarke, 1 25
James (G. P. R.). Adrian; or, Clouds of the Mind, 75
John; or, Is a Cousin in the Hand Worth Two in the Bush, 25

JULIA KAVANAGH'S WORKS.

Nathalie. A Tale. 12mo. 1 00
Madeline. 12mo. 75
Daisy Burns. 12mo. 1 00

Life's Discipline. A Tale of Hungary, 63
Lone Dove (The). A Legend, 75
Linny Lockwood. By Catherine Crowe, 50

MISS McINTOSH'S WORKS.

Two Lives; or, To Seem and To Be. 12mo. 75
Aunt Kitty's Tales. 12mo. 75
Charms and Counter-Charms. 12mo. 1 00
Evenings at Donaldson Manor, 75
The Lofty and the Lowly. 2 vols. 1 50

Margaret's Home. By Cousin Alice,
Marie Louise; or, The Opposite Neighbors, 50
Maiden Aunt (The). A Story, 75
Manzoni. The Betrothed Lovers. 2 vols. 1 50
Margaret Cecil; or, I Can Because I Ought, 75
Morton Montague; or, The Christian's Choice, 75
Norman Leslie. By G. C. H. 75
Prismatics. Tales and Poems. By Haywarde, 1 25
Roe (A. S.). James Montjoy. 12mo. 75
" To Love and to Be Loved. 12mo. 75
" Time and Tide. 12mo. 75
Reuben Medlicott; or, The Coming Man, 75
Rose Douglass. By S. R. W. 75

MISS SEWELL'S WORKS.

Amy Herbert. A Tale. 12mo. 75
Experience of Life. 12mo. 75
Gertrude. A Tale. 12mo. 75
Katherine Ashton. 2 vols. 12mo. 1 50
Laneton Parsonage. A Tale. 3 vols. 12mo. 2 25
Margaret Percival. 2 vols. 1 50
Walter Lorimer, and Other Tales. 12mo. 75
A Journal Kept for Children of a Village School, 1 00

Sunbeams and Shadows. Cloth, 75
Thorpe's Hive of the Bee Hunter, 1 00
Thackeray's Works. 6 vols. 12mo. 6 00
The Virginia Comedians. 2 vols. 12mo. 1 50
Use of Sunshine. By S. M. 12mo. 75

A Work abounding in Exciting Scenes and Remarkable Incidents.

Capt. Canot;

OR,

TWENTY YEARS OF AN AFRICAN SLAVER:

BEING AN ACCOUNT OF HIS CAREER AND ADVENTURES ON THE COAST, IN THE INTERIOR, ON SHIPBOARD, AND IN THE WEST INDIES.

Written out and Edited from the Captain's Journals, Memoranda, and Conversations.

BY BRANTZ MAYER.

One Volume, 12mo. With eight Illustrations. Price $1 25.

Criticisms of the Press.

"The author is a literary gentleman of Baltimore, no Abolitionist, and we believe the work to be a truthful account of the life of a man who saw much more than falls to the lot of most men."—*Commonwealth.*

"A remarkable volume is this; because of its undoubted truth: it having been derived by Mayer from personal conversations with Canot, and from journals which the slaver furnished of his own life."—*Worcester Palladium.*

"Capt. Canot, the hero of the narrative, is, to our own knowledge, a veritable personage, and resides in Baltimore. There is no doubt that the main incidents connected with his extraordinary career are in every respect true.'—*Arthur's Home Gazette.*

"Under one aspect, as the biography of a remarkable man who passed through a singularly strange and eventful experience, it is as interesting as any sea story that we have ever read."—*Boston Evening Traveller.*

"Capt. Canot has certainly passed through a life of difficulty, danger, and wild, daring adventure, which has much the air of romance, and still he, or rather his editor, tells the tale with so much straightforwardness, that we cannot doubt its truthfulness."—*New York Sunday Despatch.*

"The work could not have been better done if the principal actor had combined the descriptive talent of De Foe with the astuteness of Fouche and the dexterity of Gil Blas, which traits are ascribed to the worthy whose acquaintance we shall soon make by his admiring editor."—*N. Y. Tribune.*

"The general style of the work is attractive, and the narrative spirited and bold—well suited to the daring and hazardous course of life led by the adventurer. This book is illustrated by several excellent engravings."—*Baltimore American.*

"The biography of an African slaver as taken from his own lips, and giving his adventures in this traffic for twenty years. With great natural keenness of perception and complete communicativeness, he has literally unmasked his real life, and tells both what he was and *what he saw*, the latter being the *Photograph* of the Negro in Africa, which has been so long wanted. A nephew of Mr. Mayer has illustrated the volume with eight admirable drawings. We should think no book of the present day would be received with so keen an interest."—*Home Journal.*

"Capt. Canot has passed most of his life since 1819 on the ocean, and his catalogue of adventures at sea and on land, rival in grotesqueness and apparent improbability the marvels of Robinson Crusoe."—*Evening Post.*

"If stirring incidents, hair-breadth escapes, and variety of adventure, can make a book interesting, this must possess abundant attractions."—*Newark Daily Advertiser.*

"This is a true record of the life of one who had spent the greater part of his days in dealing in human flesh. We commend this book to all lovers of adventure."—*Boston Christian Recorder.*

"We would advise every one who is a lover of 'books that are books'—every one who admires Le Sage and De Foe, and has lingered long over the charming pages of Gil Blas and Robinson Crusoe—every one, pro-slavery or anti-slavery, to purchase this book"—*Buffalo Courier*

Rev. Samuel Osgood's Two Popular Books.

I.

Mile Stones in our Life Journey

SECOND EDITION.

One Volume, 12mo. Cloth. Price $1

Opinions of the Press.

"In so small a compass, we rarely meet with more Catholic sympathies, and with a clearer or more practical view of the privileges enjoyed by, and the duties enjoined, upon us all, at any stage of our mortal pilgrimage."—*Church Journal.*

"Some passages remind us forcibly of Addison and Goldsmith."—*Independent.*

"This little volume is one of those books which are read by all classes at all stages of life, with an interest which loses nothing by change or circumstances."—*Pennsylvanian.*

"He writes kindly; strongly and readably; nor is their any thing in this volume of a narrow, bigoted, or sectarian character."—*Life Illustrated.*

"His counsels are faithful and wholesome, his reflection touching, and the whole is clothed in a style graceful and free."—*Hartford Relig. Herald.*

"This is a volume of beautiful and cogent essays, virtuous in motive, simple in expression, pertinent and admirable in logic, and glorious in conclusion and climax."—*Buffalo Express.*

"It is written with exquisite taste, is full of beautiful thought most felicitously expressed, and is pervaded by a genial and benevolent spirit."—*Dr. Sprague.*

"Almost every page has a tincture of elegant scholarship, and bears witness to an extensive reading of good authors."—*Bryant.*

II.

The Hearth-Stone;

THOUGHTS UPON HOME LIFE IN OUR CITIES.

BY SAMUEL OSGOOD,

AUTHOR OF 'STUDIES IN CHRISTIAN BIOGRAPHY," "GOD WITH MEN," ETC.

FOURTH EDITION.

One Volume, 12mo. Cloth Price $1.

Criticisms of the Press.

"This is a volume of elegant and impressive essays on the domestic relations and religious duties of the household. Mr. Osgood writes on these interesting themes in the most charming and animated style, winning the reader's judgment rather than coercing it to the author's conclusions. The predominant sentiments in the book are purity, sincerity, and love. A more delightful volume has rarely been published, and we trust it will have a wide circulation, for its influence must be salutary upon both old and young."—*Commercial Advertiser.*

"The 'Hearth-Stone' is the symbol of all those delightful truths which Mr. Osgood here connects with it. In a free and graceful style, varying from deep solemnity to the most genial and lively tone, as befits his range of subjects, he gives attention to wise thoughts on holy things, and homely truths. His volume will find many warm hearts to which it will address itself."—*Christian Examiner.*

www.ingramcontent.com/pod-product-compliance
Lightning Source LLC
LaVergne TN
LVHW021308110826
845150LV00003B/515

* 9 7 8 1 4 2 5 5 5 9 1 0 6 *